D1736995

UNFETTERED

UNFETTERED

Tales by Masters of Fantasy

EDITED BY
Shawn Speakman

GRIM
OAK

GRIM OAK PRESS
SEATTLE

UNFETTERED
Copyright © 2013 by Shawn Speakman.
All rights reserved.

"Imaginary Friends" by Terry Brooks. © 1991 by Terry Brooks.
"How Old Holly Came To Be" by Patrick Rothfuss. © 2013 by Patrick Rothfuss.
"The Old Scale Game" by Tad Williams. © 2013 by Beale-Williams Enterprise.
"Game of Chance" by Carrie Vaughn. © 2013 by Carrie Vaughn, LLC.
"The Martyr of the Roses" by Jacqueline Carey. © 1996 by Jacqueline Carey.
"Mudboy" by Peter V. Brett. © 2013 by Peter V. Brett.
"The Sound of Broken Absolutes" by Peter Orullian. © 2013 by Peter Orullian.
"The Coach with Big Teeth" by R.A. Salvatore. © 1996 by R.A. Salvatore.
"Keeper of Memory" by Todd Lockwood. © 2013 by Todd Lockwood.
"Heaven in a Wild Flower" by Blake Charlton. © 2013 by Blake Charlton.
"Dogs" by Daniel Abraham. © 2013 by Daniel Abraham.
"The Chapel Perilous" by Kevin Hearne. © 2013 by Kevin Hearne.
"Select Mode" by Mark Lawrence. © 2013 by Mark Lawrence.
"All the Girls Love Michael Stein" by David Anthony Durham.
© 2013 by David Anthony Durham.
"Strange Rain" by Jennifer Bosworth. © 2013 by Jennifer Bosworth.
"Nocturne" by Robert V.S. Redick. © 2013 by Robert V.S. Redick.
"Unbowed" by Eldon Thompson. © 2013 by Eldon Thompson.
"In Favour with Their Stars" by Naomi Novik. © 2013 by Naomi Novik.
"River of Souls" by Robert Jordan & Brandon Sanderson.
© 2013 by The Bandersnatch Group, Inc.
"The Jester" by Michael J. Sullivan. © 2013 by Michael J. Sullivan.
"The Duel" by Lev Grossman. © 2013 by Lev Grossman.
"Walker and the Shade of Allanon" by Terry Brooks. © 2000 by Terry Brooks.
"The Unfettered Knight" by Shawn Speakman. © 2013 by Shawn Speakman.
All rights reserved.

Dust jacket and interior artwork by Todd Lockwood.
Copyediting and book design/composition by Rachelle Longé McGhee.

Signed, Limited Edition ISBN 978-0-9847136-4-6
Trade Hardcover Edition ISBN 978-0-9847136-3-9
eBook ISBN 978-0-9847136-5-3

First Edition, July 2013
2 4 6 8 9 7 5 3 1

Grim Oak Press
PO Box 45173
Seattle, WA 98145
www.grimoakpress.com

For those with cancer and those who stand by them

Who battle together and show no quarter

"Pain shared, my brother, is pain not doubled but halved."

—Neil Gaiman, *Anansi Boys*

"What are years to me? Like pain, they pass unnoticed."

—Jay Lake, *Kalimpura*

CONTENTS

FOREWORD
by Patrick Rothfuss

Can I be honest here? I don't read forewords.

Can I be *painfully* honest? I don't even know what forewords are *for*.

Am I supposed to somehow convince you to buy this book? Are you, even now, standing in a bookstore, reading this, your gut roiling with indecision?

That doesn't seem to make sense to me. For one thing, you can see the folks in this anthology. You've read their names on the cover. It couldn't be more impressive if it included Lord Vishnu and Optimus Prime. If those names didn't convince you, what could I possibly say that might tip you over the edge?

I mean, it is true that owning this book will make you roughly 38 percent more attractive. Its mere presence on your shelf boosts your metabolism too. And there's the fact that touching it on a daily basis is proven to cure scrofula and reverse baldness.

Seriously, what do you expect? I'm *in* the book. And I'm a professional liar. You can't trust my opinion on this matter. Of course I'd like you to buy it.

Maybe you've already bought this book, and now I'm supposed to somehow reassure you, make it clear you've spent your money wisely. Is that the point of a foreword? Am I just trying to help you stave off the chilly hand of buyer's remorse?

It seems to me that in both those cases, you'd be better served just reading the book rather than looking here for answers. I mean, honestly. We're 250 words in at this point. If you'd just skipped this foreword, you'd already be on the second page of one of the stories . . .

Well, fine. If you're here, I guess you want something else. And given that I don't know what I'm supposed to write in a foreword, I'm just going to tell you a story.

Back in 2007, my first book was published. Also in 2007, my mom died of cancer.

In 2007, I also met Shawn Speakman. I found out that he'd had cancer in the past and had beaten it. My thoughts at the time were an odd mingling of confused ("What? You can do that?") and thrilled ("Yeah! Take that, goddamn cancer!").

Then he contacted me in 2011 and told me that he'd gotten a new cancer. It's hard to describe how I felt. "Pissed off" sums it up fairly well. But there was also a sense of unfairness to it all. Nobody should have to deal with that shit twice.

When I asked for details, I was glad to hear that it was very treatable. Very beatable. I think I said something like, "Damn. That's really awful . . . but congrats on getting a really good cancer."

Those of you who have had personal brushes with cancer will understand this statement; the rest of you, probably not so much.

But there was bad news. Shawn couldn't get health insurance because he'd had cancer before. That meant his treatment was probably going to bankrupt him.

When he told me about his plans for an anthology to raise money for his bills, I said I'd be happy to give him a story. It was a no-brainer for me, as it allowed me to if not spit directly into cancer's eye, then at least glare at it angrily from across the room.

The fact that other authors have joined this anthology in such numbers shows what good folks sci-fi and fantasy authors are. I have a grudge against cancer. It was an easy choice for me. But a lot of them are merely doing this to help out a friend in a tight spot.

And by buying this book, you've helped too. Thanks for that. You're a good person.

All right, I've wasted enough of your time here. On to the stories.

Patrick Rothfuss
Author
May 2013

INTRODUCTION
On Becoming Unfettered

When I was diagnosed with cancer in 2011, fear entered my life.

But not the fear you might think.

Cancer is a frightening disease. I think it is the initial uncertainty that strikes at the soul. Will I live? Will I die? Mortality is not a topic many contemplate until it is suddenly thrust upon them. It is too late for reflection by then, the fight just to survive eclipsing everything else. In my case, I had survived a different cancer ten years earlier and I had come to terms with my mortality then. So during my 2011 bout with Hodgkin's lymphoma, those who knew me were not worried. They had seen me be a tough bastard before; they knew I would be one again.

I knew the same. I would bring my considerable emotional strength to bear and survive. I was not worried about dying.

I was worried about bankruptcy.

I knew I would be in financial dire straits from the outset. As a freelance writer and web designer, I do not have health insurance. As such, my cancer would be treated and I would receive the best in care, but that would also leave me destitute: I would likely have to declare medical bankruptcy, which would result in the fiscal ruination of the following decade. I had to do something.

After I had settled into my treatment schedule, I had lunch with *New York Times* best-selling author Terry Brooks. I have worked with Terry for fourteen years, as his webmaster and continuity editor, his friend and confidante. I asked if he'd be interested in donating a short story, the proceeds from which would go against my mounting debt.

He agreed. And added, "Why don't you contact your other writer friends?"

Time is precious to writers; words are precious to their publishers. I decided to take the risk, be vulnerable, and ask those writers a question I had no business asking. I could damage working relationships; worse, I could ruin friendships.

I had to take that risk. And when my friends selflessly began donating short stories for what would become this anthology, tears of gratitude began to replace the fear I carried. Some of the best authors in the fantasy genre rallied around me. They bolstered me during my time of hardship. In turn, I refused to dictate what their story contributions should be. I would not chain these writers with a theme or any word-count restrictions—I wanted this to be theirs as much as it was "mine."

Instead, they would be unfettered, free to write exactly what they wanted to donate.

And, in turn, I would become unfettered from medical debt.

Unfettered is an anthology filled with magic, wonderment, and hope. It is more than its combined stories, though. It is the power of friendship. Of giving. Of a science-fiction and fantasy community that protects its own. Of humanity escaping the ugliness that often plagues it to instead create a testament to the goodness found in every heart.

I am forever indebted to these writers as I am forever indebted to you readers.

As long as I am able, I will pay forward that debt.

I hope you enjoy *Unfettered*.

Shawn Speakman
Editor and Publisher
May 2013

UNFETTERED

TERRY BROOKS

Full disclaimer, right off the bat: I wrote this story back in early 1990 when Del Rey Books came to me for a piece to be included in a coffee-table book of modern fairy tales. Other contributors included Anne McCaffrey, Isaac Asimov, Lester del Rey, and half a dozen more. Since Lester was my editor and Judy-Lynn my champion, of course I agreed to contribute.

The collection was titled *Once Upon a Time,* and when it was published in 1991, "Imaginary Friends" was included.

So the story is neither brand-new nor unpublished. Of course, it has been out of print for quite a while, so at least it will *seem* new.

The idea for the story was already in my head when I was approached. For some time, I had been thinking of breaking away from the Shannara and Magic Kingdom series to write something new. I wanted to do a big, sprawling saga—another, obviously—but one that was situated in the present and in which the schematic of magic was so integral to what we know to be true about our world that it would feel entirely plausible. That meant the fantasy elements and magic devices I chose to employ had to have explanations that made them feel real to the reader.

I had envisioned this saga as a trilogy of books, all of them linked by a series of common elements, but never as a short story. However, since no one was clamoring for such an opus, I thought this would be a good chance to put something down on paper as a sort of rough blueprint of what I would one day have a chance to write in larger form.

So I wrote about Jack and his impish friend Pick and the owl Daniel and their lives together in Sinnissippi Park. Most of what I wrote in the shorter version was changed entirely in the longer. Yet I think you will find that the story stands up pretty well on its own merits.

Several years later, I would write the books that comprise the Word & Void series, but "Imaginary Friends" was the prototype. Read on, and you can discover a little about how the one led to the other.

Terry Brooks

IMAGINARY FRIENDS

Terry Brooks

Jack McCall was ten days shy of his thirteenth birthday when he decided that he was dying. He had been having headaches for about six months without telling anyone, the headaches being accompanied by a partial loss of vision that lasted anywhere from ten to twenty minutes. He hadn't thought much about it since it only happened once in a while, believing that it was simply the result of eyestrain. After all, there was a lot of homework assigned in the seventh grade.

But ten days before his birthday he had an attack as he was about to go out the door to school, and since he couldn't very well ride his bike in that condition or stand around pretending that nothing was wrong, he was forced to admit the problem to his mother. His mother made an immediate appointment with Dr. Muller, the family pediatrician, for that afternoon, sat Jack down until his vision cleared, then drove him to school, asking him all the way there if he was all right and calling him "Jackie" until he thought he would scream.

She returned promptly when school let out to take him to

his appointment. Dr. Muller was uncharacteristically cheerful as he checked Jack over, even going so far as to ruffle his hair and remark on how quickly he was growing. This was the same Dr. Muller who normally didn't have two words for him. Jack began to worry.

When the doctor was finished, he sent Jack and his mother over to the hospital for further tests. The tests included X-rays, blood workups, an EKG, and a barrage of other examinations, all of which were administered by an uncomfortably youthful collection of nurses. Jack endured the application of cold metal implements to his body, let himself be stuck repeatedly with needles, breathed in and out, lay very still, jumped up and down, and mostly waited around in empty, sterile examination rooms. When the tests were all done, he was sent home knowing nothing more than he had when he arrived beyond the fact that he did not care ever to go through such an ordeal again.

That night, while Jack was upstairs in his room fiddling with his homework and listening to his stereo, Dr. Muller paid a visit to his house. His parents didn't call for him, but that didn't stop him from being curious. He slipped down the stairway to the landing and sat there in the dark on the other side of the half wall above the living room while Dr. Muller and his parents spoke in hushed tones. Dr. Muller did most of the talking. He said that the preliminary test results were back. He talked about the body and its cells and a bunch of other stuff, throwing in multisyllabic medical terms that Jack couldn't begin to understand.

Then he used the words "blood disorder" and "leukemia" and "cancer." Jack understood that part. He might only be in seventh grade, but he wasn't stupid.

He stayed on the stairway until he heard his mother start to cry, then crept back up to his room without waiting to hear any more. He sat there staring at his unfinished homework, trying to decide what he should be feeling. He couldn't seem to feel anything. He heard Dr. Muller leave, and then his parents came up to see him. Usually they visited him individually; when they both appeared it was serious business. They knocked on the door, came inside when invited, and stood there looking decidedly uncomfortable. Then his father told him that he was sick and would have to take it easy for a while, his mother started crying and calling him "Jackie" and hugging him, and all of a sudden he was scared out of his socks.

He didn't sleep much that night, letting the weight of what he had discovered sink in, trying to comprehend what his dying meant, trying to decide if he believed it was possible. Mostly, he thought about Uncle Frank. Uncle Frank had been his favorite uncle, a big man with strong hands and red hair who taught him how to throw a baseball. Uncle Frank used to take him to ballgames on Sunday afternoons. Then he got sick. It happened all at once. He went into the hospital and never came out. Jack's parents took him to see Uncle Frank a couple of times. There was not much left of Uncle Frank by then. His once-strong hands were so frail he could barely lift them. All his hair had fallen out. He looked like an old man.

Then he died. No one came right out and said it, but Jack knew what had killed him. And he had always suspected, deep down inside where you hid things like that, that it might someday kill him, too.

The next morning Jack dressed, wolfed down his breakfast as quickly as he could, and got out of there. His parents were behaving like zombies. Only his little sister Abby was acting as if everything was all right, which was the way she always acted since she was only eight and never knew what was going on anyway.

It was Friday, always a slow-moving day at Roosevelt Junior High, but never more so than on this occasion. The morning seemed endless, and Jack didn't remember any of it when it was finally over. He trudged to the lunchroom, found a seat off in a corner where he could talk privately, and told his best friend Waddy Wadsworth what he had discovered. Reynolds Lucius Wadsworth III was Waddy's real name, the result of a three-generation tradition of unparalleled cruelty in the naming of first-born boys. No one called Waddy by his real name, of course. But they didn't call him anything sensible either. It was discovered early on that

Waddy lacked any semblance of athletic ability. He was the kid who couldn't climb the knotted rope or do chin-ups or high-jump when the bar was only two feet off the ground. Someone started calling him Waddy and the name stuck. It wasn't that Waddy was fat or anything; he was just earthbound.

He was also a good guy. Jack liked him because he never said anything about the fact that Jack was only a little taller than most fire hydrants and a lot shorter than most girls.

"You look okay to me," Waddy said after Jack had finished telling him he was supposed to be dying.

"I know I look okay." Jack frowned at his friend impatiently. "This isn't the kind of thing you can see, you know."

"You sound okay, too." Waddy took a bite of his jelly sandwich. "Does anything hurt?"

Jack shrugged. "Just when I have the headaches."

"Well, you don't have them more often now than you did six months ago, do you?"

"No."

"And they don't last any longer now than they did then, do they?"

"No."

Waddy shoved the rest of the sandwich into his mouth and chewed thoughtfully. "Well, then, who's to say you're really dying? This could be one of those conditions that just goes on indefinitely. Meantime, they might find a cure for it; they're always finding cures for this kind of stuff." He chewed some more. "Anyway, maybe the doctor made a mistake. That's possible, isn't it?"

Jack nodded doubtfully.

"The point is, you don't know for sure. Not for sure." Waddy cocked his head. "Here's something else to think about. They're always telling someone or other that they're going to die and then they don't. People get well all the time just because they believe they can do it. Sometimes believing is all it takes."

He gave Jack a lopsided grin. "Besides, no one dies in the seventh grade."

Jack wanted to believe that. He spent the afternoon trying to convince himself. After all, he didn't personally know anyone his age who had died. The only people he knew who had died were much older. Even Uncle Frank. He was just a kid. How could he die when he still didn't know anything about girls? How could he die without ever having driven a car? It just didn't seem possible.

Nevertheless, the feeling persisted that he was only fooling himself. It didn't make any difference what he believed; it didn't change the facts. If he really had cancer, believing he didn't wouldn't make it go away. He sat through his afternoon classes growing steadily more despondent, feeling helpless and wishing he could do something about it.

It wasn't until he was biking home that he suddenly found himself thinking about Pick.

The McCall house was a large white shake-shingle rambler that occupied almost an acre of timber bordering the north edge of Sinnissippi Park. The Sinnissippi Indians were native to the area, and several of their burial mounds occupied a fenced-off area situated in the southwest corner of the park under a cluster of giant maples. The park was more than forty acres end to end, most of it woods, the rest consisting of baseball diamonds and playgrounds. The park was bordered on the south by the Rock River, on the west by Riverside Cemetery, and on the north and east by the private residences of Woodlawn. It was a sprawling preserve, filled with narrow, serpentine trails; thick stands of scrub-choked pine; and shady groves of maple, elm, and white oak. A massive bluff ran along the better part of its southern edge and overlooked the Rock River.

Jack was not allowed to go into the park alone until he was out of fourth grade, not even beyond the low maintenance bushes that grew where his backyard ended at the edge of the park. His father took him for walks sometimes, a bike ride now and then, and once in a while his mother even came along. She didn't come often, though, because she was busy with Abby, and his father worked at the printing company and was usually not home until after dark. So for a long time the park remained a vast, unexplored country that lay just out of reach and whispered enticingly in Jack's youthful mind of adventure and mystery.

Sometimes, when the lure was too strong, he would beg to be allowed to go into the park by himself, just for a little ways, just for a few tiny minutes. He would pinch his thumb and index finger close together to emphasize the smallness of his request. But his mother's reply was always the same—his own backyard was park enough for him.

Things have a way of working out, though, and the summer before he entered second grade he ended up going into the park alone in spite of his parents. It all came about because of Pick. Jack was playing in the sandbox with his toy trucks on a hot July afternoon when he heard Sam whining and barking at something just beyond the bushes. Sam was the family dog, a sort of mongrel terrier with a barrel body. He was carrying on as if he had unearthed a mountain lion, and finally Jack lifted himself out of the maze of crisscrossing paths he was constructing and wandered down to the end of the yard to see what was happening. When he got there, he found that he still couldn't see anything because Sam was behind a pine tree on the other side of the bushes. Jack called, but the dog wouldn't come. After standing there for a few minutes, Jack glanced restlessly over his shoulder at the windows of his house. There was no sign of his mother. Biting his lower lip with stubborn determination, he stepped cautiously onto forbidden ground.

He was concentrating too hard on what lay behind him. As he passed through the bushes, he stumbled and struck his head sharply on a heavy limb. The blow stung, but Jack climbed back to his feet almost immediately and went on.

Sam was jumping around at the base of the pine, darting in and out playfully. There was a gathering of brambles growing there and a bit of cloth caught in them. When Jack got closer, he saw that the bit of cloth was actually a doll. When he got closer still, he saw that the doll was moving.

"Don't just stand there!" the doll yelled at him in a very tiny but angry voice. "Call him off!"

9

Jack caught hold of Sam's collar. Sam struggled, twisting about in Jack's grip, trying to get back to his newfound discovery. Finally Jack gave the dog a sharp slap on its hind end and sent it scurrying away through the bushes. Then he crouched down beneath the pine, staring at the talking doll. It was a little man with a reddish beard, green shirt and pants, black boots and belt, and a cap made out of fresh pine needles woven together.

Jack giggled. "Why are you so little?" he asked.

"Why am I so little?" the other echoed. He was struggling mightily to free himself. "Why are you so big? Don't you know anything?"

"Are you real?" Jack pressed.

"Of course I'm real! I'm an Elf!"

Jack cocked his head. "Like in the fairy tales?"

The Elf was flushed redder than his beard. "No, not like in the fairy tales! Since when do fairy tales tell the truth about Elves? I suppose you think Elves are just cute little woodfolk who spend their lives prancing about in the moonlight? Well, we don't! We work!"

Jack bent close so he could see better. "What do you work at?"

"Everything!" The Elf was apoplectic.

"You're funny," Jack said, rocking back on his heels. "What's your name?"

"Pick. My name is Pick," muttered the Elf. He twisted some more and finally gave up. "What's yours?"

"Jack. Jack Andrew McCall."

"Well, look, Jack Andrew McCall. Do you think you could help me get out of these brambles? It's your fault, after all, that I'm in them in the first place. That is your dog, isn't it? Well, your dog was sneaking around where I was working and I didn't hear him. He barked and frightened me so badly I got myself caught. Then he began sniffing and drooling all over me, and I got tangled up even worse!" He took a deep breath, calming himself. "So how about it? Will you help me?"

"Sure," Jack agreed at once.

He started to reach down, and Pick cried out, "Be careful with those big fingers of yours! You could crush me! You're not a clumsy boy, are you? You're not one of those boys that goes around stepping on ants?"

Jack was always pretty good with his hands, and he managed to free the Elf in a matter of seconds with little or no damage to either from the brambles. He put Pick on the ground in front of him and sat back. Pick brushed at his clothes, muttering inaudibly.

"Do you live in the park?" Jack asked.

Pick glanced up, sour-faced once more. His pine needle cap was askew. "Of course I live in the park! How else could I do my work if I didn't?" He jabbed out with one finger. "Do you know what I do, Jack Andrew? I look after this park! This whole park, all by myself! That is a terrible responsibility for a single Elf!"

Jack was impressed. "How do you look after it?"

Pick shoved the cap back into place. "Do you know what magic is?"

Jack scratched at a mosquito bite on his wrist. "It turned Cinderella into a fairy princess," he answered doubtfully.

"Good gosh golly, are they still telling that old saw? When are they ever going to get this fairy tale business right? They keep sticking to those ridiculous stories about wicked stepmothers, would-be princesses, and glass slippers at a royal ball—as if a glass slipper would last five minutes on a dance floor!" He jumped up and down so hard that Jack started. "I could tell them a thing or two about real fairy tales!" Pick exploded. "I could tell them some stories that would raise the hair on the backs of their necks!"

He stopped, suddenly aware of Jack's consternation. "Oh, never mind!" he huffed. "This business of fairy tales just happens to be a sore subject with me. Now about what I do, Jack Andrew. I keep the magic in balance, is what I do. There's magic in everything, you know—from the biggest old oak to the smallest blade of grass, from ants to elephants. And it all has to be kept in balance or there's big trouble. That's what Elves really do. But there's not enough of us to be everywhere, so we concentrate on the places where the magic is strongest and most likely to cause trouble—like this park." He swept the air with his hand. "There's lots of troublesome magic in this park."

11

Jack followed the motion of his hand and then nodded. "It's a big place."

"Too big for most Elves, I'll have you know!" Pick announced. "Want to see how big?"

Jack nodded yes and shook his head no all in the same motion. He glanced hurriedly over his shoulder, remembering anew his mother. "I'm not supposed to go into the park," he explained. "I'm not even supposed to go out of the yard."

"Oh," said Pick quietly. He rubbed his red-bearded chin momentarily, then clapped his hands. "Well, a touch of magic will get the job done and keep you out of trouble at the same time. Here, pick me up, put me in your hand. Gently, Boy! There! Now let me settle myself. Keep your hand open, palm up. Don't move. Now close your eyes. Go on, close them. This won't hurt. Close your eyes and think about the park. Can you see it? Now, watch . . ."

Something warm and syrupy drifted through Jack's body, starting at his eyes and working its way downward to his feet. He felt Pick stir.

And suddenly Jack was flying, soaring high above the trees and telephone poles across the broad, green expanse of Sinnissippi Park. He sat astride an owl, a great brown-and-white feathered bird with wings that seemed to stretch on forever. Pick sat behind him, and amazingly they were the same size. Jack blinked in disbelief, then yelled in delight. The owl swooped lazily earthward, banking this way and that to catch the wind, but the motion did not disturb Jack. Indeed, he felt as if nothing could dislodge him from his perch.

"This is how I get from place to place," he heard Pick say, the tiny voice unruffled by the wind. "Daniel takes me. He's a barn owl—a good one. We met sometime back. If I had to walk the park, it would take me weeks to get from one end to the other and I'd never get anything done!"

"I like this!" Jack cried out joyously, laughed, and Pick laughed with him.

They rode the wind on Daniel's back for what seemed like hours, passing from Riverside Cemetery along the bluff face east to the houses of Woodlawn and back again. Jack saw everything with eyes that were wide with wonder and delight. There were gray and brown squirrels, birds of all kinds and colors, tiny mice and voles, opossums, and even a badger. There was a pair of deer in a thicket down along the riverbank, a fawn and its mother, slender and delicate, their stirrings barely visible against the trees. There were hoary old pines with their needled boughs interlaced like armor over secretive earthen floors, towering oaks and elms sticking out of the ground like massive spears, deep hollows and ravines that collected dried leaves and shadows, and inlets and streams filled with lily pads, frogs, and darting tiny fish.

But there was more than that for a boy who could imagine. There were castles and forts behind every old log. There were railroads with steam engines racing over ancient wooden bridges where the streams grew too wide to ford. There were pirate dens and caves of treasures. There were wild ponies that ran faster than the wind and mountain cats as sleek as silk. Everywhere there was a new story, a different tale, a dream of an adventure longing to be embraced.

And there were things of magic.

"Down there, Jack Andrew—do you see it?" Pick called as they swung left across the stone bridge that spanned a split in the bluff where it dropped sharply downward to the Rock. "Look closely, Boy!"

Jack looked, seeing the crablike shadow that clung to the underside of the bridge, flattened almost out of sight against the stone.

"That's Wartag the Troll!" Pick announced. "Every bridge seems to have at least one Troll in these parts, but Wartag is more trouble than most. If there's a way to unbalance the magic, Wartag will find it. Much of my own work is spent in undoing his!"

Daniel took them down close to the bridgehead, and Jack saw Wartag inch farther back into the shadows in an effort to hide. He was not entirely successful. Jack could still see the crooked body covered with patches of black hair and the mean-looking red eyes that glittered like bicycle reflectors.

Daniel screamed and Wartag shrank away.

"Wartag doesn't care much for owls!" Pick said to Jack, then shouted something spiteful at the Troll before Daniel wheeled them away.

They flew on to a part of the park they had not visited yet, a deep woods far back in the east central section where the sunlight seemed unable to penetrate and all was cloaked in shadow. Daniel took them down into the darkness, a sort of gray mistiness that was filled with silence and the smell of rotting wood. Pick pointed ahead, and Jack followed the line of his finger warily. There stood the biggest, shaggiest tree that he had ever seen, a monster with crooked limbs, splitting bark, and craggy bolls that seemed waiting to snare whatever came into its path. Nothing grew about it. All the other trees, all the brush and the grasses were cleared away.

"What is it?" he asked Pick.

Pick gave him a secretive look. "That, young Jack Andrew, is the prison, now and forever more, of the Dragon Desperado. What do you think of it?"

Jack stared. "A real Dragon?"

"As real as you and I. And very dangerous, I might add. Too dangerous to be let loose, but at the same time too powerful to destroy. Can't be rid of everything that frightens or troubles us in this world. Some things we simply have to put up with— Dragons and Trolls among them. Trolls aren't half as bad as Dragons, of course. Trolls cause mischief when they're on the loose, but Dragons really upset the apple cart. They are a powerful force, Jack Andrew. Why just their breath alone can foul the air for miles! And the imprint of a Dragon's paw will poison whole fields! Some Dragons are worse than others, of course. Desperado is one of them."

He paused and his eyes twinkled as they found Jack's. "All Dragons are bothersome, but Desperado is the worst. Now and again he breaks free, and then there's the very Devil to pay. Fortunately, that doesn't happen too often. When it does, someone simply has to lock Desperado away again." He winked enigmatically. "And that takes a very special kind of magic."

Daniel lifted suddenly and bore them away, skying out of the shadows and the gray mistiness, breaking free of the gloom. The sun caught Jack in the eyes with a burst of light that momentarily blinded him.

"Jackie!"

He thought he heard his mother calling. He blinked.

"Jackie, where are you?"

It was his mother. He blinked again and found himself sitting alone beneath the pine, one hand held out before him, palm up. The hand was empty. Pick had disappeared.

He hesitated, heard his mother call again, then climbed hurriedly to his feet and scurried for the bushes at the end of his yard. He was too late getting there to avoid being caught. His mother was alarmed at first when she saw the knot on his forehead, then angry when she realized how it had happened. She bandaged him up, then sent him to his room.

He told his parents about Pick during dinner. They listened politely, glancing at each other from time to time, then told him everything was fine, it was a wonderful story, but that sometimes bumps on the head made us think things had happened that really hadn't. When he insisted that he had not made the story up, that it had really happened, they smiled some more and told him that they thought it was nice he had such a good imagination. Try as he might, he couldn't convince them that he was serious and finally, after a week of listening patiently to him, his mother sat down in the kitchen with cookies and milk one morning and told him she had heard enough.

"All little boys have imaginary friends, Jackie," his mother told him. "That's part of growing up. An imaginary friend is someone whom little boys can talk about their troubles when no one else will listen, someone they can tell their secrets to when they don't want to tell anyone else. Sometimes they can help a little boy get through some difficult times. Pick is your imaginary friend, Jackie. But you have to understand something. A friend like Pick belongs just to you, not to anyone else, and that is the way you should keep it."

He looked for Pick all that summer and into the fall, but he never found him. When his father took him into the park, he looked for Wartag under the old stone bridge. He never found him either. He checked the skies for Daniel, but never saw anything bigger than a robin. When he finally persuaded his father to walk all the way back into the darkest part of the woods—an effort that had his father using words Jack had not often heard him use before—there was no sign of the tree that imprisoned Desperado.

Eventually, Jack gave up looking. School and his friends claimed his immediate attention, Thanksgiving rolled around, and then it was Christmas. He got a new bike that year, a two-wheeler without training wheels, and an electric train. He thought about Pick, Daniel, Wartag, and Desperado from time to time, but the memory of what they looked like began to grow hazy. He forgot many of the particulars of his adventure that summer afternoon in the park, and the adventure itself took on the trappings of one of those fairy tales Pick detested so.

Soon, Jack pretty much quit thinking about the matter altogether.

He had not thought about it for months until today.

He wheeled his bike up the driveway of his house, surprised that he could suddenly remember all the details he had forgotten. They were sharp in his mind again, as sharp as they had been on the afternoon they had happened. If they had happened. If they had really happened. He hadn't been sure for a long time now. After all, he was only a little kid then. His parents might have been right; he might have imagined it all.

But then why was he remembering it so clearly now?

He went up to his room to think, came down long enough to have dinner, and quickly went back up again. His parents had looked at him strangely all during the meal—checking, he felt, to see if he was showing any early signs of expiring. It made him feel weird.

He found he couldn't concentrate on his homework, and anyway it was Friday night. He turned off the music on his tape player, closed his books, and sat there. The clock on his night-stand ticked softly as he thought some more about what had happened almost seven years ago. What might have happened, he corrected—although the more he thought about it, the more he was beginning to believe it really had. His common sense told him that he was crazy, but when you're dying you don't have much time for common sense.

Finally he got up, went downstairs to the basement rec room, picked up the phone, and called Waddy. His friend answered on the second ring, they talked about this and that for five minutes or so, and then Jack said, "Waddy, do you believe in magic?"

Waddy laughed. "Like in the song?"

"No, like in conjuring. You know, spells and such."

"What kind of magic?"

"What kind?"

"Yeah, what kind? There's different kinds, right? Black magic and white magic. Wizard magic. Witches brew. Horrible old New England curses. Fairies and Elves . . ."

"That kind. Fairies and Elves. Do you think there might be magic like that somewhere?"

"Are you asking me if I believe in Fairies and Elves?"

Jack hesitated. "Well, yeah."

"No."

"Not at all, huh?"

"Look, Jack, what's going on with you? You're not getting strange because of this dying business, are you? I told you not to worry about it."

"I'm not. I was just thinking . . ." He stopped, unable to tell Waddy exactly what he was thinking because it sounded so bizarre. After all, he'd never told anyone other than his parents about Pick.

There was a thoughtful silence on the other end of the line. "If you're asking me whether I think there's some kind of magic out there that saves people from dying, then I say yes. There is."

That wasn't exactly what Jack was asking, but the answer made him feel good anyway. "Thanks, Waddy. Talk to you later."

He hung up and went back upstairs. His father intercepted him on the landing and called him down again. He told Jack he had been talking with Dr. Muller. The doctor wanted him to come into the hospital on Monday for additional tests. He might have to stay for a few days. Jack knew what that meant. He would end up like Uncle Frank. His hair would fall out. He would be sick all the time. He would waste away to nothing. He didn't want any part of it. He told his father so and without waiting for his response ran back up to his room, shut the door, undressed, turned off the lights, and lay shivering in his bed in the darkness.

He fell asleep for a time, and it was after midnight when he came awake again. He had been dreaming, but he couldn't remember what the dreams were about. As he lay there, he thought he heard someone calling for him. He propped himself up on one arm and listened to the silence. He stayed that way for a long time, thinking.

Then he rose; dressed in jeans, pullover, and sneakers; and crept downstairs, trying hard not to make any noise. He got as far as the back porch. Sam was asleep on the threshold, and Jack didn't see him. He tripped over the dog and went down hard, striking his head on the edge of a table. He blacked out momentarily, then his eyes blinked open. Sam was cowering in one corner, frightened half to death. Jack was surprised and grateful that the old dog wasn't barking like crazy. That would have brought his parents awake in a minute. He patted Sam's head reassuringly, pulled on his windbreaker, and slipped out through the screen door.

Silence enveloped him. Jack crossed the damp green carpet of the backyard on cat's feet, pushed through the bushes at its end, and went into the park. It was a warm, windless night, and the moon shone full and white out of a cloudless sky, its silver light streaming down through breaks in the leafy trees to chase the shadows. Jack breathed the air and smelled pine needles and lilacs. He didn't know what he would tell his parents if they found him out there. He just knew he had to find Pick. Something inside whispered that he must.

He reached the old pine and peered beneath its spiky boughs. There was no sign of Pick. He backed out and looked about the park. Crickets chirped in the distance. The baseball diamonds stretched away before him east to the wall of the trees where the deep woods began. He could see the edge of the river bluff south, a ragged tear across the night sky. The cemetery was invisible beyond the rise of the park west. Nothing moved anywhere.

Jack came forward to the edge of the nearest ball diamond, anxious now, vaguely uneasy. Maybe this was a mistake.

Then a screech shattered the silence, and Jack caught sight of a shadow wheeling across the moonlight overhead.

"Daniel!" he shouted.

Excitement coursed through him. He began to run. Daniel was circling ahead, somewhere over the edge of the bluff. Jack watched him dive and soar skyward again. Daniel was directly over the old stone bridge where Wartag lived.

As he came up to the bridge he slowed warily, remembering anew the Troll's mean-looking eyes. Then he heard his name called, and he charged recklessly ahead. He skidded down the dampened slope by the bridge's west support and peered into the shadows.

"Jack Andrew McCall, where have you been, Boy?" he heard Pick demand without so much as a perfunctory hello. "I have been waiting for you for hours!"

Jack couldn't see him at first and groped his way through the blackness.

"Over here, Boy!"

His eyes began to adjust, and he caught sight of something hanging from the underside of the bridge on a hook, close against the support. It was a cage made out of stone. He reached for it and tilted it slightly so he could look inside.

There was Pick. He looked exactly the same as he had those seven years past—a tiny man with a reddish beard, green trousers and shirt, black belt and boots, and the peculiar hat of woven pine needles. It was too dark to be certain whether or not his face was flushed, but he was so excited that Jack was certain that it must be. He was dancing about on first one foot and then the other, hopping up and down as if his boots were on fire.

"What are you doing in there?" Jack asked him.

"What does it look like I'm doing in here—taking a bath?" Pick's temper hadn't improved any. "Now listen to me, Jack Andrew, and listen carefully because I haven't the time to say this more than once!" Pick was animated, his tiny voice shrill. "Wartag set a snare for me and I blundered into it. He sets such snares constantly, but I am usually too clever to get trapped in them. This time he caught me napping. He locked me in this cage earlier tonight and abandoned me to my fate. He has gone into the deep woods to unbalance the magic. He intends to set Desperado free!"

He jabbed at Jack with his finger. "You have to stop him!"

Jack started. "Me?"

"Yes, you! I don't have the means, locked away in here!"

"Well, I'll set you free then!"

Pick shook his head. "I'm afraid not. There's no locks or keys to a Troll cage. You just have to wait until it falls apart. Doesn't take long. Day or two at most. Wouldn't matter if you did free me, anyway. An Elf locked in a stone cage loses his magic for a moonrise. Everyone knows that!"

Jack gulped. "But, Pick, I can't . . ."

"Quit arguing with me!" the Elf stormed. "Take this!" He thrust something through the bars of the cage. It was a tiny silver pin. "Fasten it to your jacket. As long as you wear it, I can see what you see and tell you what to do. It will be the same as if I were with you. Now, hurry! Get after that confounded Troll!"

"But what about you?" Jack asked anxiously.

"Don't bother yourself about me! I'll be fine!"

"But . . ."

"Confound it, Jack! Get going!"

Jack did as he was told, spurred on by the urgency he heard in the other's voice. He forgot momentarily what had brought him to the park in the first place. Hurriedly, he stuck the silver pin through the collar of his jacket and wheeled away. He scrambled out of the ravine beneath the bridge, darted through the fringe of trees screening the ball diamonds, and sprinted across the outfields toward the dark wall of the woods east. He looked skyward once or twice for Daniel, but the owl had disappeared. Jack could feel his heart pounding in his chest and hear the rasp of his breathing. Pick was chattering from somewhere inside his left ear, urging him on, warning that he must hurry. When he tried to ask something of the Elf, Pick cut him off with an admonition to concentrate on the task at hand.

He reached the woods at the east end of the park and disappeared into the trees. Moonlight fragmented into shards of light that scattered through the heavy canopy of limbs. Jack charged up and down hills, skittered through leaf-strewn gullies, and watched the timber begin to thicken steadily about him.

Finally, he tripped over a tree root and dropped wearily to his knees, gasping for breath. When he lifted his head again, he was aware of two things. First, the woods about him had gone completely silent. Second, there was a strange greenish light that swirled like mist in the darkness ahead.

"We are too late, Jack Andrew," he heard Pick say softly. "That bubble-headed Troll has done his work! Desperado's free!"

Jack scrambled up quickly. "What do I do now, Pick?"

Pick's voice was calm. "Do, Jack? Why, you do what you must. You lock the Dragon away again!"

"Me?" Jack was aghast. "What am I supposed to do? I don't know anything about Dragons!"

"Stuff and nonsense! It's never too late to learn and there's not much to learn in any case. Let's have a look, Boy. Go on! Now!"

Jack moved ahead, his feet operating independently of his brain, which was screaming at him to get the heck out of there. The misted green light began to close about him, enveloping him, filling the whole of the woods about him with a pungent smell like burning rubber. There was a deadness to the night air, and the whisper of something old and evil that echoed from far back in the woods. Jack swallowed hard against his fear.

Then he pushed through a mass of brush into a clearing ringed with pine and stopped. There was something moving aimlessly on the ground a dozen yards ahead, something small and black and hairy, something that steamed like breath exhaled on a winter's morning.

"Oh dear, oh dear," murmured an invisible Pick.

"What is it?" Jack demanded anxiously.

Pick clucked his tongue. "It would appear that Wartag has learned the hard way what happens when you fool around with Dragons."

"That's Wartag?"

"More or less. Keep moving, Jack. Don't worry about the Troll."

But Jack's brain had finally regained control of his feet. "Pick, I don't want anything more to do with this. I can't fight a Dragon! I only came because I . . . because I found out that . . ."

"You were dying."

Jack stared. "Yes, but how . . . ?"

"Did I know?" Pick finished. "Tut and posh, boy! Why do you think you're here? Now listen up. Time to face a rather unpleasant truth. You have to fight the Dragon whether you want to or not. He knows that you're here now, and he will come for you if you try to run. He needs to be locked away, Jack. You can do it. Believe me, you can."

Jack's heart was pounding. "How?"

"Oh, it's simple enough. You just push him from sight, back him into his cage, and that's that! Now, let's see. There! To your left!"

Jack moved over a few steps and reached down. It was a battered old metal garbage can lid. "A shield!" declared Pick's voice in his ear. "And there!" Jack moved to his right and reached down again. It was a heavy stick that some hiker had discarded. "A sword!" Pick announced.

Jack stared at the garbage can lid and the stick in turn and then shook his head hopelessly. "This is ridiculous! I'm supposed to fight a Dragon with these?"

"These and what's inside you," Pick replied softly.

"But I can't . . ."

"Yes, you can."

"But . . ."

"Jack! You have to! You must!" Pick's words were harsh and

clipped, the tiny voice insistent. "Don't you understand? Haven't you been listening to me? This fight isn't simply to save me or this park! This fight is to save you!"

Jack was confused. Why was this a fight to save him? It didn't make any sense. But something deep inside him whispered that the Elf was telling him the truth. He swallowed his fear, choked down his self-doubt, hefted his makeshift sword and shield, and started forward. He went quickly, afraid that if he slowed he would give it up altogether. He knew somehow that he couldn't do that. He eased his way warily ahead through the trees, searching the greenish mist. Maybe the Dragon wasn't as scary as he imagined. Maybe it wasn't like the Dragons in the fairy tales. After all, would Pick send him into battle against something like that, something he wouldn't have a chance against?

There was movement ahead.

"Pick?" he whispered anxiously.

A shadow heaved upward suddenly out of the mist, huge and baleful, blocking out the light. Jack whirled and stumbled back.

There was Desperado. The Dragon rose against the night like a wall, weaving and swaying, a thing of scales and armor plates, a creature of limbs and claws, a being that was born of Jack's foulest nightmare. It had shape and no shape, formed of bits and pieces of fears and doubts that were drawn from a dozen memories best forgotten. It filled the pathway ahead with its bulk, as massive as the crooked, shaggy tree from which it had been freed.

Jack lurched to an unsteady halt, gasping. Eyes as hard as polished stone pinned him where he stood. He could feel the heat of the Dragon against his skin and at the same time an intense cold in the pit of his stomach. He was sweating and shivering all at once, and his breath threatened to seize up within his chest. He was no longer thinking; he was only reacting. Desperado's hiss sounded in the pit of his stomach. It told him he carried no shield, no sword. It told him he had no one to help him. It told him that he was going to die.

Fear spread quickly through Jack, filling him with its vile taste, leaving him momentarily helpless. He heard Pick's voice shriek wildly within his ear, "Quick, Jack, quick! Push the Dragon away!"

But Jack was already running. He bolted through the mist and trees as if catapulted, fleeing from Desperado. He was unable to help himself. He could no longer hear Pick; he could no longer reason. All he could think to do was to run as fast and as far from what confronted him as he could manage. He was only thirteen! He was only a boy! He didn't want to die!

He broke free of the dark woods and tore across the ball diamonds toward the bridge where Pick was caged. The sky was all funny, filled with swirling clouds and glints of greenish light. Everything was a mass of shadows and mist. He screamed for Pick to help him. But as he neared the bridge, its stone span seemed to yawn open like some giant's mouth, and the Dragon rose up before him, blocking his way. He turned and ran toward the Indian burial mounds, where the ghosts of the Sinnissippi danced through the shadows to a drumbeat only they could hear. But again the Dragon was waiting. It was waiting as well at the cemetery, slithering through the even rows of tombstones and markers like a snake. It was waiting amid the shrub-lined houses of Woodlawn, wherever Jack turned, wherever he fled. Jack ran from one end of the park to the other, and everywhere, the Dragon Desperado was waiting.

"Pick!" he screamed over and over, but there was no answer. When he finally thought to look down for the silver pin, he discovered that he had lost it.

"Oh, Pick!" he sobbed.

Finally he quit running, too exhausted to go on. He found himself back within the deep woods, right where he had started. He had been running, yet he hadn't moved at all. Desperado was before him still, a monstrous, shapeless terror that he could not escape. He could feel the Dragon all around him, above and below, and even within. The Dragon was inside his head, crushing him, blinding him, stealing away his life . . .

Like a sickness.

He gasped in sudden recognition.

Like the sickness that was killing him.

This fight is to save you, Pick had told him. The Elf's words came back to him, their purpose and meaning revealed with a clarity that was unmistakable.

Jack went a little bit crazy then. He cried out, overwhelmed by a rush of emotions he could not begin to define. He shed his fear as he would a burdensome coat and charged Desperado, heedless now of any danger to himself, blind to the Dragon's monstrous size. To his astonishment, the walking stick and the garbage can lid flared white with fire and turned into the sword and shield he had been promised. He could feel the fire spread from them into him, and it felt as if he had been turned to iron as well. He flung himself at Desperado, hammering into the Dragon with his weapons. Push him back! Lock him away!

The great gnarled shapes of the Dragon and tree seemed to join. Night and mist closed about. Jack was swimming through a fog of jagged images. He heard sounds that might have come from anywhere, and there was within him a sense of something yielding. He thrust out, feeling Desperado give way before his attack. The feeling of heat, the smell of burning rubber, the scrape of scales and armor plates intensified and filled his senses.

Then Desperado simply disappeared. The sword and shield turned back into the walking stick and garbage can lid, the greenish mist dissipated into night, and Jack found himself clinging to the shaggy, bent trunk of the massive old tree that was the Dragon's prison.

He stumbled back, dumbstruck.

"Pick!" he shouted one final time, but there was no answer.

Then everything went black and he was falling.

———

Jack was in the hospital when he came awake. His head was wrapped with bandages and throbbed painfully. When he asked, one of the nurses on duty told him it was Saturday. He had suffered a bad fall off his back porch in the middle of the night, she said, and his parents hadn't found him until early this morning when they had brought him in. She added rather cryptically that he was a lucky boy.

His parents appeared shortly after, both of them visibly upset, alternately hugging him and scolding him for being so stupid. He was still rather groggy, and not much of what they said registered. They left when the nurse interceded, and he went back to sleep.

The next day, Dr. Muller appeared. He examined Jack, grunted and muttered as he did so, drew blood, sent him down for X-rays, brought him back up, grunted and muttered some more, and left. Jack's parents came by to visit and told him they would be keeping him in the hospital for a few more days, just in case. Jack told them he didn't want any therapy while he was there, and they promised there wouldn't be.

On Monday morning, his parents and Dr. Muller came to see him together. His mother cried and called him "Jackie" and his father grinned like the Cheshire Cat. Dr. Muller told him that the additional tests had been completed while he was asleep. The results were very encouraging. His blood disorder did not appear to be life-threatening. They had caught it early enough that it could be treated.

"You understand, Jack, you'll have to undergo some mild therapy," Dr. Muller cautioned. "But we can take care of that right here. There's nothing to worry about."

Jack smiled. He wasn't worried. He knew he was okay. He'd known it from the moment he'd pushed Desperado back into that tree. That was what the fight to lock away the Dragon had been all about. It had been to lock away Jack's sickness. Jack wasn't sure whether or not Pick had really lost his magic that night or simply let Jack think so. But he was sure about one thing—Pick had deliberately brought him back into the park and made him face the Dragon on his own. That was the special magic that his friend had once told him would be needed. It was the magic that had allowed him to live.

He went home at the end of the week and returned to school the next. When he informed Waddy Wadsworth that he wasn't dying after all, his friend just shrugged and said he'd told him so.

Dr. Muller advised him to take it easy and brought him in for the promised therapy throughout the summer months. But his hair didn't fall out, he didn't lose weight, and the headaches and vision loss disappeared. Eventually Dr. Muller declared him cured, and the treatments came to an end.

He never saw Pick again. Once or twice he thought he saw Daniel, but he wasn't certain. He looked for the tree that imprisoned Desperado, but he couldn't find it. He didn't look for Wartag at all. When he was a few years older, he went to work for the park service during the summers. It made him feel that he was giving something back to Pick. Sometimes when he was in the park, he could sense the other's presence. It didn't matter that he couldn't see his friend; it was enough just to know that he was there.

He never said anything to anyone about the Elf, of course. He wasn't going to make that mistake again.

It was like his mother had told him when he was little. A friend like Pick belonged only to him, and that was the way he should keep it.

PATRICK ROTHFUSS

THIS STORY IS SOMETHING OF AN EXCEPTION FOR ME.

Actually, that's a vast understatement. The truth is, there's nothing about this story that's normal for me.

Normally I write multilayered epic-meta-fantastical thingers that clock in at a quarter million words or more.

This story has a single plot, and it's only about seventeen hundred words.

Normally it takes me a long time to finish something—months if not years.

I wrote this story in a single day.

Normally I miss deadlines like a storm trooper misses Jedi.

But I actually got this story in to Shawn *months* ahead of when I said I would.

Normally I revise like . . . well . . . like a Rothfuss, really. I take a story through dozens if not hundreds of revisions before I'm happy with it.

But once I was done with this story on that first day, it was really, really finished. I changed about eight words and that's it.

The story itself is a little odd. It's from an odd perspective, and it covers a vast scope of time. The main character is odd. The language is odd. I've read it out loud a couple times, and I've found the sound of it to be . . . well . . . odd. Rhythmic. Almost like a chant.

For all that, I have to say I'm a little proud of it.

Anyway, that's all I'll say. I don't like trying to explain my stories. Either you'll like it, or you won't. You're entitled to your opinion either way without me trying to tell you what to think.

Patrick Rothfuss

HOW OLD HOLLY CAME TO BE

Patrick Rothfuss

In the beginning, there was the wood.

It was strong wood, and old. And it grew beside a stream, by a tower all of stone.

There was warm sun, which was good. There were climbing vines, which were bad. There was wind, which was neither. It merely made leaves turn and branches sway.

There was also the lady. She was neither. She came to the tower. She turned the earth and made a garden. She cut the other trees and burned them in the tower.

But the holly tree she did not cut. The holly grew and spread its branches in the open space. And that was good.

———

There was summer, which was warm. There was winter, which was cold. There were birds, which were neither. They built nests and sometimes sang.

There was also the lady. She was neither warm nor cold. The holly grew beside the stream, its branches spreading dappled shade.

The lady sat beneath the holly reading books. She climbed the holly, peering into nests. She leaned against the holly, napping in the dappled shade.

These things were neither. None of them were warm or cold. None of them were good or bad.

————

There was day, which was light. There was night, which was dark. There was the moon, which was both light and dark.

There was a man. He was both. He came to the tower. He and the lady sat beneath the holly. They were both beneath the holly. They were both.

The man said to the lady. The man showed to the lady. The man sang to the lady.

The man left the tower. The lady left the tower. They both left the tower. Both.

————

The garden grew. The garden, left untended, changed. The garden grew and changed and then the garden was no more.

The tower did not grow. The tower, left untended, did not change. The tower did not change and stayed.

The holly grew. It did not change. It stayed.

————

The lady came to the tower.

She cut a branch of holly for a wreath, which was bad. She rooted up the climbing vines and tore them from the branches, which was good. She turned the earth and made a garden, which was neither.

She sat beneath the holly reading books and wept. She sat beneath the holly in the sun and wept. She sat beneath the holly in the rain and wept. She sat beneath the holly and the moon and wept.

These things were neither.

She sat beneath the holly and she sang.

She sat beneath the holly and she sang.

She sat beneath the holly and she sang.

The Lady sat beneath the holly, which was good. The Lady wept, which was bad.

The Lady sang, which was good. The Lady left the tower, which was bad. The tower stayed, which was neither.

The holly changed, which was both.

The holly stayed. There was a stream, which was beautiful. There was wind, which was beautiful. There were birds, which were beautiful.

The Lady came to the tower, which was good. She turned the earth, which was good. The Lady sang, which was beautiful. There were tomatoes, and the Lady ate them, which was good.

The Lady sat beneath the holly reading books, which was beautiful and good.

There was sun and rain. There was day and night. There was summer and winter.

The holly grew, and that was good. The Lady sat upon his gnarled roots and fished, and that was good. The Lady watched the squirrels play among his leaves and laughed, and that was good.

The Lady turned her foot upon a stone, and that was bad. She leaned against his trunk and frowned, and that was bad. The Lady sang a song to holly. Holly listened. Holly bent. The Lady sang and branch became a walking stick, and that was good.

She walked and leaned on him, and that was good.

The Lady climbed into the highest reaches of his branches, looking into nests, and that was good. The Lady pricked her hands upon his thorns, and that was bad. She sucked the bright bead from her thumb, and slipped, and screamed, and fell.

And holly bent. And holly bent. And Holly bent his boughs to catch her.

And the Lady smiled, and that was beautiful. But there was blood upon her hands, and that was bad. But then the Lady looked upon her blood, and laughed, and sang. And there were berries bright as blood, and that was good.

The Lady spoke to Holly, which was good. The Lady told to Holly, which was good. She sang and sang and sang to Holly, which was good.

The Lady was afraid, and that was bad. She watched the water of the stream. She looked into the sky. She listened to the wind, and was afraid, and that was bad.

The Lady turned to Holly. The Lady laid her hand upon his trunk. The Lady spoke to Holly. Holly bent, and that was good.

The Lady drew a breath and sang a song to Holly. She sang a song and Holly burrowed deep into the earth. She sang a song and all along the stream there sprung new holly from the ground. She sang and all around the tower climbed new holly. She sang and up the tower grew new holly.

The Lady sang and they were both. Around them both there grew new holly. New holly spread and stretched and wrapped the tower. New holly grew and opened groves of leaves against the sky. She sang until no tower could be seen, and that was good.

The Lady stood beside Old Holly, smiling. They looked out at their new-grown holly grove, and it was good.

Old Holly stood beside the stream and watched the land below. He stood beside the edge of his new grove and felt the earth below and knew that it was good. He felt the sun upon his leaves and knew that it was good.

The wind brushed up against him. The wind was bad. He bent. He bent his boughs against the tower window.

The Lady came to stand beside him. She looked upon the land below. There was a hint of smoke upon the sky. Far away were shapes that moved across the hills.

There were great black wolves, with mouths of fire. There were men who had been bent halfway into birds. They were both, and bad.

Worst of all there was a shadow bent to look as if it were a man. Old Holly felt the ground beneath the last grow sick, and try to pull away.

The Lady stepped behind his trunk. She was afraid. She peered out at the land below. The shapes came closer, which was bad.

Old Holly bent. Old Holly bent toward the Lady.

The Lady looked at him. The Lady looked upon the land below. The Lady laid her hand upon his trunk, and that was good. The Lady asked. Old Holly bent again.

The Lady sang. She sang Old Holly. She said to him. She said her words. She said.

Old Holly bent and he became a man. He was both, and it was good.

The Lady sang, new holly bent and it became a spear, and it was good.

Old Holly bent his boughs and took the spear. Old Holly stretched his roots and strode across the stream. Old Holly struck the wolves and pinned them to the earth. He bent his boughs and brought another spear. They bit at him, and that was neither. He clutched the men bent into birds, and pulled at them, and tore them all apart.

And last there came the shadow thing, and it was bad. When it moved across the ground he felt the earth attempt to crawl away. It sickened and it shrank away from contact with the shadow thing.

Old Holly bent his boughs again, and brought a spear, its wood of living green. Its blade as bright as berry blood. This he drove into the shadow thing, and held it to the earth, and watched it howl and burn and die, and this was good.

Old Holly came back to the tower, and it was good. The Lady smiled and sang to him, and it was good. The Lady looked upon his wounds. She wept, and sang to them, and then he bent, and that was good.

The Lady said that she must leave, and that was bad. She said she would return, and that was good. She said that it was dangerous, and Old Holly stretched his roots to stand across the stream.

The Lady shook her head. She said to stay. She said to stay here with the tower. She said to keep it safe for her return.

Old Holly stretched his roots until he stood beside the tower. His Lady went inside. She came outside. She said goodbye.

Old Holly bent, and from a branch, he made for her a walking stick of green wet wood. Old Holly bent, and from his boughs, he wove a crown for her, all bright with berry. Old Holly bent, and as he was a man, he brushed her cheek with his own bark-rough hand.

The Lady wept, and laughed, and left. And that was both and neither and all and other.

Old Holly stayed. The tower stayed. Old Holly stayed beside the tower. Old Holly all around the tower.

Old Holly stayed, and that was good.

The summer left.

The winter left.

The garden left.

Old Holly stayed, and that was good.

The bones of the wolves left.

The roof of the tower left.

The glass in the windows left.

Old Holly stayed, and that was good.

The stream left.

The tower left.

Old Holly stayed.

Tad Williams

As is usual even with a short, purposefully lighthearted story, several things led to "The Old Scale Game."

First off, I love buddy pictures and buddy stories. Most of us do. Mismatched buddies, better still. Nothing original there, but you've got to start somewhere.

I also have a thing for the idea of retired dragonslayers. I mean, if what you do is kill dragons, there's going to be a point where you get too old to ply your trade. (That's if you're good. If you're not, you've already been charbroiled a long time ago and the issue is academic.) I mean, it's dire, hard work killing a full-grown dragon. At least I assume so, not having done it myself recently.

And last, there was a film from back in the early '70s, if memory serves, with Lou Gossett and James Garner, about a couple of pals—one black, one white—pulling a scam whereby the white one pretends the black one is a runaway slave he's caught, so he takes him to the authorities and earns the bounty, then sneaks back and helps his friend escape, and they split the money and then go do it again somewhere else.

Actually, I falsely remembered the title as *The OLD Skin Game*, but even when I realized it, I left the "Old" in, because it adds to the sort of we're-having-fun-here feeling. Once these ideas bumped into each other, they began to turn into something, and I had to start figuring out how to make it all happen, who'd be in it, and also how to end it. Fortunately for me, as the story went along it took a decidedly not-quite-historical turn (although I threw in a lot of real English locations because they it gave it the right feel, and because English place names are just inherently amusing for some reason) which made it easier to come up with an extremely silly but (at least for me) satisfying ending for all involved.

And the rest is, if not history, I hope a pleasant next ten or twenty minutes of your life.

You're welcome.

Tad Williams

THE OLD SCALE GAME

Tad Williams

"Flee or be broiled to crackling! Those are your only choices!" The monster rustled in the depths of the cave. Its voice was loud because it was large, and dry because centuries of breathing deadly fire had roughened its throat.

"Neither, if you please." The man in armor waited as patiently as he could, hoping he was far enough back from the entrance that he would not actually broil if the tenor of conversation failed to improve. "I wish to discuss a proposition."

"A *what?*" The outrage was unfeigned. "I had heard that there were knights abroad in this miserable modern age who practiced such perversities, but I never dreamed I should ever suffer such a foul offer myself! Prepare to be radiantly heated, young fool!"

"I am not remotely young, and I don't think I'm a fool either," the knight said. "And it's not that kind of proposition. Ye gods, fellow, I haven't even seen you yet, not to mention the smell of you is not pleasing, at least to a human being."

When the dragon spoke after a longish silence, there was perhaps a touch of hurt feelings in its voice. "Ah. Not that kind of proposition." Another pause. "How do I know that when I come out you will not attempt to slay me?"

"If I felt sure I could slay you, I wouldn't be here talking. I give you my word as a knight that you are safe from me as long as you offer me no harm."

"Hmmmph." That noise, accompanied by a puff of steam, was followed shortly by the sound of something long and scaly dragging itself over stone as the dragon emerged from the cave. The knight noted that, although the great worm had clearly seen better days, his scales dingy and nicked, his color decidedly less than robust, he was still quite big enough and probably quite hot enough to keep negotiation more appealing than attack.

"I am Guldhogg," declared the worm, each word echoing sonorously across the hillside. "Why do you seek me? Have you grown tired of living?"

"Tired of starving, to be quite frank, and even recreational drinking is beginning to lose its charms." The knight made a courtly bow. "My name is Sir Blivet of no fixed address, until recently a retired (and impoverished) dragon slayer. This was not a happy state of affairs—in fact, I had recently begun to consider a serious return to strong drink—but lately it's worsened. I've been dragged out of retirement by the people of Handselmansby in order to destroy you—they offered me a rather interesting sum . . ."

The dragon reared to nearly the height of the treetops. "You coward! You have foresworn yourself!" He made a rumbling noise, and a cloud of fire belched from his jaws, but before the stream of flame had gone more than a few feet Guldhogg began to cough. The fire flickered and died. A puff of steam, more wisp than cloud, floated up into the morning sky. "Just a m-m-moment," the dragon said. "Give me a chance to c-c-catch my breath, f-foul knight." He had stopped coughing, but had begun hiccoughing instead. At each explosion another steampuff spun lazily into the air. "Honestly, I will broil you very . . ." *Hiccough.* "I will . . ." *Hiccough.* "Broil you very thoroughly . . ." Again, a hiccough.

"Noble Guldhogg, most vintage of worms, spare me this tosh." Sir Blivet sat down on the ground. He had not even drawn his sword. "The people of Handselmansby may not know you are old and unwell, but I do. You could no more broil me than you could earn a cardinal's red hat from the pontiff of Rome."

"*Knight of a dog!*" The dragon drew himself up once more. "Hmmmph. I mean: *Dog of a knight!* Perhaps I do have a bit of a problem with my flame just now, but I can still destroy you! Have I not my claws and teeth, or at least most of them? Can I not fly, with a fair tailwind and occasional stops for rest? Do not think me so easily defeated, insulting and unkind human person."

"I agree, mighty Guldhogg. You are still a formidable foe, even in your age and infirmity."

"Yes! Yes, I am!" The dragon leaned forward, his great yellow eyes narrowing. When he spoke, he sounded a bit worried. "Am I really such a laughingstock? The time was once when Guldhogg's name was enough to set women screaming and children crying."

"And it still is," said Sir Blivet. "The . . . falloff in your skills is not widely known. In fact, the only reason it's known to me is because I did a little investigation as I was trying to think of some way I could avoid fighting you. Because . . ." Blivet removed his helmet, revealing hair and beard that, although it could have been called salt-and-pepper, contained far more salt than pepper. Furthermore, although the hair on his head might once have covered a large territory, it had now largely conceded the front and top of the knight's scalp and was retreating rather hurriedly toward the back of his head. "As you can see—and which contributes not a little to the unhappy state of my own affairs—I am not so young myself."

Guldhogg squinted. "By my great scaly ancestors, you aren't, are you?"

"No. I really didn't want anything to do with this whole thing, but poverty makes powerful arguments."

The beast shook his long head. "So despite what the advancing years have done to you, Sir Knight, you decided to attack a poor old dragon. For shame, sir. For shame."

"Oh, for the love of my good Lord Jesu!" The man in the tarnished suit of armor shook his head in irritation. "Don't you listen? I just *said* I don't want to fight you. In fact, I would like to offer a bargain—a mutually beneficial bargain, at that. Will you pay proper attention?"

Guldhogg's eyes narrowed again, but this time it seemed to be in careful thought instead of suspicion. At last the great worm nodded.

"I will listen, Sir Knight."

"Call me Sir Blivet. Or even just Blivet. After all, we're going to be working together."

The wealthy burghers of Handselmansby, an up-and-coming market town whose Chamber of Commerce had aspirations to make it another Shoebury, or even a Thetford, threw a small celebration for Blivet at the Rump and Hock Inn, with a no-host mead bar and finger foods.

"Handselmansby is grateful for your courage and prowess, good sir knight," said the mayor as he handed over the promised bag of gold. "But if you destroyed the terrible worm Guldhogg, where is its carcass?"

"Ah," said Blivet. "Yes. You see, although my last blow was a mortal one, the fell beast had just enough strength to fly away, leaking blood and fire in what I promise you was a very unsurvivable sort of way."

As the knight reached the five-mile post on the road out of Handselmansby a large shadow dropped from the sky and landed with an awkward thump beside him. It took Guldhogg a few moments to catch his breath before he could speak—he clearly hadn't done much flying in recent years. "So it went well? They gave you the money?"

"Yes. And I have already divided it in half." Blivet showed him the sacks and offered him one. "Here is your share."

Guldhogg spilled some gold into his immense clawed forepaw. "Lovely. I haven't had any of this shiny stuff for a bit. Not quite enough to lie on top of, of course, but better than nothing." He sighed. "The only problem is, of course, now I've got nowhere to keep it. Having been driven out of the Greater Handselmansby Area, I mean. Where my cave was."

Sir Blivet nodded. "I agree, that is unfortunate, but I'm certain you can find a new home somewhere else in the greater Danelaw. In fact, I'll need to find a new place myself, because otherwise once the news of my successful dragon slaying spreads I'll have people banging on my door every week with new quests. I doubt I shall be so lucky again in finding a reasonable partner, and I no longer have any interest in *real* anti-monster combat—those days are far, far behind me. To be honest I want only to find a small but regular source of income so I can settle down and enjoy my golden years. Maybe I'd even take a wife . . ."

Guldhogg looked a bit hurt. "You seek a new and reasonable partner, Sir Blivet? I would like to think of myself as more than just reasonable—in fact, I flatter myself that I gave more than was even bargained for. Did I not spout fire most impressively above the treetops so the townsfolk could see how fierce was our battle? Did I not bellow and roar until the welkin itself shook as if it were fevered? And now I am without a home and except for this gold, just as in want of an income as you are."

"I've never really known what a welkin is, so I'll take your word on that part," Blivet said politely. "But otherwise you are completely correct, honorable Guldhogg: you were a more than amenable opponent, and should we ever find ourselves in a position to do something like this again . . ."

After a long silent interval had passed, the dragon cleared his throat, loosing a tiny, hot cumulus. "You seem to have stopped in mid-sentence. Did you forget what you were going to say?"

"No. Come along with me for a while," says Blivet, climbing up into his saddle. "I have just had an idea I would like to discuss with you, but I would prefer we were not observed here together, counting the people of Handselmansby's money."

Over the next few years, East Anglia and the Danelaw were beset with a terrible rash of dragonings. Although no citizens were killed, a great deal of property loss occurred, especially the theft of sheep and other edible creatures. The famous dragonslayer Sir Blivet found himself in constant demand from Benfleet all the way up to Torksey and beyond. Even the King of York asked Blivet to intervene when a particularly unpleasant monster (called the Wheezing Worm by the frightened townsfolk) took up residence in Kirkham Gorge. The veteran dragon-foe was able to drive the creature out again in only a matter of days, and was rewarded handsomely by the king for it, at which point the knight modestly quit York again.

Oddly, as these new boom years for monster hunting continued, they did not seem to benefit other dragonslayers quite as much as they did Sir Blivet. When Percy of Pevensey and Gwydion Big-Axe came searching for the beasts who were causing so much unhappiness in the East Midlands, they could find scarcely a trace, despite Sir Blivet's willingness to tell them exactly where to look. The two great western wormhunters rode away disappointed, as did many others. Only Blivet seemed able to locate the beasts, and soon he could scarcely rid one area of its wormish scourge before being called to help another dragon-troubled populace, often quite close by. It seemed the dragon peril was spreading, and the knight spent far more time on his horse than under a roof.

"To be honest, Guldhogg, my friend," Blivet admitted to the dragon one day in their forest camp, "I'm getting a bit tired of this whole dodge." They were taking a break, having just finished adding their latest fees to a pile of chests and caskets so heavy with coin they now needed a horse-drawn wagon just to haul it all from town to town and vale to vale. "Not that it hasn't been fun."

Guldhogg nodded as he nibbled on a side of mutton. "I know what you mean, Bliv, old man. I wonder if we don't need to expand our territory a bit. I swear I'm seeing the same peasants over and over."

"Well, one peasant does look much like another," Blivet explained. "Especially when they're pointing up and screaming. They're like foot soldiers that way."

"It's not just that. I think some of them recognized me during the last job. A family that must have moved here from Barrowby—you remember Barrowby, don't you?"

"Where you stole the chancellor's horse out of his stable and left the bones on his roof?"

"That's the place. Anyway, when I flew over the town here yesterday, spouting fire and bellowing, I heard this fellow originally from Barrowby shout, 'I've seen that bloody dragon before!' Quite rude, really."

"Indeed." Blivet stared at his pile of gold where it sat on the wagon. He frowned, considering. "So you recommend pastures new?"

"Seems like a good idea. Don't want to push our luck."

But Blivet was tugging at his beard, still troubled. "Yes, but as I was saying, Guldhogg, it goes further than that for me. I'm a bit weary of all this tramping around. The idea of moving on to the south, or out to the West Midlands . . . well, to be honest, I think I'd rather have some peace and stability—maybe even find a nice woman my age and settle down. We've made almost enough money. One more job should secure both our financial futures." He paused. "In fact, I believe I can even see a way we might fulfill both tasks at once—a last top-up of our bank accounts as well as a permanent residence for both of us! How is that for dispatching several birds with one projectile?"

"A home for both of us? I'm touched, Blivet. But how?"

"The thing is, although you are by far the most profitable of them, you're not the only beast who has been making things difficult for folk around here. This is Tenth Century England, after all—a few years ago I could scarcely stand up and stretch without nudging a wyvern or a griffin or somesuch. They've all gotten a bit scarcer now, but there are still a good few other monsters scattered around the island."

"Of course," says Guldhogg. "I know that. It's one of the reasons people don't seem surprised when I keep turning up in new places pretending to be a different dragon than the last time. Honestly, Blivet, you sound as though you're unhappy there are still a few of us left."

The knight leaned close, although there was nobody in sight for miles across the windswept heath. "Just a few miles down the road, near Fiskhaven by the coast, dwells a terrible ogre by the name of Ljotunir."

"What a strange name!" said Guldhogg.

"Yes, well, the point is, he's apparently a nasty fellow who's got the town of Fiskhaven all upset. I'm told it's a lovely place, clean sea air, several very nice beachfront castles going for rock-bottom prices since the collapse of the dried herring market. And Ljotunir is tough but not invincible. He's about twelve feet tall and quite strong, of course, but not fireproof . . . if you see where I'm going."

"No," said Guldhogg a bit sourly. "No, Bliv, my dear old bodkin, I'm afraid I don't."

"Simple enough, Guld, my reptilian chum. We can't settle down because everywhere we go, I make a big show of driving you away or even killing you. That means you can't very well hang around with me afterward. But if we can drive away this ogre together . . . well, we'll be paid handsomely again, but this time *you* won't have done any harm, so we'll *both* be able to stay on in Fiskhaven. We can buy a castle and land, settle down, and enjoy the fruits of our partnership—" he gestured to the heavily laden wagon, "—in peace and quiet, and even more importantly *in one place,* as befits individuals of our mature and sensible years. No more tramping."

"And what am I supposed to eat?" asked Guldhogg. "After all, it is devouring the local livestock that usually makes me *dracona non grata* in the first place." The great worm suddenly grew fretful. "You don't really think my presence is noxious, do you, Blivvy? I mean, we've known each other a while now. You can speak sooth."

"You are lovely company," the knight said firmly. "Only the shortsighted, the dragon-bigoted, or the just plain rude would suggest otherwise. But you didn't let me finish describing my plan, which includes provision for your sustenance. We have money, Guldy. Once the ogre has been dispatched, we will settle in Fiskhaven and become farmers! We'll buy sheep and raise them. You may eat as many as you need, as long as you leave the little ones to grow up into bigger ones—then there will always be more sheep to eat. That's how farming works, you know."

"Really? That's marvelous!" Guldhogg shook his great scaly head. "What will they think of next?"

The battle with the terrible ogre Ljotunir raged for days, ending at last in the hills high above Fiskhaven, so that the whole of the vale rang with the sounds of combat. When it was over and Sir Blivet was about to go down to the town and collect his ogre-slaying money, he noticed that Guldhogg looked preoccupied, even sad.

"What's wrong, dear old chum?"

"It's the ogre. He's so miserable!" Guldhogg nodded toward Ljotunir, who was sitting against the trunk of an oak tree, making loud snuffling sounds.

Blivet took off his heavy helmet and walked across the clearing to where Ljotunir sat—the tree was leaning alarmingly from the weight. The monster's cheeks were indeed wet with tears. "What ails you, good sir ogre?" Sir Blivet asked. "Are you regretting having settled for a one-quarter share? You understand that the risk of this business is ours, don't you? And that we have built up our reputation over several years? But perhaps instead you are mourning your lost reputation as an unbeatable and fearsome giant?"

"It's not that, and it's not the money." Ljotunir sniffed and wiped his face with a kerchief the size of a tablecloth. (In fact, it *was* a tablecloth.) "It's . . . well, I don't really have any place to go anymore. I agreed to this because I didn't want to fight. Frankly, I haven't been myself the last century—I have the cruelest sort of aches and pains in my joints from this seaside air, Sir Knight, and the noise of the wind keeps me from sleeping most nights—but I'm still very fond of the place. Where will I go now? How will I live?" Alarmingly, the giant burst into tears again, his sobs shaking a nest full of bewildered young squirrels out of the leaning oak and onto the ground.

"Here now," Blivet soothed him. "Surely your share of the reward money will be more than enough to purchase you a lovely stone hut in the wilderness somewhere. Perhaps you should move farther north—I hear that the arctic air of the Orkneys is lovely and dry, which should be easier on your infirmity."

"Dry, yes, but cold enough to freeze the berries off a basilisk!" said the ogre cheerlessly. "That would play hob with my joints, now wouldn't it?" Again his chest heaved.

"Oh, look at the poor fellow!" Guldhogg said, coming up. "He's so sad! His little face is all scrunched up! Isn't there anything we can do?"

Blivet examined the sobbing giant, whose "little face" was the size of the knight's war-shield. At last Blivet sighed, turned to the dragon, and said, "I may have a solution. But first I'll need that cask of ale."

"Really?" asked Guldhogg, who was interested to see what odd human thing Blivet would do next. "What are you going to do with it?"

"Drink it," the knight said. "Most of it, anyway."

Sir Blivet had just realized that if he wanted to make his friend Guldhogg happy, they were going to have to let the now-homeless ogre join them—which meant that, once again, they would be moving on in the morning.

It didn't seem too bad at first. Ljotunir's presence meant that Guldhogg could take the occasional week off from menacing townsfolk, leaving that strenuous chore to the Ljotunir, and that they could even go back to some localities they had already scourged of dragons (well, one dragon, anyway), but which would now need their help with ogre infestations. But Blivet himself was not getting any days off, and they were doing a great deal of tramping from county to county.

Guldhogg couldn't help noticing that the knight drank a great deal of ale every night before falling asleep now, or that his conversation, quite expansive only a few weeks earlier, was now reduced mostly to, "Forsooth, whatever."

And things were getting worse.

News of the confidence game that Blivet and Guldhogg were running in the middle of England had begun to spread around the island—not among the townsfolk who were its targets but the within the nation's large community of fabulous, mythical, and semi-imaginary animals. These creatures could not help noticing that two very large members of their kind, a dragon and an ogre, had found a way not only to survive, but also to thrive. As word of this breakthrough got around, Blivet and his friends soon found that everywhere they went they were getting business propositions from various haunts and horrors down on their luck or otherwise in need of a change.

"I know it will be a bit hard on us, Blivet old friend," said Guldhogg. "But I can't help it—I know how these creatures *feel*. It's been a long, bad time for mythical monsters, and it's only going to get worse when the Renaissance shows up in a few hundred years."

"But we can't use all of them," Blivet protested. "What right-thinking town council is going to hire a knight to slay a couple of cobbler's elves?"

"We can find work for them. Say, look at your boots, Blivvy. Wouldn't you like to have those re-soled?"

Blivet sighed. "Pass me that ale, will you?"

Before the year had passed, Blivet and Guldhogg had added to their enterprise (mostly at the dragon's urging) a cockatrice, a pair of hippogriffs who were passionately in love with each other and had decided to run away from their hippogriffic families, plus an expanding retinue of shellycoats, lubber men, bargests, and suchlike other semi-mythical folk. What had once been a compact, convenient man-and-dragon partnership was becoming a sort of strange covert parade traveling from county to county across the center of England.

Guldhogg had hoped the added numbers would make their business easier, because they could now revisit places they had already saved several more times (and not only from ogres or chimeras, but also from less-feared but still unpleasant fates, like a long and painful season of being harried by bogbears). Any gain in income, however, had been offset by the need to keep their gigantic, semi-mythical menagerie hidden, on the move, and—most importantly—fed as they crossed back and forth across the English midlands.

The biggest problem, of course, was that Blivet himself had simply grown weary of marching from town to town, pretending to kill things. He may also have been slightly depressed to find that instead of revering him as a noble dragonslayer, his countrymen now viewed him as little more than a jumped-up exterminator, chasing shellycoats and leprechauns away as if they were so many rats.

Guldhogg noticed that Blivet was becoming less and less interested in keeping the now massive operation hidden. The movement of their troop from city to city was threatening to become more parade than stealthy exercise. Already a few humans had joined their train, giving the whole thing more of a feeling of a holiday fair than a serious moneymaking enterprise. Even a dragon could see that it was only a matter of time until some of the townsfolk realized just how badly they had been cozened.

And Guldhogg wasn't the only one who could see what was coming: Blivet had begun buying his ale in bulk.

The irony, not lost on Guldhogg, was that they could probably have made more money selling the local people tickets to see all the strange animals—they were all happy enough to dump considerable sums at ragged local fairs—but Blivet and the dragon had to work from dawn until long after midnight each day just getting their charges fed and keeping them moving; any greater degree of organization would have been impossible.

Then a narrowly averted tragedy in Smethwick, when a family of werewolves left the troop to hunt for supper and ran into a children's crusade, finally made it clear to Guldhogg that things had to change. (The near-catastrophe just seemed to make Blivet even more thirsty.)

The dragon recognized that his knightly friend was at a serious crossroads, probably one more septic basilisk bite away from leaving the now-sprawling enterprise behind in search of a calmer life. Guldhogg was an old dragon, and although he was long past his own mating days, he also recognized his friend had a need for nurturing companionship of the sort that even a vast army of bog-bears, ogres, and camelopards could not provide.

Two of the newest members of the troop were articulate ravens, raucous, sly, and clever. In exchange for a few shiny articles out of Guldhogg's now large collection, they agreed to undertake some work for him, hunting the highways and byways of Late Dark Ages Britain for a situation that met the dragon's specifications.

One day, while the troop was camped by the River Derwent to water the selkies, the ravens returned with the news Guldhogg had been waiting for.

"Haunted Forest?" Blivet looked doubtfully at the sign (and perhaps slightly unsteadily, since he had already been into the ale that morning). Even from the outskirts, the forest the sign announced looked likely to breed nightmares. The trees of the wood grew extremely close together, and they were also extremely large and old, casting such deep shadows that it was almost hard to believe there was turf beneath them. The location beneath lowering mountains was stone silent, and the air of the little valley, far from civilization but close to a major thoroughfare, was dreadful enough to put even the basilisks off their breakfasts (truly not an easy thing to do). "Looks nasty. What monster lurks in here?" the knight asked. "And even if it might be of use to our venture, why should *I* go look for it instead of you or Ljotunir or one of the other large creatures? I haven't fought anything dangerous for real in years."

"Yes, but you are the best judge of monstrous character," Guldhogg said soothingly. "We all admire your judgment. We also agree your ideas are the finest and most useful."

Blivet gave him a skeptical look. "Really?"

"Oh, absolutely. Especially when you're not drinking too much."

The knight scowled. "You haven't answered my question. What monster lurks in this unhallowed place?" He shivered a little in the chilly wind that seemed to whistle out of the forest itself rather than from anywhere else.

"Some kind of she-creature," said Guldhogg offhandedly. "I couldn't say for certain."

"And how can anyone care about this she-creature, out in the middle of nowhere?" Blivet looked around. "Honestly, Guldhogg, who would pay to have it dispatched? There isn't a town within twenty furlongs of this place." In truth, to Blivet, the dragon seemed a bit nervous. "Are you sure this is the right forest?"

"Oh, absolutely. And there are excellent reasons for you to go in there," said Guldhogg firmly. "Absolutely, there are. I'll explain it all later, Blivvy. Go on, now. I'll be right here, listening. Call if you need me."

Sir Blivet gave the dragon a last dubious look, then banged down the visor of his helmet, took his lance in his arm, and spurred forward into the trees, perhaps thinking that the sooner he could get this over with, the sooner he could get back to the companionability of an ale-cask, which required no monster-bearding as a price of friendship.

The forest was just as dire inside as it appeared from the outside, shadowed and silent, with the webs of huge but not presently visible spiders swaying in the breeze. Sir Blivet felt as if eyes were watching him at every step, and he had just about decided that he was going to return to the camp and declare the she-beast unfindable when someone called him.

"Sir Knight?"

He turned, his stomach suddenly sour with unease. A robed figure stepped from the shadows and out onto the deer track his horse had been following. "Who are you?" he asked, trying to remember the boldly fearless tone he had been able to summon easily in his younger days, before he knew any better. "Are you in need of assistance?"

"I could be," the stranger said. "Are you Sir Guldhogg?"

"Sir Gul . . ." Blivet shook his head in confusion. "No. Guldhogg is a friend of mine, but . . ." He peered at the shrouded figure, but it was hard to make out much of the face in the hood.

"I am in fact Sir Blivet, semi-fabled dragonslayer. Who are you?"

"I am the She-Creature of Haunted Forest." The newcomer threw back her hood, revealing herself to be a quite attractive short-haired woman of mature years, slender of neck and discerning of eye.

"You are the she-creature?"

"Well, I'm really more of a witch." She gave an embarrassed laugh. "But when I first moved here several years ago, I spread the rumor of a dangerous and deadly beast in these woods so that I would be left alone. People have a tendency to get obsessed with witches, and before you know it they're looking you over for third nipples and hunting for kindling—you know what I mean. But I'm afraid I did the job a bit too well." She shrugged and indicated the dark forest. "Everybody moved out. Even the people in the nearby towns all migrated in fear. So here I am."

"So here you are." Blivet knew it wasn't the most sensible thing to say, but he was a bit taken aback by the unexpected fairness of the she-creature's face, and her modest but sensible speech. "But why, exactly?"

"Because I live here." She gave him a look that suggested she did not think highly of his intellect.

"No, I mean, why am *I* here?" Blivet was beginning to wish he'd waited until later in the day before starting on the ale. "No, that's not right either. What I mean is, why did you and . . . and Sir Guldhogg arrange this meeting?"

"Ah. Fair question." She smiled. "Who do you think a witch's customers are, Sir Blivet? People. You want them to fear you, to be impressed by you, but you don't want them to actually *leave*, because then who is one going to make love potions for? Whose sick calves and sick babies is one going to cure? For whom is one going to tell the future with cartomancy or tea leaves?"

"Ah, I see what you mean about that, I suppose. But this meeting . . ."

"Guldhogg opened the negotiations by raven. A good idea, since the local lord abandoned the place along with the peasants and the forest-folk, which means I haven't been getting a lot of mail in the old way."

"Oh, I see," said Blivet, who was now convinced he didn't see anything at all. "Opened negotiations."

"Mr. Hogg told me that you and he and the rest of your . . . guild? Organization? Anyway, that your lot had been offered a tidy sum of money to come and dispatch the She-Creature of Haunted Forest, and that he felt honor-bound to let me know you were on your way. So I wrote back to him and offered him a business proposition, instead."

Ah. Now it all made a bit more sense, Blivet decided. "Business. Yes. So, have you a lot of gold?"

She laughed again. Blivet couldn't help noticing she was actually rather pretty—in a serious, mature sort of way—and even prettier when she was amused. "Ye gods, no!" said the witch. "I haven't a ha'penny. How would I, with all of my customers gone to Rutland County and points south? No, I haven't got any money at all. Walk with me now, and let's talk about this."

Blivet dismounted, although he couldn't quite see the sense of it. Still, he found himself willing to spend more time in the company of this attractive woman. She had a personality that wasn't what he would have expected from a witch. "But if you haven't any money, what are we going to talk about? I mean, business-wise?"

Now it was her turn to shake her head. "Silly man. As if gold was the only valuable thing in the world. My name is Hecate, by the way. Named after the goddess."

"Pleased to meet you, Mistress Hecate."

"I don't have a cent—but I am the owner of this forest by fee simple. I did a favor for the local lord—cured his daughter of the pox—so when he moved out (well, fled, really) he gave it to me, mostly to keep me from undoing his daughter's cure, I suspect." She cleared her throat. "Which means I am, as is sometimes said, *cash-poor but land-rich*, handsome Sir Blivet, and I would like to offer you and Sir Guldhogg a mutually beneficial alliance."

It took them a year and a surprisingly large fraction of their savings to build a fence around the forest, which although not large was still a forest. Workers had to be trucked in by wagon for all the jobs that couldn't be performed by redcaps and hunkypunks. Then they needed another year for clearing and building, with the result that the Dark Ages had almost ended by the day the grand opening finally arrived.

"I still don't think it's fair," the dragon was saying in a sullen tone. "After all, it was my idea. I led you to each other. I arranged it all, more or less. And you're still going to call it Blivetland?"

"Don't sulk, Guldhogg," said Hecate. "You haven't seen the surprise yet."

"He's always that way," said Sir Blivet. "He doesn't drink, either."

"And neither should you," said Guldhogg, still grumpy.

"Don't be mean, Guldy," the witch said. "My Blivvy's been very abstemious lately."

"Too bloody busy to be anything else," the knight agreed. "Do you know how much work it was just setting up the concession stands and teaching boggarts to count?"

"Well, it was either that or putting them on display, and you know what they did when we tried that. We can't have them flinging boggart dung at the paying customers, can we?"

"Well, I think it's time for us to get out and meet the public," Blivet said. "Come on, Guldhogg. I've got something to show you."

Considering how deserted this entire stretch of the north had been only a couple of short years ago, it was quite impressive to see the crowds lined up hundreds deep all along the great fence, waiting to enter through the massive front gate. The dragon was all for letting them in immediately—"Money is burning a hole in their pockets, Blivet!"—but the knight forbade it until a last chore had been done.

"Just pull this rope," he told the dragon. "Go on, old chum, take it in your mouth and yank."

Guldhogg, who had been gazing with keen regret at the carved wooden sign over the gate, the one that read "Blivetland," shrugged his wings and pulled on the rope. An even larger sign, this one painted on canvas, rolled down to hang in plain view of the entire assembly.

"Oh," said Guldhogg, sounding quite overcome. "Oh, is that . . . is that really . . . ?"

"Yes, silly, it's you," said Hecate, elbowing him in his substantial, scale-covered ribs. "Well, except we're calling you 'Guldy Hogg,' because it sounds friendlier." She and Blivet and Guldhogg looked up at the gigantic sign rippling in the spring breeze, with its huge and colorful painted representation of Guldhogg himself, face stretched in a friendly grin. "It's everywhere, you know," she said.

"What is?"

"Your picture, silly. You're the official mascot of Blivetland. We have Guldy Hogg souvenir tunics, tea towels—even hats!" She took one of the latter from behind her back and handed it to Sir Blivet, who put it on with only the smallest show of reluctance. The protruding nostrils of the dragon face on the hat looked almost like the round ears of some bizarre rodent. "It's a wonderful likeness, Guldy!" cried Hecate. "So handsome!"

As Guldhogg stared at his own face perched atop his friend's head, the gates of Blivetland opened and the first crowd of paying customers pushed their way in, hurrying forward into the forest to see Griffin Island and Nessie's Cove and ride on Guldy Hogg's Wild Wing Ride, which consisted of large tubs whirling around on ropes, the whole thing powered by Ljotunir the ogre spinning a sizeable potter's wheel assembly with his strong and astoundingly ugly feet. Excited people seemed already to have filled every festive corner of the forest, and the vendors were already selling small beer and Goblin Goodies hand over fist.

The sound of money clinking into Blivetland's coffers put the three founders in a very benign mood.

"Isn't this better than tramping around the country?" asked Hecate. "We stay here and the country comes to us!"

"But I thought I was going to be allowed to retire," growled Sir Blivet. "Instead, you will work me into my quickly approaching grave."

"Nonsense. You and Guldy only have to put on two brief shows a day—well, three on Saturdays—and he's the one who has

to do all the costume changes, pretending to be all the other dragons you slew."

"They were all him anyway!" the knight protested.

"Well, everyone loves to see the two of you. It wouldn't be
the Merriest Place on Ye Olde Earth if you pair weren't pretending to try to kill each other at one and four every afternoon." She
leaned over and kissed Blivet's whiskery cheek. "And just think—
no more traveling!"

After that, Guldhogg decided he wanted to try a funnel
cake, so they set off toward the Faerie Food Courte together—the
knight, his lady, and his best friend. The sounds of fable being
turned into coin rose all around them, a seemingly basic exchange
but with an additional dividend of happiness to all parties. Even
in the tenth century, that made for a pretty good state of affairs.

Carrie Vaughn

YEARS AND YEARS AGO, I JOINED A WRITING GROUP AND GOT FEEDBACK on the very first novel I wrote. (Never published, this novel lives quite contentedly in my trunk.) One of the critiques insisted that I had written the story from the wrong character's point of view. Instead of writing about the powerful wizard, the intrepid knight, or the mysterious enchantress (yes, this novel was a pretty standard traditional fantasy adventure quest, which might at least partially explain why it didn't sell), I had written the novel from the point of view of the farmer's widow, who inadvertently joins the quest. Why would anyone want to read about *her*, this person said.

Well, *I* did. That was kind of the point, I remember thinking. To tell a standard fantasy adventure story from the point of view of someone who *isn't* powerful. I mean, that idea worked pretty well for Tolkien. To me, the farmer's widow was interesting because she was a fish out of water in this world of magic and adventure, and she had the strongest emotional arc—her beloved husband dies on the first page, and by the end of the book she has to learn to be okay with that while the world is falling to pieces around her.

I still really like the ideas in that first novel. And I still really like writing about the least obvious characters. "Game of Chance" isn't a standard fantasy adventure, but it does have a bit of magic, and it's got another unlikely main character who may not be the most powerful person in the room, but she's interesting all the same. And she still has the potential to change the world.

Carrie Vaughn

GAME OF CHANCE

Carrie Vaughn

Once, they'd tried using sex to bring down a target. It had seemed a likely plan: throw an affair in the man's path, guide events to a compromising situation, and momentum did the rest. That was the theory—a simple thing, not acting against the person directly, but slantwise. But it turned out it *was* too direct, almost an attack, touching on such vulnerable sensibilities. They'd lost Benton, who had nudged a certain woman into the path of a certain Republic Loyalist Party councilman and died because of it. He'd been so sure it would work.

Gerald had proposed trying this strategy again to discredit the RLP candidate in the next executive election. The man couldn't be allowed to take power if Gerald's own favored allies hoped to maintain any influence. But there was the problem of directness. His cohort considered ideas of how to subtly convince a man to ruin his life with sex. The problem remained: there were no truly subtle ways to accomplish this. They risked Benton's fate with no guaranteed outcome. Gathering before the chalkboard in their warehouse lair, mismatched chairs drawn together, they plotted.

Clare, sitting in back with Major, turned her head to whisper, "I like it better when we stop assassinations rather than instigate them."

"It's like chess," Major said. "Sometimes you protect a piece, sometimes you sacrifice one."

"It's a bit arrogant, isn't it, treating the world like our personal chessboard?"

Major gave a lopsided smile. "Maybe, a bit."

"I think I have an idea," Clare said.

Gerald glanced their way and frowned.

Much more of this and he'd start accusing them of insubordination. She nudged Major and made a gesture with her hand: *Wait. We'll tell him later.* They sat back and waited, while Gerald held court and entertained opinions, from planting illegal pornography to obtaining compromising photographs. All of it too crass, too mundane. Not credible. Gerald sent them away with orders to "come up with something." Determined to brood, he turned his back as the others trailed to the corner of the warehouse that served as a parlor to scratch on blank pages and study books.

Clare and Major remained, seated, watching, until Gerald looked back at them and scowled.

"Clare has a different proposal," Major said, nodding for her to tell.

Clare ducked her gaze, shy, but knew she was right. "You can't use sex without acting on him, and that won't work. So don't act on him. Act on everything around him. A dozen tiny decisions a day can make a man fall."

Gerald was their leader because he could see the future. Well, almost. He could see paths, likely directions of events that fell one way instead of another. He used this knowledge and the talents of those he recruited to steer the course of history. Major liked the chess metaphor, but Gerald worked on the canvas of epic battles, of history itself. He scowled at Clare like she was speaking nonsense.

"Tiny decisions. Like whether he wears a red or blue tie? Like whether he forgets to brush his teeth? You mean to change the world by this?"

Major, who knew her so well, who knew her thoughts before she did, smiled his hunting smile. "How is the man's heart?"

"Yes. Exactly," she said.

"It'll take time," Major explained to a still frowning Gerald. "The actions will have to be lined up just so."

"All right," he said, because Major had proven himself. His voice held a weight that Clare's didn't. "But I want contingencies."

"Let the others make contingencies," Major said, and that made them all scowl.

Gerald left Clare and Major to work together, which was how she liked it best.

She'd never worked so hard on a plan. She searched for opportunities, studied all the ways they might encourage the target to harm himself. She found many ways, as it happened. The task left Clare drained, but happy, because it was working. Gerald would see. He'd be pleased. He'd start to listen to her, and she wouldn't need Major to speak for her.

"I don't mind speaking for you," Major said when she confided in him. "It's habit that makes him look right through you like he does. It's hard to get around that. He has to be the leader, the protector. He needs someone to be the weakest, and so doesn't see you. And the others only see what he sees."

"Why don't you?"

He shrugged. "I like to see things differently."

"Maybe there's a spell we could work to change him."

He smiled at that. The spells didn't work on them, because they were outside the whole system. Their spells put them outside. Gerald said they could change the world by living outside it like this. Clare kept thinking of it as gambling, and she never had liked games.

They worked: the target chose the greasiest, unhealthiest meals, always ate dessert, and took a coach everywhere—there always seemed to be one conveniently at hand. Some days, he forgot his medication, the little pills that kept his heart steady—the bottle was not in its place and he couldn't be bothered to look for it. Nothing to notice from day to day. But one night, in bed with his wife—no lurid affair necessary—their RLP candidate's weak heart gave out. A physician was summoned quickly enough, but to no avail. And that, Clare observed, was how one brought down a man with sex.

Gerald called it true. The man's death threw the election into chaos, and his beloved Populist Tradition Party was able to hold its seats in the Council.

Clare glowed with pride because her theory had worked. A dozen little changes, so indirect as to be unnoticeable. The perfect expression of their abilities.

But Gerald scowled. "It's not very impressive, in the main," he said and walked away.

"What's that supposed to mean?" Clare whispered.

"He's angry he didn't think of it himself," Major said.

"So it wasn't fireworks. I thought that was the point."

"I think you damaged his sensibilities," he said, and dropped a kind kiss on her forehead.

———

She had been a normal, everyday girl, though prone to daydreaming, according to her governess. She was brought up in proper drawing rooms, learning how to embroider, supervise servants, and orchestrate dinner parties. Often, though, she had to be reminded of her duties, of the fact that she would one day marry a fine gentleman, perhaps in the army or in government, and be the envy of society ladies everywhere. Otherwise she might sit in the large wingback armchair all day long, staring at the light coming in through the window, or at sparks in the fireplace, or at the tongue of flame dancing on the wick of the nearest lamp. "What can you possibly be thinking about?" her governess would ask. She'd learned to say, "Nothing." When she was young, she'd said things like, "I'm wondering, what if fire were alive? What if it traveled, and is all flame part of the same flame? Is a flame like a river, traveling and changing every moment?" This had alarmed the adults around her.

By the time she was eighteen, she'd learned to make herself presentable in fine gowns, and to arrange the curls of her hair to excite men's interest, and she'd already had three offers. She hadn't given any of them answer, but thought to accept the one her father most liked so at least somebody would be happy.

Then one day she'd stepped out of the house, parasol over her shoulder, intending a short walk to remind herself of her duty before that evening's dinner party, and there Gerald and Major had stood, at the foot of the stairs, two dashing figures from an adventure tale.

"What do you think about, when you look at the flame of a candle?" Gerald had asked.

She stared, parasol clutched in gloved hands, mind tumbling into an honest answer despite her learned poise. "I think of birds playing in sunlight. I wonder if the sun and the fire are the same. I think of how time slows down when you watch the hands of a clock move."

Major, the younger and handsomer of the pair, gave her a sly grin and offered his hand. "You're wasted here. Come with us."

At that moment she knew she'd never been in love before, because she lost her heart to Major. She set her parasol against the railing on the stairs, stepped forward, and took his hand. Gerald pulled the theatrical black cape he'd been wearing off his shoulders, turned it with a twist of his wrists, and swept it around himself, Major, and Clare. A second of cold followed, along with a feeling of drowning. Clare shut her eyes and covered her face. When Major murmured a word of comfort, she finally looked around her and saw the warehouse. Gerald introduced himself and the rest of his cohort, and explained that they were masters of the world, which they could manipulate however they liked. It seemed a very fine thing.

Thus she vanished from her old life as cleanly as if she had never existed. Part of her would always see Gerald and Major as her saviors.

Gerald's company, his band of unseen activists, waited in their warehouse headquarters until their next project, which would only happen when Gerald traced lines of influence to the next target. The next chess piece. Clare looked forward to the leisure time until she was in the middle of it, when she just wanted to go out and *do* something.

Maybe it was just that she'd realized a long time ago that she wasn't any good at the wild version of poker the others played to pass time. She sat the games out, tried to read a book, or day-dreamed. Watched dust motes and candle flames.

The other four were the fighters. The competitive ones. She'd joined this company by accident.

Cards snicked as Major dealt them out. Clean-shaven, with short cropped hair, he was dashing, military. He wore a dark blue uniform jacket without insignia; a white shirt, unbuttoned at the collar; boots that needed polishing, but that only showed how active he was. Always in the thick of it. Clare could watch him deal cards all day.

"Wait a minute. Are we on Tuesday rules or Wednesday?" Ildie asked.

Fred looked up from his hand, blinking in a moment of confusion. "Today's Thursday, isn't it?"

"Tuesday rules on Thursday. That's the fun of it," Marco said, voice flat, attention on the cards.

"I hate you all," Ildie said, scowling. They chuckled, because she always said that.

Ildie dressed like a man, in an oxford shirt, leather pants, and high boots. This sometimes still shocked Clare, who hadn't given up long skirts and braided hair when she'd left a proper parlor for this. Ildie had already been a rebel when she joined. At least Clare had learned not to tell Ildie how much nicer she'd look if she grew her hair out. Fred had sideburns, wore a loosened cravat, and out of all of them might be presentable in society with a little polish. Marco never would be. Stubble shadowed his face, and he always wore his duster to hide the pistols on his belt.

A pair of hurricane lamps on tables lit the scene. The warehouse was lived-in, the walls lined with shelves, which were piled with books, rolled up charts, atlases, sextants, hourglasses, a couple of dusty globes. They'd pushed together chairs and coffee tables for a parlor, and the far corner was curtained off into rooms with cots and washbasins. In the parlor, a freestanding chalkboard was covered with writing and charts, and more sheets of paper lay strewn on the floor, abandoned when the equations scrawled on them went wrong. When they went right, the sheets were pinned to the walls and shelves and became the next plan. At the moment, nothing was pinned up.

Clare considered: was it a matter of tracing lines of influence to objects rather than personalities? Difficult, when influence was a matter of motivation, which was not possible with inanimate objects. So many times their tasks would have been easier if they could change someone's *mind*. But that was like bringing a sledgehammer down on delicate glasswork. So you changed the thing that would change someone's mind. How small a change could generate the greatest outcome? That was her challenge: could removing a bottle of ink from a room change the world? She believed it could. If it was the right bottle of ink, the right room. Then perhaps a letter wouldn't be written, an order of execution wouldn't be signed.

But the risk—that was Gerald's argument. The risk of failure was too great. You might take a bolt from the wheel of a cannon, but if it was the wrong bolt, the wrong cannon . . . The variables became massive. Better to exert the most influence you could without being noticed. That didn't stop Clare from weaving her thought experiments. For want of a nail . . .

"I raise," Major said, and Clare looked up at the change in his voice. He had a plan; he was about to spring a trap. After the hundreds of games those four had played, couldn't they see it?

"You don't have anything." Marco looked at his hand, at the cards lying face up on the table, back again. Major gave him a "try me" look.

"He's bluffing." Ildie wore a thin smile, confident because Major had bluffed before. Just enough to keep them guessing. He did it on purpose, they very well knew, and he challenged them to outwit him. They thought they could—that was why they kept falling into his traps. But even Major had a tell, and Clare could see it if no one else could. Easy for her to say, though, sitting outside the game.

"Fine. Bet's raised. I see it," Fred countered.

Then they saw it coming, because that was part of Major's plan. Draw them in, spring the trap. He tapped a finger, the air popped, a tiny sound like an insect hitting a window, that was how small the spell was, but they all recognized the working of it, the way the world shifted just a bit, as one of them outside of it nudged a little. Major laid out his cards, which were all exactly the cards he needed, a perfect hand, against unlikely—but not impossible—odds.

Marco groaned, Ildie threw her cards, Fred laughed. "I should have known."

"Tuesday rules," Major said, spreading his hands in mock apology.

Major glanced at Clare, smiled. She smiled back. No, she didn't ever want to play this game against Major.

Marco gathered up the cards. "Again."

"Persistent," Major said.

"Have to be. Thursday rules this time. The way it's *meant* to be." They dealt the next hand.

Gerald came in from the curtained area that was his study, his wild eyes red and sleepless, a driven set to his jaw. They all knew what it meant.

"I have the next plot," he said.

Helping the cause sometimes meant working at cross-purposes with the real world. A PTP splinter group, frustrated and militant, had a plan, too, and Gerald wanted to stop it because it would do more harm than good.

Easier said than done, on such a scale. Clare preferred the games where they put a man's pills out of the way.

She and Major hunched in a doorway as the Council office building fell, brought down by cheap explosives. A wall of dust scoured the streets. People coated in the gray stuff wandered like ghosts. Clare and Major hardly noticed.

"We couldn't stop it," Clare murmured, speaking through a handkerchief.

Major stared at a playing card, a jack of diamonds. "We've done all we can."

"What? What did we do? We didn't stop it!" They were supposed to stop the explosion, stop the destruction. She had wanted so much to stop it, not for Gerald's sake, but for the sake of doing good.

Major looked hard at her. "Twenty-nine bureaucrats meant to be in that building overslept this morning. Eighteen stayed home sick. Another ten stayed home with hangovers from overindulging last night. Twenty-four more ran late because either their pets or children were sick. The horses of five coaches came up lame, preventing another fifteen from arriving. That's ninety-six people who weren't in that building. We did what we could." His glare held amazing conviction.

She said, "We're losing, aren't we? Gerald will never get what he wants."

So many of Gerald's plans had gone just like this. They counted victories in lives, like picking up spilled grains of rice. They were changing lives, but not the world.

"Come on," he ordered. "We've got a door."

He threw the card at the wall of the alley where they'd hidden. It stuck, glowed blue, and grew. Through the blue glare a gaping hole showed. Holding hands, they dove into it, and it collapsed behind them.

"Lame coach horses? Hangovers?" Gerald said, pacing back and forth along one of the bookshelves. "We're trying to save civilization."

"What is civilization but the people who live within it?" Clare said softly. It was how she said anything around Gerald.

"Ninety-six lives saved," Major said. "What did anyone else accomplish?" Silent gazes, filled with visions of destruction, looked back at him. The rest of them: Fred, Ildie, and Marco. Their jackets were ruffled, their faces weary, but they weren't covered with dust and ragged like Clare and Major were. They hadn't gotten that close.

Gerald paced. "In the end, what does it mean? For us?" The question was rhetorical because no answer would satisfy him. Though Clare thought, it means whatever we want it to mean.

Clare and Major never bothered hiding their attachment from the others. What could the company say to disapprove? Not even Gerald could stop them, though Ildie often looked at her askance, with a scowl, as if Clare had betrayed her. Major assured her that the other woman had never held a claim on him. Clare wondered if she might have fallen in love with any of the men—Fred, Benton, or even Marco—if any of them had stood by Gerald to recruit her instead of Major. But no, she felt her fate was to be with Major. She didn't feel small with him.

Hand in hand, careless, they'd leave the others and retreat to the closet in an unused corner of the warehouse's second floor, where they'd built a pallet just for them. A nest, Clare thought of it. Here, she had Major all to herself, and he seemed happy enough to be hers. She'd lay across his naked chest and he'd play with her hair. Bliss.

"Why did you follow Gerald when he came for you?" she asked after the disaster with the exploded building.

"He offered adventure."

"Not for the politics, then? Not because you believe in his party?"

"I imagine it's all one and the same in the long run."

The deep philosophy of this would have impressed her a few years ago. Now, it seemed like dodging the question. She propped herself on an elbow to study him. She was thinking out loud.

"Then why do you still follow him? You could find adventure without him, now that he's shown you the way."

He grinned sleepily and gathered her closer. "I'd wander aimlessly. His adventures are more interesting. It's a game."

"Oh."

"And why do you still follow him? Why did you take my hand the day we met?"

"You were more interesting than what I left behind."

"But I ask you the same question, now. I know you don't believe in his politics. So why do you still follow him?"

"I don't follow him. I follow you."

His expression turned serious, frowning almost. His hand moved from her hair to her cheek, tracing the line of her jaw as if she were fragile glass. "We're a silly pair, aren't we? No belief, no faith."

"Nothing wrong with that. Major—if neither of us is here for Gerald, we should leave. Let's go away from this, be our own cohort." Saying it felt like rebellion, even greater than the rebellion of leaving home in the first place.

His voice went soft, almost a whisper. "Could we really? How far would we get before we started missing this and came back?"

"I wouldn't miss the others," she said, jaw clenched.

"No, not them," he said. "But the game."

Gerald could fervently agitate for the opposite party, and Major would play the game with as much glee. She could understand and still not agree.

"You think we need Gerald, to do what we do?"

He shook his head, a questioning gesture rather than a denial. "I'm happy here. Aren't you?"

She could nod and not lie because here, at this small moment with him, she was happy.

One *could* change the world by nudging chances, Clare believed. Sometimes, she went off by herself to study chances the others wouldn't care about.

At a table in the corner of a café—the simple, homelike kind that students frequented, with worn armchairs, and chessboards and pieces stored in boxes under end tables with old lamps on them—Clare drew a pattern in a bit of tea that dripped from her saucer. Swirled the shape into two circles, forever linked. In front of the counter, a boy dropped a napkin. The girl behind him picked it up. Their hands brushed. He saw that she had a book of sonnets, which he never would have noticed if he hadn't dropped the napkin. She saw that he had a book of philosophy. They were students, maybe, or odd enthusiasts. One asked the other, are you a student? The answer didn't matter because the deed was done. In this world, in this moment, despite all the unhappiness, this small thing went right.

This whole thing started because Gerald saw patterns. She wondered later: Did he see the pattern, identify them because of it, and bring them together? Was that his talent? Or did he cause the pattern to happen? If not for Gerald, would she have gone on, free and ignorant, happily living her life with no knowledge of what she could do? Or was she always destined to follow this path, use this talent with or without the others? Might she have spent her time keeping kittens from running into busy streets or children from falling into rivers? And perhaps one of those children would grow up to be the leader Gerald sought, the one who would change the world.

All that had happened, all their work, and she still could not decide if she believed in destiny.

She wouldn't change how any of it had happened because of Major. The others marveled over Gerald's stern, Cossack determination. But she fell in love with Major, with his shining eyes.

"We have to do better, think harder, more creatively. Look how much we've done already, never forget how much we've done."

After almost a decade of this, only six of the original ten were left. The diehards, as mad as Gerald. Even Major looked on him with that calculating light in his eyes. Did Gerald even realize that Major's passion was for tactics rather than outcome?

"Opportunities abound, if we have the courage to see them. The potential for good, great good, manifests everywhere. We must have the courage to see it."

Rallying the troops. Clare sighed. How many times had Gerald given variations of this speech in this dingy warehouse, hidden by spells and out of the world? They all sounded the same. She'd stopped being able to see the large patterns a long time ago and could only see the little things now. A dropped napkin in a café. She could only change the course of a few small lives.

"There's an assassination," said Gerald. "It will tip the balance into a hundred years of chaos. Do you see it?"

Fred smiled. "We can stop it. Maybe jam a rifle."

"A distraction, to throw off the assassin's aim."

"Or give him a hangover," Major said. "We've had great success with hangovers and oversleeping." He glanced at Clare with his starry smile. She beamed back. Fred rolled his eyes.

"Quaint," Gerald said, frowning.

The game was afoot. So many ways to change a pattern. Maybe Clare's problem was she saw them as people, not patterns. And maybe she was the one holding the rest back. Thinking too small. She wasn't part of *their* pattern anymore.

This rally was the largest Clare had ever seen. Her generation had grown up hearing grandparents' stories of protest and clashes (civil war, everyone knew, but the official history said clashes, which sounded temporary and isolated). While their parents grew up in a country that was tired and sedate, where they were content to consolidate their little lives and barricade themselves against the world, the children wondered what it must have been like to believe in idealism.

Gerald's target this time was the strongest candidate the PTP had ever put forward for Premiere. The younger generation flocked to Jonathan Smith. People adored him—unless they supported the RLP. Rallies like this were the result. Great crowds of hope and belief, unafraid. And the crowds who opposed them.

Gerald said that Jonathan Smith was going to be assassinated. Here, today, at the rally, in front of thousands. All the portents pointed to this. But it would not result in martyrdom and change, because the assassin would be one of his own and people would think, *our parents were right,* and go home.

Clare and Major stood in the crowd like islands, unmoving, unfeeling, not able to be caught up in the exhilarating speech, the roaring response. She felt alien. These were her people, they were all human, but never had she felt so far removed. She might have felt god-like, if she believed in a god who took such close interest in creation as to move around it like this. God didn't have to, because there were people like Gerald and Major.

"It's nice to be saving someone," Clare said. "I've always liked that better."

"It only has to be a little thing," Major said. "Someone in the front row falls and breaks a bone. The commotion stalls the attack when Smith goes to help the victim. Because he's like that."

"We want to avoid having a victim at all, don't we?"

"Maybe it'll rain."

"We change coach horses, not the weather." But not so well that they couldn't keep an anarchist bomb from arriving at its destination. They weren't omnipotent. They weren't gods. If they were, they could control the weather.

She had tried sending a message about the government building behind Gerald's back. He would have called the action too direct, but she'd taken the risk. She'd called the police, the newspapers, everyone, with all the details they'd conjured. Her information went into official records, was filed for the appropriate authorities, all of which moved too slowly to be of any good. It wasn't too direct after all.

Inexorable. This path of history had the same feeling of being inexorable. Official channels here would welcome an assassination. The police would not believe her. They only had to save one life.

She wished for rain. The sky above was clear.

They walked among the crowd, and it was grand. She rested

her hand in the crook of Major's elbow; he held it there. He wore a happy, silly smile on his face. They might have been in a park, strolling along a gentle river in a painting.

"There's change here," he said, gazing over the angry young crowd and their vitriolic signs.

She squeezed his arm and smiled back.

The ground they walked on was ancient cobblestone. This historic square had witnessed rallies like this for a thousand years. In such times of change, gallows had stood here, or hooded men with axes. How much blood had soaked between these cobbles?

That was where she nudged. From the edges of the crowd, they were able to move with the flow of people surging. They could linger at the edges with relative freedom of movement, so she spotted a bit of pavement before the steps climbing to the platform where the demagogue would speak. A toe caught on a broken cobblestone would delay him. Just for a second. Sometimes that was enough to change the pattern.

"Here," she said, squeezing Major's arm to anchor him. He nodded, pulled her to the wall of a town house, and waited.

While she focused on the platform, on the path that Jonathan Smith would take—on the victim—Major turned his attention to the crowd, looking for the barrel of a gun, the glint of sunlight off a spyglass, counter-stream movement in the enthusiastic surge. The assassin.

Someone else looking for suspicious movement in a crowd like this would find *them*, Clare thought. Though somehow no one ever did find them.

Sometimes, all they could do was wait. Sometimes, they waited and nothing happened. Sometimes they were too late or early, or one of the others had already nudged one thing or another.

"There," Major said, the same time that Clare gripped his arm and whispered, "There."

She was looking to the front where the iconic man, so different than the bodyguards around him, emerged and waved at the crowd. There, the cobblestone—she drew from her pocket a cube of sugar that had been soaked in amaretto, crumbled it, let the grains fall, then licked her fingers. The sweet, heady flavor stung her tongue.

Major lunged away from her. "No!"

The stone lifted, and the great Jonathan Smith tripped. A universal gasp went up.

Major wasn't looking to the front with everyone else. He was looking at a man in the crowd, twenty feet away, dissolute. A troublemaker. Hair ragged, shirt soiled, faded trousers, and a canvas jacket a size too large. Boots made for kicking. He held something in his right fist, in a white-knuckled grip.

This was it, the source, the gun—the locus, everything. This was where they learned if they nudged enough, and correctly. But the assassin didn't raise a straight arm to aim. He cocked back to throw. He didn't carry a gun, he held a grenade.

Gerald and the others had planned for a bullet. They hadn't planned for this.

Major put his shoulder to the man's chest and shoved. The would-be assassin stumbled, surprised, clutched the grenade to his chest—it wasn't active, he hadn't lit the fuse. Major stopped him. Stopped the explosive, stopped the assassin, and that was good. Except it wasn't, and he didn't.

Smith recovered from his near-fall. He mounted the platform. The bodyguard behind him drew his handgun, pointed at the back of Smith's head, and fired. The shot echoed and everyone saw it and spent a moment in frozen astonishment. Even the man with the grenade. Everyone but Major, who was on the ground, doubled over, shivering as if every nerve burned.

Clare fell on top of him, crying, clutching at him. His eyes rolled back, enough to look at her, enough for her to see the fear in them. If she could have held onto him, carried him with her, saved him, she would have. But he'd put himself back into the world. He'd acted, plunged back into a time and place he wasn't part of anymore, and now it tore him to pieces. The skin of his face cracked under her hands, and the blood and flesh underneath was black and crumbling to dust.

She couldn't sob hard enough to save him.

Clare was lost in chaos. Then Gerald was there with his cloak. So theatrical, Major always said. Gerald used the cloak like Major used the jack of diamonds. He swept it around the three of them, shoving them through a doorway.

But only Clare and Gerald emerged on the other side.

———

The first lesson they learned, that Major forgot for only a second, the wrong second: they could only build steps, not leap. They couldn't act directly, they couldn't be part of the history they made.

So Jonathan Smith died, and the military coup that followed ruined everything.

———

Five of them remained.

The problem was she could not imagine a world different from the burned-out husk that resulted from the war fought over the course of the next year. Gerald's plan might have worked, bringing forth a lush Eden where everyone drank nectar and played hopscotch with angelic children, and she still would have felt empty.

Gerald's goal had always been utopia. Clare no longer believed it was possible.

The others were very kind to her, in the way anyone was kind to a child they pitied. *Poor dear, but she should have known better.* Clare accepted the blanket Ildie put over her shoulders and the cup of hot tea Fred pressed into her hands.

"Be strong, Clare," Ildie said, and Clare thought, easy for her to say.

"What next, what next," Gerard paced the warehouse, head bent, snarling almost, his frown was so energetic.

"Corruption scandal?" Marco offered.

"Too direct."

"A single line of accounting, the wrong number in the right place, to discredit the regime," Ildie said.

Gerald stopped pacing. "Maybe."

Another meeting. As if nothing had happened. As if they could still go on.

"Major was the best of us," Clare murmured.

"We'll just have to be more careful," Ildie murmured back.

"He made a mistake. An elementary mistake," Gerald said, and never spoke of Major again.

The village a mile outside the city had once been greater, a way station and market town. Now, it was a skeleton. The war had crushed it, burned it, until only hovels remained, the scorched frames of buildings standing like trees in a forest. Brick walls had fallen and lay strewn, crumbling, decaying. Rough canvas stretched over alcoves provided shelter. Cooking fires burned under tripods and pots beaten out of other objects. What had been the cobbled town square still had the atmosphere of an open-air market, people shouting and milling, bartering fiercely, trading. The noise made a language all its own, and a dozen different scents mingled.

Despite the war and bombing, some of the people hadn't fled, but they hadn't tried to rebuild. Instead, they seemed to have crawled underground when the bombardment began, and when it ended they reemerged, continued their lives where they left off as best they could, with the materials they had at hand. Cockroaches, Clare thought, and shook the thought away.

At the end of the main street, where the twisted, naked foundations gave way and only shattered cobblestones remained, a group of men were digging a well into an old aquifer, part of the water system of the dying village. They were looking for water. Really, though, at this point they weren't digging, but observing the amount of dirt they'd already removed and arguing. They were about to give up and try again somewhere else. A whole day's work wasted, a day they could little afford when they had children to feed and material to scavenge.

Clare helped. Spit on her hands, put them on the dusty earth, then rubbed them together and drew patterns in the dust. Pressed her hands to the ground again. The aquifer that they had missed by just a few feet seeped into the ditch they'd dug. The well filled. The men cheered.

Wiping her hands on her skirt, Clare walked away. She was late for another meeting.

"What is the pattern?" Gerald asked. And no one answered. They were down to four.

Ildie had tried to cause a scandal by prompting a divorce between the RLP Premiere and his popular wife. No matter how similar attempts had failed before. "This is different, it's not causing an affair, it's destroying one. I can do this," she had insisted, desperate to prove herself. But the targets couldn't be forced. She might as well have tried to cause an affair after all. Once again, too direct. Clare could have told her it wouldn't work. Clare recognized when people were in love. Even Republic Loyalists fell in love.

"What will change this path? We must make this better!"

She stared. "I just built a well."

Marco smirked. "What's the use of that?"

Fred tried to summon enthusiasm. They all missed Major even if she was the only one who admitted it. "It's on the army now, not the government. We remove the high command, destroy their headquarters perhaps—"

Marco said, "What, you think we can make earthquakes?"

"No, we create cracks in the foundation, then simply shift them—"

Clare shook her head. "I was never able to think so big. I wish—"

Fred sighed. "Clare, it's been two years, can you please—"

"It feels like yesterday," she said, and couldn't be sure that it *hadn't* been just yesterday, according to the clock her body kept. But she couldn't trust that instinct. She'd lost hours that felt like minutes, studying dust motes.

"Clare—" Gerald said, admonishing, a guru unhappy with a disciple. The thought made her smile, which he took badly, because she wasn't looking at him but at something the middle distance, unseen.

He shook his head, disappointment plain. The others stared at her with something like fascination or horror.

"You've been tired. Not up to this pressure," he explained kindly. "It's all right if you want to rest."

She didn't hear the rest of the planning. That was all right; she wasn't asked to take part.

She took a piece of charcoal from an abandoned campfire. This settlement was smaller than it had been. Twenty fires had once burned here, with iron pots and bubbling stews over them all.

Eight remained. Families ranged farther and farther to find food. Often young boys never came back. They were taken by the army. The well had gone bad. They collected rainwater in dirty tubs now.

And yet. Even here. She drew a pattern on a slab of broken wood. Watched a young man drop a brick of peat for the fire. Watched a young woman pick it up for him and look into his eyes. He smiled.

Now if only she knew the pattern that would ensure that they survived.

When they launched the next plan—collapse the army high command's headquarters, crippling the RLP and allowing the PTP to fill the vacuum, or so Gerald insisted—she had no part to play. She was not talented enough, Gerald didn't say, but she understood it. She could only play with detritus from a kitchen table. She could never think big enough for them. Major hadn't cared.

She did a little thing, though: scattered birdseed on a pool of soapy water, to send a tremor through the air and warn the pigeons, rats, and such that they ought to flee. And maybe that ruined the plan for the others. She'd nudged the pattern too far out of alignment for their pattern to work. The building didn't collapse, but the clock tower across the square from which Fred and Marco were watching did. As if they had planted explosives and been caught in the blast.

Too direct, of course.

She left. Escaped, rather, as she thought. She didn't want Gerald to find her. Didn't want to look him in the eye. She would either laugh at him or accuse him of killing Major and everyone else. Then she would strangle him, and since they were both equally out of history she just might be able to do it. It couldn't possibly be too direct, and the rest of the world couldn't possibly notice.

Very tempting, in those terms.

But she found her place, her niche, her purpose. Her little village on the edge of everything was starting to build itself into something bigger. She'd worried about it, but just last year the number of babies born exceeded the number of people who died of disease, age, and accident. A few more cook fires had been added. She watched, pleased.

But Gerald found her, eventually, because that was one of his talents: finding people who had the ability to move outside the world. She might as well have set out a lantern.

She didn't look up when he arrived. She was gathering mint leaves that she'd set out to dry, putting them in the tin box where she stored them. A spoonful of an earlier harvest was brewing in a cup of water over her little fire. Her small realm was tucked under the overhang formed by three walls that had fallen together. The witch's cave, she called it. It looked over the village so she could always watch her people.

Gerald stood at the edge of her cave for a long time, watching. He seemed deflated, his cloak worn, his skin pale. But his eyes still burned. With desperation this time, maybe, instead of ambition.

When he spoke, he sounded appalled. "Clare. What are you doing here? Why are you living in this . . . this pit?"

"Because it's my pit. Leave me alone, I'm working."

"Clare. Come away. Get out of there. Come with me."

She raised a brow at him. "No."

"You're not doing any good here."

She still did not give him more than a passing glance. The village below was full of the evening's activities: farmers returning from fields, groups bustling around cook fires. Someone was singing, another laughing, a third crying.

She pointed. "Maybe that little girl right there is the one who will grow up and turn this all around. Maybe I can keep her safe until she does."

He shook his head. "Not likely. You can't point to a random child and make such a claim. She'll be dead of influenza before she reaches maturity."

"It's the little things, you're always saying. But you don't think small enough," she said.

"Now what are you talking about?"

"Nails," she murmured.

"You have a talent," he said, desperately. "You see what other people overlook. Things other people take for granted. There are revolutions in little things. I understand that now. I didn't—"

"Why can't you let the revolutions take care of themselves?"

He stared at her, astonished. Might as well tell him to stop breathing. He didn't know how to do anything else. And no one had ever spoken to him like this.

"You can't go back," he said as if it was a threat. "You can't go back to being alive in the world."

"Does it look like I'm trying?" He couldn't answer, of course, because she only looked like she was making tea. "You're only here because there's no one left to help you. And you're *blind*."

Some days when she was in a very low mood she imagined Major here with her, and imagined that he'd be happy, even without the games.

"Clare. You shouldn't be alone. You can't leave me. Not after everything."

"I never did this for you. I never did this for history. There's no great sweep to any of this. Major saw a man with a weapon and acted on instinct. The grenade might have gone off and he'd have died just the same. It could have happened to anyone. I just wanted to help people. To try to make the world a little better. I like to think that if I weren't doing this I'd be working in a soup kitchen somewhere. In fact maybe I'd have done more good if I'd worked in a soup kitchen."

"You can't do any good alone, Clare."

"I think you're the one who can't do any good alone," she said. She looked at him. "I have saved four hundred and thirty-two people who would have died because they did not have clean water. Because of me, forty-three people walked a different way home and didn't get mugged or pressed into the army. Thirty-eight kitchen fires *didn't* reach the cooking oil. Thirty-one fishermen did *not* drown when they fell overboard. I have helped two dozen people fall in love."

His chuckle was bitter. "You were never very ambitious."

"Ambitious enough," she said.

"I won't come for you again. I won't try to save you again."

"Thank you," she said.

She did not watch Gerald walk away and vanish in the swoop of his cloak.

Later, looking over the village, she reached for her tin box and drew out a sugar cube that had been soaked in brandy. Crumbling it and licking her fingers, she lifted a bit of earth, which made a small girl trip harmlessly four steps before she would have stumbled and fallen into a cook fire. Years later, after the girl had grown up to be the kind of revolutionary leader who saves the world, she would say she had a guardian angel.

JACQUELINE CAREY

SOMETIME IN THE MID-1990S, I AWOKE FROM A VIVID DREAM THAT involved a barren, rocky shore bursting forth in a profusion of roses. The image haunted me, and I incorporated it into a short story titled "The Martyr of the Roses." Although the story failed to find a home at the time, it sketched out the rough beginnings of a complex theology and a map of the world that I went on to explore in detail in Kushiel's Legacy, the series of alternate historical fantasy novels that launched my career.

At some point, I fully intended to capitalize on the success of Kushiel's Legacy and put the story back on the market, but as I continued writing the series, I made creative decisions that rendered the story noncanonical. It became a literary curiosity, the spark of inspiration that no longer fit within the framework of the narrative it engendered. And while I wanted to share it with my readers, I didn't know what the right venue for it might be.

When Shawn Speakman contacted me regarding this anthology, I knew I'd found it. Over the years, Shawn has done so much to connect fellow fantasy writers and fans. Donating this literary curiosity is the perfect way to give thanks to Shawn for the wonderful service he provides with The Signed Page, and to give my own readers a never-before-seen glimpse into the origin of Terre d'Ange.

Just don't ask me how House L'Envers ended up on the throne, because I honestly don't know.

Jacqueline Carey

THE MARTYR OF THE ROSES

Jacqueline Carey

Chrétien L'Envers sat on a window ledge in an empty tower room in the ancestral home of the House of Drozhny. From this lofty perch in the estate of the longtime governors of the city of St. Sithonia, the Dauphin of Terre d'Ange contemplated the quality of the light, which was unlike any other he had ever seen. Such things made travel worthwhile. In the south of Caerdicca Unitas, where he and Rikard Drozhny had spent two years together at the University in Tiberium, the sun sometimes beat like a hammer upon the hard-baked earth. This light was as intense, yet vaster, far vaster; no hammer, this, but an anvil. It flattened the harsh terrain and rendered the whole of St. Sithonia, with all her crags and crevasses, oddly two-dimensional.

They said in Vralia for three months a year the sun never set.

"Angelicus?"

Chrétien turned his head, smiling at his friend's usage of the old nickname. "Yes?"

With two glasses of wine forgotten in his hands, Rikard Drozhny stood in the doorway and blinked, struck dumb for the thousandth time at the sight of his D'Angeline comrade, whose pale hair in Vralian summerlight shone the precise hue of gold reflected on a drift of winter's snow. "I brought wine. But we should leave soon, unless you want to ride."

"I'm sorry. Is it customary to walk?"

"It is, actually." Trust a D'Angeline to be sensitive to nuance even in the midst of a reverie. "The Prince-Protectorate himself walks when he comes to make his pilgrimage. With," he added, "a very large, well-armed escort."

"Ah."

"Yes, well. Rumour has it that this year's will be the largest ever."

Chrétien raised his elegant brows and swung one booted foot. "What will your father do?"

Rikard shrugged, thrusting a wineglass toward Chrétien. "What can he do? He's the Governor of St. Sithonia, he's sworn to uphold the Prince-Protectorate." Their eyes met in silence as Chrétien accepted the glass. "Think what you will," Rikard said softly, "But my father will stand or fall with Janos Vraalkan because he can do more for Vralia as the Governor of this city than he can as a dead man."

"I know."

"Do you?" He laughed without humor. "Angelicus, how could you possibly understand? You're the first D'Angeline to even set foot in Vralia in my lifetime."

"I know you. And you're the first Vralian to attend the University in its lifetime," Chrétien said equably, smiling at him. "So."

"I know, I know." Rikard's mouth twitched in a reluctant answering smile. "So. And here you are." No one, he thought, was going to mistake Chrétien for a devout Vralian tradesman paying his respects to Sithonia today.

"I'm trying, Riko, truly." Chrétien sipped his wine. "I do my best to understand. Vralia is very different for me."

"My father thinks you're a spy." The words came out blunt and unexpected, and Rikard flushed a dull red from his hairline to his throat. Faint frown lines appeared between Chrétien's brows.

"Does he, then?" His eyes, which were in shadow a violet so dark as to appear almost black, held Rikard's. "Do you?"

"Of course not." Rikard's tongue suddenly felt thick and stupid. "No." His heart pounded, as it always did when Chrétien looked directly at him like that. "If Terre d'Ange wanted to send a spy, it would hardly be *you*."

"No?" Chrétien murmured, his tone mild. "Why not me?"

Rikard shook his head in denial and looked away. "The Dauphin? No. It's too much to risk. Anyway, it doesn't matter." He took a long draught of wine. "There's nothing to be seen here that I haven't told you a dozen times over in the cafes of Tiberium."

"But it's getting worse." Chrétien lifted his goblet, examining the workmanship. Light flooding the window behind him shone through the red Caerdicci wine and stained Rikard's face incarnadine. "Isn't it?"

"Yes," Rikard said, "it is." He was silent, thinking even an outsider had to notice the Prince-Protectorate's troops swarming in St. Sithonia, countermanding his father's orders, reacting with excessive force to any display of dissent.

And there was dissent; oh yes, indeed, there was dissent.

"Well." Chrétien drained the last of his wine and set down the glass, vaulting from the window ledge with customary grace. "I know you won't accept it," he said, touching Rikard's face with his fingertips, "but there will always be sanctuary open to you in Terre d'Ange nonetheless."

Rikard's cheek burned where Chrétien had touched it. He closed his eyes as Chrétien moved past him, curbing the familiar surge of resentment and desire. What do they expect of us, he wondered, what do they expect? Ichor runs in their veins even after a thousand and more years. So many centuries they've lived for beauty in Terre d'Ange, they've even *bred* for beauty in the Houses of the Night Court—what good is it except to make the rest of us miserable?

"We should leave, then? I do want to walk."

Rikard opened his eyes and stared blankly in Chrétien's direction. The fair brows arched again, the beautiful lips smiled.

"To the shrine. Remember?"

"Yes." He finished his own wine. "I remember."

Outside, with the vast sky stripping away the intimacy of enclosed spaces, it was easier.

"Come here," Rikard said, halfway down the Governor's Hill, leading Chrétien off the paved road. They clambered up a promontory of rock that scraped their hands but afforded a northern view. "I'll give you a history lesson they don't teach at the University." He pointed to a narrow pass still filled with snow, etched in white between the fir-green and granite peaks of the mountains. "The Pass of Sithonia. That's where she came through the mountains."

"Name of Elua! Alone and on foot?"

"With a dinner plate wrapped in rags under her arm. No one expected her to get so far." Rikard hunkered down and pitched a flake of rock, listening to it bounce and rattle down the crags. "It worked, you know. The Profaners thought it was the Wheel of Vral. They tracked her for twenty leagues."

"All the way to St. Sithonia." Chrétien gazed southward at the distant blue mirror that was Lake Khirzak, on the stony shores of which Sithonia had danced her way to martyrdom.

"It wasn't called that then. It wasn't called anything, there was nothing here but a fishing village with no name. That was over four hundred years ago."

"I know." He crouched on his heels beside Rikard, adjusting the battered scabbard that hung at his side with the ease of long practice. "I still say she went to a damnable lot of work, dying to protect a lifeless chunk of bronze, Riko."

Rikard tossed another chip, eyes crinkling with amusement. "Yes, well, you wouldn't much care for it, Angelicus. It's not very pretty."

Removing the wide-brimmed hat that Rikard had lent him to disguise his D'Angeline features, Chrétien shook out his fair hair, damp with heat and exertion, thinking how little his friend understood of the true nature of beauty. "The House of Drozhny has Vraling blood, doesn't it?"

"My great-grandmother was a Vralsturm." Rikard considered

the distant pass. "Tadeusz Vral believed he and his bloodline were appointed by God to unify and rule this nation. He made a covenant, Angelicus, and the Wheel of Vral is a symbol of it. The Profaners wanted to oust the Vralings and destroy the secular influence of the Church. How better to do it than by destroying the very symbol of that covenant?" He shook himself, glancing sideways at Chrétien. "Primitive stuff, eh? Come on, let's go. Lesson's over. Put your hat back on."

"I'm coming." In a series of swift, economical movements, Chrétien twined his hair into a braid and wound it into a coil. Jamming the hat down on his head, he rose to follow Rikard.

The streets of St. Sithonia were narrow. Most had been carved out of the rock where paths occurred by nature and tended to unexpected twists and jags. There was a crude, raw strength in this land, Chrétien thought; the bones of the earth, thrust naked into the unforgiving air. The faces of the Vralians were like that too, rugged bones jutting close to the skin.

"Of course, Sithonia did more for the Vralings than she knew," Rikard observed as they negotiated the winding streets crowded with pilgrims and tradesfolk.

"Meaning . . . ?"

"Meaning her miracle has grown very profitable over the centuries. You know that Janos Vralkaan wants to institute trade with foreign nations?"

"Yes, of course." The words came naturally. He was the heir to just such a foreign nation; of course he knew, it was his duty to know such things.

"He needs money to develop industry. The Vralian Orthodox Church tithes seventy percent to the Prince-Protectorate."

A half-step behind Rikard, Chrétien closed his eyes and winced, forcing his tone to lightness. "And St. Sithonia contributes her share, eh?"

"They say that as her strength failed her on the shore of Lake Khirzak, and the flame of her life waned and guttered, she danced. In praise of God, in thanks for His allowing her to protect the Wheel of Vral from the Profaners, she danced." Beneath the overhanging eave of a butcher's shop, Rikard glanced at him, his expression unreadable. "Vralia and God cannot be separated. The War of the Profaners proved it," he said flatly.

"You believe?"

"On the stony shore of Lake Khirzak, in sight of her pursuers and assorted fishermen, Sithonia cast down the plate she had carried so far and danced upon the shards, upon the shore, until her feet bled. And as her dance faltered, her spirit ascended; and as her body crumpled to the ground, the naked rocks burst forth with a profusion of roses," Rikard said. "How can one not believe?"

Chrétien grinned. "Need we review Anastimus' *Logic of Doubt?*" he asked. Rikard laughed, and they continued walking.

"No," he said. "It's not that. There is belief and belief; I'm not sure what I believe. But there is also faith, which is a different thing. And what I said about Vralia and God, that's true."

The foot traffic increased as the city fell behind them and the steep terrain gentled into slopes. How strange, Chrétien thought, for a country to be rooted in such a fierce, violent faith—to be wholly governed by it. Even in Terre d'Ange, where nobles of the great houses trace direct descent from Elua and his Companions, we know better. Blessed Elua cared naught for thrones, nor for mortal politics. No civilized nation could survive such single-mindedness, and yet Janos Vralkaan the Prince-Protectorate seeks to use religion as his whipping horse, driving Vralia into trade status astride its back. What shall Vralia become if he succeeds?

And worse, if he fails? What then?

Uneasy at the thought, Chrétien abandoned it as the vista of Lake Khirzak opened before them. The lake was flat and vast, too wide to see across. It was flanked along one side by the forest that rolled down from the mountains like a dark green carpet. The air above the water shimmered with heat-bands and the water itself was a blue so intense it made one's eyes ache.

On the shore was a crowd of Vralians milling about like peasants at a fair, pressing close around an empty stretch of the shoreline. There was nothing else to be seen.

"The shrine of St. Sithonia," Rikard announced, his voice devoid of inflection.

People streamed past them in either direction, but Rikard had stopped and showed no inclination to continue. A few people touched their brows, recognizing the Governor's son. He gave them no sign of recognition. Chrétien waited.

A lone figure stepped onto the empty shoreline and began a series of strange, capering gyrations silhouetted against the intense blue of Lake Khirzak.

"What is it?" Chrétien asked at length.

"He's trying to trace the Steps of Sithonia. Her footprints are embedded in the rock, you see." Now Rikard merely sounded tired. He removed his hat and wiped the sweat from his brow. "No one's ever succeeded. Still, they pay for the chance to try." He replaced his hat. "Come on."

Even in the simple act of walking, Rikard noticed, Chrétien elicited glances from the Vralian passersby. He moved—could not fail to move—with the unearthly grace of a D'Angeline prince, bred in the bone since Elua wandered the earth, and trained into the sinew from birth. The wide-brimmed hat, the plain shirt of white linen, the grey woolen trousers, rag-wrapped hilt of his sword, and worn boots could not disguise it.

"You should try the Steps," Rikard said.

Chrétien shook his head. "Not I."

A scant fifty yards from the shrine, half a dozen vendors had set up booths where they shamelessly hawked their wares. They paused before a table covered with crudely cast bronze ikons of St. Sithonia, ranging from the demure to the downright erotic. Chrétien picked up one of the latter and examined it.

"According to some legends, Sithonia was a novice at the Abbey St. Ekaterin. According to others," Rikard said dryly, "she was a repentant prostitute. You should buy one. A souvenir."

Chrétien shook his head again and placed the ikon of Sithonia back on the table, earning a glance of sharp annoyance from the vendor. Even as he set it down, a woman of middle years with a red kerchief tied about her head elbowed her way past him and seized the figurine.

"For aid in matters of love, madam." Clad in the black robes of a priest, the vendor addressed her in unctuous tones. "For aid in matters of love, pray to St. Sithonia at sunrise and sunset for seven days." He picked up a small stoppered vial, pulled out the stopper and wafted the bottle beneath the woman's nose. "For best results, rub three drops of this upon the feet of Sithonia each time you pray. Attar of roses, all the way from Terre d'Ange."

"No," said Chrétien. Rikard, who had taken his arm, froze.

"Does the young lord profess expertise in matters of love or in matters of prayer?" the priest-vendor inquired, his voice taking on acidic edge. Chrétien plucked the bottle from his hand and sniffed the contents.

"Neither," he said, handing the bottle back. "But this oil was never distilled in Terre d'Ange."

"And how . . . ?" the priest-vendor began, still acid; and then Chrétien tilted his head slightly so that sunlight pierced the shadow beneath the brim of his hat, illuminating his features. The vendor's mouth ceased speaking and gaped.

"Chrétien!" Rikard hissed, dragging his friend away, indiscriminate of the jostling crowd.

As soon as they were in the clear, Chrétien shook him off and said abruptly, "I'm sorry."

He sighed. "You know how it is with luxury items. The name alone adds half a florin to the price, true or no. It was the same in Tiberium, Angelicus."

"One never gets used to hearing the name of one's country taken in vain, that's all."

For a moment, Rikard said nothing.

Once, when they were all staggering-drunk, Chrétien had fallen into an argument with a Caerdicci rug merchant who insisted his wares were genuine D'Angeline. Chrétien had drawn his sword and slashed every rug in the shop into pieces no larger than a man's palm. No one had dared lay a hand on him. It was forgiven, of course, because he was the Dauphin of Terre d'Ange and because his father's bursar made good on the damages.

Rikard had never understood why he'd done it.

"I know what you mean," he said now, "but never mind. Let's see the shrine." He plunged into the thickest of the throng then, forging a path through the vendors' stalls until they had a clear view of the holy site.

The empty stretch of shore was cordoned off with twisted ropes of sun-faded velvet. Aside from the crowds, there was not much to see but the still blue water blazing under the white sun and the hummock of grey stone that lined the shore. A series of slight indentations, vaguely foot-sized and stained with a sanguine pigment, were impressed upon the barren rock.

"The Steps of Sithonia," Rikard murmured in Chrétien's ear. "Or mineral deposits. Take your pick."

His voice seemed to come from a great distance, for the Dauphin of Terre d'Ange was envisioning gone the ropes, the crowds, the ubiquitous priest-vendors; gone, all gone, until there was only the harsh, splendid sprawl of the Vralian landscape, the wide, blue-burning eye of the lake and the martyred stone, forever branded with Sithonia's bloody footprints. Trying to imagine how she must have felt, Chrétien shuddered and lifted his face to the bright, cruel sky. His heart expanded and his eyes welled with sudden tears.

And then one of the Sithonian pilgrims broke his reverie, pushing out of the crowd to thrust a handful of coins into the purse of the priest-vendor who kept the shrine.

The shrinekeeper drew back a rope and admitted the aspirant onto the sacred stone. The man hitched up his trousers, murmuring under his breath; prayer or instruction, it was impossible to tell. He placed his feet carefully on the first two Steps.

"What happens if he succeeds?" Chrétien whispered.

"He won't."

One, two, three Steps; a turn, then several quick steps, then a spinning lunge and the man lost his balance, overcompensated, and set a foot down on bare stone. His shoulders slumped. The crowd sighed.

"Do you think it could be done?" Rikard asked Chrétien, who shrugged.

"By a D'Angeline master of dance? Yes and no. Oh, we could probably devise something that would trace the Steps, but the odds of duplicating Sithonia's dance are one in ten thousand."

"Truly?" Rikard sounded surprised. Chrétien glanced at him.

"You can't choreograph exaltation," he said, and Rikard stared at the crimson-patterned stone, frowning.

When it came, the wordless shout seemed to shatter the hard, bright air. Rikard was half-aware, as he turned, that he had been hearing for some time a muttering disturbance behind them; he was half-aware too, as a second shout, awful and despairing, ripped across the sky, that Chrétien had already whipped about, begun to draw his sword and paused, shoving it back into its scabbard.

The terrible sound came from a young man, scarce past adolescence, who stood with his legs astraddle on a tall, jutting boulder at the eastern edge of the shrine. Even as Rikard watched, he threw back his head and shouted again, the cords in his throat swelling visibly with the raw force of it.

"Ikon-breaker," someone behind Rikard muttered fearfully.

Several of the Prince-Protectorate's troops emerged at a run from the distant edge of the forest, their black and silver uniforms in stark monochromatic contrast to the stony terrain.

"Vral protect us!" said another voice. "It's Miodrag the Cobbler's son. He's lost his wits!"

Rikard spun about, saw the woman who had spoken and caught her wrist. "What's his crime? The cobbler's son, what's his crime?"

She blinked in fear, wrenched her wrist from his grasp and backed away from him, but someone else, a tall man with the black-pored face of a coal miner, answered. "Killed two Vralkaani soldiers. They'd come to take his father to debtor's prison."

"Vralkaani? Why?"

The miner's eyes were bleak. "Cobbler was in debt to the Church. Wife was dying. He purchased healing prayers on credit. Wife died anyway. He couldn't honor the debt."

"Here? In St. Sithonia?"

"Aye."

Rikard cursed.

"The cobbler died too," a second man added. "Blow to the head. The Vralkaani beat him when his boy escaped."

On the boulder, the cobbler's son cried aloud, "Sithonia!" His hands knotted spasmodically into fists, his eyes were wild and full of sunfire. Except for a ragged breechclout, he was naked, begrimed and thorn-scratched.

———

Left to himself while Rikard questioned onlookers, Chrétien thought, ah, Elua; this one, he is not calling on the saint only, he is calling on the city, he is calling on them all. Shivers raced over his skin.

"Hear me, Sithonia, for I will soon be dead! You, who were once a savior of Vralia, have become its whore!" With another wordless cry, the cobbler's son leapt from the boulder. The crowds parted before him. "You!" His finger pointed, his arm swung, encompassing the crowd. "All of you. Blasphemers!"

In a few swift strides, he crossed to the nearest booth, set a shoulder to it, and heaved. Shelves laden with fine enamel work crashed to the ground, graven images shattering.

"Here is your truth," the cobbler's son said bitterly. "Broken faith." He grasped shards of the broken ikons with both hands. "Sithonia did not die that you might bear children," he said, almost gently, extending one hand to a young woman who shrank back from him. His fist clenched about the shards, and blood dripped to the ground. "Nor that you might be made young," he said to an elderly man leaning on a crutch, and clenched the other fist. His blood ran in scarlet ribbons. A sound like a moan rippled through the crowd.

"No! Sithonia died to keep the Wheel of Vral from the Profaners!" the youth cried, and dashed the shards to the ground.

The Vralkaani soldiers had covered half the distance between the forest and the shrine. People began to back away from the cobbler's son, away from the shrine, away from the booths. With a howl of rage, the soldiers' quarry swept his arm across another booth, sending rows of statuettes to their demise.

And then he turned and grasped the velvet cords that sectioned off the Steps of Sithonia. The muscles of his back and arms strained visibly as he hauled the ropes and the posts that anchored them loose from their moorings, and hurled them into the still blue depths of Lake Khirzak.

With a splash, the tangle of ropes and posts sank into the water and disappeared. The cobbler's son faced the crowd, holding out his bleeding hands, his eyes now strangely tranquil. His naked chest, smeared with grime and shining with sweat, heaved from his exertions.

Name of Elua, but he's young, Chrétien thought in anguish. How can they just stand, how can they bear to watch? I will never, until my death, understand this country.

"Once Vralia served the glory of God," the cobbler's son said quietly. "Now God serves the glory of Janos Vralkaan, and we are all Profaners."

In the silence that followed, the troops of the Prince-Protectorate arrived. No one spoke.

"Get back!" the soldiers' captain shouted at the crowd, his badge flashing on the front of his cap, silver braid winking on its brim. "Back!" He unslung his musket, and his men followed suit. Four of them took warning aim at the crowd. The other five trained their muskets on the cobbler's son, alone and half-naked on the shore.

Rikard stood rigid in the crowd. Chrétien's hand locked onto his upper arm, nails digging into his flesh. "*Do* something!" he hissed. "You're the Governor's son!"

"I can't," Rikard murmured. He looked at Chrétien with eyes full of despair. "He killed Vralkaani soldiers, don't you see? It doesn't matter why. There's nothing I can do; it would be treason."

The captain raised his hand. His troops waited motionless.

"Fire," the captain said.

They did.

One ball caught the cobbler's son in the right shoulder, spinning him around and making the other shots go wild. He staggered, raising a hand to his bleeding shoulder.

"Oh God," Rikard whispered. The cobbler's son had just traced the first three Steps of Sithonia.

"Reload," said the captain. "Fire."

Two more shots struck the youth, driving him, spinning, half-falling, each faltering step tracing one of St. Sithonia's crimson footprints. "No," Rikard heard himself saying, "No, no, no." His arm was numb from the pressure of Chrétien's grip.

"Reload," said the captain again. "Fire."

The cobbler's son lifted his eyes to the sun.

When the final volley struck him, his body jerked like a puppet's, wildly, flailing; it was impossible that he kept his feet, bleeding from more than half a dozen fatal wounds; impossible that every staggering step he took was tracing, continued to trace, each and every one of the Steps of Sithonia. And yet he did.

In silence, the captain lowered his hand.

In silence, the cobbler's son crumpled and fell to the stones.

In silence, the barren, blood-stained rocks brought forth a profusion of roses, wild and crimson.

They lingered only for a moment, blossoming in glorious billows of scarlet and vermilion, twined with glimpses of thorns and green vines; then they withered, faded, and passed from existence, leaving behind only the body of the cobbler's son, pale and motionless on the shore.

"Take him," said the captain, his jaw clenched on his disbelief. Faces blank with shock, the soldiers moved to obey. And for the second time that day, a tremendous shout split the sky; not raw and anguished, this, but a gilded trumpet-peal of denial.

"NO!"

With an awful feeling of recognition, Rikard realized that there was only one throat in Vralia that could have uttered that sound. Before he could comprehend the flash of movement to his left and the absence of the death grip upon his arm, he saw.

Between the cobbler's son and the soldiers stood Chrétien L'Envers, the Dauphin of Terre d'Ange. His sword gleamed beneath the merciless sun. His hat had blown off. His hair had come loose from its casual braid and it shone like a noonday star. His face, naked in its beauty, seemed to blaze with a terrible light in the harsh Vralian landscape.

"Do you dare?" he asked the captain, smiling a deadly smile. Sunlight ran like water down the length of his sword. "Do you dare?"

Now, only now, people began falling to their knees; some gasping, some wailing. Three of the soldiers threw down their muskets. Oh God, Rikard thought like a man waking from a dream; they've never seen a D'Angeline, they're not sure he's human; and why should they, after all, when he's not—not wholly? Oh God, Angelicus, you shouldn't be out there alone, not here, not in this matter. It is our grief, our shame, our loss.

With his heart in his throat, he stepped forward.

"I am Rikard Drozhny, the Governor's son," he announced. Heads turned in his direction. The captain of the Prince-Protectorate's troops stared at him. "You have killed your man, sir," Rikard said. "His body, I think, belongs to St. Sithonia."

No one spoke. Feeling a hundred and more eyes upon him, he walked past the captain, past the Vralkaani soldiers, past Chrétien onto the shore.

On the barren stone, Rikard knelt and gathered the body of the cobbler's son into his arms. Slack and lifeless, it weighed heavy. The face was calm and unmarked despite the body's terrible wounds. Rikard stood. The youth's head and legs dangled. The body was heavy, heavy as stone, but he could carry it all the way to Vralstag if he had to, to the foot of Vral's Throne itself. He looked around him at the staring faces full of hunger and need.

"To the Church of St. Sithonia," he said, and began to walk, carrying the body of the cobbler's son. One by one, the people of

Sithonia stood. They cleared an aisle for Rikard Drozhny and the burden he cradled. They reached out as he passed, touching the body of the cobbler's son, murmuring, weeping. They fell in beside him, forming a procession.

And behind them, Chrétien L'Envers guarded their passage.

One by one, the remaining soldiers of the Prince-Protectorate lay down their weapons and fell in with the procession. Left behind on the shore with the bright D'Angeline apparition, the captain dropped to his knees and buried his face in his hands.

———

Chrétien L'Envers, the Dauphin of Terre d'Ange, sat alone at the writing desk in his guest room in the ancestral home of the House of Drozhny, reading the words of the letter he had just composed.

"Dear Father," the letter stated, "Fondest greetings from your eldest son, the errant traveler. May I hope that it gladdens your heart to read that I am well, and expect to be home in some six weeks' time with full many a tale to tell. The darkless nights of a Vralian summer are a wonder to behold, though in truth I would not trade them for the moon and stars of Terre d'Ange, and there are no nightingales to be found in the whole of Vralia nation."

He read these words and no more, staring beyond the page into the flame of his single candle. The other words did not matter. Encrypted into this brief paragraph was message his father awaited.

Civil war imminent. Cease all trade negotiations immediately.

With steady hands, Chrétien folded the letter and inserted it into an envelope. He held a taper of sealing wax in the candle-flame and allowed one precise drop to fall upon the envelope, then stamped it with the impress of his signet ring.

Within a few days' time, he estimated, it would no longer be safe for him in Vralia. His role in what had transpired at Lake Khirzak remained a mystery to the populace, but there were Vralian nobles who knew that the Dauphin of Terre d'Ange was visiting his fast friend Rikard Drozhny, the Governor's son. Word of this was bound to reach Janos Vralkaan. The Prince-Protectorate had already proved himself amply capable of adding two and two in the literal sense; doubtless he was capable in the figurative sense as well.

The Dauphin of Terre d'Ange would make, among other things, an admirable hostage.

Rikard wanted him to stay, of course, but Rikard understood. They had spoken some, though not much, of the cobbler's son and the events at the shrine.

It had changed things between them.

"Why did you do it?" Rikard had asked, anguish and bewilderment in his voice. "I thought you were only here to . . . *Why,* Angelicus? Armed with a sword, against muskets! You might have been killed, you know. You might well have been killed."

"Ah well," Chrétien had murmured, gazing at Rikard across the vast rift that separated them. "And you wonder why we cultivate beauty? It too is a weapon, my friend, and one that cuts both ways."

Rikard was a hero among the common Vralian people. His father reviled him publicly and grieved with him privately. When the war came, they would be on opposite sides, Vralings by blood the both of them. Whichever side won, the House of Drozhny would be there to serve Vralia.

Vralia and God, Chrétien thought, picking up the gold medallion that Rikard had given him; a talisman of St. Sithonia, of course. The gold gleamed coldly in the candlelight.

"You can't tell me you've no need of a souvenir now," Rikard had said with a nonchalance that fooled no one, averting his gaze to hide the emotion it held.

The talisman was embossed on one side with the Wheel of Vral and on the other with a full-blown rose. Chrétien closed his hand on the medallion and clenched his fist until the gold edges bit into his flesh, a pain he welcomed. His pale, shining hair fell forward to curtain his face.

Alone in his room, the Dauphin of Terre d'Ange wept.

PETER V. BRETT

THE FOLLOWING STORY, "MUDBOY," STARTED OUT AS A PART OF MY Demon Cycle series from Del Rey Books. When I add a new POV character to the series, I try to take the reader back into their childhood, reintroducing the demon world through their eyes and showing the pivotal events in their life that led them to become the person they are in the central story line.

Briar was a great addition to the series, and I had originally intended for the following story to be the introduction to my third book, *The Daylight War.* It would have been the first part of a three-act play on Briar's young life, spanning the ten years or so before he encountered Leesha and Rojer on the road to the Hollow.

But I quickly saw how the character might grow unchecked. I kept having more and more ideas for Briar's own tale, and they were largely separate from the main story line of the series, to the point where it might become a distraction.

So I cut the section I had written, meaning to save it for a Demon Cycle novella like the others I have done for Subterranean Press. When Shawn asked me to contribute a story to *Unfettered,* I knew it would be a perfect fit.

I will eventually write more of Briar's adventures, but in the meantime, please enjoy this little tale. I am thrilled to finally be able to share it, and in such prestigious company!

Peter V. Brett

MUDBOY

Peter V. Brett

Summer 323 AR

Briar started awake at the clanging.

His mother was banging the porridge pot with her metal ladle, the sound echoing through the house. "Out of bed, lazeabouts!" she cried. "Breakfast is hot, and any who ent finished by sunup get an empty belly till luncheon!"

A pillow struck Briar's head. "Open the slats, Briarpatch," Hardey mumbled.

"Why do I always have to do it?" Briar asked.

Another pillow hit Briar on the opposite side of his head. "Cause if there's a demon there, Hardey and I can run while it eats you!" Hale snapped. "Get goin'!"

The twins always bullied him together . . . not that it mattered. They had twelve summers, and each of them towered over him like a wood demon.

Briar stumbled out of the bed, rubbing his eyes as he felt his way to the window and turned up the slats. The sky was a reddish purple, giving just enough light for Briar to make out the lurking shapes of demons in the yard. His mother called them cories, but Father called them *alagai*.

While the twins were still stretching in bed waiting for their dawn vision, Briar hurried out of the room to try and be first to the privy curtain. He almost made it, but as usual, his sisters shouldered him out of the way at the last second.

"Girls first, Briarpatch!" Sky said. With thirteen summers, she was more menacing than the twins, but even Sunny, ten, could muscle poor Briar about easily.

He decided he could hold his water until after breakfast, and made it first to the table. It was Sixthday. The day Relan had bacon, and each of the children was allowed a slice. Briar inhaled the smell as he listened to the bacon crackle on the skillet. His mother was folding eggs, singing to herself. Dawn was a round woman, with big meaty arms that could wrestle five children at once, or crush them all in an embrace. Her hair was bound in a green kerchief.

Dawn looked up at Briar and smiled. "Bit of a chill lingering in the common, Briar. Be a good boy and lay a fire to chase it off, please."

Briar nodded, heading into the common room of their small cottage and kneeling at the hearth. He reached up the chimney, hand searching for the notched metal bar of the flue. He set it in the open position, and began laying the fire. From the kitchen, he heard his mother singing.

> *When laying morning fire, what do you do?*
> *Open the flue, open the flue!*
> *Leaves and grass and kindle sticks strew,*
> *Then pile the logs, two by two.*
> *Bellow the coals till the heat comes through,*
> *And watch the fire, burning true.*

Briar soon had the fire going, but his brothers and sisters made it to the table by the time he returned, and they gave him no room to sit as they scooped eggs and fried tomatoes with onions onto their plates. A basket of biscuits sat steaming on the table as Dawn cut the rasher of bacon. The smells made Briar's stomach howl. He tried to reach in to snatch a biscuit, only to have Sunny slap his hand away.

"Wait your turn, Briarpatch!"

"You have to be bold," said a voice behind him, and Briar turned to see his father. "When I was in Sharaj, the boy who was too timid went hungry."

His father, Relan asu Relan am'Damaj am'Kaji, had been a *Sharum* warrior once, but had snuck from the Desert Spear in the back of a Messenger's cart. Now he worked as a refuse collector, but his spear and shield still hung on the wall. His children all took after him, dark-skinned and whip thin.

"They're all bigger than me," Briar said.

Relan nodded. "Yes, but size and strength are not everything, my son." He glanced to the front door. "The sun will rise soon. Come watch with me."

Briar hesitated. His father's attention always seemed to be on his older brothers, and it was wonderful to be noticed, but he remembered the demons he had seen in the yard. A shout from his mother turned both their heads.

"Don't you dare take him out there, Relan! He's only six! Briar, come back to the table."

Briar moved to comply, but his father put a hand on his shoulder, holding him in place. "Six is old enough to be caught by *alagai* for running when it is best to keep still, beloved," Relan said, "or for keeping still when it is best to run. We do our children no favors by coddling them." He guided Briar onto the porch, closing the door before Dawn could retort.

The sky was a lighter shade of indigo now, dawn only minutes away. Relan lit his pipe, filling the porch with its sweet, familiar scent. Briar inhaled deeply, feeling safer with his father's smoke around him than he did from the wards.

Briar looked about in wonder. The porch was a familiar place, filled like the rest of their home with mismatched furniture Relan had salvaged from the town dump and carefully mended.

But in the false light before dawn everything looked different—bleak and ominous. Most of the demons had fled the coming sun by now, but one had turned at the creak of the porch door and the light and sound that came from the house. It caught sight of Briar and his father, stalking toward them.

"Keep behind the paint," Relan warned, pointing with his pipe stem to the line of wards on the planks. "Even the boldest warrior does not step across the wards lightly."

The wood demon hissed at them. Briar knew it—the one that rose each night by the old goldwood tree he loved to climb. The demon's eyes were fixed on Relan, who met its gaze coolly. The demon charged, striking the wardnet with its great branchlike arms. Silver magic spiderwebbed through the air. Briar shrieked and ran for the house.

His father caught his wrist, yanking him painfully to a stop. "Running attracts their attention." He pulled Briar around to see that indeed, the demon's gaze was turned his way. A thin trickle of drool, yellow like sap, ran from the corner of its mouth as it gave a low growl.

Relan squatted and took Briar by the shoulders, looking him in the eyes. "You must always respect the *alagai*, my son, but you should never be ruled by your fear of them. Embrace your fear, and step beyond it."

He gently pushed the boy back toward the wards. The demon was still there, stalking not ten feet away. It shrieked at him, maw opening to reveal rows of amber teeth and a rough brown tongue.

Briar's leg began to twitch, and he ground his foot down to try and still it. His bladder felt about to burst. He bit his lip. His brothers and sisters would never tire of teasing if he went back inside with a wet pant leg.

"Breathe, my son," Relan said. "Embrace your fear and trust in the wards. Learn their ways, and inevera, you will not die on *alagai* talons."

Briar knew he should trust his father, who had stood out in the night with nothing but his shield and spear, but the words did nothing to stop the churning in his stomach, or the need to pee. He crossed his legs to help hold back his water, hoping his father wouldn't notice. He looked at the horizon, but it was still orange with no hint of yellow.

Already, he could see his brothers rolling on the floor with laughter as his sisters sang, "Pissy pants! Pissy pants! Water in the Briarpatch!"

"Look to me, and I will teach you a Baiter's trick," Relan said, allowing the boy to step back. His father toed the wards instead, looking the wood demon in the eye and returning its growl.

Relan leaned to the left, and the demon mimicked him. He straightened and leaned to the right, and the wood demon did the same. He began to sway slowly from side to side, and like a reflection in the water, the demon followed, even as Relan took a step to the left, then went back to his original position, then a step to the right. The next time he took two steps in either direction. Then three. Each time, the demon followed.

His father took four exaggerated steps to the left, then stopped, leaning his body back to the right. Instinctively, the demon began stepping to the right, following the pattern, even as Relan broke it, resuming his steps to the left. He reached the far side of the porch before the demon caught on, letting out a shriek and leaping for him. Again the wards flared, and it was cast back.

Relan turned back to Briar, dropping to one knee to meet the boy's eyes.

"The *alagai* are bigger than you, my son. Stronger, too. But," he flicked Briar's forehead with his finger, "they are not smarter. The servants of Nie have brains as tiny as a shelled pea, slow to think and easy to dazzle. If you are caught out with one, embrace your fear and sway as I have taught you. When the *alagai* steps the wrong way, walk—do not run—toward the nearest succor. The smartest demon will take at least six steps before growing wise to the trick."

"*Then* you run," Briar guessed.

Relan smiled, shaking his head. "Then you take three deep breaths. It will be that long at least before the demon reorients." He smacked Briar's thigh, making him wince and clutch at his crotch, trying to hold the water in. "*Then* you run. Run as if the house were on fire."

Briar nodded, grimacing.

"Three breaths," Relan said again. "Take them now." He sucked in a breath, inviting Briar to follow. He did, filling his lungs, then breathing out with his father. Again Relan drew, and Briar followed.

He knew it was meant to calm him, but the deep breathing only seemed to make the pressure worse. He was sure his father must be able to see it, but Relan gave no sign. "Do you know why your mother and I named you Briar?"

Briar shook his head, feeling his face heat with the strain.

"There was once a boy in Krasia who was abandoned by his parents for being weak and sickly," Relan said. "He could not keep up with the herds they followed to survive, and his father, who already had many sons, cast him out."

Tears began to stream down Briar's cheeks. Would his father cast him out as well, if he wet himself in fear?

"A pack of nightwolves that had been following the herd were frightened of the family's spears, but when they caught the boy's scent, alone and unprotected, they began to stalk him," Relan continued. "But the boy led them into a briar patch, and when one of the wolves followed him in, it became stuck in the sharp thorns. The boy waited until it was caught fast, then dashed its head in with a stone. When he returned to his father with the wolf's pelt around his shoulders, his father fell on his knees and begged Everam's forgiveness for doubting his son."

Relan squeezed Briar's shoulders again. "Your brothers and sisters may tease you for your name, but wear it proudly. Briar patches thrive in places no other plants can survive, and even the *alagai* respect their thorns."

The need to empty his water did not go away, but Briar felt the urgency fade, and he straightened, standing with his father as they watched the sky fill with color. The remaining demon faded into mist, sinking into the ground before the first sliver of the sun crested the horizon. Relan put his arm around Briar as they watched sunrise shimmer across the surface of the lake. Briar leaned in, enjoying the rare moment alone with his father, without the shoving and teasing of his siblings.

I wish I didn't have any brothers and sisters, he thought.

Just then, the sunlight struck him.

The others were stacking their dishes, but Dawn had left plates for Briar and Relan. Briar sat alone with his father, and felt very special.

Relan bit into his first strip of bacon and closed his eyes, savoring every chew. "The *dama* used to tell me pig-eaters burned in Nie's abyss, but by the Creator's beard, I swear it a fair price."

Briar mimicked him, biting into his slice and closing his eyes to savor the grease and salt.

"How come Briarpatch gets to eat after sunup?" Sky demanded.

"Yeah!" the twins echoed at once. If there was one thing they agreed with Sky about, it was bullying Briar.

The smile fell from Relan's face. "Because he eats with me." His tone made it clear further questions would be answered with his strap. The old strip of leather hung on the wall by the mantle, a warning all the Damaj children took very seriously. Relan used the strap to whip his mule when it refused a heavy load, but he had not hesitated to take it to Hardey's backside the time he threw a cat in the lake to see if it could swim. They all remembered their brother's howls, and lived in terror of that strap.

Relan paid his other children no further mind, taking a second slice of bacon on his fork and laying it on Briar's plate.

"Boys, go feed the mule and get the dump cart hitched," Dawn said, breaking the tension. "Girls, you've got laundry to do while I tend garden. Git to it." The children bowed and quickly filed out, leaving Briar alone with his father.

"When a boy first stands before the *alagai* in Krasia, he is sent to spend the following day in prayer." Relan said. He laughed. "Though I admit when I tried it, I soon grew bored. Still, it is wise to think on the experience. When you are done helping your mother pick herbs, you may take the rest of the day to walk in the sun."

A day to do whatever he wished. Briar knew what to say, though the words seemed insufficient. "Yes, Father. Thank you, Father."

"You were very brave today, Briar," his mother said as they weeded the skyflower bed. Briar felt his face flush in embarrassment, thinking of how he had nearly peed in his pants.

He shook his head. "I was really scared."

"That's what brave is," Dawn said. "When you're scared, but keep your wits about you. Your father says you held up better than your brothers."

"Really?" Briar asked.

"Really." Dawn narrowed her eyes. "You stir trouble by tellin' 'em I told you that, though, and it'll be the strap."

Briar swallowed. "I won't tell anyone."

Dawn laughed and put her arms around him, squeezing tightly. "Know you won't, poppet. I'm so proud of you."

"Mistress Dawn!" a call came, breaking the moment. Briar looked up to see Tami Bales running up the road. Tami was only a year older than Briar, but the Damaj children weren't allowed to play with the Baleses since Tami's father, Masen, called Relan a desert rat at the Solstice festival. Relan would have broken his arm if the other men hadn't pulled them apart.

Tami's dress was splattered with mud and red with blood. Briar knew bloodstains when he saw them. Any Herb Gatherer's child did. Dawn ran out to meet the girl, and Tami collapsed in her arms, panting for breath. "Mistress . . . y-you have to save . . ."

"Who?" Dawn demanded. "Who's been hurt? Corespawn it, girl, what's happened?"

"Corelings," Tami gasped.

"Creator," Dawn drew a ward in the air. "Whose blood is this?" She pulled at the still-damp fabric of the girl's dress.

"Maybell," Tami said.

Dawn's nose wrinkled. "The cow?"

Tami nodded. "Stuck her head over the pen, blocking one of the wardposts. Field demon clawed her neck. Pa says she's gonna get demon fever and went for his axe. Please, you need to come or he'll put her down."

Dawn blew out a breath, shaking her head and chuckling. Tami looked ready to cry.

"I'm sorry girl," Dawn said. "Don't mean to belittle. I know stock feels like part of the family sometimes. You just had me thinking it was one of your brothers or sisters got cored. I'll do what I can. Run and tell your pa to hold his stroke."

Tami nodded and ran off as Dawn turned to Briar. "We'll need sleep draught . . ."

"Skyflower and tampweed," Briar nodded.

"Cut generously," Dawn said. "Takes a lot more to put down a cow than a person. We'll need hogroot poultices as well."

Briar nodded. "I know what to get." He ran off to gather the cuttings while his mother got her implements ready.

"You'll have to wait a bit before your walk, poppet," Dawn said as they headed down the road to Masen's farm.

"It's okay," Briar said. "I want to help."

They could hear Maybell's bleats of pain long before they arrived. The heifer was lying on the dirt floor of the pen, neck wrapped in heavy cloth soaked through with blood. Masen Bales stood nearby, running his thumb along the edge of his axe. Tami and her siblings crowded around the cow protectively, though none were large enough to stop their father if he decided it was Maybell's time.

"Thanks for coming, Gatherer," Masen said. His eyes narrowed at the sight of Briar, and he spit some of the tobacco he was chewing. "I meant to put the animal down quick and sell her to the butcher, but the kids begged me to wait 'til you came."

Dawn nodded, pushing through the crowd and lifting the cloth to look at the animal's wounds, three deep grooves in Maybell's thick neck. "It's good you did. This ent too bad, if we can stave off the infection." She turned to the crowd of children.

"I'll need more cloth for bandages, buckets of clean water, and a boiling kettle." The children looked at her blankly until she clapped her hands, making them all jump. "Now!"

As the children ran off, Briar laid out his mother's tools and began crushing the herbs for the sleeping draught and poultices.

Getting the animal to drink was difficult, but soon Maybell was fast asleep, and Dawn cleaned out the wounds and inserted a thin paste of crushed herbs before stitching them closed.

Tami stood next to Briar, horrified. Briar had seen his mother work before, but he knew how scary it must seem. He reached out, taking her hand, and she looked at him, smiling bravely in thanks as she squeezed tightly.

Masen had been watching Dawn work as well, but he glanced at Tami and did a double take, pointing his axe at Briar. "Ay, get your muddy hands off my daughter you little rat!"

Briar snatched his hand away in an instant. His mother stood, moving calmly between them as she wiped the blood from her hands. "Ent going to need that axe anymore, Masen, so I'd appreciate you not pointing it at my boy."

Masen looked at the weapon in surprise, as if he'd forgotten he was holding it. He grunted and dropped the head, leaning it against the fence. "Wasn't going to do anything."

Dawn pursed her lips. "That'll be twenty shells."

Masen gaped. "Twenty shells?! For stitching a cow?"

"Ten for the stitching," Dawn said. "And ten for the sleep draught and hogroot poultices my rat son made."

"I won't pay it," Masen said. "Neither you nor your mud-skinned husband can make me."

"I don't need Relan for that," Dawn said, smiling, "though we both know he could make you. No, all I need is to tell Marta Speaker you won't pay, and Maybell will be grazing in my yard before tomorrow."

Masen glared. "You ent been right in the head since you married that desert rat, Dawn. Already cost most of your patients. Lucky to get cow work these days, but that won't last when folk hear you're charging twenty shells for it."

Dawn crossed her arms. "That's Mistress Dawn to you, Masen Bales, and now it's twenty-five. Call one more name, I'll go see Marta right now."

Masen began muttering curses, but he stomped off to the house, coming back with a worn leather bag. He counted the smooth lacquered shells into Dawn's hand. "Fifteen . . . sixteen . . . seventeen. That's all I got right now, *Mistress*. You'll have the rest in a week. Honest word."

"I'd better," Dawn said. "Come along, Briar."

The two of them walked down the road until they came to the fork, one way leading to their home, the other to the rest of town.

"You run off now, Briar. Enjoy the sun for a few hours. I'll see you at supper." Dawn smiled and pressed a handful of shells into his hand. "In case you want to buy joint of meat and a sugar candy."

Briar felt a thrill as he made his way into town, running his fingers over the smooth lacquer of the shells. He'd never had money of his own before, and had to suppress a whoop of glee.

He went to the butcher shop, where Mrs. Butcher sold hot meat pies and laid a shell on the counter.

Mrs. Butcher looked at him suspiciously. "Where'd you get that shell, Mudboy? You steal it?"

Briar shook his head. "Mother gave it to me for helping her save Tami Bales's cow."

Mrs. Butcher grunted and took the shell, handing him a steaming pie in return.

He went next to the sugarmaker, who fixed a glare on Briar the moment he came into the shop. His look did not soften until Briar produced a pair of shells to pay for the candies he collected from the display, all wrapped in twisted corn husks. These he stuffed in his pockets, eating the meat pie as he walked back out of town. The sun was bright on his shoulders, and it felt warm and safe. The memory of the wood demon snarling at him seemed a distant thing.

He walked down to the lake and watched the fishing boats for a time. It was a clear day, and he could just make out Lakton in the distance, the great city floating far out on the lake. He followed the shoreline, skipping stones across the water.

He stopped short, spotting a pair of webbed tracks in the mud left by a bank demon. He imagined the frog-like creature leaping onto the shore and catching him with its long sticky tongue. The tracks made him shiver, and suddenly he had to pee desperately. He barely lowered his pants in time, thankful there was no one to see.

"Brave," he muttered to himself, knowing the lie for what it was.

Late in the afternoon, Briar hid behind the house and pulled out one of the sugar candies. He unwrapped the treasure and chewed slowly, savoring every bite as his father did with bacon.

"Ay, Briarpatch!" a voice called. Briar looked up to see Hardey and Hale approaching.

"Where'd you get that candy?" Hale called, balling a fist.

"We get to haul trash all day, and he gets extra bacon and candy?" Hardey asked no one in particular.

Briar froze. His mind ran through all the things he might say, but he knew none of them would make any difference. His brothers were going to knock him down and take the candy, promising worse if he told their parents.

He ran. Over the woodpiles, quick as a hare, and then cut through the laundry lines as his brothers charged after him. Sunny and Sky were collecting the clean wash in baskets, and he barely missed running into them.

"Ay, watch it, Briarpatch!" Sky shouted.

"Stop him, he's got candy!" he heard Hardey cry. Briar dodged around a hanging sheet and kept low as he doubled back around the house, running into the woods out back.

He could hear the others close behind, and made for the goldwood tree where the wood demon rose. Briar had climbed the tree a hundred times, and knew every knot and branch. He swung up into its boughs like he was a wood demon himself, then froze and held his breath. The others ran by, and Briar counted fifty breaths before he dared move.

There was a small hollow where the branches met. Briar packed the candy in dry leaves and left it hidden there, praying to the Creator it would not rain. Then he dropped back to the ground and ran home.

At supper, his brothers and sisters watched him like a cat watches a mouse. Briar kept close to his mother until bedtime.

No sooner than the door to the tiny room the three boys shared was closed, Hale and Hardey pinned him on the floor of their room, digging through his pockets and searching his bed.

"Where'd you hide them, Briarpatch?" Hardey demanded, sitting hard on his stomach, knocking the breath out of him.

"It was just the one, and I ate it!" Briar struggled, but he was wise enough not to raise his voice. A shout might get his brothers the strap, but it would go worse for him.

Eventually the boys gave up, giving him a last shake and going to bed. "This ent over, Briarpatch," Hardey said. "Catch you with it later, you'll be eating dirt."

They were soon asleep, but Briar's heart was still thumping, and out in the yard, demons shrieked as they tested the wards. Briar couldn't sleep through the sound, flinching at every cry and flash of magic. Hale kicked him under the covers. "Quit squirming, Briarpatch, or I'll lock you out on the porch for the night."

Briar shuddered, and again felt an overwhelming urge to empty his bladder. He got out of bed and stumbled into the hall to find the privy. It was pitch black in the house, but that had never bothered Briar before. He had blindly fumbled his way to the curtain countless times.

But it was different tonight. There was a demon in the house. Briar couldn't say how he knew, but he could sense it, lurking in the darkness, waiting for its chance to pounce.

Briar could feel his heart pounding like a festival drum and began to sweat, though the night was cool. It was suddenly hard for him to breathe, as if Hardey were still sitting on his chest. There was a rustling sound ahead, and Briar yelped, literally jumping. He looked around and it seemed he could make a dim shape moving in the darkness.

Terrified, he turned and ran for the common room. The fire had burned down, but a few pumps of the bellows had an open flame, and Briar fed it carefully from the woodbox until it filled the room with light.

Shadows fled, and with them the hiding places of the demons. The room was empty.

Baby Briar, scared of nothing, his brothers and sisters liked to sing. Briar hated himself, but his leg would not stop shaking. He couldn't go back to bed. He would piss the covers and the twins would kill him. He couldn't go down the hall to the privy in the dark. The very thought terrified him. He could sleep here, by the fire, or . . .

Briar slipped across the common to the door of his parents' room.

Never open the door if the bed is creaking, his mother had said, but Briar listened closely, and the bed was quiet. He turned the latch and slipped quietly inside, closing the door behind him. He crawled up the center of the bed, nestling himself between his parents. His mother put her arms about him, and Briar fell deep asleep.

It was still dark when he awoke to screaming. His parents started upright, taking poor Briar with them. All of them took a reflexive breath, and started to cough and choke.

There was smoke everywhere. His parents were both touching him, but he couldn't see them at all. Everything was a gray blur even worse than darkness.

"Down!" his mother croaked, pulling Briar with her as she slid off the bed. "Smoke rises! The air will be better by the floorboards." There was a thump as his father rolled out of bed on the far side, crawling over to them.

"Take Briar out the window," Relan said, coughing into his hand. "I'll get the others and follow."

"Into the night?!" Dawn asked.

"We cannot stay here, beloved," Relan said. "The wardposts in the herb garden are strong. It's only twenty yards from the house. You can make it if you are quick."

Dawn grabbed Briar's hand, squeezing so hard the boy whimpered. "Wet the towel by the washbasin and put it over your mouth to hold out the smoke."

Relan nodded and put a hand on her shoulder. "Be careful. The smoke will draw many *alagai*." He kissed her. "Go."

Dawn began crawling for the window, dragging Briar after her. "Take three deep breaths, Briar, and then hold the last. Keep it held until we're out the window, and as soon as we hit the ground, run for the garden. You understand?"

"Yes," Briar said, and then coughed for what seemed forever. At last the wracking ceased, and he nodded to his mother. On the third breath, they stood and Dawn threw open the shutters. She lifted Briar in her arms, swung her legs over the sill, and dropped to the ground with a thump.

As Relan had warned, there were demons in the yard, flitting about through the drifting smoke. Together, they ran for the garden before the corelings caught sight of them.

Dawn stopped up short once they crossed the garden wards. "You stay here. I need to help your father with the others."

"No!" Briar cried, gripping her skirts. "Don't leave me!"

Dawn gripped Briar's shirt tightly with one hand, and slapped his face with the other. His head seemed to flash with light, and he stumbled back, letting go her skirts.

"Ent got time to baby you right now, Briar. You mind me," his mother said. "Go to the hogroot patch and hide there. Bruise the leaves and rub them all over your body. Cories hate hogroot. Even the smell of it makes them sick. I'll be back soon."

Briar sniffed and wiped at his tears, but he nodded and his mother turned and ran for the house. A wood demon caught sight of her and ran to intercept. Briar screamed.

But Dawn kept her head, doing the same dance Relan had done that very morning. In a moment, she had the coreling stumbling left as she ran to the right, disappearing back through the window.

Feeling numb, like he was in a dream, Briar stumbled over to the hogroot patch. He rolled in the thick weeds, tearing off leaves and rubbing them on this clothing and skin. As he rubbed the leaves into his pants, he found one leg soaked through. He had pissed himself after all. The twins would never stop teasing him once they saw.

He cowered there, shaking, as his family's cries echoed in the night. He could hear them calling to one another, bits of sentences drifting on the night smoke to reach his ears. But no one came to the garden, and moments later, the night began to brighten, the gray smoke giving off an evil, pulsing glow. Briar looked up, and saw the ghostly orange light came from the windows of the house.

The shrieks of the demons increased at the sight, and they clawed the dirt impatiently, waiting for the wards to fail. A wood demon struck at the house, and was thrown back by the magic. A flame demon tried to leap onto the porch, and it, too, was repelled. But even Briar could see that the magic was weakening, its light dimming.

When a wood demon tried the porch, the wardnet had weakened enough for it to power through. Magic danced over the demon's skin and it screamed in agony, but made it to the front door and kicked it in. A gout of fire, like a giant flame demon's spit, coughed out of the doorway, immolating the demon. It fell back, shrieking and smoldering, but a pack of flame demons had made it through the gap by then and disappeared into the house. Their gleeful shrieks filled the night, partially drowning out his family's dwindling screams.

Hardey stumbled out the side door, screaming. His face was dark with soot and splattered with gore, and one arm hung limply, the sleeve wet with blood. He looked about frantically.

Briar stood up. "Hardey!" he jumped up and down, waving his arms.

"Briar!" Hardey saw him and ran for the garden wards, his usual long stride marred by a worsening limp. A pair of howling flame demons followed him out of the house, but Hardey had a wide lead, and it seemed he would make it to Briar in the hogroot patch.

But Hardey hadn't cleared half the distance when a wind demon swooped down, digging its clawed feet deep into his back. Its wing talons flashed, and Hardey's head thumped to the ground. Before the body even began to fall, the wind demon snapped its wings and took to the air again, taking the rest of Hardey with it. Briar screamed as the demon vanished into the smoky darkness.

The flame demons shrieked at the departing wind demon for stealing their prey, but then leapt onto Hardey's head in a frenzy. Briar fell back into the hogroot patch, barely turning over in time to retch up his supper. He screamed and cried, thrashing about and trying to wake himself up from the nightmare, but on it went.

It grew hotter and hotter where Briar lay, and the smoke soon became unbearable. Burning ash drifted through the air like snowflakes, setting fires in the garden and yard. One struck Briar on the cheek and he shrieked in pain, slapping himself repeatedly in the face to knock the ash away.

Briar bit his lip to try and stem the wracking coughs, looking around frantically. "Mother! Father! Anybody!" He wiped at the tears streaking the ash on his face. How could his mother leave him? He was only six!

Six is old enough to be caught by alagai *for running when it is best to keep still,* Relan said, *or for keeping still when it is best to run.*

He would burn up if he stayed any longer, but as his father said, the fire was drawing demons like dung did flies. He thought of the goldwood tree. It had hidden him from his brothers. Perhaps it could save him again.

Briar put his head close to the ground and breathed three times as his mother had told him, then sprang from hiding, running hard. The swirling smoke was everywhere, and he could only see a few feet in any direction, but he could sense demons lurking in the gloom. He raced quickly over the familiar ground, but then somehow ran into a tree where he was sure none should be. He scraped his face on the bark, bouncing and landing on his back.

But then the tree looked at him and growled.

Briar slowly got to his feet, not making any sudden moves. The wood demon watched him curiously.

Briar began to sway back and forth like a pendulum, and the demon began rocking in unison, moving like a tree swaying in a great wind, to keep eye contact. It began to step with him, and Briar held his breath as he moved two steps, then back, then three steps, then back, then, on the fourth step, he kept on walking. A moment later, the demon shook its head, and Briar broke into a run.

The demon shrieked and gave chase. At first Briar had a fair lead, but the wood demon closed the gap in just a few great strides.

Briar dodged left and right, but the demon kept pace, its growls drawing ever nearer. He scrambled over the woodpile, which was already beginning to smolder, but the demon scattered the logs with a single swipe of its powerful talons. He skidded to a stop by his father's refuse cart, still loaded with some of the items Relan and his brothers had salvaged from the dump.

Briar dropped to his hands and knees, crawling under the cart. He held his breath as the demon's clawed feet landed with a thump right in front of him.

The wood demon lowered its toothy snout to the ground, snuffling about. It moved to the hollow, sniffing the roots and dirt. Briar knew the demon could reach under and fish him out, or toss the cart aside easily, but perhaps that would give him enough time to run out the other side and get to the tree. He waited as the snout drew closer, coming just a few inches from him.

Just then, the demon gave a tremendous sneeze, its rows of sharp amber teeth mere inches from Briar as the mouth opened and snapped shut.

Briar bolted from hiding, but the demon, gagging and coughing, did not immediately give chase.

The hogroot, Briar realized.

A small flame demon, no bigger than a coon, challenged him as he drew close to the tree, but this time Briar didn't try to run. He waited for the demon to draw close, then flapped his arms and clothes, creating a cloud of hogroot stink even in the acrid night. The demon heaved as if sick, and Briar kicked it, sending it sprawling as he ran on. He leapt to catch the first branch and swung himself up into the tree, hiding in the boughs, before the demon could recover.

Briar looked back and saw the windows of his house blazing like the hearth, flames licking out to climb their way up the walls.

The hearth.

Even from this distance, the heat could be felt, smoke and ash thick in the air, making every breath burn his lungs. But even so, Briar's face went cold. His leg twitched, and he felt it warm as his bladder let go what little it had left. In his mind, he could hear his mother singing.

> *When laying morning fire, what do you do?*
> *Open the flue, open the flue!*

How many times had he laid that fire? His father always closed off the chimney flue after the evening fire burned down. In the morning, you had to open it . . .

"Or the house will fill with smoke," he whispered.

A minute ago, Briar had been feeling quite brave, but that was over. *Brave is when you're scared*, his mother said, *but keep your wits about you.*

Whatever Briar was, he wasn't that.

He dug in the hollow where the branches met, finding his hidden trove of sugar candies, and let them fall to the ground as he began to weep.

I should have just shared.

PETER ORULLIAN

I HATE WATCHING SOMEONE SUFFER. I HATE THE FEELING OF HELPLESSNESS it evokes in me when there's little I can do to help. Perhaps that's why my story here got longish, when it was supposed to be shortish.

On many of Shawn's chemotherapy days, I went and sat with him. Just to chat. Keep him company. Maybe take him a taco, if he thought he could stomach it. I know he appreciated it. But at the end of the day, my offering felt small. Because, I'd eventually head home after surreal conversation in which he spoke about his chances of beating cancer. Or not.

It reminds me of a dark novel I wrote once (a hard one to write, and one I've never tried to publish) that grew out of this idea: The pain and helplessness of watching someone you love die. I wrote a whole concept album around it, too—also unreleased. Maybe that's why when Shawn shared the idea of *Unfettered*, and invited me to write for it, I went at it with reckless abandon. I needed to do something more. Needed to say something this time. (That whole *this time* reference is a long story for another day.)

So I poured myself into it. For weeks. Things that matter to me converged on the page: family, loyalty, friendship, authenticity . . . music. I began telling a story set in the universe of my series, The Vault of Heaven. It's the story of two men, one old, one young, each putting his music-craft to use in very different ways.

I imagine you've heard the adage, "Music has charms to soothe a savage breast." Well, the phrase was coined by William Congreve in his play *The Mourning Bride*:

Musick has Charms to sooth a savage Breast,
To soften Rocks, or bend a knotted Oak.
I've read, that things inanimate have mov'd,
And, as with living Souls, have been inform'd,
By Magick Numbers and persuasive Sound.
What then am I? Am I more senseless grown
Than Trees, or Flint? O force of constant Woe!
'Tis not in Harmony to calm my Griefs.
Anselmo sleeps, and is at Peace; last Night
The Silent Tomb receiv'd the good old King;
He and his Sorrows now are safely lodg'd
Within its cold, but hospitable Bosom.
Why am not I at Peace?

I can't even begin to unpack those lines in this short intro. But I'll tell you this: It's no accident that the central song of power in my music magic system is known as The Song of Suffering. And I'll tell you that music in this story sometimes soothes, sometimes moves inanimate things. It has to do with numbers (more of that in Book Two of my series). And it has to do with the notion of absolute sound. And harmony. And resonance. To calm grief. One way or another.

So, thank you, Shawn, for the opportunity to write this story. It's helped me strike an inner chord. One I still hear.

Peter Orullian

THE SOUND OF
BROKEN ABSOLUTES

Peter Orullian

Maesteri Divad Jonason gently removed the viola d'amore from its weathered sheepskin case. In the silence, he smiled wanly over the old instrument, considering. *Sometimes the most important music lessons feature no music at all.* Such was the case with this viola, an old friend to be sure. It served a different kind of instruction. One that came late in the training of a Lieholan, whose song had the power of *intention*. This instrument could only be understood when the act of making notes work together had long since been any kind of challenge. This viola made fine music, too, of course— a soft, retiring sound most pleasant in the shades of evening. But this heirloom of the Maesteri, generations old now, taught the kind of resonance often only heard inwardly while standing over a freshly dug barrow.

Behind him, the door opened, and he turned to greet his finest Lieholan student, Belamae Sento. The young man stepped into the room, his face pale, an open letter in his hand. Divad didn't need to ask the contents of the note. In fact, it was the letter's arrival that had hastened his invitation to have Belamae join him in this music chamber.

"Close the door, please." Softly spoken, his words took on a hum-like quality, resounding in the near-perfect acoustics of the room.

Belamae absently did as he was asked. The wide-eyed look on his face was not, Divad knew, amazement at finally coming to the Chamber of Absolutes. Although such would have been normal enough for one of the Lyren—a student of the Descant—it wasn't so for Belamae. Not today. Worry and conflict had taken the young man's thoughts far from Descant Cathedral, far from his focus on learning the Song of Suffering.

"You seem distracted. Does finally coming here leave you at a loss for words?" He raised an open palm to indicate the room, but was really just easing them into conversation.

Belamae looked around and shook his head. "It's less . . . impressive than I'd imagined."

Divad chuckled low in his throat, the sound musical in the resonant chamber. "Quite so. I tend not to correct assumptions about this place. Could be that I like the surprise of it when Lieholan see it with their own eyes. But the last lessons in Suffering are plain ones. The room is rightly spare."

The walls and floor and vaulted ceiling were bare granite. In fact, the only objects in the room were four instruments: a box-harp, a dual-tubed horn, a mandola, and the viola Divad held in his hands. Each had a place in an arched cutaway at equal distances around the circular chamber.

He held up the viola. "What about the instruments? What do they suggest you might learn here?"

Belamae looked around again, more slowly this time, coming last to the viola. He concluded with a shrug.

"Aliquot stringing," Divad said, supplying the answer. "It's resonance, my boy. And leads us to *absolute sound*."

Belamae nodded, seeming unimpressed or maybe just overly distracted. "Do we have to do this today?"

"Because of the letter you've received," he replied, knowing it was precisely so.

The young Lieholan stared down at the missive in his hands, and spoke without raising his eyes. "I've looked forward to the things you'd teach me here. We all do." He paused, heaving a deep sigh. "But war has come to my people. We're losing the fight. And my da . . . I have to go."

"Aliquots are intentionally unplayed strings that resonate harmonically when you strike the others." He held up the viola and pointed to a second set of seven gut strings strung below those the bow would caress.

Belamae looked up, an incredulous expression on his face.

Divad paid the look no mind. "A string vibrates when struck. There's a mathematical relationship between a vibrating string and an aliquot that resonates with it. This is usually in unison or octaves, but can also come in fifths. We've spoken of resonance before, but always as a way of understanding music that must be *heard* to have a resonant effect."

"Did you hear me?" Belamae asked, irritation edging his voice. "I'm leaving."

"Absolute sound," Divad went on, "is resonance you feel even when it's *not* heard."

"My da—"

"Which is what makes this instrument doubly instructive. You see, we play it in requiem." He caressed the neck of the viola, oiled smooth for easy finger positioning. "Voices sometimes falter, tremulous with emotion. That's understandable. So just as often, we play the dirge with this. And the melody helps to bring the life of a departed loved one into resonance with those they've left behind. Like the sweet grief of memory."

Belamae's anger sharpened. "In requiem . . . You knew my da was dead? And you didn't tell me?"

Divad shook his head. "You're missing the point. There is a music that can connect you with others in a . . . fundamental way. As fundamental as the sound their life makes. And once you find that resonant sound, it surpasses distance. It no longer needs to be heard to have effect."

The young Lieholan glared back at the older man. Then his

132

brow relaxed, disappointment replacing everything else. "You're telling me not to go."

"I'm telling you you're more important to them here, learning to sing Suffering, than you would be in the field as one more man with a sword." He offered a conciliatory smile. "And you're close, my boy. Ready to understand absolute sound. Nearly ready to sing Suffering on your own."

Belamae shook his head. "I won't ignore their call for help. People are dying." He glanced at the viola in Divad's hands. "They wouldn't have sent for me if it was my sword they wanted. But you don't have to worry; I know how to use my song."

"And what song do you think you have, Belamae? The song you came here with?" His tone became suddenly cross. "Or do you pretend you can make Suffering a weapon? That is not its intention. You would bring greater harm to your own people if that's why you go. I won't allow it."

"You're a coward," Belamae replied with the indignation only the young seem capable of. "I will go and do what I—"

"You should let your loss teach you *more* about Suffering, not take you away from it." Divad strummed the viola's strings, then immediately silenced them. The aliquots hummed in the stillness, resonating from the initial vibration of the viola's top seven strings.

The two men stood staring at one another as the aliquots rang on, which was no brief time. Divad knew trying to force Belamae to stay would prove pointless. Crucial to a Descant education was a Lieholan's willingness. Especially with regard to absolute sound. But if he could get Belamae to grasp the concept, then perhaps the boy would be convinced to remain.

Divad reached into his robe and removed a funeral score penned specifically for this viola. It was a challenging, complex piece of music, made more difficult by the seven strings and their aliquot pairs. Even reading it would stretch his young protégé's skill. Divad had written it himself in anticipation of this very meeting, knowing sooner or later Belamae would learn of the trouble back home. Its theme was separation, constructed in a Maerdian mode that hadn't been used for centuries. It made use of minor seconds and grace notes as central parts of the melody. A listener had to wait patiently for a passage or phrase to resolve, otherwise the note selection might be interpreted as the performer misplaying the piece.

Learning to play it would be its own kind of instruction for the musician, precisely because of the instrument's aliquots.

Divad handed the piece of music to Belamae. "Read this when you think you're ready to hear it." He gently tapped his young friend at the temple, suggesting he be in the right frame of mind when he did so.

Then, more gently still, he handed Belamae the viola d'amore. He wanted this Lieholan to know the heft of it, to run his hands over the flaws in the soundboard, to ask about the intricately carved earless head above the pegbox, to pluck the top-strung gut and listen for the resonating strings beneath . . .

Belamae received the instrument as he had the sheet music, giving it a moment of thoughtful regard. But almost immediately a sneer filled his face, and he slammed the viola down hard on the stone floor, shattering it into pieces.

The crush and clatter of old wood and the twang of snapped strings rose around them in a cacophonous din, echoing in the Chamber of Absolutes. Divad's stomach twisted into knots at the sudden loss of the fine old instrument. The d'amore wasn't crafted anymore. It was as much a historical artifact as it was a unique and beautiful instrument for producing music. And of all the aliquot instruments, it had been his favorite. At Divad's mother's wake, his own former Maesteri had played accompaniment on this viola while Divad sang Johen's "Funerary Triad."

He sank to his knees, instinctively gathering the pieces. Above him he heard the viola bow being snapped in half. The instrument's destruction was complete. Divad's ire flashed bright and hot, and escalated fast. His hands, filled with bits of spruce and bone points still tied with gut, began to tremble with an urge he hadn't felt in a very long time.

With what composure and dignity he could maintain, he gently laid the splintered viola back down and stood. "You ungrateful whoreson. Get out of my sight. And by every absent god, pray I don't forget myself and strike the note of your life. Mundane as I might now find it."

He then watched as Belamae left the room, his student having failed to even try and understand absolute sound. Or perhaps the failure had been Divad's. Belamae hadn't been ready, he told himself. That much was true. But Divad hadn't had a choice. He'd known the lad would feel duty-bound to return home. Still, he never imagined it would go this way. Looking down again, he grieved at the ruin of a beautiful voice—the viola—broken, and appearing impossible to mend.

Morning frost crunched under my boots as I crossed the frozen field. Several weeks of barge, schooner, overland carriage, and bay-mount had brought me from Recityv to within walking distance of the battle staging area. And more importantly, the captain's tent. I'd left within the hour of my last meeting with Maesteri Divad, which still played in my mind like a vesper's strain sung by an unpracticed voice. All sour notes misplaced by bad intonation.

I was able now, finally, to leave the memory of it alone, though. Mostly because of the dread that began to fill my gut. I didn't know what to expect. I'd hoped to see my ma first, and my sister, Semera. To have some news. To offer some comfort. Probably to receive some of the same. But long before reaching Jenipol, I'd been intercepted by two tight-lipped drummel-men. It's easy to spot men who make percussion a trade—their arms show every sinew. They escorted me here. That had been an alarmingly short ride. Our enemies had pushed deep into the Mor Nations.

The last twenty paces to the tent, my escorts fell back. That didn't do much for my state of mind. I paused a moment at the tent flap, noting where the frost had condensed into droplets from the heat inside the tent. Then I took a long breath and went in.

The air carried the musky smell of warm bodies after a fitful night beneath thick, rough wool. That, and the odor of spent tallow. Four men sat staring down at a low table in the light of two lamps burning a generous amount of wick. They all looked up at me as though I'd interrupted a prayer.

As I started to introduce myself, the man farthest back nodded grimly and said, "Belamae. I didn't think you'd come. Or I should say, I didn't think the Maesteri would permit it."

His name escaped me, but not his rank—this man held field command. I could tell by the deliberate and careful scarification on the left side of his neck in the form of an inverted T. Four horizontal hash marks crossed the vertical line. They weren't formal signifiers of rank. The Inverted T was a kind of music staff—an old one, a Kylian notation. The number of lines across it indicated the number of octaves the man had mastered. Which would include complete facility in all scales *and* modes across each. It was breadth as well as depth. More than simply impressive. A second scar-line beneath the bottom one meant he could make good use of steel, too.

The men at his table had similar neck scars, but all with one fewer hash. One of these craned his head around, the act seeming to cause him considerable pain. I could see that he'd lost the service of one eye but took no care to cover the wound. A flap of lid hung like a creased drape over the hole.

The one-eyed man looked me up and down the way a tiller does a draft horse just before plow season. "Doesn't look like much. Neck is thin. Skin's soft. He's not used to making sound on open air. He'll quit in three days. Doesn't matter if he's Karll's boy. I don't believe none in loinfruits."

A third man looked on, carefully appraising, but in a different way. The fellow looked up for a moment, as though framing a question. When he stared at me, his gaze was focused, the way Maesteri Divad's became when he watched for truthful answers and understanding. "Do you want a sword?"

I stared back, somewhat puzzled. "That's not why you sent for me."

The last man at the table did not speak, but instead invited me forward with a nod. As I drew close, I saw what the four had been studying. Not terrain or position maps. Not inventory manifests.

Not even letters of command and inquiry sent from the seat of the Tilatian king.

Across the table were spread innumerable scores. These leaders of war were sifting sheet music to prepare for the day's battle. In my few years away from home, I'd learned this was uncommon. The Tilatians might be the only people to do it, in fact. And even among my own kind, it hadn't been done in more than three generations.

Coming a step closer, and as I looked into the faces of the men around the table, it wasn't the carefree good humor of conservatory instructors that I saw. Lord knows I'd come across a cartload of those in my travels as a student from Descant Cathedral. No, these were sober-minded men, reviewing the language of song written for an unfortunate purpose. The tent held the cheerless feel of an overcast winter sky.

Sullen, I thought. *Bitter maybe. But sullen for sure.*

"Nine of ten bear steel into battle. There's no shame in that." The field leader sniffed, refocusing on a score laid out in front of him. "But you're right. That's not why we ask you here. Sit down."

I pulled forward a thin barrel and sat next to the captain, as he set before me a stack of music. "What?"

"I'm Baylet. This is Holis, Shem, and Palandas. These," he gently tapped the scores piled loosely before me, "are airs we send to the line. Tell us which one you'll use."

A chair creaked as Holis, the man with one eye, leaned forward, turning a bit sideways to have a good view of the stack.

"We've already selected morale songs to encourage those who carry steel," Baylet added. "Holis has a good eye for that."

The men exchanged scant looks of mirth, as if the joke were as tired as the men themselves.

"Shem's put aside for later a song of comfort and well-being. Something he wrote himself."

"Calimbaer," I muttered, recalling the class of Mor song that accompanied medical treatment.

Baylet looked across at Shem. "He's also found a good sotto voce for Contentment."

I knew that class of song, too. Two classes really. Sotto voce, an incredibly difficult technique to master, in which singing happened almost under the breath. But *Contentment* . . . it was a type of song sung to one who is beyond help, one who can only be given a spot of peace before going to his final earth.

Holis and Shem produced the music Baylet had spoken of, and dropped it on top of the pile before me. I fanned them out and began to scan. The morale song read like a blaze of horns—written for four voices with two soaring lines above a strong set of rhythmic chants beneath. I could hear the mettle and resolve in my mind as I tracked the chord progressions.

Shem's Calimbaer was an elegant piece composed of few notes, each with long sustain. The movement was languid and would be rendered in a thick legato.

But it was the sotto voce piece that really got to me. I sat poring over the note selection, which made brilliant use of the Lydian and Lochrian modes, the composition effortlessly transitioning between the two. It had me taking deep relaxing breaths. Parts of the melody, even just scanning them, instantly evoked simple, forgotten memories. In those moments, I recalled the marble bench on which I sat the first time I kissed a woman. How cool it had been to the touch, contrasted with the heat in my mouth. I then remembered kneeling in my mother's garden, dutifully clearing the weeds, when I spontaneously created my first real song, or at least the first one I could still recall. And last to my mind came the memory of lying awake, scared, in my first alone-bed, until I heard the comforting, safe sounds of adult voices talking in the outer room.

Baylet swept those selections aside and tapped the original stack again. "Mors who have *influence* in their voice." He gave me a pointed look. "Mors like you. Have each been sent to different lines so that only the Sellari will hear their song. And suffer by it."

The field leader then began to hum a deep pitch, a full octave lower than any note I could reach. The sound of it filled the tent. He gently lifted the topmost score, written on a pressed parchment, and placed it in my hand. When he stopped singing the single note, the silence that followed felt wide and empty, like the bare-limb stretches of late autumn.

He let that silence hang for a long moment before saying, "This is what they will sing today. They have already set out. You should choose quickly."

It wasn't the urgent request or the song he'd sung or the lingering sotto voce that left me in a panic. I put the score aside and began to leaf through the rest of the stack. While I got the impression that the chests I saw in the shadowed corners of the tent carried more music, the fifty or so here would prove to be enough.

Some were reproductions on newer, cleaner paper that still smelled of ink. Most of these were Jollen Caero songs, very old. Jollen was a composer thought to have come down out of the Pall when my Inveterae ancestors had escaped the Bourne. Any other time, I would have liked to study these longer; the melodic choices were as unpredictable as the vocal rhythms. Other selections had been transcribed on parchment that looked like it had seen the field before—ratted edges and smudges where dirty thumbs had held them. Many of these were as interesting as the Jollen songs but for an entirely different reason: their composers were not generally known. And until now, I'd never seen the full scores—only snippets had survived in the forms of childhood rhymes and song-taunts. Seeing the full context for phrases I'd sung here and there all my life left me feeling a bit ashamed and naive.

Before I'd left to study with the Maesteri at Descant, I could have read maybe half of these scores. Back then, I was fluent in six different types of music notation. Now I could read more than thirty. Some of the music here was just that, music only. No lyrics. The Lieholan singing these scores was free to sing them using vowels of his choosing, so long as he didn't attempt to sing actual words.

Other songs in the stack were nothing more than lyrics, but so familiar that any Lieholan worth his brack would know them. The harder part with these came in the language. They hadn't been translated. I counted at least four different languages: early Morian, a difficult Pall tongue, lower Masi, and a root language

we knew as Borren. Most Lieholan would perform these phoneti-
cally, singing words they didn't understand. For my part, having
spent four years at Descant, where language study went along
with music training, I could make out the meaning in the lyrics.
These were terrifying words. There'd been little effort at rhyme
in them. The worst was a litany of tragic images with no narrative
or resolution. It might have been the darkest thing I'd ever read.
Something I couldn't *unread*.

I scanned from one sheet to the next, moving from standard
Mor notation, to the subdominant axis approach typified on the
necks of the men around me, to a symbol-centered system that
referred to a mandola neck, to the more elegant Petruc signifier,
where slight serifs and swoops on a handful of characters gave the
singer all the information he needed to render the pitch. I liked
the Petruc system best. Those delicate strokes could be added to
written language, allowing the lyrics to become the central part of
the piece, while subtle Petruc ornamentation on its letters carried
the melodic direction. Originally, it had been created as a code,
back during the War of the First Promise.

Probably the most interesting music, though, was a pair of
songs written in an augmented Phrygian mode. They were unat-
tributed, but the parchment was old and the Sotol music notation fading some. This music would require vocal gymnastics to
carry off, and two voices besides. Though separately composed,
they were clearly a call-and-response orchestration. In my mind
I could hear where notes sounded together and where vocal runs
built tension on top of beautifully dark counterpoint. I wanted to
sing this song, whose first bridge was the only portion I had ever
heard, and then only the caller side of the arrangement.

All of them I'd heard or sung, if only in part. But the familiarity was precisely the problem and the thing that alarmed me.

When I'd made sure there was nothing *un*familiar, I looked
up and locked eyes with Baylet. "You haven't brought the Mor
Refrains with you?"

Holis laughed, the squint of his eyes as he did so pinching the
lid of his eyeless socket into a pouch of skin. "I see now. You think

that's why we called you back. To sing the Refrains. Ah, sapling, we've had it more bitter than this, and not fallen to such foolish desperation." His one remaining eye widened, the way it might if he'd happened on some realization. "But your asking tells us something about you, I think."

The captain knocked on the tabletop once to silence them. "The field men have already marched. Are you rested enough? And is there one of these you know by rote?"

My heart ran cold. They meant to send me to the field . . . today. I stood there, struck dumb for a long moment before nodding.

Baylet seemed satisfied and stood. He motioned for me to follow, and I'd just started after him when a hand caught me tightly by the wrist. I looked down to find Palandas holding me. His grip seemed unusually strong for a man his age.

"The best song, when singing the end of someone, is the one you can make while watching him die." He moistened his lips with his tongue. "That'll be one you must know awfully well, my young friend. Since your voice will have to carry on when the rest of you would rather not."

Palandas held me until I nodded my understanding, which I did without any idea what he really meant. He let me go, and I followed Baylet through the tent flap and south across the frozen field. The promise of sun had grown in the east as a faint line of light blue.

We gathered our mounts at the tree line, and the field leader led me south and east through an elm and broad-pine wood. For the better part of a league we rode. As the trees began to thin, he pulled up and dismounted. I slid from the saddle and stood beside him. The shanks of our mounts steamed in the morning chill.

Finally, I couldn't hold it back any longer. "Why haven't you brought the Mor Refrains? The letter I received made it sound dire."

"War is always dire," he said flatly.

"I came through Talonas, Cyr, and Weilend. All burned. All empty. My history isn't strong, but I don't remember us ever losing three cities to those from across the Soren." My breath plumed before my face as I spoke. "Asking me to leave Descant. I assumed you needed someone—"

"Your training is complete then?" Baylet asked, one eyebrow arching.

"No," I admitted. "But the Refrains haven't been sung in so long. I assumed you'd want someone—"

"The Refrains have *never* been sung." His voice held a pinch of reproach. "The first Mors brought them out of the Bourne to *keep* them from being sung. Which the Quiet would surely have done, if they'd ever gotten their hands on them."

"It's why the Sellari come," I said, stating the obvious. "It's why they've always come. If we fail, they won't hesitate to sing them."

Baylet turned to face me. His stare chilled me deeper than the frigid air. "Then don't fail." He pointed ahead. "Twenty Shoarden men wait for you at the tree line."

Shoarden men. As a child, I'd thought Shoarden simply meant "deaf." Later, when I began to study the Borren root tongues, I learned that it meant "to sacrifice sound."

"Shoarden," I muttered to myself.

"Most Lieholan aren't skilled enough to have their song resonate with a specific individual or . . ." he looked away to the south, where the Sellari camped, "group or army or . . . race." He looked back at me. "It's a technique of absolute sound. A technique you'll possess once your training at Descant is complete. Until then, your song affects any who hear it. So, some of the men sacrifice their hearing in order to guard Lieholan in the field. They take the name Shoarden. Today, I've assigned twenty such men to you. Beyond the tree line, a thousand strides or so, the Sellari eastern flank is camped. They'll come hard. Don't let them through."

He'd apparently said all he meant to say, and quickly mounted.

I struggled to remember the thing I'd wanted to ask him. A hundred questions about the Refrains clouded my mind, but I mentally grasped it before he rode away. "My da."

Baylet held his reins steady, staring ahead. "His sword sang, Belamae. Any man who stood beside him in battle would say the same." He then turned to look at me. "Karll was a friend. Proud as hell of you. He'd be angry with me for sending for you. But a son has to . . . Quiet and Chorus, son, if I'd lost my da I'd want to return murder on the bastards. Thought you'd want the same opportunity. Besides that, we need you. We're outnumbered . . ." His eyes, if it was possible, looked suddenly stonier. "Don't fail."

It was a command. But it was also a plea. The desire to step into the breach for my people filled me like a rush of warm wind. It's hard to explain that feeling. The other thing that was true was that Baylet had put the perfect words on the quiet reason inside me that had brought me here: *return murder on the bastards.* I wasn't proud of that feeling, but I couldn't deny it either. And in the end, I didn't find a thing wrong with it.

I started for the tree line before Baylet kicked his mount into a canter. I did not pause when the twenty Shoarden men fell in around me. I did not pause when I came in sight of the first Sellari scout. I did not pause.

And when a hundred, two hundred of the invaders lined the far meadow, coming on with a steady stride, I recalled the music I'd reviewed that morning in the company of four grim men. A dozen of those songs I knew backward and forward. Three times as many other songs I had full command over: lyric, phrasing, rhythm, and melody. Songs that might suit the kind of destructive influence that filled my heart at that moment.

But as the enemy came within earshot, none of these would do. And when I filled my lungs and opened my mouth, only one song came to me. The fifth movement of Suffering: War.

It was a rough-throat song. As all the line-songs shown to me that morning had been. Maesteri Divad liked to smile and say it was "controlled screaming, cultured hollering." That made as much sense as anything else. The intent of these songs was destruction, aggression. Rasping the voice gave it a scouring, abrasive sound. It conveyed violent intent.

I filled my mind with anguish for my da. I recalled the words of the Song of Suffering's War passage. And I let it all burn inside me. Suffering wasn't meant for this purpose, but I was way past caring about that. I let myself feel indignation and hatred against those who had burned my countrymen.

And then I let it all pour from me in a stream of pounding

vocal rhythms that shot out like a succession of iron-gloved punches. I didn't know what would happen, but I'd studied *intention* in my Lieholan training. That's a far cry from saying I'd mastered it. But on this chill morning, mine was clear.

The first few Sellari were ripped off their feet and sent crashing hard upon the frozen earth. I'd later remember the puffs of my own hot breath on the cold air as I shouted out Suffering's War music, which had been meant for protection. I'd instinctively found the way to make that music a weapon. It was the difference between winning and not losing; between merely drawing breath and gasping it in after a mad dash. It actually taught me a practical lesson on *intention* in a way my Descant study of the principle never had.

At the far end of the great field, hundreds more Sellari appeared in full dress, rushing forward. The Shoarden tightened their circle around me, taking out runners my song didn't seem to affect. When I saw that these runners' ears had been cut off, I realized the Sellari had Shoarden of their own.

The sight of them only deepened my anger. The song itself began to live inside me in a way it never had at Recityv. The feeling was strange. It buoyed me up. But I was simultaneously aware that it was being fueled by some part of me that I wouldn't get back.

I didn't care.

I lengthened my stride. The next notes rushed up past my throat into the natural cavities behind my nose and cheeks, becoming a bright, powerful scream that I shrieked into the morning light. Thirty more had flesh ripped from their face and hands. I heard necks pop, and saw heads cock at unnatural angles, and then bodies falling to the hard earth.

Every attack made me stronger. And sicker it seemed. Though strangely, the burn of aggression kept me moving forward, each screamed musical line felling more of the others. I was soon walking over the bodies of Sellari, eager to take them all down.

I never got that far. The ill feeling soon outbalanced the vengeance, and I struggled to even take a breath. Before I knew it, the Shoarden had picked me up and were rushing me back across the great field ahead of the chasing Sellari. I blacked out to the sound of rushing feet pounding over brittle ground.

He'd laid the broken pieces of the viola out across his worktable like pieces of a puzzle. The sun bathed Descant's lutherie, a haven where Maesteri Divad spent as much time as he could afford. Putting his hands to use in repairing broken instruments helped him think. Occasionally he crafted something new. But he much preferred mending what was broken. It allowed him to maintain his sense of an object's intrinsic worth.

As he sat surveying the wreckage, he breathed deeply the scents of birch woodshavings, willow blocks aging nicely against the outer wall, and the Tamber steel of chisels and planes and fine-tipped paring knives. In the sunlight, motes lazed through the stillness, moving ever so slowly.

The viola's single-piece flat-back had taken too much damage from Belamae's smashing of the instrument. It would have to be replaced. The same was true of the side pieces. Divad picked up the inside blocks and soundpost, which appeared intact. He stress-tested them, gently trying to snap them with his fingers. They seemed fine, until two of the blocks broke where hairline cracks gave way. Those might have been there before Belamae's outburst. Regardless, he resolved to replace all these, too. The gut strings, of course, had all snapped. Those would be easily replaced; Divad knew a good abattoir that specialized in gut drawn from young prairie sheep. That would be one element of repairing the viola where he'd use new material.

The tail, bridge, and neck had all cracked visibly. The bone points, pegbox, pegs, and scrollhead were all salvageable. And the fingerboard—a beautiful length of ebony—remained in perfect condition. That didn't surprise him; ebony was strong.

It was the soundboard that worried him most. Besides being the face of the instrument, it was the piece most crucial to producing the sound of the instrument itself. Wood selection would be everything in its repair. But he loved the challenge of it. The work of carefully piecing this fine old viola back together would be a welcome distraction from the predicament of there being too few Lieholan to sing Suffering. It might also take his mind off the investigation the League of Civility had begun to make of Descant and its Maesteri.

Divad sighed heavily in the quiet of the luthier shop, then smiled to himself. *Living would mean nothing without burden.*

With that thought, he got up and crossed to the racks of wood used for building and repairing woodwinds and stringed instruments. An entire shelf of bird's-eye maple sat in the cool shade on that side of the room. The shelf tag indicated that it had been cut in the forest of Pater Fol one hundred fifty-eight years ago. That'd do nicely for the back. He also found a shelf of willow taken from the Cantle Wood in Alon I'tol. This wood was fresher, a few years old, but would do just fine. It was lightweight, strong, and difficult to split—perfect for the blocks, which took a lot of stress.

As for the soundboard, Descant kept two shelves of old-cut red spruce. They had several different harvest years of the wood, all from the Mor coastal alps: sixty-one years old, one hundred twelve years old, and a short shelf with a tag reading H.G. 481. H.G., Hargrove, was the current age, so named for the poet. This spruce harvest was almost two hundred ninety years old. More than good.

But when it came to repair, Divad went on instinct as much as anything else. Every other component *felt* right: the bird's-eye maple, the willow, the remaining bits that hadn't taken any damage. But for the soundboard . . . he'd have to keep looking. This was no ordinary instrument. He knew of no replica. It accompanied the Johen triad. It was his best tool for teaching the resonance of absolute sound. The soundboard wood needed to be tried and tested. Regardless its age, any wood he had here in his shop would be like a sapling that bends and pulls free in a rough wind.

But Divad had no ready answer for where next to look. He had savvy contacts in the timber trade, of course. They might have suggestions for him. And he knew other luthiers in the city, as well as several more in the eastlands. But he tired at the thought of having to journey to call on them. And he couldn't afford to be away from Descant anyway. So, he went where he always did when he needed to think.

He shrugged into his cloak and slipped through the streets of the Cathedral quarter and into a lesser-known performance tavern called Rafters. Coming here was a holdover from the time before he, himself, had entered Descant to train. Lulling conversation over a mild glass of wheat bitter always mellowed him to the point of inspiration.

Rafters was on a small lane far from the nearest major thoroughfare. Committed drinkers rarely found their way here, since there were closer places to start their binge. And they wouldn't have come for the music, since music didn't factor much in a drinker's decision on where to begin. But musicians were a different tribe.

There were numerous performance taverns in Recityv. And truth be told, for the most part anyway, they were all unofficial audition halls for Descant. While Suffering lay at the heart of the cathedral's purpose, there were hundreds of music students there who would never lay eyes on its music. Some harbored dreams of one day singing Suffering or maybe becoming Maesteri themselves. But most of them understood the reality of those aspirations, and had come to the Cathedral for its unequaled music training. Musicians who cared about the craft all wanted admission. However, there was no formal process for that. Divad could accept a petition to become Lyren from anyone for any reason. Belamae had shown up from Y'Tilat Mor four years ago and done nothing more than hand him a self-drawn diagram of the circle of fifths and shared with him a model for altering it to produce a lovely dissonance. It had also been nice to learn he could "sing from his ass," as the saying went. The kid had one hell of a voice.

Over time, and in the absence of a defined path, Recityv performance taverns had become the best way to build recognition for musical prowess. On any given night, Divad might hear a lap or floor harp, kanteles, psalteries, lutes, flutes, zithers, horns, cellos, violins, hand drums, chimes. And those who sang:

soloists, ensembles, choirs, duets, tenors, altos, contraltos, sopranos, and so on.

The taverns on the main roads were pay-to-play. Musicians actually handed over a fee to the proprietor for fifteen minutes of stage time. The going rate stood at three plugs. The larger houses got four.

Rafters didn't take money for stage time. But you didn't just show up and have your name added to the stage-side slate, either. In rare instances, you could play something for Ollie, the proprietor-bouncer-barkeep-and-gossip-curator, in private impromptu auditions. He'd been known to let an act or two play on raw talent alone. But most of those who took the stage had earned the respect of other established musicians. And they had followings of their own that came specifically to hear them play. Such clientele were less likely to wind up in a brawl or putting illicit hands on barmaids. Ollie curated his crowds as much as he did good rumors.

Which wasn't to say it didn't get lively at Rafters. Divad took great pleasure in watching the musicians' skill whip the crowds here into a frenzy. It reminded him that music had a power all its own, well before the gifts of a Lieholan's intention gave it influence.

He arrived ahead of the evening crowd. Regulars had already staked out their places—Chom, who'd been a promising violinist before a mill accident took his hand; Jaela, who cared mostly for the vocalists, having abandoned her own musical ambitions years ago when Divad let her know she was tone-deaf; Riddol and Mack, a pair of genial-enough fellows, as long as the music proved truly satisfying—they were fair but harsh critics. Divad nodded to them all, receiving enthusiastic acknowledgments—Maesteri in the house meant players would push themselves tonight.

He climbed onto his stool at the far end of the bar near the stage, and rubbed a bit of weariness from his face. Much as the prospect of rebuilding the viola excited him, another part of him felt the constant pull of worry and regret over Belamae's departure. Odds were the lad would not survive his country's war. A damn shame, that.

Before he could spend too much energy on the dismal thought,

Ollie stood before him, a damp towel slung over his shoulder, ready to mop up a spill.

"Wheat bitter tonight?" Ollie gave him a close look. "Or are you here to drink heavy. Push out some of what's botherin' ya?"

"What makes you think something's bothering me?" Divad replied.

Ollie just gave him an are-you-serious look.

"Wheat bitter'll do." Divad glanced up at the stage-side slate. "Who you got tonight?"

"Madalin is back in the city. She wants to sing something she wrote herself while down in Dimn. She won't preview it for me. Told her she can live or die by it then. She'll probably bring the house down. Woman's got lungs."

Divad nodded. "That she does. I see Colas. Is he playing alone?"

Ollie gave a wry smile. "Oh that. Yeah, Senchia took a lover. Her lines have gravitated to droning chordal roots. Colas is better off without her. He's striking too hard though. I think he's trying to fill up the same amount of sound without her. He'll figure it out. He's slinging new wood, too."

The reference reminded Divad of his reason for coming to Rafters: to think, ponder how to tackle the viola soundboard. While he got himself refocused, Ollie slid a glass of So-Dell light grain in front of him.

"Tell me how that does ya." Ollie smiled with bartender satisfaction. "Came in about a cycle back, but it's a full nine years aged. Wheat was threshed late that season, full ripe kind of taste, if you follow."

Divad took a sip, and his brows rose in pleasant surprise. "Enough of those and *I* might sing tonight."

"You're not on the slate," Ollie said, half kidding. The man liked things planned and proper, but he'd put his towel to a name and write Divad in if he got serious about it.

"I see Alosol is singing last," Divad said, taking a healthier draught off his glass.

"Still the best voice not to be taken into Descant," Ollie observed, giving him a mock judgmental glare.

Alosol had an immense following, and for good reason. He had more control and range in his tenor voice than almost any vocalist in Recityv. Problem was, he knew it. There was a smidge too much conceit in the man. Maybe more than a smidge. But that took nothing from his sheer ability. He could sustain a note three octaves above speech-tone, and do it as softly or with as much volume as another singer would his first octave. Divad didn't have a student that wasn't envious of Alosol's gift, save maybe Belamae.

"Put in with the Reconciliationists," Ollie added, conversationally. "Best acquisition those religionists have had in some time. I imagine they weep when he sings the Petitioner's Cycle over at Bastulen Cathedral. Shame."

Divad said nothing. He'd denied Alosol's several requests for admission to Descant. The man had Lieholan in him, all right. And Divad would have liked to take him in. But as important as talent was, being teachable mattered more. Alosol carried himself with a callow arrogance, the kind that smacked of someone who thinks he's got the world figured out.

"Speaking of religionists," Ollie said, running the towel over the bartop by habit, "listen to this. I was laying up some of that there wheat bitter in the cellar, keeps the temperature right, you see. But I'm running out of room down there. So I'm moving shelves, and I find a cellar door I hadn't noticed before. A closet. Inside, there are maybe eight crates sealed tight. Dust on 'em as thick as carpet. And what do I find inside?"

He waited on Divad to guess.

"More bitter?"

"You lack imagination," Ollie quipped, proceeding with his discovery. "No, hymnals. And some other papers, besides. Turns out, before this place was Rafters, it was a chantry. Don't you just love that?"

Divad smiled over the top of his glass. He did, in fact, love that. The idea that these walls had been a devotional songhouse of sorts, even before becoming a tavern, tickled him for no good reason.

"To a new kind of sacrament, then," Divad said, hoisting his bitter. And part of him meant it. Songs sung in memoriam were

150

damn important. Suffering itself took that theme more than once.

Ollie didn't drink. He tasted all his stock, but he never finished anything. 'I'll keep my wits, thanks,' he was fond of saying. But he took his bar rag and pretended to clink glasses with Divad.

"That's not the half of it," he went on, gleefully. "That stage, the balcony balustrade . . . my dear absent gods, even this bar," he chuckled, "altar and pews, all of it."

Divad drank down half his glass and nodded his amusement. Just then, the first musician of the night began. Divad swiveled in his seat to find a young woman slouching at the rear of the stage. Her first notes were hesitant, like a child stuttering. The melody—a mum's lullaby known as "Be Safe and Home Again"— hardly carried past the first table.

The first musicians of the night were those Ollie thought had talent, but who had little reputation yet. They played mostly to empty seats.

Beneath her timid first notes, though, Divad heard what Ollie surely had. He got the young girl's attention with a simple hand wave. When she looked over, he straightened up tall on his barstool, threw out his chest, tilted back his chin, and took an exaggerated breath to fill his lungs. He then narrowed his eyes, and screwed onto his face a look of confidence. The young girl nodded subtly, mid-phrase, and at her next natural pause, drew a deep breath, stepped forward on the stage, and threw back her head and shoulders. The diffidence of her tone vanished. A clear, bright sound transformed what had been a plaintively beautiful lullaby into a clarion anthem of hope.

Now that's teachable.

The rest of the night only got better. As music flowed from one to the next, Rafter's filled to standing room only. Between acts, conversation buzzed with anticipation for the next performer. Divad would turn back toward the bar to try and avoid too many inquiries about Descant admission. Mostly that failed. But he did it anyway.

During one of the brief intermissions, an overeager percussionist sidled up close to him. To announce himself, he began to beat on the surface of the bar. With one hand he set a beat in four-four, while with the other he tapped increasingly faster polyrhythms: three-four, five-four, six-four, seven-four. He then repeated the entire cycle at double the tempo. It was rather impressive, actually. But when the young man reached out a hand in greeting, he knocked over Divad's third glass of wheat bitter. The amber liquid washed over the bar, giving the worn lacquer new shine.

Ollie appeared out of nowhere with his rag, and began mopping up the spill. Some of the bitter remained in shallow grooves scored into the bar.

The indentations looked familiar somehow, and Divad sat staring, thoughts coalescing in his mind. All kinds of songs had passed across this bar, ribald tunes, laments, fight and love songs (which he thought shared more in common than most other types), dirges. And those melodies had risen from strings and woodwinds and horns and countless voices.

And all that just since it had become Rafters. What about its years before that? Divad found himself grinning at the idea of countless songs for the dead sung here when it had been a chantry.

It got him thinking about sonorant residue—the idea that exposure to music could create subtle changes in the fabric of physical reality. The notion found its roots in the Alkai philosophies of music. To Divad's ear, the evidence was something you could hear in old, well-used instruments, and in the music of musicians who'd spent their lives listening, teaching, performing. *It got in you*, as was said. Not an elegant way to express it, but it got the point across.

Ollie had nearly finished drying the bar, when Divad caught his rag-hand. He tapped the bar. "What's this made of, my friend?"

Ollie's brow furrowed. He then produced a paring knife from his apron, bent down behind the bar, and a moment later stood up. In his fingers he held a thick curl of wood, presumably carved from the underside of the bar. He handed it to Divad, while continuing to stare at it with newfound interest.

Divad turned the shaving over in his fingers twice, inspecting the grain. He gave Ollie a quick glance, then put the curl of wood to his nose and breathed in deeply. He knew that scent like he knew the sound of his own voice. He turned his attention back to Ollie, grinning widely in spite of himself.

"I have a proposition for you, my friend."

I shivered, and sweat dripped from my nose. I sat alone in a tent, huddled under three layers of rough wool blankets. The fire in the middle of the space leapt higher than was probably safe, but I kept adding more wood. I couldn't seem to get warm. The cold emanated from somewhere inside me. It felt as if I'd drunk a pitcher of iced water too fast, and was now experiencing the chill of it in the pit of my stomach. I'd downed several mugs of hot tea that hadn't helped a jot.

There wasn't really any mystery in it, either. I'd tried to repurpose Suffering. It had been an arrogant thing to do. And I was feeling the effects. The worst of it might be that I hadn't done much good. A few moments of song, a few dead Sellari, and then they'd carried me back from the line. It was embarrassing, really. They'd sent for me at Descant, like some bright hope. And I'd managed only a few passages of song for them.

I was able to let the failure go, though. Selfish to worry about my failing. I needed to figure out what I'd done wrong.

Suffering had nine passages:

Quietus
The Bourne
The Placing
Inveterae
War
Self-Destruction
Vengeance
Quiet Song
Reclamation

My first thought was that I'd chosen the wrong passage to sing. Aligning the right song to the right singer for the right encounter had been a Tilatian art of war since they'd escaped the Bourne. Perhaps I should have asked Baylet to assign me one of the songs I'd reviewed last evening.

But I quickly let go of that argument. I'd sensed that War had been the right air. In truth, there might be many *right* songs for any one moment on the line. Much of the choice of song had to do with the confidence a Lieholan had in the music. That hadn't been the problem for me, though. Something else, then.

Maybe it's as simple as the fact that I've never sung with this intention *before.*

That made sense. But it was also a depressing thought. It could mean I'd be no use to Baylet or our people. Or it could mean I'd wreak no vengeance for my da. The very thought of it brought a new wave of shivers. And in shivering, I happened on a new, entirely unpleasant idea. Maybe in turning Suffering into a song to suit my own need, a need to harm, I'd opened up a darker part of myself. An untested part. Like an unused muscle that, when overworked, tires quickly, making a man sweat and retch.

Could also be that the rough-throat technique itself had been my failing. Twice as hard as pure vocalization if it's done correctly. But I'd thought it would be second nature to me. Besides toying with it now and again back at Descant, I'd grown up hearing it a fair bit.

Whatever the reason, I'd failed to make Suffering the right kind of song to take to battle. And as I sat shivering, what worried me most of all was that I just wasn't cut out for this. I took another sip of strong sage tea, and was bending nearer the fire when Baylet ducked into my tent.

"Not a good day," he said right off.

I swallowed my tea and said nothing.

He sat across the fire from me, knitting his hands together. The scar on his neck caught the firelight in flickers of orange and shadow. "What did you sing?"

"Something from Suffering," I replied, looking down into my mug. "I thought the power of it would transfer . . ."

"Suffering?! Dear Lords of Song, you're crazier than your

father." There was a soft chuckle. "I'm going to assume your Maesteri wouldn't approve."

"He might laugh, given how well it went." I wiped the sweat off my face. "And you might wind up disappointed you brought me here."

Baylet stared at me through the flames. "I already told you. I brought you back as much for you as I did for me."

"Ah, right. For my da. I imagine he'd be proud, too," I said with no small measure of sarcasm.

"You have a gift, Belamae, no question about that. But so do a hundred others just like you. I've no delusion that one voice will tip the scales in our favor. And you letting your failure color your sense of your father's pride is foolish. It's not honest either." He paused a long moment. "You probably failed because you're still looking at things for what they are."

"And what are they?" I asked.

Baylet pinned me with a thoughtful stare. But he never answered my question. The silence that stretched between us became uncomfortable. I shivered the whole time, inching closer to the fire so that my knees had grown hot.

Finally, he broke the silence. "Why Suffering? Was that your plan the whole time?"

I took up a stick and poked at the fire, causing sparks to be scattered up in the heat. "I think it probably was. Not the specific passage. But it's the one music none of the rest here know." I pointed vaguely toward the staging area with my stick. "And Suffering . . . there's a lot about it that makes sense here."

Baylet listened, never looking away from me. "And yet you told me your training wasn't complete. What do you know about absolute sound, then?"

The question didn't seem conversational. He was asking for a reason, and it had to do with more than just today's disappointment.

"A little," I answered. "Maesteri Divad tried to show me before I left. But I wasn't terribly receptive."

As I said it, I began to wonder if Divad had been coaching me, preparing me, for when I arrived here. Surely he'd known I wouldn't stay in Recityv. He could judge a stranger's intention from body language and the first word out his mouth. And he'd known *me* for four years.

"Absolute sound is the last principle of music you must master before you can sing Suffering the way it was intended." Baylet's eyes grew distant, staring across the flames. "And at their core, the Mor Refrains are written with the same principle in mind. There's more to them than that, but you can think of them in that way." His eyes focused on me. "Which is why we didn't bring them with us; why we never do."

I fought to remember what Maesteri Divad had said the last time we'd spoken, argued. Anything to help me pull myself from the music illness that had gotten inside me.

"And I still stand by that," Baylet said, though his voice didn't sound convincing. "But you . . . I need to tell you something. Things have changed during your four days—"

"Four days. What are you talking about?"

Baylet gave a weak smile with one corner of his mouth. "You slept straight through the first three. While you did, the Sellari changed their strategy." His eyes then widened with new understanding. "It makes sense now. They must have realized you'd sung Suffering."

"What makes sense?" I threw back my blankets, worry getting the better of me.

"All the Sellari coming at us now, on all fronts, are like our own Shoarden men. Our songs don't stop them." He scrubbed the stubble on his cheeks. "They don't hear us. We are reduced to steel alone . . . And we're outmanned five to one."

I felt a heavy pressure in my chest. "It's my fault," I muttered. "For trying to sing Suffering."

Baylet stood. "Timing is a hell of a thing, Belamae. If you'd had more training at Descant, the Sellari wouldn't need to hear your song for it to beat them down." He laughed bitterly. "That's not a fair thing for me to say. The use of song that way is precisely why the Mor Nation Refrains are held safe. Never sung."

Baylet then pulled a sword from beneath his own cloak and

laid it on the ground. He stared at it for a moment before standing and leaving, not saying another word.

I sat listening to the crackle of fire, and watching the dull gleam of orange flame on the hilt of the blade. If I was no good with Suffering, I was utterly inept with a sword. In fairness, I hadn't spent any real time cultivating a feel for one. It would be as foreign to me as playing a new instrument.

Like a viola.

New shivers claimed me before I managed to crawl my way to my travel bag. Inside, I found the hollow oak tube I'd carried with me from Recityv. I pulled off the fitted plug on one end and gently removed the score Maesteri Divad had given me the last time we met. I carefully unrolled it, and scanned the music staff.

Scordatura.

Of course it would be this kind of notation for the viola d'amore. As I pored over the melody, I began to realize why Divad had given it to me.

I read and reread it for hours, and jumped when my tent flap was pushed back. Baylet poked his head inside. "The Sellari are pressing their advantage."

His eyes found the sword where he'd laid it down. I ignored the invitation and shrugged out of my blankets entirely. I stood, felt a bit woozy, but forced myself to follow him into the dark hours of night. As we went, I kept hearing the song my Maesteri had given me.

Scordatura. *Mistuned.*

Beyond the window of Divad's lutherie, heavy rain fell, causing a distant hum of white noise. Now and then a gust of wind pushed drops against the glass, adding a plinky *tep, tep* rhythm to the music of the storm. It was late, well past dark hour, as he sat smoothing the piece of old spruce. He moved the rough horsetail back and forth with the grain, adding another rhythm to the music of the rain.

As much as he liked the still, warm moments of morning in

his luthier rooms, nighttime, when Descant slept, could be just as enjoyable. And the sound of hand tools applied to wood to shape and refine, simple as it seemed, put him at peace. Perhaps molding an instrument that did not ask questions (as Lieholan incessantly did) had a certain appeal.

Whatever the reason, working with his hands felt good. It reminded him that he lived a unique life, a privileged life. It also reminded him that it had not always been so.

He finished smoothing the piece of Ollie's bar that would become the viola's top, and removed it from his bench dog and vise. Using a rasp, he filed the edges to conform perfectly with his original trace, and set to purfling the piece with a thin border. He finished that up, and added more oil to his lamp before setting to the most important part of reproducing the viola soundboard.

Before beginning, he took a deep breath of the spruce-and-maple scent that lingered in the air. This, too, he loved. The smell had a settling effect. Then he bent over the original instrument, which he'd carefully pieced back together with some hide glue. It would never hold together over time, but it gave him a good sense of what the top had looked like before Belamae shattered it.

He ran his hands carefully, lovingly, over every fraction of it, lingering on the original imperfections it had received here and there. Marks, dents, scrapes. He felt these for depth, length, ridges. He needed to understand them entirely.

He repeated the whole process twice more, then placed the new, smooth top back into his bench dog and vise. He picked up a fine-tipped taper punch with a rounded end. Methodically, working from the tail of the original instrument forward, he found the first mar in the wood, ran his fingers over it several more times. Then he turned his attention to the new wood. He'd never found wood inflexible or difficult to work with. For him it was as potter's clay. Just holding it gave him comfort. Particularly if that wood was on its way to becoming an instrument of some kind. Especially then.

When he felt ready, he began to score the new spruce top in the same place, and to the same depth and form as the broken viola. He worked slowly, applying a little pressure, compared the new mark to the old, then applied more pressure. He repeated this process until they seemed to him identical. Then he found the next imperfection, and worked that one.

He wanted everything as close to the original as possible, because he knew that all things affected the sound an instrument made.

The soundboard would vibrate when played. It transferred more sound than the strings alone. That was its whole purpose. It was key to the tonality of the instrument. And it all began with the wood itself. Spruce was stiff and light, growing slowly in alpine climes. It produced a lovely timbre. The age of the wood mattered. The manner of that aging mattered. The thickness of the soundboard also mattered. The walnut oil, as well. For Divad, there was also sonorant residue—the songs the wood had already *heard*. It was like a good chili. You never finished making it. You simply kept adding beans and peppers and corn and loin cuts. And the richness of the blend deepened as days went by. Good chili pots were never empty.

And past all that, an instrument received its share of wounds. Sometimes they were the result of careless hands, dropping something on the instrument or mishandling it in some way. Other times, the anger of a musician would have him lashing out. This almost always came from impatience with his own facility or technique. Still, it was often taken out on the instrument. More wounds. And then, of course, time takes its own toll. The smallest imperfection in the wood or the luthier's assembly of the instrument would result in changes that affect its sound, if only in the smallest degree.

And with more time, all those practically inaudible changes would accrete to something audible, giving each instrument its own voice, a rich blend of resonances that could never be duplicated.

Divad meant to reproduce *this* viola in as much detail as humanly possible. To get back its voice. It mattered. And later into the night, when he fingered a long deep scar in the original instrument's wood, he began to remember why.

With one hand holding forward her cowl, his sister, Jemma, held something out to him. "Take it," she said.

They stood on the west side of Descant in the shade of mid-evening. A pleasant after-rain freshness filled the air.

"What is it?" Divad asked, knowing very well what she proffered. He'd been at Descant only a year, but in that year his life had gotten busy. He hadn't been home in months. Whenever she came, her gift was the same.

Into his hand, Jemma dropped a pomegranate, its skin dry and pocked. Around it a note had been wrapped after the fashion of his father, who sold damaged fruit on the edge of the merchant district, where street carts were permitted. His and Jemma's gifts on their name days and any other special occasion had been the same—father's best piece of fruit with a handnote as wrapping.

"Will you visit soon?" Jemma now used both hands to keep her cowl carefully in place.

Divad opened the note, which basically asked the same question, along with words of fatherly pride over Divad's being one of the select few admitted to Descant.

"I'll try," he said. "You don't know what it's like, though. There's so much to learn. Any time away puts me behind."

Jemma nodded inside her cowl. "Mother misses your laughter after supper. Especially since the harvest came in light."

That caught Divad's attention, if only for a moment. "Father's still selling what the merchant houses won't though, right? The older produce. The houses haven't taken that business back in, have they?"

"No," she replied, "but they may as well. There's not much left by the time it reaches father's carts. And what of it there is, he has to sell at less than half, it's so picked over."

"And you? You're well?" he asked.

She simply stared ahead. She stepped toward him and gave him a light hug with one arm, then turned to go. He said goodbye, and caught a brief glimpse of her face in the light of a clothier shop as she stepped past him. He should have stopped her to ask about the discoloration— or was it a shadow?—but she gave him little time and he was eager to get back to his study. If the pomegranate wasn't completely desiccated, *it would make a fine treat to accompany the memorization of the mixolydian mode.*

Divad's fingers began to tremble with the memory. He put the taper punch down, flexed his hands several times, then shook them to get the blood flowing. He sat back and drew several deep breaths. While waiting for his tool-hand to feel normal again after so long pinching the iron, he reached out with this other hand and again traced the scar in the viola's face.

It had gone much deeper than simply marring the lacquer. This gouge had gotten into the wood, and had torn along the sound-board for the length of two thumbs. It was by far the viola's worst scar. *Before Belamae shattered it.* His student might have been the one who slammed the instrument down, but Divad felt responsible. Just as he was responsible for this older scar in the viola face.

Divad looked away to the window, allowing the sound of the rain beyond to fill him. But try as he might to avoid it, the memory of the next time he saw Jemma rose like a specter in his mind.

The Cathedral quarter had once been the high district in Recityv. Now, it was maybe a hair's breadth better than a slum. The smells of bay rum sold by the cask, old urine-soaked straw and rotting mud, and unwashed day laborers filled the air. Jangly music drifted from the windows and open doorways of performance taverns. And children too young to be on their own either panhandled or waited with cunning eyes to pick the pockets of the unsuspecting.

Divad, oblivious to it all tonight, made his way through the streets to a familiar tavern. He needed a glass of wheat bitter to sip while he continued to struggle with the notion of attunement—a concept introduced to him that afternoon during a lecture on acoustics.

As he ambled toward the back corner, he passed a seated woman who kept her eyes lowered. At the edge of her table rested an empty mug. He'd nearly passed her when he realized who she was, and stopped abruptly.

"Jemma? What are you doing here?"

His sister's eyes flicked up to him with a mix of concern and embarrassment. She regained her composure within the time of a single breath. "Same as you, I would guess. Resting. Trying to shake off some of the street. Thinking."

He smiled and sat down opposite her.

"At home, it was strong tea and the stump behind the house." She returned his smile.

"Here it's wheat bitter and the stool in the corner," he said. "What about you? What are you drinking?" He pointed to her empty mug.

"Nothing. I'm fine," she replied rather quickly.

Divad nodded, recognizing when not to press too hard. "How's Father? Mother? Has the market gotten any better?"

When she met his eyes he noticed the same discoloration he remembered seeing . . . was that a year ago? But hadn't it been on the other side of her face?

"Father's selling road fare beyond the city wall now. The merchant houses haven't had fruit for him to vend in months."

A heavyset man with a ponderous belly that rolled over his belt like a water bag sauntered up to their table. "You going to buy the lady a drink? Or talk to her all night?"

"This is my brother," Jemma said evenly, without looking up.

Divad caught a twinkle of delight in the man's eye. "It's like that then. Well, I–"

"Go away," Jemma said flatly.

She sighed and pulled her empty mug back toward her. The heavy man huffed something under his breath and trundled away. Once he was gone, Divad ordered a glass of Kuren wheat bitter and set to explaining about acoustic attunement, and the parts he was struggling to understand. All the while Jemma nodded and smiled patiently. And though she seemed quite weary, she listened and asked questions. Later, they spoke of small things as only a brother and sister can.

Divad couldn't recall what, beyond attunement, he'd jabbered about that night with Jemma. The details were lost to him. But he remembered how it had felt to slip back into that unself-conscious kind of chat that didn't have to be about anything. Just talk for its own sake.

It had felt rather like the rain tonight. Soft, lulling. And yet, his hands continued to shake. It was the memory itself that unsettled him. A memory marked by this scar in the wood. To try and settle his nerves, he began to hum. He recalled a particular tune Jemma had been fond of. Then he picked up the taper punch again, holding it firmly but not too tightly.

Before he could begin, he heard the sound of steps behind him in the shop. "Maesteri?"

Divad remained poised, irritated yet also grateful for the intrusion. "Back here."

A third year Lyren stepped into the light of his lamps. There was a long moment, while Sedri, a woman gifted with a powerful alto voice, surveyed the tabletop. "Are you gouging a new sound-board?"

He let out a sigh, realizing she wouldn't be simply shooed away. Sedri was nigh onto fifty, coming to Descant after decades in the performance taverns. Despite her age, she could be as trusting as a child. But her many years had made her rather fearless, an important quality for someone doing the kind of singing he'd been teaching her.

He nodded for her to sit beside him. Then he gathered in her inquisitive stare, her original need of him apparently forgotten. "If you could go back," he began, fixing an instructive metaphor in his mind, "if you could back and do it again, would you spend those thirty years singing in smoke-filled taverns?"

She never averted her eyes, which, far from being sleepy at this forsaken hour, burned with the shrewdness of age. "You mean would I trade the smoke that has gotten into my vocal timbre."

Divad nodded. "You came by your craft a hard way. And those long nights airing out your songs through tabaccom haze has surely damaged your vocal chords. Given you some lovely alto tones, to be sure, but mostly given you a smoky sound."

She gave him a questioning look.

"That's not criticism," he added. "Your control and vocal strength are equal to or better than Lyren half your age. But . . ." he trailed off, forming his question more accurately, "if you could have the same facility in your voice, but have back the clarity, would you take it?"

After a moment, her face bloomed into a thoughtful smile. "No. I earned this tone."

He put a hand on her shoulder. "Just so. For my viola here, I'm doing my damnedest to be sure she has all the smoke and haze in her voice that she had before she was broken. Now, you get some sleep. You've a lesson on vocal dynamics tomorrow, and the regimen is an athletic one."

Sedri stood up.

"By the way, what was it you wanted when you came in?" Divad asked.

She smiled down at him. "I had a question about attunement. But I think I'll hold onto it for now."

When her footsteps had completely receded, Divad turned back to the new soundboard—his hands steady as wrought iron— and continued to scar the viola.

The smell of pine resin was strong in his parents' home. His father took in a plug every cycle for hauling away the carpenter scraps, which they'd always burned in their fireplace. The scent might have been a perfect welcome if Divad hadn't returned for Jemma's wake.

Six mourners—three of them unfamiliar to him—sat with his father and mother in the foreroom of their home. On the floor in front of the hearth lay a simple casket. The wood shape held an awful finality. Seeing it, Divad gasped. He hadn't been home in four years. Hadn't seen Jemma in . . . was it a year? More?

Time got away from him while he was concentrating on his studies. And until now, he'd given little thought to what he'd left behind.

He put down the viola case he carried, and went to his father. He struggled to find the right words. Really, his best response to this would be found in his music. He settled on, "I'm sorry." The words were entirely too small for the feeling inside him, inside this room. His mother reached up, still holding a kerchief, and grasped his wrist. Tortured eyes pleaded with him to do something.

"Oh Divad . . ." Her voice quavered. "We had no idea. We thought she took a laundry job. Her few coins . . ." She couldn't continue.

He looked at his father. "What happened to Jemma?"

The shame Divad saw rise on his father's face was terrible to see.

Such a look of helpless failure. The man's own skin looked heavy on his bones.

His father softly cleared his throat. "*Jemma took to beds to earn coin, Divad. The kind of man that would pay her . . . liked to use his fists. It's my fault, son. I should have been able . . .*"

Divad began to feel a cascade of grief overwhelming him. Grief for Jemma; for his mother's broken heart; for his father's feelings of shame and failure; for his own absence during it all. He looked down at the top of the casket. Pine.

Before he realized what he was doing, he retreated to his instrument, unclasped the case, drew out the viola, and began to play without bothering to resin his bow or tune. He escaped into the only song that came to mind, "If I'm Reminded."

The sweet sound of his viola filled the room. It held the unique qualities of both eulogy and sympathy. Long mournful notes resonated beneath his fingers as he played for Jemma. As he did, the story of her life fell into place: the discoloration in her face when she'd handed him a pomegranate; his father's loss of his cart-trade; an empty mug at the edge of a table—a signal he hadn't understood until now; Jemma's lack of beauty, and the only kind of man willing to pay her—one who sought to brutalize as part of pleasure-taking.

He should have seen it before. He shouldn't have been so absorbed in his music that he failed to see or help. He began to hate himself for blathering on about his lessons while she waited on the prospect of a few plugs in exchange for being beaten while giving up her maiden box.

His music had gotten in the way. And yet even now he used it to find refuge from a pine overcoat and the anguish of people he loved but had rarely seen in four years. Refuge from his own shame.

Sometime during the chorus of his song, his grip loosened. His bow and viola slipped from his hands and fell, crashing against the wood scuttle.

Divad's hands became still. His left forefinger had come to the end of the original scar. His right hand remained poised with the taper punch near the surface of the new soundboard. The mark was complete; as nearly identical as he could make it. The one gouge in the antique instrument that utterly belonged to him.

His leaving for Descant to study music had meant one less wage earner to support the family. He couldn't have known the produce trade would wane, any more than he could have imagined his sister would take to the mattress to help earn coin. Jemma had never said a word. Not to him, and not to his parents. Her modest contribution had helped them continue to survive.

"If only I had been there," he muttered to himself, "instead of here."

Music, even the learning of music, had begun to mean something different after that. He no longer took it for granted. And he did his damnedest to put it after his family in his list of priorities. That had meant late-hour repair for fiddle players and the like, who were willing to pay a Maesteri to fix up their decrepit instruments. He'd started to become accustomed to the wee hours sitting in this very shop. And every plug or jot he earned made its way to his father, no matter how healthy the cart-trade was at the time.

As the rain continued to whisper beyond the window, he nodded to himself. The soundboard was done. But he didn't, just yet, stand to leave. Instead, he remained in the company of wood smells and old spruce, thinking about smokiness.

The Sellari prisoner sat bound to the trunk of a tall poplar tree. I'd asked Baylet for a deaf one, like our Shoarden men. He'd assured me this one could not hear. The man appeared to have been severely beaten—for information, I assumed. The blood on his face had dried in the cold night air, and his chin hung slack so that his sleeping breath gave out slow tendrils of steam in the moonlight.

I stood a ways off, considering what I must do.

The lesson in the score given me by Divad had become clear. Scordatura was a kind of music notation used for altered tunings, as the viola d'amore usually had. That particular instrument was rarely tuned in fifths. In fact, it might employ twenty or more different tunings, each one to suit the individual piece. The various tunings made it possible to play chords and individual notes that weren't playable using conventional tuning.

Scordatura told the musician how to tune his instrument and where to put his fingers. But *not* what note to expect.

Some called it finger notation. On the page, the music appeared to be dissonant, filled with minor seconds. But because the strings were tuned differently, scordatura notation merely indicated finger position, the possible note combinations were unique.

That night I realized what scordatura could teach me about absolute sound, song with absolute value. That's why Divad had given me this piece of music in the Chamber of Absolutes. Trying to make sense of the notes proved frustrating, until I let myself simply consider where my fingers would rest on the strings, not knowing which note would sound, but trusting that the right one would.

Like scordatura tuning, singing a note with absolute value meant finding the right *place* inside a thing to resonate with, regardless of the note. If I meant to produce music that could stop Shoarden men, it would have to be of the absolute kind. I needed to figure out how to resonate with some part of them even when they could not hear me. I needed to go beyond my training, and figure out *where* to play these Sellari, the song of them.

In a real way, I'd be playing them like a scordatura-tuned viola d'amore. And the song that came out of me would resonate inside them as though they were aliquot strings.

I gave a weak but grateful smile, thinking of Maesteri Divad. He'd been trying to help me, even as he'd tried to convince me to stay. Perhaps he'd known I would come here to fight, regardless. But I still had to find that Sellari string to play. And looking back at the captive, I decided how I would do it.

As I approached him, the frozen ground crunched beneath my feet, the sound of it loud in the night. The Sellari couldn't hear me, so I tossed a small stone at his chest. His slack mouth slowly closed, and his eyes opened. He looked up at me, seeming to gauge whether or not he'd be beaten again. After a moment of silent regard, I allowed myself to become attuned to the figure sitting before me. To hear the song of him.

I began by focusing on his wounds, understanding how physical pain would feel in my own face and neck. Then I recalled the feeling of being restrained and threatened—a particularly worrisome moment I had suffered at the hands of a gang of five street brawlers the year I arrived at Descant. Then I summoned the images of the fallen from this very war, both theirs and ours.

Like a string being drawn across by a long bow, I began to feel the first notes of resonance between us.

In my mind, I identified musical phrases, performing mental turns in a descending Lydian scale to suggest surrender and helplessness and the simplest fear for self. And I let the look in the other's eyes, the vaguest hope of returning to his own loved ones, sweeten a bitter musical signature that rumbled inside me.

It wasn't the memories or thoughts themselves that brought us together, but their residue. The combinations of like things produced a kind of vibration we both shared.

I was attuned. I could hear the song of him. But what I had never done, never been taught to do, was sing that absolute value. Though now, I had a model for it. A scordatura model.

Rather than define the note or song I might sing to find a resonance inside him, I concentrated on a sense of him, the emotional fabric that made him who he was. And when that crystallized in my own mind, I opened my mouth and let come whatever most resonated with that sense.

I had never before made or even heard the sound that followed. It began as a low pitch that shifted so subtly that it lived in the space between notes. In those first few moments, the Sellari's ravaged lips curled into a smug smile; he must have thought he was safe from my song. But mere moments later, his brow tightened, creasing into several deep ridges. Concern rose on his face, his eyes darting from my mouth to my eyes and back.

I modulated a fourth up, then another minor third, singing with a glottal tone like the muggy feel of air thickened with rain. As I did, the Sellari's lips began to tremble, and a single runnel of blood issued from his nose.

He shook his head in confusion and worry, and pulled at his

bonds in panic. I then began a steady pulsing change in pitch, letting each new note come without forethought, landing in a modal set unlike anything I'd ever heard—part Aeolian, part Dorian. But never rushed, and never loud.

When the Sellari looked back at me, abandoning his effort to break his bonds, the fear was so palpable I could feel it. This was the moment of resignation that precedes some final pain or gasp. But this Sellari's pain was less about the fear of not living another day, and more about what he left behind: days he would never spend in the company of a son and daughter; regret for failing to do something he wished he'd made time for; the forgiving smile of his wife.

I sang his absolute value, resonated with him at the most fundamental level, and caused a violence inside him that tore him apart. He appeared to try and scream, but he could only tremble and sweat and suffer as my song undid him.

Finally, in a darkly beautiful moment, the resonance was complete. That's when I stopped, and he collapsed. The sweat and blood that coated him steamed in the moonlight. I felt both triumphant and sick inside, my own sense of attunement fading. But in those moments of song, I had found the place of the Sellari, that fingering a Lieholan could use to target the song of an entire people.

It was a broad and bloody thought. And once I'd found it, I began to weep. It was not a song I should know. The moral weight of that knowledge stole my strength and turned my legs to water. I fell to the mulch of rotting poplar leaves and sat there, smelling their autumn brown and the scent of cold soil.

Divad turned the length of Pemam wood slowly over the alcohol flame. He'd been at it for three painstaking hours. He carefully heated each thumb-length of the bow-stick over a small clay pot filled with sour-mash-soaked gauze. Using a strong wheat whiskey served a whimsical notion he couldn't explain. He was also of the opinion that the spent wheat alcohol infused the bow with the grace seen in an unharvested wheat field brushed by a slow wind.

Then he put the heated section to the camber, bending it gently before placing it on the edge of the flat bench. With a caliper, he measured the distance from the benchtop to the upper edge of the bow. For best performance, the bow camber needed to follow a gently increasing arc.

He turned a fair hand as a bowmaker, and had made countless bows in his day. The viola bow, in particular, proved to be a favorite, though, as its three extra finger-lengths over its violin counterpart allowed for a greater-than-usual variety of breaks and spreads. He'd fit it with a wider ribbon of horse hair, too—two hundred fifty strands. But the gradations he worked through now were the thing. They needed to be precise so that the bow remained equally flexible from tip to handle.

He sight-checked his work with a wooden template, too, though he preferred the exact measurements he got with his caliper.

Lesser luthier shops rushed through bow construction. They missed this crucial bit. Divad liked to tell his impatient students that: *The viola, it is the bow.* His overemphasis on the need for precision in its construction would, he hoped, mean they'd take care in all parts of making an instrument. It was true, though, that a well-made bow had a marked effect on the timbre of the instrument. More than anything else, he thought it gave the player a better hand at legato. Easy, fluid transitions in a piece most pleased his ear, so he didn't mind spending extra time to craft a proper bow.

He was in the process of bending in the delicate center-most section when indelicate footsteps crossed the luthier shop threshold.

"You'd best have a powerful reason for charging in all clumsy-like," he grumped. "You know this is delicate work up here."

"I think you can take a rest," came an unfamiliar voice. There was a calm but commanding tone in it, as from one who feels sure he'll be obeyed.

Divad released the pressure on the camber and looked under his armpit to see three men from the League of Civility entering his workshop. They weren't bustling, really. But they might as well have been, compared to the easy manner he instructed Descant members to use when coming into this place. The League liked to say of themselves that they *served the common interest.* Their emblem of four interlocking hands, each clasping the wrist of the next in a quadrangle-like circle, seemed comically obvious. Though the modest chestnut brown of their cloaks did just as good a job of conveying *common* while also setting them apart in uniform fashion.

He put the bow down gently and turned, wiping his hands on a dry cloth dusted with talc. "How can I help you gentlemen?"

The lead man slowed up, beginning to walk the line of instruments hanging from pegs in various states of repair. He ran a finger across each as he passed, the motion one part intimidation and another part casual familiarity. Close behind the other two Leaguemen came three Lyren, their arms outstretched as if they'd been beseeching their guests to slow down. Divad held up a hand for them to relax.

"Just some questions. Nothing that has to become contentious." The Leagueman's lips showed the barest of grins.

"Sounds harmless," Divad replied. "Always glad to educate. Shall we go and have a seat. I can offer you some—"

"What is it you do here?" the man asked.

Divad looked around. "I should think it's somewhat obvious. I repair instruments."

The man offered a soft chuckle. "You've wit. Please answer the question you know I asked."

"Fair enough." Divad leaned back against his workbench. "I teach music. And for some—those who have the gift—I teach *intentional* music. Most likely you call these folks Lieholan. It's as good a name as any, I guess."

"And these Lieholan, their job is singing a song that you would have us believe keeps us safe from mythical races, yeah?"

"A rather cynical way to describe it." Divad again wiped his hands of the sweat that had begun to rise in his palms. "If I look ahead of your questions, I suppose I'd say that what we believe on that score is ours to believe. And it doesn't cause a wit of harm to the League, or the people for that matter. May even lend some hope to weary—"

"Ah, see, that's the arrogance I expected." The Leagueman crossed to a near bench—the one where the glued viola rested beside a mostly reconstructed new one.

The stranger's nearness to the instrument made Divad panicky. "Does the regent know you're here? Or is this less . . . *official?*"

Something changed subtly in the man's face. And it surprised Divad. The Leagueman's demeanor actually became less guarded, less scrutinizing, as he began to run his fingers along the unfinished viola. "Let me start over," the man said. It was a masterful change in manner. One Divad would have fallen for if he hadn't been changing the tone of his own voice to color vocal performance for the better part of thirty years.

Divad played along. "I'd like that. I'll admit to being a mite weary. So, truly, how can I help you?"

"I think maybe there's too much mystery around what Descant does these days," the man said. His tone was almost apologetic, as though he were on a forced errand. "I've been asked to invite several of your singers of Suffering back to help explain it to us." He smiled magnanimously. "I'll tell you something else. I'll wager when it's done, we find ourselves more kin than kessel."

Divad kept from smiling. *Kessel* was an Ebonian word that meant 'separated,' but most folks used it to mean 'enemy.'

"I'll be glad to accompany—"

"Not you," the man said abruptly, then raised his hands as though to revise his own terseness. "That's not how I meant that. I'd imagine you have a good handle on your purpose. It's those you teach that we need to talk to."

Divad began to lose patience. "Is this a trial of some kind? Because if it is, I'll want a letter with the regent's seal."

The man's stare narrowed, though his grin did not falter. "No. Not yet. But mind you, a man might wonder about the person who frets over being invited to explain himself."

"No," Divad said flatly. "You have no authority to insist. And none of us is freely going with you. We can talk here, if you'd like. Beyond that, I'll have to ask you to leave."

The man's genial manner fell away entirely. He stood glaring at Divad with calculating eyes. Then he turned to look back at the unfinished viola. He picked it up in both hands with a delicate kind of grace. The room fell silent and taut with expectation.

"It's fine work," the man said. "My father was a fair hand with a knife. Though he used his skill to gut sea trout and coalfish, and mend nets and loose deck planks."

"Sounds like a decent fellow," Divad offered.

The Leagueman nodded. "He was. Up until I was nine," he replied cryptically. He then began to wave the viola by its neck, his agitation slightly more manic. "Your students. They're free to choose whether to go, yes?"

"Of course," Divad said, tracking the instrument worriedly as the Leagueman began to use it to point around the room.

"What about you," he said, jabbing the viola toward the Lyren near the doorway. "Nothing preventing you from leaving, is there?"

The Lyren shook their heads rather emphatically.

He turned back to Divad, being sure their eyes locked. Then he raised his arm, and began to swing the viola down toward the workbench. Divad felt that sinking feeling again. His first thought was a random one: that instrument bows were historically a weapon, and how he wished just now he had the former kind. On the heels of that thought, song welled up inside him. It had nearly burst forth when the Leagueman stopped his swing and rolled the viola onto the tabletop. It fell harshly but remained unbroken.

The room hung in a stunned silence at the Leagueman's forbearance. After a moment he stepped close to Divad, an obvious attempt at intimidation. The smell of rain-soaked wool was strong.

"You don't recognize me, do you," the Leagueman said, his voice deep and soft and accusatory.

Divad shook his head. "You have my apology if I should."

The man leaned in so that his lips were near his ear. Softly, he began to hum a chromatic scale. When he reached the upper end of his middle register, his voice broke over the passagio—the natural transition point in the vocal chord between middle and upper registers. It was a difficult transition to master. But absolutely necessary for advancement at Descant.

It wasn't the break that brought the man's name to mind, though. It was the timbre of his rich bass voice. "Malen."

He'd spoken the man's name without thinking, and drew back to look him in the eye. Years ago the young man had simply left Descant, after struggling for the larger part of a year to learn how to sing over the passagio.

"You needn't have left," Divad said, offering some consolation. "We'd have found a way."

Malen smiled bitterly. "And I'd have believed you. They all do." He reached down and picked up the bow Divad had been shaping. "Still using sour mash, I see."

"Let me pour you a drink. Settled nerves make better music."

"You and your music metaphors. A teaching technique, yeah? Well, Maesteri, you then are Descant's bow." He tapped the side of Divad's neck with the length of Pemam. "And you play each Lyren for the fiddle he is."

Divad felt some compassion for the man. Each musician hits several potential break points—passagios of a different kind—that they either work through or are defeated by. But Divad's sympathy quickly turned to anger. He didn't like being threatened. Less so here within the walls of Descant. And least of all in the peaceful confines of his lutherie. "Don't retaliate against us because you failed here. Or are *you* still being played, only the fiddler now is the League Ascendant?"

Malen brought the unfinished bow up between them, and began to slowly bend it, holding Divad's defiant gaze while he broke the Pemam stick in two. The two Lyren at the threshold gasped.

"Maesteri?" he said, "I'm not asking permission. Four of your Suffering singers will come with me. We have some questions we'd like answered. If we find everything here is aboveboard," he gestured around to mean Descant, "they'll be back soon enough. And because I'm fair-minded, I've left you two Lieholan to sing Suffering. Just in case I'm wrong that it is all myth."

He grinned and departed unceremoniously, leaving Divad breathless with anger. When Malen left the cathedral, Geola, Harnel, Pren, and Asa left with him.

It wasn't a quarter hour before another visitor came to Descant's doors. This time it was the young regent, in her seat less than a year. She explained that the League had twisted a new law, the Rule of Impartiality—meant to prevent treachery. Under its provisions they were broadly questioning various affiliations throughout Recityv. She'd heard they were coming here. And she apologized for arriving too late to help.

"What can I do?" Divad asked.

The young regent, Helaina was her name, answered, "Come with me."

He put out his alcohol flame, doused his lamps, and pulled on his cloak. He gave brief instruction to Luumen, the senior of the two remaining Lieholan to whom he was leaving Descant while he was away. Then he hastened into the street, and struggled to keep pace with the purposeful gait of his regent.

Anger and worry twisted in his gut. He caught her eye and asked, "Can they really do this?"

She gave him a reassuring wink. "Not while I'm around," she said, and if it was possible, strode faster still.

I never made it to the line. After singing the Sellari to death, I crawled back to my horse, and eased my way to my tent. I'd found an absolute sound, and the weight of it proved difficult to bear. Some songs were heavy. Knowing them was like shouldering a yoke of brick. Suffering was that way. Suffering was an absolute song. Its passages swirled in my mind now that I better understood its underpinning.

Near dawn, Baylet slipped into my tent again. He sat beside the sword he'd given me, which remained untouched. After a long moment he spoke wearily. "We lost two thousand men tonight."

I'd have thought there'd be a tone of indictment in his voice.

But really he was just tired. Tired in his body. Tired somewhere deeper.

As I sat with him, we both kept our own observances for the unspeakable loss. Sometime later, while he stared away southward, he said, "You killed the Sellari."

It wasn't something I wanted to talk about. I said nothing.

"You found a way to sing death to a Shoarden man. We need your help."

Phrases of Suffering began to repeat themselves in my head. "I'm not sure I can."

"Because you can't? Or because you won't?" If Baylet hadn't been so weary, there might have been some impatience or indignation in his tone. As it was, mostly the question rang of disappointment.

It's how my father might have sounded, were he here to ask me the same. But I wouldn't have had any better answer for him. The best response I had was to keep silent.

Baylet shut his eyes and pinched their inner corners as his face tightened in a moment of frustration. When he let go, he tapped the sword beside him as one who's accepting the way of things. But rather than leave me alone, he said, "While you work through your personal grief, do me one last favor."

I gave him an expectant look, preparing for a barrage of insults. Instead, he stood and ducked out through the tent flap. A bit reluctantly, I followed. To my surprise, he neither rushed nor led me south. At an almost leisurely pace, our horses walked north and a smidge east. Moment by moment, the world awakened, near to dawn as it was. Animals skittered in the underbrush, birds began to call against daybreak in that soft way that keeps morning peaceful.

Several leagues to the west, the tips of the Solden range showed the sunlight gradually working its way down the mountains as the sun rose in the east. Before it reached the valley, Baylet stopped. I came up beside him and looked out over a vast field riddled with humps of freshly dug earth. There might have been eight hundred that I could see. In the distance, the field sloped away from us.

"I told you before. We're losing the war." Baylet took a deep breath, one that sounded like acceptance.

The graves of soldiers, then, I imagined. Unmarked barrows of the thousands who had fallen. It was a grim thing to see.

"The histories tell of the Sellari. Of the devastation when they lay hold of a place or people." Baylet surveyed the field left to right before continuing. "Rough hands, Belamae. They've no interest in servitude. They're glad to make sport of the living before putting them down for good. That'll mean indignities for families before the blessing of death."

"We could retreat north—"

"And leave the Refrains for the taking, you mean."

I shrugged. "Sounds like that's going to happen sooner or later."

The field leader became reflective. "Maybe. But trying to move so many so fast . . . and the Sellari would follow. The feud is an old one. It goes beyond the Refrains."

I'd not heard of this, and Baylet didn't offer to explain. So I let it pass.

"Rough hands," he said again. "They're coming. I don't have anything to stop them." He surveyed the field from right to left this time. "They knew it. And they did not wait . . ."

That's when I realized what I was truly looking at. Not the graves of his men. But killing fields. All Mor nation children were taught a simple, dreadful lesson when they reached their twelfth name day. If invasion should come, and defeat appear inevitable, our people would not wait for cruel foreign hands to take our lives. By our own hands, we would go to our last sleep with quiet dignity.

"There are at least a dozen more killing fields." Baylet's tone was filled with self-loathing. "They've begun to lose hope. By every abandoning God, this is too much!"

The field leader's voice boomed out over the field in long rolling echoes.

I wanted to say something. I wanted to say I would try. But my mind felt like an open wound that even a stir of wind would sear.

Baylet rode forward before I could find any words. I followed again, and soon we were navigating carefully between the graves. I noted the awful sight of patches of earth not much longer than the length of my arm. My mind conjured images of mothers offering their babes what they thought of as a mercy. If I'd felt disheartened before, if I'd thought I was too far from shore, now I felt lost and empty in a way only one song had ever taught me.

Before I could run that song through my mind, Baylet stopped and dismounted. I did the same. We stood together as the sunlight finally touched the field where we were. Our shadows fell across a pair of graves.

"I don't understand what it's like to sing an absolute," he began. His voice sounded strangely prayerful in that day's first light. "I've read the music of countless composers who've tried to write it down. Black scores. The kind whose melodies never go out of your head, though you wish they would." He shook his head slowly. "But they're just approximations. The ability to actually do it . . . it'd be a burden. A lot like keeping the Mor Refrains is a burden, I suppose. I'd like you to know, before I sent for you, my petition to the king for access to the Refrains was denied."

It seemed obvious now that all along Baylet had meant for me to find and sing the Sellari absolute. I felt duped. But I didn't have the energy for anger, and simply nodded.

Later, as the field began to warm in the sunlight, I asked, "Why are we here?"

He continued to stare down at the two graves. "Some by tincture. Others by rope. And more by blade drawn across blood veins."

Then it dawned on me. We must be standing over the barrows of his family. He fought for Y'Tilat Mor. He fought for his men. But after it all, he fought for those closest to him.

"I'm sorry," I offered.

For the first time, he looked up from the graves, giving me a look that passed from puzzlement to understanding to sympathy in a breath. "No, Belamae. We honor your mother and sister this morning."

My stomach tightened, and I felt instantly shaky. Baylet put a hand around my shoulders. Some faraway part of me thought again of how the field leader was orchestrating, influencing my decisions. But I'd have wanted to know. And no matter when or where, I'd have felt the same.

I drifted in a haze for I don't know how long, while grief pounded at my chest with its insistent rhythms. I couldn't keep from picturing ma and sa putting a knife to their own flesh. I felt their powerlessness and despair. And the dignity with which they went to their final earth, avoiding rough hands that—if things were left unchanged—would surely come.

Without realizing it, the words and melodies that had been circling in my mind started to come out. The sixth passage of the Song of Suffering: Self-Destruction, which was sung about the Inveterae condemned to the Bourne, countless of whom had taken their own lives rather than go to that awful place.

I sang the lament, gathering quiet strength with each phrase.

I lent it a measure of absolute value.

And I wondered if in so doing, somewhere ma and sa felt my song, though like Shoarden men, they would never hear it.

The streets of the Cathedral quarter were just beginning to come alive with the night arts. Confidence men sized up marks; sheet women angled for lonely men with spare coin; performance taverns were opening their windows, using music as a lure to drink and be entertained. More than a few packs of bearded men stood wearing hard looks, spoiling for fights. Through all this, Divad lead his four Lieholan.

For the better part of two straight days, he and Regent Helaina had argued with League leadership, clarifying the Rule of Impartiality, describing the workings of Descant Cathedral, growing angry. They'd had to involve the Court of Judicature, which helped but also delayed his students' release. By the time the League set them free, the thuggish treatment they'd received was visible on their faces in dark and purpled spots. They were exhausted, but alive.

Divad hadn't had time to put the ordeal into any kind of

rational context yet. After a hot bath, warm meal, and night of uninterrupted sleep, he'd need to do that. They turned onto the quarter road that lead to the cathedral's main entrance. No sooner had they come in direct sight of Descant, than the door was opened and three Lyren began gesturing urgently for them to hurry.

He broke into a run, his cloak seeming suddenly overlarge and cumbersome. Behind him, the slap of Lieholan shoes on paving stones followed close. He darted through crowds, around wagons and carriages and riders. He climbed the cathedral steps two at a time. One of the Lyren, Waalt, grabbed his arm and began to run with him, guiding him, pulling him along.

"What is it?" Divad asked, breathless.

"Luumen fell ill with autumn fever a day ago." Waalt pulled him faster.

Divad understood immediately. "How long?"

"Almost three entire cycles." Waalt's voice cracked with desperate worry.

"Dear merciful gods."

Luumen was the more experienced and stronger of the two Lieholan he'd left behind. Ill with fever, she would not have entered the Chamber of Anthems to sing Suffering. Which meant Amilee had been singing Suffering by herself.

"My last sky," Divad whispered, and pushed his legs to go faster.

It took nearly nine hours to sing Suffering's nine movements. After singing the cycle, the Lieholan was spent, and needed two days' rest to fully recover. There'd been occasions when one vocalist sang part of a second cycle. But it was rare, and always came at great personal cost to the singer. Amilee had been at it for not just two full turns, but nearly three . . .

Casting a look backward, he called commands. "Pren, prepare yourself." Pren's bruises were the worst, but he was also the strongest Lieholan Descant had since Belamae's departure. The young man stripped off his robe mid-stride, and began to run vocal scales as he maneuvered up beside Divad. "Asa, fetch a Levate." Divad didn't hold much hope that a physic healer could help, but he'd be prepared in any case.

The sound of their racing feet filled the cathedral halls. The flames of wall lamps fluttered with their passage. Lyren watched them go by with grave looks in their eyes.

Moments later, Divad pushed open the heavy oak doors to the Chamber of Anthems. Amilee was on her hands and knees, unable to hold her head up, singing toward the floor. Her voice sounded like corn husks brushed together by summer storm winds. She had almost no volume left. But the perfect acoustics of the rounded chamber lifted the delicate song she could still make, and gave Suffering life.

Pren picked up the melody line just a pace or two inside the door. When Amilee heard it, she did not look up at them, but simply ceased singing and collapsed on the stone floor.

Divad swept the girl up and carried her straight through the chamber and out the opposite door. He cut left to the nearest bed-chamber and went in. He laid her gently on the coverlet, while Harnel fetched a pillow for her head.

Amilee's eyes fluttered open. "Maesteri," she said with a bruised voice.

"Save your words," he admonished. "Gods, I'm sorry, my girl."

He had to hold at bay renewed anger at the League, who had put them in this situation. His growing hatred for them would not help this courageous young woman.

She shook her head in a weak motion. "I didn't lag," she whispered.

Divad's pride in the girl swelled, tightening his throat with emotion. But he managed a low sweet tone, to course gently through her. Help him see, or rather, feel. So that even then, he knew she would not live. If her wound were of the flesh, he could render a song of well-being. But Suffering drew on a different part of a Lieholan's life. And of that, she had expended too much. It was remarkable that she had anything left. But it was not enough for him to resonate with.

Oh child.

As she lay dying, Divad found strength enough to put away his ill feelings for the League. He sat beside her and took her hand

and sang a song of contentment. Slow and low, he poured out his love and admiration for the girl. He watched as the pain in her eyes and brow slowly relaxed.

And before she let go, he leaned in close, so that no one would hear the question he asked of her. When she nodded, she looked grateful and at peace.

Divad resumed his melody and sang until her hand grew cold. It was a dreadful thing to feel the song go out of a person for good. To feel the vacancy, the silence, that replaced what once was the resonance and melody of a life. His voice faltered more than once as he sang into the emptiness she left behind. He would have liked to play his viola for her, but it was still missing its strings.

Four days after Amilee went to her final earth, Divad sat again in the warmth and silence of morning sunlight inside his workshop. Motes danced slowly in the shafts of light, reminding him that even in silence there's a kind of song that stirs the air. These last few days he'd been preparing gut for his viola. Now, all that remained was to string the instrument.

Gut was best taken from the animal while the body is still warm. It needed to be stripped of fat and placed in cold water. Later, it would be transferred to wine or a solution of lye to help remove any last unwanted matter that still clung to it. Strips were cut to length, twisted together in various numbers to create different pitches, and rubbed with almond or olive oil to prevent them from becoming brittle.

Divad had thoughtfully done all this, and now picked up the first length and began stringing the repaired viola. One by one he fixed the aliquot strings to their bone points, and ran them up through the neck to their pegs. When he'd finished the resonant gut, he did likewise with the playable strings.

Next he tuned the instrument. Never rushing. Turning the peg as he thumbed each string to find the extended tuning for the first song he intended to play on the salvaged viola. The sounds of the tuning were somehow muted in the morning stillness, almost as if the air was resisting the sound.

When the instrument was finally ready, he sat back, regarding the fruits of his labor. The work had been tedious and filled with reminders. Both things were part of the process, something he knew from experience. But he felt satisfied that he had done well, and smiled genuinely for the first time in many days.

In every part, there'd been meaning. That mattered. From the spruce top harvested from a performance tavern bar, to the gut that Amilee had willingly surrendered from her own body. This last element might prove to be the most important, Divad thought. If there was truth to his notion of sonorant residue, then a piece of Lieholan that had sung Suffering might make this incarnation of the viola better than its predecessor. To teach resonance and play for the fallen, he could think of nothing better.

When the moment felt right, he took up the viola, and the bow he'd completed the prior day, and stood in the light of the window. There, he drew the bow across the gut, fingering the first notes of "If I'm Reminded." He then muted the top strings, and listened intently as the aliquots continued to resonate in the silence that followed.

A long time, he thought, and smiled. *A long time since I've heard this song.* Later, when the resonating strings ceased to hum, he would play it for Amilee. He'd play it finally for Jemma. For now, though, he stood still, allowing the aliquots to ring, and learning something more about resonance.

It was not dawn when I arrived at the line. Midday had come and gone.

It was not the start of battle. They'd been fighting for hours.

It was not ceremonious. I simply found the front of the line and started to sing.

I sang the song of them. And almost without thinking, I blended the absolute value of the Sellari with a passage of Suffering—Vengeance.

Before my training at Descant, my experience with the word, even the idea of *vengeance,* came mostly from pageant wagon plays. Now I realized they'd treated the notion rather too simplistically. And I thought I understood why. Either the players didn't themselves really know. Or, if they knew, they believed most folks would be better off remaining ignorant on the topic. For that, I wouldn't blame them.

Then later, under the tutelage of the Maesteri, as I learned Suffering, my understanding of vengeance grew by half. But it was still a clean thing, theoretical. It remained a nearer cousin to the pageants, where vengeance sounded like melodrama, performed by a player wielding a wooden blade, wearing a silly mask, and moving in exaggerated motions. If it had a sound, it was that of a recalcitrant child screaming, "I'll get you back."

My Sellari song of vengeance was nothing like this. It was blind and messy. It pulsed with hatred. It knew nothing of justice or balance or *making something even.* And if my other recent songs had been rough-throat, this sounded as though I'd just gargled with crushed stone. I half expected my throat to start bleeding.

So I walked into their midst, unhurried, letting the song out. It was like playing a great chord, strumming a thousand strings. Ten thousand. Some men simply fell. Others began losing blood from every orifice. The flesh of many sloughed from the bone. Wails of anguish filled the air. There came the sound of countless bodies thumping onto cold ground. Some made a few retreating steps before the song got inside them.

Bright red blood spilled across the vast field.

It was a terrible song. And it was also mine. Since at his core it was resonance.

The property of resonance in sounding systems serves as a metaphor for love. One system can be set in motion by the vibrations of another. Two things, people or strings, trembling alike for one another.

That was one of the first Predicates of Resonance. The awful, practical knowledge I added to it was this: there were many resonances that could cause a man to tremble; love was but one of them.

With each note, my song grew stronger, feeding off itself,

swelling as a wave traveling a broad ocean. I had no idea which of my enemies actually heard me sing, but it didn't really matter. Even if it wasn't heard, this song was felt.

When I finally stopped, I had no idea how long I'd been singing. It might have been a few long moments. It might have been hours. An eerie silence fell across the vast field. Not a single Sellari stood between my countrymen and the far tree line.

But there came no feeling of relief or triumph. The desire for vengeance still surged inside me. That's when I learned the hardest truth about vengeance: it had no logical end, served no real purpose, except perhaps to delay grief. Vengeance was just an inversion of loss; or maybe its cowardly cousin.

But it did have consequences.

Though I'd survived its singing, the song had done something to me. I knew it when the first Mor congratulated me. I didn't feel happy that this fellow would return to his family. Instead, I wondered and worried whether I'd saved a Mor who would bugger his son or beat his wife or ignore a daughter who only sought his approval. The cynicism ran deep, painful. It sickened me. And I instinctively knew that the only relief I'd find for this new pessimism was to continue singing the song.

Dear absent gods, give me someone to hate.

That prayer seemed to find an answer. Two hundred strides away, at the long tree line of poplar, hundreds of fresh Sellari emerged, striding purposefully toward us. In their midst, four Anglan draft horses pulled a broad flatbed wagon bearing a spherical object two strides in diameter.

I felt an eager smile creep onto my face, and I began to close the distance between myself and this new crop. To their credit, the second-wave Sellari came on bravely, as though they hadn't seen how I'd sung down those whose bodies I now trod on in my haste. I wanted to be closer this time. I wanted to watch them suffer as they went down.

Sea-crossing bastards killed my father. Forced ma and sa to . . . Inveterae filth, I will shatter the bones inside you. No, that is too good an end. I will find the point of resonance in your shank-given race and will make it your misery, show you the end of your women and children, their slow despair. I will break your hearts before tearing away your flesh.

With that, I rushed forward. I could hear the sound of running steps trying to keep pace with me—the Shoarden men assigned to keep me safe. But I cared none for that. When I was five solid strides from the Sellari, so that I could see the lines in their faces, I began to sing the shout-song again. I lent it a new intention, infusing it with the menace of hopelessness, like the sound of a screaming parent when she finds her child dead by her own hand. I knew such a sound from many years ago—that memory came back with a vengeance of its own.

I watched, eager to see the look in their eyes as they felt that deep ache before I broke their bodies.

But nothing happened. None paused or flinched or grimaced. They just kept coming on in the face of my song.

I was nearly upon them when I realized why.

This new brigade was dressed like Sellari, carried the same slender arcing sword. They'd even painted the same black band around their eyes. But they weren't Sellari. They strode with the swagger of mercenaries who lived for the opportunity to kill. Their grip and motion with their blades made it clearer still. They were not tense or overeager. A frightening casual readiness marked them. These were Holadai, fortune-swords. My Sellari song was useless against them.

More than that, each next note became more painful to sing. I tried to modulate the song, switch modalities, shift its intention, but nothing helped. And I watched in a kind of stupor as one of the Holadai reared back and threw a heavy hammer at me. I saw it come, and knew the aim was true. But stunned by the deception of this mercenary force, I couldn't move. The iron hammer hit me hard in the chest, where I felt ribs crack.

It knocked the wind from my lungs and drove me to my knees. Two pair of boots came into view, swords swinging casually. I saw them rise up out of my field of vision, and sensed they'd soon end my pain.

Then a flurry of footsteps rushed in around me. The clash of steel rang sharply against the sky. A Mor fell dead beside me, as did a Holadai. Then a spray of something warm and sticky caught me in the face. I fought to take a breath, but still could not. Around me more of my countrymen fell hard to the cold ground, as Holadai grunted and fought through their own wounds.

When at last I gasped a painful stuttering breath, I took in the coppery smell of blood. I grew blind with rage, and pushed myself to my feet. I fixed my eyes on this new enemy and summoned a different song. When I let it go, the air shivered with the harsh sound of it. The rasping noise tore at everything, shrieking through the minds and bodies of the Holadai.

As they began to drop, new forms took their place. My song caught in my throat to see that these replacements were a mix of Sellari and Holadai Shoarden. They wore menacing grins as they rushed toward me.

Fine trickery, you damned wharf-whores!

A stabbing pain fired in my thigh. I looked down to see an arrow protruding from my trousers. Around me, my Shoarden men were falling in alarming numbers. Frustration mounted inside me. I staggered backward a few paces. Another arrow caught me in the shoulder. This one I reached up and ripped out, feeling its barbs pull at my flesh.

The number of Sellari and Holadai became overwhelming. I didn't know how to help myself or my countrymen. But I had to do something. On instinct, I started to sing. *At the end of it, get the sound out,* I remembered Divad saying—the lesson an old one.

I began with a dire shout-song, a rough-throat cry I simply made up as I went. Then every third beat I switched, singing the song of the Sellari. I sang faster, the two songs beginning to come in a strange syncopation. And each time I changed, different men screamed, different bodies dropped.

I felt another hammer strike me. But it seemed somehow far away, and only hit me in the elbow—maybe breaking it, but that pain felt distant, too.

The real pain came each time I sang the notes of the Sellari song. The large sphere, now twenty strides away, amplified the music and reflected it back toward me. It didn't deflect the song from striking at the hearts of the Sellari. But it more than doubled the personal cost of the resonation I felt. The pain grew fast, much the way one's palm begins to burn when held close above a candle flame.

But I did not stop. The alternating songs wove in and out of one another, reminding me of waves rolling onto a shore and back.

Then, again, sometime later, all motion stopped. Heaps of bodies lay across the field, some stacked three deep around me. When I ceased to sing, silence returned to the world.

My face and hair, and all my clothes were drenched with blood.

I thought I heard the distant song of mockingbirds in the poplar trees. I couldn't be sure. My ears rang with the remnants of my own music. In those first moments of stillness, my cynicism, and the terrible ache that only singing destruction would assuage, began to plague me again. So once more, I wished for someone to hate. Looking far ahead, I saw several thousand Sellari stepping tentatively from the shadows. I started to smile. Then stopped.

Walking slowly toward me, across the bloodied field, came a line of Sellari women . . . and children.

At this new sight, I felt my mind break. That was the only way I could explain it.

Behind them strode fresh Sellari bladesmen and archers.

I watched them come, sensing an awful truth. This was not simply an invasion force. They'd come to occupy the Mor Nations, bringing with them their families, which they'd now turned into a walking shield.

A distant pluck and hum sounded, like a chorus of cellos being tuned. A moment later the sky darkened with arrows whistling toward us. Questions vied inside me. Could I let fly my own weapon, and sing the Sellari song into the bodies of the innocent? On the other hand, could I let them rain down death on my own people?

My struggle seemed endless, but in truth lasted only a moment. I felt my song rising, and hated myself for it.

Belamae?

The name came at me as though I stood at the bottom of a deep, dry well.

Belamae? It's over. Can you hear me?

I felt my body being shaken, but ignored it, my song touching my vocal chords, ready to be loosed.

Belamae? A sharp crack on my cheek stalled my song, and I was suddenly staring into Baylet's concerned eyes. "Are you all right?"

Confused, I slipped to one side, looking south to the line of poplar trees. Nothing. The field still lay quiet with thousands of the dead. But there were no archers. No women. No children.

"You found their song," Baylet said, his voice solemn.

I only nodded, slowly realizing that my mind had conjured a need to sing out Vengeance again. *Oh dear merciful music, what I was prepared to do.*

I fell to my knees and buried my face in my hands, weary, ashamed, relieved . . . changed. Song had become something I would never have imagined. A burden.

I also thought I finally understood what it would truly take to sing Suffering.

And I meant never to do it.

When the Descant doors were pulled open, Divad looked out on an emaciated, disheveled figure. If he hadn't been told in advance, he might not have recognized Belamae. But it would not have been because his returning student looked as if he hadn't eaten in weeks or that his cloak was tattered and reeked of his unbathed, filthy body. Rather, his face was changed, his aspect. The useful intent in his eyes had gone away.

Everything about him gave Divad the feeling that he'd come here only because he didn't know where else to go. Belamae made no attempt to enter, or speak. He didn't even look up, simply staring downward, his hands hanging at his sides.

He looked too fragile to embrace, so Divad gestured him inside. The heavy doors closed with a deep, resounding boom. In the lamplight, he hummed a very low, very soft note. It was brief, but enough to resonate with the change that had gotten inside his prodigy. He gave a sad smile that the boy did not see, and turned, motioning Belamae to follow.

He walked slowly, without speaking, knowing that the soft resonant hum of Suffering that could be heard in the very stone of Descant would reacquaint the lad with the purpose of this place. That'd be a good start to righting his sense of things. The boy had a form of what the early Maesteri called *Luusten Mal*. Sound poisoning. It was a rather simplistic way of referring to it, but accurate in its own way.

Divad considered returning to the Chamber of Absolutes, where he'd first tried to impart a sense of absolute sound by way of aliquot strings and the viola d'amore. Instead, he turned down a different hall, and went up four levels by way of a spiral staircase, where the granite steps had been worn enough to resemble thin smiles.

Eventually, he led Belamae into his eastern-facing lutherie. He came to the worktable where he'd spent so many hours over these last many cycles, carefully repairing the instrument his student had destroyed.

He lingered a moment in the clean scent of spruce shavings made by recent work with a hand plane—he'd begun a mandola as a gift to a prospective Lyren he'd denied admission. But the viola was the reason for coming here. It rested on a three-legged stand very like an easel. He gently picked it up and turned toward the lad.

With slow deliberateness he stepped forward, watching as realization dawned in Belamae's face. He saw shame pass to surprise, to wonder, then to delight. That last came as little more than a faint smile, not unlike the surface of the stone steps they'd just climbed.

Relief held in his prodigy's eyes more than anything else, though. And he liked the look of that. It made every moment of remembrance and backaching work bent over his table worth the pain. But there was still an emptiness in the boy. He could feel it, like the reverberating resonance felt in the head of a tightly covered drum.

As he stared at Belamae, the right thing to do occurred to him. He extended the viola to him again, as he'd done what seemed like many cycles ago. Belamae tentatively reached for the instrument. But before his student could take it, Divad whipped it around and brought it crashing down on the hard oak surface of his worktable. The viola strings twanged, the spruce split and splintered, the body smashed into countless pieces, and the neck ripped in three parts. The soundboard he'd labored over lay in ruins. He felt a pinch of regret over it.

But his own loss was nothing compared to the shock and horror that rose on Belamae's face. It looked like the boy had been physically wounded. His mouth hung agape, his hands held out, palms up, as if beseeching an answer to the violent, incomprehensible vandalism.

"My boy," Divad said, his voice softly intoning some reason to all this. "Won't you help me collect the pieces. We'll see what's salvageable."

"Maesteri?"

Divad smiled warmly. "Instruments can be mended, Belamae." He tapped the lad's nose. "Come. We'll see about this together. I've decided I rather like this part of instrument care."

He began to hum a carefree tune, as they gathered in the shattered viola.

R.A. Salvatore

I'VE NEVER SHIED AWAY FROM ADMITTING THAT MY WORK IS CONNECTED to the trials of the real world or to the journey of my life. Indeed, I consider writing my way of making sense of the world, my—if you will—spiritual journey. My characters are sounding boards. I put them under pressure, bounce impossible situations against them, and in a weird way try to learn from their reactions.

Writing also gets me through the dark times. With this particular short story, however, there was yet another dimension added to that psychological mix: putting some of my own emotional baggage to rest.

I was an athlete growing up, but in the sandlot. When the movie of that name, *The Sandlot*, came out, my old pal Rusty called me up and said, "Bobby, you have to see this! It's us!"

And it was. We played more baseball growing up than any kid in Little League today. Every single day, we came home from school, threw our books on the table, grabbed our gloves and bats, and rushed down to the open lot at the back of the cemetery. Four of us would play "hit the bat" for hours at a time. Hundreds of swings, hundreds of catches, hundreds of throws.

Life was good.

Then we had to go and play—or "perform"—for the adults, and life was not so good. I was a shy kid, and due to circumstance, I wound up with a coach in a less-than-ideal situation. One thing led to another, to another, to another. The coach humiliated me in front of the team, and it just went downhill from there.

So I quit. I did. And it hurt like hell. And it hurt more when I saw the crestfallen look on my Dad's face.

So I resolved to fix it. When Babe Ruth tryouts came around the following year, I got up to bat and knocked the adult who was pitching right off the mound with a line drive. I hit one off the right field fence. I left the field dancing on air. I had nailed it.

And I didn't get drafted. In essence, my baseball "career" was over.

I never understood it until years later, when my barber, who had a son a year younger than me, told me that my Little League coach, who had moved up that year with his sons, had blackballed me at the draft. I was a troublemaker, you see, and so the coaches crossed me off their draft list.

The profound idiocy of an adult doing something like that to a little kid haunts me to this day. I was incredibly shy, but I was also top of my class academically, *never* in trouble, and could play baseball, football, hockey, and basketball pretty well. In the sandlot, I was the team captain, the pitcher, the diamond quarterback . . . in the organized world, I was intimidated by the scowling, judgmental adults, and had gotten on the wrong side of a vindictive man indeed.

I don't know how different the rest of my middle and high school years might have been except for this one incident (no, I have no illusions that I would have been a pro athlete!). The kid I threw passes to (because I had a better arm) in the sandlot became the star quarterback of the high school team. My aforementioned friend Rusty starred in baseball in a small college.

And I was the shy kid who did everything he could to stay invisible until graduation.

I know my story is nowhere near unique—not even rare. As my own kids were growing up, I often told my wife, "I wouldn't want to be a kid today," and I meant it, and mean it. When I was a kid, we played. We made up our own rules to fit the sandlot dimensions, settled our own arguments, and didn't look over our shoulders to see the disapproving glares from adults. By the time the '90s had rolled around, the young players lived under a microscope of adult supervision and domination, and far too often under the control of adults who cared not at all for the kid, but only for the "player," because that player was their way of reliving the dream.

"The Coach with Big Teeth" is not a fantasy story. It is the sad reality of far too many shy and overwhelmed ten-year-olds.

R.A. Salvatore

THE COACH WITH BIG TEETH

R.A. Salvatore

"This is what it's about," Coach Kaplan said to Assistant Coach Tom in a throaty voice, caught somewhere between a cheer and a growl, and loud enough so that his team could hear him clearly. "This is what makes all those hours of practice worth it!" He stood at the edge of the dugout, putting him less than a dozen feet from first base, while the Panthers' coach, similarly positioned at the end of his own dugout, was closer to third.

Kaplan's enthusiasm was hard to deny, even for these kids, who hadn't taken Little League very seriously, or at least hadn't shown enough intensity to make their coach—and in many cases their parents—happy. Especially now, when the championship was on the line and neither of the teams, as so often happened in a league where pitchers hit batters nearly as often as the strike zone, had busted out into any substantial lead.

The tension in the air had mounted all through the first three innings, shifting gradually from nervousness to sheer excitement as many of the initial jitters dissipated. This was familiar. This was what they knew. And they could do it—maybe.

Like everyone else in the park, Lenny Chiles McDermott, or LC, as he preferred, wanted to win. He knew that he wouldn't play much of a role in any victory, just as he had pretty much been the invisible outfielder all year long, but he wanted to win, and in the event his team pulled off that miracle, LC would savor his trophy as much, if not more, than the "real" ballplayers on Tony's Hardware Mariners. A sporting trophy, however earned, would validate LC once and for all.

Small for his age, and timid, LC had never felt at home on the team. Sure, he was a smart kid, and truly likeable, but the things he was interested in weren't the things that made a ten-year-old popular. He read three books a week, real books, novels that rarely came in at under three hundred pages, but he couldn't talk about those with his friends, who simply didn't understand the value of plain old words; nor could he expect good grades to get him any-thing more than teasing from his fifth-grade classmates.

But a baseball trophy!

A pop-up ended the top-of-the-fourth rally that brought the Mariners back even with the Telecable Panthers. The Mari-ners had done well, had scored four runs, but that easy out had left runners on second and third. Coach Tom clapped his hands eagerly, and told the guys, "Hold 'em now and get 'em in the fifth!" He patted Rusty, the pitching ace, on the back as the tall young-ster rushed past, heading for the mound.

Coach Kaplan slapped his hands together loudly and turned toward the bench, but kept turning, as though he didn't want the team to see the snarl that was lifting the corner of his mouth.

LC, so often on the bench and going nowhere in a hurry, did notice the feral expression, but was hardly surprised. He noticed, too, that Ben Oliver, the kid who had choked, was quick to retrieve his glove and skip out to the field, consciously avoiding eye contact with Coach Kaplan. LC didn't blame him; Coach Kaplan had a strange look to him when he was mad. He was a big, muscular man, an intimidating sight indeed, particularly to one of LC or Ben's stature. His eyebrows were thick, as was his curly black hair and mustache, and his complexion was dark. The combination was ominous, especially since he always seemed to need a shave. His eyes, too, were dark, but to LC the most striking thing about the large man was his jawline, square and huge, and filled with equally huge white teeth.

The Mariners' players took the field, leaving LC sitting on the bench with Mikey Thomas, who had played his mandatory two innings at second base, and Joey DiRusso, who would have been on first base had he not broken his elbow on the Tarzan swing. Boy, had Coach Kaplan turned red when he learned that news! "What were you doing on the Tarzan swing a week before the playoffs?" he had howled at poor Joey. Joey's father had done little to protect his son from the coach's outburst and, in watching that scene, perceptive LC got the feeling that the man considered Kaplan's outrage a great compliment to his son's baseball ability.

After all, Kaplan wouldn't have yelled if he hadn't cared, and he wouldn't have cared, would even have been pleased, if Joey had not been an asset to the team.

LC had sighed then, and he sighed now, wishing that he could change places with Joey, wishing that it had been his father who had taken Kaplan's outburst as a compliment.

And now Joey, wearing jeans and his Mariners shirt, got to watch the game from the bench, with no pressure. LC could see the combination of embarrassment and sheer frustration in the boy's brown eyes. He wanted to tell Joey not to worry about it— he himself had long ago gotten over the embarrassment of sitting on the bench, but there was really very little that a sixty-five-pound fifth-grader could say to comfort a hundred-and-five-pound sixth-grader.

Very little.

So LC went back to watching the game, or to watching his feet, crossed at the ankles, as he swung them back and forth under the bench, just brushing the dusty dirt. He looked up in time to see the Panthers' Ryan Braggio (boy, did the name fit!) strike out, and it wasn't until the loudness of the cheers registered that he realized it was the third out of the inning. The Mariners had held, one, two, three, and LC's trophy loomed a little bit closer.

Rusty's home run, a hard ground ball that rocketed through the hole between first and second, then hopped the right fielder's glove and rolled all the way to the rough at the base of the fence, put the Mariners up by two, had Coach Kaplan and Coach Tom hooting and backslapping, and had the parents in the stands on this side shouting with joy, while those fans across the way sat quietly, with only an occasional shout of encouragement for the despairing Panthers.

Momentum is a tentative thing in baseball, though, and it shifted dramatically when the next Mariners' batter ripped a line drive that would likely have gone for at least a double, but for the marvelous diving grab by the Panthers' shortstop.

Now the howls and cheers came from across the field.

"All right, keep up. Keep up!" Coach Kaplan implored his players even as the next batter took a called third strike.

"We need a hit now," LC heard the oversize man whisper to Coach Tom. "We gotta get Matt up this inning." Both men turned subtle glances LC's way, and the boy understood what was happening. He hadn't been in yet, and the rules said that he had to play in at least two innings, that he had to be on the field for at least six of the opposing team's outs. And that meant he had to go into the game soon. He would go to right field, of course, replacing Matt Salvi, the on-deck hitter. Which meant that if Matt Leger didn't get on base now, LC would have to lead off the sixth.

Matt Leger walked; Coach Kaplan breathed a sigh of relief. LC took the insult to heart. Why hadn't the coach asked him to go in now, to bat for Matt Salvi? What difference did it make which of the two worst hitters on the team made the last out this inning? LC, too intelligent for his own good, understood the truth of it, and that hurt him even more. Kaplan hadn't put him into the game because the coach simply hadn't thought of it. The rules said that every player had to play for six of the opposing team's outs. Period. And Kaplan would play by the letter of the rule, whatever the intention of the rule, to avoid a forfeit. Other than that, he never gave LC a moment's consideration.

"Give it your best swing, Matt!" Coach Tom said as Salvi

approached the plate. Kaplan snorted. He wasn't expecting much, LC realized, and was probably glad when Matt Salvi struck out. Kaplan's team was leading by two runs going into the bottom of the fifth, and they would have their leadoff hitter, who almost always got on base, starting the sixth.

Coach Kaplan didn't even have to say it. He just looked at LC and nodded. They both knew where he was going.

LC heard Kaplan tell Rusty to "keep it in on the righties and out on the lefties." It made sense; a right-handed batter would likely pull an inside pitch to left field, and a left-handed batter would have a hard time getting the bat around fast enough to hit an outside pitch into right field. Coach Kaplan was trying hard to keep the ball away from LC.

LC could accept that. He just wanted the trophy, the validation, and for this season to be over, to be the stuff of proud talk and not terrifying reality. He could live out the big play in his fantasies, could hit the last-inning homer, or make the game-saving catch doing a somersault over the outfield fence. He wanted that, like any kid would, but the greater probability of his making an error was simply too frightening.

"Keep it in on the righties, out on the lefties," he mumbled under his breath as he crossed the infield stone dust to the thick grass of the outfield. "Or better still, Rusty, strike them all out."

Rusty did just that, in order, to end the fifth inning.

Coach Tom greeted the players with high fives as they returned to the bench, though the only Mariners who had even touched the ball that half of the inning were Rusty and Tony, the catcher. Coach Kaplan's smile, meanwhile, was ear-to-ear, those huge teeth shining against his dark complexion. The situation looked good indeed: two runs up, last inning, and the top of the order coming to bat. That was Billy—Billy Socks, they called him, because it was said that he would often run right out of his shoes. LC had never actually seen this amazing phenomenon, because he wasn't really a part of Billy's social group, and he didn't believe it at all. Still not wanting to be chastised, or worse, he yelled for "Billy Socks" right along with the rest of the Mariners.

Billy hit the first pitch up the middle, a looping, soft liner. The team went crazy, Coach Kaplan howled, and apparently, all the excitement got to Billy Socks, because he never stopped at first. The Mariners and their fans were surely surprised, but the Panthers' players were not.

Billy Socks was out by ten feet as he tried to get to second base. LC noted that he still had both of his shoes on as he walked dejectedly back toward the dugout.

When the next batter hit a ground ball right to the first baseman, who scooped it up, dropped it, and still had plenty of time to step on the bag for the out, Kaplan's toothy smile was long gone. The Mariners could have put the Panthers away this half of the inning by scoring a few runs, but that chance was slipping through their little fingers.

LC figured that he wouldn't be getting up to bat. He had been hoping that he would, figuring that if they got all the way through the order anyway, if eight other batters had come to the plate before he stepped up to bat, his ups couldn't really be vital. Even if there had been two outs with the bases loaded, three other runs would have had to score and the lead would be five, not two. So the situation, if LC did get the chance to bat, would be safe enough. Maybe he would walk, or even manage a hit, and then he would truly be part of the team, not just a benchwarmer. Maybe he would close his eyes and swing as hard as he possibly could, and hit the ball over the fence!

Yeah, a grand slam, and then he would be a part of Billy Socks's crowd, and then he—

The boy glanced around nervously, wondering if his private fantasy was being openly observed by his teammates. He noticed then that he was sweating. LC hoped that he would get the chance to bat; he was terrified that he would have to bat.

Those conflicting thoughts grew stronger when Ben Oliver made up for his last choke by ripping a hard grounder that was bobbled by the Panthers' first baseman. Safe at first.

That brought up Tony, the catcher, the cleanup hitter. "Tony Boomboom," who had once hit a ball so far over the center field fence that it had dented the hood of Kaplan's pickup four rows back. Kaplan had never fixed that dent, displaying it on his truck proudly, as if it were a testament to his coaching prowess.

The first pitch was way outside: it was obvious that the Panthers' pitcher was wary of Tony, but with dangerous Rusty on deck, there was little that he could really do. The next pitch came in high and hard and Tony nailed it, launching it sky-high. All the Mariners' fans leaped to their feet. At least a dozen yelled, "Get outta here!" or "See ya later!"

But it was too high, way high, so high that lumbering Tony, who was even slower than LC, was nearly at second base when the Panthers' left fielder leaned up against the fence and caught the ball.

Momentum was a funny thing, and so, to LC, was the way that this entire side of the field suddenly drooped back down at the exact moment the people on the other side of the field leaped up, as though some underground wave had sucked all the energy on the Mariners' side and pushed it underground into the waiting legs of the Panthers' fans.

LC chuckled at the thought, but wisely coughed to disguise his mirth. He took up his glove and started for the field along with the rest of the Mariners. Coach Kaplan stopped them and brought them into a huddle, counting heads and coming up one short. He yelled out to Joey DiRusso and waited until the frustrated youngster joined them, then spent a long moment dressing Joey down for his lack of team spirit.

Right after that Kaplan confused LC, although most of the others didn't see any irony in it, when he told the players taking the field to win this one "for Joey."

You mean the kid with no team spirit? LC thought, and he chuckled again, and this time it was okay because it seemed like he was joining in with the rising cry for the Mariners.

Here it was, bottom of the sixth. Last inning, trophy on the line. It took a while for play to begin, because Tony had made the last out and now had to put on all of his catcher's equipment. Each passing second seemed interminable to everyone in attendance, but worst of all to LC, who only wanted it all over with so he could breathe again.

Finally Tony came trotting out of the dugout, slipping on his catcher's mask and glove as he went. LC tensed and patted the pocket of his glove hard; the first Panther batter was a lefty, which made it far more likely that the ball would be hit to right field. LC hoped that Rusty would strike the kid out, or keep the pitches so far outside that the kid couldn't possible pull anything to right. At the same time that he was hoping the ball wouldn't be hit his way, however, LC was fantasizing that the ball would indeed be hit his way, and that his incredible diving catch would make the first out!

His fantasy was shattered by a yell from Coach Kaplan, one of those animal howls, aimed directly at LC. The boy looked up to see the man waving him over to left. He didn't understand, even put a finger against his chest as if to say "Me?" but then he noticed Billy Socks, the left fielder, jogging his way.

LC got it; Coach Kaplan was shifting him over to left field while the left-handed batter was at the plate. LC felt itchy suddenly, felt as if all the eyes in the world were boring into him. He didn't really want the ball hit to him—was surely afraid of that—but for Kaplan to so obviously be attempting to keep it away from him . . .

LC trotted across the thick grass, not able to look in toward the dugout and stands, feeling ashamed and humiliated. Most of all, he couldn't possibly look his father in the eyes. He could almost hear the relieved sighs of those people in the stands near his dad, quietly congratulating Kaplan for his cunning coaching. What would those sighs and whispers do to his father?

As he crossed near second base, LC heard Kaplan call to Rusty to keep it "high and tight." Now they could pitch the lefty aggressively, because a well-hit ball wouldn't wind up anywhere near LC.

The young boy wanted the game over; he wanted to take his trophy, earned or not, and go home.

Rusty came in high and hard with the pitch. The lefty hit a shot down the first base line, into the outfield. He took the turn at first, but had to go back, for speedy Billy Socks fielded the ball cleanly and threw it on one hop to second base.

The next Panther batter was right-handed; LC started back toward right field before Coach Kaplan even motioned to him. He noticed, too, that Coach Kaplan and Coach Tom were nodding to each other, confirming that they had done well in shifting LC out of right field.

It took seven pitches, including one foul ball that landed dangerously close to the right field line, but Rusty managed to strike the kid out.

Up came the third Panther of the inning, another lefty.

Rusty brought his glove to his belt, ready to throw; LC tensed. His breathing would not steady.

"Time!" yelled Coach Kaplan, his hands up high, waving as he neared the first-base line. He yelled out angrily to Billy Socks and to LC, as though they should have understood and executed his strategy without being told. The pair swapped places again.

The batter eyed LC every step of the way. He glanced out toward left field, then to his bench, where his coach was nodding subtly. LC didn't miss it—the Panthers had figured out that he must be very weak in the field, and so the batter was going to try to come his way.

Rusty's pitch came in tight, too tight for the lefty to hit it the opposite way, and the result was a soft liner right back to the pitcher. Rusty grabbed it and fired to first, hoping to catch the runner before he could get back to the base.

"He's out!" cried Coach Kaplan, looking for a double play. Half the Mariners howled, thinking the championship won.

But the umpire was right on the spot, his hands wide to either side. The runner had gotten back to the bag before the throw.

LC knew he could relax again for a few minutes. With typical intensity, Coach Kaplan got into it with the ump, shouting and screaming, kicking dirt and pointing repeatedly toward first base. Several of the Mariners piped in, the better players mostly, and many of the fans on both sides made sure that their perspective on the play was heard as well. Never mind that those fans were at least thirty feet away, with a chain-link fence between them and the play. Never mind that the ump, alert and moving toward first base before Rusty had even turned to throw the ball, couldn't have been more than ten feet from the bag, with a perfect angle to see the diving runner's hand and the catch by the Mariners' first baseman.

Before he left the field, the argument futile as always, Coach Kaplan motioned angrily for LC to get back to right field.

And so the boy watched, far out of the play, as Billy Socks raced for the next batter's line drive to left-center, watched and fantasized that it was him, not Billy, as Billy dove for the ball.

And missed.

The center fielder headed it off, though, making a great play, and fired it back toward the infield. The Panthers' coach took no chances and held the lead runner at third base, while the batter, the game's tying run, chugged in easily to second.

Coach Kaplan called time-out again, this time going out to the mound for a talk with Rusty. After a few tense moments, with Kaplan growling and kicking dirt, the man stalked back to the edge of the dugout. He managed to get in another insult at the umpire as he went, complaining that the runner had been out on the line drive and that the game should be over.

On Kaplan's orders, Rusty walked the next batter intentionally, loading the bases, resulting in a possible force-out at every base.

LC could hardly find his breath. Five batters had come to the plate; the game should have been over, one way or the other, by now! The fans on both sides were going wild. The Panthers shouted at Rusty, who just rubbed down the ball and let fly a wad of spit in the general direction of the Panthers' bench, glaring at the next batter as the kid dug in at the plate.

All LC cared about was that this batter was big and strong and right-handed, which meant he wouldn't be likely to hit the ball anywhere near right field!

Rusty's first pitch popped into Tony's glove with the sound of a firecracker. Strike one.

The next pitch was too far inside, nearly clipping the kid on the hands, and the third pitch, too, was a ball. It bounced in the dirt, and only a smothering grab by Tony prevented all three runners from advancing.

The Panthers' batter ripped the next one down the left field line, foul.

LC breathed a little easier. Not only did the kid now have two strikes, but Rusty was working him inside, and he seemed quite willing to pull the ball to the left.

Rusty fired; the batter swung.

LC and all the Mariners nearly jumped for joy, for the ball went right by the hitter. There was a moment of confusion, of the sheerest tension LC had ever known.

The kid wasn't out; he had foul-tipped the pitch and Tony hadn't held on to it.

The situation only got worse when the next pitch came in too tight again. Ball three—full count.

LC hated this game.

Rusty rubbed down the ball. The entire park seemed to go eerily silent. Three balls and two strikes, two outs, tying run on second, winning run on first.

Rusty went into the windup and let it fly. All three base runners took off. Rusty had to get this one over, couldn't afford to tease the kid inside again. The ball came in waist-high over the *outside* part of the plate. LC saw it all as if in slow motion: the batter's puffy cheeks, the great exhalation as the bat came around and connected.

And then, suddenly, the ball was in the air, soaring high into right field.

LC's glove came up immediately—all the inexperienced ballplayers did it that way, putting the glove above their heads as if it were an umbrella. LC was all alone then, just him and the ball, and he heard nothing but the sound of wind in his ears as he ran back, back, and toward the line.

Five short steps put him under the peaking fly ball, he thought, with plenty of time to spare, for the ball had been hit so high.

And then it was coming down, down, spinning and falling. LC shifted back a bit more. Since a right-handed batter had hit the ball to right field, it was tailing toward the line, spinning like one of Rusty's patented curveballs.

But LC was there, in position. Down came the ball, right into his glove.

And out it spun, rolling up his index finger and hopping back into the air. LC felt as if he were in a dream, moving slowly, too slowly. He could count the stitches on the rotating ball, could see its arc as it rose above his head. His short legs pumped for all his life, cleats grabbing at the turf, propelling him forward. He dove straight out, trying to get to the ground before the ball landed.

He did get down fast enough, but his arm wasn't long enough; the fingers on the vinyl Kmart glove his father had bought him for his first year of baseball weren't long enough! The ball hit the ground just beyond his reach and rolled tantalizingly away from him.

LC knew that he was in trouble. The runners had taken off with the pitch. One run was in, maybe two, and the winning runner was nearing, or rounding, third. LC scrambled to his feet, took a running stride, then glanced back and saw his doom.

The third run, the winning run, was halfway home; he couldn't possibly pick up the ball and throw it to the infield in time!

He looked at the ball as though it had betrayed him. He heard the screams of delight from the third base side of the field, the Panthers' side of the field.

Kaplan howled. Still the world seemed to turn in slow motion. LC's gaze went over his shoulder, to his teammates, to the coach with big teeth, down the line to the stands behind first base. He wanted his father, but something was wrong. He couldn't even pick out the man, for all the fans, the fathers and mothers, the little sisters, even, seemed to change. They got hairy in the face, like Kaplan, blond hair becoming black.

And their jaws, every one! Square and huge, opening to show those monstrous teeth, unleashing those feral howls. LC stood openmouthed as they came down from the stands in a pack, swirling like flowing water as they came through the fence gate just down the line from the Mariners' dugout. Only then did LC glance back to the field, to his teammates and two coaches, all looking like Kaplan, all charging his way!

The terrified boy turned to run. He started right, but then realized that the center fielder had cut him off that way. Back to the left went LC, screaming and crying, his legs seeming to move impossibly slow, the howls growing closer, closer. He slammed into the four-foot fence and threw his chest over, scrambling to get his legs up.

Billy Socks got there first, clawing at LC, tearing the boy's Mariners shirt with two-inch fingernails. Other hands joined in, grabbing and pinching, clawing viciously. LC hung on for all his life, screaming denials, and tried to kick out. But he was pulled back into the mob, taken down on the grass, thrown on his back right beside the settled baseball.

Despite their frenzy, they took their time in tearing him apart. A hundred scratches, a hundred trickles of blood. LC tried to grab onto something, and blindly latched his fingers through Tony Boomboom's catcher's mask. Then he screamed, more loudly than he ever had before, for Tony Boomboom promptly bit off one of his fingers. LC looked at the large boy, the mask on crooked, no longer fitting the now-elongated jawline. Blood spurted from the stub onto Tony's face, but it only seemed to excite the vicious boy-creature more.

LC looked back up just in time to see Kaplan's—the real Kaplan's—face descending, mouth opened impossibly wide, wide enough to cover LC's entire face. And then the hands were back, beating him, clawing him, ripping him.

Nearly blinded by agony, LC turned his head and somehow looked back down the line, to the fence entrance, to the one Mariners' fan who hadn't transformed, who hadn't come after him.

His father, standing with hands in pockets.

The man walked away.

The coach with big teeth tore out LC's heart.

TODD LOCKWOOD

I LEARNED TO DRAW BY MAKING MY OWN COMIC BOOKS. THROUGHOUT my childhood I wrote as well—in my mind I saw movies or TV shows. Love of *story* compelled me to become an artist, but it was a choice that left half of my desire unfulfilled.

In 2005, I began work on a book of dragons. At first I imagined a coffee-table book of art, but soon she who inspires the written word stirred. She's a demanding muse, but has such a comely form . . .

Before I knew it, the book of art inspired a cast of characters, a history, a landscape. A story demanded to be told. I spent most of the following years studying and bettering my craft. Shawn had opportunity to read my manuscript before I sold it to a publisher—we'd already combined forces on other projects. When he invited me to submit a story to *Unfettered*, I leapt on the chance to reveal a bit of backstory, a snippet of ancient history from my world.

Todd Lockwood

KEEPER OF MEMORY

Todd Lockwood

Daen screamed until the monster's teeth crushed ribs against ribs. Blood poured from his lungs, a bright flower unfurling on the pavestones.

He bolted upright. A tree root scraped his back as he tried to crab backward, but his feet were entangled in his blanket. He sat still, surprised to feel moss and short grass under the heels of his hands. A soft hush surrounded him, the landscape shrouded in fog that deadened sound and confused distance, rendering trees and stones into ghostly shadows of themselves. Panting, he rubbed his face with pale fingers and blinked away the blur in his eyes. His sweat grew cold in the damp air.

Gods, what a dream! It wasn't the first time he'd died in his dreams. Not the first time by a long stretch. The details were familiar: towers of acrid smoke and blinding flame, a tumult of screams, clashing metal, and bellowing rage. But he'd never before faced the Dahak itself, the monstrous, sentient dragon whose armies terrorized his city of Cinvat. Many priests insisted that the Dahak was a High Dragon—something far greater than the beasts Cinvat's warriors rode into combat. True or not, the beast in this dream was bigger and more terrifying than any dragon he'd ever seen.

He shook his head to evict the last ghosts of his nightmare. He was in the mountains, in the fog. The wet mist must have put out his fire in the night. His third night—and he still hadn't found any cinderblack for Mer, his master, the Keeper of Memory.

Cinderblack. Mer had sent him up the mountain to find the dark berries of the cindervine for the priests. They needed the cinderblack for their inks, for the magic that they hoped would help turn the fortunes of war. With it they tattooed sigils of strength and stamina into the flesh of the warriors and their dragon mounts. The science was young but promising; the staying power of the cinderblack inks allowed for greater complexity and nuance.

Daen wasn't a warrior, he was an acolyte of the temple, and they didn't fight. Most acolytes assisted the priests who graved the sigils onto the skin of those who fought. They tended their wounds, or delivered them to their pyres on the rare occasion when their bodies made it home. He knew war, if only from a distance, from seeing its aftereffects: the broken, the dismembered, the maimed who'd returned on their dying beasts; the grieving wives and mothers, the wailing children . . .

Daen's task as Mer's acolyte—one of four—was markedly different. As the Keeper of Memory, Mer had dedicated his life to preservation of the city's long history. Daen studied in Mer's library, and hoped to be his successor. Already the entire history of Cinvat resided in Daen's head, after years of hard study and drill and rote memorization. He knew the name of every man who had fallen, every dragon mount that failed to return. He committed every one to memory, scribed each into a record book that he kept with him at all times—

He sat up straighter in panic—*where was his record?*

Daen untangled the blanket from his legs and jumped to his feet.

His basket nestled in the elbow of a tree root, empty of all but his meager food supply. *Foolish! I must have kicked it in my sleep and sent it rolling.* His toothscrub and pens lay nearby. The box containing his flint and steel had spilled into a puddle.

A fine Keeper of Memory he would be one day; he couldn't even keep track of his most important possession! He imagined his master's scornful rant, felt the sharp crack of the old man's hand on the back of his head. He was Mer's best student; he knew that. But he couldn't lose his first record book in the mountains—his very first personal entry into the great Library of Cinvat. That would be disaster.

He scanned about quickly, shook out his blanket, raked through wet grass with his hands. It wasn't here. His search became frantic. Not under the bushes, not in the puddle. Could it have landed in his fire? With sinking stomach he poked at it, but the wood wasn't even completely burned. Surely a piece of the book would remain if it had. At last he picked up his basket, and there between the tree root and a hummock of moss lay the small, leather-bound book. With a sigh of relief, he brushed it off and held it to his chest. When his heart stopped pounding he kissed the book and stuck it in his tunic.

Taking a deep breath, he shrugged off his shame at panicking and acting like a child.

Cinderblack. The very thought of berries made his belly grumble. On Waeges' Day, the autumnal equinox, there would be autumn berries everywhere—but the cinderblack were rare, and not for eating. He pulled a knotted cloth out of his basket and opened it. Less than half a loaf of his waybread remained, and the cheese was gone. Unhappily, he broke off a small knob of bread and bound the rest up again. Water shouldn't be hard to come by, but he would wait to drink until he found a stream where he could refill his waterskin.

Daen slid the straps of the basket over his shoulders. It bounced lightly on his back. Too lightly. *Don't return until your basket is full*, Mer had told him.

He set out.

This late in the season, cinderblack would be hard to find. He'd found none on the southern exposures of the nearest slopes, so he set a course along a ridge for the next mountain southward, hoping for success on its north face where cooler temperatures and limited light delayed the harvest.

Light glimmered in wan diffusion, the sun little more than a patch in the fog. Soon, Daen realized that he was lost, but he maintained his southern path. Pine trees replaced ash and birch and oak, moss gave way to grass, dirt to stony outcroppings. He knew he'd gained altitude.

He stepped into an open space suddenly, surprised to find paving stones beneath his feet. The glowing air revealed silhouettes of crumbled wall and toppled pillars surrounding a small courtyard. It might have been a fortress, or a temple, with a commanding view of the valley on a clear day. The sun brightened, acquiring a hard edge, though he could still look directly at it. For the first time that morning, he became aware of smells—crisp pine, wet earth, and damp stone. It seemed as if this place defied the gloom, a small island of light and life. A brief gust of air caused an old leaf to chitter across the stones, then the mist swirled, parted.

A statue appeared out of the fog. At first its subject eluded him—he saw only a tangle of roping sinew and claws and wings, pitted and worn beneath a cloak of moss. But as he studied it, two dragons emerged in realistic detail, a white one above and a black one below, locked in battle. The closer he looked, the more masterful the artifice became. They seemed almost alive.

But their forms were exaggerated, not like the dragons men rode into war. Certainly they must be depictions of High Dragons. He hurriedly fished his record book out of his tunic. He should sketch a picture of this. His eyes were drawn morbidly to the black beast below. The Dahak was said to be a High Dragon, like this one . . . but the white one? In all of Cinvat's stories was there—

"Hello."

Daen jumped, barely keeping hold of his book, and spun to see a young girl stepping cautiously out of the forest and onto the courtyard, staring. She might have been six, possibly seven. Dark eyes and hair, simple homespun attire, carrying a small basket. She paused and cocked her head with a beguiling half-smile on her face, as if waiting for him to answer before she came any closer.

"H-Hello . . ."

"Who are you?" she asked, approaching again, tentatively.

He looked around himself—for *what* he didn't know—feeling awkward at having been surprised, pleasantries the furthest thing from his mind. Mer often scolded him for being tongue-tied, or for saying the exact wrong thing at the exact wrong time. He tucked his book away and straightened his tunic self-consciously. Only when she stopped again, a few feet away, did he find his wits to reply. "I . . . my name is Daen. And you . . . you're . . . er . . . your name—?"

"I'm Maia." She smiled. "What are you doing here?" Her accent was odd, clipped, unlike any he knew.

"I . . . well, I was admiring this sculpture here. Can you tell me anything about it?"

She scrutinized the statue behind him, her head tilted and her mouth twisted sideways. "Well . . . it's very old. It shows two High Dragons fighting, one is black and the other is white. The white one wins. Mother likes to come here on Menog's Day to lay dried flowers under it. But I don't remember why . . . that's really all I know."

High Dragons! She said it so casually. Daen squatted down to bring his eyes to her level. She backed up a step, so he shrugged the basket off of his back and sat on it. "I'm surprised to see it, that's all. I've never heard of this place, though it's so close to my city. It's a very elegant statue, isn't it?"

She cocked her head at him, brows pinched. "You talk funny."

He smiled. "No, *you* talk funny!"

She grinned back at him. "Where is your house?"

"I'm from Cinvat . . . that way." He gestured vaguely in the direction that he thought might be west.

"I've heard of that, but I don't know where it is. Is it a big village?"

"I should hope you've heard of it. It's a city—the biggest in these parts, until you get to the coast. Trenna is on the coast and it's the biggest city I know of."

"Tren-na . . ." She shook her head slowly. "I don't know that name. It must be very far away."

"Not so terribly far, really. Have you ever seen a big city?"

"No. Just my village, Riat."

"And where is that?"

She pointed back and to her right, more or less southeast. "That way, on the cliff. My father is the broodmaster there."

Broodmaster. An unfamiliar term. "Are you here alone?"

"No. I'm here with my mother and Grus."

"Grus . . . is that your sister?"

She laughed briefly, a melodious sparkle of sound. "No! Grus is Mother's dragon!"

"Her dragon! You have a dragon?"

Maia studied him through squinted eyes. "Of course we do. We have six dragons—three breeding pairs. I told you: my father is the broodmaster."

Dragon breeders? So close by and he had never heard of them before? Surely the Council knew every breeder for leagues around. Perhaps he had wandered farther off his course than he realized, or Maia and her mother traveled a long way on their dragon to be here. Six dragons would scarcely compare to the hundreds bred in the aeries of Cinvat, but in such times as these, every dragon qit mattered. He fished his record book out of his tunic, fumbled his pen and a bottle of ink out of his basket.

Maia's eyes grew round. "What is that?"

"This is my record book. I write everything important in here."

"Are you going to write *me* in there?"

"I most certainly am. You and your mother and . . . Grus, did you say her name was?"

Maia nodded happily, pleased to be accorded such importance.

His hand hesitated before making a mark, though. He didn't know how far off his trail he might have wandered in the fog. He drew a quick map of the valley and the surrounding peaks and ridges, put an X as a best guess, then added some notes about the statue and Maia. "I suspect some of the elders would like to visit your father and meet Grus. Is your mother nearby?"

Maia nodded again.

"May I meet her?"

The girl's brow pinched into a frown, her lips puckered in thought. "I don't think she will see you."

216

Daen pulled upright. "Why ever not?"

She crossed her arms. "You don't belong here."

Daen felt indignation rising, but he struggled with the voice of Mer in his head, warning him to stay polite, to consider his words wisely. Even as he swallowed his anger, the girl said, "Why are you here really? Not just to look at statues. Are you *lost?*"

Perceptive child. He slumped and nodded. "Yes, I admit that I am a little bit lost. The fog disoriented me . . ." He shrugged. "I'm supposed to collect berries for the priests."

Her face brightened, if only a little. "We're gathering berries too! We come here sometimes to picnic, but today we're gathering berries for the Waeges' Day banquet." She held up her little basket as proof. He now saw that it was full of dark red bunchberries.

"So you are! Do you know where to find the best berries?"

She nodded. "Where you're from . . . you get to eat berries?"

"Of course, sometimes. I'm looking for a very specific kind of berry, though. Do you know cinderblack?"

"Nooo . . ." Said like a question.

"They're very dark, not shiny like some berries. They grow in the shadows, on vines with blazing red leaves. Do you know of these?"

"Do you mean charberries? They're not very good. Birds and faerie dragons like them, but that's 'cause they swallow them whole. Then their poop stains never come clean."

Daen leaned forward in excitement. "That sounds right. Yes! Do you know where some are, right now?"

She nodded again, slowly. Apprehension now seemed to jostle with her interest, so he pulled back. "Can you show me? I would be very grateful."

She scrutinized him for a moment. "Why do you want those awful things? I can show you good berries."

He considered how to answer such an innocent question. He could invent something simple, but he suddenly felt concern for this wilding child and her family. Her guileless curiosity put an unexpected lump in his throat. She deserved the truth. She should know the truth. "We are hard-pressed by the Dahak's forces, and we need every advantage we can get—"

She looked truly puzzled now. "You're *pressed*? Like squashed?"

She didn't understand at all. How could she not have been touched by war? Were they so isolated that the Dahak hadn't found them yet? It seemed impossible.

"No . . . Yes. The Dahak squeezes us. All of us. We need the . . . charberries because they make the best ink for the priests. The best inks make the strongest gravings."

She nodded. "My father has gravings."

"Does he? Is he a warrior?" He stood, and she took a step back, shaking her head.

"Maia—our people are at war, and whether you realize it or not, you are in great danger. The Dahak won't stop until its armies have taken everything. Have you seen strange and horrible armies, with dragons that are . . . dark and misshapen?" He reached out to her, but she took another step back. Was it possible that her family had already been turned? Is that why Maia's mother might refuse to meet him?

"If you're at war, why are you here gathering berries?"

Her voice in that moment seemed wiser than her years, her face so pinched with distrust that Daen regretted his surge of honesty. "It . . . It's my duty. They are needed. Please, Maia . . . Can you show me where the berries are?"

She pointed to the west without taking her eyes off of him. "Up there, in the rocks."

"Thank you! And now, may I meet your mother? I would love to talk to her . . ."

Maia shook her head again. "She won't see you. You should go back where you came from. I think you're scaring me."

"Maia, no! I'm not scary . . . I . . . I'm scared *for* you. I really need to talk to—"

"I think I should go now." She turned and headed into the forest, into the mist.

"No! Please don't go! Maia—wait!" He stuffed his pen and his record book into his tunic, stoppered his ink and poked it in too, then snatched up his basket and followed after. He suddenly found himself surrounded by soft gray shadow, as if the edge of the courtyard defined a boundary between light and gloom.

The fog had swallowed her. It still lay thick under the trees, but he thought he heard footsteps and cracking twigs ahead. "Maia! Please don't go! Please take me to your mother!" He stopped to listen for her, but the dense air muted all sounds. Beneath this canopy of shadows he felt disoriented again, and cursed himself for a fool.

"Maia!"

Not even an echo.

"Please!"

Surely her mother would have heard his shouts, even in this fog. "Maia's mother—if you can hear me, please answer!"

He waited long minutes for some sort of response—a shout, returning footsteps, the beat of a dragon's wings. But the air only grew heavier, the silence more dense.

And what if her family *had* been turned? For whom did her family breed dragons? He shuddered to think that he stood here shouting out his position, inviting his own doom.

He turned to retrace his steps back to the statue in the ruins, his hands shaking and his feet numb. He needed to reclaim his sense of direction. After several minutes of tramping, he knew that he had missed it somehow. He took a bearing on the brighter patch of sky where the sun dwelled, then started a circular path, expanding with each turn, in hopes of coming across the statue in the courtyard again.

When the bright patch neared its zenith, he abandoned the effort. If it could be found, he most certainly would have found it by now.

What had happened here? He trudged through the wet undergrowth toward the ridge the girl had indicated, watching each approaching shadow with supernatural fear until it confirmed itself as a tree or log or pile of stone. He touched them as he passed, to be certain of their solidity. Shaking, he drew his tunic closer. A strange, arcane glamour permeated this mist, something dark and elusive that teased him with statues, and with images of little girls, who then vanished without trace.

The voice of young Maia repeated in his head, again and again, *If you're at war, why are you here gathering berries?* Why had Mer sent him into the mountains? He'd be far more useful recording events in Cinvat.

"Oh Asha, Source of All Truth, without doubt I am the most miserable servant you ever endured."

Almost as soon as the words were out of his mouth, he stumbled upon a thick patch of cindervine growing out of the cracks in a rock outcropping. The leaves blazed with their autumn colors, the vines laden with cinderblack, dripping with dew.

He fell to his knees and bowed his head. "Praise to the Source for showing mercy to this humble fool. I terrorize myself with imagined dangers, when all along you only mean to show me what I seek." A tear of thanks melted into the dampness collecting on his skin. He emptied the contents of his basket—pens and ink and flint box—wrapped them together with the bread in his parcel, and poked it all into his tunic. Then he slung his waterskin on his shoulder and set to filling the basket with fruit. Soon it was heavy enough that it no longer bounced on his back. He sat with the basket resting on the ground behind him long enough to make an entry in his book:

> *Waeges' Day, 207th y. 4th Age: Huge patch of cinderblack on the high ridge east of Cinvat, possibly one day (?) on a direct path. Revealed to me by Asha, Source of all Truth, through the auspices of a young girl, Maia, whom I met in a courtyard previously unknown to me. This was a singularly strange event; I pray one day to retrace these steps, to find the ruins and the girl again.*

It wasn't the thorough sort of entry that would please Mer, but it would have to do. He hefted his load and started west, slightly north, downhill toward his home. Earlier than he expected to, he descended out of the clouds into familiar terrain of oak and moss.

The sight of Cinvat's domes and towers gleaming in scattered beams of sunlight quickened his heart and added length to his stride. He couldn't wait to deliver his bounty, glad to leave behind him the mists that shrouded the uplands.

Soon he hailed the city guard, who swung a gate beside the eastern portcullis open for him to enter, and he hurried through crowded streets toward the Temple Library. As the throng jostled and bumped him in passing, Daen felt an edge, an urgency that troubled him. He slid into a doorway to watch and listen.

Everyone moved with unusual haste. A troop of foot soldiers marched past in double-time. Dragons bearing mounted warriors circled overhead in greater numbers than was normal. Expressions were fearful, voices clipped or strident. Panicked conversations jumbled together in his ears, but he listened, taking mental notes the way he'd been trained to do, planning ahead to the entries in his record.

He heard "armies" and "battle" and "Dahak" again and again.

Finally he grabbed a courier by the sleeve as he passed. The boy spun about with fear rather than annoyance or anger in his face.

"I beg pardon, young sir, but can you please tell me why everyone's in a panic?"

The boy peeled Daen's fingers from his sleeve, shaking his head in stunned negation. "Haven't you heard? Trenna has fallen. The Dahak comes." And then he dashed away.

The world descended into fog again, a cloud of shocked disbelief. Trenna, fallen! How was that possible? Trenna defended Cinvat's western approach from . . . Daen leaned against the doorframe with his basket of berries until balance returned.

Shining Trenna by the sea, fallen!

Unsure what else to do, he let rote guide him. He slid down the wall to a sitting position and pulled his writing materials out of his tunic. Opened his book on his lap. Fumbled the bottle of ink open. His hands shook so violently he couldn't put nib of pen into ink. When it splashed on his book and leg, he dropped the bottle and it shattered on the cobbles.

What am I doing? Asha, forgive my addled brain . . .

He struggled upright and closed his book, vaguely aware that the wet ink would stick those two ruined pages together. His pen lay forgotten in the doorway as he staggered out into the traffic again.

Movement seemed to sharpen his mind, and he hurried his pace—through the middle streets crowded with carts and soldiers to the Temple District, where the circle of Truth, representing the Cycles and Asha, surmounted the great brass Dome of the Temple. Up the long stairs to the huge arched doors of the Temple Library, with the shadows of mounted dragons crisscrossing his path. Blindly past the tattooed sentries who mumbled his name, their alarmed questions failing in his ears. Into the vast hall where skylights above threw slanted beams across the dusty vault. Past ranks of tables normally covered with stacks of books and baskets of scrolls, crowded with students and scholars and peasants alike, but now starkly empty. To the great desk that served as both barricade and gateway to the legions of bookcases beyond, where Mer turned toward him, eyes bright above wire-rimmed spectacles, with a gaze that shifted from worried to horror-stricken.

"Daen! By the Source! What are you doing here?"

Panting, Daen removed the basket from his back and set it on the desktop. Black juice dribbled out of it like ichor. No doubt his tunic was stained too. It would never come out. He started to apologize, scrubbing ineffectually at the liquid with his fingers, but Mer hobbled around the desk and took him by the shoulders.

"My boy, my boy! Oh Gods, what have I done? You should not be here." The old man drew him close with arms like sticks, but sinewy and strong.

"But . . . I don't understand . . . I have done what you asked. I've brought cinderblack for the priests—"

"Yes, and a good bounty it is." A tear escaped from his master's eye. "But I didn't expect you to find *any*. My hope was that you would be gone for a long while and might escape the coming storm. Escape with and preserve everything you have committed to memory about Cinvat."

Daen's heart sank in his chest, pounded against his ribs. "Why didn't you tell me that? Why would you send me out on . . . on a fool's mission?"

The old man took Daen's face in hands dry as paper and studied him, his gaze shifting from eye to eye. "I didn't know for certain that it would happen. I only acted as a precaution against rumor. You are my brightest pupil, but you are honest to a fault—I didn't want you to go forth in alarm, spreading news that would turn to false gossip. My hope was that you would return eventually, the rumors would be proven false, and we might laugh over my needless fears—but that in the worst event, you would be safe, you who contain everything . . . everything."

"Master . . . if I had known . . ." His stomach twisted at his master's words. He *was* honest to a fault. He'd scared a little girl this morning when she might have led him to new allies. He hung his head.

"No, don't blame yourself." Mer released him. "Not your folly, but mine. I sent you because our history lives in your brain like in none of the others. If rumor were to prove true, you might survive to put it all to pen once more and rescue Cinvat's place in time. But now, because I played coy with the truth, here you are, successful and thorough as always . . . Asha, forgive me . . ."

Daen watched his master's face sort through pain, then sorrow, then anger that settled with outthrust chin on firm resolve. "It's not yet too late. You've returned in time to help me finish a task. Come. I have been moving the most important tomes to the vaults, where I hope we can wall them up before the hour grows too late."

"What about these . . ." Daen indicated the basket of cinderblack.

Mer waved him off. "I'll send a boy to collect them and take them to the priests, and well done, my son, well done. But think about them no more."

The Keeper of Memory hobbled around the desk and into the maze of tall wooden bookcases. Daen followed, with one backward glance at the basket leaking indelibly on the desk of the Great Library.

Gaps decimated the rows of books, many shelves vacant entirely. "You have been at this already, I see. Where are Tolec and Barth? And Jennia? Are they helping?"

Mer paused and turned toward him, peering over his eyeglasses. His face drew long. "I sent them away this morning when the rumors became truth, with instructions to get as far from Cinvat as they could, not to return until they know all is safe . . . If ever. The more of you who escape, and survive, the better chance Memory has."

He turned away again.

Daen swallowed and hurried after. They passed row upon row of volumes Daen had read or copied or repaired. Here were the chronicles of the Conquest of Lannaris, followed by the story of the Lascarion Peacemakers, and the Trials of Lautern. He saw that Mer had already removed the oldest and the newest of each copy, preserving both the ancient original and the most recent translation, leaving those of middling age to chance.

A painful lump filled his throat. So much would be lost, even if he escaped with all his memories intact and the vaults escaped plunder.

Mer stopped before a shelf containing the volumes of the Third Age, and pulled out several books without delay. "Here, my boy." He dropped the volumes into Daen's waiting arms, stacking them until Daen whimpered. He added one more, grabbed the last and largest two for himself, then started down the row again. "This way. Quickly now!"

The stairs to the vaults were old beyond reckoning, artifacts left from the original library built in centuries past. They represented the original hall, around which the city had risen layer by layer, until now the ancient ceiling was below the level of the streets. Daen caught himself against the wall several times when his feet slipped on the smooth, rounded steps. They emerged into dank gloom where torches burned fitfully in sconces along the walls. Shelves of stone staggered away into darkness, arrayed like miniature rowhouses in the poorest quarter of the city. Mer plucked a torch from a sconce and led the way down one of the narrow avenues. Daen stumbled after.

At last they climbed a short stair into a smaller room, with a rounded ceiling decorated in ancient mosaic. More tiles peeked from the walls, between the books that filled every corner. Stacks upon stacks of books. Every horizontal surface bore mountains of ancient tomes in leather and cloth, wood and paper. Piles supported planks of wood, with more piles atop that, baskets of scrolls tucked into every void. There was scarcely room to walk between them, but there was order nonetheless. Bits of paper stuck out here and there with notes penned in his master's careful hand.

"Put them here, my son." Mer set his tomes gently on a low bench, and Daen managed to place his beside them without toppling the entire stack. Then Mer produced a note from the pocket of his robes and stuck it into one of the volumes. "There are a few more books to gather, but first I want to show you something important."

He pointed to the lintel of the door by which they had entered. "Do you see this great slab of stone here? This is how the vaults will be sealed if worse comes to worst." Daen felt a touch of nascent panic at what might follow. Mer continued. "This wheel here," and he indicated a large metal ring like a cartwheel set in the wall beside the door, "when turned completely to the right, will release a cascade of sand within the walls. A counterweight will fall, releasing the stops that hold this stone up. It will crash down and seal this chamber against any assault."

Daen considered that, allowing in his mind that a man might turn that wheel and still escape before the sand ran out and the door fell.

"Now come with me over here."

Mer wormed his way through piles of books to the opposite side of the room, where Daen saw an identical arrangement of door and wheel. Mer slapped the stone doorframe "The passage you see beyond this door winds under the streets to the northern foothills of the mountains. In a last resort, this will be our escape route. We'll drop this door behind us . . . and pray that the mountains aren't crawling with the Dahak's minions." He said the words with great calm, but his eyes were wide and bright.

Daen could only nod.

"Now let us go and collect the last of the books."

When they returned to the great hall of the Library, they heard screams from the city.

Daen ran to the doors, with Mer hobbling after. The sentries stood in ready pose, looking out with their halberds lowered. One of them turned, his face ashen, and raised a hand to stop Daen from going to the door.

"What . . . ?"

"It has begun," said the sentry, voice cracking. "You should go back—"

"No! I must see. I'm a student of the Keeper." Daen shoved his way past and into the doorway. "I should see and take notes, make a record . . ." His voice failed when he looked out over the city.

Mounted dragons swarmed over the outer defenses, a tidal wave breaching a sea wall. A black cloud of winged terrors snatched soldiers and civilians up into the air, tore them apart, flung the pieces, returned for more. Their riders dropped nets to snare men and drag them from the ramparts, or threw pots that shattered into flame in the city below. Dragons landed in cleared areas; extra skirmishers dismounted bearing swords and crossbows. Cinvat's defenders gave battle—dragons grappled with dragons in midair; their riders fired crossbows and swung swords. Warriors ripped from harnesses plummeted to their deaths. Beasts toppled from the sky with broken necks or crippled wings. A dragon corpse crunched onto the stairs not thirty feet away and rolled loosely over, revealing half a mangled rider still strapped to the saddle.

A groan of shock escaped Daen. When Mer clutched his shoulder he jumped.

One of the sentries pushed them backward so forcefully that Daen had to catch Mer in a stumble. "Get inside! We are barring these doors . . ."

They pulled the doors closed, doors that had stood wide in welcome Daen's entire life. Ornate brass latches rotated shut with a clatter. The bar fell into its braces with a heavy thud.

"Come, my son." Mer's voice was strangely calm. He pulled Daen by a sleeve. "We have a task to finish."

There came a boom on the door that rattled its hinges and echoed around the great hall.

"Hurry, now!" Mer led Daen to the big desk, went around to the back, and reached underneath. As he struggled with something, Daen noted the basket of cinderblack where he'd left it, the rivulet of black juice now puddling on the floor.

Mer wrestled three large tomes onto the desktop. Daen recognized them immediately. One was a student's primer in the history of Cinvat. Not a detailed record, but complete—a best, single repository of Cinvat's story. Another was a discussion of philosophy that had guided the creation of Cinvat's representative style of governance. The last was a book of poetry, an omnibus of the most beautiful and inspiring works of art from several ages. Tears came to Daen's eyes, for he knew why Mer had set these three aside. When he looked to his master's face, the old man nodded sadly.

"If all else fails, these must escape," he said.

Something large struck the doors again, followed by scratching and shouts. The sentries—only three of them, Daen saw—positioned themselves in a line across the entry. The doors flexed inward; the bar groaned under the strain. One of the sentries looked back, flinching as the door boomed again, but then waved them away. "Go! You can't stay. Bless you, Keeper, for your service. May Asha keep you."

Then something long and wide, but flat, like a gigantic curved blade, pushed through the space between the doors, destroying one of the latches. It swept upward, and the bar flew off its braces and thudded to the floor. The doors burst inward, hinges bent and latches shattered. The sentries cowered in a rain of wood splinters and metal shards. A dragon's silhouette filled the opening, before a towering column of flame and smoke in the city beyond. As it tucked its leathery wings close and entered, the

227

torchieres revealed its monstrousness. Black armor replaced its top frill, bolted to the midnight scutes of its long arching neck. A dark helmet covered its head, with only slits for the eyes to peer out of. In place of paws on its forelimbs it instead walked on the tips of two long, curved blades, strapped to the upper leg and bolted to the scales.

Runnels of fresh blood bathed those blades.

The sentries charged, but the beast reared up and its weapons slashed out, longer than the reach of a halberd. The men were cut in half with a single scissor-like motion.

Mer whispered in Daen's ear, "Sweet Asha! Boy, collect the books and follow me."

But a deep voice froze them. Daen hadn't noticed the rider before this moment, strapped into an ornate saddle atop the dragon, clad in black armor with a huge flat sword on his back. "Keeper of Memory!" he said, "The Dahak has sent me to find you . . . with a gift." He reached behind into a saddle-borne chest and withdrew three objects, then hurled them into the hall.

Three heads crunched onto the marble paving and rolled into view. Mer moaned in horror and started toward them, but Daen held him back. It took him but a moment to know Tolec, Barth, and Jennia, the other students whom Mer had sent away this very morning.

Daen gathered up the books as Mer began to wail. Foot soldiers poured in through the doors to either side of the dragon, which reached down to gobble up pieces of dead sentry. Shaking with terror, Daen grabbed Mer's sleeve and dragged him into the forest of bookcases.

The clatter of metal-shod feet chased them. Daen glanced back once to see soldiers in black leather and dull armor clambering up the shelves, knocking books off, setting torches to the dry paper. Orange light bloomed. Shouts and laughter followed.

Mer sobbed as Daen dragged him to the stairs and down. Through the vaults, with the clamor of pursuit close behind, to the smaller chamber where the books were hidden. Torchlight slashed and flickered from a dozen sources as the pursuit closed in.

Trembling, Mer attacked the wheel that would release the great lintel stone. Daen set the three books aside and joined him, but Mer struck his hands away. "No! Boy, you must go! Now!" When Daen hesitated, Mer slapped him full across the face. "GO!"

Cheek stinging, tears flowing freely, Daen gathered the books again and started across the chamber, wending a cautious path through the stacks of tomes. The wheel creaked behind him, and he heard a muffled rasp, as if insects ran within the walls—the sand flowed. The big lintel stone rumbled and growled like the cough of a giant, and Daen looked back. Soldiers with torches and swords sprinted across the chamber beyond, but the lintel hadn't dropped, not yet. Mer struggled with the wheel, and Daen hesitated again. "Master . . . ?"

"Go, boy! Curse you if you do not leave. You are the Keeper of Memory now. Go!"

Daen ran to the far door, knocking piles of books over in his haste. He set his load aside and grabbed the other wheel, pulling with all his strength. It resisted his efforts at first, but then moved with a lurch, stuck again, and finally spun freely. Shaking with fear, he gathered his books and darted through the door even as the lintel began to grind and chatter slowly downward.

He looked back.

The far door was still open, the big lintel stone jammed in its descent. Soldiers poured into the chamber, knocking piles of books aside, swords leveled. Flames erupted from ancient paper. When Daen saw him last, Mer crouched in the midst of the gathered history of Cinvat with an armload of books clutched to his chest, a skirmisher's sword raised above him. Even as the stone lintel dropped, Daen heard his sorrowful cry cut short.

The thunder of the door's closing echoed through the blackness that followed.

Goulish taps and scratching came from the other side. Daen screamed at the sounds, willing them to stop, then succumbed to anguish, shivering and sobbing for several minutes in the dark. But Mer's voice in his head scolded him for being emotional and selfish. He braced himself with several deep breaths, then stood and felt about until his hand encountered the stone wall. Leading carefully with his toes, he started down the corridor, guided only by touch.

"I will keep your memory, Mer," he whispered to himself.

Time crawled in the utter night of the tunnel. Drips punctuated skittering noises and the echoes of his scuffling footsteps. He struggled with his own mind, resisting images that scorched his inner eye, repeating endlessly—a monster slicing through soldiers in a single movement; the faces of Tolec, Barth, and Jennia, both in life and in death; Mer cringing beneath a falling sword. Books burning.

Accompanying the images, Mer's last words to Daen—*You are the Keeper of Memory now.*

What would he do? Where would he go? Trenna was taken, Cinvat overrun. What cover or comfort would the surrounding wilderness give him? He'd been less abandoned and alone in the fog this morning . . . had it really only been this morning?

A memory of laughter made him pause in his tracks—the little girl, Maia, with her dark eyes and innocent curiosity. There were people in the wilds who didn't know of the Dahak, were still untouched, perhaps less than half a day away. Vulnerable, but they had dragons. An alarm could be raised, word spread. He might be flown to safety, and the memory of Cinvat saved.

With hope kindled in his heart, Daen hurried forward, anxious now to find the end of this tunnel. Shortly, his toes struck stone, and feeling with his free hand, he discovered stairs going up. When his head bumped on a ceiling of stone, he set his books down and felt about with his hands. Hinges here, and a latch! He studied it with his fingers until he knew how to work it, threw it back, and pushed up. The door resisted. He pushed harder and it swung up a few inches.

The light of a ruddy sunset stung his eyes—after his long trek in the darkest night of his life, it illuminated trees and boulders like a noonday sun. He pressed the door higher, observing a metal rod hinged to the edge that swung down beside him. He used it to prop the door open as he ducked back inside, gathered up his books, then crawled out into the world once more. Around him lay a small stone courtyard ringed with low benches, but with wild terrain beyond.

The surrounding light shifted and moved unnaturally—not the glow of sunset at all. A low roar filled his ears. Turning, he said, "Sweet Asha . . ."

From eastern gate to far western wall, the city burned. Towers of flame and smoke swirled into the starless void from every quarter. Even as he watched, the roof of the Library collapsed in a fountain of sparks and cinders. On the pinnacle of the Temple dome, the circle of Truth, of the Cycles and of Asha, stood bare against the curtain of fire.

Daen watched in shock for several minutes, as buildings crumbled and the inferno grew higher. Dragons still circled above, but the combat had ended. Cinvat was lost.

Daen swallowed his grief. Two thousand years of conquest and refinement and culture now survived only in these three books, and in his memory. He had a mission, and a destination in mind. He fished his record book out of his tunic and flipped through its pages to find the map he had drawn this morning, with an X to mark his best guess at the location of the courtyard and the statue, where he had met an enigmatic little girl.

The map wasn't there.

He flipped back through the book the other direction. But it wasn't to be found. There were two pages stuck together toward the back. Surely . . .

When he peeled them apart, they were blank other than the stain that bound them, and he remembered spilling ink as he sat in a doorway just a few hours ago. But he knew he'd seen the statue, walked upon the pavers, and spoken with a curious wilding child.

A deep, mournful gong sounded from the Dome of the Temple at that moment, reverberating through the valley and off the surrounding peaks. Daen's eyes snapped up in time to see the dome list, the walls beneath it disintegrate. It thundered down into a maelstrom of flames, giving out one last enormous peal as it cracked. The Circle of Asha disappeared in a plume of fire and smoke that shot into the sky. Screams of despair sounded from the city.

All of it hauntingly familiar. Too familiar: his dream of death this very morning.

As the beat of giant wings filled the air around him, a dreadful thought struck Daen, and he swiped the pages of his record forward and backward in vain hope. The map was not there. Nor were there missing pages where it might have been. He had never made any such accounting in his record.

The only chronicle he found with today's date stunned him:

> *Waeges' Day, 207th y. 4th Age: Sun bright and warm.*
> *Stumbled upon a huge cache of cinderblack. Mer will*
> *be pleased.*

He read it twice, pulse throbbing in his ears.

But he *remembered* wandering through fog to a stone courtyard, where he spoke to a mysterious little girl. He'd asked to meet her mother. "I don't think she will see you," she had replied.

As black dragons settled down around him with weapons bolted to their limbs, bearing armored warriors on their backs, he realized the bitter, horrifying truth. He knew it as certainly as he knew his name. A rare gift of Truth, from Asha, perhaps.

And when the High Dragon, the Dahak, sculled to a landing before him, all doubt was erased. Bigger than any dragon he'd ever seen, so black as to reflect no light at all, its wings like a chasm across the heavens revealing the farthest, lightless void, it stepped toward him. Where its giant talons trod, the grass curled and blackened.

The monster from his dream, but also the black dragon from the sculpture.

KEEPER OF MEMORY, it said, in his mind, its lips not moving at all, SEE HOW MEMORY DIES. Then it bent its head down, plucked the three books off the paving where he had laid them, and swallowed them whole.

Daen cried out in hopeless agony, knowing that his failure was absolute, the story of Cinvat lost forever. Knowing he had relived the final day of his life over and over again, unaware, condemned by his remorse to a nightmarish limbo he would inhabit for eternity . . .

Until, after a millennium, a child wandered into the path of his mournful spirit, a child who could see him and speak with him, who interrupted his endless torment with a glimmer of Truth, in a courtyard so distant in time from his failure that a statue had been erected and its story all but forgotten while he repeated . . . repeated.

Would he even remember this revelation if . . . when he woke again? If he could find the girl again, could he somehow give her the history that was about to die with him—that *had* died with him—or was he doomed to echo this tragedy, unknowing, until the end of creation? It was the slimmest hope of redemption, perhaps not a hope at all.

But he realized something else, and with it came a strange serenity. The statue depicted two High Dragons in battle, one white, one black. *The white one wins,* the girl had said to him.

Even as the jaws of the Dahak opened and descended toward him, he knew that this was all a phantasm, a memory of events long past.

"You have already fallen," he said.

The Dahak faltered for an instant at this ghost whispering to a memory, and a ripple coursed through its wings of night. Then it took Daen in its teeth and crushed ribs against ribs until blood poured from his lungs onto the pavestones, like a bright flower unfurling.

BLAKE CHARLTON

TOWARD THE END OF MY MEDICAL SCHOOL PEDIATRICS ROTATION, I WOKE in an on-call room from a nightmare about a very sick little girl melting into a cloud of light. I had gotten to know her parents well, particularly her father. It had been a tumultuous year for me, spent in hospitals up and down the San Francisco Peninsula, filled with languages ranging from Spanish to Samoan, and punctuated by strange sights alternately disgusting and beautiful. The people I met haunted me, especially the father of this girl. I will never forget his eyes as he watched his daughter.

I should have spent any free time I had studying or working on my Spellwright trilogy, but instead I found myself haunted by a new story that would try to capture something of what I had seen during the year. One rare day out of the hospital, the following story spilled out of me onto the page in very rough form. I showed it to a few people and realized that it would require more polishing than I had time for. So it sat on my hard drive while I finished medical school and pressed ahead on my novels. But when Shawn asked me if I had a story for an anthology to help him recover from all that cancer had put him through, I knew I had to revive the story and try to get it right.

Blake Charlton

HEAVEN IN A WILD FLOWER

Blake Charlton

The baby girl floated around the water pump as a small, radiant cloud of light. She illuminated the nearby ferns and made the darkness beyond her darker.

Joaquin Lopez put his bucket down. He was a tall, thin man. Early forties. Dark eyes and hair. He pressed a shaking hand to his mouth, wondered if he had the balls to gather in the girl. He looked to the sky for a heaven but saw only stars between redwood branches.

He called to Luis and Collin. When the boys came out of the cabin, he told Luis to fetch a sheet and Collin to go to town for the doctor. Collin was old enough that he turned and ran, but Luis stood staring. "Papá," he asked, "what is it?" Now that Collin was gone, they spoke in Spanish.

"Only a baby. You looked the same. Get the sheet."

The boy went and Lopez stepped closer. The baby didn't seem to notice. Tendrils of her indigo light curled around a water drop forming on the pump's spigot. The drop fattened and fell, dispersing her into a corona. She made a crackling sound, like pine needles burning. Something in the sound reminded Lopez of childish laughter. "Nena," he asked, "have you come to stay?"

The nimbus paused. Another drop grew from the spigot, and she coalesced around it. Lopez crept forward until he was standing next to her. The drop fell. Again the corona, again the soft crackling laughter.

Luis came back with the sheet. Lopez took it and wondered if he should wait for Robert. It'd be safer that way. This wouldn't be so bad for Robert. A familiar, dark, and doubtful mood began closing in around Lopez.

"Papá?" Luis whispered.

Lopez stared distractedly into the nimbus. A trill of irritation had interrupted his doubts. He didn't want to wait anymore, to do the careful thing anymore. Maybe this would be the last time he came across a baby girl.

"Papá," Luis repeated, then switched to English. "Daddy, what's wrong?"

Lopez started. "Nothing's wrong," he murmured, made up his mind. To hell with caution. He draped the sheet around the baby. She didn't seem to mind, but when he pulled her upward, some of her tendrils gathered around a water drop. He waited for the drop to fall, and then gathered the rest of her into the sheet.

"Oh, oh, Nena, it's okay, it's okay," he whispered in Spanish and carried her back to the cabin. Even wrapped in the blanket, she lit up the lowest redwood branches. Then Lopez noticed that his hands glowed. A shiver of fear ran down his body.

He had the balls after all.

"Papá," Luis asked, "where did she come from?"

"From a heaven. All reincarnated babies come from a heaven, just like you did. She's your sister now. Maybe she was your sister in your last life too."

"But you didn't come from a heaven, Papá?"

"I wasn't reincarnated. I was born."

They walked into the cabin. "Will she stay?" Luis wanted to know.

"Hopefully. Light one of the candles in the dresser."

"What is the girl called?" Luis asked while trying to do what he was told.

Lopez laid the baby on his bed. "We don't name reincarnated babies for two years. We'll just call her Nena until then."

The boy was fumbling with candle and flint, but Lopez could see by the faint light now radiating from his hands and forearms. He unlocked the closet, fetched his Remington and set it against the wall. His daughter had formed a body and head, but her face was still a cloud of light.

"Why don't we name reincarnated babies for so long?"

"Because they might still go back to their heaven."

"I don't want her."

Lopez lifted Luis onto the bed and looked into his eyes. Luis wasn't a Latino like his father; he was a Hindú, probably. "Mijo, there are so few girls on earth that being a brother will make you very important. You'll like her."

The boy looked at the baby dubiously.

"I was glad you stayed," Lopez added.

"But I was a boy."

"Even though you were a boy, I was glad."

"Is she going to take you back to her heaven?"

"Everything's going to be fine."

"I don't want you to die, Papá."

"I'm not going to die," Lopez said and pressed his lips together. They were trembling. But just a little. He looked at his son. Better tell him the truth. "I won't die, Luis, unless she does."

By the time the doctor's footsteps sounded on the porch, the baby had consolidated. Dr. Lo stood an inch under six feet. Wide shoulders. Tanned complexion. Thick white hair combed neatly back. He was some mix of Chino and Gringo, like many emigrants from the Francisco Ruins. Dr. Lo set a pistol down on the nightstand and sat on the bed.

"She's a girl?" Lopez asked in English.

"Let's find out," the doctor said and took the baby into his lap.

As he examined her, she began to cry. A sound like flowing water. "A healthy reincarnated baby girl," he announced when finished. "Congratulations."

Lopez took her back. "You think Señora Jenner would come down to see her?"

"The Jenner outfit moved to the Eureka Camps last month. One of her people up there gave birth."

"Like . . . natural?"

The doctor nodded. "The mother's reincarnated, but she delivered a girl. Only natural born baby girl I've heard about in ten years, maybe more. It's a miracle, really. Story goes she was carrying wood when her water broke. She walked home and caught her daughter without a whimper."

Lopez fretted his baby's swaddling. "It's too bad. With Señora Jenner gone, the closest woman must be . . . I don't know."

"You mean it's too bad Señora Jenner took Señorita Jenner with her. She was a pretty one. But word of your daughter will get around. I'm sure your daughter will bring you what you're after. Now, it's time I examined you."

Afterward Dr. Lo sat across from Lopez. "The glow on your arms won't last much longer. It's nothing to worry about."

"I'm her father now?"

"You are."

Lopez picked up the baby. "How long 'til we know if she'll stay?"

"Likely after the first three days. But there are reports of children as old as fourteen years going back."

The baby began to cry, this time with the wail of a corporeal infant. Lopez asked, "If she does go back, how will I die?"

"Sometimes a seizure, sometimes the heart stops."

Lopez nodded.

"How are you holding up?"

"It's only been a few hours."

"You could have waited for Robert. He's reincarnated, yes?"

"He is, but he's also trading down on the coast. Nena might have hung around long enough for him to get back, but . . ." He looked back to his daughter.

"She's beautiful."

Lopez flattened his daughter's downy hair.

"Forgive my prying, but what made you pick her up?" Dr. Lo asked. "The chance to find her a mother, yes?"

"That's part of it, but . . ." His voice trailed off. Why had he done it? Now it seemed like a foolish, impulsive thing. He changed the subject. "Do you think she'll stay?"

"I think she will."

"Is there anything else I can do? Anything that might help convince her to stay?"

"Try not to think about what will happen if she goes."

In the morning, Robert returned on their horse. He was a stocky Gringo with a dark blond beard and a bald head the sun turned pink. Long ago, Lopez's niece had married Robert's brother, making him family. The niece had died in childbirth, but Robert and Lopez had been friends ever since, running the same outfit for near fifteen years.

When Lopez showed Robert his new daughter, the other man was clearly jealous. "Wolfy, why didn't you wait for me?" Robert asked through a teasing smile. "Worst she could do to me would be drag me to my heaven."

"Daaad!" Collin said and punched Robert's leg.

Robert ruffled his son's blond hair and then looked look at Lopez. "Seriously, Wolfy, what came over you? I didn't think you had the huevos."

"Yeah, well, turns out I do."

"Good man," Robert said. "Well, when word gets out about your daughter, you'll have to fight the women off with a stick." He cooed into the baby's face. Man and girl smiled at each other. Robert wasn't going to stay jealous for long; it wasn't in his nature.

"Hot damn, poontang! Una niña!" Robert said as he straightened and turned to Collin and Luis. "Boys, get the bags inside. We'd better tidy up; we'll be expecting company of the *feminine* kind!"

Later Collin and Luis got into a shoving match. Lopez broke it up and took his boy onto the porch. A brisk ocean wind rushed through the redwoods. They sat on the steps.

Luis scowled at his toes. "Collin says you're chickenshit because you weren't reincarnated." Luis spoke in sullen English; sometimes he did that when angry with his father.

"Mijo, I don't know what will happen to me when I die. It makes things uncertain."

"Papá, why weren't you reincarnated?"

Lopez sighed. How to explain to a child? "Way back when, there were many people in the world, as many women as men. But when the heavens came, the world fell apart. It happened south of here, in the Valley of Melted Sand, where the smartest people had a technology magic that made the heavens. You were one of the men who made the heavens."

"I was?"

Lopez nodded. "So was your Uncle Robert and Collin and anyone else who's reincarnated. All that happened a hundred years ago."

"I'm older than you, Papá?"

"Much older."

"How do the heavens work?"

"No one knows any more. After the reincarnated people went into the sky, the mightiest nations made war on the heavens, but you all sent down a plague of very tiny machines that got into naturally born humans so we can't make many children and hardly no girls. That's why your sister is special."

"I still wish you hadn't found her."

Lopez pointed at the moonless night sky, the host of stars. "You see that stretch of stars that twinkle more than the others?"

"I see it."

"They are twinkling more because they are shining through one of the heavens. That particular heaven is called the Floating Bridge. It was passing over when we found you. Your sister

242

might be from there too. When you leave this world, maybe you two will go back there together."

"What if I don't want to go?"

"You don't have to anytime soon."

"Why did I come back down from the heaven, Papá?"

"No one knows why you all come back. My guess is that it's a bit like camping."

"Camping?"

"Sometimes you'll go with me and Uncle Robert to the coast and we'll sleep in tents and hunt deer. We don't have to do that. We got a cabin with a stove. But we like sleeping on the beach and drinking from streams and hiking up mountains."

Luis frowned with concentration. "Because it reminds us of what it was like back before we built cabins or used stoves?"

"Exactly what I think. You got tired of being clouds and thinking lighting. You wanted to hear thunder again and remember sunsets and tamales and mosquitoes and laughter. So you reincarnated yourselves."

Luis thought about this. "Why are baby girls so dangerous?"

"No one knows exactly why, but any man who picks up a reincarnating baby girl is bound to her through a special infection of small machines. If the girl dies, the father dies. So now all fathers have to be very good about protecting their daughters and keeping them well fed and healthy."

"So why does Collin say you're chickenshit? You picked up the girl."

Lopez sighed. "I am scared of dying."

"You're scared because you won't go to a heaven?"

"I won't go to one of your heavens. I won't go where you will go."

The boy hugged his arm.

Lopez continued. "I might go somewhere else or I might just go out like a candle flame. No one knows."

Luis didn't say anything.

"But for now everything's going to be fine."

"I wish you could come with me when I go up there."

"So do I."

Two days later, in the late morning, Lopez was working in the root cellar when he heard Robert call out. He took his daughter up to find Robert crouching on the patio, the Remington laid across his knees. The boys were nowhere to be seen. Robert gestured uphill. Two men were standing on the path as it came out of the redwoods. One held the halter to a shaggy palomino. A pale woman sat on the horse's back. She raised a hand. When Lopez did the same, she and her group approached.

"That the baby girl?" the Gringa asked. She was maybe fifty, short and slender. Her light brown hair was tied into a tight bun. It made her long forehead seem longer.

When Lopez said the baby was his daughter, the woman introduced herself and the two men. One was her brother. The other—a younger man with a shotgun in the crook of his arm—was her husband. Both men studied him. "We're all reincarnated, and I've raised two reincarnated girls. I got enough left in me for one more."

Lopez cleared his throat. "I appreciate that, ma'am."

"You'll let me be her mother?"

Lopez looked from her to the two men. "Can't say."

The Gringa changed to stilted Spanish: "No se puede decir, o usted no va a decir? Estás esperando a una muchacha para levantar su falda?"

Lopez answered coldly in English: "A daughter deserves a family."

"A daughter deserves a father who thinks north of his navel. I've raised two girls."

"This homestead can't feed three more. There's an abandoned cabin a mile on toward the ocean. Maybe you could join our outfit."

The woman looked from her brother to her husband. "Maybe. We'll take a look."

Lopez pointed to a path. "One mile. Can't miss it."

She didn't move. "Tell me, Dad, is it true you're natural born?

He nodded.

She laughed. "Hell of a gamble, Dad, hell of a gamble just to get under a skirt."

That evening Robert sent Collin down the path with a dinner invitation. The boy came back with a report of an empty field. Robert snorted. "You scared her off, Wolfy! We can't have you scaring off all the ladies with *delicate* sensibilities."

Lopez scowled. "She was no good."

———

A week later a man and a woman appeared on the path from town. Both carried rifles. He, short and stout, stood straight and wore a grave expression under a comically floppy leather hat. A thick bush of kinky white hair spread down his back. She was taller, with dark hair pulled back into a tight braid.

Lopez called for Robert and walked out to meet the strangers. At first, he thought they might be Latinos. But closer up he looked like a Polinesio, she a Gringa. Or maybe she was Middle Eastern. He couldn't tell.

"You the natural-born man who picked up a baby girl?" the stocky man asked.

Lopez nodded.

His grave expression split into a smile. "Did the same thing twenty-two years ago. This is my daughter, Lani. She'd like to be a mother to a baby girl."

Lopez studied the woman. In her early twenties, she was neither slender nor solid. Her well-defined arm muscles suggested that she was no stranger to work. She nodded to him. Her eyes were quick and seemed intelligent.

The father spoke again. "Perhaps we could stay a few days. She doesn't eat much, and I'm handy in the fields."

Lopez looked at him. "Perhaps. Set your rifles down and meet the rest of the outfit."

Robert was waiting, the Remington leaning against the railing beside him. In the doorway, Collin held the baby and whispered to Luis. They met the newcomers on the porch steps.

The father's name turned out to be Joe. "Simply Joe. No other names." They had come up from the Santa Cruz Mountains. Lopez had known that there were several Polinesio outfits in those parts. They hadn't had a natural birth in seven years. Hence Joe's long journey up the peninsula, across the Golden Gate, and into the redwood forests to help his daughter find a daughter of her own.

When Collin brought the baby closer, Lopez watched Lani. Her brown eyes seemed to drink in the swaddled form. But her mouth tensed. Stiffly, she folded her arms. "Would you like to hold her?" Lopez asked.

Then she was focusing on him. "Not just yet. I don't want to get my hopes up."

The group went into the cabin. Lani never looked at the baby, but she was aware of the infant at all times. To her, the baby was like a bright fire that she didn't have to see to know where it was.

Four days later and a few hours past midnight, the baby woke Lopez with a sputtering cry. He picked her up, and she vomited down his sleeve. Her cloth diaper was wet with watery stool. She was warm, fussy.

Lopez felt dizzy, couldn't get enough air into his lungs. He rocked his daughter, terrified that there was too much pain in this world for her and that she would go back to her heaven. His hands tingled, and orange spots swam across his vision.

Someone sat on the bed next to him. He was so sure that it was Lani that he jumped when Joe spoke. "First time Lani got the shits, I was so nervous I didn't shit solid for a week either." He laughed. "You just lay down. This baby girl isn't leaving yet."

Lopez obeyed and the spots left his vision. He and Joe took turns trying to feed the baby and changing her diapers. Joe insisted the baby wasn't going back to her heaven. When Lopez asked how he knew, the old Polinesio only shrugged. Lopez fell asleep briefly but woke in a sweat. Stepping onto the porch, he discovered morning fog so thick he couldn't see the barn.

It made him think of his old life in Bodega Bay. For a year he had had a lover, a younger man named Alejandro who spoke mostly Spanish but sometimes murmured in Chinese in his sleep.

Lopez remembered his cottage amid eucalyptus. He remembered the day he had decided to leave, Alejandro's angry words, the relief to be going.

In the growing morning light, Lopez felt darkness being draped around him. The old feeling he had fought before. He was going to die, perhaps not in that hour or even in that year, but he was going to die far too soon. No one could go with him. All his memories of eucalyptus groves and ruined cities and old lovers would vanish. He grabbed the porch railings and tried to breathe more slowly.

The cabin door creaked. He turned to see Lani, nightgowned and barefoot. He stood up straight and tried to slow his heart. She paused, as if she might go back inside. But when he gestured for her to come closer, she eased the door shut and went to the railing.

"I'm sorry if we made it hard to sleep," he said.

"I would have helped with the baby, but Daddy told me not to."

Lopez looked out into the fog.

She said, "He said it'd be hard on you, raising a girl."

"He did it for you."

"I often wish he had been reincarnated—" she said, then seemed to interrupt herself. "Not for my sake. I just never realized what he went through by picking me up."

"He's glad he did so."

"This is hard on you."

He tried to smile. "It's embarrassing."

She laid her hand on his but didn't say anything.

The warmth of her palm sent goose bumps running up his arm. He wanted to say something but didn't know what. The moment stretched on, and he felt as if he were not really himself, as if it were someone else's hand she was touching.

At last he said, "You should go to the baby."

She turned to him. Her eyes, searching his, seemed to be asking a question.

He nodded.

She left.

Dr. Lo diagnosed the baby with a viral infection. Nothing to worry about. And, indeed, the baby improved over the next few days. But still Lopez suffered bouts of a racing pulse, ragged breathing, a sensation of darkness closing in.

Then, on a cold evening, Lani hung a curtain at one end of the cabin to separate Lopez's bed from the rest. She lay beside him, smiled in the half light, slipped out of her blouse. She joined him the next night and all the nights after.

The next Sunday, Luis came back from town with a black eye. He had picked a fight with an older boy. When Lani asked if she could help, Luis yelled at her. In the following days, Lopez left the baby with Lani and took Luis to work in the fields. Joe was happy to join. Luis was sullen and didn't talk much, but he stopped picking fights and was polite to Lani.

Time passed. The morning fog burned off earlier and earlier until one night it failed to roll in at all. There followed crisp end-of-winter days that filled the forests with slanting light. Lani made peace with Luis when she bribed him with a bit of honeycomb. For Lopez, life regained a bearable rhythm. Each day's work exhausted his worry, set him to anticipating the night with Lani. In the mornings, he watched Lani sit with the baby in sunlight, their two expressions of contentment.

The cadence of days broke when large flat-bottomed clouds drifted in from the south. For a week, the outfit worked under cathedrals of air, billowing higher. Then came long, rolling sheets of rain.

Confined indoors, the outfit became relaxed, talkative. At first they filled the hours by mending clothes, filling a chink in the roof, that sort of thing. But when the rain persisted, they lapsed into long conversations or card games played with an ancient, shabby deck.

Lopez, Luis, and Collin were in a competitive game when a voice sounded from outside. Robert led the men onto the porch to discover a lone figure on horseback. A rifle, wrapped in leather, was tucked into the saddle. The rain was so loud that Robert had to yell to be heard. When the newcomer answered, Lopez realized she was a woman. Her hair was cut short. She wore a man's riding coat.

When Robert invited her in, she dismounted and stepped onto the porch. Her black hair had whitened around her temples. She called herself Melisa and came from a ranching outfit in the Central Valley. Her English was fluent but her cadence suggested she'd be more comfortable speaking Spanish.

When she said she was searching for the outfit with the new baby girl, Lani stepped onto the porch with her daughter and a cool stare. The newcomer only laughed. "Don't worry, Señora. I've raised five boys; I don't need to be a mother again. I'd be happy just being an aunt to a girl."

Melisa was a handsome woman—long nose, high cheekbones, laughing eyes made more prominent by the few wrinkles around them. When Robert helped her out of her drenched coat, Lopez noticed that her breasts filled her blouse with curves impressive for any age. When Robert offered to help put up her horse in the barn, Lopez felt a sting of jealousy.

When the rain stopped three days later, Robert took Collin and Melisa to examine the abandoned cabin a mile toward the ocean. The next morning, they took half the supplies and inhabited the old homestead. At first Lopez felt an emptiness of his cabin; the bouts of darkness-closing-in increased. But he saw Robert and Collin in the fields, and Melisa spent most days with Lani and the baby.

Rain followed by weeks of clear skies covered the land with thick green grass. The baby suffered chicken pox, reducing Lopez to a nervous wreck until the spots disappeared. Then the days became warmer and warmer until, abruptly, the rainy season ended.

Word got around that the Lopez outfit boasted three female members and only five male. It had become a small, reincarnated piece of the ancient world. In town, men treated Lopez, Robert, and even the boys with respect.

When the summer fog began to roll in during the nights, Collin saw three strangers camping near their homestead. Robert and Lopez went out with rifles. Even at fifty feet, they looked like a rough lot, skinny and poorly clothed. Lopez suggested they talk. "All right," Robert grunted and fired a shot above their heads. "That's what I have to say."

The strangers leapt into chaotic action, firing two shots while retreating. The next day, there was no sign of them.

The land dried out, turning the waist-high grass to golden brown. One night the baby spiked a fever so high she had a brief seizure. Panicked, Lopez ran the baby up to the doctor's house. Dr. Lo put her in a cold bath and gave her a spoonful of bitter medicine. Though fussy, she passed the rest of the night without trouble.

Lopez, on the other hand, fell asleep next to Lani on the doctor's guest bed and dreamt of being endlessly shoved into a sack made of scratchy, hot fabric.

Summer ended. On a trip to the coast, Robert discovered a baby boy floating above a tidal pool filled with spiny sea urchins. He brought the baby back to Melisa, who seemed neither excited nor upset about raising another boy.

One morning, when they were mucking out the stalls, Robert told Lopez, "When I first picked up the baby, I thought I'd name him Jacob. My favorite uncle was named Jacob." He paused. "For a while, I thought I was going to name the boy *after* Uncle Jacob."

"Now you think the baby *is* your Uncle Jacob?"

"I'm certain of it. It's the strangest feeling, you know?"

"No, hermano, I don't. I envy your certainty."

The winter rains came, and again the world was covered with thick green grass. The baby girl began to speak simple words and stand on her own. She had a tangled halo of black curls. She giggled and shrieked with joy when Lopez would spin her about, hold her upside down. The boys wanted to be held upside down too. It was a good time.

When the rains stopped, Lani missed her monthly and the outfit began to hope that she was pregnant. Joe especially was proud. But midway through the fourth month, she had a dull pain in her belly and then bled profusely.

Afterward, she said she felt fine but didn't want to talk about it. Joe had a harder time. When working in the fields, he felt a pain in his chest. Then during the hot, languorous nights of the late dry season, Joe drank too much in town. He woke up on the way home, a sour taste in his mouth. The next day he ran a fever, coughed up dark phlegm, complained of horrible chest pain. Lopez sent the boys for Dr. Lo. But during a coughing fit, Joe passed out. He fluttered in and out of consciousness for half an hour. Then he died.

They buried Joe in a clearing east of the cabin. Lopez was the only naturally born person left in the outfit. He held Lani and she wept. The folds of unseen darkness closed around Lopez's mind. Nothing had changed since he had picked up the baby girl. His death was closer now than it had been before. The events of the last year—the work, the sex, the long and beautiful days—were only distractions from a final terror. For a moment, he hated Lani and Robert because they knew what would happen to them after death, while he had to die into such uncertainty.

But Lani's despair was real, her need pressing. Twice her soft crying woke him at night. The comfort she took in him helped. Slowly the days regained their cadence. It helped to pick up his daughter and son, spin them around, hear them laugh. Summer's morning fog dissolved into bright autumn mornings, darkened into winter rains. On the second anniversary of their daughter's reincarnation, Lani and Lopez named her Olivia.

Even at two years old, Olivia was talkative, mostly in English but also Spanish and a little Samoan. By three, Olivia was ordering Luis and Collin around. They spoiled her, just as everyone else in the outfit did.

Shortly after Olivia's fifth birthday, Lopez came out of the cabin and saw her jumping off the barn roof and onto a pile of tarps while the boys cheered her on. Lopez thought his heart was going to stop. Despite the harshest discipline he and Lani could muster, Olivia showed no repentance.

"What was she in her first life?" Robert wondered one day.

"Warrior queen of the technology magicians?" Lopez said while massaging his temples. "Hard to imagine her adding her mind to a heaven without taking over the whole fucking thing."

Robert's newest son, and perhaps favorite uncle, was growing fast. But on one foggy morning when Melisa was holding him on the porch, the baby stopped breathing and dissolved into luminescent green light and floated off into the white air.

Melisa had lost three other boys this way. She seemed unaffected and spent more and more time with Lani caring for Olivia, but Robert fell into a dark mood for nearly a month.

At nine years old, Olivia had mastered the air of sweet-talking her father into letting her stay up late or into buying something for her at the store. In town, the men teased Lopez. He never admitted how much he enjoyed it all.

But then Olivia talked her Aunt Melisa into teaching her how to ride, even though her father had forbidden it. She was caught only when she fell off at a gallop and broke her leg. This sparked a shouting match between Lopez and Melisa, then Lopez and Robert. For a tense few days it seemed as if the outfit might split.

During Olivia's immobile convalescence, Lopez tried lecturing, cajoling, and pleading to inspire caution in his daughter for her own sake, for her mother's sake, and—goddamn it—for his sake. She agreed to be more cautious but never apologized.

Two years later, Luis told his father he'd be leaving. Lopez had seen it coming. Olivia admired Collin, now a levelheaded young man. It was clear to everyone that if Collin stuck around, he would one day marry Olivia. Luis, on the other hand, had nothing to keep him in a small outfit deep in the redwoods.

Olivia threw a fit, screaming and crying for three days. Everyone else in the outfit still spoiled her, but now her brother would not. Two days after Luis left, Lopez heard crying from Olivia's bunk and went to sit with her. "Mija," he said, taking her hand, "you'll see him again."

She hugged him close.

When she turned fifteen, Olivia was five feet and nine inches tall. Her eyes were wide and childlike, her body slender. Her curly black hair cascaded down her back. Lopez knew she was a Gringa, but still found himself comparing her smile and long hair to his mother's.

In the early dry season, Olivia convinced Collin to take her to town and then, for a laugh, slipped away. A man caught her alone behind the tailor's shop. He was a squat old trader named Jimson. He owned a mule caravan that ran goods up from the Petaluma trading outfits. He held her against the wall and ripped her blouse. She bit his thumb hard enough to draw blood and then rammed her knee into his testicles.

While Jimson was doubled-over and vomiting, she went into the tailor shop and showed the owner what Jimson had done to her shirt. She also told him that Jimson's penis was as small as a five-year-old boy's. Collin took her back to the homestead. By the time Lopez and Robert came marching back into town with rifles, Jimson had left for Petaluma. For the next two weeks, neighbors visited the Lopez outfit to hear Olivia tell her story. She told it well.

A few months later, when the summer seemed nothing but dust and heat, Lopez found Olivia on the path up from the ocean. Her shins and forearms were covered with bruises. At first he worried someone had attacked her. But when she denied it, he asked if she had been cliff-diving with Collin. After a telltale pause, she denied this too.

Lopez sent her home and went looking for Collin. He found the young man helping his father clear land behind their cabin. After a few questions, Collin confessed to the cliff-diving.

Back in his own cabin, Lopez found Lani fretting over their daughter's bruises. They kept Olivia in bed for three days. The bruises faded but she developed a nose bleed that didn't stop for an hour. Lopez walked her up to town. Dr. Lo listened to their story and examined Olivia for a long time, drew blood from her arm, disappeared into a back room. He came back with a tight expression. Lopez felt as if his heart had fallen into ice water. "What is it?"

"I believe there are too many immature blood cells in Olivia's blood."

Lopez blinked. "What does that mean?"

"With the equipment I have, I can't be certain. It could be nothing."

"Or," Olivia asked, "I might have something bad?"

"We can't jump to conclusions."

Lopez felt darkness closing in. "What's the worst it could be?"

The doctor looked at Olivia as he said, "Cancer."

On the way back to the homestead, Olivia stopped and covered her face. Lopez put his arms around his daughter. At first her shoulders shook and the only sounds she made were sudden inhalations. Then came wailing, and she clenched his shirt in her fists. He felt nothing. No panic, no dread, no darkness closing in. Nothing. He rocked slightly and made the same shushing sound he had made when she was a baby. "It's okay, Nena. Oh, oh, it's okay."

When she was done crying, he still felt nothing.

Lopez felt as if the air had been replaced by a drug so thin and so light it flowed across a body like wind and filled the lungs, removing all sensation. He was himself and not himself as he led his daughter by the hand to their cabin.

Lani met them at the door. He told her what the doctor had said, and she shook her head. "He wasn't sure. He said he wasn't sure."

Dr. Lo had told Lopez about several doctors in Sebastopol that could make or rule out a diagnosis of leukemia. Lani wanted to go there with Lopez and Olivia, but they both agreed that traveling with two women might prove too great a temptation for the worst sort of men to resist. So they decided Lopez and Olivia would leave the next day. Until they returned, Lani didn't want to talk about it.

Lopez and Olivia sat on the porch. He took his daughter's hand. She squeezed it. "Papá?" She was studying him. Her expression was flat, exhausted. "How are you?"

"Fine, fine, mija. Don't worry about me."

"But if I have cancer, then so do you."

"You can't worry about me. I don't feel . . . anything just yet."

She laid her head on his shoulder and he put his arm around her. "I'm worried you'll have one of your panics."

"I won't."

"Promise?"

"Promise."

They sat in silence, watching the shadows stretch. When Lani called them in for dinner, she did her best to cheer them up. It worked, a little. Lopez was hungry. He couldn't remember ever feeling hungrier.

The next morning, they rode through bleaching dry-season sunlight to reach Sebastopol at dusk. Lopez bought a dinner of sausages and dumplings. They lit two candles in a cathedral that seemed to be both under construction and falling apart. They camped on the town's edge, beside a lemon tree.

At dawn he took Olivia to the address Dr. Lo had given him. It was an old mission-style building, plaster flaking. The nurse took them up to a wide room with two rows of beds. Hours passed, punctuated by different doctors who questioned and examined Olivia before vanishing.

Finally a doctor explained that blood came from bone marrow. To see if something was wrong, they had to stick a needle into Olivia's hip. She bravely agreed, squeezed her father's hand when they did the horrible thing. Lopez thought he heard a crunch; it felt as if the sound came as much from his chest as from her hip.

Afterward, Olivia cried silently while he brushed her hair back. "Mija, mija," he murmured. Gradually her breathing slowed. Midday heat crawled into the room. Olivia slept.

In the evening, they talked about what might be happening on the homestead while he sat on her bed. They must have dozed off, for when he opened his eyes again they were sitting in a square of moonlight.

In the morning, one of the younger physicians appeared wearing an expression of practiced, perhaps genuine, concern. "You have the bone marrow test back?" asked Olivia.

The doctor sat down. "I am sorry, but the results are consistent with leukemia."

Olivia buried her face in her father's stomach. He sat down and wrapped an arm around her. "Can it be cured?" he asked.

The young doctor exhaled. "Long ago it was often cured, four out of five cases. But back then there were many more drugs."

"And you don't have all of those drugs now?"

"We don't have any of them. Not here. There is one drug left that comes from a wild flower, a kind of periwinkle, from an African island named Madagascar."

Lopez cleared his throat. "You don't grow that flower here?"

"The only place left that grows it is the hospital in the old university." He looked at Lopez with searching blue eyes. "Can you take her down the peninsula? Often the Bridge People take sick children across without fee. We can write you reports. The drug you should ask for is called vincristine."

"I'll take her. Her mother's people are from down around there."

The doctor nodded and left. Olivia wasn't crying. She took his hand and pressed it to her cheek. "Papá," she said.

"Nena," he whispered.

There was nothing left to say.

The moment she saw her husband's face, Lani began to cry. That evening, Lopez and Robert worked out how he and Collin could tend to the outfit's fields. At dawn, Lopez and his wife took their daughter, two rifles, and a horse, and they left.

It seemed like a story Lopez's mother would tell—a quest for a magical flower that would save a girl's life. Periwinkle. Vincristine. Old technology. Old magic.

After two days they reached the Old Freeway and joined the traffic of mule caravans, travelers, drifters. A few men eyed

Lopez and his two women. They also eyed his rifle.

Two days later they reached the Golden Gate. Fog obscured all but the tops of its towers. All the fabled gold had fallen off, leaving only rust and patches of orange paint. Lopez wondered at how it must have shone in the lost world.

A hundred yards before the ancient monument, one of the Bridge People with wild brown hair and a long aluminum spear stopped them. When Lopez showed him the papers from the Sebastopol doctors, the man looked at Olivia and waved them past.

The bridge was riddled with holes. In some places nearly half the concrete had fallen out. Beneath these gashes swirled white air obscuring a view of the long drop to twisting currents.

On the other side, Lopez paid a few Bridge People to guide them through the city of crumbling streets, rusting cars, hollow-eyed men standing around oil drum fires. Toward night, their party reached the city's southern edge and looked back at the sunset glittering on decaying buildings shrouded in fog. "It's beautiful," Olivia said from horseback. "It must have been even more beautiful."

"You don't remember it?"

"In my last life?"

"Everyone in the heavens was from the Valley of Melted Sand. You've seen it before. You'll see it again."

"Papá, are you angry at reincarnated people?"

"No, no." He gave her shoulder a squeeze but then pulled his hand back, worried that he might bruise her.

She continued to look out at the city, her expression softening. She had been growing up so fast, too fast for Lopez. Now she had discarded the joy and petulance of childhood for . . . Lopez couldn't say what exactly. She hadn't suddenly become an adult, but now she carried an air of solemnity, which she never had before.

"I think . . ." she said, her tone experimental, "I think I had this cancer in my first life. I must have been cured and grown up to become one of the technology magicians who made the heavens."

"Maybe."

"But in every reincarnation since then, I might have died of the cancer."

"Or maybe you were cured each time. Maybe you'll recognize the hospital and you'll say 'Hey, doctor, do this or that because that's what worked last time.' And they're going to groan when they see you've come back because they know you'll end up running the place."

She laughed and the solemnity hanging about her evaporated. She gave him her bright, mischievous smile and said, "Maybe."

As they continued down the peninsula, Lani pointed out landmarks that she remembered from childhood. That night they camped by San Andreas Lake. The next morning, in the blue hour before dawn, Lopez woke to pee among the bushes. On the way back, he saw Olivia sitting by the shore. The water was so smooth that the lake had become a mile-wide mirror. He sat beside her.

"Papá," she said, her face miserable. "I'm not going to remember the hospital. I don't want to go."

He took her hand. "Mija, it'll be okay. It's just scary."

"It is, but . . . not for the reason you think. I mean . . . it's frightening because of what they might do to me and because you might die." She paused. "It's not scary because I might die."

He nodded. "You'll go to your heaven. You're not scared about that. That's good." For the first time since Dr. Lo had suggested she might have cancer, Lopez felt an emotion twisting in his heart, something hot.

"I mean . . . I mean . . ." Olivia started to say.

He let go of her hand.

The hospital was smaller than Lopez expected. Three stories tall and circular, it enclosed a small garden of poppies and a pool of green water. Most of the glass windows had been replaced by paper screens. In every room, at least one small rectangular window was left open. Lopez started when he realized that this was to provide an escape for reincarnates returning to their heavens.

In the midmorning, Lopez and Olivia sat in a room on the third floor. He stood by the window and looked down on the poppies. Olivia sat on a bed, fussing with her gown. They had seen several nurses and three physicians. He had lost track of how many times he had told their story. No one seemed to know if they could get vincristine or if it could cure Olivia.

Lani was down in the hallways, talking to her relatives. Most of her old outfit had come down from the hills to see Olivia. They were powerfully built Polinesios who lavished their cousin Olivia with embraces and soft words in English and Samoan.

A knock sounded at the door before it swung open. An older doctor—black man, thin wreath of white hair—came in and sat down. He wanted to talk about how difficult it would be to take vincristine. "It might make your fingers and toes numb or your hair fall out," he said. "And if you have a lot of cancer cells, it might hurt your kidneys."

"You don't think we should give her the drug?" Lopez asked.

"I want you to be aware of the options."

"What are the options?" Lopez asked, his voice more heated than he had intended.

"We can treat any discomfort you two might have before you return to your heavens."

"You two?" Lopez repeated.

"You are my patient as well."

"I'm not reincarnated."

The doctor blinked. He hadn't known. "I see. That complicates things." He paused. "But please consider, without the old technologies, vincristine can be dangerous."

"So if the cancer doesn't kill me, the drug might?" Olivia asked. She glanced at her father. "Might kill us?"

"We have to deal with a lot of uncertainty. You will want to talk it over."

After the doctor left, Lopez sat on Olivia's bed. "What are you thinking?"

"Nothing."

After a while Lani returned. Lopez reported what the doctor

had said. "We have to try," Lani said and looked from Lopez to Olivia. "Why wouldn't we? We have to try. If we don't, both of you will die."

Olivia flinched and Lopez looked away.

"What's going on with you two?" Lani wanted to know.

"Nothing," Olivia said.

He agreed.

They started vincristine injections the next morning. Olivia had to spend the day drinking as much water as she could stand. The drug would kill many of her cancer cells, releasing toxic chemicals that had to be filtered out by her kidneys.

In the late afternoon, Olivia began to vomit. The doctors gave her a shot of something that reduced her nausea but made her groggy. She fell asleep soon after sunset.

Lopez and Lani walked down to the ground floor to talk. An electric light shone in the room with the sickest patients. "How much longer?" Lani asked.

"Four weeks," he said numbly. "Then they need to look at her bone marrow again."

Lani went back up to sit with Olivia. Lopez remained, standing at the edge of the fluorescent light. Something was breaking open inside of him. The numbness that had been sustaining him was being filled with something that made his fists clench and his throat tighten.

All the toil and action of his life—love and fear for his daughter, admiration for his wife, the long journey through the ruined city filled with fog—were only distractions. Now he felt as if everything he perceived was not real but rather had been painted onto the emptiness that his death, closer now than ever before, would deliver him into. He had to die, and die soon, while his wife would continue to live. He would go into unknown darkness, while his daughter would float up to her technological heaven.

He paced around the hospital trying to dissipate the anger that coursed through his veins like a drug. An hour passed as if it might be endless, and still his hands trembled. He went up to Olivia's room. Lani was sitting at the bedside, stroking her daughter's hair. He went to stand by the window. After a moment, Lani went to him and slipped her arms around his waist, hugged him close.

He tried not to stiffen.

Another week, another vincristine injection. Even though the doctors gave Olivia the medication to stop vomiting earlier in the day, she spent most of that afternoon heaving. The next day the doctors said there was too much nitrogen in her blood, meaning her kidneys were being damaged. They had to give her less vincristine.

In the hospital, most every hour seemed the same. In the hospital, there was no sense of the dry season progressing. No sense of season at all.

One morning, Olivia found small black nests on her pillows. She cried silently, then cried harder when Lani cut the rest of her hair off. Two more weeks passed, each with the horrors of treatment. Then they took another sample of Olivia's bone marrow.

The next day a new doctor knocked before opening the door. He stuttered when he said that the bone marrow showed almost no improvement. Even so, they couldn't increase the vincristine dose without destroying her kidneys.

"So what are our choices?" Lani asked.

"Continue treatment and hope there's a change." He paused before quickly adding, "That would be unlikely."

"Or?" Lani asked.

"Stop and make sure she's comfortable."

Lani shook her head. "But there's no hope with that option."

The young physician looked at his lap and said they would want to talk it over. Trying not to hurry, he hurried out of the room.

Lopez looked at his daughter, her shaved head. She was staring at her palms. "Lani," he said, "we can't keep putting her through this."

Olivia began to cry.

Lopez clenched his jaw. He had done it at last. Of course he had. They had forced him to say it. To say anything else would have been monstrous.

Lani hurried to her daughter. She argued with Lopez until she realized that Olivia was trying to interrupt her. "I want to stop. I'm sorry. I'm sorry." She was mumbling through her tears. "I want to stop. I'll go to heaven."

Lani grew quiet.

Five hours later, they gathered their things and walked down and out of the hospital into the dry-season sunlight.

In the first weeks, Olivia regained her vigor. Her gaunt face filled out again. After three weeks, she was running about with her cousins.

Lopez worked in the fields with his in-laws. He liked most all of them, but he felt out of place at the large gatherings. He would leave when the conversation shifted into Samoan.

This far down the peninsula, the fog never made it over the mountains. So, working under blue skies, Lopez felt darkness locked around his mind. At times he again suffered the sensation that the world had been painted onto emptiness made tangible.

As the dry season grew old, Olivia ran with her cousins less and less. She looked pale to Lopez and was often short of breath. This didn't stop her from climbing trees or swimming in the nearby reservoir. Once or twice she had nose bleeds that would take an hour or two to stop, but she rarely felt ill.

Sometimes Lopez would see her walking about with her cousins, and he would boil with rage at his daughter and wife, at anyone reincarnated, at their privilege.

More often, he was frightened by how intensely alone he would be in his last few moments before death. No one could be with him when he died, even if they were standing beside him. He would draw his last breath and look at their faces, at the painted-on reality. Impossibly, the eternal moment of his life would end.

One morning just after breakfast, Olivia stumbled and fell on some steps. At first it seemed that she had only bruised her knee. But within an hour, the joint swelled to the size of a grapefruit.

Lopez felt himself going numb again. It was almost a relief. Here was a crisis. He didn't have to feel, just do.

Lopez took his wife and daughter down to the hospital. They put Olivia in a small room on the second floor. She began to shiver, said that bad memories were giving her chills.

A new doctor examined Olivia, explained that the cancer kept her from making the cells needed to stop bleeding. Maybe she had just bumped her knee and was bleeding into it. But she was also running a fever. He drew some blood, gave her some pills, asked them to stay the night.

An hour passed. Then two.

Olivia continued to shiver. Lani covered her with a few blankets. No one spoke. When the doctor returned, he looked grave. "Her fever is worse. I'm worried the cancer has limited her ability to fight infections, but we have given her the best medicine we have for that."

"I'm sure it's nothing," Lani said. "It's nothing."

An hour later, Olivia began breathing quickly, her skin cold and clammy. The nurses hovered around her. The doctor returned.

Time seemed to be passing faster and faster. Olivia felt hotter. As the sky outside their window darkened, her words became confused.

Lopez sat on her bed, breathing too fast, his heart kicking his rib cage. Black spots appeared before his eyes. He tried to stand but found himself on the floor. Then Lani's face was before him. She was begging him to get up. He tried harder to slow his breathing but couldn't.

Suddenly two nurses were lifting him up. One put a chair under him. Slowly the spots cleared from his vision and he could think more clearly.

"Daddy." Olivia said from her bed. "Daddy, I'm sorry." Her voice was unsteady, her words slow. With effort, Lopez scooted his chair closer so he could take her hand. It was cold. Lani was crying.

"Daddy, I'm sorry you picked me up."

"No, no," he said automatically. In truth, he both wished he had not gathered her in and was so very grateful that he had.

The doctor returned. Now he paid as much attention to Lopez as to Olivia. "Mr. Lopez," he said, "your daughter's getting worse."

The words made his heart kick harder. The world was spinning. Outside it was night. Someone behind him was talking in a low voice. Lani sometimes replied. Sometimes she would sob.

A doctor was by his side again. "Mr. Lopez, should we give you something for the anxiety?"

He couldn't answer.

Then there were hands on him, something sharp in his arm.

Lani stood beside him, holding his hand. When he looked at her, he could hear. "Don't leave me. Don't leave me."

Suddenly he realized what it must be like for her to have to stay behind while he and Olivia died. Suddenly he knew how hollow the world would be for her, his wife, the woman who had traveled through the ruined city and across the crumbling bridge to find him and their daughter in the redwoods.

He felt sorry for her.

He tried to say something but his lips were clumsy, his tongue unresponsive. But he was breathing slowly now. He thought of his faraway son, of Collin and Robert, of Olivia's face when as a little girl she had begged for a sweet. Something like warmth but not warmth was pouring through his body. He seemed to sleep . . .

Lani shifted in her seat, and Lopez saw his daughter lying in her bed. Her chest rose and fell only a little. In the candlelight, her face was pale. Her chest rose and fell a little less, a little less. And then. Not at all.

Her skin began to shine.

Lani shrieked.

Lopez clumsily grabbed his wife's hand. *No llores, Nena. No llores.* Don't cry.

Olivia grew brighter. At first white, then faintly violet. She melted into a cloud of indigo.

Lopez fell back into his chair. The world at the periphery of his vision began to dim. His daughter drifted toward him and then over him, toward the window, toward her heaven.

The glory of her light, a shining universe in miniature, filled his vision. The baby girl he'd found drifting about the water pump. He hadn't truly known why he had picked her up. Now he knew, truly knew.

The darkness at the edge of his vision gathered faster and faster, and so in his last moments, Joaquin Lopez marveled at his daughter's luminosity.

DANIEL ABRAHAM

I DON'T ACTUALLY WRITE A LOT OF HORROR STORIES, AND THE ONES THAT I do, I'm usually not aware that they're horror stories when I'm writing them. I mean, sure, it may be a little dark. But most of the time, I'm just following some idea wherever it goes and seeing what comes of it.

Not with "Dogs."

When Shawn approached me with the idea of *Unfettered*—total freedom to write whatever I wanted!—my initial thought was "Sure, I'd love to." My second thought was "Well, I'm boned." No constraints at all is a terrible way to start a project.

Eventually, I did find something, though. It was sparked by a couple conversations I was following online and a particularly grim study about sexual violence on college campuses. They came together in a single visual image, like a scene from a particularly unpleasant movie. And also as an idea.

In the old days, writers would sometimes write a story in public as a kind of stunt. I wanted to do something like that with this story, and Shawn—gentleman that he is—let me. So here in your hands is the final draft of "Dogs." The whole process of building it is outlined at: www.danielabraham.com/2012/02/01/the-dogs-project-introduction.

On the up side, at least I knew going in that it was horror.

Daniel Abraham

DOGS

Daniel Abraham

"Well, you've used a lot less morphine today," the nurse said, tapping the feed with her thumbnail. "Keep this up and we'll have you out of here by the weekend."

"Go dancing," Alexander joked.

"That's the spirit, my man."

The nurse adjusted something in the suite of machines beside the bed, and the low, chiming alert stopped for the first time in an hour. The sounds of the hospital came in to fill the void: the television in the next room, the murmur and laughter of nursing station shop talk, monitor alarms from all along the ward, someone crying.

"I'll get you some more ice," the nurse said, taking the Styrofoam cup from the little rolling bed table. "Be right back."

He tried to say thank you, but it was hard to focus. His mind didn't feel right, and his body was a catalog of pains that he didn't want to associate with. They'd saved his toes, but in five days, he'd only glimpsed the complication of red flesh and black stitching that was his leg. The muscles of his abdomen were compromised.

That was the word the surgeon had used: *compromised*. As if there had been some sort of agreement, some give-and-take. The fluid draining from his gut had seeped down, feeding deep, bloody bruises on both his thighs, and filling his scrotum until it swelled up to the size of a grapefruit, the skin tight, hot, painful, and discolored. Strangely, the punctures on his neck where the dog's teeth had held him were the least of his injuries and the quickest to heal.

The nurse stepped back in, put the cup where it had been. Firm white foam holding crushed white ice.

"Up and around in no time," she said.

"You bet," Alexander said and lifted the cup to his lips. The cold comforted him. It was like a water-flavored sno-cone: a kid's treat with all the sweetness gone. He remembered something about the ancient Greeks thinking the afterlife was like that, just the same as life, but with all the sensation and color turned to gray. That's how he knew he wasn't dead. The pleasures might all be gone, but the pain was exquisite.

After the nurse left again, Alexander thumbed the morphine drip. A few seconds later, the pain lost its edge, and the tightness in his throat went a little softer around the edges. He closed his eyes and let the nightmares come play for a while—dreams of formless dread and shame, more like an emotional cold sore than a real dream—and when he woke, Erin was there. Sandy hair. Sun-scarred face. She was wearing a lumpy flight jacket that made her look massive.

"Hey," Alexander said.

"Hey, you. You're looking better."

"This is better?"

"There was some room for improvement," she said. This was what they did. Joked, like if they laughed about it, nothing would have happened. It felt dishonest, but Alexander didn't have words for the things that wanted to be said. Even if he did, he didn't want to put it on her. She was dong so much for him already. They had been friendly acquaintances before. She was the newest draftsman in the office. He was the guy who checked the prices and specifications on materials for the architects. She'd watched

Dickens for him when he went to his father's funeral the year before, and it seemed like that was enough to make a little bond between them. No one else from the office had even visited. "I got your mail in. Pretty much just bills, ads, and credit card applications. Figure it's all stuff that can wait."

"Thanks for that," he said, pulling himself slowly up to sitting. His crotch shrieked in pain, and for a moment he thought the skin around his scrotum had popped open like an overcooked hot dog. It only felt that way. "How're the salt mines?"

"The usual. Too many projects in not enough time. Joey's covering for you, but he takes twice as long with everything. Everyone's looking forward to getting you back in," Erin said. "There's a collection to get you a welcome-back present, but don't tell 'em I spilled the beans."

"Just glad they remember who I am."

On the intercom, a professionally calm voice announced, "Code seven in the pediatrics lobby." Code seven meant someone was dying. Someone was doing worse than he was. He felt a pang of guilt for taking the bed space, the doctors' attention. He wasn't dying.

"Brought a surprise for you," Erin said with a grin, and unzipped the flight jacket. "Had to smuggle him in, right?"

Dickens's head popped out, nose black and wet and sniffing wildly. His expressive eyebrows shifted anxiously back and forth, but he didn't bark or growl. When he saw Alexander, he tried to scramble out of the half-zipped jacket, his legs and paws flailing wildly. Erin grunted as she lifted the dog up and set him gently on the bed.

"Hey, boy. Did you miss me?" Alexander said, trying to keep the tone of his voice gentle and happy, the way he would have with a child. Dickens looked up at him, eyebrows bunched in worry, then at Erin, then back again. The sniffing sounded like hyperventilating. "It's all right, boy. It's okay."

But the dog, hind legs shaking, only looked around the room, distress in his eyes. Distress, and a question he couldn't ask and Alexander couldn't answer.

It had happened on the walk from his apartment to the bus stop. The morning air was clean and crisp. The leaves of the trees still held the rich green of summer, but the morning chill was autumn clearing its throat. Running late, Alexander trotted along the familiar streets the way he did every morning. Past the corner deli with its hand-drawn signs, past the dog park where he'd take Dickens to run on the weekends, past the little strip mall with the head shop that never seemed to be open and the Laundromat that always was. There was a meeting scheduled for ten o'clock with the interior designer. He had the pricing on three different brands of paint, and was waiting on the technical specifications of the fourth. Alexander's mind ran, preparing for the day ahead.

The dogs started following him at the park, and at first, he saw them but didn't particularly take note. There were three: a buff-colored hound with long, loose ears and a joyful canine smile; a Dane cross, broad-jawed and tall; and a bull terrier whose white fur was so short that the pink of its skin showed through. They were facts of the landscape, like the grass pushing up from cracks in the sidewalk and the smell of garbage from the Dumpster.

As Alexander cut across the parking lot, one barked, a high, happy sound. The Dane ran in front of Alexander, blocking his way. When he tried to walk around it, the big dog shifted into his path again and growled, and Alexander thought it was being playful. Running claws tapped against the pavement behind him.

Even when the first bite tore into his leg, the pain blaring and sudden, Alexander didn't understand. He reached for his calf, thinking that something had gone wrong, that there'd been some sort of accident. The bull terrier leaped away from him. Blood reddened its muzzle, and its tail wagged. Alexander tried to walk, but his foot wouldn't support him, the tendon cut. Bitten through. The fear came on him like he was waking up from a dream. The parking lot seemed too real and suddenly unfamiliar.

"Hey," he said, and the smiling hound lunged at him, yellow teeth snapping at the air as Alexander danced back, lost his

balance, fell. A white minivan drove by, not pausing. The bull terrier jumped forward, and Alexander tried to pull his foot away
from it. The Dane stepped over to him, bent down, and fastened
its teeth around his throat. The thick saliva dripped down the
sides of Alexander's neck, and for a moment, all four of them were
still. When Alexander lifted his hand toward the Dane's muzzle, it
growled once, faintly—almost conversationally—and the jaw tightened. *You live if I let you live.* Alexander put his hand back down.

The attack began in earnest, but he didn't get to see it happen.
The only thing in his field of vision was the side of the Dane's
head, its sharp-cropped ear, the curve of its eye, and beyond that,
the clear blue of the sky. Teeth dug into Alexander's leg, into his
arm. One of the dogs stood on his chest, its weight pressing down
on him, bit deep into the softness of his belly, and then shook
its head back and forth. The pain was intense, but also distant,
implausible. Intimate, and happening to somebody else. It seemed
to go on forever.

The Dane growled again, shifting its grip on Alexander's
neck. Its breath warmed Alexander's ear. The smell of its mouth
filled his nostrils. The voices of hound and terrier mixed, growls
and yips and barks. Violence and threat and pleasure. Something
bit into this foot, and he felt the teeth scraping against the small
bones of his toe. A pigeon flew overhead, landed on a power line.
Another bite to his belly, and then something deep and internal
slipped and tugged. The dogs had chewed through the muscle
and were pulling out his intestine.

I'm going to die, Alexander thought.

And then it was over. If there had been something that
stopped it—a shout or the sound of a car horn—he hadn't heard it.
The grip on his throat just eased, the assaulting teeth went away.
Alexander looked down at the slaughterhouse floor that his body
had become, the ruins of his blood-soaked clothes, the pink loop
of gut spilling out onto the asphalt. The hound with its friendly
face and permanent goofy smile trotted to his head and hitched
up its hind leg. Its testicles seemed huge, its red, exposed pizzle
obscene. Urine spattered Alexander's face, thick and rank.

Then they were gone, pelting down the street away from him. They barked to each other, their voices growing softer with distance until they were just part of the background of the city. Alexander listened to his own breath, half expecting it to stop. It didn't. Another car drove by, slowed, and then sped away. He felt a vague obligation to scream or weep. Something. The pigeon launched itself from the wire above him and flew away, black against the bright sky.

Some time later, he thought to pull the cell phone from his pocket and call 911. The blood made dialing hard.

The effort of going home exhausted him. The effort of being home. Alexander had spent weeks in his nightmare, and all his things waited for him, unchanged. It was like walking into his room in his parents' house and finding all his books and clothes from high school still where he'd left them. The artifacts of a previous life.

Erin had stacked the mail neatly on the dining table. Alexander sat there, his new aluminum cane against his leg, and went through it, envelope by envelope. Dickens capered and danced and brought his old fetch toy, a ragged penguin. Alexander only had the energy to toss it halfheartedly across the apartment a few times, and Dickens seemed to recognize his lack of enthusiasm. The little dog hopped up on the couch with a sigh and rested his head on his forepaws for the rest of the evening.

In the morning, Alexander took Dickens on a quick walk around the block, focusing on getting out to the street and back again as quickly as he could, trying not to feel anything more than impatience. Then he fed the dog, fixed himself a cup of coffee and a piece of toast, and called a taxi to carry him to work. The indulgence wouldn't work as an everyday occurrence, but for his first day back to the office, he didn't want to push.

And, secretly, it meant one more day before he had to walk down past the strip mall, past the parking lot. Better to spend a few dollars and treat himself gently. There would be plenty of time to face unpleasant memories later, when he had more strength.

As soon as he sat down at his desk and turned on his computer, guilt pressed against him. Eight hundred unread e-mails tracking back to that day. Messages from people he'd worked with for months or years with subject lines like "Third attempt" and "I'm running out of time here." His morning wove itself out of apologies and lists of deadlines that had already passed. He tried to lose himself in the cost of roofing tiles and the weight tolerances of flooring.

The physical therapist had given him exercises to do throughout his day, gentle stretches that would help to keep the scars from adhering where they shouldn't, would get him back as much range of motion as possible. It wouldn't be all it had been, but mostly. Probably. Enough. He had his toes on a thick hardback book to gently stretch the reattached tendon when Michael from bookkeeping popped his head in the office door. Alexander felt a flush of embarrassment that bordered on shame.

"Alexander. You got a minute?"

"Sure," he said, pushing the book under his desk with a toe. "What's up?"

"Little thing," he said, and ducked back out. Alexander took up his cane and followed.

It could have been worse. It could have been the whole staff. Instead, there were just four of them: Michael, Robin from HR, Mr. Garner, and Erin. They didn't half fill the breakroom, and the little tray of cupcakes, with one frosted letter on each, spelled out WELCOME BACK. Everyone smiled. The sweetness of the cakes went past mere sugar into something artificial and cloying, and Alexander got a cup of the bitter work coffee to make it bearable. Mr. Garner joked about how badly things had fallen behind without him. Robin said it was all just awful without ever quite saying which *it* she was referring to. Erin stayed politely quiet, a sympathetic look in her eyes saying *I warned you they were going to do something.* Alexander sat on the metal folding chair, nodding and smiling and trying to be touched and grateful. When it was over, he went back to his office, leaning on the cane more than he had before. He could feel the sugar crash coming and the coffee left him jittery. Probably the coffee.

He tried to catch up on his e-mail, but it was too much. In the end, he composed a little canned response that he could copy into the reply field whenever he needed to: "I'm very sorry for my late response, but I have been out of the office for a medical situation and have only just returned. Please rest assured that my full efforts and attention are on this issue, and I will be back on track shortly." It wasn't even a lie, quite. The bland, conventional phrasing would have annoyed him before. He'd hated the insincerity and falseness of etiquette that everyone knew was just etiquette. Now, it felt safe and familiar. Something happened, but it was over now. He was moving on. He was putting it in the past. Everything that had happened could be put in a box marked "medical situation" and the lid nailed shut.

"Hey," Erin said. "Sorry about that."

"Well. Can't say you didn't warn me."

"They mean well."

"I know," Alexander said. "And I appreciate the thought, it's just..."

"Yeah."

She stood, neither in the room nor out, her expression friendly. The moment stretched just a little too long. If Alexander wasn't looking to talk, it wasn't an invitation. If he did want to, then it was.

"They didn't find them," Alexander said. "The dogs? They never found them."

Erin stepped into the room, sat in the chair beside Alexander's desk. Alexander's fingers hovered over his keyboard, then folded into fists and sank slowly to his lap. A telephone rang in someone else's office.

"It bothers you," Erin said.

"I keep thinking about how they're still out there, you know?" Alexander said. "I think maybe the pound picked them up and put them down and never knew they were the ones. Or maybe they were a pack that was just moving through the city and didn't really belong here. Or maybe . . ."

"Or maybe they're still out there," Erin said, speaking into the pause. "Maybe they belong to people in the neighborhood. Maybe they're sleeping on one of your neighbor's couches."

"Like that," Alexander said. He felt his hands shaking a little, but he couldn't see the tremor. "I don't know how we do it."

Erin took a breath and let it out slowly.

"You get people, you get dogs," Erin said. "Strays, yeah. But pets. People love their pets. Seriously, there are probably more dogs in this town than cars."

"I know. I've had a dog my whole life. At least one. It's not like I expected them to—"

"That's not what I meant," Erin said. "We've always lived with predators. Before dogs were dogs, they were wolves. I mean, that was a long-ass time ago, but they were *wolves*. And no matter what, some of them are always predators."

"Yeah," Alexander said.

"Most of them aren't, though. Most dogs go through their whole lives and never bite anyone. And how many therapy dogs are there, right? Seeing-eye dogs. Companion dogs. Most dogs are good."

"About how many, do you think?"

"I don't know. Four out of five?"

"So for every ten dogs you see . . ."

"Yeah. A couple."

The air conditioner hummed. Someone walked past Alexander's door, bitching about the copy machine. On the street, a truck lumbered around the corner, its brakes screeching metal against metal. Erin leaned forward, her elbows on her knees. Alexander was afraid she would reach out, touch his shoulder or his knee, but Erin only waited.

"I don't know how we do it," Alexander said again, more softly.

The afternoon was the worst. The pain ramped up a little, but more than that, Alexander's mind seemed to fall into a haze. The documentation he was working on seemed to mean less and less, the price and weight tolerance for one set of hinges started to look the same as the one before. The information didn't fit the allotted spaces, and Alexander couldn't remember how to make AutoCAD resize them. He tried to walk to the bathroom without his cane, which turned out to be optimistic. Everything felt too hard, too forced, like something he should have been able to do but couldn't. By three o'clock, the exhaustion robbed him of anything resembling productivity. He sat at his desk making a list of everything he had to do instead of doing it. Eventually, the hour hand moved far enough that he could go home without it feeling like a rout. He called for a taxi. Next week would have to be different. He'd feel better.

At the apartment, Dickens leapt and bounced, running in a tight circle the way he had since he was a puppy. Alexander collapsed on the couch, closed his eyes. When he heard nails scratching at the front door, he shifted his head, opened his eyes. Dickens looked at him, at the door, at him again. He needed to go for a walk. It was almost more than Alexander could stand. He swallowed his exhaustion and his fear and forced himself back up.

Everything was normal. Everything was fine.

The week passed slowly, old patterns slowly remaking themselves in slightly altered forms. He took himself to the lunch bar at the side of the fancy steak house across from the office. Meetings became more and more comprehensible as he put together what he'd missed during his time in hospital. His still-healing wounds bothered him less; he found ways to move and sit and stretch that worked with the new limitations of his body. Every morning and evening, he allowed himself the luxury of a taxi, swearing that this would be the last, that he'd get back to being responsible with his money next time, and then changing his mind when the next time came.

He hadn't thought to dread Sunday until Sunday came.

The late morning light spilled in through his bedroom window, making spots of white too bright to look at on the bed. The night before had been a movie streamed off the Internet, a couple rum-and-cokes, and a bag of Cracker Jacks for dinner. Between that and skipping his evening stretches, his body felt tight and cramped, the complex of scars in his belly and down his thigh pulling at his healthy flesh like something jealous. Lolling at the edge of sleep, he smelled the hound's rank piss, but the illusion faded as he came to, leaving only a bright panic behind it. Dickens lay at the foot of the bed, black eyes focused on Alexander. Even perfectly still and trying not to disturb, the delight and excitement showed in the little dog's eyebrows and the almost subliminal trembling of his body. Even then, the penny didn't drop for Alexander until he sat up and Dickens leapt off the bed and ran, nails clicking against the wood, for the front door.

It was Sunday morning, and Sunday morning was the dog park. Alexander rubbed the back of his hand against his eyes as Dickens raced from the front door to the bedroom to the door to the bedroom. Dread spilled in his chest like ink, but he pulled himself up from the mattress and forced a smile.

"Yes, I know," he said to Dickens, capering at his feet. "I have to put some clothes on, right?"

Dickens's bark was high and joyful. Alexander brewed himself a cup of coffee, showered, pulled on his sweats and sneakers. Without meaning to drag things out, he still didn't reach for the leash until almost one o'clock in the afternoon. Cool air tightened Alexander's skin, and the trees that lined the streets were giving up their green for red and gold and brown. It wouldn't be many more days before some wind came and knocked the dry leaves into the gutters, but they still held on for now. Dickens strained at the leash, choking himself a little with eagerness. Alexander focused on breathing, staying calm. They'd gone to the dog park hundreds of times. This wouldn't be any different. He'd take Dickens through the gate, let him off the leash, and wait, visiting with the other people there or reading the news off his phone, while the dogs ran and jumped and chased each other. Then, eventually, Dickens would trot back to him, scratch at his shin, and they'd go home together. The same as always. The same as ever.

Half a block from the park, the first sounds of barking reached him. Alexander's body reacted like a sudden onset of the flu; his hands went cold, and he started to sweat. Nausea crawled up the back of his throat. Dickens tugged at the leash, pulling him on, and he set his teeth and forced one foot ahead of the other until they were at the gate. Inside, half a dozen animals ran in a pack over the grass and mud. Red tongues lolled from mouths filled with sharp ivory teeth. Muscles bunched and released along the flanks of a Doberman pinscher, the animal's claws digging at the turf, throwing bits of mud and grass behind it. They were all so fast. Their barking was joyful and rich and inhuman. Bestial. Alexander's vision dimmed at the sides. Narrowed. His heart was tripping over too fast. His breath shook like a storm.

Dickens scratched at the green-painted iron gate, both fore-paws working too fast to follow, then looked back at Alexander, expectant. Confused. Alexander gagged, the taste of coffee and vomit at the back of his mouth. He stepped back, dragging Dickens with him.

"Come on boy," Alexander said, the words shuddering. "Let's go. Let's go home."

Dickens set his feet on the sidewalk, head low and pulling back against the leash. Alexander yanked harder than he'd meant to, and the little dog sprawled. Dickens's eyes registered surprise, then confusion, then hurt. Alexander turned, his teeth gritted tight against the nausea, his arms and legs shaking, and pushed for home. After the first few steps, Dickens stopped pulling back on the leash, but he didn't dance or caper anymore. Just walked along behind, his gaze never rising above knee height.

———

Alexander sat at the little kitchen table for a long time, his hands on his thighs. His mind felt empty and raw. Sandblasted. Dickens didn't come near, didn't press his nose into Alexander's lap. Instead, he curled up on the couch where he wasn't supposed to be and looked away. The sun shifted, the angles of the shadows growing thinner, the light turning darker and red. Near sundown,

Alexander became aware that his bladder was screamingly full, pulled himself up to standing, and made his way back to the bathroom. He sat on the toilet, head in his hands. Guilt and shame and a bone-deep exhaustion made the early evening feel like midnight. If it hadn't been for the autonomic demands of his body, he'd have sat still as a stone until morning.

He took a shower, the hot water making his skin pinker, the pale scars white by comparison. When he got out, he stood in front of the mirror for a long time, his gaze tracing what damage could be seen. The bedroom clock told him it was just past seven, and he had to check his phone to convince himself it was true.

Dinner was a frozen serving of butter chicken run through the microwave until the apartment smelled rich with it, and a glass of ice water. There were sitcoms on TV, so he sat there, letting other people's laughter wash over him, and joining in by reflex. Before, he would have gone out to a bar, maybe. Gotten together with friends. Tried his spotty luck with his online dating service. Every option seemed impossibly hard. And more than that, dangerous. If he did something, he might lose the quiet numbness in his head, and he still wanted it. Still needed it.

By the time the evening news came on, he felt almost like himself again. Still fragile, but himself. He cleaned the dishes, put on some music. He needed to get up a little early. He was going to take the bus, and he wanted to leave a little extra time to walk there.

Dickens hadn't moved except to shift from time to time. Alexander knew he should have made the dog get down from the couch, but that little breaking of rules seemed important; an apology for the shortcomings of the afternoon. After all, if one pattern had changed, maybe they all had. Maybe everything was up for grabs. Alexander finished cleaning, put a bowl of food down for Dickens, and listened to the soft sounds of the dog eating. He wasn't looking forward to the walk that would follow. It was cold outside now, and dark. When the little steel bowl was clean, Dickens walked over to the leash and looked up at him.

Alexander hadn't meant to hesitate, but it was there. That little half beat that marked the difference between enthusiasm and reluctance. Dickens sighed and went back to the couch.

"No, hey," Alexander said. "Come on, guy. It's walk time."

Dickens hopped up, curling himself in toward the armrest with his tail tucked under him. Alexander picked up the leash.

"Come on. It's okay. We'll just go and—"

His fingertips touched the familiar fur of Dickens's back. The little dog whipped around, teeth snapping. Alexander took a fast step back, staring down at Dickens. The world seemed to go airless. The small tufted eyebrows showed resentment and guilt. Grief. Or maybe they didn't and Alexander was seeing them there because he'd have seen them anywhere, everything in the world a sudden mirror.

"Okay," Alexander said and put the leash back where it belonged. "All right, then."

Dickens sighed and turned away again, muzzle to the armrest, back to the room. Alexander went to the bathroom in silence, brushed his teeth, changed into the old sweats he used for pajamas. He didn't sleep for a long time, and when he did, it was a thin, restless kind of sleep. He woke in darkness to a dry sound. It came again. Nails, scratching at something. Once, and then a breath, and then again. It wasn't the sound of any activity, just a message. He got up, walking out the front room. Dickens sat in front of the door, one forepaw lifted. As Alexander watched, he scratched again, then turned to look up, sorrowful. Alexander felt a thickness in his throat.

"Hey, guy," he said, pretending not to understand. "What's up?"

Dickens scratched the door.

The moment seemed to last forever until it was suddenly over. Alexander turned the dead bolt, pulled open the door. The street was blackness with occasional dull orange streetlights. It smelled like rain coming and the chill of autumn. Dickens licked the top of Alexander's foot once, then trotted out, nails ticking against the pavement like hail. Alexander watched until Dickens went into the pool of light under one of the lamps and into the darkness on the far side, then closed the door and sat up, waiting. When dawn came, he understood that Dickens wouldn't be back. He'd put up "Lost Dog" flyers, he'd make trips to the pound to look through cages for the familiar face. The only thing he wouldn't do was find him. The world was broken, and he and Dickens had both been wrong to expect that the old pieces would still fit.

In the morning, he called for a taxi.

"You're looking for a dog?"

The man behind the counter seemed amused, but Alexander couldn't guess why. Outside, the street traffic was thick. Cars and busses and pedestrians locked in the perpetual daily struggle of lunchtime at the edge of the business district. Inside the pet shop, birds shrieked and complained, and puppies yapped. The display cages ran down the wall, little rooms the size of closets with stainless steel bowls for food and water, oversize cushions to rest on, and in each one at least one dog. The walls facing the shop's main room were thick plexiglass, scratched and pitted but clean.

"Thinking about it," Alexander said, the words rich with shame. *I want a dog that didn't know me before. One that doesn't expect anything.*

In the days since Dickens left, he'd found himself looking at pet shops and animal rescues online like he was testing to see whether a wound had healed by pressing on it. More and more in the past week, he'd found himself daydreaming at work or at the office, thinking how he could have done things differently or telling himself that it was the change that had made the difference. A new dog would never know what kind of person he'd been before, and so wouldn't be disappointed in who he was now.

"You thinking more companion or protection?" the man asked as he came out from behind the counter.

"I . . . I don't know," Alexander said.

"Had a dog before?"

"Yeah," Alexander said. "Always. Since I was a kid."

"Me too," the man said. He was a few years older, with graying stubble and jowls. His eyes were dark brown approaching black, and he seemed almost dog-like himself. "My mother had a dog before she had me. There's pictures of me when I couldn't walk yet, dragging on old Hannibal's ears."

Alexander felt his gut tighten a little at the idea. A baby, soft-skinned and awkward, and standing over it a dog, yellow teeth and black eyes.

"Must have been a sweet animal," Alexander said.

"Hannibal? Hell yes. He was great. The whole time he was alive, no one broke into our house, and it wasn't a great neighbor-hood. But no one messed with our place."

"I meant with you. When you were a kid."

In the cell nearest them, a small terrier lifted his brown-and-tan head, looking at them with curiosity. The man chuckled.

"Oh, he kept me in line, all right," the man said. "I pushed things too hard, he'd let me know. Didn't take any crap, that dog."

Alexander walked slowly along the wall, looking in at the dogs as he passed. An Australian shepherd with one pale blue eye barked and wagged and barked again. A bloodhound cross eyed him with an expression of permanent sorrow built into its breed like a poker face. Alexander couldn't guess what it might be thinking. Or what it would do if it were free. The room was feel-ing oddly warm. Sweat dampened his neck.

"Nothing in this world will love you like a dog," the man said with the air of repeating something everyone knew, everyone agreed on. "Loyal. Best protection there is. Better than a burglar alarm, you know that? And anyone messes with you, dog'll be right there beside you."

"Yup," Alexander said. *Unless*, he thought.

But most dogs were good. Most never bit anyone. He counted the cells. Two, four, six—up to fifteen. If Erin was right, about three of them would be predators. A dozen good dogs and three predators.

"You feeling all right?" the man asked.

A bulldog sat by the plexiglass, looking out. Its flat face with the loose black lips and lolling red tongue looked insectile and obscene. In the corner of his eye, Alexander caught a sudden flash of motion, but when he turned, the animal was behind its transparent wall. Thick-shouldered, wide-faced, its tail cutting through the air behind it in pleasure. For a moment, it was the hound with its permanent smile, and Alexander's throat was tight.

"Seriously," the man said again. "You all right? You're looking kind of pale."

"I've always had dogs," Alexander said. "You know? Always."

"Yeah," the man said, but his voice was polite now, distant. He'd seen something in Alexander that he knew wasn't right, even if he didn't know what. Alexander pushed his hands deep into his pockets and nodded. In their cages, the dogs licked themselves and slept and barked. Twelve of them were probably fine. Good dogs.

"Thanks," Alexander said. "I've got to think about it. Talk to the landlord. Like that."

"Sure," the man said. "No trouble. We'll always be here."

We'll always be here, Alexander thought as he stepped back into the reassuring press of humans of the sidewalk. The man hadn't meant it as a threat.

The downtown streets were thick with bodies, each one moving through its own peculiar path, its own life. Alexander hunched down into his clothes, hands in his pockets, and head bowed trying to seem like one of them. Trying to seem normal. And maybe he was. Maybe the thick-bellied man with the navy blue suit and gold tie was just as worried about seeming strange. Maybe the woman driving past in her minivan had the same sense of almost dream-like dislocation. The kid bent over the bicycle weaving through stopped cars at the intersection might be riding hard and fast so that no one would see the tears in his eyes or ask him to explain them.

A bus huffed by, throwing out a stinking wind of exhaust. The cars started moving again, following the autonomic signals of the stoplight. Alexander paused at the corner, waiting his turn. Across the street, the glowing red hand meant he had to wait. A little crowd gathered around him—an older man with skin the color of

mahogany and close-cut hair the color and texture of snow clinging to stone, a woman in a tan business suit with the empty stare
of boredom, a man Alexander's age tapping at his smartphone and
glancing up occasionally to make sure the world was still there.

A dog barked. The sound of pure threat.

Alexander's heart raced. He turned his head. A white sedan
idled at the curb, waiting for the same light to change. The
woman behind the wheel had straight-cut hair and makeup that
was starting to wear thin. In the back seat, the dog stood, teeth
bared at the window. Its gaze was on Alexander, and with every
bark, every snap of its jaw, it lunged toward the thin sheet of glass
a little. Flecks of saliva dripped from its raw, wet lips, and its tail
wagged with pleasure at the threat and anticipation of violence.
There was an empty child's car seat behind it, a clawed hind paw
digging into the cloth upholstery. Alexander glanced away. The
others were ignoring the dog; the older man looking out at the
traffic light, the young one at his phone. The woman noticed Alexander looking at her and pointedly didn't look back. They were in
some other world. Some different reality where a predator wasn't
an arm's length from them. Alexander looked away, kept his head
down. Dogs didn't jump through car windows. They didn't attack
people on the street. They waited until you were alone.

The red didn't turn. And it didn't turn. And it didn't turn. The
dog shouted at him, wordless and unmistakable. It wasn't just barking. It was barking at *him*. It knew him, knew his scent. It wanted
him. The motion at the corner of Alexander's vision drew him
back. The car's back window was smeared with something clear
and viscous. The teeth snapped white, tearing at the air. Ripping it.

The light changed. The red palm became a pale walking figure, the light went green, and the sedan pulled away, dog still
barking as it went. Alexander walked into the street, carried by
the flow of bodies more than any impulse of his own. By the time
he reached the far corner, the sedan had vanished, woman and dog
and booster seat. The thought came with a strange detachment: A
child probably rode in that seat every day, to school and back from
it, with that dog sitting at the far window. He wondered what the

woman at the wheel would do if the kid ever started screaming.

In the office, Alexander sat at his desk, his glazed eyes on the monitor. There were words, projects, windows open that held all the information that was supposed to be his life. All he could see were teeth. After an hour, he got up and went to the back storage room where he could sit on a box of printer paper and wait for the dread to pass.

He didn't hear Erin's footsteps, only her sigh. Alexander looked up. She was in the doorway, a handful of pale green printer paper in her hand, a grim expression on her face. Alexander tried to smile. Tried to wave hello. His body wouldn't comply.

"Rough day," Erin said. It wasn't a question.

Alexander felt a tear on his cheek. He hadn't realized he was weeping.

"I can't do this," he said. His voice was weak. Erin squatted down next to him, carefully not touching.

"Do what?"

"Any of it."

Erin nodded.

"Feels like that sometimes, doesn't it?"

"How am, how am, how am I supposed to ignore it? How am I supposed to pretend it didn't happen?"

"Or that it won't happen again," Erin agreed. "That was the worst part for me."

Alexander looked into Erin's waiting eyes. Her smile was sorrowful. She put down the handful of paper, pale green spreading on the floor, leaned forward, and took the bottom of her shirt in her hands, pulling the cloth up until the bare skin of her belly and side were exposed. The scars were white and ropey, and they pulled at the healthy skin around them, puckering it. Alexander couldn't imagine the wounds that had created them, and then, for a second, he could.

She let the hem of her shirt fall. In the silence, the distant sounds of the office—voices, the hum of the air conditioner, the groan of a printer—could have come from a different world. She shifted the fallen pages with her toe, the paper scraping against the floor with a sound like dry leaves rattling down a gutter. The smell of overbrewed coffee slipped in from the breakroom, familiar and foreign at the same time.

"So how'd you do it? How did you get to where you aren't scared all the freaking time?"

Erin's smile drooped a little, tired with the effort.

"You're making an assumption," she said. "Just hang in there. It'll get easier."

"But not better," Alexander said.

"But not better."

Living without a dog felt strange. It felt wrong. It felt better than living with one. Maybe later, Alexander told himself, it would get easier.

Days passed and flesh knitted. The last stitches came out, and the low, gray skies of winter settled in. Thanksgiving came and went, and Christmas began its low, flat descent. He had nightmares sometimes, but less often. He had moments of profound and crippling fear that came like bad weather and then moved on. His doctor put him on antidepressants, and they seemed to help some.

The morning he didn't call a taxi was a Wednesday. He'd been online the night before, looking at his bank balance, and when he woke up, he just didn't make the call. He drank his coffee. He ate his eggs. He walked out into the cold, biting air with a scarf wrapped around his neck. The dog park was empty, the grass brown and dead, the trees leafless. Walking across the parking lot where it had happened was like going back to an old elementary school; the place was so much smaller than he remembered it. It was like someone had come and taken the old place away and brought in a scale model. The fear he'd expected didn't overwhelm him. It was just asphalt and sidewalk. It didn't mean anything. Or maybe everything it meant he carried with him anyway, so the location added nothing. He reached the bus stop with its green roof and advertising poster walls for the first time, pleased with the accomplishment, and spent the whole day at work exhausted and unable to concentrate. He wound up staying late to finish things he should have had done before his afternoon coffee break.

The evening streets were dim and empty, the daytime world of downtown already closed down. A dull red between the sky-scrapers to the west marked where the sun had been. The shop-front displays glittered and shone for nobody. Alexander pushed his hands into his pockets and scurried toward the bus stop, his mind already skipping ahead to a cup of hot chocolate liberally spiked with rum and an early bed. Maybe he could see if anyone had left a message for him online. Or if there were any decent movies on. At the stop, he sat on the formed plastic bench and pressed his hands between his thighs. The city had put a program-mable sign marking the time until the next bus, and he watched it count down to nothing and reset without any actual bus arriving. A few cars hissed by.

The dog came out from an alley to his left, its claws clicking on the pavement. The blackness of its coat seemed to defy the light. It trotted down the street toward him, moving in his direc-tion with a distracted air. A mastiff. A rottweiler crossed with something huge. No fat cushioned its skin, and the muscles work-ing under the fur were as large as a man's. Its breath steamed past stained teeth. Alexander pressed himself against the back of the bench, heart racing, the metal taste of fear in his mouth.

The dog angled toward him. The clicking of its claws was unnaturally loud, drowning out the sounds of traffic. At the curb, it sat, looking into the street as if it was waiting for the bus too. It turned to look at Alexander, its black eyes expressionless. For a single, horrible moment, Alexander imagined he saw blood on its muzzle. The dog chuffed once and bent down to lick itself, the unself-conscious intimacy threatening and obscene. Alexander could already feel its teeth on his neck, smell its piss in his face, even though it hadn't so much as growled at him.

Four out of five, Erin said. Only two in ten ever bit anyone. Ever mauled anyone.

Lights glowed white and red and green in the growing dark.

Any moment now, the well-lit bus would lumber around the corner. Safety would come. The streetlights changed and cars moved past, hurrying away on their own errands, oblivious and uncaring as birds. The dog stopped its obscene licking and looked up at Alexander again.

The dog's broad head bent forward a degree. The bus didn't come. The dog grunted, not a bark, not a growl, just a sound low in its throat, and Alexander smiled at it, trying to act like he wasn't scared, trying to imagine how someone who wasn't scared would be. The seconds stretched out into years.

"Good doggie," he said, his voice weak and thin as a wire. "Good doggie, good doggie, good doggie . . ."

KEVIN HEARNE

For quite some time I've been fascinated by the old Grail legends that developed in several countries of western Europe but today are largely associated with England. The legends illustrate how our stories and beliefs evolve over time, for the Grail originally had nothing to do with the Christian mythology that got stapled onto it in later iterations.

Modern scholars have filled many pages trying to figure out the pagan origins of the grail, most notably Jessie L. Weston's *From Ritual to Romance* that inspired portions of T. S. Eliot's *The Waste Land*. Since several scholars have suggested that the grail was of Celtic origin and in fact may have been Dagda's Cauldron—a far cry from the cup of Christ—I could not resist the opportunity to explore that idea in "The Chapel Perilous."

The Chapel Perilous is a feature of many grail legends, a final challenge that the questing knight must face before he's ready to see the Fisher King, the keeper of the grail. Though the details vary from version to version, it's definitely not a place of peace; it's uniformly creepy, often surrounded by a graveyard and suggesting an abandonment of faith more than anything else.

This anthology offered me the chance to help out a friend and indulge my penchant for mythological geekery, so I took it. Hope you enjoy this glimpse into the past of Atticus O'Sullivan before he became the Iron Druid.

Kevin Hearne

THE CHAPEL PERILOUS

Kevin Hearne

Stories are sometimes born in fire, but regardless of origin they always live around fires and grow in the telling. If bellies are full and the veins pulse with a flagon or two, why then, all the better for the story. Sometimes, as a Druid, stories are expected of me. People just assume I'm a part-time bard as well.

<Atticus, tell us a tale we haven't heard before,> Oberon said. We were taking a break from training by camping on the Mogollon Rim near Knoll Lake. After cooking fresh trout over our campfire for dinner, we were relaxing with hot cocoa and roasting marshmallows.

"You want a story?" I said aloud. My apprentice couldn't hear my hound yet; she was still four years away from being bound to the earth and practicing magic. To be polite and include her, I sometimes spoke aloud to Oberon by way of inviting her into the conversation.

"Usually he wants snacks," Granuaile said. "I'd go for a story, though. It's a nice night for one."

<Listen to the clever apprentice,> Oberon said.

"All right, what are you in the mood for?"

<I want one where a ne'er-do-well wolfhound meets the fluffy poodle of his dreams and they take a magic carpet ride to sing perfectly orchestrated duets until they land in a field of heather, and there's a man there who looks like Uncle Jesse from *The Dukes of Hazzard* and another man who looks like Hank Williams Jr. who says he's got a pig in the ground and—>

Granuaile didn't hear any of that, so she spoke over him and offered her own suggestion: "I want a story where you took part in an historical event—a famous one."

"All right." I paused to think and plucked a gooey marshmallow off a steel stake before answering. "How about the quest for the Holy Grail?"

<Nuh-uh!>

"No way!" my apprentice said. "You weren't a Knight of the Round Table!"

"No, absolutely not," I agreed. "But the Grail legends didn't start out as highly Christianized tales about Arthur and Lancelot and so on. They were based on the adventures of one man—a Druid, as it happens—and then that story got changed, the way stories do, in the telling and retelling of it around hearthfires and campfires like this one."

Granuaile crossed her arms. "So you not only know the original story of the Grail, you're telling me you actually found it?"

"Yes. It was my quest."

She still thought I was bluffing. "Who gave you the quest?"

"Ogma of the Tuatha Dé Danann."

"All right, fine. And what was the Grail? I mean, it couldn't have been the cup at the Last Supper or anything, right?"

"No, that whole business with Joseph of Arimathea and the cup of Christ was a later addition. Hell, King Arthur's story was pulled almost entirely out of Geoffrey of Monmouth's ass. There were about six hundred fifty years separating the events themselves and the first written account of them that survived to the modern day. Plenty of time to screw everything up and fabricate large portions of it. What the poets eventually called the Grail was Dagda's Cauldron, one of the Four Treasures of the Tuatha Dé Danann, which could feed an army and never empty—it was an all-you-could-eat forever sort of deal."

<Okay, now that sounds interesting.>

"You went on a quest to steal Dagda's Cauldron and that got turned into the quest for the Holy Grail?"

"Sort of. Somebody else stole Dagda's Cauldron. It was my quest to steal it back."

"So who were you? Lancelot? Galahad?"

"No, stories about those guys got created later. I was the lad who went galloping around the country telling everyone my name was Gawain."

Granuaile shook her head in disbelief. "Okay, sensei, let's hear it," she said.

<Make sure you don't leave out what was in the cauldron,> Oberon added. <And how the dogs got so full they almost exploded. Hey, there *are* dogs in this story, right?>

The Tuatha Dé Danann are loath to put themselves in harm's way when someone else can be harmed in their stead. With this in mind, in 537 AD, Ogma approached me on the far reaches of continental Saxon territory with a task he thought I'd find attractive. It wasn't the first time he had asked for my services; he'd asked me to raid the Library at Alexandria once because he'd foreseen its destruction.

"Some bloody Pictish git has stolen Dagda's cauldron and taken it into the western territory of the Britons," he told me. He was referring to what would eventually become Wales; at this time the Britons there were just beginning to form their Welsh identity. "But he's spread some sort of arcane fog across the area, preventing us from divining his precise location and from shifting directly there. We need someone who can go in there and take the cauldron back."

"And I was your first choice?"

"No, we've sent some others in as well."

I noticed the "we" but didn't comment. "Other Druids?"

"Aye, there are few enough of you left, but there were a couple willing to go."

"Sounds bereft of entertainment or profit to me," I said.

"Did you not hear me, lad? We can't see into the area and can't shift there. Considering that you've been on the run a good while now, does that not hold some attraction to you?"

He was hoping I'd jump at any chance to escape the eyes and ears of Aenghus Óg, the Irish god who wanted me dead, but I shrugged. "It sounds like I'm trading a god who wants to kill me for a mad Pict with a giant pair o' balls and some magical talent. One's not necessarily better than the other."

Ogma laughed. "Fair enough. But you'll be earnin' my gratitude on top of it. The Dagda is me brother, you know."

"I thought I earned your gratitude already for that favor I did you down in Egypt."

"True. But this would be *more* gratitude."

Unspoken was the certainty that my refusal would mean *less* gratitude.

"All right. Get me a good horse and a proper kit from Goibhniu so that I look like I deserve respect. Shift me as close as you can and point me in the right direction. I'll make up the rest as I go."

"Attaboy," Ogma said and clapped me on the shoulder. "I'll see you soon."

It was a week before I saw him again, but he had the promised armor from Goibhniu and a fine horse for me to ride. There were also provisions for the both of us. I changed happily into my kit, feeling optimistic for the first time in months, and then we shifted through Tír na nÓg to a spot near the old Roman road leading west from Gloucester. It was raining heavily.

"I'd forgotten the rain here," I said. "And you didn't remind me, did you?"

Ogma ignored my complaint and pointed west. "Go that way."

"How far before Aenghus Óg won't be able to sense my magic or divine my location?"

"Not far at all. You'll sense the change once you pass through it. My advice is to make friends with your horse before you do. I've heard they spook easily in there."

"What can you tell me about the Pict?"

Ogma shrugged. "He's mean and ugly."

"Right. Onward then."

Ogma wished me well and shifted back to Tír na nÓg, leaving me alone in the rain.

The horse snorted and looked at me uncertainly. I approached him calmly and petted his neck, slowly introducing my consciousness to his, so that he would pick up on my emotions and vice versa. What I got in response was much more than that.

<Oh, good,> the horse said. <You're one of them.>

I was startled to hear his voice in my head. *One of who?*

<One of the humans who can hear me.>

Where did you learn language?

<Goibhniu taught me.>

It appeared that Ogma had taken my request quite literally; he'd not only gotten a kit from Goibhniu, but the smith god's personal horse. And it was because of this experience that I began to teach my animal companions language from that time forward.

I am called Gawain, I said. *Do you have a name?*

<Apple Jack. Quite fond of apples, you know. I don't suppose you have any?>

I checked the provisions and found a significant store of apples in one of the saddle bags. I removed one and offered it to Apple Jack.

<Thanks,> he said, taking it from my fingers with his lips and then crunching down. <I think we'll get along just fine. Just one more thing. When I smell things that scare me, you have to either kill them or let me run away. Because you heard that guy who brought me here. Since I'm a horse, I spook easily. Deal?>

Well, it depends on what scares you. I can't commit to a blanket statement like that. What if you get scared by the scent of an attractive woman?

<I have been reliably informed that there are no attractive women outside of Ireland. If you see one here, then it must be a witch and you should either kill it or run away.>

Goibhniu has trained you very well.

<He had a lot of apples to secure my attention.>

I'll bet he did. I threw my leg over Apple Jack, gathered the reins, and gave him a friendly slap or two on the neck. *Let us sally forth, my good horse! Follow the road west. To danger and glory!*

<Are those villages?>

Danger and glory? No. I was being dramatic.

<Please stop. That could get us in trouble.>

Point taken.

We plodded forward because one does not trot, canter, or even manage a respectable walk in such weather. In less than a mile, however, the character of the rain changed. Instead of a proper downpour with respectable drops, it became a splattery, aggressive mist that couldn't decide which direction to fall. It whipped me in the face from both directions and did its best to fall into my ears and leap up into my nostrils. It argued with cold, implacable determination that there was no clothing I could wear that would allow me to be even mildly comfortable. And something else happened in terms of pressure; my ears popped. We must be under the fog that Ogma had mentioned.

The temperature dropped as well and the trees along the road did not seem to be the sort that would hide a band of merry men. They rather offered a surplus of gloom and rot underneath their canopies. The sky was nothing but a diluted wash of ink, gray swirling brushstrokes of moisture. I felt miserable and unwelcome and began to wonder if I had made an imprudent decision. Apple Jack expressed similar sentiments. Repeatedly. We were slowly turning into frozen avatars of anxiety. Dreadsicles. Doompops.

The forest rustled at nightfall. Growls from predators and shrieks from prey were followed by cracks and wet squelching noises and very loud chewing sounds. I built us a makeshift shelter between two trees, binding fallen branches into a rough roof that bridged the gap and kept off the worst of the rain.

<Can you just go ahead and build me a stable?> Apple Jack asked. <Or how about surrounding us with a nice stockade?>

This will do just as well, I said, building a fire underneath the

roof. *I've asked the local elemental to keep the hungry animals at bay.*
Now all you have to worry about are unnatural predators.

<Hey, what? What kind of predators?>

Ghosts. Witches. Goblins. The usual.

<The usual?> Apple Jack tossed his head and stamped nervously. <Goblins are the usual here?>

Hey, calm down—

<That puny fire won't protect me from goblins! Have you *seen* a goblin before, Gawain? Tiny eyes but large teeth and nostrils. They wear horsehide leather! ME-hide leather! Let's get out of here!>

Settle down! There aren't any goblins! I was only joking!

Apple Jack's ears flattened against his head and he showed me his teeth. <You are NOT funny.>

Sorry. I know it's spooky out there but we're not in terrible peril yet. I'm sure that's a few days down the road at least.

<Still not funny.>

I got him a couple of apples and a bag of oats to atone for my teasing and I spent some time brushing him down. I told him the legend of the Fine Filly Fionnait, the white mare of Munster, and that comforted him enough so that we could both get some sleep. Before shaking out my wet blanket, however, I spent a wee bit of time modifying the sole of my right boot. I cut a hole in it so that I would still be able to maintain contact with the earth and draw on its magic, but hopefully it would not be the sort of thing that people would notice or, failing that, remark upon.

The rain stopped sometime during our slumber, but promptly began again in the morning once we emerged from our temporary shelter.

<It's a conspiracy,> Apple Jack said. <They want mold to grow in my ears.>

Who are they?

<Them.>

Usually I'm the paranoid one.

<Why? You have a sword and opposable thumbs. I can only run away and look delicious to predators. Paranoia is my specialty.>

I'm guessing you're not Goibhniu's war horse.

Aside from the rain and our collective fears, we had little to complain about that day. In the afternoon we chanced upon an inn with a stable and decided to call the day's ride early. We weren't in a terrible hurry and a bit of comfort would be welcome. After I'd put Apple Jack up in a nice stall with plenty of feed, it occurred to me that I hadn't seen anyone taking the road out of the area. No one had passed me in either direction. Yet the stables were quite nearly full, which meant the inn—called the Silver Stallion, according to the shingle outside—must be packed with travelers. Perhaps they were all waiting for the rain to end?

No. That's not what they were doing. I quickly discovered that the reason no one was leaving the area toward Gloucester was that they couldn't.

"Here's another one!" a salty old codger said when I walked in the door. "Welcome to hell, good sir."

I quickly scanned the inn. It didn't look hellish, nor did anyone's body language suggest that they were going to give me hell. The customers simply looked depressed as they lounged at tables and benches with flagons of ale and stared at plates of half-eaten cheeses.

"Thank you," I replied, keeping my voice low. "Why is this hell, though? I missed it."

"We're condemned to stay here for eternity," the old man explained, "and it's certainly not heaven." Medieval logic.

"You can't leave when you want?"

"Oh, sure, you can leave. But you'll be back. Take the road toward Gloucester and you'll find yourself right back here. I've gone to Gloucester three times now, only to arrive back at the Silver Sodding Stallion each time."

"What happens if you keep going west?"

"West?" The man practically barked at me. "Why'd you want to go that way?"

The old man's raised voice drew eyes to me. I shrugged and said, "I suppose because I'm poorly informed. What's wrong with the road to the west?"

"Bloody awful doings down at the Viking trading post.

Sveinsey, they call it, down there on the Gwyr peninsula, but fuck if anyone knows what that means."

I laughed along with him at that, even though I knew it meant Sveinn's Island in Old Norse—which was simply called "Norse" then. Today the place is called Swansea.

"How bloody awful are we talking about?" I asked.

"It's a long story, and me tongue is like a slug left out in the sun."

"Ah. Allow me to buy you a drink, then?"

"Kind of you, sir. What's your name?"

I introduced myself as Gawain, which many people heard, no doubt, especially since I spoke their language with a noticeable accent. Conversation in the dining area was subdued and people probably noted that my kit marked me as a knight of some means. The old man offered his hand and told me his name was Dafydd. We bellied up to the bar and I ordered two flagons of mead. I also made inquiries about staying the night and the innkeeper shook his head. "No rooms left. Not unless you want to stay in the stables."

"The stables it is, then."

Once the old man had slaked the worst of his thirst, he told me merrily of death and ruin in the west.

"Some daffy Pict with his face pierced a hundred times has come into Sveinsey and bollixed up the entire kingdom. Haven't seen the sun in three months. The rain never lets up—never enough to flood, mind, but nothing ever gets a chance to dry out either. Crops are collapsing from root rot and you have poxy mushrooms bigger than an ox's cock sprouting up all over the place. Cows and sheep are shitting themselves until they die, am I right?" He looked at the innkeeper and nearby patrons for corroboration. A couple of half-hearted grunts set him off again. "Pastures of them just spread out in the mud for the sport of crows. The smart people moved out a few months ago when they saw there wouldn't be any fucking food, but it's a hard thing to give up one's land after fighting over it and sweating over it year after year."

"So did the people who moved earlier get out? They weren't trapped like you?"

"Aye, they made it out. This magic fence he's put up has only been in effect for a month now. Good King Cadoc is off praying about it, God bless him, but I don't see what good it's doing when the Pict is sitting there building defenses. Bloody sorcerer says he's got his own king there now at Sveinsey."

"Begging your pardon, but I've been away for a good while. What kingdom am I in right now?"

Dafydd laughed at me, and a few of the patrons listening in joined him. "What kingdom, you say? How does a knight not know where he is?"

I shrugged. "I travel a lot. Just came across from the continent not long ago. Borders shift and kings die all the time. Hard to keep track after a while."

"Well, that's true enough. You're in Glywysing. Who is your lord?"

"I don't have a lord," I said, but immediately saw that the assembled men wouldn't accept such a state of existence. "I'm looking for one," I added. "A righteous one. My last lord was slain by the Saxons."

A round of cursing and spitting greeted this revelation, and as an enemy of the Saxons, I was instantly their friend. Someone offered to buy my next drink.

"How are you surviving if you can't get new supplies in?" I asked, shooting a glance at the innkeeper. He scowled and picked up a flagon that needed polishing.

"Lads have been helping out," he said. "They go hunting. Plenty of game hereabouts. But it's all meat all the time now. That and drink, because I had quite a few kegs in storage. Ran out of flour so there's no bread. Haven't seen a vegetable in three weeks."

"That's a sailor's diet, that is," Dafydd said. "We're going to turn pasty and die weeping if we can't get out of here."

"Well, what about the Pict?" I asked. "Isn't he facing the same problem?"

"Oh, no," Dafydd said, shaking his head. "He's got something special there at his wee little fortress. He's trying to turn it into a proper castle, you know—but bugger that, what I keep hearing

302

is that he has some kind of infinite supply of food. It's a magic *graal*, you know. Take food from it and more appears. He can feed everyone in his fortress just fine, and plenty of people have joined him to get their three squares a day, you bet. But meanwhile the land is dying around him, spreading east from the Gwyr peninsula and maybe north and west, too, I don't know. Haven't heard from anybody out there."

"So nobody is heading to Sveinsey anymore? Or even in that direction?"

"Only the evil and the stupid."

I raised an eyebrow. "The evil?"

"Pagan bastards. Druids. There was one in here about seven days ago, and another a couple weeks before that. Tattoos on their arms, you know."

That was why I'd asked Ogma for a full kit. The time when Druids earned respect wherever they walked had passed, and it was getting to the point where we couldn't even walk around freely without harassment or outright violence. I nodded and asked, "They went to join the Pict?"

"No, not join him. They thought they could bloody do something about him. I wished them well in that regard, but they haven't come back and we still can't get to Gloucester, so they've had all the effect of King Cadoc's prayers, which is to say, no effect at all."

Abruptly I no longer felt like drinking with those men. They had told me all I needed to know, and nothing would follow except personal questions and the exchange of lies. Blending in with the converted populace wasn't difficult so long as I kept my tattoos hidden, for the rules were simple in the early Church of the time: praise Jesus, and if you ran into anyone who didn't do the same, attack the weak and shun the strong. The social camouflage was easy to maintain but wearying on the spirit. I thanked the men for their company and excused myself to look after my horse, may the Lord bless and keep them and destroy all evil.

I brushed Apple Jack down and fed him and settled in to wait out the night, resolving to get an early start in the morning. I wanted to strip and dry out my kit but the necessity of maintaining my Christian façade made that impossible. Whenever someone entered the stables I knelt and clasped my hands and made a show of prayer. No one interrupted my pious devotion.

The rain renewed with a vengeance in the morning, determined to erode my substance away and chap my hide. Big fat drops spanged off my helmet and slapped against my leathers. I kept my head down for most of the time and trusted Apple Jack to follow the path. After a soggy lunch under the partial shelter of an ash tree, we longed for the dry comfort of the stable at the Silver Stallion.

An hour's numbing march after lunch brought a surprise. I wiped rain out of my eyes at one point and Apple Jack shook his head to accomplish the same end. Refocusing on the road, I saw a structure ahead that I had missed before.

"Wait," I said aloud, and Apple Jack stopped. "How did I not see that?"

<You mean that building surrounded by a graveyard?>

Yeah, that's what I mean. It looks like a chapel. The cross on the roof was a bit of a giveaway. It wasn't a cathedral or even a regular meeting house; it was a small gray stone-and-mortar job put together in such a way as to suggest that the mason had been in a hurry. Tombstones leaned left and right in the sodden earth and completely surrounded the chapel, giving the yard the likeness of stained and broken teeth. It was the most morbid house of worship I'd ever seen.

<I didn't see it either. Maybe it was camouflaged? I have seen Druids do that before.>

Oh, that's true. That must be what happened. There must be another Druid around here somewhere, and that's good.

<Nothing smells good though. I smell death.>

How much? Is this just a vague uneasiness or do you actually smell rotting flesh through all the rain?

<I suppose it could be coming from the graveyard. But there's something not right about it. Oh well, we're just going past, right?>

No, I think we need to check it out.

<I think we need to live.>

Come on, it's just a chapel in the middle of a graveyard. Buried bones can't hurt you. There's probably someone friendly inside.

<What if that's the lure? It's not a place of refuge; it's a spider's web, Gawain! There's a murderer inside who has a convenient graveyard to bury us in! Have you thought of that?>

Um. No.

<Well, you go say hi then, and I'll stand out here and guard the supplies.>

I dismounted and fed him an apple before casting camouflage on myself and my kit and drawing Fragarach from its scabbard.

A low fence that marked the boundary of the hallowed ground had a single open gate that led into the graveyard and pointed to a narrow path between the graves. Once I passed through it, I saw that the door to the chapel was ajar. Candles could be seen burning inside. I began to think maybe Apple Jack had the right idea when I saw that the door was ajar because somebody's head on the floor wouldn't let it close.

The head was still attached to a body, but it was a dead body with blue unblinking eyes staring at the door frame. It didn't look like a member of the clergy; he was wearing a simple tunic of dyed blue cloth. I couldn't tell anything more about him, including the cause of death, without getting closer and perhaps opening the door further to investigate.

But there might be someone waiting behind that door.

There could also be an archer waiting in ambush behind one of the gravestones. I dismissed that as unlikely almost as soon as I thought of it; ambushers rarely like to settle in for their long waits in the rain. Whoever killed this man was either long gone or still inside. I was betting the killer was still inside, or else he would have cleaned up the scene a bit.

The sound of falling rain prevented me from hearing anything else, but the same noise would disguise my approach. I crept closer until I was on the doorstep and could peer through the opening. I saw a bit more of the body. The right forearm and hand were draped over the man's belly. They were covered with Druidic tattoos like mine.

I stepped back and considered. The floor of the chapel was stone and once I entered I would be cut off from the source of my magic. I was still centuries away from the creation of my bear charm, and our bodies can only store a little magic for a limited time, so I'd be able to walk in there with one spell and maintain it for no more than a couple of minutes before I'd be tapped out. The gamble would be choosing a spell. I tried to reason it out, because Druids are not easily killed but someone had clearly succeeded quite recently. If I went in camouflage, the killer would still see the door opening and might indeed be waiting for just such a signal. Speeding myself up would normally serve me well, but that advantage would be negated if I didn't know from which direction the ambush would come and realized it too late. I opted for strength; if something zapped me or attacked after I entered, I would do my best to wrestle myself outside where I could tap into more of the earth's magic. The dead Druid on the floor might have been trying to accomplish the same before he died. I resolved to keep close to the door if I could.

<You've found a dead body, haven't you?> Apple Jack's voice said in my head.

Yes.

<But you're going in anyway.>

Yes.

<I don't understand why you're in charge when you are incapable of making decisions in your own self-interest. "Oh, look!" you say. "A slain human! Instead of running away from this obviously perilous chapel, I think I'll stick my neck in and see if it gets chopped off!">

If I die, you have my permission to run away. Hush now and let me think.

Apple Jack had a point. There was no need for me to go in. Dagda's cauldron wasn't in there. But thanks to the bloody Romans and the spread of monotheism, there were precious few Druids left and I felt obligated to avenge this one if I could.

I paused for a full minute to listen. I heard nothing but the white noise of water on stone. I dissolved my camouflage and whispered a binding that would strengthen my muscles; I drew as much power as I could hold and then kicked the door open, charging in and looking behind it. No one there. I looked up; no one waited to drop on me from the rafters. I crouched and surveyed the rest of the chapel, cautiously sidestepping back toward the open door. It was a single chamber. There was an altar in the back of the chapel surrounded by candles, and a body rested on it: a second Druid, his tattoos clearly visible, and his arms folded over his torso and clutching a sword like a soldier.

"Hey, lad," I called. "Wake up." He didn't move. His chest remained still, bereft of breath.

Dafydd's claim that two Druids had left the Silver Stallion in recent weeks came back to me. Apparently they'd both met their end here. But how? I didn't want to be Druid number three and I was operating on too little information. I backed out the door, grabbed the Druid lying there by his tunic, and dragged him outside with me for a proper investigation. The chapel was simply too creepy; someone had lit those candles recently, and I doubted the dead men were responsible.

I knelt beside the Druid in the rain. He had no visible head wounds—not even bruising. A purpling of the skin low on the right side of his throat, however, made me look for more; on the left side were four more marks. This Druid had been choked to death by a single large hand. Perhaps it had been gauntleted—but that hardly mattered. I'm sure the Druid hadn't meekly accepted his strangulation. He must have fought back but it had done him no good. There was enormous strength behind those telltale bruises.

My hand trailed up to my neck and I speculated on how much protection the chain mail would offer against a hand like that. Probably very little.

I wondered if the Druid on the altar had been killed the same way. It was probably safe to investigate since the owner of the giant hand was obviously not in the chapel at present.

Stepping back inside, I noticed most of the candles around the altar had been snuffed out, presumably by the wind circulating through. The only illumination now came from the pillar of wan light cast by the open door, largely occluded by my own shadow, and a single candle in front of the altar. I was halfway to the altar when the strangeness of it upset me. If the wind had snuffed the candles, the one that was still burning would have been the first one to blow out. So what had put them out . . . ?

Movement drew my eye to the lower right corner of the altar. A huge disembodied black hand and forearm crawled toward the final candle using its fingers. The hand was an unnatural carbon black, scarred and pitted like volcanic rock. It pinched out the candle with its thumb and forefinger, and then I lost it in my own shadow.

It had no trouble finding me, however, as I backstepped. It scrabbled inhumanly fast across the floor and gripped my leg, not to halt my progress but rather to climb up one finger at a time. I hurriedly swiped at it with my left hand to knock it off, but it must have been waiting for just such a reaction, for it somehow caught my fingers, spasmed, and flipped itself onto my forearm, now much closer to my throat. It knew which direction that lay, for it immediately began to inch its way up my arm with ropelike finger movements.

My panicked brain suggested that I cut off my own arm with Fragarach to prevent the hand's advance. Its enchanted blade would slice through armor as easily as skin. But after my logic had its say in the next fraction of a second, I thought of something else. *"Freagroidh tú!"* I said, pointing my sword at the hand and activating the primary enchantment, which would force the target to tell the truth. But I didn't want to talk to the hand; I wanted the secondary effect, which prevented the target from moving more than a few inches from the point of the sword while under interrogation. Move the point, and you effectively move the target. I directed the point at the floor in front of me, and the hand was yanked magically from my arm and placed under firm control a comfortable distance away. I watched it writhe and struggle to break free of the spell for a few seconds while I caught my breath and tried to slow down my heartbeat. It was too repulsive to bear for long, however, and I began to saw off the digits, starting with the thumb. Once disconnected from the palm, they ceased moving.

The arm still tried to attack me with all five fingers missing, so I stabbed it through the back of the hand and it finally slumped inert on the floor.

Before I could sigh in relief, the Druid on the altar stirred and sat up, vacant eyes swiveling to face me. His feet slapped the cold stone as he advanced, sword raised. His movements lacked grace and his jaw hung slack.

It was evidence—if the hand hadn't provided enough—that I was dealing with a true necromancer, and I'm not ashamed to say I turned and ran out of there, calling for Apple Jack to meet me at the gate. The other Druid was on his feet outside and managed to trip me as I passed. Mud and turf rippled all around; the dead were rising from their graves. A heavy hand closed around my leg; I swung Fragarach behind me and the grip fell away. I scrambled for purchase in the mud and tore down the path toward the gate as fists erupted from the graves nearby.

<I told you we should have run, but no, you don't have any horse sense.>

Yes, well, you might find me more willing to listen from now on.

I had to decapitate one of the raised dead at the gate, but otherwise I had fled in time to avoid the crush of them. I looked back from the saddle as Apple Jack galloped away and saw that the milling creatures did not leave the fenced area around the graveyard. I blinked rain out of my eyes and when I refocused, the chapel was gone. It was as if it had never been there. I didn't know how I'd convince anyone it ever existed, for what would I say—"My horse saw it too"?

The rain stopped soon after I left the chapel. The waterlogged landscape abruptly turned into a dried-up wasteland of red rock and pale straw skeletons of plants. Trees like scarecrows scratched at a cloudless blue sky. I looked behind me and saw only more of the same; the verdant forested path had vanished like the chapel.

Which was the illusion? My kit was still damp and Apple Jack was thoroughly wet, so I chose to believe the desert was a lie.

It didn't feel that way after a few more hours on the trail, however, once I'd completely dried out and started to bake. A necromancer who was also able to either control weather or my perceptions like this was indeed a formidable opponent. But every step I took confirmed that he was precisely the type of opponent Druids were tasked to take down. He was doing serious damage to the environment here, not by polluting or mining or anything conventional, but through magic.

The wasteland went on for days. It would have killed anyone who wasn't traveling with a keg of water. I periodically bent down to the earth, asked it to part for me, and water welled up for Apple Jack and me to drink. Still, I tried to look thirsty when we rode into Sveinsey. The people there were getting their water from the River Tawe. The markets were unsurprisingly bare of fresh vegetables, though there were some wormy apples here and there. There was plenty of fish to be mongered, but as Dafydd had observed, it was a sailor's diet. Except that somewhere in the fortress they had Dagda's cauldron. The *graal*.

There was an upper limit to the number of people it could feed; at some point, there was only so much food that could be scooped from a magical container per day. But the Pict's plan was becoming clear: With a nearly impassable desert surrounding Sveinsey and no land nearby to pillage, an army was going to have a tough time getting here, and laying siege would do them no good when he could feed his people in the keep indefinitely with Dagda's cauldron.

The keep wasn't complete yet, but it was taking shape, and the walls of the fortress looked like they had been shored up and thickened. It sat upon the river's edge and there was no doubt a well inside that afforded them plenty of water.

Some judicious inquiries with a fishmonger here and an apothecary there revealed that the captain of the guard was looking for a few good knights to join the crew.

"You look like you can dish out a good fonging," the apothecary said as he measured out some herbs that I would use for purposes beyond his ken. He squinted at me sideways. "The pay is good and so is the food, I hear. The Fisher King is generous to his subjects, even though he be plagued by some terrible pestilence."

"The Fisher King?"

"Aye. Quite an upstanding chap as far as kings go. The bloody Pict on his elbow is a nightmare, but thank the tits of all the saints, he's not in charge."

"Where can I find the captain?"

"Inquire at the fortress first," he said, "but check the pubs along the docks if you don't find him there."

I checked along the docks first, primarily to give myself cover; I wanted the captain to think I arrived by sea rather than braved the wasteland. After picking a suitable ship—it was a busy port— I searched for a stable to house Apple Jack. If I'd come across to Sveinsey on ship, it would be unlikely for me to arrive on horseback.

In Apple Jack's assigned stall, I knelt down and touched the earth with my hand and made contact with the local elemental. It was understandably distraught at what had been happening in the area and relieved that a Druid had finally made it far enough to possibly address the problem. I asked for its help: I'd been think- ing of how I could access magic for a longer period of time when cut off from the earth. Could it charge up a stone or gem, perhaps, with enough magical energy that I could still craft a few bindings?

//Not stone// it said. //Metal / Silver or gold / Stores magic best//

//Gratitude// I replied. //Query: Craft silver storage talisman for me?//

//Affirmative / Contact with skin required//

After some additional back and forth, a rough silver cross pushed up from the earth into my hand, imbued with enough magic for several spells. Social camouflage again: If I cast any magic, it would be seen as a miracle performed by the Christian god. All I had to do was whip out the cross and give praise for my deliverance. I stowed it in a belt pouch for easy access.

Four men-at-arms challenged me at the gate to the Sveinsey fortress—the soon-to-be castle. The captain was in attendance, a middle-aged veteran with more salt than pepper in his beard. He saw me as a threat at first since my armor was better than his, but once I humbly begged leave to join the guard, follow his lead, and serve his lord, he relaxed somewhat.

"Why are you here?" he said.

"I came in on the last ship from the Frankish lands."

"Fine, but why sail to Sveinsey, boy?"

I never get tired of being called "boy" by men who are hundreds of years younger than I am.

"I heard about the Fisher King across the channel. Kind and generous and yet invincible."

"You heard about the Fisher King across the channel? Come with me. I think he would be very interested to hear the details."

He led me through the gates and into the fortress, past halls hanging with tapestries and maids keeping the stone swept.

"It's near time for the evening meal," the captain said. "I'm sure they can find a place for you at the table. Always enough food to go around, of course."

The great hall was a festival of tapestries and seven-branched candelabras. Long tables with simple benches were placed end-to-end on one side; the other side was curiously bare, and everyone sat facing the blank space, which I began to suspect would be the scene of some entertainment forthwith.

The middle table was furnished with high-backed chairs rather than benches, and there sat a pale man with heavy-lidded eyes dressed in luxurious furs. A huge golden cross dangled about his neck and a simple golden circlet rested on his head. He seemed uninterested in the food before him. To his left sat a couple of noblemen, and to his right sat a man who could be none other than the Pict. The entire right half of his face was covered in tattoos that undoubtedly served a magical function, just as mine did. Perhaps thirty silver bars pierced his face on the same side; he must have heard about silver's magical properties as well, so I could expect him to be fairly juiced. Still, I wasn't terribly worried. No one had attempted to take away my sword yet, and that gave me confidence—that, and my own silver store of magic.

The Pict wore greasy dark hair down to his shoulders and his beard had been shoved through silver circlets so that it fell like a dark stalactite down to his sternum. It was to him, not the presumed Fisher King, that I was led. Dagda's cauldron sat plainly before him; serving women were loading up plates as high as they could manage and walking them down the tables to serve guests. Since it was far more food than any one person could eat, a small pack of dogs waited behind them for the bonanza of leavings that would no doubt ensue. And yes, Oberon: there were sausages.

"Counselor," the captain said, addressing the Pict by what must be his title. "This knight has come from the Frankish kingdom, where he says he has heard of the Fisher King." The Pict looked up at me but the Fisher King did not stir at the mention of his name.

"Has he now?" The Pict's voice was mellifluous and light; I had rather expected something reminiscent of sulfur and bone shards. "And you are?" he asked me.

"Sir Gawain, at your service," I replied.

"Excellent. You can serve me by joining us for dinner. I would like to hear how you heard of the Fisher King in the land of the Franks." He turned to the nobleman to his right. "Lord Gwynedd, might you do me the great courtesy of making room for this knight?" A shuffle of chairs, an additional one produced for me, and I was seated within choking distance of the Pict who'd stolen Dagda's cauldron. Though I couldn't be absolutely certain that he was also the necromancer that had turned Wales into bloody bollocks, he certainly looked the part. The captain excused himself to return to his post.

A serving maid placed a heaping plate in front of me and said, "Counselor, dinner is served."

"Ah. Thank you. 'Tis your cue, my liege." The Fisher King roused himself from his stupor and said grace before everyone began to eat. Everyone said amen and then the Fisher King slumped back in his chair.

"Is the king not well?" I asked.

"His appetite is a bit off right now," the Pict said. "You may call me Domech," he added.

"Thank you," I replied.

"Tell me how you came to hear of the Fisher King," he said. I spun him a story of how I had heard of a land wasted but a castle in the middle of it saved by God because the Fisher King was so faithful.

"I wanted to serve such a man, and so I came here to offer my sword."

"A man of faith, are you?"

"Tremendous faith, sir. Let me show you this cross given to me by a lady I saved from the Saxons." I took the silver cross from my pouch and brandished it over my plate. "If you say a small prayer each evening it protects you from the very demons of hell." I spoke the words that would bind my vision to the magical spectrum. It was Old Irish, of course, and bloody Domech recognized it.

"That sounded like the speech of Druids," he said, frowning at me. "Are you a Druid, Sir Gawain?"

At this point I'm sure he expected a denial. I actually expected to issue one. Instead my left arm whipped up and I smashed him in the face with my studded leather bracer. The back of his head hit the chair, stunning him, and I pushed mine back to give myself room and stood. The assembled diners gasped in shock and some angry exclamations wafted my way. I gave Domech another punch in the mouth to prevent him from speaking a spell and then checked out the Fisher King in my magical sight.

He wasn't alive. That explained the loss of appetite. He had plenty of dark spells wrapped around him, however, some of them clearly bound with Domech, and other wisps of smoky malevolence that seemed to radiate in every direction until they disappeared at the walls. Domech was definitely a necromancer.

"Right," I said, pulling out Fragarach. There wasn't time to analyze the situation with a room full of armed nobles and guards who would shortly be after my head. I made sure the Fisher King lost his first, since he wasn't using it anyway. It was telling that he hadn't moved, even though his most trusted counselor had been whacked in the face—twice—in close proximity. I swung Fragarach through his neck and it tumbled onto the table; there was no blood. The shadowy spells around him dissipated.

Domech jerked as if I'd hit him again and the screaming began. I checked my rear to see if anyone approached from that quarter and found the nobles cowering in a satisfactory manner. The lesser folk and the maids tore at their hair in terror as they fled the hall. There were guards running my way, however, and I was quite clearly the bad guy from their point of view.

"No!" Domech cried, his eyes fixed on the head of the Fisher King. "He was chained to the land!"

No wonder the land had died out so quickly; Domech had bound it to a dead man. With the Fisher King gone, the land would be able to recover on its own—so long as the Pict didn't do it again.

Domech had more than earned the death sentence according to Druidic law; he'd been draining the life out of an elemental while cloaking his activities beneath a fog. There wasn't a Druid alive who wouldn't slay him for what he'd done, and I felt honored to get to him first. Unfortunately, he ducked under the swing of my sword and trapped my arm across my body before I could take a backswing. Magic swirled amongst the silver bars in his face and blood dripped from his ruined nose. His right hand grabbed me between the legs and then he lifted me bodily over his head, *throwing* me over the table into the clear space of the hall.

"Kill him!" he demanded, and pointed at me in case the guards hadn't figured out I was a public nuisance.

A slim wee man like him shouldn't have been able to pick me up and toss me. He was using the earth's energy in the same way a Druid would to boost his strength. Except he'd stolen all that energy, leeching it through the Fisher King.

The minions in leather boots weren't any trouble. Fishing out the silver cross, I used some of the stored magic in it to bind the leather on the insides of their calves together and they collapsed to the stone floor. Some landed less gracefully than others.

I couldn't do the same to Domech; he had fashioned some kind of ward against my bindings. He couldn't affect me directly with his magic either, since necromancers are incapable of affecting the living except through the dead. I used some of the juice to increase my speed and strength instead and charged him.

For all the power he had leeched, Domech was still at a disadvantage and he knew it. He wasn't armed or armored and there weren't any dead people in the hall he could use for his own ends. He did, however, have some big fucking chairs he could throw at me. I leapt over the first one but the second knocked me down. He was on top of me before I could regain my feet, his left hand pinning my sword arm to the floor while his right tried to grasp my throat. I prevented that by sweeping my left arm out, dropping the cross, and then I locked onto his neck—a rather skinny one—and began to squeeze with all I had. He could have grabbed me in turn, but instead he clawed at my arm and tried to break my grip. His damned nails ripped at my forearm and he bruised me, but he wasn't enough of a fighter to know anything about pressure points or how to break bones.

"That black hand of yours got two Druids this way in the chapel," I said through clenched teeth. "You know the one I mean, Domech? The wheel keeps turning, doesn't it?"

He couldn't answer me. I crushed his trachea and his hands fell slack as the strength left him. I rolled him off me and saw that there was still plenty of magic centered on his head. As a necromancer, he might have rigged his own resurrection, so I removed the Pict's head and tossed it into the hearth to burn. I didn't need my magical sight anymore, so I dispelled it.

More guards streamed into the hall, including the captain, alerted by the panicked dinner guests. The lads on the floor couldn't decide whether to plea for help or to urge their friends to get me. It was time to make my exit, so I picked up the silver cross and hurried to the nobles' table. Dogs had leapt on the tables to chow down since the humans had left all that perfectly good food there to cool. One of them was feeding directly from Dagda's cauldron and couldn't believe his good fortune. He snapped at my arm when I tried to take the cauldron but discovered that his teeth didn't fare well against chain mail.

"Go on, you're full," I said, and he allowed me to take the cauldron without any more fuss. I upended it to turn off the infinite refill and then camouflaged it, my kit, and myself with the remainder of the magic stored in my cross. I sheathed Fragarach as the dismayed shouts of the guards echoed in the hall. Carrying the cross in my left hand and the cauldron—or the Grail—in my right, I did my best to hurry past them with a minimum of noise.

It's tough to sneak around in armor, but they were helping me out by loudly asking each other where I went.

Once out in the unpaved courtyard where I had access to the earth, it was a simple matter to maintain my camouflage and slip past the guards at the gate. I retrieved Apple Jack from the stable where I'd left him and set off across the wasteland toward Gloucester. Weather patterns returned to normal and the elemental was showing the first signs of recovery with the necromancer truly dead. You'd never know today that the area around Swansea had been a desert for a few months.

I didn't see the Chapel Perilous, as it came to be known, on my way back. Most of the lads had cleared out of the Silver Stallion by the time of my second visit and I was able to get a room. There were only three people there, in fact—myself, the innkeeper, and one other—and it was with them that I shared the story of what happened, the quest for the magic *graal*. From there the story was told and retold through the centuries until poets like Chretien de Troyes finally started to write them down.

Ogma was waiting for me on the trail to Gloucester the next morning. I returned Dagda's cauldron to him and he thanked me. I told him about Domech and what he'd done, the dead Druids at the chapel, and he was grateful that I had dispatched the Pict as well.

"What would you have of me?" Ogma said. "I owe you some favor for what you've done."

"I'd like to stay out of Aenghus Óg's sight for a while, if you can manage it."

He gave me a hunk of cold iron and told me to wear it as a talisman. "It won't completely shield you from divination but it will make it more difficult to pinpoint your location. And I've recently linked a new part of the world to Tír na nÓg. Feel like learning a new language?"

I told him I did. After bidding farewell to Apple Jack, Ogma shifted me east of the Elbe River, where the Slavic people were emerging as a distinct culture. And that was how I, as Gawain, came to be immortalized in legend.

Granuaile dropped her eyes to the fire after I finished and said, "Wow."

<What kind of review is that? Specific praise is always better, so here is mine: I liked the bit where the dogs ate on the tables,> Oberon said.

Thanks, buddy.

My apprentice looked up from the fire. "Are necromancers common?"

"Quite rare, actually, outside of video games. Domech was one of the worst, but I was able to surprise him. If he'd had time to run the fight his way, I don't think I would have made it."

"That's where you got the idea for your cold iron amulet, isn't it?"

"Yes, that gave me the idea. The silver cross gave me the idea for the charms, and Apple Jack is the reason I have a talking hound today." I scratched Oberon behind the ears. "Ogma did me quite a favor by sending me on that trip."

<Did you get to try any of the food in Dagda's cauldron on the way back to the Silver Stallion?>

Of course I did.

<Well, was it tasty?>

Meat and potatoes in the most delicious gravy I've ever had, Oberon. I still dream about it.

<Oh, that's even better than the proverbial pig in the ground! I'm going to go to sleep now and see if I can dream about it too.>

Good night, Oberon.

<Good night.>

"That story actually made me a bit hungry," Granuaile said. "Anybody up for a snack?"

Oberon leapt to his feet, tail wagging. <I meant to say good night after the snack,> he explained.

I smiled at him. *Understood.*

MARK LAWRENCE

When Shawn invited me to drop a short story into his super-thology, I said yes immediately. I had quite a few short stories going spare.

When he asked if it could be a story based on my Broken Empire trilogy, a Jorg story, that gave me pause. I've always written short fiction as stand-alone. It allows more freedom. To write a short story that used established characters in an established world and yet that delivered something self-contained in a few thousand words and didn't require the reader to have first read *Prince of Thorns* . . . that was a significant challenge.

In the end I enjoyed the attempt!

Mark Lawrence

SELECT MODE

Mark Lawrence

They call me a monster and if it were untrue the weight of my crimes would pin me to the ground. I have maimed and I have murdered and if this mountain stood but a little higher I would cut the angels from their heaven. I care less for accusations than for the rain that soaks me, that runs down every limb. I spit both from my lips. Judgment has always left a sour taste.

"Keep moving!" And he strikes me across the shoulders. The staff is thick and polished from hard use. I imagine how he'll look when I make him eat it. Avery, they call him.

There are five left to guard us now, twenty when they found us on the Orlanth Road. A man like the Nuban doesn't give up easy but two against twenty are poor odds, especially when one of the two is a child. He surrendered before the Select had even drawn their horses up around us. It took me longer to reach the same decision, hampered by my pride.

"Pick it up!" The stick catches me behind the knee and I stumble, loose rocks scattering beneath my feet, rolling away down the steep path. Rope chafes at my wrists. We exchanged our weapons for rope, but at least those odds have narrowed. They set only five men to take us into the mountains for judgment. Two against five are the best odds I've had in a while.

The Nuban is ahead of me, huge shoulders hunched against the downpour. If his hands were unbound he could throttle four of them while I fed Avery his staff.

Back on the Orlanth Road the Nuban had shrugged off his crossbow and let it fall. Set his short sword on the ground, leaving only the knife in his boot against the chance of discovery.

"One black as the devil and the other's not thirteen!" Avery had called out when they surrounded us, horses stamping, tails flicking.

A second rider leaned from his saddle and slapped Avery, a cracking blow that set the white print of his hand on a red cheek.

"Who judges?" A thin man, gray, but hard-eyed.

"The arch, Selector John." Avery pushed the words past clenched teeth, his scowl on me as if it were my handprint on his face.

"The arch." And Selector John nodded, looking from one man to the next. "The arch judges. Not you, not I. The arch speaks for heaven." He rode between us. "And if the man, or this boy, are Select then they will be your brothers!"

And now the pair of us walk, soaked, freezing, beaten toward judgment on the mountain, wrists bound, and with Avery's staff to encourage us on and four more of the Select to see we don't stray from the path.

I choose each step, head down, rain dripping from the black veil of my hair. I wonder at this arch of theirs, puzzle how an arch could judge, and what it might say. Certainly its words have power. The power to bind Selector John's disparate band together and hold them to his command.

"If you are Select you will ride with me," he had said.

"If not?" the Nuban rumbled.

"You won't."

And that seemed to be all that underwrote the Select, feared across the north counties of Orlanth, famed for their loyalty and discipline. Men taken at random from the road and judged in secret, bound by nothing but the good word of some arch, some relic of the Builders no doubt, some incomprehensible toy that survived their war.

The water runs in rivulets between my boots, their frayed leather black with it.

"Hell—" Avery's cry turns into something inarticulate as his slip turns into a sprawl. Even his staff can't save him. He lies for a moment, embracing the mountainside, stunned. As he starts to rise I skip forward and let myself fall, letting the whole of my weight land behind my knee as it hits the back of his neck. The sound of bone breaking is almost lost in the rain. With bound hands pressed to his back I manage to stand before the others reach me. Avery does not stand, or move, or complain.

Rough hands haul me back, a blade at my throat, colder than the wind. John stands before me, a hint of shock in pale eyes unused to such expression.

"You murdered him!" he shouts, fingers on the hilt of his sword, closing on it, opening, closing.

"Who judges?" I shout back and a laugh rips its path from me.

I slept until my ninth year, deep in the dream that blinds us to the world. The thorns woke me. They gave me sharp new truths to savour. Held me as my little brother died, embraced me for the long slow time it took my uncle's men to kill my mother. I woke dark to the world, ready to give worse than I got.

"I will see this arch and listen to its pronouncement," I say. "Because if it speaks for heaven then I have words of my own to speak back."

Deep in the cloudbank lightning ricochets, making the thunderheads glow, a flat light edging the slopes for a heartbeat. The rain hammers down, pricked with ice, but I'm burning with the memory of those thorns and the fever they put in my blood. No absolution in this storm—the stain of sin is past water's touch. The wounds the thorns gave turned sour, beyond cleansing. But heaven's arch waits and suddenly I'm eager to let it speak of me.

The hand on John's sword spasms open. "Let's go." A curt nod, scattering water, and he strides off. I follow, impatient now, the slope seeming less steep. Only the Nuban spares a backward glance for Avery, still hugging the slope, and a second one for me, watchful and beyond reading. The glow of my small victory fades, and not for the first time it's the Nuban's silence rather than his words that make me want to be better than I am.

Another of the Select takes up the rear guard. Greb they call him. "Watch your footing," I say. "It gets slippery."

We crest the lip of a valley and descend into shadows where the wind subsides from howls to complaint. The light is failing but where the trail snakes down the slope I can see something is wrong. I stop and Greb stumbles into me, cursing.

"There's something wrong with the rain." I stare at it. Across a wide swath the rain seems to fall too slowly, the drops queuing to reach the ground and making a grey veil of falling water.

"Slow-time." John says, not turning or raising his voice.

Greb kicks my calf and I carry on. I've heard of slow-time. Tatters of it wreath the Arcada mountains, remnants from when the Builders broke the world. We discovered the same thing, the Builders and me; if something shatters your world then afterward you find the rules have changed. They had the Day of a Thousand Suns. I had the thorns.

I follow the Nuban into the slow-time, a band of it two or three yards wide. From the outside the rain within seems to fall at its leisure. Passing into the region all that changes is that now *only* where I'm walking are things right. Ahead and behind the rain powers down as if each drop were shot from a ballista and would punch holes in armour. And we're through. Greb's still wading through it behind me, moving like a street-mummer, slower than slow, until he's free and starts to speed up. The slow-time sticks to him, reluctant to release its prisoner, as if for ten yards it's still clinging to his skin before finally he's walking at our pace once more.

We advance and a shoulder of rock reveals the strangest sight. It's as if a bubble of glass, so clear as to be invisible, has been intersected by the mountainside. Rain streams off it, turned from its path by unseen currents. At the heart of the half-sphere, close to the ground, a wild blue light entices, part diamond, part promise. And all about it statues stand.

"Idiots." John waves an arm at them as we pass. "I can understand the first one being trapped, but the other seven?"

We're close enough to see they're not statues now. Eight travellers, the closest to the light dressed in fashions seen only in dusty oil paintings on castle walls. Flies in amber, moths drawn to the light of the fire in which we burn. What world will be waiting for them when they think to turn around and walk back out?

"Do all time-bubbles have a handy warning light at the centre?" I wonder it aloud but no one answers.

I glance back at them once before the distance takes them. All of them held there like memories while the days and months flicker past outside. I have time-bubbles in my head, places I return to over and again.

When I killed my first man and left the Healing Hall in flames, sick with poison from the wounds the hook-briar gave, it was Father Gomst who found me. Memory takes me to that tower-top where I leaned out, watching the flames spiral and the lanterns moving far below as Father's guards hunted me. We stand on that tower, trapped in those minutes, we two, and often I pass by, pausing to study it once more and learning nothing.

Father Gomst raises both hands. "You don't need the knife, Jorg."

"I think I do." The blade trembles in my grip, not from fear but from what the fever puts in me. A sense of something rushing toward me, something thrilling, terrible, sudden . . . my body vibrating with anticipation. "How else would I cut?"

"Give it to me." He doesn't reach for the knife. Around his neck a gold cross, and a Builder talisman, a fone, the ancient plasteek fractured, part melted, chased with silver like the church icons. He says God hears him through it, but I sense no connection.

"The thorns wouldn't let me go," I tell him. Sir Jan had thrown me into the middle of the briar. The man had slabs of muscle, enough to tear the carriage door off and throw me clear before my uncle's soldiers caught us. A strong man can throw a child of nine quite a way.

"I know." Father Gomst wipes the rain from his face, drawing his hand from forehead to chin. "A hook-briar can hold a grown man, Jorg." If he could truly speak to God he would know the judgment on me and waste no more words.

"I would have saved them." The thorns hid me in their midst, held me. I had seen little William die, three flashes of lightning giving me the scene in frozen moments. "I would have saved them." But the lie tastes rotten on my tongue. Would anything have held William from me? Would anything have held my mother back. Anything? All bonds can be slipped, all thorns torn free. It's simply a matter of pain, and of what you're prepared to lose.

Greb jabs me and I'm back on the mountain. The stink of him reaches me even through the rain. "Keep moving." It's as if he didn't even see me kill Avery for the same damn thing. Judgment . . . I'm ready for it.

———————

"Here." John raises his hand and we all stop. At first I don't see the arch, and then I do. A doorway rather than an arch, narrow and framed by the silver-steel of the Builders. It stands on a platform of Builder-stone, a poured surface still visible beneath the scatter of rocks. Twenty yards beyond is a pile of bones, an audience of skulls, some fresh, some mouldering, all cleaned of flesh by the dutiful ravens. "What happens if we're not Select?" Dead men's grins answer the Nuban's question.

John draws his sword, an old blade, notched, the iron stained. He goes to stand beyond the arch. The other three men take position around it, and Greb, who took over Avery's position as Jorg-poker, pulls his knife. "You, big man. You're first."

"When you pass through stand still and wait for the judgment.

326

Move and I will kill you, without the mercy of the ritual." John mimes the killing thrust.

The Nuban looks around at the faces of the Select, blinking away raindrops. He's thinking of the fight, wondering where his chance will come. He turns to me, making a single fist of his bound hands. "We have lived, Jorg. I'm glad we met." His voice deep and without waver. He walks to the arch of judgment. His shoulders almost brush the steel on either side.

"Fail—" The arch speaks with a voice that is neither male or female, nor even human.

"Move aside." John gestures with his blade, contempt on his face. He knows the Nuban is waiting his chance, and gives him none. "You next." The Nuban is secured by two Select.

I step forward, watching the reflections slide across the Builder-steel as I approach. I wonder what crimes stained the Nuban. Though he is the best of us you cannot live on the road and remain innocent, no matter the circumstance that put you there. With each step I feel the thorns tearing at me. They can't hold me. But they held me on that night the world changed.

"Judge me." And I step through. Ice runs down my spine, a cold fire in every vein. Outside the world pauses, the rain halts in its plunge for an instant, or an age. I can't tell which. Motion returns almost imperceptibly, the drops starting to crawl earthward once more.

"Faaaaaiiiiilllllllu—" The word stretches out for an age, deeper than the Nuban's rumble. And at the end it's snatched away as if a knife sliced the throat it came from.

I believe in the arch. I deserved to fail, because I am guilty.

Even so.

"Join your friend." John waves his sword toward the Nuban. His voice is wrong, a touch too deep.

"The rain is too slow," I say. The quick-time is fading from me but still the arch's effects linger. I step back through the arch. God made me quick in any event, God or the Devil, and the Builders made me quicker. This time the arch had no comment, but before the Select can close on me I step through once more.

Again the cold shock of transition. I ignore the arch's judgment and dive forward, wrapped in quick-time, trailing it with me. John hardly flinches as I sever the ropes around my wrists on the sword he is so kind as to hold steady for me.

"Sssssseeeeeellllect m—" While the arch speaks I take John's knife from his belt and cut him a new smile. And before the blood comes I'm off, sprinting toward the Nuban. I'm still quick, but less so as I reach him and stab the first of his guards through the eye. I twist the blade as I pull it free, grating over the socket. The Nuban breaks the second man's face with the back of his head.

I chase Greb down. He runs although he has the bigger knife, and he thinks I'm as old as thirteen. My arm aches to stick John's blade into the man, to sink it between his shoulders and hear him howl. But he sprints off a drop in the half-light before I reach him. I stop at the top and look down to where he sprawls at broken angles.

Returning to the arch, I take slow steps. The rain comes in flurries now, weakening. The cold is in me at last, my hands numb. The Nuban is sat upon a rock by the bone pile, checking his crossbow for damage. He looks up as I draw near. It's his judgment that matters to me, his approval.

"We failed." He nods toward the arch. "Maybe the Builders have been watching us. Wanting us to do better."

"I don't care what they think of me," I say.

His brow lifts a fraction, half puzzled, half understanding. He puts the crossbow across his knees. "I'm as broken a thing as my gods ever made, Jorg. We keep bad company on the road. Any man would look good against them." He shakes his head. "Better to listen to the arch than me! And better to listen to neither of us." He slaps a hand to his chest. "Judge yourself boy." He looks back to his work. And more quiet, "Forgive yourself."

I walk back to the arch, stepping around the corpses of the Select. I wonder at the ties that bound them, the bonds forged by the arch's judgments. Those bonds seem more pure, more reasoned that the arbitrary brotherhood of the road that binds me to my own band of rogues, links forged and broken by circumstance. A yard from the arch I can see my reflection warped across the Builder-steel. The arch called "fail" for me, condemned me to the bone pile, and yet seconds later I was Select. Did I validate myself in the moments between?

"Opinions are well and good," I tell it. I have a rock in my hands, near as heavy as I can lift. "Sometimes it's better not to speak them." I throw the rock hard as I can and it slams into the cross support, breaking into jagged pieces.

I set a hand to the scar left on the metal.

"*FAIL*ure to connect," the arch says.

And in the end the arch has the right of it.

DAVID ANTHONY DURHAM

My daughter, Maya, has loved and lost many cats. There was Boyboy, who went out one rainy Massachusetts night and never came back. In all likelihood, his was a grisly demise. Girly died of a heart attack at a vet's office in Colorado Springs. A couple years later, the suave and debonair Dolphino felt called by the wild and disappeared into it. And then Melio, that scrappy street kitten from Fresno . . . let's just say that Melio went to Maine. That's no place for a Californian. We now have two very alive cats, Percy and Mungo. We're doing our best to keep them that way.

Maya had a bond with each of these lost pets. I will never forget the wail of grief when she heard of Girly's death, or the glazed look in her eyes that lasted for weeks after Dolphino disappeared. They're sad memories, but they're ones that will forever be part of the childhood she's now growing out of fast.

Shawn Speakman asking me to contribute a story to his anthology coincided with the run-up to Maya's thirteenth birthday. Prompted by him, I came up with a story that in many ways is for my daughter. I gave it to her on her birthday, a handmade version that I bound myself. And then I offered it to Shawn as well. Kind guy that he is, he accepted it.

Expect no mad sorcerers, warrior princesses, or fantastical monsters in this story. This one is about a ghost cat named Michael Stein. He's a clever cat, one that doesn't let his unfortunate death stop him from giving an amazing gift to the girl he loves.

David Anthony Durham

ALL THE GIRLS LOVE MICHAEL STEIN

David Anthony Durham

"I don't know how much more of this I can take," Michael Stein said.

"Indeed," Pax sighed. "It breaks my heart. She just has to get through it, though. They always do, eventually."

"But look at her!" Michael Stein said. "She's . . ." He couldn't think of the word. "She's . . ."

"Inconsolable?" Pax offered.

The *her* was Lucy, and she did indeed look inconsolable.

She lay on her bed, crying. It had been three days since the incident, but she hadn't gotten any better. Her parents tried to soothe her. They let her miss the last few days of middle school, saying the summer would just have to begin early. They even proposed getting a new kitten.

Michael Stein had been a bit put out by that, but he had nothing to worry about. Lucy wouldn't hear of it. The very suggestion ripped a sob of grief out of her. She refused to leave her room. She refused to take her friend's phone calls. She wouldn't read any of her detective books. She wouldn't even look at the shelves with the cat books, of which she had quite a collection. Usually, she spent hours each evening drawing feline forms in all their glory. Not anymore.

Looking up at her from the floor, Michael Stein said, "I've tried everything."

He really had. Michael Stein had pulled out his full arsenal of techniques to cheer Lucy up. He had whipped himself back and forth across her ankles when she stood. He climbed on to the bed with her and kneaded the stuffed penguin she was attached to for some reason he couldn't fathom. He curled up beside her and suckled on the edge of her old blanket. He even brushed his head on her chin and fired up the rumble of his full-on purr. Normally, that fixed just about any problem she had—even problems with boys.

"You're having a classic grief reaction," Pax said, licking his forearm. "You'll get through it. You'll be all the wiser for it. Like me."

Michael Stein wished that Pax would quit with the old and wise act. He was annoying. But he was also right. Michael Stein couldn't fix this. Even during the best days of his life, he had only been a medium-size tabby cat. Now . . . well, now he was a dead medium-size tabby cat. A ghost of his former self.

Before he died, Michael Stein had lots of opinions about the dead cats he'd met. He'd spoken to plenty of them. All cats did. They see things that humans don't, including the ghosts of departed cats. Michael Stein had found the sulky way they moped through their human's homes kinda pathetic. They could go anywhere! Do anything! They weren't bound to their humans. They didn't need to coax food out of them or rely on them to change the litter. All of those physical needs were gone. Instead, they lingered on as pure vaporous energy. Considering that, why did they all stick around the same houses, watching the same lives of the people they'd lived with before they died?

He used to argue about this with Pax, who was the ghost of an old cat that had belonged to Lucy's mother when she was girl. He'd died like thirty years ago! But the old geezer was still hanging around. He seemed to think the afterlife should consist of nothing more than lying curled in a ball at Lucy's mother's feet. The woman didn't even know he was there! What was the use of that?

Michael Stein had been sure that when he died he'd get up to all sorts of adventures. Once he was freed of any dependence on his humans he'd just take off. See ya. Been nice. Thanks for the catnip. He'd explore the world.

But that was before he died. Now, he wasn't so sure. A few days in the afterlife, and Michael Stein was starting to think he had misjudged the virtues of being dead.

The whole ghost body thing wasn't as much fun as he'd expected. He didn't have to worry about getting hurt or killed anymore, but he couldn't feel or smell or touch the world the way he used to. The things he thought he'd so enjoy about being dead just didn't live up to his expectations.

He'd always wanted to go right out onto the tiniest little tree branches in pursuit of the chickadees that seemed to think the entire garden belonged to them. When he was dead, he figured, he'd be light as a feather and could go anywhere they did. That was true. Problem was that when he got out on really thin branches his body would sink through them. He'd gotten right up beside a bird once, only to watch in frustration as the branch slipped through his body and he floated down to land in the bird pond.

Worse still, he couldn't actually touch the birds. He'd stalked a few his day first as a ghost. It was great right up until that last moment when his vaporous form crashed down upon the unsuspecting birds without having the slightest impact. Sometimes, when he'd really splattered them good, the bird might feel just enough to get a little nervous and fly away. It was terribly unsatisfying.

More importantly, there was Lucy and all of her crying. If he could step back in time and change things, he would. He wouldn't sneak out that fateful night. He wouldn't focus all of his attention on that rabbit den. He'd have kept his wits about him, and the beast—he was never sure what exactly it was—wouldn't have pounced on him. One moment he was about to sink his claws into a juicy rabbit. The next, something had caught him in its jaws. End of story.

He was philosophical about it. Every cat had to go at some time. His time had just come. At least it happened so fast he didn't feel any pain. And he had died a hunter's death. *Live by the claw, die by the jaw*, he'd always said.

Still, it seemed very, very important that Lucy not be so sad. He'd always liked her, even if he never took her declarations of love for him too seriously. She had called him the "best cat ever" hundreds of times. He'd thought nothing of it. Now he realized just how much he'd meant to her, and how much she meant to him.

The situation was insufferable. Michael Stein decided to do something about it.

"You're going to do what?" Pax asked. He lifted his head from its resting place on Lucy's mother's foot. She was sorting through bills on the kitchen table, completely oblivious to the ghost cat's affections.

"I'm going to see the Catfather," Michael Stein said. "Lots of cats do it. That's what he's there for—to hear our grievances and help us out."

"You won't find it's as easy as that. Catfathers are movers and shakers when they're alive, but . . . You do understand that you can't go to a living catfather, don't you?"

Michael Stein hadn't thought of that. "You sure?"

"Trust me, I've been dead a lot longer than you. You're not part of their constituency anymore. It's a catfather ghost for you. And those . . ." Pax lifted one of his white paws, licked it, and ran the paw over one of his black ears. He couldn't actually touch it, but old habits were hard to break. "They're really rather useless."

Michael Stein doubted that. He had an idea about what he was going to ask the Catfather for. He almost said it, but he didn't want Pax to laugh at it. Instead, he just said, "Still, I'm going to try."

Pax shrugged. "Suit yourself, but what you *should* do is accept the way things are. Act like the rest of us do."

"You mean sit around on your human's feet?"

"You always have to have the last word, don't you?"

Michael Stein didn't think that was fair. He also couldn't help but have the last word. "Lounging around invisibly doesn't do anybody any good."

"You'd be surprised," Pax said, with an air of import that annoyed Michael Stein.

Before Michael Stein could try again to have the last word, Lucy's father trod down the stairs, having just come from Lucy's room.

"She any better?" Lucy's mother asked.

"Not really. She cried herself to sleep. She's going to have puffy eyes in the morning." Sighing, he added, "She really loved that cat."

Lucy's mother looked up from her bills and stared wistfully out the open window. She said, "All the girls loved Michael Stein."

"Good grief!" Lucy's father said. "If I'd known it would be this bad I wouldn't have agreed to keep him in the first place."

"With Michael Stein, it's better to have known love and lost it than to never have loved at all," Lucy's mother said. "I was miserable when my old cat, Pax, died, but that was only because I loved him. I still do. Sometimes I think of him and it almost feels like he's in the room with me. You know that feeling?"

Lucy's father said, "Nope. I can't say that I do." He grabbed the trash bag from the bin and stomped outside with it.

Pax purred and looked pleased with himself. "See? Didn't I tell you? Why don't you just curl up beside Lucy and do what you can to comfort her?"

"That might be fine for other cats," Michael Stein said, "but I say there can be more to death than that."

The Catfather's headquarters was in the same backyard that it had been in when the Catfather had still been alive. Michael Stein had never called on him before, but he'd known where he lived. Every cat knew that. He was surprised at how many cats were already there when he arrived. Seemed like half the town had crammed into the yard, between the lawn furniture and the shed and all around the raised garden beds. All of them had problems they were hoping the Catfather could solve for them.

When he gave his name at the back gate, the Catfather's secretary looked up from his notepad, one eyebrow cocked. "What kind of name is Michael Stein? For a cat, I mean."

"Oh," Michael Stein said awkwardly, "I don't know. I was only a kitten when my humans chose it."

The secretary raised his other eyebrow.

Truth is, Michael Stein knew exactly where his name came from. Humans thought it was a pretty strange name for a cat too. Lucy's mother had to tell the story of how she came up with it on more than one occasion.

Michael Stein was a guy Lucy's mom had a crush on in high school. He was half-Filipino and half-Jewish. "A crazy mix," Lucy's mom had said, "but the result was dreamy." She claimed that all the girls at school had a thing for him. Because of all the attention he got, Lucy's mother only admired him from afar. In her junior year science class she got paired with him for a series of projects. They worked well together, but she didn't let on for a minute about how she felt. And that was that. Unrequited love. Life moves on.

Or so she'd thought until the night of her twentieth high school reunion. Michael Stein was there, looking as dreamy as ever. He ran a successful software design firm with offices in Boston and Munich. He was married with three kids, a dog, two cats. He liked foreign films, ran 10k marathons, and had hand built a wood-fired pizza oven in his backyard. He drove a Prius. He was everything Lucy's mother had dreamed he'd become.

Much to her surprise, he confessed to having had a crush on *her* in high school. He'd never said anything because she'd seemed so indifferent to him. Leaving the reunion, Lucy's mother cursed her younger self as a fool.

About a week after that two things happened on one fateful day. One, Lucy's mother had a fight with Lucy's father, and two, she found a kitten. Mad at her husband, she brought the kitten home for Lucy, announcing that his name was Michael Stein, the one that got away. And that was that. Michael Stein had always felt a little weird about it. When Lucy's mother called him in at night, he was never sure if she was calling for him, or for her long lost high school love.

"Michael Stein! Where are you, Michael Stein . . ."

So that was the story. It all seemed like too much personal information to give the secretary. Michael Stein tried, "Humans . . . What's a cat to do?"

This seemed to sit well with the secretary. He let both eyebrows drop and motioned in the air with his paw—the cat equivalent of saying *Amen, brother!* He said, "Humans are mad. That's true enough. So what do you want to see the Catfather about?"

One awkward question right to another.

"It's policy," the secretary said. "I have to screen out the nuts."

Michael Stein had the sudden fear that maybe that would include him. He didn't see any choice, though, so he revealed the situation that brought him here.

The secretary didn't look moved. "Sorry, but there's nothing—"

Michael Stein didn't want to hear the end of that sentence. He blurted out, "If the Catfather would just give her *the gift*, everything would be all right!" It was a lot to ask, he knew, but the Catfather had the power to do it—the power to allow Lucy to see cat ghosts.

"That's what you're going to ask him to do?" the secretary said. "Give a girl *the gift*? In the whole history of the human/cat relationship, only a handful of humans have ever been given *the gift*. Ghandi had it. That whole nonviolent resistance thing? A cat idea. Eleanor Roosevelt had it, too. Talked her husband through the Great Depression with a cat ghost council. Bet you didn't know that." The secretary squinted.

No, Michael Stein hadn't known that. "So humans having *the gift* is a good thing, right?"

"It can be, but Napoleon had it too. Conquered most of Europe before a double agent ghost cat convinced him that invading Russia in the winter was a good idea."

"There are ghost cat spies?"

"Don't say you heard it from me," the secretary said. "Anyway, your Lucy's circumstances don't merit this sort of intervention. It needs to be for the greater good, not just to get a girl to stop crying. And you don't want to waste the Catfather's time. If you annoy him you could get banished from his district."

"Banished from his district?"

"You know what that would mean, don't you?"

Michael Stein did. If he got banished from the district he wouldn't get to stay with Lucy anymore.

"So what are you here for?" the ghost cat ahead of Michael Stein asked. She was a ginger kitten with large, expressive eyes.

Michael Stein looked through the kitten at the queue of cats strung out along the cement path up toward the back porch, where the Catfather held court. He was trying to work out the speech he was going to deliver. It had to be a good one, something that would set him and Lucy apart from whatever the other cats were asking for.

The kitten blinked and waited.

"It's personal," Michael Stein said.

The ginger kitten didn't take offence. She also didn't take the hint. "I'm here about Fiona. She's the kitten that lives in the apartment I used to live in. Her humans are going to get her declawed."

Michael Stein hissed.

"It's a crime against nature, right?" the kitten asked. "They tried to do it to me. I scratched them up and jumped out the window. That was a mistake. Our apartment is on the seventh floor. It's why I'm like this now." She waved a paw, indicating her translucent body. "They got a new kitten and I heard them talking about taking her to the vet for the procedure. That's what they call it. The procedure. Fiona doesn't believe me. She's too innocent. Can't even conceive of being clawless."

Michael Stein had a hard time conceiving of it himself. Nothing could be worse for a cat.

"I tried to get her out of there," the ginger kitten said, "but they keep her locked up in the apartment. No easy way in or out."

"What do you think the Catfather can do about it?" Michael Stein asked.

"I don't know. He couldn't do anything last time, but he said to come back."

"You've spoken to him already?"

"Yep. Fifteen times."

Michael Stein felt his hopes take a dive. "You've been here fifteen times, but he hasn't helped yet?"

"Not yet."

A voice behind them said, "He hasn't helped any cat, really. Not since he died." The speaker was a dark gray longhair. "I knew the Catfather when he was alive. He was a serious dude. Cats listened to him. He got things done. That all changed when he died. He's pretty depressed, really."

"None of us have figured this afterlife stuff out," the flame-tipped Siamese in line behind the longhair said. "We're all return customers. This your first visit?"

Michael Stein nodded.

"Wow," the Siamese said, "a first-timer. Sorry, kid. Get used to disappointment."

By the time his turn to address the Catfather came, Michael Stein had heard more hard-luck stories than he cared to remember. Everyone had their own tale, and Michael Stein couldn't claim that Lucy's happiness mattered more than all the others. His paws trembled with nervousness as he realized he wasn't at all sure what he was about to say.

"This one calls himself Michael Stein," the secretary said, checking his clipboard. "Wait until you hear what he wants from you. Crazy kid."

"Michael Stein," a low, deep voice said, "my secretary says you're a bit mad. I do hope that's not the case."

The Catfather. In life he'd been a mythic cat. Not only was he a

341

bulky Maine Coon, one of the largest breeds of domestic cats. Even more, he'd been born with six toes on each of his front paws. He was famed as a hunter. Mice, rabbits, rats, squirrels: you name it; he'd caught it. He used to stalk the deer that came onto the high school fields at night. In his youth, he'd fought epic battles with other powerful cats. Even the local dogs granted him a grudging respect after a story went around town that he'd chased a Doberman up a tree. Michael Stein found that hard to believe. But, regardless of the exact facts, the Catfather had certainly been impressive.

He still was. He reclined in his basket. One enormous paw draped over the rim, claws just slightly visible. Even though they couldn't do damage anymore, those claws made Michael Stein nervous. The Catfather stared at Michael Stein through his one good eye. The other eye was milky white, a battle wound.

"What brings you before me today?" he asked.

Michael Stein realized he'd been staring open-mouthed. He had to do better than that. He was Michael Stein, after all, and he was doing this for Lucy. He said something he hadn't expected to. "Catfather, most impressive of cats, I come to you with a humble proposal."

"Is that so?" the Catfather asked. "I thought you were going to ask for something."

"Well, yes . . . but I'm also offering something!" Michael Stein hadn't known he was going to say that, but once he did he knew what he was going to propose. To make it work, though, he had to spell out a few things first.

Pacing in a slow circle, Michael Stein tried to sound confident, an older cat than his years. "I haven't been dead a long time," he said, "but I've learned some things already. For one, it's not fun being dead."

"Tell me something I don't know," the Catfather said, crossing his paws.

"But the reason it's not fun is different than I thought at first. The sad thing isn't not having a body and claws and teeth. I mean, that's a bummer, but that stuff just doesn't matter quite the same way anymore. Something else matters."

"Yeah, and what's that?"

"The living people we care about. Living humans. Living cats. Everyone that comes here asks for something for somebody else. Somebody living." Michael Stein pointed at the ginger kitten. "You came because of a kitten you're worried is going to get declawed. You're not here about what happened to you. That's history. You came here because life goes on, and it's filled with dangers for the ones you still care about. And you . . ." He found the long-haired cat. "You're here because the nurse looking after your old human isn't taking care of her properly."

The longhair looked positively dejected. "It's a tragedy."

"Of course it is," Michael Stein said. "And you're tired of seeing your human boy get picked on by bullies."

The Siamese cat agreed. "They take his lunch money everyday, but he never complains. He's a brave little trooper."

"So, what I'm saying is that the gift of death is also the tragedy of it. The gift is that we come to care about others more than we ever used to. The tragedy is that we can't do anything to help them. We're powerless to do anything but just linger, watching."

"You're depressing me, kid," the Catfather said.

Michael Stein turned back to him. He knew now just what he was going to propose. It all made sense. He said, with great gravity, "Yes, but what if it didn't have to be that way? What if there was a way to solve all our problems?"

"See," Michael Stein said, "look at all those detective books."

He and the Catfather stood side by side, having just walked through the wall into Lucy's room.

The Catfather let his good eye roam over the shelves. "She's read all of those?"

"Each and every one. She knows all about sorting out problems and solving crimes. And she's read those too." He pointed a paw at another shelf. "Those are all books about cats."

"All about cats, huh?" The Catfather sounded impressed.

"And the cat drawings and posters," Michael Stein prompted.

343

"Yeah, I see them." It would've been hard for the Catfather not to see them, plastered over every inch of the walls like they were. He hopped up on to Lucy's bed and walked up the sleeping girl's side. After studying her face, he concluded, "Puffy eyes."

"From crying." Michael Stein sat on his haunches. "So, it's like I said, Lucy knows two things—cats and detective stuff. What more could you ask for?"

The Catfather nodded grudgingly. "You sure it won't make her crazy? Most humans wouldn't want to have their minds blown this way. Remember, it's irreversible. It will be with her for life. *The gift* could be too much for her."

"Lucy is the sanest human I know. If you do this for her you won't regret it."

"I better not," the Catfather said. "You're sure she'll keep her part of the bargain?"

"Absolutely," Michael Stein said, looking at Lucy's sleeping face. "I'm sure of it."

"If this doesn't go the way you claim it's gonna . . ."

"It will," Michael Stein said. "You've got my word on it."

"The word of a dead cat?" the Catfather asked.

Michael Stein smiled. "There's nothing more sacred."

After the Catfather left, Michael Stein curled up beside Lucy and waited through the dark hours of the night. The Catfather hadn't done much. He just placed a kiss on each of Lucy's puffy eyelids and mumbled some words that Michael Stein hadn't quite heard. And that was it. Would it really be enough?

Michael Stein tried to be patient, but the waiting got to be too much for him. "Lucy," he said. "Hey, Lucy, can you hear me?"

Lucy's eyes opened. She blinked and sat up. She stared at Michael Stein for a long moment, looking confused. She brought her fists to her eyes and rubbed them, and then looked at him again. "Michael Stein?"

She looked surprised, amazed even, but she didn't look like

she was at risk of losing her mind. Michael Stein decided it was safe to take things a step further. "The one and only," he said.

"You can talk! You sound just like I thought you would." Lucy lunged forward and flung her arms around him. She couldn't embrace him like in the old days, but since she could see him it was different than before. Her arms cradled him as they had in life. He did his best to fit perfectly within them. "You're the ghost of Michael Stein," she said.

He fired up his purr.

Lucy inhaled a surprised breath, and Michael Stein knew that she could hear him purr. That made him very happy.

"I know this just a dream," Lucy said. "I love it anyway. I don't want to wake up."

"It's no dream, Lucy," Michael Stein said.

She drew back and stared at him, and he told her the whole story.

Well, almost the whole story . . .

"There's one catch," Michael Stein said when he couldn't avoid the topic any longer.

Lucy frowned. "What's that?"

"I should probably show you. Let's go outside."

The porch and the porch steps and the sidewalk all the way down the street were filled with ghost cats. Big ones. Little ones. Gingers and tabbies. Black cats and Siamese and longhairs and mixes of every variety. Even one Egyptian hairless. And a one-eyed Maine Coon, who looked both distinguished and grave.

"Do you see them?" Michael Stein asked.

"Do I ever! Are they all . . . well, I mean . . . are they all like you?"

"Yes," Michael Stein said, "they're all ghosts. But for cats, being dead doesn't mean we end or go anyplace or anything like that. We stick around near the ones we love." He felt a little guilty for ever thinking that he *wouldn't* stick around, but Lucy didn't need to know that. He didn't want her to ever think he wanted to leave. He didn't even feel like the same cat anymore. "And that's the thing . . ."

Lucy looked like she wanted to rush out into the throng of cats, but she held back. "What's the thing?"

"The problem is that we ghost cats can't help the living. Humans don't even know we're around. Living cats know about us, but they don't exactly listen." Michael Stein realized he was talking about himself just a week ago, but he kept going. "So, in return for allowing you to see me, I said that you would hear ghost cats' problems and help them. Sometimes a crime has been done. Sometimes one is going to be done. Sometimes it's just an injustice that needs a living human to deal with it." Michael Stein swallowed. "I said that you would be that person."

"You mean . . ." Lucy said, "that I'm a detective for dead cats?"

"You could think of that way, I guess."

"Awesome!" Lucy whispered. "This is like the best job imaginable! And I've got all summer . . ."

She stepped through the door and fell right into conversation with the ginger kitten. Michael Stein felt a great deal of relief, though he also knew that he had changed more than just what she was going to do with the summer. *The gift* would be with her for life. He'd have to talk about that with her sometime. But today he was just pleased to have her back.

Lucy turned around and mouthed the words, "I love you, Michael Stein."

Michael Stein couldn't help it. He started to purr. He realized that his relationship with Lucy hadn't ended with his death. Instead, it was just beginning.

A voice beside him startled him. It was Pax. He had a way of sneaking up, all silent like. "So," he said, "I reckon this means you'll be staying around. Told ya."

For once, Michael Stein didn't try to have the last word.

JENNIFER BOSWORTH

I HAVE A SOFT SPOT FOR MINIONS. LACKEYS. HENCHMEN. THE sycophantic underlings who make a good villain great. Who would the Joker be without his flunkies? Hans Gruber without his crack team of gun-toting criminals? Sauron without his Uruk-hai?

And, in my debut novel, *Struck*, the villain, Rance Ridley Prophet, would have been a lost and lonely soul without his twelve adopted Apostles, particularly the twins, Iris and Ivan.

In recent years, we've gotten to delve into the origin stories of some of pop culture's favorite villains. Darth Vadar. Magneto. And now Norman Bates and Hannibal Lecter. But we rarely get to go behind the scenes with their trusty minions.

For this reason, I decided to more closely examine the origins of Iris and Ivan, fiercely loyal followers of Rance Ridley Prophet. Who were they before Rance adopted them? What was it about their lives, their experience, that primed them to become his true believers?

And, most importantly, what is in the heart of a minion?

Jennifer Bosworth

STRANGE RAIN

Jennifer Bosworth

Iris knew her mother didn't love her, had maybe never loved her, not the way a mother is supposed to. There was something broken in Anita Banik. Maybe it happened when Iris's father left Anita for another woman (or several) while she was hugely pregnant with twins, her stomach extruded three feet in front of her, the skin stretched taut as a balloon about to pop. Or maybe it had more to do with the complicated birth that nearly killed Anita, and had ravaged her body so that she could never have another child. Not that she seemed to want the ones she already had.

Iris and her identical twin, Ivan, had once been more than identical. They had been joined, literally, at the hip, and down the thigh as well. Conjoined twins, separated at birth. They were a cliché, but Iris didn't care. She loved looking at the pictures of her and Ivan as newborns, before the surgery that sliced their fused flesh and removed them from one another. Iris had asked Ivan once if he ever wished the doctors had left them how they were. Nature had intended them to enter the world as one body. Maybe that's how they should have remained.

Ivan had thought she was kidding. He laughed and said sarcastically, "Oh, yeah, that would have been great. Life would be one never-ending three-legged race."

Iris laughed along with her twin, and then excused herself to go to the bathroom so she could wipe at her eyes before Ivan noticed she was crying. With the door locked, she unzipped her pants, pulled them down, and examined the soft, pebbly scar that stretched from her hip to the top of her knee. Sometimes she imagined she still felt Ivan attached to her, a phantom limb amputated against her will.

When Ivan laughed off her question as too ridiculous to be considered, Iris should have taken it as a sign of things to come. She should have been prepared for the day when her twin would tire of her company and need . . . more.

Iris knew her mother didn't love her, would probably never love her. But she expected her brother to love her forever. Her, and only her.

Ivan made his pronouncement the spring before they were to start high school. They were fifteen, but Ivan was already six foot two, and Iris was hot on his heels at five foot eleven. With their pale skin and colorless eyes, Iris was already dreading how inconspicuous they would appear in a new school. Sometimes she stared into the bathroom mirror and spat the word "freak" over and over again to get used to the sound of it being hurled at her. To build up a tolerance.

"I'm going to try out for football," Ivan told Iris one afternoon, leaning against the wall across from her bed, his arms crossed defensively over his chest as though anticipating her reaction, an involuntary burst of laughter she immediately regretted. She couldn't help herself, though. The idea of lanky, bookish Ivan with his delicate, almost feline features and his porcelain skin playing football was a joke.

A joke Ivan didn't think was funny.

"Oh, come on," Iris said when he scowled at her. "You can't be serious."

"Dead serious, actually," Ivan said.

Iris took a moment to digest this development so she could figure out the best way to bring her twin back to reality.

"Why?" she finally asked, so she'd know what to argue against.

Ivan shrugged his narrow, pointy shoulders. "Why does anyone play football? To make friends. Be on a team. Be a part of something."

He might as well have slapped her. "You *are* a part of something."

He stared at her blankly, clueless. Iris felt the back of her throat begin to burn.

"You and me," she said. "You're a part of us. We're our own team. You don't need a bunch of meathead jocks to give you that. You were born with it."

Ivan sighed and turned to leave her bedroom. He stopped with his hand on the doorknob. From the kitchen, they could hear their mother crashing around, probably looking for another bottle of the cheap booze she loaded up on each week. Iris wondered if they could buy alcohol in bulk at Costco. Of course, then they'd have to get a Costco membership, but it might still save them some money, which they needed. Anita had been fired (she preferred to say laid off, but that wasn't the truth) three months ago. Money was tight. She liked to remind them of that at least once a day, even though she never gave them any money. Iris used the cash she earned babysitting to pay for lunches and school clothes, and more often than not to buy groceries for all three of them. She was lucky their neighbor paid her fifteen bucks an hour and liked to go out a lot, otherwise they'd all starve.

"Mom's drunk again," Ivan said, speaking more to himself than to Iris, but she responded anyway.

"Yeah, the sun must have risen this morning."

Ivan looked back at her; his eyes were like those of a person at a funeral. Watery. Fighting to maintain control.

"We're not normal, Iris," her twin said.

She nodded, sort of proud. "I know."

"I want to be normal."

And then came the news that stole Ivan from her. He didn't even tell her himself. She had to find out in the worst way possible. From their mother while she was blackout drunk.

It was summertime, the heat in their house oppressive. The air had weight, slowed everything down. The air conditioner had died, and Anita said they didn't have the money to get it fixed. Iris assumed that was why Ivan had been spending so much time away from the house.

Then she started to notice he was getting a tan, and that his waify, garden hose arms had filled out a bit. She wanted to ask her twin if he'd been working out at the gym, if maybe she could join him, even though she hated working out. But she was lonely. Iris did not have friends. She'd never needed them, because she'd always had, and always would have, her brother. Why bother with superficial relationships when she had such a unique bond with another human being? How could any other friendship compare?

Iris was in her room one evening, reading something she couldn't pay attention to and wondering when Ivan would be home and what, if anything, there would be to eat for dinner, when Anita burst through the door. She had a bottle of five-dollar rotgut vodka in one hand and a piece of paper in the other.

Iris sat up, dropping her forgettable book, suddenly afraid. Her mother had never hit her, but she was vindictive. Anita reveled in emotional torture when she could find a way to get at the twins, like it was revenge for them being two people, for ripping her insides apart in their attempt to vacate her body.

Anita waved the piece of paper in Iris's face. "Oh dear, oh dear, oh dear. He didn't tell you, did he?" Though she was stumbling around the room like she was on a ship going through rough waters, her voice was surprisingly clear. Not a trace of her usual drunken slur. She was obviously trying hard to be articulate, over-pronouncing each word. She didn't want Iris to miss anything.

"Guess what this is. It is a fucking bill for the football gear your brother is going to need next year. Ha! Who knew that delicate little boy of mine would ever become a jock. I expected him to spend a lot of time in locker rooms, but, you know . . . on his knees." She cackled at her joke. She'd been insinuating that Ivan was gay since he was eight years old and she had caught the twins playing dress up as each other. Ivan looked just like Iris when he put on her dresses, but after Anita ridiculed him, he never wanted to play that game again.

Iris snatched the paper from her mother's hand and read it carefully to be sure. She had to be sure.

And now she was.

Outside, her window lit up as heat lightning flashed somewhere close by. The thunder wasn't far behind.

She was awake when he came home, sitting in the armchair in the dark, like a wife waiting up for her cheating husband. It was raining by that time, and Ivan came through the door dripping. He shook his hair like a dog. Iris could smell him, but he didn't smell like her brother. He smelled like sweat and grass and mostly like betrayal.

When Ivan saw her, he froze. "Mom?"

Their mom had passed out an hour earlier, luckily in her own bed, which was not always the case. Most of the time she never made it farther than the couch or the kitchen table.

"It's me," Iris said.

"Iris?" He sounded confused. "What . . . what are you doing?"

Outside, lightning flashed again, so close it was blinding. Iris could feel the electricity in the air, especially along the scar on her hip and thigh. The skin there tingled with hundreds of tiny shocks. The scar had always been the most sensitive part of her body.

Iris shot to her feet and brandished the equipment bill at him the way their mother had brandished it at her. "You keep secrets from me now?"

He didn't take the paper, only glanced down at it and then away, obviously ashamed.

As he should be, Iris thought.

"How could you do this to me?" she demanded.

"What?" Ivan brought his gaze to hers, and she was startled to see that his shame had already disappeared, and in its place was only fire and defiance. "What did I do to you? Huh? Did I get in the way of you having a life of your own? No, that was you! Did I try to hold you back from something you wanted to do because of my own selfishness? Nope, that was you, too! Tell me, twin, what did *I* do to *you*? Tell me!"

He was shouting into her face now. Ivan had never shouted at her. He'd always been so calm and thoughtful and composed. Now he was a jock. Worse, a jock with a temper.

Iris realized suddenly that tears were pouring down her face. She wiped at them furiously. She didn't know whom she was angrier with, Ivan or herself. He was right, she'd tried to hold him back from what he wanted. But only because she assumed he thought like she did . . . that there was no one else in the world with whom he could share the kind of bond he had with her. So why bother? Why bother with other people at all?

Iris's scar buzzed like a doorbell. She pressed her palm against it to try to calm its insistent tingling. She spoke softly. "Do you ever feel your scar humming . . . or, or begging, like you took something away from it, and it wants you to give it back?"

When she dared look at Ivan, she wished she didn't. He backed away from her, holding up his hands, as though in surrender. Or fear. That was the answer.

No.

He was afraid of her.

Her twin did not feel the same connection to her that she did to him. Maybe when the doctors separated them, they took more out of her and gave it to Ivan. Or maybe it was all in her head, this undying twin-bond she'd only imagined.

Ivan's look of apprehension turned to pity, and he reached for her. "Sis," he said, but Iris slapped his hand away. She bolted for the door, and was through before he could stop her. She ran from the house, out into the rain. Her scar—that huge scar that spanned from her hip to her knee, an irregular, pinkish landscape as wide as her hand that looked so rough but felt, to her fingertips, like velvet—burned like it had been doused in acid.

Iris didn't even get to the sidewalk before a crooked arm of white light stabbed straight through the top of her head and stopped her in her tracks.

For a moment, Iris's entire body was on fire the way her scar had been a moment before.

Then the burning consumed her, and it was all that she was.

"Iris! Iris, wake up! Please be okay. Please be okay. I'm sorry for what I said. Please be okay!"

She knew the voice better than any other. It was Ivan, calling to her from far away. But when she opened her eyes, he wasn't far away. His face was above hers. Her gaze was drawn past him, though. Something loomed above him. Above them both. A black mass of what she first mistook to be smoke. But then she felt the raindrops on her face, raindrops that were not coming from the sky, because the clouds far above had cleared. Only this black cloud remained, hovering no more than ten feet off the ground.

Iris sat up, and then immediately wished she hadn't. Her head felt like it had been removed from her neck, dropped on the cement from twenty stories up, and then returned to her body. Even the raindrops falling from the low black cloud, light as they were, felt like hammer blows when they tapped her skull. She wished the strange little cloud would stop spitting on her, hurting her.

As soon as she thought it, the rain stopped.

"Oh my god . . . Iris, your hair."

Iris raised a shaking hand to touch her hair, and found that there wasn't much *to* touch. What was left on her scalp was brittle and smelled like smoke.

"Can you stand?" Ivan asked. "No, that's a bad idea. I should call an ambulance."

"Don't," Iris snapped. "We can't afford an ambulance. Anyway, I'm fine."

"How can you be fine? You've been struck by lightning. I saw it happen."

"Oh, don't worry. I believe you." Iris winced as she tried to stand. Her head screamed mercy. "I felt it."

She wobbled on her feet, and her brother helped to keep her steady. Something crumbled into her eyes. She picked at her lids and came away with a dozen singed eyelashes.

"They'll grow back," Ivan said, trying to sound reassuring. "I'm taking you to the hospital. You need to at least get checked."

Iris shoved him away, remembering the reason she'd run out into the rain in the first place. "No. I wouldn't want to get in the way of you having a life. Besides, I'm sure you'll be spending plenty of time in the hospital over the next three years after you get pummeled by 'roided-up human bulldozers."

Though her head felt as though it might crack open like an egg and spill out the scrambled yolk of her brain, Iris walked on her own back inside the house. She didn't realize the dark cloud had followed her inside until she was in her bedroom. She lowered herself onto the mattress she'd slept on since she was five (she'd peed the bed on it a number of times back then, but her mom refused to buy a new one) and when she lay back, she saw it. The black mass bunched above her. She reached up and raked her fingers through it. The cloud looked so substantial, so dense and tangible, but it was no more solid than a thought.

"Rain," Iris said, and the cloud contracted, as though experiencing a muscle spasm. Then she felt droplets of water land on her face. She opened her mouth and took them on her tongue. Her skin felt hot, fever-sick, and the coolness of the rain was a small relief.

She let the cloud rain on her as she went to sleep, and when she woke, it was still drizzling, and her old mattress was soaking wet. Iris decided to throw it out and get a new one, even if she had to use the money she'd saved for new school clothes to do it.

She didn't really need clothes for school, anyway. The point of starting school every year with a new wardrobe was to make the best first impression possible. But when Iris looked in the bathroom mirror and took in her new image, she realized the only kind of impression she'd be making was a shocking one.

Her hair and eyelashes had fallen out. Her scalp, where the lightning had struck her, was etched in a veiny red mark the size of her fist.

But when Iris stripped off her wet clothes to take a shower, she found that the scar she shared with Ivan was gone, as though it had never been.

Wearing a hoodie pulled up over her head even though it was a muggy ninety-five degrees, Iris rode her bike to the library the next day. She told her cloud to stay home, and it did, tucking itself into a corner of the room. Iris loved that the cloud did what she told it to do. At least she had control over one thing in her life. But she wanted to understand *why*. Why had it appeared after she was struck by lightning, and why did it obey her?

There was a one-hour-per-person limit for using the library computers, but Iris begged the librarian for more. The librarian, a black woman with yellowing corneas and wires of gray protruding from her braids, peered at Iris suspiciously across her desk. Iris could tell she was wondering about the hood.

"I got a really bad haircut," Iris told her.

The librarian's hard stare melted into a sympathetic smile and she handed Iris another password. "I'm sure it's not as bad as you think."

Iris thanked her and returned to her search, reaching under her hood to touch her smooth scalp. It was not as smooth as it had been that morning. Already a light fuzz of hair had sprouted. Iris was surprised. Her hair had never grown particularly fast.

By the time she had exhausted the librarian's patience with her overuse of the Internet, Iris had discovered three things about lightning and people who were struck by lightning that she considered applicable to her situation.

1. Lightning is one of the most mysterious forces on the planet, and no one really understands it.

2. Aftereffects of being struck by lightning range from but are not limited to: death, burns, amnesia, personality disorders, blindness, deafness, learning disorders, and changes in brain function. Cases where being struck by lightning has healed a person of a virus or degenerative illness have also been recorded.

3. Being struck by lightning sometimes leaves behind a veiny, red Lichtenberg figure on the skin. Lichtenberg figures fade shortly after a person has been struck.

A week later, the Lichtenberg figure on Iris's scalp still had not faded, but she could no longer see it because her hair had grown in to cover it.

Her hair, once a drab color of dishwater blonde, was now white tinged with the slightest hint of yellow, as though she had bleached it. Her eyelashes had yet to grow back.

Iris didn't care. School started in a week, and she just didn't care. Maybe she wouldn't even go. It wasn't like her mom would make her. Come to think of it, Iris hadn't even seen Anita Banik in a few days. Her mom went on occasional benders like this. She'd be gone for three days or a week. In truth, Iris preferred her mom out on a drunken bender to being drunk at home. It was simpler that way, and Iris had exhausted her ability to worry about her mom a long time ago. Anita always turned up eventually, whether the twins wanted her to or not.

At first, after Iris was struck, Ivan worried over her. He tried to talk her into going to a doctor. Iris ignored him. She felt fine. Better than fine, actually. She had more energy than she used to. She felt stronger. She hardly needed to sleep anymore. She lay awake at night and turned her black cloud on and off, letting it rain on her for just a moment, and then commanding it to stop. She directed it around the room, and it always did as she instructed, hovering here, then there. Changing shape for her. Splitting into two and then merging back together.

But sometimes Iris touched the place on her thigh where her scar used to be, and she felt a crippling pang of loss. She wondered if there was anything she could do to repair things with Ivan. To make them like they used to be.

Someone was at the door. Knocking instead of ringing the bell. Iris couldn't remember the last time anyone had come to their house. Maybe Anita had lost her key.

But when Iris opened the door, she found not her mom, but a man. A man with long white hair and clouded eyes, dressed from head to toe in white. His face was smooth and tan, and he smiled at Iris, though she doubted he could actually see her through his heavy cataracts.

He held out a hand and Iris saw, on his palm, a veiny red marking. A Lichtenberg figure like the one etched on her scalp.

"Iris Banik," the man said in a voice made for radio, it was so fluid and polished. The voice of someone who'd spent most of his life speaking, and had perfected the art. "May I beg a moment of your time? I have traveled a long way to meet you."

Iris shook her head, confused. "Why?"

"Because you're unique, and I have need of you. We have great work ahead of us."

Her instinct should have been to slam the door in the stranger's face. Instead, she gave him her hand and shook, and the second her skin touched his, she felt a jolt of energy surge through her and wind its way up her arm.

When he spoke again, his lips did not move, but his voice, like a radio broadcast, was in her head, static and all.

It is time to leave this life you've known. A new life awaits you. A new family.

A new family?

Iris waited for her scar to tingle at the idea of leaving her twin behind. But then she remembered that her scar was gone. She was no longer half of a whole. She was alone.

Instead of the tingling along her now nonexistent scar, Iris felt a sort of humming pressure inside her mind. The man in white fixed her with his filmy eyes.

I can give you what you desire. I can forge a new bond between you and your twin. A bond that can never be broken.

Iris opened the door wider and allowed the man inside. When they were alone and the door was closed, he put his hands on the top of her head, and the humming pressure returned. He made everything turn white. He made everything make sense.

After that, Iris understood what needed to be done. The man in white would help her do it.

"There's a storm headed this way," the man in white told her before he left. "You know what to do."

"Put him in the path of the lightning," Iris said, her own voice sounding dreamy and disconnected from her body. She didn't feel like herself anymore. The man in white had done something to her, she realized, but not something bad. At least, she didn't think so. He had simply made her feel calm, and cleansed, and certain of the course of action she must take.

But a worm of doubt wriggled beneath this layer of certainty. "What if the lightning doesn't want him?" she asked.

"It will," the man in white said. "God told me it would be so, just as He told me where to find you. You and your brother belong with me and mine."

"What about our mother?" Iris asked. "She might not want to let us go."

The man in white smiled and answered without speaking.

She has been dealt with. You will not see her again.

Iris knew she should have cared about this, but she didn't. All she cared about now was doing what the man in white told her to do, because that would give her what she wanted.

It would give her Ivan back.

She couldn't wait for Ivan to come home. What if the storm passed before he arrived and she missed her opportunity? She called Ivan's cell phone, but he didn't pick up. Still, she knew where to find him. At the high school, practicing with the team he'd wanted so badly to be a part of.

But they were about to get a new family, a new team. The man in white had promised. He had said they had work to do. Great work in the name of God. Iris had never thought much about God. She'd always believed in her and Ivan, and that was enough. But Ivan had abandoned her, and only the man in white's God could bring him back.

Iris brought her dark cloud along as she rode her bike toward the high school, but she commanded it to rise higher into the sky so no one would notice it following her. She searched the sky for the storm the man in white said was coming, but the clouds were as white as his hair. The only dark cloud belonged to Iris, a stain on snowy floating mountains.

When she arrived at the high school—an institution she now knew she would never attend—she found the football players finishing up practice on the field. She parked her bike next to the bleachers and watched, trying to pick her brother out of the tangle of uniformed, grass-stained boys on the field. She spotted him quickly. He was taller than most of the other boys, even the seniors. Iris realized after only a few minutes of watching that he had talent. He could throw the ball with startling accuracy. And when he took off his helmet at the close of practice, Iris saw her twin smiling in a way he never did at home. He looked happier than she'd ever seen him, basking in male camaraderie as his teammates slapped him on the back or pounded fists with him.

Then Ivan saw her leaning against the bleachers, and his smile disappeared. He looked around at the other departing players, and Iris realized he was nervous about his new friends seeing his freak of a sister with her lashless eyes and head of ice-colored bristle.

Iris didn't give her twin the option of joining the other players.

She strode out onto the field and met him there. Glancing up, she saw her dark cloud trailing her, fifty feet up.

"What are you doing here?" Ivan asked.

"I have to tell you something," Iris said. "Mom's not coming home. She was driving drunk and caused an accident. She's in the hospital now, and after that she'll be going to jail because people got hurt. Oh, and we're going to lose the house."

Ivan's eyes grew round as she spoke. His helmet hung like a stone in his right hand, and he dropped it on the grass so he could rub his hand over his face, as though by doing so he could scrub away reality.

Reality. The reality was that the man in white had told Iris about their mom and the house. Then, after he left, Iris received a phone call from a police officer, informing her of the accident. Iris didn't need proof about the house. If the man in white said they were going to lose it, then they were going to lose it.

Ivan surprised her by suddenly kicking his helmet. It flew across the grass.

"Why can't my life ever be good for two seconds?" he wailed. His face was red, and his eyes filled with angry tears. He fell to his knees in the grass and hung his head. His hands lay in his lap, palms facing up, as though waiting for someone to place a gift in them.

Iris lowered herself to the grass in front of her twin and settled her hands in his. He gripped them tight and looked at her, tears streaming from his eyes. "I'm sorry for the things I said to you. I didn't mean them. We have to stick together," he said. "Always."

They were the words Iris had been waiting to hear.

It was time for the storm she was promised.

She turned her face to the sky, spotted her dark cloud. Saw it growing, staining the white cotton clouds that hung above them, turning them black.

"We should go inside," Ivan said, worry in his voice. "I read somewhere that people who've been struck by lightning once are more likely to be struck again."

He tried to rise, but Iris held him where he was, clenching her fists tighter around his. She felt far away, like a part of herself had risen with her cloud.

"Stay with me," she said. "Forever."

A burst of rain spattered them. "Seriously, Iris, we need to—" That was all Ivan had a chance to say before lightning split the air and found him.

Iris was still holding her brother's hands when the lightning entered his shoulder. She felt their skin go molten like metal and fuse them into one being, the way they'd been born. The way they were meant to be.

ROBERT V.S. REDICK

SOME STORIES LIVE WITH YOU GENTLY, AND RIPEN AFTER SANE AND steady work. Others rage out of the forest and cross your threshold and sink their teeth into your leg. "Nocturne" was of the latter sort.

I was living in Cali, Colombia; my first novel was still no more than a collection of voices; my movements were hampered by the violence surrounding the city and the epidemic of kidnapping-for-ransom that made travel a high-anxiety affair. I suppose all sorts of things were high-anxiety then: my career, my marriage, my day-to-day life in that beautiful, mad boomtown.

Then one night I dreamed "Nocturne," or at least its climax: a shockingly detailed and specific dream that left me astonished and afraid. For the next month my life grew simpler. I had to tell this story. It would not relax its jaws until I did so.

I wrote obsessively, and revised with patience, and then (alas) slipped "Nocturne" into a box. I never sought to publish the story. What was I waiting for? Perhaps a signal as clear and certain as the original impulse to write the tale? If so, that's what Shawn has provided, and for this I'm very grateful.

Robert V.S. Redick

NOCTURNE

Robert V.S. Redick

There are windows we struggle not to look through, scattered among all the houses of our lives. Here is one: a boy slick with chilly sweat, skeleton-thin, tube-trussed, mouth opening and closing like a fish on a pier. His eyes, somewhere unfathomable; his room filling with flowers.

Perhaps he sees the great aunt at his bedside, frail and silent, fighting to keep the blanket about his chin. Perhaps he stares into delirium, into the dream from which he cannot wake: a fat man has hooked him through the gills, and laughing cheerful murder, reels in his prize. The man's face changes minute by minute; his laugh and his absolute power do not.

You are forgiven if you doubt the next hypothesis; the author himself has been drawn to it as reluctantly as the boy to that unattractive brute. Perhaps minds cleansed of the film of rationality do sometimes sharpen. Perhaps that's all it takes.

Consider a window in a deep stone wall. Gaping, glassless, big shutters banging in a storm. Lean inside. A cavernous room, rows of steeple-backed chairs, moonlight on a lustrous floor. Moist tongue of wind uncoiling room to room, odor of bloodwood and marsh myrtle, blackness, a threshing of waves. And kneeling before a lifeless hearth, a young man, shivering: Anton Cuza, alone in Tchavodari Palace.

He is in command of the situation: for indeed, despite the squalor of the moment, he also commands the palace. A very mixed blessing, he thinks. Christ, but my hand is cold!

The hand, his left, fishes for wood chips in an iron urn. The urn is slippery with kerosene, painfully cold. His mind swims with the vapors, until a sharp pain shocks him awake. The fuel has touched a scratch on his wrist. He spits and curses, but in fact he is almost grateful for the pain, its clarity and warmth.

He thinks: I must get warm like that, now, all over. Oh damn this wood! For the logs are green, and shrug off flame with sharp cat hisses. Anton is slight, shallow-chested, and mortally afraid of the Spanish influenza, its death march through the Romanian lowlands.

The Great War is over; much of Europe is electrified. Women in Bucharest cook on iron coils that blaze red at the twist of a dial; even the Turk dangles a bulb from his ceiling. But no cables have yet braved the Danube marshes, and the truck that brings gas and food to the palace has gone south with the Măgar and his army, prowling the Bulgarian frontier.

"That damn fool Ionel!" their commander bellows at each return, failing to find his palace bathed in a twentieth-century glow. "Does he want the Second Division maintained like a levy of serfs forever?" These are theatrical rages, destined to be gossiped up and down the coast, reminding everyone that the Măgar may speak with contempt, if he pleases, of the Unifier of Greater Romania. Some say he and Bratianu are friends; others that they are bitter rivals, that the Măgar could take Bucharest if he chose. Whatever the truth, last year his tantrums won him a telegraph wire, threaded apologetically over the swamps from some distant terminal in the Carpathian ice. No one but Anton ever uses it. Forever left behind (consumptives are easy prey for Bulgarians), he taps a midday report to the capital, boils wheat grist with ham, paces to keep warm.

The logs wheeze, exude a yellowish steam. He wrings his hand at them; drops of kerosene cry *pff!*—accomplishing nothing. Disgusted, he pulls together the last wood chips and stuffs them into the iron cradle of his torch. With his clean right hand he strikes a match. The torch bursts to life, a gag bouquet from a magician's sleeve.

"Hooray!"

Anton does not mind shouting, even at foolishness. He is at home.

Somewhere above, wind scours the chimney. Moonlit ash rises like some otherworld snow; his torch trembles. Anton cradles it to his chest.

"A storm tonight. Just our luck." He presses the torch into a wall mount. "Not to worry. We'll fix things, won't we?"

Of course he will, but only by fastening shutters against this crazy wind: a tedious job. "No choice about it, though. That's all right."

He picks his way across the great hall. Pelts conspire to trip him: red fox, ferret, wolverine, a huge black bear with claws and head intact, agate eyes watchful. The Măgar has a passion for animals quite absent in his warden. He returns from Black Sea excursions with chained lynx, birds of prey astonished under leather hoods, grizzled elk heads limed for mounting.

And every kind of dog! Even now, just audible over the wind, he hears their furious noise. Like a mercenary barracks, the kennel stands removed (but sufficiently visible) from the main gate of the palace, a nightmare space of snarls and excrement and flung bones. That howler, now: is that the Airedale, who leaps so fast the eye cannot follow? Or the Rhodesian devil, heaped with muscle to the point of deformity and raised on a diet of black flesh and beatings, until even a passing dark shirt opens the faucets of its bloodlust?

Anton is glad to think of the salt marsh and swollen Danube between him and the Măgar's eye.

He shuffles past the kitchen, its dangling Posnr hams, forbidden French chocolates. The splay-footed master staircase. The

369

snicker of lowered visors on suits of mail at attention since the fifteenth century, the maid's thorny broom propped insolent against one iron shoulder. And last, and most precious: the door of the library. *His* library, he always thinks. A portal to a kinder universe.

Soon, he tells the door. Wait for me.

His thoughts race: these storm-shutters, now. I've never bothered with them before. It's never been so *cold*. Will my hands make music, or just go numb?

Very much preoccupied with this last thought, he flips past the sighing curtain, and all at once stands gulping in the bitter strength of the gale.

The palace wall cleaves straight down upon a cliff. Below is the Black Sea—roaring, angrier than he has ever seen it, a rabid infinity of foam. The land is broken and cruel, rock and slime and more rock and more slime, and directly before him a livid gash: a fissure astoundingly deep and wide. Over and into this wound in the rocks the surf is pouring, exploding skyward, rushing back with a monstrous slurp to cascade again.

No less than a typhoon. But that crack, that canyon in the breakers—why can he not remember it? Surely it is named and known?

You are addled, Anton. If you're not careful you'll forget your name.

The rain has not arrived, but he sees it coming, a gray net dragged by thunderheads. There is the moon, too: also grossly huge. Never in his life has it loomed so large, not even at harvest, bloodshot on the world's rim. And gripping the cornice, Anton begins to consider the moon's intentions.

Do they not say that it commands the tides, after all? Of whose making this unnatural surf, if not the moon's? Could it be seeking, in some private malevolence, to tug the sea's wide lip over the land, over the palace itself, as an impatient nurse tugs bedclothes over a child's head?

He has read of corals and anemones, and teeth of sharks, fused in the Carpathian foothills, millions of years old. Where had the shore stood then? How many meters of soundless sea assured the

Black that *this* land, here, was forever hers? How long had she suffered no other's touch on this deep-sea shelf, none but the moon's, gently exciting her, lifting her waters, smoothing the glide of her round-eyed children? When had men come, hooking those children through the gills?

Can they hate—the moon, and natural things?

The cold light ambles on the surf; the wet wind claws with nails of salt.

Then Anton laughs, his intensity at once merely comic. He grins at the storm, the moon, the white-toothed waves. They are beautiful.

"You are beautiful! Tell me: how will my sonata go tonight, eh? A sign for the suffering artist? No? Nothing?"

Throwing the bolt on the last shutter of the great hall, he feels instantly warmer. The gale drops to a whisper: these walls so thick that melon-sized shot from Russian cannon lie still undiscovered in the stone, they say. He returns to the hearth, where his torch rubs orange fins together, glad to see him. Its warmth runs up his arm and across his chest. But once out of the wall socket, the flame still cowers, writhes, and he knows the wind has not conceded him the palace.

Too many windows, he thinks angrily. Too many rooms from which the day's faint heat has bled already. Night fell—an hour ago?

Three hours?

It doesn't matter. He will secure the upper galleries and then shut himself in the library. His library! Beloved nucleus, smelling of tallow and camphor, stalagmite heaps of candles on the maple desk. He *must* hurry and get there, before he loses everything. Before fatigue and chill rob him of his gift, those galloping harmonies, the wild something in his blood.

Then he stops, amazed. Why has the maid gone to bed, and the palace in such a state? Where is the porter? Did they seek his permission to retire?

Irritated, he turns abruptly into the Paris room. Here as always he checks himself. The chamber is fragile, intimate: tables on does' legs, bowls of lacquerwood and antique silver, a tea service set out for visitors who never come. Anton feels a trespasser here, even though the maid crosses the room day and night. Does she sense what he does—the trembling of a thousand crystal minnows in the chandelier, the narcotic murmur of the divans in their dust-shrouds, a room tossing in its sleep?

He crosses gingerly to the far corner, where a stair curls tightly down to the maid's chambers. He leans over the rail. No light whatsoever reaches his eyes from below.

"Tatiana!"

She is a long time answering, a mumbled acknowledgment that might be, "Your mercy."

"You ought to know to fasten the shutters, little mother, or do you want us all to freeze? And really, you haven't left me so much as a warm coal. Come up now, we must see to the galleries at least."

She says nothing, and Anton waits a very long time for the first drag of her clubfoot over the granite floor. Her candle is barely visible, a salamander-shine in a dark pool.

"It's truly cold, Tatiana." He does not know what else to say. He knocks against a tea table, turns with a scowl, rushes from the room.

On the great stair his temples throb, his footsteps ring loud and individual. Yet another open window at the landing, where he pauses for breath. He snatches at the wind-whipped curtain, tugs it aside.

Here is the west yard, scrubbed clean of straw and cigarettes by the gale, the fountain's spray tossing far beyond its basin. Under the hay wagon, a lone gull shudders from foot to foot, looking as if it wishes to speak up against its circumstances. The flags on the parapet crack like whips.

Granite frames this yard on three sides, but the last is a tall, solid hedge. Cutting through at its exact center is an arch of laurels: the path to the memorial gardens. Just inside the arch, grotesquely large, Charonic, face like a rhinoceros beetle, frowns Wagner. Further in, Strauss's imperious arm rises over a sickly magnolia. It was the Măgar's idea: diversify the garden's populace of marble kings and generals with statues of composers. Like the older figures, these are gigantic, fawning. Not one Romanian stands among them.

Yet.

Anton looks up. In the moonlight the distant Carpathians slash the sky in two: blue-black above, midnight down to the horizon. He must smile for lovely Bicazului Pass, the corset of ice that declares the ridgeline.

But—*where are the lights of Constanta?*

The city is dark.

The entire plain is dark. A blackout.

"Oh *no.*"

He sees them, then: dull metal beads on a taut string, high over the plain. The gray wings are cruel, the bellies deep. He cannot hear the engines. Russians? Turks? He counts in a panic—ten, fourteen, eighteen—then fumbles and leaps up the last steps.

In a Spartan room on the left, half hidden beneath scraps of his own wriggling shorthand, is the telegraph key. He is tapping before his other hand has even found the crank: *wake up, wake up, Lupescu!*

Colonel Lupescu is a kind man, even when dragged from his bed, but now his response is curt.

"Talk."

Anton taps: "Eighteen maybe twenty aircraft capital blacked out heading north in file—"

"Stand by."

The distant station is silent for some minutes; Anton waits in terror. Lupescu would be confirming the blackout with Bucharest or Constanta, or verifying the planes' trajectory, or warning the army to the east. The rain begins, a soft hiss at the window.

At last Lupescu responds. "Tchavodari Palace."

"Here!"

"Anton?"

"Sir!"

"Anton, how are your studies progressing?"

"Did not copy—"

"I believe you were preparing for the conservatory."

Anton pulls back his hand, as though the key might snap at him. Lupescu cannot tap code at such speeds. No one can.

"Anton."

He pounces on the key, taps like a lunatic: "Repeat unknown aircraft northbound—"

"The viola, isn't it?"

"Constanta—"

"I don't think I ever told you I played the cello."

Anton touches nothing.

"I was really quite accomplished in my twenties. I played in Sienna before the Lady Sofia di Bali Adro. She actually cried, at the end of Schumann's Fourth."

Anton cannot transmit to any other station. He is miserably cold again.

"Are you serious about music, Anton?"

What to do? His hand gropes to the key. "Yes."

"That may be why I've never brought this up. For I'm exactly the same. Music was everything, absolutely everything I lived for. It's purely accidental, a cruel joke really, that I ended up in the army. My grandfather gave me his own violin on my eighth birthday; I played it eleven years. But something in my wrist protested the violin. The angulation, is that a word, Anton? The angulation was all wrong. So very severe, violins. But when I picked up the cello I knew I was home."

He goes on. It truly is Lupescu; Anton knows his hesitations, misspellings, the twitch that makes half his *r*'s into *d*'s. He wants to scream for a witness, but who would come? Tatiana, the lame, the slow-witted? Was she even out of bed?

"My masters presented me to *their* masters; I was universally adored. I rode to Venice on the Kaiser's train, and played when he entertained the American ambassador. I was so happy, Anton! They paid me to do precisely what I loved! But one night changed it all."

Stop, thinks Anton. *Please stop, Colonel.* But he knows Lupescu won't.

"When are your trials?"

"The ninth."

"Day of judgment! Ha! You must be ready for anything. My own—God knows I'd rather forget it—came right there, in your palace. When the Măgar was new to power, his cruelty a rumor. We didn't know what cruelty meant, we who guarded Constanta against ships that never attacked, watching Bucharest's boys tramp off to the slaughter. But we gained an education that night.

"All of us knew that the Măgar was the one voice of power east of the mountains, that he could order the symphony dissolved, could even have us shot if he wished, but what does one do about that as a cello player? He was a dandy, too, our little tyrant, a great lover of the arts. Fresh from Paris, from those five exiled years, whoring and sobbing into crystal champagne, waiting for his star to rise. As it did.

"We learned later that he had proposed to a young violinist, a student in the Sorbonne, and that she had not even rejected him, but simply told her butler not to accept his letters, not to let him in as far as the cloakroom. A great shame, a fiasco. Think of his rage—no troops at his service to storm *that* door. No view from his palace windows, no dance in the Summer Ballroom to tempt her. And every day the contempt of Parisians, certain the Danube delta was a Godforsaken land of grog halls and fever. As it is.

"He ordered our performance in the Round Hall, and it had never been more beautifully decorated, Anton, with gardenias and roses from God knows where laced round the pillars, and yellow candles in the mezzanine. Three hundred chairs for the listeners. My parents sat in the second row, behind the dignitaries. Mother wore a lily in her hair—"

Anton blinks. His mother?

"Yes, she was already ill; in fact she only lived a few more weeks. But we could not dissuade her. She sat with her piccolo in her lap, beaming: she couldn't play it any more, but believed the old thing's presence would bring me luck. The next day she threw it from her window into the canal.

"All were seated and smiling; we waited only on the Măgar.

But we waited long. A whisper raced the hall that he was taking tea, alone, in the Paris room. I've never known for sure.

"But finally he came: in dress uniform. With no one on his arm. He bowed smartly to the audience, then turned and looked at us so long and coldly that we began to fidget in sheer nervousness. Our conductor held his little ivory baton as though it burned him. Finally, instead of taking his seat, our host walked to the east entrance, and leaned with crossed arms against those big, barnlike doors, shut as always against the noise of the yard. At last he gave our horror-stricken maestro a nod.

"We played two movements of Beethoven's *Pastoral*. Bold and bright and flattering. And we were perfect. The crowd whooped, almost too loudly. The Măgar clapped as well, but his face was a chilly mask. We followed with Debussy's *Nocturnes*, and for that we earned a meager smile. Then the soloist walked forward, slowly, into the hush before Ravel.

"She was lovely, all of sixteen, vague Gypsy lines to her eyebrows. A prodigy. Our conductor pumped her arm like a hysteric; the Măgar's handshake was slow. Detaining her, he studied us once more, and this third look was positively mortal. He worshipped Ravel. We knew it, had known it for months, and right down to that pimpled pipsqueak with the silver triangle, we trembled at the thought of a bad performance. A clarinetist massaged his wrist, pouting voicelessly; the second violinist traced a cross—"

Now Anton interrupts, convulsive. "Colonel Lupescu! I don't want to know what happened. It has nothing to do with me!"

"Ah, but consider, my insubordinate fellow: we were just two floors down from where you sit now—two floors, and nineteen years. Imagine it: the excruciating absence of sound, of breath. The conductor with sweat in his eyes. His baton darts. And oh, the music! Begun awry! Whose was the sour voice? There's a shuffle of bending backs. Everyone leans steeply into the work, a ferocious concentration takes us all. And the sourness disappears. We sail smoothly over large waves, ride them out, each grace note cut like a dream. My mother sways; the Măgar closes his eyes. Ravel is a full-billowed sail.

"Then, suddenly, that little worm of poison again. His eyes snap open. It's in the woodwinds, I think, and dare a glance. There he is—that blubbering clarinetist! He has ceased playing, is squeezing his wrist in agony; he is having some sort of attack! And then the buffoon leaps up, red-faced, lurching from his row—"

"Stop!" Anton's hand is shaking.

"And the white-haired French horn player gapes at him and catches his sleeve, and the clarinetist shoves him back against the musicians behind, and the loving audience convulses in a shout of dismay—"

"I am leaving, Colonel!"

"And the soloist turns her back to the audience, hoping someone will shoot her. And my mother rises from her own chair, haggard, clutching the piccolo in her big arthritic hands, and groaning for breath. The conductor thrashes out the lost tempo with insane animation, and *then*. Anton. The final, unbearable train wreck of the strings! And the Măgar—"

"Be quiet!" screams Anton, backing to the door.

"—the Măgar has waited for this. He barks a command, and we are suddenly surrounded by dozens of guards, men with naked bayonets; they just swarm in like fleas and drive the audience out. And the Măgar throws open the door to the west yard, and in rush, I swear before God, dozens and dozens of swine—"

"No! No! No!"

"—huge hogs from that Posnr fellow—"

"Christ!"

"—men behind with German shepherds, and they are so horrified, filthy, shoving, pissing, squealing . . ."

"Bastard! Liar!"

Anton turns and runs. His one thought is that if he hears any more, he will rip the telegraph from its wiring, smash it, and later be called a saboteur. *I can still think practically*, he tells himself, on the verge of another scream. *Lupescu. Pigs. Why such horrible nonsense?*

The hallway bucks under his feet. His breastbone resonates with the storm. He gropes for reason, like a life vest he might yet slip into, but all he can think of is that gentle Lupescu has been a long, long time alone.

———

The Summer Ballroom is awash with rain: staghorn ferns weep it from high chains on the balconies; skylights thrash it upon the dance floor. Anton stands in the doorway, slowing his breath. A famous room, this, where princes and later prime ministers and dictators waltzed their wives or lovers. He tries to see them, the unapproachable ones: prim, powdered, a night in every respect opposite this one; a blushing cheek, a sextet—

He kicks away the doorstop. No heating this room.

But then, over the storm: footsteps. Someone has ducked into the dressing chambers.

"Faraz?"

In the wet moonlight, nothing. But quick footfalls echo in the rooms beyond. Anton lifts his torch, dashes through the spray, cursing. It can only be Faraz, the Shiite porter; abandoning his post to nose about the Măgar's rooms, perhaps make off with something. No one else is inside the palace gate, save lumbering Tatiana.

Anton bursts into the master dressing room, finds it untouched. But sounds tease from a room adjoining: left, right? No, behind him, the bathchambers. Water splashing into the tub! Anton leaps for the door, but hears the bolt slide home even as he pushes.

"Have you gone mad, Faraz?" Anton hurries to the other door. Also locked. He beats furiously. The splashing stops.

Now the footsteps approach his door. Knuckles rap from inside, once.

"It is for you."

"The bath? For me?"

"Don't you want to be clean?" The voice is distinctly mocking.

"Who's there?" Anton cries. "Faraz?"

"You don't know me?"

"I don't know if I know you! But no one is to run a bath without my express permission! No one is to do *anything* without my permission while our Commander is afield! And if it *is* you, Faraz, I will have you in stocks, like a common deserter, for leaving your post. Do you realize—"

"Call *me* a deserter." The other speaks with slow contempt.

"Let me in! I order you!"

The footsteps retreat.

"Come. I unlocked the door while you were bellowing."

He has indeed. But as Anton swings the door open, the other—the door on the opposite wall—crashes shut. Anton runs through the steamy chamber, grabs at the knob, pushes.

It will not budge. A foot is against it.

Anton throws his whole weight against this door, but his whole weight amounts to little. The owner of the planted foot snickers.

"Go on, laugh. You won't be laughing long."

The other obliges, laughs louder. Anton is ready to explode. But with a tremendous effort he does not. He dislikes hysteria, really. And he is on duty.

"Faraz, listen. I'm not angry. But you've got to take a message to town. We're under attack!"

"No one ordered me to run you a bath."

"What?"

"I said no one made me to do it. You might show some appreciation."

"What?"

"It wasn't easy getting that boiler lit. I did it because you were freezing to death."

Anton looks over his shoulder. The great claw-footed tub squats under billowing steam.

"I am so very cold." Anton nearly whispers, his shoulder still pressed to the door.

"We *might* pull you through—one hears of such things—if only you would cooperate. But I see you won't. Out in the storm with me, is it? Very well. The servant obeys."

He had no idea Faraz possessed such Romanian.

"I'm off. Don't you dare waste that water."

The master obeys, backs slowly to the tub, but—disaster! Faraz has pulled the plug. Less than an inch of water left. With thought-less need, he plunges his free hand into the water. The voice out-side erupts in laughter. Boots clatter down the service stair.

"Faraz!"

The pantry door slams.

"You bastard Persian!"

Hot water teases his fingers. Gone.

Anton will send a message by the tower lamp. Risky—but he can neither ignore the aircraft nor go to town himself, leaving the pal-ace in the hands of a cripple and a lunatic porter. He rushes back through the rainy ballroom. Down the windy corridor. Under the oilpaint smirks of deposed kings, freezing to death.

Lupescu's code still perforates the night:

". . . insane, don't you see, he's crazed by power, his hideous power!"

On the great stair landing, Anton leans from the window again. The rain surges in like a cold sneeze, almost extinguishing his torch, and he backs away.

"Sweet Mary and Joseph. I'm drenched."

"Beware of him!" taps Lupescu.

He turns the corner, running again. There would be a drybox and matches in the tower, in fact—

"Oh, the *tower!*" For the second time that night, he shouts in joy and triumph. The tower's huge signal lamp, it burns *hot.* Incredible that he has forgotten. But then he has not used the lamp for—six months?

A year?

He shivers up an iron staircase, six dizzying turns, and then his torch thumps on the padlocked tower door. He groans, feels his pockets.

Below, the drag of Tatiana's foot on the great stair. Her voice wavering about a melody. She enjoys the stairwell's echo, the cho-ral embrace it affords even the meanest voice. Suddenly, for no reason he can fathom, he wishes urgently to avoid her.

The key. He had quite forgotten it was in his pocket. It fits, but what now? The lock is rusted, fused. Tatiana labors up another step, singing:

> *And if you treat him as your only son,*
> *He'll cheat you 'ere the day is done*
> *And if you tender him his liberty*
> *Then far beyond your call he'll be*
> *Oh, far beyond your call he'll run*
> *And you with harvest scarce begun.*

Halfwit. Singing to the gale. And how she tortures him with that ballad. Days, weeks, until it flits about in his head like a thrush in a chimney.

> O *bitter coin of liberty*
> *For far beyond your call he'll be.*

Her candle glimmers on the wall. With a gasp, he wrenches open the lock. In a moment he has struggled into the hollow tower. The door booms shut, and Anton follows the sound up a thin ladder. Cold rungs bite his fingers; oil splatters from his torch, which he clamps awkwardly between two fingers; the climb seems endless. But at last he thrusts open the ceiling door, dangles horribly in the air a moment, and pulls himself through.

It is like wriggling into heaven. The chamber is nearly all glass, and it is the highest point between Mount Amăgire and the sea. He is between rain clouds again. Like knots of fireflies, electric storms ripple to the horizon, illuminating icy Bicazului, splashing brilliance in the troughs between slithering breakers. The capital is still dark, and even the lights of the village—his own village—are dim. But strangely, in other places his vision extends for miles: he sees stubbled wheat fields, smudges of forest, ruins.

A low fog, he reasons. Snagged on church spires, wedged into alleys. For his village creeps almost to the palace wall, spends mornings in its shadow. Anton remembers this view, reversed: all the long years he trundled to school, or wheeled sawdust from the lumber mill, or eased great butterfly-winged piano cases from his father's shop into waiting trucks—always, this tower loomed over his life. Each morning until that one on which he left for the municipal music school (certain those meager, mouse-dung halls were no more than a turnstile in his path to the Conservatory) he had craned his neck *up* to see the first sun dancing here, on this high glass pulpit.

"Posies for the mayor, poppies for the king," his sister Julita would sing, cavorting, gripping his finger. "Violets for the merchant-man with his golden ring." She waved to the soldiers above, and very rarely, they waved back. Then she would squeal with delight. She loved the tower, had no sense that generals rather than kings ruled Romania today, or of the difference between them.

Julita down there below. Grown up now, almost a woman. Invisible in the fog. He gulps down a sudden virulent melancholy. To be at his mother's table, sipping coffee sweet as molasses, watching his father chew a pipe. To dance with his sister again.

But even as he watches, the moon leaps free of a cloud, emerges round and huge, fixing the land below like a squint animal eye. Everything is abruptly visible: each street of his town, every branch in the thatched roofs. The listing Posnr mansion squats on the next ridge, over a slum of groggy stables. But the windows do not shine. Nothing shines, everything merely *appears* in the submarine light, shipwrecks at forty fathoms.

The fleet of aircraft hangs in the south sky, dwindling.

A noise: his skin crawls. The mad baying of the dogs, seeking a harmony quite impossible to so grotesque a team—but distinctly hungry. Has Faraz forgotten them?

Anton turns away from the view. Now then.

Exactly in the room's center stands the signal lamp, exquisite and huge. Its concave mirror is larger than a half-barrel; its mantel of spun asbestos like a fetal star. Anton raps the fuel tank: half full. Now he twists opens the valve and pumps vigorously, bringing the fuel to pressure. Then he touches his torch to the mantle.

The flash quite blinds him; flames singe the hair up and down his arm. He smiles, finds a socket for his torch, and steps directly in front of the mirror.

Heat!

It bathes his face, his chest, his limbs. His wet hair streams. He shields his eyes with a raised arm. Only now does he realizes how thoroughly cold he has become.

I'll never move again.

But the heat bites at the scratch on his wrist. Annoyed, he turns his back, stares at the small, irregular wound. He cannot remember where the damn thing came from.

No one responds to his lamp signal. Hardly surprising. Anton has begun to suspect an immense drill, and his part in it a test of readiness. Well, he would damn well pass. But what would they do to Lupescu?

He rolls the lamp about, inspects the world at leisure, standing so close to the flame that his chest burns through his shirt, loving it. The tide has risen over the cleft in the sea rocks, but it is still there, leviathan-like beneath the waves, troubling their charge. And from this height he sees the whole garden and its stone residents, beyond Wagner's gate: twisted Paganini, and scarecrow Prokofiev spindled between a pair of unhealthy lilacs. Farther back, yellow eyes glisten from a row of cages, mouths hang open. The dogs are watching him, like prisoners waiting to riot, tense with idiot hate.

They howl. Let them howl. Hot, hot to the edge of pain, Anton smiles over his country, his palace, his lovely Black Sea—and then he sees the girl, and shrieks aloud.

She is standing on an iceberg, making swiftly toward the palace over the waves: a young girl, with ice crystals in her hair like white jewels, and her colorless eyes brighter than these. She is regal and coldly smiling, her arms are bare and slender. He lunges for binoculars: she wears a robe of frozen teardrops, frozen baby's breath, frozen eighth notes. He thinks, *Something is going to happen to me.*

When she draws near the cliff, the clouds roll solemnly back, and one leaps rippling down to become a white stairway from her feet to the window of the tower. She starts to glide up to him, effortless, and her voice precedes her in a velvet singsong. He has never heard a thing so beautiful.

Anton touches his lamp. Its heat is distant.

She is almost to him, a girl in full flower—but her skin is the blue-white of the iceberg. Her hand is on the window. He has not unlatched it.

She pauses, and then a new, kinder smile plays on her lips. They shape two words:

Don't wait.

Her breath paints ice crystals on the glass.

Still, he does not move. He is scared out of his mind. But the beautiful girl only watches him with greater compassion. She knows everything about him. She is *for* him. She is the Empress of Antarctica's daughter.

When she breathes out, the patch of ice widens, hiding her face. But then her finger taps, and ice and glass shatter together in a cough of wind. Her blue hand reaches in and touches the latch. Halfheartedly, he moves to stop her. She flicks his arm away; it is done.

Inside the chamber her smile is more than kind. He has expected her all his life. She drops her glistening robe, reaches beneath his shirt with both spreading hands, and for a moment he feels an unbearable sweet flame as her sapphirine body presses his own.

Then he thrashes. He is sprawled over the chair, head thrown back. The window is closed, the lamp has gone out, he is bathed in a sweat turning rapidly cold. He sits up—and the world spins black. Sand and grime bite his cheek. He is suddenly on the floor.

Fumes, from the lamp! Retching, he pulls himself to his feet, throws open the window, gasps and gasps and gasps.

He has nearly been asphyxiated! And the girl?

No girl. No iceberg. Hallucination. And yet she tried to kill him.

Kill him? By opening the window?

Save him?

The Măgar has a bathrobe famous throughout Europe: a gift to his grandfather from Catherine of Russia, it is sewn entirely from the pelts of the pepper-brown coyotes of Tajikistan. Anton has never allowed himself to so much as stroke it. Now, down in the library, he tightens its sash, arranges its sumptuous collar. He tells himself that his commander owes him this much—a little comfort on a freakish night, a few hours rescued for music.

"And I don't care if you like it, you son of a toothless bitch."

In fact he would gladly stay here for days: the innermost chamber of the palace, the safest, the driest. The warmest place, too (except for the white umbra of the tower lamp, where he no longer wishes to be). No bust on the mantle, no frowning eyes. One tight door. One shuttered window, a mere slot really, through which for untold ages the librarian-priest dispensed scrolls, sermons, obituaries bound in scarlet wax.

He warms his hands on the valiant candles, cracks his knuckles, picks up his viola and bow. He makes a slow first draw.

There. The sound, the embrace of pure joy.

He moves without haste into his music. Playing in a trance, barely glancing at the manuscript. It swells, soft étude to deeper forte, a small boat borne with confident strokes to a deepening ocean. The other strings, the woodwinds, the brass are with him, he hears them all. Deep beneath the spell of the music, he smiles, dances, shouts. It is what he has waited for. They will come to their feet, they will pour him glasses of sherry. They will cheer him into his conservatory rooms.

For Anton knows that he has never played such a wonder of music; that it bespeaks, he will not fool himself, a destiny. For this his haste, for this his suffering—and now he leaps beyond the last scribbled bars, sails on through untroubled skies. He pauses, holding in an ocean of breath, to jot a phrase—

The candles cringe, spit a palsy of wax on his hands. Wind moans in the shuttered slot.

"God damn it! This heap of stone is drafty as a sty! What?"

For he thinks he hears a tongue click, a mouth he knows making sounds of disapproval beyond the window.

"Father?"

Silence.

He pulls his score back from the candles, takes one of them, steps from the library to the hall. "Dad! Is that you?"

There is no one at the slot.

He sighs. He has wrestled down every window, tied every curtain, closed the chimney flues. This obstinate draft, it should not *be*. And then he knows. The Round Hall.

Yes: the wind comes from that way. And Faraz has to have gone somewhere.

He does not want to visit that room, bearing the chalice of his unfinished sonata.

His candle dies. He swears again.

The circular performance hall is empty. Dusty candles cling to the mezzanine; brown vines rooted in cracked earthenware grip the pillars. A few chairs jumble in the corners.

As he guessed: the huge wooden doors stand open. Above them, rapine, an old wolf's head. The jaws gape, the discolored tongue cleaves to a leathery palette. Anton imagines the Măgar, young, strong, with a younger violence in him, standing below this animal with a fragile Gypsy girl, holding her hand. He lays his own upon the doors.

The smell of the farmyard, through the space between: methane, manure, rotten straw. Sounds, too: a snuffle, a porcine grunt.

Nineteen years, and he still keeps pigs. Lupescu's tale crowds his thoughts. *I hate pigs, all pigs, everywhere*, Anton thinks. *I hate them.* He slams the doors with a boom. Beyond, a sudden hysterical squealing.

He has to relight all the candles. He flexes his arms, still uneasy, but soon the walls armored with books, the dozen sentinels over his jotted score, relax him. He plays serene and strong, writes a few notes, plays on. Deep shivers, but this time only of delight. He is Anton Cuza of Romania. There will be cheers, lovers, invitations, busts.

At the window slot, very softly, a voice coughs, "No."

"Who is it?" shouts Anton. "Dad!"

More coughs. "Too florid, too *bravo*. Do you want to be known for melodrama?"

Anton fairly sprints to the window. But whoever is there has drawn to one side, so that only his breath can be seen, puffing white.

"You let me down, Anton." The voice is soft, soft. He is *almost* sure it is his father's.

"Why? How?"

"Tch, as if it needed telling. You don't even know me any more, do you? You've quit your family, your friends, your home. Chasing a dream of vanity."

"I know you—Dad." Anton stutters, wants to reach through the slot but is afraid.

"You don't. And your mother? And Julita? Ten months without a visit, without a letter. And have no doubt: they knew what they had been traded for. They saw them—painted women looking you over from the train windows, men in black finery in the dining car."

"How did you get in here? What on earth did you say to Faraz?"

"Do you give a thought to them now? Do you remember the house of your birth at all?"

"Of course I do. What, have you come all this way to accuse me of *that*?" Anton squeezes out a laugh. "I remember everything. Our morning coffee, Mother's sweetbreads, you in your woodshop, throwing hammers at the rat. It *is* you. Why don't you come around to the door?"

The other says nothing. His white breath withdraws a bit.

"I remember the wooden blocks you carved, for me and for Julita."

A faint snort.

"You never could stand to be wrong, Dad. But you are, you see. I'll remember as much as you want." Anton is crowing, no longer bending to the slot. "I remember Julita at her sixteenth birthday, the calico dress, the necklace we chose. She was the kindest, loveliest, gentlest—I remember her dancing with me, and with Enri and Zoltan from next door, while you jigged those songs on your fiddle, the only three you know. Posies and poppies. I remember her chattering about France, wanting everything French, dreaming of a trip to Provence, a ferry down the Rhône."

"It is you who dream."

"I remember my sister—"

"You read it."

"No, no. I lived it."

"You imagined living it. You read something similar."

Anton checks himself. The old man was in the foulest of moods. There was no contradicting his claims, no matter how ridiculous, when such waves of despair and contempt took hold. One could only wait, or leave.

Another cough. "You are pathetic, my son. If indeed I should call you that today. You ran from us."

"I went to school."

"You fled. Your mother had been ill. I had not sold a table in a month, a piano in five."

"It was a clammy place. My chest hurt and my nose ran."

"We had nothing to eat."

"The cows gave milk that spoiled in an hour."

"You had work. A debt to your family. You think you have a gift—what about the gifts we gave you?"

"Well I'm back—isn't that enough? I'm in the stinking army, I send you my pay."

"Late remorse. Ten months late. We had to consent to Julita—"

"Dad! Listen to me!" Anton hisses through the window. "It's not my fault you're a woodsmith, and I'm an artist. But just because I brought you here once, let you shake hands with the porter in his uniform, took you around in secret to gawk like a serf, doesn't mean that you can simply *show up and visit me*. I'm on duty! Can you imagine what could happen to us if Faraz's tongue is loose? Now I won't send you out in the storm, but you must come round here, and be quiet, and touch nothing, and in the morning be gone at once!"

Silence. His father is holding his breath.

"It's warmer in here, too," adds Anton gently.

"I'm sorry," his father murmurs.

"It's all right, Dad."

"I didn't understand."

"Forget it. Come around, let me kiss you."

"You're ill. Your mother was right."

"What?"

The door opens. It is his father, in his work clothes. Wood shavings in his beard, face lined with worry. The cold wind follows him in.

Anton is mute, still holding his viola. His father wordlessly shuts the door, comes forward, takes his son's hand. Examines it. Then he bends, and cold lips press Anton's cheek.

"Sit down, my boy."

He presses Anton down on the couch, sets the viola aside. Draws up a chair.

"Dad?"

"She said your mind was going. I didn't believe her."

"What are you talking about?"

"You're barely with me. You're somewhere else."

"No! What the hell do you mean?"

"Shhh. You say *you* showed *me* round the palace—the palace of the Măgar?"

"When he opened it to the families of the troops. Some time ago."

The old man's lips trembled. "Ah, child, it has been. Eighteen, nineteen years back. I'd forgotten. I took you there by the hand, and carried you when you tired. The Măgar was in exile, in France. And the mayor, just once, let his friends have a look at Tchavodari Palace."

Anton could weep for his addled father.

"You nearly tore the skin from my arm, you were so afraid. But later you were proud and could not stop talking about the palace, the grand dark palace, not for years. You remembered every detail, you drew pictures. Oh, how you pestered me to take you back!"

His father is rubbing his nose. Anton glances about, vaguely agitated.

"What's the matter with everyone tonight, Dad?"

The old man merely looks at him, eyes wet. Anton gives a shrill yell.

"Why did you come here if you refuse to talk to me?"

"Yes, hush! But lie down first—that's it. What shall we talk about, child?"

Around his father the room swims a bit. Anton pulls his feet up on the couch.

"I hardly know. Such a mad night. Faraz is taunting me. Colonel Lupescu's raving. I almost suffocated in the tower. And then you tell me I'm not a good son."

"You are a good son."

"But I left you for music school."

"True enough."

"And when I came back—"

"We were in a terrible way. We had let Julita—"

"But I found work again. Here. The best job in the whole town."

"No, Anton. You can't work now."

"That's very like you, Dad. Why can't you respect my efforts, why?"

"Don't sit up."

"*Why?*"

"Hush! You forget, no matter how many times I tell you. You nod, you say you remember, and then—gone again, away to your palace. God, it hurts me—" His father is actually crying, shaking Anton's shoulders. "Don't tell your mother I'm saying this. But I don't want to let you go. I want you here with us a little longer. That's why I keep telling you."

"Telling me what?"

His father is falling to pieces. "The same things. That she's with child, Julita, but he's let her go. He kept his horrible bargain with you. That you did it, you got her away from him, and we shouldn't ever have agreed to it, but we were hungry, and afraid, and you never, never wrote—"

Anton begins to scream. His father bends down, sobbing, holding his son's chin against his chest.

Hiltan Posnr, nearing sixty, ox-strong, one eye bulbous and staring, splattered with pig shit to his knees, a glob of it clinging to the brandy bottle in his hand, balances high on the groaning rail of a fence in his pig stockade like a squat, greasy-haired god. He reels a bit, but holds on. There is a small, filthy dog with a torn ear on the ground ten feet to his left. Head cocked to one side, it is staring into the pond of gray feces that surrounds them, stinking worse than the foulest reek of the sewers of Constanta. The squealing of pigs innumerable, pigs for forty hectares, rends the air.

Posnr wears an unpleasant smile.

"You think it's a sin, don't you, my nobbly nephew?"

Anton, on the edge of this sea of shit, behind a gate, says, "No, Mr. Posnr. I just think she would be happier with someone her age."

"You're smart enough to remember your manners, boy. But you're a bad bargainer. She's my wife. Your daddy gave her to me. And thanks to me, the doctor came and stilled your mother's fever, and the creditors left off sniffing round his shop."

"She's only sixteen, sir."

"My mother was."

"But today—"

"The *first* Mrs. Posnr was."

"But sir. Today—" Ridiculous, ridiculous! "—women want to marry someone close to themselves in years."

"An expert on women, Lord help us." He tips the bottle up, lurches backward. "*Glah.* Call me Hiltan. What are you here for, boy?"

Anton would like to ask Posnr the same question. He cannot fathom why the richest farmer for a hundred miles, the owner of the village's largest house and (it is said) three thousand hogs, should be perched here, high on a fence in the center of his wallow, with only a dazed dog for company, drunk enough to topple into the swill. He would like to know why this unwanted, undreamed-of brother-in-law calls him *nephew.* He would like to turn and bolt down the hill.

But Anton is not in command of the situation.

"I wrote—I came here—when I heard you had married Julita."

"'Twas more'n a month ago!"

"I was in Constanta, sir. In music school."

The fact catches Posnr's attention. His grin widens to a leer; from his throat a slobbery laugh escapes. He begins to sing, a sort of depraved caricature of a sonata. He lifts the whiskey bottle to his shoulder, stabs the air with his other hand, aping a violinist. Again he almost falls.

Anton's stomach lurches. He can only wait, nauseated and wracked with guilt. It is a gray afternoon, his eighth in the village after ten months absence. His parents' faces in the threshold of the house, dry, hope-robbed faces, are stamped on his eyes. He had known at once. Something had taken Julita away.

"We couldn't find you, Anton." His father, ashen and morose. "And what would you have done? Your mother might have died."

"And been at blessed rest." She turns back to the shadows.

Anton bellows: "You married her to an ogre!"

He does not even succeed in angering his father.

"We sent her to be his maid. She chose to marry, later." His father gestures in the doorway, impotent as death. "It was done—"

Anton can fill in the rest. To save the home. To pay the doctor. To shoulder the burden her brother dropped.

"She was always a good child," says his mother, invisible.

Then had come a week of torture: letters, unanswered. Interviews, rejected. Visits to the city magistrate, a wallow in impotence (the old fellow worried his knuckles, looked Anton over, asked, "Have you proof that your sister has been raped, tortured, or coerced to prostitution?"). No power on earth could oblige Hiltan Posnr to meet his wife's brother.

Anton had felt plunged into a bog of nightmares: Julita given to Posnr! The pig man! Rich, but foul. More powerful than anyone but the Māgar, but hated and feared. Immensely successful (his sausages chewed as far away as Paris), but still just a provincial, belching bore, withdrawn into his forty-hectare wallow, downwind from which houses had to be torn up and moved.

It is Ravel he profanes. Anton forces his hands not to clench.

Posnr glances up, still giggling. Anton's look of rage and disgust nearly finishes him. He doubles over, tears runneling both cheeks. The dog hiccups.

I could kill him! The idea flashes through Anton's mind: the hard bottle, the slippery deep shit, the hogs. But he does not want to be a killer. And what if the man overpowers him? Posnr has shoulders like smoked hams, fists like Clydesdale hooves. And I have a brain, thinks Anton. A useless brain!

"You're a vile man."

Instantly he regrets his words. Posnr lifts his head, suddenly alert, eyes predatory. "You to be talking. Who cut and ran? Who took his last pay from the mill and scurried off to study *music?* Left mother and dad to stumble through a poorly year? *Glah.* She's not been silent, my little Julita. She hates you for leaving them. She says so."

Anton turns his back on the pig man, ramrod straight. Fights for breath.

"She hates you, she hates you—"

He whirls around. "I'll do anything you ask. Please let her go home with me!"

"Not to be, boy."

"I'll work for you."

"You! You'll stoop that low for little sister, eh? Dip your toe in pigshit?"

"I'll pay you back. Everything you gave to them."

"A music school dandy." Posnr looks as if he might be sick.

"I worked in the mill for years."

"Stop it, boy. You're a runt pup, we won't argue that."

"Don't keep her, sir. I can—"

"You can be damned! She's my wife! Maybe she don't love me yet, though she hates Brother Anton more, but she'll mellow. And my Julita knows her place. I know what you think. That I'm a savage, an idiot. But I've got more brain than you, my little charmer.

I'm not as big as some in Bucharest, but in this town I'm on top. *On top!* The Măgar says it—know your place. I send him hogs. He lets me be." With a thick finger he stabs at Anton. "And you have forgotten your place, nephew, and for that you will pay a pretty coin!"

Anton does not move or speak or breathe. Posnr watches him another moment, spits, lowers his hand and his eyes. The silence pulls out. When he looks up again, his face is changed: equally cold, but over his asymmetrical eyes has settled a glaze of milky fascination.

"I had my way with her. What kept me waking nights."

Anton's whole body twitches.

"I can have my way with you, too, boy. I can say, 'Come carry me out of this shit hole,' and you will. That's what I want."

Anton only stares, bewildered. Posnr's gaze slides to the dog.

"I want you to do it now."

"And you will—"

"Now, I said."

He can't believe it. He is opening the gate, slushing over the gravel margin, and then, agonizingly slow, he puts his black buckled shoe down in the shit. His foot disappears, then the cuff of his trousers.

There is no bottom!

Posnr howls with laughter.

Anton finds solid ground at mid-calf. Balanced, he plants his other foot. Deeper. Warm below the surface. The dog yelps sharply. He feels the gray ooze in his shoe. Another step. And another.

Posnr is leering with delight. Anton tastes bile.

Another.

Posnr gurgles. Throws his bottle away. Waves his hand, in a kind of bloated lilt.

Four more steps. The buckle on his right shoe gives way.

Posnr is singing. Horrible, unspeakable.

Posies for the mayor, poppies for the king

Three. Two.

Violets for the merchant-man

One.

With his golden ring!

"Now then! Keep me clean, boy! Ha!"

Crusted boots clump Anton's thighs. Thick arms drape over the young man's shoulders. Posnr's bulk slides down, and gasping, staggering, Anton catches him, hoists him. The dog drools.

"Higher!" The brandied voice in his ear. Somehow, he nudges Posnr a few inches up his back. Turns. Pulls. His bare right foot leaps free like a wrenched stump, descends again. His left follows.

"No matter what, you don't drop me, see?"

Another step. The gate hangs open. A wet lip grazes his ear.

"You're a kind lad." Something new in Posnr's voice. Fatigue? Shame?

Then the dog growls, and growls louder. Barks, hysterical. Posnr's limbs tighten like pythons. A splashing, sucking sound from behind. Anton reels, sways, recovers.

The dog's teeth close on his wrist.

At a dead run he bursts from the library, manuscript in hand. His father shouts. The walls are failing. The moon has raised the foaming sea.

Out through the Paris room, the great hall, the foyer. Through the main doors and into the courtyard. He is scalded with rain. Dashes toward the gardens, ducks under the laurel arch.

Wagner grins, humming a deranged tune.

And then—howls. The dogs have escaped! They are ahead—no, behind in the courtyard. They will smell him.

He turns at bay between Handel and Chopin. Shadows lope among shadows.

"Faraz!"

God knows how long he's starved them.

Anton dashes on, throaty barks following. Soon he is at the very heart of the gardens, where a shallow reflecting pool churns in the rain. The wet jaws snarl in a tightening circle. He jumps into the water, thrashes to the center of the pool. His mind races: he would hide his smell. He would crouch here, motionless upon this flat disk of porphyry, be taken for a statue, he would—

Anton would never know how Julita spent her coin of freedom. He was buried in the village of his birth, in a churchyard swept by the shadow of Tchavodari Palace: as close as he ever came to the structure, save for once as a child.

He would not learn how Julita walked over the Bicazului in a fury of snow, holding the hands of two boy cousins who would abandon her in Brasov for factory jobs; would never know that she carried not only Posnr's child in her womb but eleven thousand dollars of his silver in burlap over her shoulder, between slabs of salt pork; how she caught the train from Brasov to Rijeka, Yugoslavia, crossed the Adriatic to Venice on an Italian steamer, sold the silver with perfect acumen to a dealer on the Ponte Rialto, and after a night of horrible dreams, caught the train to Paris where instinct told her, correctly, the doctor waited who would take the fetus from her womb.

Her brother never saw her skin browned by four years of sun, or the leaps that brought gasps of pleasure when she danced with the Ballet de l'Opéra. He also would not know how she fled violence again in January 1939, this time to New York, boarded a southbound train the same day, descended in Washington, danced with the National Conservatory, and married a lawyer.

Julita did not speak of Anton. In the lawyer's extended family, the deceased brother was simply a figure connected to an incomprehensibly distant time of sadness—the small, cold place from which Julita came.

But one of this brood, the lawyer's brother's son, shook hands for the first time with Great-Aunt Julita at a Christmas party in 1986, and disturbed the old woman profoundly.

The boy was a recovering anorexic. Thin as a whittled stick. Shuddering in a warm room, like his great-uncle half a century earlier on the Black Sea coast. His laughter was forced.

Julita, past seventy, knew nothing about that branch of the family—a soft-spoken, old-money clutch from Virginia. They were consistent in attaching *stabilized* to every mention of the boy: he had a stabilized diet, stabilized moods, stabilized glands. But they were consistently wrong, and two weeks later he fell into a coma, with flooded lungs and a heart murmur: galloping pneumonia.

She had quite taken to him at Christmas, liked his aberrant bookishness, in a family replete with practical men who spoke of growth funds, golf tournaments, quarterbacks, tight ends. When it seemed he might die she came alone, sparrow-small behind the wheel of a huge green Buick.

The boy thought his waking was his own death. Above him was a wrinkled angel, smiling with infinite tenderness, shrunken until she seemed almost a girl. Her hands, spread beneath his pajama shirt, burned cold through his fever. She was drying his chest with a towel.

The boy's parents slept on a couch, wretched and unwashed. Julita sat primly on the edge of the bed.

"Stay with us," she said.

"I don't remember you."

"You will."

"What's wrong with me?"

"Pneumonia."

"I dreamed I was a fish. Hooked."

"But fighting?"

"Yes. Who are you? I don't know you."

He didn't know any of them. But he sat up, stronger than he had been in weeks, and listened curiously as Julita told him who he was, and who she was. He drank some orange juice. And since his parents showed no sign of waking, she leaned very carefully on one elbow and told him the whole tale of Anton and the pig man, the little rabid dog that killed him, and the palace where his mind took refuge.

But the next day the boy suffered a relapse, and lay wheezing and muttering for three days. Julita was still there when he woke, but they were never alone, and uneasy in the crowded room, she kissed him goodbye and drove back to Maryland.

The boy recovered his health, mostly, but never a clear memory of his long illness. In fact he did not think once of his great-aunt until, in March, his father called to say that Julita had been found on the shoulder of the Annapolis turnpike, frozen stiff. The Buick was half a mile behind her in a marbled sheath of ice. It was the latest winter storm on the Maryland register.

Even then he was not inclined to linger on, far less share, her story. It had nothing to do with him, and he didn't want to be known for melodrama.

ELDON THOMPSON

But what happened to Kylac?

That was the question that dogged me more than any other upon the completion of my Legend of Asahiel trilogy. My editor asked it, my readers asked it—heck, I'd have asked it, if I didn't already know the answer. I had plans, you see, and all would be revealed in due time.

While I assured my editor that the continuation of the Asahiel story would shed light on the fate of a certain rogue assassin, she urged me to address the more immediate concern regarding one Kylac Kronus and his whereabouts following events in *The Crimson Sword*. Relenting, I realized that to do so meant giving Kylac his own spin-off series—less epic in tone and style than the Asahiel books, but an interesting challenge in itself. The larger world story could wait, I decided. In the meantime, it would be all about Kylac.

As I delved into the new project, however, it became clear to me that even these Kylac-centric books were not going to fully answer questions pertaining to his mysterious origins. His is not the sort of backstory that lends itself to hearthside anecdote, and he is not the sort of person to reveal it if it did. Some things we simply keep to ourselves.

Then Shawn invited me to contribute to *Unfettered*, and the proverbial light bulb flashed in my brain. Here it was, an exclusive location in which to tell an origin story, if you will, for this character. A tale to address the themes of courage and perseverance that seemed to me paramount in honoring Shawn as a second-time cancer survivor. I already knew most of the story and, given a place to put it, I required very little time to flesh out the rest.

For any who may enjoy it, thank Shawn for making it happen. My personal hope is that it will shed a measure of light on Kylac's attitudes and actions, and maybe even tide readers over while I strive to finish answering that persistent question . . .

But what happened to Kylac?

Eldon Thompson

UNBOWED

Eldon Thompson

The wooden rapier clattered against the sanded stones of the arena floor, its hilt coming to rest near Brie's hand. She ceased her scrubbing to consider the weapon, hunched as she was on hands and knees, then turned her head to consider *him*. Her expression accused him of madness.

"Would you see me flogged?" she hissed.

"My father has an audience with the king, and won't return before nightfall." Kylac grinned. "Call it a birthday gift."

A flush stole across Brie's freckled cheeks. He'd remembered. Just as swiftly, her familiar pout returned. "And a celebration it'd be, to see your father beat you bloody." Her gaze swept the edges of the chamber, as if expecting to find someone spying from the shadows. "Go on. I've work to finish."

With emphasis, she dipped her sponge in her bucket of dirty water and resumed her scrubbing. Kylac felt his smile slip. Mayhap her flush owed solely to her exertions. Or frustration at being interrupted. Or alarm at his proposal. Whatever, he felt suddenly foolish, having woefully misjudged her imagined reaction.

"I just thought . . ." He watched her reach her sponge blindly for her bucket, pointedly ignoring him. "I mean, you've always said—"

He stopped as the bucket tipped, bending reflexively to catch it before it spilled. She spun toward him as he did so, releasing her sponge to take up the wooden rapier by its hilt. Kylac just barely managed to slide his leg clear of its whipping arc, while righting the bucket, before sliding back a pace. By then, Brie was lunging to her feet, pressing him back farther. A skip, slide, and duck enabled him to avoid any stinging bruises, and on her fifth strike, his own practice weapon came to hand—with a sound block and swift counter that she deftly avoided, but that finally forced her to pause.

"Why, did I just catch the masterful Kylac off guard?" she taunted. Her eyes sparkled now with that fierce fire, her puffy cheeks set high and wide in a proud grimace.

"Open your stance. And straighten your toes."

"My toes are fine. You're just embarrassed that I nearly took yours."

"Your front foot is pointed toward the side wall, when your enemy is in front of you." He jabbed. She parried, realigning her footwork. "The bucket was a nice touch."

"You underestimated me." She lunged, choosing a simple combination that compensated with execution for what it lacked in creativity. "You *always* underestimate me."

"I'm better than you." Kylac blocked her advance, then fed her the same combination in reverse. "There's a difference."

"One day, you won't be. And you'll be too stubborn to see it until it's too late."

"Not before you learn to focus your attack on my centerline," he countered, slipping from side to side as her prodding strikes fanned wide. Brie's short brown locks swished about her face, causing her to puff now and again as they fell across her eyes. "You'd do well to crop that hair, too."

"And look more like you? I'd sooner not."

She nearly caught him then with one of those stabbing lunges. Like an asp she was, with that one, her reach swift and long. *Too* long, it seemed. For, as usual, she failed to return her guard in time to defend her face against a counterstrike that Kylac chose not to take. "You won't look a thing like me when you lose your ear," he admonished her instead. "And you will, if you don't remember to raise your guard when you snap back from one of those."

"Oh? Did I nearly lull you again?"

"Keep your elbow down. You're flapping like a wounded gull."

Brie just laughed, a sound so rare that it spawned a comforting warmth in Kylac's chest. She had long yearned for this—a chance to try him in the arena as though she were a fellow student, rather than a scrub girl relegated forever to sopping up their blood and sweat. But Talonar was the preeminent combat school in the city, in the land, likely in all of Pentania. With the long list of wealthy, highborn students clamoring to pay the school's prohibitive fees, Kylac's father flatly refused to make room for those who could not.

Least of all some blind pauper's eleven—no, twelve-year-old granddaughter.

It rankled his father that Kylac should waste his time sparring with her at all. But, at age thirteen, he was already the most skilled student at Talonar, and had been for the past year. So long as he kept excelling in his own lessons and exceeding every staunch expectation his father had for him, he'd been allowed his "petty diversion with the rag," as his father called her—provided, of course, he did not interfere with her chores, and they confined their after-hours play to the parks and alleys beyond Talonar's gates.

A pair of stipulations they were breaking now, obviously. But then, it was a special occasion. And truly, what was the harm? Should it come to it, the memory of that laugh would be enough to soothe the sting of a lash or two.

"Guard up," he cautioned her again. "That's twice already I might have slit your throat."

"A fine boast. Feel welcome to back it up at any time."

And so it went as they danced their dance across the arena floor: Brie letting loose some of that bridled fury of hers, and Kylac offering admonishments where he felt them most needed. In truth, she was a fine athlete, both vigorous and disciplined, with strong endurance, natural instincts, and the even rarer skill of adaptation. She wasn't as fast as him, nor as polished, but then, with her limited training time, how could she be? Even among the full-time students, he'd met only one or two others who could match him—and they each had a dozen years on him. While they stood at or near their full potential, his remained yet untapped.

"Faster," he coaxed her, and quickened his own pace, forcing her to respond. "You've got to be faster. Weight and speed—"

"Breed power," she said. "Yet you never advise I grow thicker. If I were to sprout breasts or belly, would you still fawn over me as you do?"

It was Kylac's turn to redden. As its warmth brushed his forehead, Brie launched another diving thrust. "Guard up," he reminded her in counter, this time razing her gently across the jaw.

Brie scowled. She was tiring, though neither torture nor deprivation would lead her to admit it. Nor would she ever suggest they stop. Her passion ran too strong, her pride even stronger.

"Open your stance. Guard up. Guard . . ."

He hesitated as a sudden darkness entered the arena. It might have been a cloud shouldering past the setting sun, except that this was a darkness felt, not seen. Brie pressed him as he slowed and withdrew, perceiving some unexpected advantage, mayhap, or thinking it a ruse. But it took her only a moment more to register the truth of his grim expression. Her gaze lifted past him, and she gasped, drawing to a startled halt.

"Master Rohn," Kylac acknowledged, turning toward the near entry. "Master Xarius." He bowed briefly to the pair standing within the shadowed alcove, barely more than shadows themselves.

His father stepped forward from beneath the arch, his heavy brow pinched inward, the corners of his mouth anchored low in stern disapproval. The expression itself told Kylac nothing, for it was the only look his father ever wore. But the weight of his silence felt heavy enough to crush stone.

At his shoulder stood Xarius, arms crossed, smirking coldly. His father's prized pupil and personal warder. Ever the first to taste it when Master Rohn unleashed wind, as Brie had once whispered, though far from the school's grounds. Xarius had killed for lesser insults.

"Your pardon, sir. I was only—"

"Reminding her to keep her guard up, by my hearing. Is that what you heard, Master Xarius?"

"More than once, sir," he whispered, like a hissing reptile.

"Aye. More than once. Is your pupil deaf, Master Kylac?"

"Sir? No, sir."

"Then it would seem a more stringent reminder is in order."

"Sir—"

"Remind her."

Kylac glanced at Brie, who was doing her best to control her breathing. "We were only playing."

"In this arena? You know otherwise, Master Kylac. As does she. If you would train her on this floor, you will finish the lesson."

"You have my apologies already. If I am to be punished—"

"Master Xarius, remind this new pupil of ours to keep her guard up."

"Sir," Xarius replied. He gave a crisp bow, then stepped forward, a slender shortsword coming to hand. Light from the high, open windows gleamed upon its steel surface.

Kylac felt Brie stiffen, pierced by a sudden panic. She dared not run, but knew as well as he that Xarius would maim her with no more thought than he might spend on the removal of a pebble from his boot. As Xarius advanced steadily on soundless feet, Kylac instinctively stepped in front of Brie, snatching the practice sword from her rigid grasp and thus arming himself with the pair of wooden blades.

"The fault lies with me," he insisted. He twirled one sword and tossed the other, testing their balance and heft, before raising them in a defensive cross. "If any need reminder, it is I."

Xarius scowled, the predatory glint in his eye dimming with uncertainty. He glanced back at Rohn.

Their headmaster only glared, saying nothing.

Xarius smiled, the cruelty in his eyes flaring. It was the only warning Kylac received before Xarius attacked, a second blade joining the first, whipping toward his face in a blinding flurry.

Kylac had anticipated nothing less. His own blades were

already moving, turning the strikes aside with deft twists and precise angles. He could not harm Xarius with his training weapons, allowing the elder combatant to press him with impunity. Yet it also enabled Kylac to narrow his focus, to concentrate solely on defense.

Brie shied backward, retreating toward her bucket and sponge. Thankfully, Xarius made no move to follow her. And why would he? It wasn't often he found himself with an advantage such as this against his only real rival. Kylac was not only the headmaster's son, but roughly half Xarius's age—salts in the wound as Kylac had taken to besting him regularly during their daily sessions. Given the chance to reassert himself and deliver a scar or two in lasting insult, the prideful Xarius would be determined to do just that.

Assuming he failed to simply take Kylac's head or some piece of it in trophy.

The fury of the quicksilver strikes slashing and stabbing his way left Kylac little doubt as to Xarius's preference. And by now it seemed clear he could rely on his father not to intervene. Kylac had staked this challenge. His father—his instructor—would let him live or die by it.

Thus far, his wooden swords were holding up well against the onslaught. Hewn of granitewood from the deep Kalmira, thickly lacquered and well polished with use, they were as strong as any oaken staff thrice their girth, able to withstand the lighter blades with which Xarius was most adept. Nonetheless, Kylac could feel the nicks and notches collecting along their length. Be it late or soon, his opponent's fine steel would hack and carve them to splinters, and Kylac's bones with them.

If he intended to end this in his favor, he needed to do so swiftly.

The lethal blades thrashed before him, a dicing whirlwind. Xarius was unquestionably a master—precise, poised . . . patient? Normally, yes. But as Kylac continued to weather the storm, he could sense in his adversary a gnawing frustration. He had expected a swift victory, in this instance. Denied that, and with his master looking on, Kylac could see in him the mounting need for a decisive victory—and the urgency that came with it.

So Kylac gave him the opening he sought, angling a wooden blade out carelessly wide, inviting Xarius to disarm him on that side. Xarius did so, and Kylac gave a startled yelp in feigned dismay as the practice weapon skittered away. A somewhat reckless maneuver, but also fairly obvious. He doubted Xarius would have taken the bait under normal circumstances.

In this instance, however, the next strike took dead aim at his naked wrist. Rather than shy from the advancing blow, Kylac rolled forward underneath it, trading a small cut on the shoulder of his jerkin for his pursuit of Xarius's retreating blade. His open hand grabbed for its hilt as his remaining sword stabbed hard against a nerve in Xarius's elbow, disabling his grip.

An overhead block spared Kylac's head a cleaving, and enabled him to spring up with confiscated steel in hand. By the time Brie had placed a hand to her mouth to silence her squeak of alarm at Kylac's seeming vulnerability, it was he who held the edge of a sharp blade against his opponent's throat, drawing Xarius backward into a submissive stance.

They remained locked that way for a moment, Kylac triumphant, Xarius fuming, neither making a sound. It was Rohn who finally shattered the stillness.

"I heard no one yield."

Kylac glanced at his father, then peered down into Xarius's livid face. In nine years of training together, not once had the elder fighter admitted defeat. He didn't have to. Both knew that Kylac wasn't going to slit his throat. Even if Kylac couldn't guarantee the same were their positions reversed.

Rohn, too, had seen this stalemate before, and shook his head disapprovingly. "Suffer the weak . . ." He left the sentence hanging, waiting for Kylac to complete it.

"And you will suffer their weakness."

"Again you prove soft—a softness with which you would now infect others." Rohn gestured vaguely toward Brie. "You think you've defended her this day? Shielded her with your coddling? You've enabled a deficiency. Reinforced a flaw. Fostered a failing.

You have killed her, perhaps, and do not yet know it."

Kylac didn't dare face Brie, as he wished. Instead, he glanced down at Xarius, who now wore a derisive sneer.

"We do not teach failure here," his father spat, and swept the arena with his glare. "This lesson is over."

When her work was finished, Kylac escorted Brie home as he often did, although they had crossed two plazas and the bridge on Wayfarer before he dared speak to her.

"Are you all right?"

"Are you?" she snapped.

Evidently, he had loosed his tongue too soon. "I never meant . . . I only thought—"

"I know what you thought, Kylac."

"Will you not permit my apology? My father—"

"Your father was right. I don't need to be coddled. He thinks me weak as is."

Kylac blinked. She was taking Rohn's part? He felt a stirring of indignation. "Would you have had me stand aside? Leave you to Xarius?"

"It never should have come to that. You should have obeyed your father and delivered whatever punishment I was to receive. I've no fear of bruises. Especially if Master Rohn deems them necessary."

Her assessment stung. It had been foolish of him to tempt her as he had, to goad her into breaking the rules and violating his father's trust. For that, her anger was well warranted. But to be wroth with him for accepting blame, and for shielding her . . . what sense did that make?

Rather than argue, he opted for the safety of silence, stewing privately. Next time, she could fend for herself, if so determined. Let the blood she mopped from the arena floor be her own.

Mayhap he wasn't so soft as his father feared.

They slipped through the south gates of the Blackthorn district to enter Crestmire—or the Mire, as it was more commonly

known. Stone walls, paved streets, and lush gardens quickly gave
way to thin wood slats, dirt lanes, and weedy plots littered with
filth and refuse. Homeless beggars skulked amid the shadows,
muttering to themselves or to the rats who served audience.
Brusque shouts and rough laughter echoed from the taverns and
brothels that dominated the area. Smith Jarrons was being called
a cheat again by some angry patron, while stablemaster Paresh
was berating one of his grooms.

Brie's petulant silence aside, it seemed all was in order here.

They passed a butcher's shop, a cobbler's shack, and a derelict
chandlery that had near burned to the ground more than a year
past when the proprietor, it was said, had fallen into a drunken
sleep with a lit pipe in his mouth. The ground on which it stood
edged a slough that stank of sewage, and so the structure sat, half-
collapsed, home now to mice and insects and a handful of feral
cats. Kylac spotted one of the latter, a striped tom, eyeing him
from a blackened eave.

Beyond that, as they continued to round the slough, lay a cluster of dilapidated homes, lit from within by guttering oil lamps
and evening cookfires. Aback of these farther still, tucked in amid
a swath of decaying brambles, stood a lone, tumbledown cottage
that might have been deserted for all the light that burned in its
empty windows. Someday soon, it would be, if gods there were—
though Kylac had his doubts.

Brie slowed as they neared its sagging porch, halting when
they were yet a stone's throw away. A foul breeze blowing in over
the slough seemed to cool her anger.

"I do thank you," she said, peering at her feet. "For my gift. I
quite enjoyed it."

Kylac could not say whether she was being snide or genuine—
until her big brown eyes found his, and she gave him that hint of
her lopsided smile. Like that, his own bitterness became as dry
sands swept in a wind, his angrier thoughts buried by a wash of
guilt. Though hardly the prettiest girl he'd ever caught stealing
glances in his direction, she was the only one he'd found himself
glancing back at. "Chipmunk," her crueler friends had dubbed

her as a child, making mock of her puffy cheeks, heavy freckles, and slightly bucked teeth. In truth, she hadn't fully outgrown the resemblance. But she possessed also a chipmunk's curiosity, playfulness, and athleticism. And when she gazed at him as she was gazing now—

"Bray!" the old man barked, emerging from the depths of the seemingly abandoned house. "Is that you?"

He came sniffing onto the porch like a mole, his pink nose twitching, sightless eyes clouded and milky beneath a wrinkled brow and the stray white wisps still clinging to it. His back was stooped, his joints and limbs as gnarled and crooked as the staff to which he clung. To see him curdled Kylac's blood. If Brie was a chipmunk, then she had done well, coming from such wretched stock, even a generation removed.

"Bring another viper home, did ya?" her grandfather snarled, and spat from the edge of his porch. "I can smell its venom."

"It's me, sir. Kylac."

"Don't you hiss at me, viper, or I'll give your hide a tanning that'll have you pleading for the next molting."

Kylac readied a retort, but gulped it down when Brie put a restraining hand on his chest.

"I'm coming, Grandfather." She looked back at Kylac, only to turn without a word and shuffle dutifully toward her home.

"Have you no notion of the hour?" the old man groused. "Or did the sun go and take a longer route than usual?"

"Apologies, Grandfather."

"I don't want your apologies. I want my dinner," he said, as she shuffled past him and into the cottage. To Kylac, he hollered, "Well, go on, viper. Back to your nest. I've told you before, my Bray ain't your concern."

Bray, he called her, for nagging worse than any mule. *Her name is Briallen*, Kylac wanted to shout. *Her friends call her Brie.* Instead he said, "Today is her birthday, sir."

"You fear I'd forgotten? That I can't still hear her mother's blasted wailing and her own damnable squalling from the day she was whelped?"

Within the cottage, a taper flared to life, its soft flame set to chasing shadows and no doubt sending the roaches skittering.

"Away, viper. I catch you slithering 'round my home again, I'll have your fangs."

Brie spoke not a word to him over the next week. Though Kylac saw her every day in the arena, mopping and hauling and scouring while he trained, she kept her head down and her eyes bent to her tasks. Ordinarily, she would discreetly observe him and the other combatants, learning what she could at a distance before joining up with him when both had completed their work. Instead, she made sure to finish up while he was still at his lessons, and rather than wait for him, hurried from the school grounds without so much as a nod or a glance.

Unusual behavior, though not without precedent. She got this way sometimes, become angry and aloof. On the heels of their disobedience in the arena, however, Kylac worried this time that he might be responsible. She'd forgiven him that night, hadn't she? There at the end?

Regardless, he'd learned not to pry when he found her in these moods, leaving him little choice but to wait her out. If history could be trusted, it might last days, or even weeks. In most instances, he suspected these withdrawals had to do with her grandfather's mistreatment of her. Though she'd never spoken of it, Kylac had seen the bruises, and noticed her ginger strides. He'd considered spying, to ensure her safety, but felt that would be a violation of their trust as friends. Short of that, he'd suggested she leave the old man. Her response had been that her grandfather was her only surviving family member, and she was all he had. She wasn't going to abandon him.

How much could Kylac do to help someone who claimed she didn't need it?

The question had long gnawed at him, and continued to do so. Seven days into this new episode, he could ponder little else. When at skills or studies, he would picture Brie's cold shoulder or her grandfather's age-spotted face, and feel a rush of anger. Sometimes, the emotion would work in his favor, giving him an added burst of energy against an opponent, say, or the conviction to tear through a puzzle or equation. More often, it led to some lapse in concentration that left him scratched or battered, or having to rework a failed calculation or bungled recitation. Somehow, the latter always occurred under his father's watchful eye—not that it had any discernible effect on the man's appraisal. Rohn looked upon him now, as always, as a blacksmith might a piece of brittle steel. No matter how well he performed, he could not escape the inherent flaws his father perceived in him.

He was back in the arena, demonstrating techniques for staving off a pack of assailants to a cluster of younger pupils, wishing Brie would slip even a glance his way, and half hoping his father would find another target for his chilly disapproval, when the stamp of booted feet marching in formation betrayed the unannounced arrival of an armored company. Twoscore in number, their hard leather soles drew notice from even the neophyte students, who ceased their wrestling, tumbling, and swordplay to mark the commotion.

City watch, Kylac realized, as they neared the arched entry to the arena. Advancing with grim purpose. Dorravian, the school's chief steward, hastened alongside.

"Master," Dorravian called. "I bade them halt. They claim to have a warrant."

A soldier on the left flank shoved the steward aside as the forward ranks fanned out in shell formation, as if to seal against any attempt at exit. Revealed at the heart of the regiment was Captain Traeger, immediately recognizable by the cleft in his lip. A deformity he'd been born with, though he would have others believe he'd earned it in battle. Whichever, it gave his face a permanent sneer that seemed somehow fitting for Atharvan's most notorious enforcer of civil ordinance.

"Headmaster Rohn," the captain greeted. "Pleasing it is to at last be welcomed into your hallowed sanctum."

Rohn regarded Traeger with his typical, stone-crushing glare.

"I trust this warrant of yours bears royal seal, for you to be foolish enough to invade these halls."

Traeger brandished the small scroll clutched in his gloved fist. "By special order of Royal Magistrate Aarhus," he announced with barely bridled glee.

He may as well have pronounced them all traitors to the crown, for the grim murmur that swept through the arena. All knew of Magistrate Aarhus, a ruthless inquisitor said to be little more than a torturer in silk robes. A year earlier, under pressure from powerful factions at home and abroad after a rash of escalating murders among some of the wealthiest guildmasters throughout the realms of Pentania, King Galdric had granted Aarhus commission to root out and eliminate members of the fabled Seax Lunara—a secret order of assassins rumored to have originated here in Partha centuries earlier, before the foundation stones of Atharvan's curtain wall had been laid. Most snickered at the time, suggesting that the magistrate had been set to chasing ghosts and mummers' tales, and whispering loudly that the deaths of a few high-ranking merchants and noblemen well known for their rivalries and contentions did not mean the proud city of Atharvan was infested with assassins.

In the months since, however, Aarhus and those serving him, given free rein, had somehow managed to round up and imprison or execute half a dozen confessed members of the Seax Lunara. Wherever the magistrate pointed a finger, it seemed, the guilty boiled to the surface. And with each new kill or capture, they claimed to be closing in on the order's unknown leader.

"And what purpose do you serve here?" Rohn inquired coolly. Neither his expression, nor the tenor of his voice had changed—though Kylac noted that Xarius, who'd been leading a series of advanced scaling exercises, crept close now to his father's shoulder.

"They search your chambers even now, Master," Dorravian reported from where he stood pinned against the wall.

"And the grounds entire, until we are satisfied," Traeger added.

"Should you tell us what you seek, perhaps we can aid you in your search," said Rohn.

The captain's cleft-made sneer stretched higher. "Salveris, son of Governor Tehric of Crylag, was killed last night, robbed in an alley. We have witnesses to the account that finger you, Headmaster."

That sparked another murmur among the arena's occupants. Kylac looked toward Brie, stood frozen in the far corner holding a fistful of bloodstained rags. He felt her gaze flick in his direction before pinning back like everyone else's to Master Rohn.

"Salveris," Rohn echoed. "I know the lad. As likely staggered drunk off a tavern stoop, cracked his skull, and was fell upon by scavenging urchins."

Xarius and a handful of the older students sneered or chuckled. Most of the younger students could only observe in awe.

Traeger himself was not amused. "The trail led here. The evidence we seek *will* be found here. And when it is, this little empire of yours, and the plague it breeds, will be put to the torch. And I'll be there, flame in hand, to crush the fleeing rats underfoot."

Kylac's father hadn't built this "empire," but none could deny it had flourished under his watch. While Talonar was not the only combat school in the city, it was far and away the most renowned. They did not limit themselves here to the practice of brute fighting techniques. Rather, they explored all aspects of death and injury, covering human contest with and without weapons, acids and poisons used alone and in combination, methods of stealth and infiltration overt and secretive, mental exercises of interrogation and deception and skullduggery, the effects of torture and deprivation, and more. Surgeons and healers trekked from the westernmost shores of Alson and the southernmost Kuurian peninsula to learn anatomy and the precise impact of various wounds and diseases. Foreign military commanders crossed tempest seas to share and develop battlefield tactics, siege strategies, and the logistics of troop movement. If it related in any way to the physics or psychology of warfare, it was entertained in a manner both scholarly and practical within these walls.

Given the subject, it was only natural, mayhap, to draw rumor of dealings more sinister. For decades, even before Rohn's time, the school had been accused of harboring a darker motive and purpose. Yet Kylac's father and those before him were not without powerful friends. King Galdric himself had visited the grounds and taken private lessons. Several of his personal guard had trained here, as well. Many of the city's finest pit fighters were forged in this very arena, representing a significant, ongoing investment on the part of their masters. Rivers of coin ran through these halls, breeding envy and resentment among some, but limiting those who dared to challenge Rohn with any open accusations.

Clearly, Magistrate Aarhus and Captain Traeger were beholden to no such fear.

"Your fervor is remarkable, Captain," Rohn allowed, "if ultimately misguided. The skills purveyed at this institution are tools, nothing more. What men do with those tools is their business. If some murder"—he shrugged—"others defend and save lives. Or is the blade on your own hip merely for ceremony?"

"The blade at my hip is an instrument of lawful justice, duly blessed, and held in plain view. Not some poisoned barb, secreted in shadow, to be plunged into an unsuspecting man's back for a purse of gold."

"Most are worth far less, I would say."

The ever-sneering Traeger cocked his head to one side. "Enjoy your japes. Doubtless, you believe His Majesty will save you. Not this time. The only—"

"Captain!" a watchman shouted from the fourth tier of the arena, at the mouth of a hall that led to Rohn's personal quarters. A youthful soldier, full of eagerness. He held up what looked to be a jeweled medallion. "Captain, we found it! In the headmaster's chambers."

Traeger's smile stretched so high, it seemed the cleft in his lip might tear further. At a signal, his fellow soldiers presented the tips of their pikes or swords. "Headmaster Rohn, you are hereby placed under royal arrest, for the unnatural death of Salveris, son of Tehric, Governor of Crylag. By order of Royal Magistrate Aarhus, you will attend us peacefully, or die where you stand."

Xarius drew his swords. Nearly a dozen elder students

followed his lead. Kylac found himself clutching a blade of his own, though still in its sheath. He preferred not to think of what might happen should he draw it.

Sweat beaded on the foreheads of Traeger's watchmen, while their gazes skimmed around in anticipation. The captain's own face underwent a set of contortions as he reweighed the task before him. Rohn, by comparison, stood deathly calm, unmoved, arms crossed. If he cared whether or not he—or all of them—were to die, there was no hint of it in his visage.

The standoff lengthened, the tension in the air thickening until Kylac feared it would snap like a drawn bowstring. He dared not look for Brie, but hoped she had the sense to flee when the arrow was loosed.

Then his father's eyes found his, seeming to darken at the sight of his sheathed blade.

"As you will, Captain," Rohn said, stepping past Xarius with wrists held out before him. "Let us see where this little game of yours will lead."

Before being ushered from the school grounds in manacles, Rohn pronounced Masters Vashar and Stromwell chief regents in his absence, and charged them with ensuring that operations proceeded without deviation. He did so in a booming voice from the front courtyard, with nearly the entirety of Talonar's occupants looking on, as it became clear that a sizable faction was preparing to join Kylac and Xarius in pursuit of Captain Traeger's prisoner escort. Even so, it took Master Stromwell's beefy hand and a personal rebuke from Rohn himself to collar Kylac and prevent him from following when Traeger's pikemen prodded his father through the front gates.

Only when the day's duties were finished was Kylac permitted to make his way to the royal prisons, where word held it his father had been delivered. Not surprisingly, he was denied entry by a bullish master jailor, who would allow only that Rohn was a guest in the complex's central tower—the Gilded Cleaver, as it had come to be known. A cage typically reserved for accused nobility, the jailor pointed out, bestowed with comforts beyond his father's station. Rohn's treatment would be better than he deserved.

"Even if he's innocent?" Kylac asked.

The jailor had a barking laugh. "Show me a blue-feathered pig, I'll show you an innocent man."

He fared no better the next day, or the day after that. His father would be permitted no visitors lest they be approved by Magistrate Aarhus or King Galdric himself. Rohn had counselors and advisors already working that tract—men who did little more than grumble of petitions and precedents and patience. Whispers filled the school's halls, but Kylac could find nothing substantial in any of them. Vashar and Stromwell were as blind and deaf as he. While sympathetic to Kylac's concerns, they preferred to focus on the duties they'd been assigned, and urged him to do the same.

By the third day following his father's arrest, Kylac was seriously contemplating an unauthorized incursion into the Gilded Cleaver. A perilous proposition, he knew—not only for himself, but for the damage it might do to his father's chances of formal pardon should the act be perceived as an escape attempt. And yet, how long could he stand idle when they might be torturing his father toward a confession even now?

He was deliberating privately in one of the open-air wards, working through a series of leaping and climbing exercises on the labyrinthine porcupine tree, when Brie entered the yard below with a hand rake and a pair of pruning shears. Kylac gave her a moment to retreat upon spying him there, up in the tree's highest rungs. When she knelt instead amid the hedges of evenshade and thanesbloom to one side, he knew with a spear of hope that her coming was no accident.

A series of drops, tucks, and descending flips brought him to his feet at the tree's base.

Where have you been? he wanted to demand, but had learned well enough the foolishness—and unfairness—in that. Instead, he approached tentatively, drawing to a stop a pace away, where he commenced stretching. "Been wondering when someone was going to trim those hedges."

Brie kept her gaze in the dirt. "Any word of your father?"

"Little of note. And none I can trust."

"What are you planning?"

"Who says I'm planning anything?"

This time, she spared him a look—the sort meant to remind him that she was not a fool. "The servants think him guilty."

Kylac bristled at the implication. The evidence against his father had likely been planted—quite possibly by one of his own servants. "And you among them?"

"He did not deny it, as I recall."

"My father is a fighter, not a murderer." Rohn had killed, yes, but only that one time, as far as Kylac knew—under circumstances in which most men would likely do the same. He had confessed the matter readily to his young son without any clear reason to do so, and had in no way profited from the act. Hardly the earmarks of a professional assassin.

"Your *master* sees people as mechanisms, nothing more," Brie said, as a branch snapped beneath her shears. "He speaks of us as bony frameworks, sacks of fluid, bundles of sinew. Would it truly surprise you to learn he might advance himself through the death of another?"

"He has no need of coin, as you may have noticed."

"Have you ever asked yourself why?"

Kylac felt a boiling frustration, as only Brie could spawn in him. "You sound as though you *want* him to be guilty. Would you confuse him with your grandfather, I wonder?"

He regretted the words as soon as they had escaped his lips. Too late. Brie's ears turned flaming red, and the gaze she leveled at him scalded him where he stood. "My grandfather makes no pretense at what he is, while your father . . ." She caught herself, seeming embarrassed by the outburst, as if it in some way bespoke weakness. She turned her shears back upon the hedge, her movements as terse as her words. "I only wondered if you had considered the possibility."

How could he not? Truth be told, he'd never been able to read his father as he could others. Where most men's thoughts and aims seemed easily discernible, his father had long ago erected walls too high and thick to penetrate. *Soulless*, Brie had called him before. Kylac wouldn't know. His studies here had not encompassed souls.

"I've considered it odd my father could be so clumsy, if he is all that Traeger claims. I've considered how easy it would be, as a captain of the city watch, to speak of secret witnesses and to happen upon evidence where it would be most convenient to find it. I've considered the reputation of Magistrate Aarhus, and the impunity with which his forces operate." Brie shook her head. Kylac lowered his voice. "Yet content I knew I'd be, even as my father was being arrested, to await the ruling of a tribunal, to learn if there might be any truth to these claims."

Brie's reckless pruning slowed. For a moment, Kylac ceased his stretching.

"But, Brie, it's been nearly three days. They'll let none see him. There's more to this than what we know. I can smell it."

Brie lowered her head, then turned it to face him. "The night before the arrest, I spied Xarius leaving Master Rohn's chambers. Odd, it struck me, that he should visit them at a time when he knew your father to be absent."

She might as well have doused him with a bucket of water. The piercing chill settled quickly into his bones. *Xarius.* "You're certain?" The evidence against his father . . . Could it have been . . . ? "Why did you not tell me straightaway?"

"I feared you might seek to confront him. I . . ."

Kylac snapped to his feet. "Of course I'll seek to confront him."

"It's a suspicion, Kylac. I've no proof of anything."

"So I'll be sure to inquire courteously."

There were no windows in Xarius's bedchamber, and he'd lit no taper upon retiring to his slumber. Thus, there was no glint upon the blade that Kylac set to his throat, nor gleam in his eye as it flicked open in the darkness. There were only the stiffening of

419

cords in his neck, and that small hiss of furious realization.

"Touch that bedside blade," Kylac whispered, "and your dreams this night will continue without end."

"Bold threat from a boy who wept when he butchered his first pig."

He felt Xarius reaching furtively, almost imperceptibly, in the blackness, and so opened a warning scratch along the man's neck. "The pig had done nothing to warrant it. I'm not convinced you can say the same."

Xarius seethed. "If you were not your father's son . . ."

"Fear my father, do you? With fair cause, I should think, when he learns of your part in his betrayal."

The momentary silence seemed a screeching admission. "You would accuse me, boy? I am his personal shield."

"All the more reason to hold you responsible. What did they promise you, I wonder. Wealth? Position? I thought you beyond such petty attachments."

"You waste your time, boy."

Kylac did not disagree. He'd waited until the Nightingale's Hour before breaching Xarius's private quarters. He had looked to enter on the Swallow's, earlier that afternoon, but had found a trap laid there that could only be reset from the outside. Had he attempted to set ambush within, Xarius would have known it.

So he'd come again two full hours after Xarius had retired, with the moon cresting its midnight arc, hoping to find the man sleeping. Three traps had he discovered this time, but Kylac had known what to look for, and how to disarm them without alerting his prey. Even so, the process had been slow . . . painstaking.

Successful as he'd been, he had no more hours to waste.

"Mayhap you're right. Mayhap I should kill you now and be on my way." He angled his blade higher, and pressed deeper, cutting into the soft crease between neck and chin.

It proved just enough to loosen Xarius's tongue. "Kill me, and you'll see him again only in pieces."

"The medallion found in his chambers . . . that was your work, was it not?"

"Yes."

"And the murdered nobleman?"

"I know not."

"You know not?"

"The corpse was reported to Captain Traeger, who in turn apprised Magistrate Aarhus. They deemed it an opportune chance to implicate the headmaster. So they purchased a pair of witnesses, and gave me the medallion."

Meaning Xarius had been bought some time ago, primed for the moment in which he might best be used—all the while continuing to pose as Rohn's most trusted protector. "You will testify to this at my father's trial. If you do not . . ."

Xarius's hissing laughter stopped him short. "What trial is that? The one in which they would risk a stay of execution to your father's royal ties? The one in which the magistrate and captain themselves might be exposed? No, boy, they will present the headmaster and their evidence to Governor Tehric, if they've not already, and let *him* pass judgment."

The knot in Kylac's stomach tightened. Long hailed a national hero, Tehric had been named chief general of the Parthan West Legion and later governor of Crylag not for jailing Menzoes encountered on the frontlines, but for slaughtering them in droves. None could deny that, under his command, Partha had strengthened its foothold against the northern secessionists. Yet, for all his victories and medals, Tehric was scarcely more than an upjumped warlord, a man of cruelty and vengeance.

He would not take lightly to the slaying of his son, useless as many believed that particular seed to be.

Nor would Aarhus or Traeger be made to suffer the full extent of any backlash. Rohn's favor with His Majesty, King Galdric, was not *that* great.

"Where is he?" Kylac asked. "Where is my father being held?"

"The Gilded Cleaver, by common account."

"It's *your* account I'm asking. Not even Aarhus or Tehric would torture a prisoner jailed under the king's roof. He'll be where His Majesty can disavow any knowledge or involvement."

"And if I were to reveal their location? What cause would you have to let me live?"

Kylac shook his head. What cause would there be to kill him? He might still need Xarius as a witness. Of greater value that than a corpse, which could only further impugn his father in the eyes of any judges.

Besides, as Xarius had observed, Kylac was no killer—and in no great haste to claim otherwise. Though Rohn's teachings held it to be inevitable, the slaying of a man struck Kylac as fundamentally avoidable. Not out of weakness or some vague notion of morality, but because he was so much faster, so much better, so much more skilled, that it would simply be unfair to his opponent.

In essence, too easy.

Not so with Xarius, mayhap. But, for all their differences, Xarius was the nearest he had to an elder brother, the one he'd always looked to match and then best. If a man *were* to die upon his blade, he would have to do more than Xarius had to earn it.

"I'd sooner leave you to my father's mercy," Kylac said. "But tell me where he is, and I'll tell *him* how you aided me in his rescue."

"You would seek to free him? Alone?"

"Would that I could trust you to join me."

Xarius's amusement was palpable. "The young sparrow, sniping at the tail feathers of falcons."

"Name their location, or I'll sever your useless tongue and find it myself."

"If you're so eager to die, seek them in the Cytharian Catacombs."

"Cytharia? Temple and tombs alike were sealed half a century ago."

"Were they?" Xarius taunted. "Doubtless I was misinformed."

Kylac considered. "They would not have strolled in through the temple foyer."

"Where the Dryslake forks beneath the southern promontory of Harrowridge Cemetery, behind a briar wall at the base of the ravine, lies a shaft of an ancient sulfur mine. Follow the right passage, and you'll discover the catacombs."

Mines? Catacombs? A labyrinth. "How will I know their path?"

"Neglected your tracking lessons?" Xarius sneered. "Failing that, follow the screams."

A pack of possible scenarios crowded forward in Kylac's mind, each spawning a dozen more. But seeking to untangle them all would mean a further drain of his time. "Should I learn you've lied to me—"

"Ply me no more with your threats, boy. If you would become a man, put that blade to its proper use. If not, I'll pray you survive this night, that we might settle this matter between us."

Kylac withdrew his weapon, keeping it at the ready. "I'll return with my father before sunrise. It might be wiser of you to be gone by then."

He backed toward the bedchamber door. He'd nearly reached it when Xarius's voice slithered through the darkness. "Mark me, boy. You'll spill blood this night. If not another's, then yours."

As Kylac eased across the threshold into the black corridor beyond, he found himself wondering which would please Xarius more.

He discovered the entrance to the mine precisely where Xarius had said he would, at the base of the bluff forming the promontory above, amid a forest of brambles that clawed skyward a dozen feet overhead. A thread of foul-smelling mineral water trickled from its mouth over a bed of crushed stones, forming a muddy layer at the bottom of the ravine. The signs of passage were abundant—boot prints in the mud, smears and scuffs on the dry slopes to either side, bent and broken bramble stalks, and loose stones recently overturned. Whatever company had trekked this way had made no attempt to mask its travels through the wild, scratching tangle. No fewer than six men, Kylac determined. Mayhap as many as ten.

Given time, he would have performed a more thorough inspection, attempting to better gauge the precise number of men he must face. But the Shrike's Hour drew near, the night half gone already. The only set of prints that truly concerned him were those matching the size of his father's boots, the shortened stride and scraped wedges that spanned them indicating ankle irons. Although it might have been another armored company escorting some other prisoner through this remote, uninviting region, Kylac thought it unlikely. And he didn't imagine they had dragged his father this far out of the way with the intent of ever dragging him back again.

Better that he did not tarry.

He did take a moment to search for snares at the tunnel's mouth. Finding none, he crept past the half-collapsed framework of rotted timbers, treading lightly upon the stoop of moldering deadwood branches and crushed stones, weightless as a stray breeze. As part of their training in stealth, students of Talonar were trained to walk and later race across fields of eggs. Kylac had been nine years old the last time he'd lost a race, and five when last he'd suffered the penalty of breaking a yolk.

Once inside the mine's gullet, a shortsword came to hand. He'd forged and fashioned it himself—along with the matching blade that hung from his opposing hip—under the tutelage of Vehn, the school's master bladewright. They were not the first weapons he'd crafted, but the first to pass all of Vehn's tests, thus earning him the achievement of bladewright third grade. He would have to hone his smithing skills for another ten years before he could hope to achieve second grade. So he would have to hope these served to pass the only test of true consequence.

His longsword, he'd left in his weapons closet, owing to the anticipation of close quarters. A decision that might haunt him before this night was done, but Kylac had learned to shun such misgivings. He had no intention of getting caught in any protracted duels. He intended to be swift, silent, and well gone by the time anyone was alerted to his presence.

The meager wash of moonlight that trailed him into the tunnel bled away twelve paces in. A cold, clammy darkness embraced him in its stead. Kylac eased his pace, allowing for his eyes to find what light they could. He didn't dare a flame, for the beacon it would become. Instead, his free hand traced the tunnel wall, finding chiseled stone amid patches of raw earth ushered through by piercing root tendrils. A stale and vaguely sulfurous smell drew him onward, deepening with each silent stride.

He heard the skittering of rats and beetles, and now and again brushed one or the other with his hand or foot. Worms dug amid the roots sprouting from the wall; he could tell by the way they recoiled at his touch. It became harder to advance silently, for he could no longer determine the lay of the loose rocks upon the tunnel floor. Fortunately, that ground had been largely worn smooth from the days when the mine had been in use, and covered since with mud and clay that had seeped down over the years.

The tunnel delved steadily along a mostly direct course. Kylac had counted four hundred thirty-seven paces when he felt the weight of the ceiling rise overhead and the closeness of the walls retreat. He did not require his vision to know that he had entered a larger chamber or cavern. But to map it blindly could take hours, depending on its size. And if it held multiple passages, as seemed likely, he'd have to guess as to which he should follow.

Seeing no other choice, he drew back into the tunnel to ignite a small firebrand. Alas for his cloak of darkness.

His flame spawned only a meager globe. Held near the ground, however, it served to reveal the trail of those he followed. He moved more quickly now, racing along in a crouch, brand outstretched to one side. Should he happen across any bowmen stationed in ambush, he didn't want them aiming for the light and catching his face or chest in the bargain.

The tracks took him down one tunnel and then another, each smaller and tighter than the last. Insects scurried from his light, but nothing large or loud enough to draw undue attention. For that, he was grateful. The last thing he needed was to disrupt a colony of screeching bats.

Twice he happened upon pocket caverns that looked to have served at one time as smuggler's dens. To whom, and for what riches, he couldn't say, for Kylac scurried through both quickly, pressing into the next tunnel. As intriguing as it might be to explore such hidden reaches of this ancient city, he had no time for ghosts or the traces of their past.

Upon emerging from the second, however, one of those ghosts took to following him. He did not hear or see or smell it, but felt it like a worm on the nape of his neck. A sensation he knew better than to ignore.

Someone was following him.

Xarius.

Kylac considered his options. He'd known from the outset that the elder student was unlikely to leave matters as they had in his chamber. But Kylac had hoped to move quickly enough to stay ahead of any delayed pursuit. It would seem he had failed. The question now was, how great a lead did he have? As reliable as his instincts were, he was still learning to interpret them. Xarius could be a hundred paces behind him, or a thousand. Should he hurry on, hoping to outpace the alarm? Or should he lie in wait and attempt to deal with his proud rival before becoming trapped?

By the time he found the cave-in exposing the entrance to the catacombs, Kylac's warning sense was screaming. He decided there that he dared not allow Xarius to seal off his retreat. He still had to locate his father, and knew not what condition he might find him in. Should they have to limp from this labyrinth, Xarius would descend on them like an owl on a wounded mouse.

So he turned a tight corner and set down his brand upon a burial niche, then doubled back to conceal himself within an ornamental alcove thick with inky darkness. There he waited, single blade in hand.

He heard Xarius coming, the hasty fool. The steps were small and slight and strangely distorted by the warren's walls, but Kylac detected them nonetheless. Had this been a skills test, Rohn might have had his prized student flogged.

Kylac crouched. The steps slowed. His pursuer eased across the threshold of broken stones that marked the boundary between mine and catacombs, a hooded form that Kylac sensed more than saw. He waited for it to turn the corner, to bend toward the distant pool of light. It did so tentatively, producing a long sliver of metal . . .

Kylac pounced, clamping a hand around Xarius's mouth and pressing the tip of his blade against a kidney. He might have driven deeper, given Xarius a wound to fully contemplate . . . but suddenly, everything was wrong. The body's size, scent, the way it tensed, and the tone of its startled squeak.

"Brie?"

He stepped back, aghast. Brie turned, relief reflecting in her features before being shoved aside by an indignant pout. "That hurt," she hissed.

Hurt? He had almost skewered her. "What are you doing here?" was all he could think to ask.

"To aid you, fool."

"You followed me?"

"No, lackwit, I burrowed down through one of the crypts above. Of course I followed you."

"How did you . . . ? How could you . . . ?" He watched a smug smile stretch across her face. "Brie, you have to go back."

The smile vanished. "Back? Certainly. Just as soon as we're finished here."

"It wasn't a question, Brie. Turn around right—"

"Touch me and I'll scream. I swear I will, Kylac. And draw whoever's down here on top of you, given the echo in this place."

"You're mad, is that it?"

"No more than you. I wasn't going to watch you run off and never even know what happened to you. Together, we stand a better chance." She bent to retrieve the burning brand from the burial niche. "How many of them are there, do you think?"

Kylac was livid. "Forget it. I'm hauling you straight back to the surface."

"You'll have to truss me up. And that'll take time I'm guessing we don't have, given your terrible haste to get down here."

She was correct about that much. He might render her unconscious . . . and then what? Leave her in a burial niche and hope no one found her? Pray she didn't wake and raise a stir?

"How long must you stand there gaping?" she asked him. "Master Rohn has to be wondering by now if anyone means to free him."

There would be no second chance at this—or at least, none that Kylac could risk. *Fool!* he wanted to shout. *You blind, arrogant fool!* Only, he was unsure who deserved it more, Brie or himself.

Kylac stepped toward her. Brie shied back, looking as if she might actually cry out. He glowered for a moment, then snatched the brand from her hand before she could blink.

"Stay behind me," he commanded, "and keep silent."

Brie grinned slyly. "I managed it this far."

Kylac shouldered past. "Should you get yourself killed, don't expect me to weep."

The acrid smell of smoke betrayed the outer watchman's position even before the globe of his torch was seen pushing against the darkness. Kylac snuffed his own brand and awaited the soldier's approach. The dark-bearded corporal drew to within three paces of Kylac's position before turning heel and marching back down the corridor.

Brie tugged at Kylac's arm. Her gesture bespoke confused irritation. Kylac shrugged free, motioning for patience.

The watchman marched thirty paces, by Kylac's count, reaching an intersection where he raised his torch to the left in signal. He then turned and repeated his approach.

Again Kylac restrained himself, holding back his anxious friend in the bargain, observing Darkbeard's path and cadence.

"We'll have to move quickly," he hissed at Brie when the watchman turned for a third approach. He slipped from his belt a pair of leather thongs. "Bind him ankle and wrist. Cut strips from his tabard to gag him."

Brie scowled. "Easier to slit his throat."

"As you prefer," Kylac said, and wondered if she truly had it in her.

They were silent for the final fifteen paces. As Darkbeard made his turn, Kylac rose behind him, capturing him in a sleeping hold. The startled soldier resisted for two heartbeats before slumping limply. Kylac eased the body to the ground, then stripped the watchman of cloak and helm, donning them himself.

"He's a full head taller than you," Brie observed, when she realized what he intended.

Kylac just scooped up the fallen torch while nodding toward the body, then hastened down the corridor, falling into the proper rhythm of steps as he neared the intersecting tunnel.

He kept his head low while hefting his torch in signal, raising his free hand to his chin as if to rub at a beard. He needn't have bothered. The signal he received in return was another thirty paces distant, the man who held it scarcely visible in the engulfing blackness. Kylac smirked as he made his turn back down the first corridor, pausing to inspect Brie's work. Darkbeard's throat was uncut, his bindings tight. She was still working on the gag, but when he knelt to assist, she elbowed him aside, the task in hand.

He returned to the signal junction. After hefting his torch, he found Brie on his heels. So he passed her his light and padded invisibly down the next corridor, marking the watchman's patrol path while positioning himself at its near end. When the soldier returned, Kylac disabled him as he had the first, then assumed the man's route. He left another pair of thongs with the body, and smiled to see them already put to use upon his return. He also found Brie wearing the second man's cloak and helm, both of which looked ridiculously large on her. Matched with her too-serious expression, he very nearly laughed aloud.

By the time they reached the fourth watchman, their incursion began to strike Kylac as suspiciously easy. Upon disabling the fifth, the nagging thought had blossomed into a genuine concern. As narrow as the chance might be that anyone could find or would attempt to follow Traeger's company into this subterranean labyrinth, the captain believed he was dealing with the fabled Seax Lunara. Should he not have tightened his defenses accordingly?

But they were too far committed to turn back now. If they had wormed their way into a trap, there was naught but to side-step its trigger, else respond as they could when it was sprung.

He found the sixth watchman in a stationary post at the top of a descending stair heavily lit by bracketed torches. A voice echoed from deep within, though Kylac could not discern the words. He mimicked the fifth watchman's signal to the stair sentry, then drew back along the previous route, sharing with Brie what he had seen.

"Well?" Brie whispered.

"If there's another at the base, we'll not likely be able to take him silently."

"Then we do it swiftly. How many are left?"

Kylac couldn't be sure. "Three at the least. Not more than six, I should hope."

"No more bindings, then."

Kylac took a steadying breath, then drew his shortsword. "If it's the latter, no."

"We but tread the course they set," Brie offered, keen to his hesitation.

She waited on his confirmation, so Kylac gave her a nod. "We'll approach slowly, get as close as we can. Keep your head low."

He handed her the torch, which she accepted. As they returned to the signal junction, Kylac bolted ahead without her. He was three strides into his sprint—a safe lead on Brie—before the watchman responded.

"Hathen? Krakken's blazes . . ."

His words afforded Kylac five more strides. Drawing his sword gave Kylac two more. He half-turned to holler a warning down the stairs, but managed only an inarticulate grunt as Kylac closed the remaining distance. His sword came up to block Kylac's lunging thrust. As it raised, Kylac dove low, driving a shoulder into the man's thighs and carrying them both into the torchlit stairwell.

The watchman scraped and thudded headfirst along his back, white-blond beard and colored cheeks giving him the look of a turnip. Kylac perched atop him, coiled to spring. The stair wasn't long. A gap-toothed watchman stood at its base, fumbling for a blade of his own. As the weapon came free, Kylac leapt into him, tackling him against a chamber wall.

They struck hard enough to jar the sword from Gaptooth's hand. Kylac used his blade to dislodge the soldier's helm, following with a pommel strike to the temple. Gaptooth crumpled beside his weapon, which Kylac kicked clear.

Turnip moaned senselessly, mouth bleeding, eyes glazed. So Kylac turned focus to the rest of the room. A swift survey revealed a crypt come to serve as a torture chamber, given the bladed instruments set around its torchlit walls. At the far end, his father hung half-naked from a pair of manacles hammered into the ceiling, unconscious if not dead, covered in sweat and filth.

That was all he had time to discern before Traeger and an attending watchman rounded on him with ready blades, their features flashing alarm, anger, and finally bemusement as Kylac shed his cloak and helm.

He did not wait to see what their reaction would be when Brie came scampering down the stairs, or for their companions to recover. Instead, he launched toward the attending watchman, forcing the soldier to engage. The watchman responded with a practiced thrust. Kylac deflected it high and to one side with a scissored defense, giving a twist that forced the weapon from his opponent's grasp. As it struck the stony ground, he drew a pair of shallow gashes along the soldier's wrists—a deterrent against retrieving his blade too quickly.

He heard Brie enter behind him, but did not have time to turn. Traeger's sword came at him in a sweeping arc. He ducked low to avoid its cleaving edge, then spun for a pommel strike against the back of the bleeding watchman's head, who had stubbornly bent to chase his sword despite his wounds.

I should have taken his thumbs, Kylac thought.

Thumbs dropped like a sack of grain. Brie stood over the dazed Turnip, pointing her sword at his throat.

"Eyes up!" she shouted.

A kind warning, if unnecessary, as Traeger slashed again. Kylac twisted, then ducked a sudden backswing. The next strike aimed low. Kylac sprang from the floor to the wall, somersaulting over Traeger's head to land at his back. The captain fought to whip his blade around, but Kylac pricked his ribs, causing him to reflexively hunch over that side. Kylac then dropped his own blades to latch on with a sleeping hold.

"Pleasant dreams, Captain."

Traeger sputtered furiously, then fell slack in Kylac's arms.

Kylac dropped the captain, then reached for the final handful of thongs tucked in his belt. "Bind them," he said to Brie, tossing her the leather strips.

"This one's waking," she replied, pricking Turnip's throat with the tip of her sword.

"He'd rather be trussed than dead, I'll wager," Kylac said, reclaiming his own swords while staring pointedly at the half-dazed watchman. "Have him roll over with his hands behind his waist. If he refuses, I'll carve the peak from his throat."

Turnip cowed to the threat, rolling over as commanded.

Kylac watched until the man's hands were tied, then sheathed his weapons and turned to his father. Rohn continued to hang limply from the iron chains hammered into the ceiling, head bowed against his chest. Kylac wasn't even certain he still lived.

His heart raced . . . carrying a warm flood of relief when he found his father's pulse.

"Is he . . . ?" Brie asked, as she worked at binding Turnip's feet.

Rohn's face was bruised and swollen, but did not bear any permanent injuries. Traeger had only been softening him, in preparation, mayhap, for Governor Tehric's arrival. "He lives." He took his father gently by the jaw. "Come now, Father. I need you to wake."

"What now?" Brie asked, as she moved on to Gaptooth. "I mean, where will he go?"

"We'll find a safehouse, hold him until the king hears my petition for an honest trial."

"Have you a place in mind?"

He didn't. Not yet. He needed his father to regain consciousness first.

He snapped his fingers beside Rohn's ear, then raised an eyelid, exposing the reddened orb to the light. Still his father did not respond.

"Check our good captain for a key to these manacles," he said, before deciding it might be just as quick to pick the locks. "Belay that. I'll tend to it. Just see that he's bound like the others."

The cuffs hung too high for him to access without difficulty, so Kylac moved farther back to fetch a stool. He had just picked it up when he heard Brie's startled gasp, followed by the rasp of her blade coming to hand. As he turned, he watched Traeger retrieve his own sword and throw a clumsy swipe. Brie parried it easily, and then another.

Kylac dropped the stool and reached for his blades.

Traeger managed a third strike, this one stronger and more focused. Brie deflected it as she had the others, then lunged forward with one of those lighting thrusts she executed so well, catching Traeger in the side.

"I got him!" she cried, the thrill evident in her voice.

Guard up, thought Kylac, dashing toward her on legs suddenly made of sand.

A broad grin raised her puffy cheeks. But as her fiery gaze found his, gleaming with anticipation of his approval, Kylac watched Traeger's sword slash out in counter.

She was still grinning when its tip ripped a matching smile across her throat.

Traeger lurched aside as Kylac flew past, ignoring the captain completely. He dropped his blades to catch Brie as she slid into his arms. She was still smiling when she looked up at him, sword slipping from her nerveless fingers.

"Brie?"

"I got him," she said again, a whisper now as blood pulsed from her throat.

He put his hand to her neck as if he might wipe the wound clear. But it was the smile on her face that vanished, a choking realization seizing upon her brow. Her eyes turned toward the ceiling, lids fluttering.

"Kylac . . . ?"

"I'm here, Brie. Lie still. I'm here."

Her gaze found his again, though it seemed to peer through him. She reached a hand toward his face. "You . . . You're . . ."

A sudden spasm gripped her. She clutched his arm with amazing intensity, nails gouging his flesh. "Breathe. Just breathe. I'm here, Brie. I'm here. Shards, I'm right here."

She blinked twice more before her eyes rolled back and her head sagged in the crook of his arm. "Brie? *Brie?*"

As her grip on him weakened, he clutched her all the harder, pressing his cheek to hers, where her blood smeared against his tears.

"Hypocrites," he heard Traeger say, as though from a great distance. "You sow death amid the shadows, yet weep when the harvest comes home."

Kylac opened his eyes to find the captain standing beside Rohn, blade perched against his throat. A fistful of hair kept Rohn's head upright. His father was awake now, if only barely.

"Too long has my fair city suffered your plague," Traeger spat, and there was blood in it. His abdomen glistened darkly where Brie had pierced him. "Tonight, I end it."

Kylac lowered Brie softly to the earth, gently closing the lids over her eyes. *You . . . You're . . .* He folded her palms upon her chest.

"Doubtless, another will take his place. But Magistrate Aarhus will continue to hunt you. And as each head rises, he will strike it down, until no more dare rise."

Guard up, Kylac thought. He noticed Brie's blade upon the ground, lying near his own.

"Tehric," Rohn coughed suddenly. "He'll not be pleased . . . should you cheat him of his prize."

The words proved a distraction, stealing the captain's focus, giving him pause. In that moment, a sensation like liquid ice burned up Kylac's spine, spilling into his shoulders, coursing outward through his limbs. He could not have said how it happened next, only that he willed himself forward, and his body responded. A pair of swords came to hand. His heart beat once, twice, while the physical world stood still around him. When it was done, Traeger's severed sword arm was falling toward the earth, and Brie's blade was sliding cleanly through his gaping mouth.

Too easy.

A chill ran through him as the captain's body fell. It convulsed upon the floor, its expression contorting with fury and denial, blood coughing from its ruined face. Its back arched as it flopped to one side, where it finally lay twitching.

Kylac watched, awaiting a sense of satisfaction, of triumph, of vengeance slaked. He watched until the throes had ceased, yet tasted only raw, writhing emptiness.

He continued to stand there, unmoving, while blood pooled beneath the mutilated body, spilling outward into the cracks and crevices of the floor, spreading . . .

The presence of a shadow drew his gaze toward the chamber stairwell. There stood a man in silken robes trimmed with gold, his impressive height and rigid posture giving him an austere bearing. His head was shorn, his close-cropped chin beard shaped into an arrowhead. The gilded ropes draped about his shoulders proclaimed his office.

Magistrate Aarhus.

The magistrate surveyed the scene. He seemed utterly disinterested in the pair of watchmen bound at the base of the stair, Turnip pale with fear, Gaptooth unconscious. His gaze lingered only slightly longer on Thumbs, similarly insensate, bleeding at the wrists—whom Brie hadn't had a chance to bind. He took careful note of Brie's small form, laid out peacefully, and of Traeger's, laid out in pieces. Only when his eyes found Kylac's did they cease to roam, taking hold like a raptor's talons.

Then came Xarius, slinking from the stairwell like a stray patch of darkness, rapiers drawn.

Aarhus advanced—one long, slow stride followed by another—shadowed by Xarius. Kylac found himself stepping protectively in front of his father, hefting his blades.

Aarhus stopped. Though his gaze burned with enmity, a savage grin split his features. "And you thought the boy a lost cause."

Rohn grunted, his chains clanking with movement. "I nearly had Jedrick do the deed. Loose these irons."

Kylac blinked, as confused by the strength in his father's voice as he was by the words. He half turned to find Rohn standing on his own, no longer limp in his shackles.

"A shame he didn't take Jedrick, too," said Aarhus. The magistrate stepped nearer, raking a glance at Thumbs. When Kylac snapped toward him, Aarhus stopped.

Xarius snorted. "He doesn't understand. Look at his face.

I doubt he could even tell us where he is."

"Show him," said Aarhus.

Xarius grinned before backing toward the stairs. With a reverse thrust, he put a sword through the chest of the unconscious Gaptooth. That drew a startled shout from the waxen-faced Turnip, trussed upon his belly, now fully alert.

"M-m-magistrate. My lord, I—"

A rapier through the back of his neck put an abrupt end to his plea.

Aarhus produced an iron key from a pocket within his robes. "For the master's manacles. If I may?"

Kylac could not seem to think straight. If the magistrate had come not to harm Rohn . . .

He felt his arms lowering, sagging beneath the weight of realization. He fell aside a pace, so that he could easily face his father as he did the others. "What scheme is this?"

"The elimination of a troublesome nuisance," Aarhus replied, closing the distance between himself and Rohn. A long arm reached skyward, fitting his key into the first cuff. "Captain Traeger had become quite rabid of late. I tired of holding his leash."

"Do you truly believe me so clumsy?" Xarius asked, his tone seething with mockery. "That a scrub girl could note my comings and goings? That you could penetrate my chambers, uninvited, without leaving your blood upon the floor?"

"An assignment," said Rohn, rubbing his wrists as the second popped free. "Long overdue. Master Aarhus slew his first at the age of seven."

Their words surrounded Kylac like grit in a funnel cloud . . . clawing . . . flaying . . . Traeger. They had wanted him to kill Traeger. Xarius had goaded him, set him on his way. An *assignment*, his father called it. To slay his first . . .

"I'll admit I doubted you," Rohn said, while Kylac's gaze slipped toward the dark pool in which the mutilated body of the captain of the city watch now bathed. "I feared you lacked the fortitude."

"But all men have it in them," Aarhus added, placing a reassuring hand on Rohn's shoulder. "The hunger to take a life, hold

it in your palm, and then crush it in your fist. For some, it is buried deeper, is all. But once unleashed . . ."

Kylac's gaze snagged upon Traeger's face, his cleft lip barely
noticeable now amid the red wash of his lacerated cheeks. He felt
no pride in the act, but neither did he feel remorse. Just the hollow sting of inevitability.

"The first is the hardest," said Rohn. "Those that follow will
become easier and easier."

"Those that follow?" *His* words this time, though they sounded
to him a stranger's.

"The time has come to assume your place among us, to lay
claim to who and what you are."

"Seax Lunara," Kylac whispered. Daggers of the Moon. A fable
come to light.

The magistrate inclined his head. "Aarhus Hafoc, I am known,
to those of our order."

"Xarius Talyzar."

"Rohn Mandrinc, named guildmaster of the Seax Lunara by
Ernathian Crennlok."

So the slain captain had been correct in that, as well. The rest
were puppets, his father who pulled their strings. *The servants
think him guilty . . .*

"By rite of passage," said Rohn, "choose your name."

"My name," Kylac echoed numbly. A mark of initiation. The
acceptance of an atrocity committed this night, and those they
would have him commit in the future.

"Any you wish," his father prodded.

Hafoc. Talyzar. Mandrinc. Crennlok. Old Entien names all.
Hawk. Wraith. Poison. Dread.

He glanced toward the unconscious Thumbs—Jedrick. One of
theirs, given the exchange between Rohn and Aarhus—and the
fact that Xarius hadn't killed him. Positioned here to hold Traeger
in check, most likely, should the captain have grown too fervent
in his beatings or tired of waiting on Governor Tehric's arrival. Or
had the governor's vengeful coming been merely another layer of
plotting?

It caused him to wonder vaguely at how they meant to explain away this affair. Traeger would bear the blame for all, he supposed. A zealot, acting out on a known grudge. Xarius? Coerced to plant evidence, later employed by Aarhus to free a man wrongfully detained. With Rohn perceived as a victim, no witnesses to the contrary, and Aarhus as the magistrate in charge, any who sought to press alternate accusation would be pissing against a gale. Shards, the king himself, while shocked and disappointed at these dire failings of a captain of the city watch, might actually be relieved to hear of Rohn's innocence.

His father's innocence. How could he have ever defended it? The only innocence in this chamber lay with Brie's small, still form.

Xarius scoffed. "We waste our breath. He'll never be one of us."

"Don't be foolish, boy," urged Aarhus. "Name yourself, and let us bear witness."

Should he refuse, would they seek to kill him? Would he in turn kill them? It scarcely mattered. The threat, real or imagined, would weigh as wind in his decision.

When all else was stripped away, he could not refute his actions this night. Nor would he shirk responsibility for them. He would accept them because he must, because they had branded him more surely than any moniker ever could. He would not debase himself further by cowering behind a lie.

His father's bark echoed in the stillness. "Who are you?"

Kylac looked once more at Traeger's ravaged corpse, then forced his gaze to settle upon Brie. Briallen, whose rare laugh would never again warm his heart. *You . . . You're . . .*

"Kronus," he decided abruptly. "Kylac Kronus."

He buried her the following afternoon, beneath a crude cairn he erected beside her mother's, on a remote steppe too stony for digging. The others had frowned upon his decision to carry her from the catacombs, but had done nothing to prevent it. Neither had they lent aid, ignoring him and his burden throughout the return journey. Xarius had searched his reaction early on, as they trailed past the corpses of murdered watchmen—those he and Brie had left bound on the way in. Unsurprised, Kylac had said nothing.

His thoughts had been solely with his friend, a maelstrom of emotions fueled by memory, by fantasy—crushing waves of acceptance alternating with riptides of denial. But for the ghastly rent in the flesh beneath her chin, she might have merely been sleeping, her eyelids on the verge of fluttering open. He in turn had refused to rest, holding her close even when his muscles had burned with fatigue and seized with cramp. He had no right to set her aside for personal relief. He'd hoped that if he could bear the pain, these gods he so often heard tell of would reconsider, and give ear to his silent pleas.

Yet deaf they'd remained, not only while he'd borne her hence, but as she had lain still, pale, upon the bare, unforgiving earth selected for her burial ground. She hadn't appeared to mind. At peace, she had seemed, comfortable in her endless dreams . . .

He stood vigil for some time over the mound of stones, staring numbly at the hilt of her blade where he'd planted it as a marker. This far out, it was as liable to rust as fall prey to grave robbers. He'd considered keeping it as a reminder of the blood on his hands—both Traeger's and Brie's—but had imagined Brie's scornful reaction toward anything so dramatic. It was her blade. She had died fighting with it in hand. Its final resting place would be the same as hers.

Leaving him without a longsword, since he'd already decided not to return to the gates of Talonar. Throughout the long march from the catacombs, the hard climb to this overlook, and the bloody, blistering hours of scraping together and piling cairn stones, he'd been haunted by Brie's dying moments. *You . . . You're . . .* She'd been fighting to tell him something. About himself, perchance. Some defining characteristic, or advice for his future. *You . . . You're . . .*

His father had fashioned him to be an agent of death. It seemed he had succeeded. But to what end? Like Brie's final words, it would be for *him* to decide. Whatever, it would have nothing to do with the Seax Lunara or any more of his father's secrets. Given the game that had culminated in Brie's death, he wished to learn no more from Rohn or his ilk.

Henceforth, he would be his own instrument, and not theirs to wield.

He wondered if they might hunt him, but found it difficult to envision. Rohn must have anticipated his possible desertion, yet had done nothing to prevent it. A reaction that suited him. A master smith did not dwell on a flawed piece of steel. He simply tossed it aside and went to work on the next.

The name, he would keep. Kronus. It was Brie he'd been thinking of when choosing it—of whatever demons she had lived with and stood against. Day after day, suffering, but unbroken. Undiminished. *Unbowed*. With such a name, he might seek to honor her, living as he imagined might please her, without apology or shame.

If there was more to it than that, he would learn it along the way.

He had but one more call to make. A visit that took him to the bowels of the Mire. To the stoop of a rotting shack shunned by even the most sordid inhabitants of that underprivileged district. To a creature whose mere sight curdled his blood.

"Finally got bit, did she?" her grandfather asked, once Kylac had delivered news of Brie's death. "I told the little whore to tread clear of them vipers. Girl was deaf as I am blind."

Kylac flinched, but suffered the words, stinging as they did with a measure of truth. He'd allow that Brie might have been better served distancing herself from Talonar and its machinations—from Rohn and even from Kylac. He'd allow that and more, if only the crusty old mole could manage to shed a tear. A single tear was all Kylac would demand of him, accepting it as a sign of guilt, of remorse, of confession to whatever horrors the old man had inflicted upon her.

"Well, snake?" the monster asked after a time. "What would you have of me?"

Rohn had been right. His second kill was easier to stomach than the first.

Leaving the roaches to feed, Kylac set forth.

NAOMI NOVIK

THIS STORY BEGAN ALMOST TWO YEARS AGO, WHEN THE FABULOUS ERIKA Swanson made me a plush Temeraire for my daughter to play with, and I asked her for a story prompt by way of thanks. She offered me the lovely idea of the Temeraire-universe dragons encountering early attempts at human aviation. And so when Shawn asked me for a story, I decided to write one about my *Victory of Eagles* character Perscitia bumping into a hot air balloon.

Possibly I was asking for it, given that I was writing for an *Unfettered* anthology, but I've rarely had a story so completely dig its heels in and run away in the opposite direction. I don't want to say anything much about what is in the story, as I think it's more fun to read unspoiled, but I will say that there are no balloons. A dragon or two may have snuck in, though.

Naomi Novik

IN FAVOUR WITH
THEIR STARS

Naomi Novik

He woke and did not immediately know where he was, a thick cottony taste in his mouth, bitter, and a small stinging pain near the base of his neck and at his wrists. He was secured in wide straps crossed over his chest and thighs, and his sight was badly blurred and in black-and-white; all he saw above him was a smear of gray light. He put his hands out on instinct and met cold glass only inches away from his face. Fog spread out from his fingers. He shoved on the glass in panic, then pounded against it with his fists, bare feet kicking and toes sliding uselessly against the invisible coffin-lid, his heart thundering rapidly but it refused to yield in the slightest, and a shuddering wave of exhaustion made him fall limply back against the padding underneath.

He lay there breathing, gasping. He worked his mouth until a little moisture came into it, and he swallowed. His sight began to sharpen little by little. Faint blue outlines began to become visible on the glass above him, and nearly simultaneously, his mind began to function again. He was still in the cradle. That was the ship's medical bay, outside him; he'd been awoken from shipsleep; and that meant—

He had barely an opportunity to look up and see the large implacable countdown display; then the cradle dropped abruptly, his stomach following a moment after the rest of him, and the walls of the launch channel rose around him. From instinct, he tried to brace himself against the lid as the roar and white blaze of propulsion echoed at his feet, as useless as that was; then the launch channel was blurring past and gone: the cradle was ejected out into the void, and ten million stars were turning in their stately course all around him.

The deep dark was comforting, familiar, and the weightlessness that let his body rise and press against the straps. Laurence breathed deeply and let his uncoordinated arms sink again. His body remained all but limp. How he loathed planetary landings: of course he knew the rationale for leaving the muscle relaxants in his system until he was on the ground, and a thousand statistical analyses had confirmed the sense of it, but he could not like the sensation of uselessness; he could not even work the cradle's diagnostics, his fingers thick and clumsy. He could only watch, his eyes slowly regaining focus. The cradle was curving away from the ship now: he had a final moment to see her, the *Reliant*, sleek and silver and gleaming with the star's pale yellow-tinged light behind her, and then the planet was rising in his view: vast and endless green, mazed with clouds, and four of its small moons ringed around it, sweeping gaps in a thin encircling cloud of rings and dust.

It was an awkward and a choppy landing, buffeted by the debris, and despite the stabilizers, the cradle tumbled over itself two dozen times before it struck the atmosphere: bottom first, the angry red-orange glow blooming at his feet, and the air boiling white over his lid, which gradually blackened with the heat even as gravity took a sure and steady grip upon him. He lay still helpless and now blind in his carbonized shell, falling endlessly. Reason said that he was in fact slowing, the cradle's landing systems activating; but it was difficult to cling to reason in the close and stifling dark. Though his body was yet chilled through from the long sleep, the air within was stale and hot now, and sweat began to spring out on his forehead; he was still falling.

And then, quite abruptly, he was not: a massive and unexpected jerk that flung him hard against his straps, and dropped him back again into his padding; he gasped with the jolt. Had he struck on a mountaintop, or one of the trees? His mind was still sluggish, but he remembered those vividly from the endless reams of his briefing: their vast bulk, skyscraper-high and more, the latticed network of their roots like mangroves twisting furiously into the earth. The surveyors had taken dozens of holographs, panoramic, trying to convey the scale of them, of a world that seemed built for giants.

Of course, the surveyors had failed quite thoroughly to account for that unnatural size and strength, until too late. Laurence hoped very grimly that they had not also failed to properly scan: if the cradle's systems had been given bad information about the composition of the trees, and he had run into one—but the cradle was still moving, though more gently, no longer in free fall. Laurence could not account for it; he pressed on the coffin-lid with his still-clumsy hands. The console keys glowed blue at him against the charred black, and he managed to fold all of his fingers but one down. He pressed with painstaking care one button after another: the diagnostics showed normal operation, and his elevation was decreasing rapidly; abruptly there was another thump outside, and the cradle stopped upon the ground and ceased to move.

There was a warning puff of air against the side of his neck; he held still and forced himself to relax as the needle slid in. He drew several more breaths as the purifiers washed through him, carrying away the residue of sleep and inaction; he opened and closed his fists and rolled his fingers. He had to stretch his hands fairly far apart to reach the opening controls, and then use his toes to touch the final panel at the base, an act of coordination entirely beyond the limits of any panicked thrashing, as it was intended to be.

The lid cracked and bright fresh cool air rushed in, a brisk slap to the face. The halves of the lid raised up and retracted; Laurence seized the sides of the cradle and heaved himself up sitting, teeth gritted against the near-painful heat of the metal shell, and then he looked up—and up, and up, and up: there was a dragon standing over the cradle, a dragon on a scale he had never imagined, peering down at him with narrow-slitted eyes, gleaming blue against a black and armored hide.

He stared up at it a moment; then he cleared his throat and said, voice a little hoarse and rusty, "I am Captain William Laurence—"

"I know who you are," the dragon interrupted coldly, "—you are from the Navy, and you have been sent to tell us that we ought to let you break up our home, all for this nonsense of trinium; well, I am Temeraire, the governor of this colony, and you may as well know straightaway that we will not put up with it at all. You had much better never have come."

———————————

Of course, the situation was nothing so simple. Young dragons always had a certain tendency to see matters in their most straightforward light, as Laurence well knew; he had worked alongside dragons in the Navy all his life, of course, and that had in no small measure marked him for this mission. But he had not entirely appreciated—nor, he thought, had his superiors—the very real, very marked difference between the kind of dragons which served in the Navy, and those ancient lines which had been sent to populate New Atlanta.

Levitas, a supply officer on Laurence's last command, was some five meters in length, and a ton; Yu Shi, the communications officer at Viro Station, was only three meters—although her wingspan was somewhat wider—and not half a ton. Laurence did not think there was a beast in the service more than five tons, even on the heavy-armor landing crews; and he had been thoroughly impressed on the occasion he had met one of those dragons, a monstrously built—he had thought at the time—tank-like creature, who had worn her four hundred pounds of body-plating as lightly as if it had been made of lace, and had cheerfully eaten sixty pounds of solid protein-carbohydrate mix straight from the vat in a single sitting.

The laws of nearly every settled world firmly required the

engineering of dragon eggs, of necessity; the mania for size that had possessed the dragon-breeders of the nineteenth and twentieth centuries had crowded the gene pool with tendencies toward wholly unsustainable, impractical mass. But New Atlanta was a private colony, a business endeavor aimed at the very oldest and wealthiest of dragons; the marketing Laurence had seen had promised "a pristine haven untouched by industrialization," as the sales literature had put it, "where your eggs, having been transported in the finest commercial liner available, attended by a devoted and highly trained staff of nursery personnel, will hatch and develop to their fullest and most extraordinary potential in a lush and luxurious setting, while funds you set aside for their care appreciate tax-free in guaranteed liquid instruments."

Only such a private colony could offer free and unfettered breeding to dragons, and those places were much sought-after by the small but fiercely proud coterie of aristocratic dragon lines still preserved from the era of pre-industrial combat. There had been only a thousand places sold, at a million federals each, shockingly outrageous prices even for a luxury colony; but they had sold nonetheless. To dragons like this.

As a second lieutenant, Laurence had once needed to step outside the *Goliath* mid-journey, to oversee repairs when a diagnostic system had failed; he had stood upon the hull with the slip-stream coursing past in a glittering stream and felt himself a small almost parasitical creature clinging to some immense and curving whale, dwarfed into insignificance; the present sensation was not unlike that, except the *Goliath* had never glared down at him, and bared serrated jaws in his direction, and complained of his presence.

Temeraire was not the size of a full warship, of course, but he would not have fit inside the *Reliant*'s hold, either: twenty tons at least, and forty meters long. Laurence looked down at the cradle and could see faint indentations in the casing where Temeraire had plucked it from the sky with his metal-sheathed talons, as easily as a hawk catching a squirrel.

But Laurence had stood on the *Goliath*'s hull, despite the low shrilling whine of the ship's engines and the slip-stream ready to take him off in an instant and fling him into the gravity wells, to be crushed or torn limb from limb; he had done his duty. He drew a single breath, deeply, and did not quail. "I beg your pardon," he said, "but I assure you that I have not been frivolously sent: we have reason to believe that the Bonapartists have learned of the trinium deposits as well, and if you do not have military protection you will certainly be under attack in short order."

Temeraire frowned down at the Navy officer in some irritation: he had been assured via comlink, by his aunt Lien, that he needed only be certain to surprise the fellow, and speak threateningly, to cow him into immediate departure. "Humans are not used to proper dragons, anymore," she had said, "—not *our* kind. If he is old enough, he may fall down stone dead from fear: I have seen it happen," and while Temeraire did not really care to make anyone fall down stone dead, he had relied on her assurances; he had not bothered to work out what he would do if the officer did *not* choose to go away at once, and that left the present circumstances quite awkward.

This news about the Bonapartists was also a puzzle. Temeraire knew about the wars, of course, in a distant, vague sort of way, but it was not the sort of thing that Celestials were supposed to pay attention to. He had considerably more immediate matters to attend to, in any case. The colony was not at all what had been promised, and they had all heard the promises in the shell, along with what now seemed a most unrealistic program for the careful, painstaking development of a lush and welcoming world, which had fallen apart in almost every particular. Instead they had met an unending stream of problems. It had proven impossible to establish any kind of mine at all with the equipment they had been provided, and it consumed a week to bring down even a single tree and make it usable, which in turn stifled all their hopes for agriculture.

It was very difficult to have been promised so much—and for their progenitors to have *paid* so much—and received so little. With every fresh difficulty, one felt as though one had been robbed, despite all the technical protests which the developers' lawyers and insurers made, and the laws—quite unreasonable in Temeraire's opinion—which shielded them from liability, under this supposed excuse that it was impossible to imagine every potential challenge which a colony might face. The surveyors might have tried to cut down *one* tree, or dig at least *one* small hole; they might have been a little curious what permitted the trees to grow so large, instead of merely taking a great many falsely attractive holographs.

He prided himself on how well they had risen to their challenges, but six years of effort had only been sufficient to make them halfway secure and not comfortable, and everyone's tempers were grown short. Their elephant and bison herds were not properly established despite all their best attempts, so they had to keep eating out of rationed protein vats, which left everyone hungry and disconsolate; they had not had sufficient time to establish proper schooling practices, and several dragons had even failed to learn to read before they had grown too old, from the necessity of pursuing mere subsistence. Temeraire had to write letters for them, often, to help them conceal the painfully embarrassing lack of skill. Even now they still did not have enough pavilions for everyone to sleep inside at night, which meant there were a dozen outstanding quarrels of precedence demanding his attention.

The only thing worse than having been saddled with this world would be to have it snatched out from under them after so much labor and effort: and all because of the trinium that was the source of their difficulties in the first place. Temeraire would not stand for it; none of them would stand for it, they were all in perfect agreement on *that*, if on virtually nothing else. However unsatisfactory this world, it was still *theirs*; Temeraire did not mean to see it torn quite apart, all so that a war about which he cared very little should be forwarded. But he did not in the least know what to do with this Navy fellow, and if it was not all just made-up nonsense about the Bonapartists, he was not sure what he should do if they did come.

"I suppose I cannot only leave you here," Temeraire said, feeling disgruntled: they were a good hour's flight from the capital, and the Green River was between there and here, which this tiny creature could scarcely have crossed on his own.

"I would be grateful if you did not," Captain Laurence said dryly. "I hope you will forgive my saying that stuffing your ears makes a poor kind of answer, however much you may dislike my intelligence."

Temeraire flattened his ruff, but consoled himself with the thought that it *was* sensible to bring the officer in and hear him out, not because there would be any sense to his proposals, but to know what those proposals *were*: it was surely the best way to be prepared for whatever the Navy might do. "Very well," he said ungraciously. "You had better climb up, then, and try not to fall off, for I dare say I would be hard-pressed to catch you if you should happen to do so."

Laurence could not say that he inwardly met the prospect of climbing aboard this monstrous creature with any great equanimity: and how he was to hold on, during flight, was an ominous puzzle. But he dug his survival kit from the cradle and slung it onto his back, and then hesitatingly looked up the enormous column of the foreleg: muscles larger than his body, tendons and sinew sheathed in the tiny overlapping scales of gleaming black horn, under the netting that supported the dragon's wing-bracework. Laurence took a cautious grip of one jutting spur and pulled himself up, searching for footholds as though he were creeping over a ship's hull in dry dock.

The bracework netting broadened as he climbed, attaching at last to a massive gleaming band molded to the dragon's shoulders, glittering with electronics and the thickness of Laurence's wrist; when he had managed at last to drag himself up along it onto Temeraire's back, he drew out a length of cord and tied himself onto it, as securely as he could. He took a grim hold as Temeraire said perfunctorily, "Are you ready?" and without waiting for an answer launched himself aloft.

The air came rushing into Laurence's face, cool and sweet and startlingly fragrant, full of earthy, organic musk: rot and nectar all together, the sulfurous tang of the dragon's body, all of it somehow magnificently *real* even if anyone might have called it unpleasant, if it had been offered in a scent bottle. Temeraire beat up in shocking, enormous strokes, purely physical; the wings moved past Laurence on either side like vast black sails, limned with their silvery netting, and then Temeraire turned into the wind and his bracework hummed faintly, coming online, as he launched himself forward.

The air tore from Laurence's lungs. Temeraire's body and the bracework's shielding protected Laurence from the full force of their passage, but that only saved him from being torn off, shredded; he still felt with all his body the ferocity of the wind as they shot forward through the air. He clung to the bracework and stifled an involuntary burst of wholly inappropriate, delighted laughter. He had begun as a fighter pilot, had fought in five actions and a dozen skirmishes—once even manually, during the battle of the Lilienthal Belt, when all their navigation systems had been compromised by the Tricolor virus. He had always loved the sheer intensity of a small starship, the speed and physicality of their flight; but nothing to compare with *this*: bare to the open sky, exposed, breathing real air, with the green world rolling endlessly below.

"Of course I can go more slowly, if you find you cannot endure it," Temeraire said, the voice amplified and coming from the neckband.

"No," Laurence said; he felt himself grinning like a child. "No; I thank you, I am perfectly at ease."

He could with pleasure have stayed aloft for hours. Temeraire swept with dazzling speed and skill between the massive treetops, the shining trunks like the polished columns of some endless cathedral; Laurence pulled on one of his gauntlets from the kit and reaching out blindly caught one leaf as they tore past a branch: it was wider across than the breadth of his shoulders, the veins gleaming faintly silver, the translucent skin mottled green, with one irritated creature rather like a starfish clinging to the underside, perhaps trying in some slow, slow way to digest a scrap of it. "How long a flight have we?" Laurence asked, letting the wind take the leaf away again, when they passed the next tree.

"Only half an hour more," Temeraire answered him, more cheerfully. Perhaps the flight was improving his temper; Laurence could scarcely imagine any irritation that could survive this experience, although perhaps it was less remarkable to a dragon. "That is the Green River, over there," Temeraire added, and Laurence, looking, saw it first merely as a great canyon-like break coming in the treetops, a wide chasm, until they came overhead.

It was astonishingly broad: on another world, in more welcoming soil, it would surely have long since carved itself a deeper passage; here, however, fifty million years had only sufficed to make and slowly widen a gentle indent, that nevertheless gathered runoff to itself. The far side was visible only because they were aloft, and even then only by the upper boughs of the trees that stood there. Masses of green leaves floated upon the surface in great mats, small saplings rooted upon the largest and a few, trapped against the curve of the river, had become veritable islands.

Laurence looked, breathtaken and dazzled; in either direction the river ran through the towering heights of the trees in immense silence, unbroken by birds, by cicada-hum; only a soft endless whispering noise of water running.

He and Temeraire were the only things in sight moving with mortal speed. He knew the youngest of the trees, those the height of yearling oaks, were a century old; the giants were a million years and more. They conquered the unforgiving earth with patience, slow sipping of nutrients by degrees. Those few native living things that were mobile moved only a little, and then carried by the wind; this was not a world that encouraged haste.

"I suppose," Temeraire said, heavy with scorn, turning his head back to look at Laurence, "that the first thing you will say of the river is you think we ought to dam it up."

"At the moment," Laurence said honestly, "I only think it lovely; but I suppose that you would dam it, somewhere, if you could. *Can* it be done?"

"Oh," Temeraire said, sounding a little mollified. "Well, no; we did try, but it is just too shallow. We cannot really carve a basin, so the water only runs off, and the trees drink it up so quickly if it gets anywhere near them that it is no use. We have set up some turbines, anyway," he added, "but they do not do very much good. There are no falls anywhere."

Laurence felt his great sigh, the dragon's sides belling out and the hide rising beneath him. He looked and saw a glitter of metal and light, in the distance along the river's length, and asked, "Are those the turbines there?" Even as he asked, he knew it wrong; those were not turbines.

"No, they are much farther north," Temeraire said. "That is the capital, where we are going, although what those lights are—" He paused mid-air: his wings described an endless circling wave in the air, while his bracework hummed.

The lights came again: a flickering pattern of green and gold. "Scatter guns," Laurence said abruptly, cold. The Bonapartists had somehow beaten him here.

Temeraire flung himself as quickly as he could down the river: the guns were flickering again, and as he drew nearer he could hear their faint singing whine, and more dreadfully the acrid, terrible smell of burning plastics. He had never before pressed his bracework to its limits, much less beyond.

"*Reliant,*" the Navy officer was saying upon his back, "this is Captain Laurence; answer, if you please." There was a low anxious note of worry deep in his voice. "*Reliant,* please respond," and then he shook his head and dropped his arm, a grim expression on his face. "I do not think they could have managed to corrupt or block my connection to the ship. Not without having taken her. What grade is your planetary shield?"

"The very highest, of course," Temeraire said. "It is up to primary-world standards; you cannot suppose our families would have consented to anything less."

"And you are self-sufficient?" Laurence asked. "They cannot starve you out?"

"I suppose not," Temeraire said dismally, although he by no means relished the idea of going back to a diet entirely from the vats. "But they will surely try and destroy those at once," he added anxiously, "and our power supplies, and bring down the shield itself: everything is in the capital." He pressed on for more speed, but Laurence reached forward and lay a hand upon his neck, restraining.

"Governor—I beg you listen to me: they will certainly have at least one gunship for aerial support. You cannot come in underneath their fire, or they will bring you down as soon as you are within range. Does your bracework have any stealth capabilities?"

"Whyever should it?" Temeraire said, beating on. "It is not as though I had ever needed to hide from anyone; oh! How dare they come here." He was deeply infuriated, and he did not care in the least that the Bonapartists would try and shoot at him: he would not merely stand by and see their colony wrecked, and torn apart. Perhaps he might dodge their attacks—

"Then you must have more elevation," Laurence said, "and as far as possible, keep to the cover of the trees until you can get a clear run at the gunship: if you can get us aboard, they cannot shoot us, not once we are among them."

Despite his distorting wrath, Temeraire could not deny that this sounded like highly reasonable advice; he angled himself aloft and beat up and up, the air thinning to unpleasant degrees and making for cold and difficult flying: but he persevered, darting among the silvery thicket of branches, thin enough at this height that they yielded to him, bending if he caught against one, until he caught sight of the capital.

It did not really deserve the name of capital or even of city: they had only a tiny clustered handful of real buildings, all of them quite small—Temeraire could only just fit through the doors of the main warehouse, and not at all into the defense center; that was Perscitia's domain. These buildings were ringed by the more skeletal frames of the sleeping-pavilions they had managed to erect—nearly all of which were presently wreathed in flames: their marvelous silken hangings, brought all the way from Earth, were smoking into ruin. Temeraire hissed in fury, trembling; it was not to be borne.

But Laurence had been quite right, there was indeed a gunship, a simple boatlike oval hovering, with half a dozen men and two smallish dragons aboard it. A boiling storm of black smoke below them illuminated in flashes as they continued to fire the guns.

"Seven o'clock from their center," Laurence said. "They are only twenty meters from the tree cover: wait until the rear guns have fired next, and then make the attempt."

Temeraire saw at once what he meant, and dropped himself spiraling through the thicker branches until they were on a level with the boat; another glittering cascade of fire went off, and this close Temeraire could see the cartridges themselves: long thin silver casings with their green running lights blinking like cold, cruel eyes as they plumed with yellow-gold smoke and darted down, looking for something to destroy. As soon as they had gone, he flung himself across, his bracework straining, and the entire boat shrieked like a living thing as he came down upon it.

The soldiers recoiled, shouting, bringing up their guns; but Temeraire roared at them in fury, wings and ruff spreading wide, and the two dragons quailed back, fumbling their weapons. He lashed his head forward on instinct and seized the larger by the throat, shook her violently; he felt the sharp taut strands of her bracework scraping against his teeth with a horrid sound, and she shrilled in pain. He threw her off the platform, sweeping several of the men away with her body; the rest of them leapt of their own accord, chutes opening up like blossoms as they plummeted away into the ruin they had created, and the other small dragon darted after them.

"Perscitia!" Temeraire cried over his comlink, "can you hear me at all?" He dug his talons into the edges of the madly rocking platform and looked over the side, but he could see nothing below of her, or any of the others who worked at the capital ordinarily: there were four of them, all of them smaller than this very platform;

they had surely been taken by surprise, quite vulnerable.

The platform made low whining noises, and he could feel a grinding of steel beneath him, but it did not cease firing. "They will certainly have disrupted your networks," Laurence said, sliding down from Temeraire's side and darting to the platform's controls. "One moment—"

He drew off the cover and was tearing cables out by the handful, with great abandon; at last the firing stopped, but a moment later the platform went listing even further over and then abruptly plummeted. Temeraire snatched Laurence up and flung himself off and free; the platform fell away end over end beneath them until it smashed with a roar of foam half into the river, upside down, and yellow flames erupted out of its belly in massive spurts.

Temeraire put Laurence back up onto his neck and circled warily around while the officer latched himself back onto the bracework. At first glance the capital looked dreadfully, plastic smeared in great blackened puddles over everything, any exposed electronic equipment a shattered sparking tangle of wire and shards of metal, but Temeraire was heartened after a moment to see that beneath the mess, the buildings they had so laboriously raised, built from the native trees and mortared with a concrete they had mixed from the riverbed sand, were quite undamaged.

The enemy soldiers were collecting themselves on the ground, regrouping; there were some twenty men altogether, and five dragons, none of them very substantial, and all were looking warily up in his direction. "We must withdraw to cover again," Laurence said. "They are putting together a chain-gun there, and your bracework is unarmored; you cannot take a shot from that gun—"

"If you are quite certain they do not mean to surrender," Temeraire said, "I will not let them finish it; even if they *are* so very small, I suppose they are larger, and better armed, than Perscitia and the others; I cannot consider that I am going against the natural order of morality to defend—"

"You are not!" Laurence interrupted. "But their small-arms fire will pierce you if you come close enough to bowl them over again: you can see they have taken up defensive positions."

"I do not need to come very close," Temeraire said, and wheeling away into a wide circle, gathered his breath, in steady gulps, swelling out his chest; he dived toward the strike force, and opening his jaws, let the shuddering thunder of the divine wind come bellowing out of him, the smaller trees ringing like struck bells as their branches trembled and clashed against one another. The men in the front ranks collapsed, blood dripping from their faces beneath their helmets; the dragons crying out fell to the ground. The gun emplacement fell, its nose crumpling against the ground, explosions of white dazzling electrical light bursting along its sides, cartridges detonating like tiny bombs; and as Temeraire swept over, he lashed out with his hind legs, smashing the rest to pieces.

"My God," Laurence said, in something between astonishment and dismay; he had never heard of the like, an entire heavy-armor strike force brought low by one dragon. Temeraire was wheeling back up again, away from the wreckage; Laurence twisted around to look down at the smoking rubble and the soldiers sprawled raglike in the remnants of their gun post. Certainly Temeraire had possessed the advantage of surprise, but the sheer magnitude of destruction was extravagant.

"*Now* do you suppose they will surrender?" Temeraire said, circling back.

"If they remain capable of it," Laurence said.

They landed again behind the emplacement, and Laurence secured the few surviving soldiers one after another: they were all of them in a bad way, ill and most of them visibly concussed, pupils wandering and eyes bloodshot, confused; he supposed there was some sort of brain damage there, and shuddered to see it. The dragons all huddled, flinching away from Temeraire, flattening themselves to the ground instinctively when he leaned toward them. Laurence began to think that perhaps the old breeders had not been entirely so absurd as he had always been taught to think them.

Temeraire nosed at the smoldering buildings anxiously, and

abruptly a blue dragon—not half his size, though larger than any of the soldier beasts—thrust a head out and said, "Oh! Thank goodness you are here; have you cleared out those wretched soldiers, then?"

"I have, naturally," Temeraire said, preening a little. "Laurence, this is Perscitia; I dare say she can tell us what has happened to your ship: he is that Navy officer," he added, turning to Perscitia, "and he is not so dreadful as I supposed he would be: he knows a great deal about fighting—not, of course, that fighting is anything so very splendid, at all."

"I should say not," Perscitia said. "Only look at what they have done to all our instrumentation, and our equipment! I suppose everything is ruined that we did not have under cover; it is beyond bearing. As for his ship, if you mean the Navy vessel that was up there—"

"Was?" Laurence said sharply.

"Oh, it is still up there," Perscitia said, "but they have surrendered: the Bonapartists brought a cruiser."

That was ominous indeed. "If they have a cruiser, they will have more than one landing strike force," Laurence said to Temeraire urgently. "Have you other installations critical to keeping up the shield?"

"There is the secondary generator, on the southwest continent," Temeraire said, "but our six Longwings live directly by it, so I don't suppose they will have had any luck, unless there are a great deal more of them than there were here."

Perscitia was already orchestrating a small army of robot hands, which had trooped out of the building behind her, to resurrect the communications; very shortly a message had been received confirming that the strike force had been sent, and dispatched in what Laurence gathered was a somewhat gruesome manner. "But they would not listen," one of the Longwings, named Lily, said, sounding quite bewildered that a fully equipped Bonapartist heavy armor strike force should have dared to persevere in the face of ground resistance, "and those guns were terrible—Temeraire, Excidium is badly hurt; we must have the full medical unit here straightaway—so once we realized how dangerous they were, we went aloft and spat on them from there; I am afraid it was quite indiscriminate, and they are all of them mostly dead. We ruined a great deal of our own gear, too, and we cannot touch anything or go into the encampment, but fortunately the housing was not harmed, so the shield is perfectly secure at present."

"So there is no need for any more fighting, at present?" Temeraire said—sounding, Laurence thought, rather wistful.

"No," Lily said, with a like tone of regret.

"Sir," Laurence said, "I entirely appreciate the Navy's interest in this matter, but having spoken with the governor, I cannot offer you the least hope of persuading the dragons to relinquish the planet; nor do I consider it even a desirable course of action. We should have to divert at least a first-rate to adequately defend the system from orbit."

"And you in all seriousness expect me to believe that a handful of untrained, largely unequipped dragons, the better part of them from antiquated and oversized breeding lines, are going to be a sufficient ground defense instead?" Admiral Roland regarded him with marked skepticism.

"I might point out that they have already turned aside two incursions," Laurence said, "although I grant you, we cannot rely on the Bonapartists not to find ways to address their advantages; but supplying their want of equipment and training will surely be the more efficient solution—not to mention," he added, "that any alternative should certainly involve having to remove them by force ourselves."

He went outside after his conversation—he suspected his suggestions had been better received for lack of any really palatable alternatives, than for his own qualities of persuasion—and found Temeraire loitering outside, in as innocent a manner as a dragon the size of a dreadnought could manage, which was not wholly successful. He looked at Laurence when he had come out and said, with an attempt at coolness, "So I suppose that now we have settled the Bonapartists, you mean to press us again to let you quarry the planet."

"As it happens," Laurence said, "to the contrary: Admiral Roland wishes me to inform you that the Navy will send you some proper armor: we hope that if we can make you a sufficient bar to possession, the Bonapartists will be induced to give up their attempts to seize the planet, and you may proceed with your development as you like."

"Oh! That is very handsome of her," Temeraire said, sitting back on his haunches. "That is quite more than I had looked for; we will be very glad for the armor. I suppose I do not need to bargain with you, then."

"I beg your pardon?" Laurence said.

"Well," Temeraire said, "I have persuaded—that is, we have all talked it over together, and we think if you will give us some better tools, that there is no reason we might not extract perhaps a ton of trinium every year: Perscitia is of the opinion it would be quite manageable, without doing anything untoward, or making a ruin of things. So, if you like—we will give you the trinium, and you will give us more armor, and perhaps some more silken hangings, and send us some more elephants: we hope you may find it a reasonable exchange."

"Good Lord," Laurence said, "I should say so; but—" He hesitated; of course for the Navy's sake, he ought merely to take it, straightaway; a ton of trinium a year would represent nearly a quarter of the entire Commonwealth's supply. "But I think I must tell you," he said, reluctantly, "that such a quantity of trinium will certainly encourage the most hostile intentions on the part of the Bonapartists: they will be far less likely to leave you unmolested. You will require more armor and more weaponry as well—a secondary shield at the least, and you must prepare for regular incursions; not merely attempts at invasion but raids, to seize whatever trinium they might lay their hands on; you may also be sure that they will fund piracy against you as well. You will have to devote considerable effort to meeting their offensives, and to training as well."

"Pirates? Are you sure?" Temeraire said, his ruff pricking up, before he hastily cleared his throat and said with a tolerable attempt at carelessness, "But that does not matter: we have agreed we think it very poor-spirited of us to refuse to mine the trinium, only because we were afraid, which we aren't at all; and certainly we must be prepared for them to make attacks in the future, regardless. Even though, naturally, under most circumstances we would prefer by far to devote ourselves entirely to scholarly pursuits, one must be prepared to make sacrifices."

"That is very handsome of you," Laurence said, beginning to be amused. "Well, if you are quite certain, I can assure you that Admiral Roland will be delighted to accept, and I am confident there will be no difficulty in making you a fair exchange, nor in equipping you suitably."

Temeraire rubbed a talon over his forehead, pleased, and then cleared his throat, a peculiar deep rumbling noise. "But I suppose *you* will be leaving again, straightaway," he said. "Once your ship has been repaired."

"That, I am afraid, will be some time," Laurence said. "The *Reliant*'s systems have been thoroughly compromised: she will have to be hauled to dry dock and purged. I have been seconded to you as a military advisor for the moment, if you will have me; Admiral Roland thought I might be of some use to you." He had known, as he sought the assignment, that it was unwise: having allowed himself to be grounded, as it were, he might well not receive another ship. But aside from a sense of duty—he had felt the need they had of such an advisor, even before Temeraire had outlined to him their intentions—he found he could not leave this world without reluctance; there was work to be done here, and in an honorable company.

Temeraire's ruff flared momentarily. "Oh, yes," he said, "—that is, I am very glad to hear it, Captain; your assistance has been very useful to the colony; do you suppose," he added, abandoning his pretense at formality, "that we might take a survey together, of our settlements? I should like at once to take consideration of our defenses."

"With all my heart," said Laurence.

461

ROBERT JORDAN & BRANDON SANDERSON

THIS IS A DELETED SEQUENCE FROM THE FOURTEENTH AND FINAL WHEEL of Time book, *A Memory of Light*. As such, it contains some minor interior spoilers for that book—and it might not make a ton of sense to you if you haven't read the Wheel of Time.

However, if you *have* read the Wheel of Time (particularly the final book), I'd suggest that you read this sequence now and go no further in the introduction. The commentary here will be more meaningful to you if you've read the sequence first, I believe.

I pitched this series of scenes to Team Jordan with the knowledge that the scenes were on shaky ground from the start. We knew Demandred was in Shara, and we knew some of what he'd been up to. I wanted to show a glimpse of this. However, Robert Jordan—in interviews—had said that the stories were never going to show Shara, at least not in any significant way.

I felt that he hadn't ruled out the possibility of a glimpse of Shara—he had only implied that nothing major would happen there on screen. Team Jordan agreed, and I set to work writing these scenes. My goal was to show a different side of one of the Forsaken. Demandred had been building himself up in Shara for months and months, overthrowing the government (Graendal helped with that, unwittingly) and securing his place as a figure of prophecy and power.

He had his own story, which could have filled the pages of his own Wheel-of-Time-like series. He had allies and enemies, companions who had been with him for years, much as Rand, Egwene, and company had found during their adventures in the west. My goal was to evoke this in a few brief scenes, at first not letting you know who this "Bao" was. I wanted to present him sympathetically, at least as sympathetically as a man like him could be presented. It would only be at the end of the sequence that the reader realized that Bao was indeed Demandred, and that everything he was doing here was in preparation for destroying the heroes.

It was also important to me that we see Demandred for what he is—an incredibly capable man with a single overriding flaw.

Everything about him, including his ability to feel affection, is tainted by his supreme hatred of Lews Therin. The narrative was to hint that it never had to be that way. He could have made different choices. Of all the Forsaken, I find Demandred the most tragic.

The sequence accomplished these goals—but it did so too well. In threading this sequence into the rest of *A Memory of Light*, we found that the Demandred scenes were distracting. The worldbuilding required to make Shara distinctive felt out of place in the last book, where the narrative needed to be focused on tying up loose threads rather than introducing a multitude of new questions.

Harriet—Robert Jordan's widow and editor of every Wheel of Time book—felt that the scenes' evocation of an entire untold series of books was too overwhelming. It didn't feel enough like the Wheel of Time. If this had been book eight, that would be wonderful—the scenes would add variety to the series. In book fourteen, however, they offered a taste of something that would never be sated, and served only to make promises we could not fulfill.

My biggest worry in cutting these sequences was that Demandred's arrival later in the book would feel abrupt. However, test readers didn't feel this way—Demandred as a character had been a proverbial gun on the mantel long enough that everyone was waiting for him to show up. His arrival felt dynamic to them, rather than unexplained.

So, in the end, we left these scenes on the cutting room floor. I'm quite fond of them, and do consider the general outline of events within to be canon. However, the specifics of the worldbuilding are *not* canon. We cut these scenes before Team Jordan's Maria Simons, queen of continuity, had a chance to go over them with her fine-tooth comb.

I hope you enjoy this last taste of Wheel of Time storytelling. Thank you for reading.

Brandon Sanderson

RIVER OF SOULS

Robert Jordan & Brandon Sanderson

Bao slipped into the Oneness as he sat with legs crossed, surrounded by darkness.

During his youthful studies, he had been required to seek the Oneness in the midst of a crashing storm, while being towed on a sled behind a horse, and finally while enduring the pain of a hot coal against his skin. He had once considered that training to be extreme, but life had since required him to find the Oneness during war and agony, during tempests and earthquakes. For today, for this moment, a dark quiet room would do.

The Oneness was lack of emotion. Bao took all of his feelings—all of his thoughts, all that he *was*—and pressed them into a single point of darkness in his mind. That darkness consumed the emotion. He felt nothing. He thought nothing. He did not sense satisfaction at this, for there could be no satisfaction in this state. He was the Oneness. That was all.

The tent flap lifted, allowing in filtered sunlight. Bao opened his eyes. There was no surprise when he saw Mintel. One could not be surprised in the Oneness.

466

A thought did hover on the edges of his consciousness. The thought that this man should have been miles and miles away.

"How?" Bao asked, releasing the Oneness.

Mintel stepped forward. It had only been six months since Bao had seen Mintel, but the old man seemed to have aged a decade. His face was all folds and furrows, like a tablecloth taken in two hands and crumpled together. Completely bald, he wore a short beard, all gray. Though he walked with a cane, his steps were sure. That was good to see. Mintel might have grown old, but not frail.

"I rode the *caprisha* through the City of Dreams, my son," Mintel said, taking Bao by the arm.

"Dangerous."

"I could not miss this day."

"I would not have had you lose your soul to come see me."

"Not just to see you," Mintel said, smiling. "To see the fulfillment of prophecy, after all of these years. To see the coming of *angor'lot*, the True Destiny. No, I would not risk the City of Dreams for my son alone, but to attend the crowning of the Wyld . . . I would risk anything."

"Not a crowning yet," Bao said. Emotions were insignificant. "Not unless I survive."

"True, true. You held the Oneness when I arrived?"

Bao nodded.

"You came to me knowing the Oneness already," Mintel said. "Sometimes I wonder if I've taught you anything at all."

The bells rang outside, distant. Bao looked toward the tent flaps, outlined faintly with light. "It is time."

"So it is."

After years of preparation, it was time. Bao looked at the man who had adopted him. "I came here for this, you understand," Bao said. "For this only. I did not expect it to take years. Attachments are irrelevant. Only this matters."

Mintel's smile broadened, lines spreading from his eyes and mouth. "To want, to receive, to understand." It had the way of a quote about it, likely one of the proverbs of Kongsidi, the great servant. Mintel was *abrishi*, after all.

"And that means?" Bao asked.

"All men want something," Mintel said. "All men receive something. Not all men understand the nature of what they have received. You came to us for one purpose, but it was not the purpose that the Grand Tapestry planned for you. That is not uncommon."

Bao flexed a hand, then pulled off his glove. The back of his hand had been scarred with a terrible burn in the shape of a circle, with three sinuous hooked knives stabbing out from the center toward the perimeter, their tips turning until they blended with the line outside.

"If I survive this day," Bao said, holding up his hand, "I will do with my power things that some will call evil."

"Good, evil," Mintel said with a wave of his hand. "These words are the words of the *ulikar*, the outsiders. Our ways are not theirs. Our ways are not *yours*. We are only concerned with what must be done and what must not be done."

"As the Tapestry unravels . . ." Bao said.

"As the Tapestry unravels," Mintel said, "so the lives of men unravel a little each day until we reach our end. You have come to us, as prophecy said. Our lives have been chosen for us up until this moment, this time. From today, fate will no longer be decided. We give our lives to you. It was what we were created to do, since the days of the very first Sh'botay. Go, my son. Go and be victorious."

Bao pulled his glove back on, then strode out into the light.

Bao pulled his horse to a halt at the lip of Abyrward. The massive rent in the ground spread out for what had to be leagues, though the people here did not use that term. It had taken him months to understand their complex measurements of distance, weight, and time. He still had to call in a member of the counters' guild any time he wanted to be certain of a calculation.

Mintel rode at his side. The ancient man had spent most of the trip with his eyes closed in meditation, as was the way of the *abrishi*. No man—not lord, not bandit, not slave—would interrupt an *abrishi* in meditation. A man would rather take his own hand off at the wrist than risk the unfavorable fate caused by such an action.

As the horses stopped, Mintel's eyes fluttered open. He breathed in deeply, and Bao knew that he was appreciating the grand sight. It was one of the most beautiful in nature. Short kingdom trees lined the edge of the rift. Though other places in the Inner Land were filled with dead trees only, here in this sacred place, they grew vibrantly. Their bright green leaves were the food of the silkworm, a symbol of the Inner Land as old as the symbol that had been burned into the back of Bao's hand.

The trees were in bloom, the blossoms hanging in clusters on short stalks below the leaves. The air smelled sharply of pollen. In front of the trees, the ground fell away into the deep chasm, the strata of rock making stripes on the walls. A stream ran down below. *Angarai'la*, the River of Souls. It was there that Bao hoped to find the object of his long search.

Around him, the Freed moved up to the chasm's lip. That was the name they had taken for themselves. Bao had given the men shirts, and they had ripped them into strips and tied them around elbows and knees. They moved like animals as they reached the chasm and looked down, not speaking, bare backs to the sky, feet unshod. The tattoos on their backs and shoulders wrapped around their necks, then formed into claws or barbed branches below the chins. Their heads seemed to be held from below by the tattoos.

"Where is Shendla?" Mintel asked.

"She will come," Bao said.

And she did, right on time. As the sun reached its zenith behind the clouds, Bao picked out her crew moving up the side of the chasm from below. Slender and dark of skin, Shendla wore woodsman's clothing. Thick boots, a rugged coat. She carried two long knives strapped to her back, handles up over her shoulders. Bao had never seen her in a skirt, and didn't care to.

She reached the top of the chasm, then bowed to him, not

pausing to drink or rest despite the long climb. "The way is prepared."

"No man entered the shrine?" Bao cautioned.

"None. We only scouted the path for you, Wyld."

"Not Wyld yet," he said, climbing down from his horse.

"Ha!" said one of Shendla's companions. Torn had a wide smile and wore his beard in two thick, knotted braids, one down from either cheek. "You are surely the most humble conquering despot this world has known, Bao. You will execute a man for failing you, but you will not allow us to give you the title you seek?"

"To take the title I do not yet have," Bao said, "is to dishonor it, Torn. I will walk *Angarai'la* and enter the Hearttomb, where I will face—and kill—its guardian. Until I return, I am not the Wyld."

"Then what are you?" Torn asked.

"Many things."

"I shall create for you a title to use until you return! Wy-dain!"

The term was not lost on Bao. The language they called *isleh*, or Ancient, had little left in common with the Old Tongue that Bao knew. However, during his time with this people, he had begun to piece it together. *Wy-dain* was a pun on *Wy-eld*, or *Wyld*. *Wy* meant slayer, and *Wy-dain* roughly translated to "slayer of boredom."

Mintel chuckled at that, ancient eyes alight. Shendla smiled.

"No smile?" Torn asked, inspecting Bao's face. "Not a hint of one?"

"Lord Bao does not laugh, Torn," Shendla said, a possessive hand on Bao's shoulder. "His duty is too heavy."

"Oh, I know, I know," Torn said. "That doesn't mean I can't try. Someday I will break that mask of yours, my friend. Someday!" Torn laughed, taking a canteen from one of his servants and drinking its contents down.

"My time has come," Bao said. "I will descend. Camp here and wait for my return."

The Freed gathered around him, but Bao seized the One Power and pointed. "Wait!" he commanded. They responded only to direct—and forceful—orders. Like hounds. The feral men pulled away, climbing up onto a nearby incline and huddling down to await his return.

Shendla still held his arm. A tiny broken piece of him was fond of her touch and wished for it to linger. That disturbed him. It had been . . . long . . . since he had felt an emotion such as that one.

"I see trouble in your eyes," she whispered.

"Walk with me a moment," he said, leading her toward the path down into the chasm. Bao turned his head and saw that Mintel watched them go with a curious, yet patient, expression. The old man then closed his eyes and entered meditation. The man would meditate until Bao returned, eating nothing, taking only occasional sips of water. Mintel gave no farewell, and Bao had expected none. The old man closed his eyes to Bao, then would open them to the Wyld—come at long last into the world.

Once they were a short distance away, Bao stopped Shendla with a hand on her shoulder. "I know you would come with me," he said to her softly. "You cannot."

"Let me at least walk you to the opening below," she said. "I know the path. I—"

"I must walk it alone," Bao said, stern. "You *know* this. If I am to bring your *angor'lot*, I must follow the prophecies exactly. 'He descends alone and dies, returning to us reborn.' You will wait."

She drew her lips into a line. She did not like being told what to do, but she *had* given him her oaths.

"What bothered you, above?" she asked.

Bao turned, looking down the chasm, toward the River of Souls below. "Torn called me friend."

"Is he not your friend?"

"I do not have friends," Bao said. "And I certainly did not come here to find them. I seek the prize, and the prize alone. I will have the cup's power, Shendla. Nothing else matters to me. Surely all of you can sense that. I long ago lost the capacity for affection."

"You say things such as that so often."

"They are true," he said. "Tell me honestly. You cannot look in these eyes of mine and see anything but death and coldness."

He turned to her, and she stared into his eyes.

"No," she said. "That is not what I see at all."

"Bah!" he said, pulling away from her. "You are fools, all of you. I don't care for your prophecies! I speak the words so I can control you. How can you not see this?"

"You have come to save us," she said. "You break us free of fate's chains. You did not know the prophecies when you first came—you have said so yourself—but you fulfilled them anyway."

"By accident."

"Releasing the enslaved, declaring all men free? That was an accident?"

"I did it to create chaos!" he said, turning.

"You have brought us unity," she replied. "You have brought us glory. The Dragon has come, Bao. Every man and woman in this land can feel it. He will try to destroy the world, and only you can stop him. There is a *reason* you have done what you did. The Tapestry . . . shall I call it by your word? The Pattern? It has brought you, and once you step into that cavern below, we will be freed from fate and be made our own people again."

Darkness within, Bao thought. *She is so earnest. She believes it.*

And . . . did he? Two years in this land. Was he starting to believe? Had he accidentally found in this place the very thing he'd so long sought?

"The others always hated me," he said to Shendla. "They named me *ulikar,* and spat at me. Not you. You followed me from the start. Why?"

"You do not want the answer to that," she said, meeting his gaze. "It will weigh upon you."

How well she knew him.

"I . . ." he found himself saying. "I will . . . protect this people, if I can." Darkness within! He did believe. Only just a little, but he did believe.

"I know," she whispered. "Go. I will wait here for you."

Bao let his eyes linger on her, hearing Torn laugh as he told a story above. Then Bao summoned the Oneness and stepped down the path.

Bao kicked out the campfire. He had started it with the One Power, but now—in the light of morning—it seemed to be wise to avoid channeling. He did not know what awaited him inside *Rai'lair*, the Hearttomb. The guardian was said to be something ancient, and there were many ancient things that could sense channeling.

He continued on his trek. His sleep had come fitfully these two nights of his journey. Perhaps he should have Traveled directly to the entrance of the cavern, but that would have been . . . cheating. A piece of him laughed that he thought of it so. What cared he for such rules?

Strangely, he did care. More and more, he *wanted* to be the Wyld to this people. They were a means, a tool, but a man could treat his tools well. Too many of Bao's associates would break or cast aside a tool once their interest waned.

He stepped up beside the River of Souls. It did not look like much, more a stream than a true river, if a fast-moving one. The babbling noises it made accompanied him down the long decline, always his companion. At times, its noises sounded like whispers. Perhaps that was where it had earned its name.

He filled his canteen from it. Only the Wyld could drink its waters, and he wanted to taste them as soon as he achieved his goal. Eventually, he saw the maw of the Hearttomb opening before him. He checked the sun. Still early in the day. Could he be done and return in time? By prophecy, he was supposed to return from the pit at sunset on the third day. How would the people react if he fulfilled their prophecies in all other ways, but then failed to do so in time?

He arrived at the point where the river descended into the cavern. The stone face of the rock here was worked into the shape of a man and a woman kneeling, heads bowed. And . . . was that the image of a chora tree, carved behind them? Time had worn the rock face deeply; he could not make it out for certain.

He seized the One Power and entered the cavern. Amazingly, the inside was overgrown with foliage. Ferns and saplings lined the river as it ran into the darkness. Bao frowned, then spun a web to create a light for himself. Better to risk a small amount of channeling than to continue forward in the dark.

He anticipated the plants vanishing as he went deeper, but they did not. Against all logic, they continued; they bloomed, though the land above was in the Great Lord's grip.

So, Bao thought, walking deeper, *the tomb's guardian is one of the Nym?* He had not expected this.

One of the vines at his feet moved.

Bao channeled, releasing a blast of fire at the vine. The fire hit, but it had an unexpected effect—where the web touched the vine, more sprouted out. The room started to shake.

Ahead of him, the darkness trembled, and his light shone on the interior of a horrible maw that stretched from floor to ceiling. Needle-sharp teeth stood in array all the way down its greenish throat. What looked like insectile arms broke up through the twisting plants, long and slender, reaching for him.

Bao cursed, unsheathing his sword. During these last two years he had honed his skill back into top form, and he now considered himself the equal of any man. As those arms came for him, he hacked and sliced, weaving between them in the ancient sword forms. He separated the insectile arms at the joints, leaving them twitching on the ground.

He now knew what he faced. Somehow, a juvenile jumara must have crawled into this cavern and gone through its pupation and transformation. The resulting Shadowspawn was too large to squeeze back out; he saw only its mouth and some of its tendrils and spines. Jumara strengthened when the One Power was used against them.

Aginor, I hope you burn, wherever you are, Bao thought. He had always hated these creatures.

He snarled, and charged the beast. As he ran, he used weaves to lift chunks of rock up into the air, then burned them molten in the blink of an eye and sprayed the jumara's maw with melted rock. The thing screamed, the rock trembling as the creature pulled away from the end of the tunnel, revealing that it crouched in an enormous cavern. Its mouth had been pressed against the tunnel's entrance near the ceiling of the cavern, to devour anything that tried to enter the cave.

Bao's foot hit the lip of the rock at the end of the tunnel and he threw himself out into the cavern, using a blast of Air to hurl himself forward. The enormous jumara reared beneath him, the "vines" proving themselves to be the tentacles that surrounded its mouth, the insectile arms the spines that grew from its maw. It was easily a hundred feet long, pushed up against the side of the cavern, its enormous clawed legs clinging to the rock.

Bao raised his sword and dropped through the air toward the thing.

———

Bao hauled himself to his feet, gasping, covered in blood from the jumara'nai. Its heart continued to thump, its body splayed open in places, crushed by rocks in others. Bao stumbled, then retrieved his sword from the rocks where he'd dropped it near the stream that ran through the cave.

Behind him, the beast's heart finally stilled. Bao leaned against a rock, ignoring his bruises and cuts. Darkness within. The thing had nearly had him. He *hated* the monsters he could not fight directly by channeling. Bao was convinced that Aginor had created them not to be part of the Shadow's armies, but because of a twisted desire to see just how terrible a beast he could make.

Bao summoned light. The cup had better be in there. If it was not . . .

He crossed ground overgrown with plants. Between them peeked the bones of fallen heroes who had tried to best the cavern's champion. A jumara was nearly immortal unless slain; they could live for millennia in hibernation, only eating when something touched one of their spines or tentacles.

Bao shook his head, thinking of how easily these heroes must have fallen. Even with the One Power, even with centuries of training at the sword, he had nearly become another meal—and he had fought jumara before. He knew where to strike.

Sword out, Bao reached the other side of the cavern. Here, upon a natural stone dais, he found the plants grown together into what seemed a kind of face or head.

"So I was right," he said, kneeling beside the face. "I thought the Nym had all died."

"I . . . am not of the Nym . . ." the face said softly, eyes closed. "Not any longer. Have you come to give me rest, traveler?"

"Sleep," Bao said, channeling Fire and burning away the creature. "Your service is at an end." The plants on the dais writhed, then shriveled, drawing back.

Upon the dais, the withdrawing plants revealed an object of gold. Bao could see why the people of this land had called it a cup, though it was not truly one. He had spent two years seeking it, slowly teasing its location from old accounts, myths, and stories. He picked it up, reverent.

A short time later, he left the cavern and stepped into *Angarai'la*, the River of Souls, to wash off the blood of the fallen guardian, and drank deeply of the cold water. That done, he walked to his pack and removed the golden rod, as long as his forearm, that he had carried in it. A short distance below the end, the metal splayed out into a disc shape.

He took the "cup" and slid it down onto the rod, the two locking into place. How enraged he'd been when he'd found the rod, thinking his quest done, only to find that the *sa'angreal* had been separated into two pieces!

Now they were whole again. He took a deep breath, then channeled through the rod.

The One Power rushed into him, flooding him. Bao cast his head back, drinking it in, and laughed.

Laughter. How long had it been since he had laughed? This land, these experiences, had brought mirth back to him somehow. He exulted in the power. What he held was no cup, but the second most powerful *sa'angreal* ever created for a man to use. *D'jedt*, known simply as the Scepter during his time, had been so powerful that it had been kept locked away during the War of the Power.

This . . . this was a grand weapon, greater than *Callandor*.

Holding it, Bao felt powerful, invincible. He found himself running back up along the river, and did not grow fatigued.

He ran through the rest of that day. The hours passed as if in the blink of an eye. At sunset, he burst up the last few feet of the trail, bearing his prize. He raised it up high over his head, striding to where he had left Shendla.

She waited there still, sleeping in the very spot where he had left her. She rose, then immediately went to one knee before him.

The Freed scrambled down from their hillside above. He did not fail to notice that the female Ayyad, dressed in black robes with white tassels, had arrived to watch for him. Two hundred of them waited with the gathered nobility that Bao had appointed. In a wave, they fell to their knees as Shendla had, leaving only Mintel, who sat at the top of the path with legs crossed as he meditated.

"Mintel!" Bao announced, walking up to Shendla and reaching down to her shoulder. "Open your eyes to *angor'lot*! The day has come at long last. I name myself the Wyld. Your dragonslayer has come!"

The people began to cheer him, and Shendla looked up. "You smile," she whispered.

"Yes."

"You have accepted it?" she asked. "Your role among us?"

"Yes."

He noticed a tear roll down her cheek, and she bowed her head again. He had come among them as a stranger. And oh, what power he had found, far more than he had ever anticipated. The Scepter was merely a beginning.

Mintel cried out, standing, eyes opening. "Hail the Wyld! Hail him and bow! He who shall save us from the Dragon, who shall prevent the death of the land and bring us to glory! Hail Bao! Hail our king!"

The cries of the people rose to the heavens above. Bao drew in power thirstily, and fully embraced what he had become. Two years ago he had started on this course when he had decided to impersonate a slave among the Sharans. After that had come the revolution, which he had led almost by accident.

Through it all, he had sought one thing. Through earning the allegiance of the Ayyad—won at a terrible price—and gaining the fervent loyalty of the Freed. Through the chaos of revolution and vanished monarchs, through the solidification of a kingdom beneath him.

Through it all, he had sought this one object for a single purpose. *Finally, Lews Therin,* thought Bao—once named Berid Bel, and later called Demandred, now reborn as the savior of the Sharan people. *Finally, I have the power to destroy you.*

MICHAEL J. SULLIVAN

THE CHARACTERS OF ROYCE AND HADRIAN CAME TO ME DURING MY self-imposed ten-year hiatus from writing. After crafting twelve novels and spending a decade getting nowhere, I had determined that publication was hopeless, and I had vowed never to write creatively again. But they kept invading my mind, and as hard as I tried to silence them, I finally gave in, on one condition: that I would write a book that *I* wanted to read and forgo any thoughts of publication. What a fun time I had bringing these two rogues to life. My wife decided to circumvent my plans and got the books published, and hence Riyria was born.

The six books of The Riyria Revelations were released by Orbit in three two-book omnibus volumes, and while I thought that would be the end of Royce and Hadrian, readers clamored for more. Because I didn't want to "tack on" to a carefully choreographed ending, The Riyria Chronicles were born to explore adventures that occurred during the twelve years the pair were together before Revelations began.

The short story I've provided is a Chronicles tale. It takes place after the events of *The Rose and the Thorn* and before those of *Theft of Swords*. Even so, it's a stand-alone story and no prior experience with any of my books is required to enjoy it to its fullest.

Crafting a work for *Unfettered* was quite a daunting experience. I wanted to help Shawn and his cause, but how could I not be intimidated by the esteem of the authors I'd be sharing the pages with? Like Riyria, I hope that I rose to the challenge, and that you'll be entertained by "The Jester," a story of adventure, bonds of friendship, and a recognition that the choices we make dictates the future we find.

Michael J. Sullivan

THE JESTER

Michael J. Sullivan

Hadrian discovered that the most fascinating thing about plummeting in total darkness wasn't the odd sense of euphoria instilled from the free fall or the abject terror derived from anticipating sudden death, but that he had the opportunity to contemplate both.

The drop was that far.

The four had plenty of time to scream, which they did the moment the rope had snapped. Hadrian wasn't sure if Royce yelled. He couldn't hear him—and doing so wasn't in his partner's nature—but Wilmer would have drowned him out anyway. The pig farmer was so loud that his shrieks ricocheted off the stone walls and bounced back before any of them hit the water. Whatever air they had left was driven from their lungs by the vicious slap and suffocating cold.

The impact would have hurt anyone, and Hadrian already had a broken leg. He nearly blacked out from the pain. Maybe he did, if only for an instant, but the immediate plunge into ice-cold water woke him. Just deep enough. Hadrian pushed off the bottom with his good leg and hoped he would reach air in time.

Normally weighed down by three swords, this was the first time he was happy to have lost two—not so much lost as one having been shattered and the other devoured.

He broke the surface with a gasp.

"Hadrian?" Royce called.

Turning, Hadrian spotted his friend, bobbing. The soaked hood collapsed over his head, as if a bat hugged his face.

"Still alive," he yelled back.

A flurry of splashing near him suggested neither Wilmer nor Myra could swim. Wilmer had never impressed Hadrian as athletic in any way. Given that walking had proved difficult for the pig farmer, swimming might be as impossible as flying. Similarly, Hadrian imagined Myra's past experience with bodies of water would have been limited to lying in a brass tub while servants added scented oils and refilled her wine cup.

"There's a blue light behind you," Royce pointed out after peeling off his hood. "Looks like the edge of the pool is just ten feet or so. Can you make it?"

Hadrian turned and spotted the eerie glow coming from the cavern wall. Royce was right. The edge of the little lake was close. The subterranean pond was less a basin and more a stone fissure filled with water—likely with straight sides. The ice-cold pool sapped Hadrian's strength, freezing his muscles and strangling his breath. A death trap.

"I can try," Hadrian replied, still struggling to keep his head above the surface. Over his shoulder he called out, "Myra? Wilmer? You okay?"

"Forget about them," Royce said. "Get yourself out."

Hadrian struggled to see in the dim light. He could hear both Wilmer and Myra gasping, coughing. "I don't think they can swim."

"Not my problem—not yours either. Get to the edge."

"If you won't help them, I—"

"You'll what? Help them drown?" Royce asked. He was somewhere behind Hadrian, somewhere in the dark, hardly making a sound. "You'll be lucky to get out alive on your own."

Royce was right, but when had that ever mattered? "I'll do what I can."

"All right, all right!" Royce barked, the familiar frustration in his voice. "I'll help them. But get yourself out. I can't save everyone."

Hadrian swam as best he could, happy to be wearing leather and wool rather than chain mail. While down to only one sword, the two-handed spadone strapped to his back was still the biggest and heaviest he owned. His left arm, numb and useless, hung limp. The distance wasn't far, just a few kicks away, but he only had one good leg. At least the cold water soothed the burns on his back, and—if the pool wasn't putrid—it might help clean the claw marks raked across his chest.

Working as best he could, Hadrian swam until he reached the ledge. He hung for a moment, catching his breath. Then, using his elbow for leverage, he lifted and rolled onto the stone floor, carefully avoiding the burns on his back and the cuts on his chest. He lay on his side, panting, feeling the water drain from his clothes.

Opening his eyes, Hadrian saw they were in yet another massive chamber of the never-ending cave complex. How many were there? How deep did they run? How long could they keep going? They must have been a week underground. All the food they had brought was gone, but Royce still carried some of the wolf meat.

They all would have died if it hadn't been for Royce. Not that his partner cared about Wilmer or Myra. They had stopped being important when the level of danger exceeded the twenty-five gold tenents Myra had offered them to serve as escorts. After only the first night inside, Hadrian had been convinced Royce would have abandoned the fee, along with Myra and Wilmer, if doing so would have caused a magic exit to appear. As it was, Hadrian worried what would happen when the wolf meat ran out.

They must be at the bottom. The *roots of the mountain*—that's what was written on the map; that's how the jester described the heart of the Farendel Durat range. Hadrian had always considered mountains to be beautiful—but learned this was only true from the outside and from a distance. On the inside, they proved terrifying.

The others crawled out of the inky pool, shivering in the faint glow emanating from the cluster of gems embedded in the cave wall. Myra looked dead, the blue light draining her skin of color, thin hair plastered flat. Upon first meeting, she had been lively as a rabbit and spoke so quickly they had needed her to repeat everything. Lying on the stone, coughing, shivering from the wetness, the widowed wife of the candle merchant looked more her age. Somewhere in her thirties, or maybe older, she was finally sapped of the insatiable drive that had powered her. The exhaustion showed in her eyes, a blurry, unfocused stare. She was a dormouse, caught too far from her hole by a bright light. She wanted it to be over—they all did.

Wilmer lay facedown a few feet away. Never more than a rag, his thin, homespun tunic—blackened on one side and bloodied on the other—had become the stained road map of where they'd been. Wilmer was still coughing, still spitting. That scream of his must have cost a lot of air. He'd likely swallowed water on the way up.

"Nice place, this," Hadrian said and grunted, trying to shift position. "I think we should stay awhile."

Royce knelt beside him, panting. "I'll ask the innkeeper for extra pillows and blankets."

"Tell him I'll have the special—the special is always the best."

Royce pulled up Hadrian's shirt to examine the burns and the claw marks.

Hadrian saw him grimace. "Oh—nice bedside manner, pal. Why don't you just pull my cloak over my face and recite something religious."

"If I knew anything religious, I might."

"Did we get away?" Myra asked.

No one answered.

Hadrian was afraid to—afraid to jinx what little luck they found by hitting the pool instead of jagged rocks. Gods looked for such hubris when deciding where to step, and so far good fortune had been scarce.

Of the group, Royce showed the least wear. His hood and cloak had survived without a tear, although he did have a nasty-looking cut across his forehead. His expression was sullen, but that was normal for Royce. It was only when he smiled that Hadrian worried.

Royce turned and cocked his head, like a dog listening. Always the first sign, the early indicator that life was about to get ugly again. Over the course of their underground journey, Hadrian had come to see his friend as a canary in a mine. He wished he could have been surprised to see his friend's expression darken, but by then he would have been more astonished to discover they were safe. A second later, Hadrian heard the distant banging for himself. A long, familiar, striding rhythm that sounded like a god beating out a cadence using thunder as a drum.

"Nope," Royce finally told Myra, as he helped Hadrian to his good leg.

"Why doesn't it stop?" Wilmer cried. "Why doesn't anything in here *ever* stop?" He was slapping the floor with his palms, fingers spread out.

The banging became hammering and then pounding as the sound grew nearer.

"Go! Go! Go!" Royce shouted, and they were up and running again. Hadrian limped, using his partner as a crutch.

Wilmer also struggled, his side still bleeding. The stain around the snapped arrow shaft had grown almost up to his arm and down to his hip. In contrast, Myra made better time, her wet skirt hiked to her thighs, modesty abandoned in favor of survival. They ran the only way possible, the only way they could see—toward the light.

"Door!" Royce shouted. Abandoning Hadrian, he raced ahead. Reaching it first, he knelt, as if proposing marriage.

Of course it was locked. He expected nothing less from that miserable place. Hadrian had never seen a lock that Royce couldn't open, but they were in a race. The frightening bangs of giant footfalls became terrifying booms. Hadrian chanced a look but couldn't see it. The thing was still in the darkness, and his imagination just made the panic more justifiable.

"Open!" Royce announced, and they raced through. Shoving the door closed behind them muffled the thunderous steps but also blotted out the light. Hadrian heard Royce twist the lock then the sound of a board sliding into place.

"We need a light," Myra said.

"You're the candle maker!" Wilmer shouted.

"Everything is wet."

"Give me a second," Royce said.

Outside, the thundering steps closed in.

Sparks flared several times before a flame developed, revealing Royce. Kneeling on the floor, he blew into a pile of gathered debris. Myra pulled candles out of her pack and began lighting them.

She must have a million in there.

Before setting out, Myra had possessed eight separate bags of luggage—some with hats, another with makeup, and several filled with fancy gowns. An entire bag had been devoted to uncomfortable shoes. Hadrian had persuaded her to leave most of them behind. His argument had become irresistibly convincing when everyone refused to help carry her load. She had kept only a single knapsack with food, water, the map pieces, and candles. As she opened her pack this time, Hadrian realized all that remained were the pieces of map and the candles.

Flickering light revealed an octagonal chamber the size of a barn. Chisel marks revealed a room carved out of the mountain— the handiwork of the jester.

Had he done this all himself?

It seemed impossible that anyone could hew a hall from solid stone. Dwarves were legendary for their mastery of such things, but Hadrian had long since been convinced the jester hadn't worked alone. Even so, it must have taken years.

In the center of the chamber, a chest the size of a wagon sat on a stone dais. Built of steel with brass corners and coin-sized rivets, it was secured by a formidable padlock. On the far side of the room stood another door, also cast from steel with its own massive lock. The last remaining item was an iron lever and the thick chain that connected it to the keystone holding up the arched ceiling.

Royce was busy shoving another brace across the door they'd entered, and with the light of Myra's many candles, Hadrian could see it was old and rotted. The door itself was an even greater concern. The iron hinges were rusted, the wood grooved from worms and termites. As the pounding grew closer, they all backed away, staring with anticipation at the rickety door that had become their castle gate.

"Better open that other door, Royce," Hadrian said.

"Wait!" Myra shouted, and all of them froze. "It's another choice."

Hadrian looked to Royce.

"I think she's right. We'll get to choose only one." His partner said, shaking his head in disgust. "By Mar, I hate this short bastard. First Manzant prison and now this—I'm really starting to develop a dislike for dwarves."

"So it's another trap?" Hadrian asked.

"What are we gonna do?" Wilmer's voice was rising in octaves again. The man was a human teakettle always on boil.

BOOM!

Something hit the little door and it shook, kicking out a cloud of dust.

Wilmer screamed.

"Shut up!" Royce ordered, and Wilmer clamped both hands over his own mouth.

"This is all *his* fault," Myra said. "We were doing fine until he screamed and announced us to everything in the area. He screams at everything! We should never have brought him."

"We had to," Hadrian said. "He had the last piece of the map. Besides, Wilmer only started screaming because you turned that statue to the left and made the floor disappear."

Myra smirked. "I didn't have a choice. Have you forgotten about the snakes? And Royce wasn't doing anything."

"I was busy trying to stop the walls from closing in," Royce said absently, his sight fixed on the chest, and if Hadrian had to guess, the lock. Anything requiring a key must be like a loose tooth to his partner. "And stopping them was more important than a few snakes."

"A few? Where'd you learn to count?"

BOOM!

Hadrian felt the impact through the floor that time, and it made one of Myra's candles wobble. "We've got a choice to make, people." Hadrian leaned against one of the carved walls. "Door, chest, or lever?"

"We came here for the treasure," Myra pointed out. "We have

to open the chest, or what was the point of all this?"

"How can you even think that?" Wilmer shouted. He alone faced the little wooden door. "That—that *thing* is out there. A tiny door won't hold it! But that one might." He pointed across the room. "We gotta get to the other side now!"

"You're just panicking." Myra dismissed him with a wave of her hand that the farmer didn't see. Nothing could pry his sight from the entrance.

"'Course I'm panicking!" Wilmer balled his hands in fists. "Panicking is what a body does in a spot like this!"

"Why did you even come?" Myra shook her head in disgust and moved away from Wilmer—or was it the door she was getting distance from? Perhaps she was heeding the old adage that one doesn't need to outrun a monster, just the terrified pig farmer and the guy with the broken leg. Whatever her motives, Myra began following Royce as he approached the chest. She was careful not to pass him and stepped only where he had. She wouldn't make that mistake again.

"And here I thought you was a smart lady," Wilmer responded to Myra's rhetorical question. "You said you had the rest of a map leading to some amazing treasure. Why in Maribor's name do you *think* I came along?"

"Royce?" Hadrian called to him. "What's your choice?"

The thief didn't answer. Instead, he tilted his head once more, and Hadrian thought his heart might stop. This time, however, the familiar scowl didn't appear.

"What is it?"

"It's quiet," the thief told them.

They all turned to look at the little door and waited. Hadrian was holding his breath without realizing it until he had to take another. By then it was obvious Royce was right. It was quiet. The pounding had stopped.

Hadrian limped closer to the door. Placing a hand on it, he felt the bristles of the stressed wood where it had begun to snap. He listened. Nothing.

"What does that mean?"

Royce shrugged. "I don't even know what the blazes that thing is out there."

"Well, it don't like us," Wilmer said, his voice down an octave. Turning to look at Myra he added, "And that weren't *my* fault. It was *yours*."

Myra looked embarrassed and turned away. Setting her pack down on the stone dais in front of the chest, she drew her wet hair out of her face and softly said, "I don't like spiders."

Royce, who was on the dais studying the lock, turned and shook his head in disbelief. "Are you joking?"

"No, I'm deathly afraid of them."

"Anyone is," Hadrian said, "when they have teeth and are as big as a river barge."

"Well, there you have it. I'm vindicated." Myra sat down and began pulling more candles out of her pack. They were all the same. She must have had a backroom filled with the things.

Myra was even odder than Wilmer, who Hadrian felt could best be described as *challenged*. A well-to-do widow of a candle baron, she had packed up the family carriage and headed off for fame and glory by spelunking for treasure. Chandlers—*wax* chandlers especially—supplied the rich and the church with light, making them both wealthy and respected. He couldn't imagine why she would trade all that for this insanity. Early on, Hadrian had called her the Queen of Wax and received a nasty glare. Maybe Myra wasn't happy with her inherited candle empire, or perhaps she simply wanted to try lighting one at both ends.

"You shouldn't have run," Wilmer told her.

With an armload of candles, Myra moved deeper into the room, establishing new lights as she went. "I'm sorry, okay? But I had no idea that crossing that blasted river would make the wolves attack."

"It didn't," Hadrian said, feeling the pain in his back. "They were just trying to get away from the fire, and of course you were still holding that cursed amulet."

Myra turned. "We don't know for certain it was cursed," she said, drawing sharp looks from all of them. "Okay, maybe it was."

Myra paused, one arm cupping a host of little beeswax sticks to her breasts, the other holding a lit candle. "Oh—but wait. Then I don't understand. What woke that thing up?" She gestured at the door with the hand holding the candle, and it went out. She sighed miserably and began walking back to the nearest flame.

"I would suspect the explosion did," Royce said, then added with remembered frustration, "proving me correct that you never feed ravens, no matter how much they beg." He glowered at Wilmer, who quickly looked away. Turning to Hadrian he asked, "How's your leg?"

He shook his head. "Hurts."

"Broken?"

"Pretty sure."

"Listen," Wilmer pleaded, raising his arms in desperation. "Can we just decide what we're gonna do? I don't understand why we can't just have Royce unlock this big, beautiful, iron, Maribor-blessed fortress door. Wouldn't you rather have that standing between us and whatever that thing is?"

"Might be a demon," Myra offered, as she delicately placed a candle on top of the treasure chest.

"Demons aren't real," Royce said.

"You're so sure, are you?"

"Allow me to rephrase. It would seem unlikely."

Exhausted, Hadrian sat on the floor and continued watching Myra place another candle, this one on a ledge near the metal door. The room was almost bright.

"We won't get out of here alive—I just know it," Wilmer grumbled, and Myra made a clucking sound that was audible even from the back of the room.

Royce finished examining the chest and moved through the rest of the chamber, nimble as a cat and peering in every corner. Granted, he didn't have a broken leg, nor had he been burned or clawed, but still, Hadrian marveled at Royce's stamina. He'd even outlasted Myra, a feat Hadrian had once thought impossible.

How long has it been?

Hadrian straightened his back and felt the pain in his shoulder and the stab in his leg. This job was feeling much too similar to the Crown Tower, the first mission he and Royce had done together. It had nearly killed both of them. More than six years had passed since forming their little thieves-for-hire business, which they named Riyria—an elvish word for two. This job felt a lot like that one, and it wasn't the first time Hadrian suspected they wouldn't live through this ordeal. It wasn't even the first time that day.

Wilmer sat only a few feet away, hunched on the floor, his head between his knees. He rocked and muttered to himself—maybe singing, or possibly praying. With Wilmer, it was hard to tell. The farmer's hair hung in the way, obscuring his face. When he wiped his cheeks, Hadrian realized the man was crying.

Wilmer was an easier clam to open than Myra. They'd seen his home. Calling the little hovel a shack would be flattery. A more accurate assessment would be to say he had two pigsties. He lived alone—not just in his hovel, but because his farm was in the middle of nowhere. From what little Wilmer had said, Hadrian guessed he, his mother, and the pigs used to live somewhere else but were driven out into the wilds—something Wilmer had done. Then his mother had died, leaving him with only his pigs. Hadrian imagined they had become more like children or siblings than livestock. Wilmer must have been desperate to have left them. Maybe he expected they would only be gone a day or two.

"Wilmer, how in the world did a pig farmer get one of the map pieces?" Hadrian asked. "I thought only nobles of the old empire received them."

"That's true," Myra answered for him. "His piece was given to Governor Hilla, whose descendants are now the Kenward family. Turns out his mother worked for the Kenwards once."

"Lord Kenward thought me mum was special," Wilmer said.

"I bet he did." Myra smirked. "When he died, Kenward left the map section to her. Maybe he thought it was funny."

"It weren't funny. That map is cursed." Wilmer sighed, then turned so that the lights illuminated the arrow in his side. "That fall snapped the end off. Don't really hurt much though—not if I don't move."

"Then don't move," Royce said.

"Shouldn't we pull it out?"

"No." Hadrian held up a warning hand. "You'll bleed like a spigot, and we don't have any more bandages. That shaft is working like a cork in a bottle."

"That's another thing," Myra said, returning from her lighting expedition to look at Wilmer. "Why aren't you dead? Anyone else gets hit by an arrow, they die—you don't even stop talking."

"Just lucky, I guess." Wilmer looked up at the ceiling, which appeared ready to cave in. "I don't think our chances are very good. None of us will survive this place. Thing is—it's all a joke, ain't it? I mean, that dwarf made jokes for a living, right?"

"He was the imperial jester," Myra said.

"If this is a joke, it isn't funny." Royce walked back to them. "I can't find any other way out besides that steel door. No way to continue forward, at least. We could go back the way we came in, but I don't think that's wise."

"So the choice is still the door, the chest, or the lever," Hadrian said.

"The door is the only thing that makes any sense," Wilmer insisted.

Myra shook her head in frustration and pretended to pull her own hair. "What in Maribor's name do you know about sense? The door isn't the answer. It's way too obvious."

"You think pulling that lever and bringing the roof down is the smart thing to do?" Wilmer asked with a sarcastic tone. "Because that *definitely* ain't obvious."

She glared at the farmer. "That's also obvious—obviously stupid. Although I'd almost like to, just to see you crushed under a mountain of rock."

"But what would be the point of opening the chest?" Hadrian asked. "We'd still be trapped. All the gold in the world won't help."

"No one said a thing about gold," Myra replied. "The legend says the emperor's jester stole, and I quote, *'the most valuable thing anyone could ever possess.'* You people have such small imaginations. We're talking about the ancient Novronian Imperial Palace here. The greatest empire the world has ever known. They conquered the dwarves and elves and forced them to pay tribute for centuries. The jester was probably once a dwarven king they had enslaved. And everyone knows how dwarves hoard precious gems. The old empire also had wizards so powerful they could move mountains and redirect rivers. The bloody Rhelacan itself might be sitting in that chest."

"What's that?" Wilmer asked.

"No one really knows; a weapon of some sort that won the war against the elves. I'm just saying whatever is in that chest might be magical and could give us the power to escape these caverns. We might be able to lop the whole top of the mountain off and just walk away."

"What do you think, Royce?" Hadrian asked.

"I'm wondering where the battering ram went," he said. His partner was focused on the little wooden door and seemed more bothered by it than before.

"Back to that hall of scary lights, I hope." Wilmer was up and walking, not heading toward anything, just pacing in a circle. His still-wet feet left a damp trail. He stopped in his orbital trek and glanced around. "When you think about it, this is the nicest room we've found so far."

"That's what frightens me," Royce said, then once more tilted his head.

"Not again," Hadrian muttered. "What is it?"

"Water," Royce said before running off to the far side of the room, grabbing one of Myra's lighted candles on the way.

They all watched as he climbed the rear wall. From that distance, Royce appeared to be little more than a shadow. His trek was so fast and fluid that he could have been some dark liquid spilling uphill. When he reached the top corner, he set the candle on a ledge and they all saw the problem. Water was leaking from a crevice near the ceiling. A column of dark streaks discolored the stone below it. The room looked like it was weeping.

"So?" Wilmer said. "It's just water—right?"

"Yeah," Royce replied. "But it wasn't there before."

BOOM!

This time the impact didn't come from the little door, and they heard a pop near the rear wall, which turned the trickle into a spray.

"Oh how nice, Royce," Myra said. "Your friend is back. Must have heard you were missing him."

"Not my friend," Royce replied. "But it looks like he was off causing mischief. Maybe you're right. Maybe he is a demon."

BOOM!

The rear wall cracked, and more water surged in. It hissed under pressure, kicking out a rooster tail far enough to spray the side of the metal chest. Hadrian wondered if there might be some river or lake above them. Perhaps they had traveled far enough west to be under the ocean itself. The force of the water looked likely to win the battle against the walls, but even if no more breaching occurred, the floor was solid stone, and there was no drain.

Hadrian said, "We have almost an inch of water gathering here."

"All right, that settles it. I'm ordering you to open that chest," Myra told Royce, who looked at her and raised an eyebrow. "Look, I hired you—so do what I say. You two were supposed to be an accomplished pair of thieves—"

"Technically, he's the thief," Hadrian said. "I've never made that claim."

"No—you're right, Viscount Winslow assured me you could fight. *Good with a blade,* I think he said. Only I haven't seen anything out of either of you to prove your worth. You couldn't even steal the map piece. How hard could that have been? He's a pig farmer, for Maribor's sake. He lived in a shack on a lonely road in the middle of nowhere. He didn't even have that many pigs! You had three swords, and you're twice his size. You should have just killed him and taken the map."

Royce looked at Hadrian and raised both hands palms up, as if to say, "*See?*"

"Is that how you got the other pieces?" Hadrian asked Myra.

The woman stopped. The rush of the water was loud, but he knew she'd heard him. Still Myra hesitated, turning slowly. "What?"

494

"You said that an old man *gave* you the other pieces, but did he? Did he just give them to you?"

Hadrian could see it on her face—she was considering lying. Any other time, anywhere else, she probably wouldn't have hesitated. He had long suspected Myra was a good liar but buried deep under a mountain in a sealed room filling with water, she must have realized there wasn't much point.

"He was an old man and dirt poor," she replied. "Figured a rich widow could be persuaded to finance an expedition for a quarter of the recovered treasure—a quarter! He had seven of the eight map pieces and told me Wilmer had the last."

"Did you poison him?" Royce asked. There was no accusation in his tone, merely professional curiosity.

"I run a candle shop not an alchemy store."

Royce shrugged. "It's just a common choice for women."

"Maybe for the women in your social circle, but all I had on hand was a lot of hot wax."

This made Wilmer grimace, shocked Hadrian, and even Royce looked impressed.

Myra rolled her eyes. "What kind of person do you think I am? I smothered him with a pillow while he slept." She folded her arms and huffed. "So why didn't you kill Wilmer?"

"You know I'm right here!" the pig farmer yelled.

BOOM!

The room shuddered once more. Dust rained from the ceiling, and all of them looked up to see if some new and more immediate disaster was about to befall them. When the stones hanging over their heads remained unaffected, the party shared a communal sigh.

"I asked Royce not to," Hadrian said.

"He's annoying that way," Royce added.

"It wasn't necessary. Wilmer offered his piece in exchange for a fair share. His only condition was to come along."

"And Maribor's beard, was that ever a mistake," Wilmer said. "Might have been better if you *had* killed me." He looked at the thief. "Would have been quick and painless, right?"

Royce shrugged. "Sure, why not."

"At least it would have been over and done with. These last few days have been the worst of my life."

"Coming from you, that's really saying something." Myra sloshed over toward Royce through ankle-deep water.

The tight bun on top of her head had come loose, and her hair cascaded over her shoulders, making Myra look like some fairy-tale swan princess. Lines of gray frosted darker locks, lending her a mystical quality—then again, Hadrian might have lost more blood than he realized.

"I should have hired someone else. Viscount Winslow told me you had escaped from the Manzant salt mines, and I got too excited. You just don't find many people who have experience with dwarven constructions. But this whole trip has been a complete disaster. You've done a pathetic job."

"We're here, aren't we?" Royce said. "And you don't even have a scratch."

"Oh, I have plenty of scratches. I can assure you."

"What are you complaining about?" Wilmer asked, pointing at the arrow in his side.

"And if Hadrian hadn't killed those wolves, you'd—"

"And how about when I caught your shoe?" Wilmer said. "You'd be nearly barefoot if it weren't for me."

She looked at him incredulously, then turned back to glare at Royce. "Okay, fine, but none of that matters if we drown down here." Myra looked down. Several of the map pieces and an armada of candles had escaped her pack and were floating on the surface. "I'm telling you the way out is some sort of magical item hidden in that chest, so once more I'm ordering you to open it!"

BOOM!

The creature had returned to the little door, and the two braces bucked and threatened to splinter. The water was nearly knee deep.

"Okay, forget it," Myra said. "I'm begging you to open it."

"We don't *need* the treasure," Wilmer yelled. "We *need* to get out! It's one of them tests, ain't it? You're just letting your greed get the best of you. If we open the chest, there could be some kind of explosion that traps us." He looked up at the ceiling. "Maybe kill us too."

"You know, there's really no reason to believe we have only one choice," Myra said.

"You were the one who suggested it," Hadrian reminded her.

"I know, and maybe it's true, but maybe it isn't. Everything up to this point could have been designed to frighten us away. We might be able to just open the chest, grab the treasure, unlock the door, run out into the beautiful mountain meadow where we left our horses, and all live happily ever after."

"Are you still drinking that stuff?" Royce asked.

"No!" she shouted. Then a melancholy looked crossed her face. "Hadrian threw away the last bottle that the faerie king gave me." She shot Hadrian a wicked stare.

"How many times must I tell you," Hadrian said. "That thing wasn't a faerie king, and what you were drinking certainly wasn't wine."

BOOM!

The room shook, and a good-sized chunk of rock punched out of the wall. The spray of water became a torrent.

"Time's up," Royce said, as the water began to rise at an alarming speed.

"Open the chest!" Myra shouted.

"For the love of Maribor, open the door or we'll all die!" Wilmer cried.

Royce turned to Hadrian and in a low voice asked, "What would you do?"

Hadrian looked at the chest, which supported one of the few remaining undisturbed candles; most of the rest had been snuffed out by the rising water. Then he glanced at the giant steel door and finally at the lever and the chain leading to the ceiling where the keystone held everything in place. "I think Wilmer is right."

"The door it is," Royce said.

"No, that's not what I meant." Hadrian shook his head. "I mean he was right about not opening the chest. Only a greedy person would do that, and I'm starting to think the jester set this whole thing up to make a deliberate point. So the answer won't be greed."

"Right—so we open the door," Royce waded a step forward, through waist-deep water, reaching for his tools.

"No, not the door. Only a coward would choose that door."

"You aren't planning to fight that thing out there, are you? Because I don't think you're up to it."

"No, that's not what I'm suggesting."

"So, what *are* you suggesting? And I would appreciate it if you hurried the explanation. We're running out of time," Royce said.

Wilmer and Myra nodded their agreement as they waded closer to hear Hadrian over the frothy roar.

"Think about it. The dwarf stole the treasure, and then tore the map into eight parts. He had the pieces delivered to the nobles who he'd been forced to entertain for years. I suspect dwarves know a lot about greed. I'll bet most of those nobles, and their descendants, hunted and killed each other over the centuries while collecting the pieces. Just like Myra did. But we've been through this place. It would have taken a legion of dwarves to make. Consider what kind of mastermind created it. Do you think the jester was just some clown?"

"No time for questions, just tell us, okay?"

"I think you were right, Myra. The dwarf *was* special—a noble or king perhaps. Maybe he had been hauled to the imperial court to be humiliated by a bunch of greedy cowards—and this—all this is his revenge. The right choice isn't the chest or the door."

Royce's eyes tracked from the chest, to the door, and finally to the chain that led to the lever, which by then had disappeared below the water's surface.

Royce smiled. "Only a *fool* would pull the lever."

"Exactly."

Royce moved to where the chain disappeared. Hadrian joined his friend, which was easy since he was floating.

"Wait!" Myra shouted. She was looking up and swam deeper into the shadows of the room. Between the rising water and the growing dark, Hadrian lost sight of her. "There's a key hanging from the ceiling right above the chest now! Look! The banging must have made it slip down."

"There's one above the door too!" Wilmer shouted, swimming away and disappearing into the growing darkness as another candle hissed out.

Royce ignored them and started to reach down.

"Wait," Hadrian told him, then shouted. "Come back! We're pulling the lever!"

Hadrian noticed the water rising frighteningly fast. *Did one of them do something to cause that?* He couldn't tell, couldn't see them. Wilmer would be at the door by then all the way on the far side. Myra was likely in the center of the room, just a few dozen feet away, but the water had already snuffed out almost all of the candles. When it reached the ceiling, and the last one went out, they would never find their way back. Even if they knew how to swim, it would be impossible with only a single breath of air. Still he waited while the water level consumed chain links, ticking out the seconds.

"Can you hear me?" Hadrian yelled.

"They aren't coming," Royce said, looking impatient as the two bobbed closer to the ceiling.

"Do it!" Hadrian shouted.

"You sure?"

"No, but do it anyway."

"Good enough for me."

Royce disappeared below the surface.

The chain stretched taut. The keystone was yanked free and fell into the froth. Hadrian braced himself for the ceiling's collapse, but none of the other stones moved.

"It's an exit!" Royce shouted the moment his head broke the surface. "Take a breath and swim!"

"Broken leg. Bad arm. And I can't see in the dark the way you can. Maybe you should just—"

"Shut up and hold your breath."

The water rose, and the last candle was snuffed out as the room topped off. Hadrian had seen no sign of Myra or Wilmer.

He struggled to find the hole in the darkness, his fingers fumbling over rough stone. Grabbing him from behind, Royce shoved Hadrian into the opening where their heads broke the surface. With the room below filled, the water had nowhere else to go and surged up the narrow shaft, bubbling, frothing like a fountain and lifting the two up with it.

"Did you see them?" Hadrian asked. "Did you see Myra or Wilmer?"

From somewhere above, a white light shone enough for Hadrian to see Royce's face. He was grimacing. "The door and the chest were both open."

"And? Did they get out?"

"In a way, I suppose. Wilmer's head was smiling at least."

"What about Myra?"

"You don't want to know."

They spilled out into another chamber, where the water filled a basin that formed a small pool. When the water rose high enough to reach the chiseled edge, it stopped.

The light came from the full moon overhead. They were in a beautiful domed chamber with a crystal roof that allowed the moonlight to illuminate the interior. The space was circular and in the center was the unmistakable shape of a stone coffin. On the far side, Hadrian saw a door, which lacked any sort of latch, lever, or knob. In the very center was a tiny keyhole.

The chamber, vast, flat, and sparsely adorned, possessed an unexpected atmosphere of tranquility. Unlike any room they had visited since descending into the jester's cave, this space felt safe, even hallowed.

Royce and Hadrian glanced at each other, then back at the center of the pool they had just climbed out of. They waited. The surface remained undisturbed except for a single candle that floated, listing to one side. Beyond that, not even a bubble. It could have been a mirror. Slowly they got up. Royce lent Hadrian an arm, and together they made their way out of the pool.

"Look." Royce pointed out magnificent carvings in the stone walls surrounding the chamber. "This joker just had all kinds of time, didn't he?"

Hadrian was still looking back at the water.

"If either of them had been at the lever while we were at the door or chest, they wouldn't have hesitated," Royce said. "Myra would've jumped at the chance to rid herself of us, ensuring she got all the treasure, and Wilmer didn't have the courage to wait."

As much as Hadrian wanted to deny it, Royce was right. They had made their choices.

With his partner's help, they moved to the coffin. Etchings similar to those Royce had pointed out adorned its side. Some of the markings appeared to be writing, but not in a language Hadrian could read. "Pretty," he said, wiping off the dust.

Together they lifted the lid.

Inside lay a small body, wrapped and decayed. At his head was a multicolored hat with bells, at his feet, a silver box. Royce carefully removed the little container, took a step away, and set it down beneath a shaft of moonlight. The box had no lock, just a simple clasp and hinge. Tilting the lid back, they found the interior lined with fine blue velvet. Inside rested a small stone tablet and a key. Carved into the stone were four sentences that Hadrian could read.

> *Cowardice and greed will drown one's soul.*
> *The greatest treasure a person can possess is freedom.*
> *I stole mine by playing the fool.*
> *Now, so have you.*

Royce took the key and, with Hadrian in tow, placed it in the lock. A single click echoed. The door swung open, revealing a mountain trail and a starry night.

Hadrian looked behind them.

"What?" Royce asked.

"We should put the box back."

"Why?"

Hadrian shrugged. "Just seems right. After all we went through with the jester. I feel we owe it to him."

Royce shook his head. "The little monster tormented us for days—tried to kill us—came damn close."

"He just wanted justice, or to put it in your language, revenge."

"That's fine, only *we* never did anything to him. We weren't even after the treasure. It was just a job."

"Maybe that's why we got out."

Royce sighed. "Give me the damn thing." He replaced the box, closed the coffin, and rejoined Hadrian, who waited leaning against the door. Outside, the night air was sweet with the scent of pine.

Hadrian gave Royce a surprised look when he returned.

"What?"

"I didn't expect you'd really put it back," Hadrian admitted, as he wrapped an arm around his friend and the two stepped out, letting the door close behind them.

Royce shrugged. "I owed you."

"Owed me? For what?"

Royce pulled his hood up, covering his features as the two limped out into a lovely summer's night. "I would have picked the chest."

Lev Grossman

LIKE ALL STORIES, THIS ONE HAPPENED FOR SEVERAL REASONS, NOT JUST one. It was, as they taught me in high school social studies, *overdetermined*.

So for example, this story happened because I read George R.R. Martin's *A Clash of Kings*, and I liked the character Strong Belwas. I liked him so much I decided to steal him and give him a new name ("Vile Father") and use him in a story of my own. It also happened because I had recently become a father again, and my own father was ill, and I was dealing with a lot of father-related issues, and I liked the idea of somebody having a big fight with a guy named Vile Father.

This story happened because I was coming to the end of the Magicians trilogy, and before it was over I wanted a chance to write a bit more in the vein of what might loosely be called epic fantasy, à la Fritz Lieber. I wanted to show Fillory in full flood, in the late-afternoon sunlight of a great age of adventure. Also, I wanted to display a little more of the biodiversity of Fillory, hence a mixed army that includes, among other things, manticores and hippogriffs and fairies and giants.

It happened because I wanted to write a scene from Eliot's point of view, and more importantly, I wanted to show Eliot displaying the seriousness of purpose that I knew he was capable of. I wanted him to put his life on the line, and even more seriously, his dignity, because there was something even more important to him than that.

Most of all—and there's nothing more important than this—I wanted to write this story because I thought it represented the playing out of tensions and forces that were already implicit in the world of Fillory, in a manner consistent with the logic that governs things in that world.

In other words, it happened because that's what would have happened.

Lev Grossman

THE DUEL

Lev Grossman

The Lorian champion was a squat fellow, practically as wide as he was tall, and apparently of some slightly different ethnic background than most of his compatriots. The Lorians were Vikings, basically, Thor types: tall, long blond hair, big chins, big chests, big beards. But this character came in at about five foot six, Eliot would have said, with a shaved head and a fat round Buddha face like a soup dumpling and a significant admixture of some Asiatic DNA.

He was stripped to the waist even though it was about forty degrees out, and his latte-colored skin was oiled all over. Or maybe he was just really sweaty.

The champion had a gut hanging over his waistband, but he was still a pretty scary-looking mofo. He had a huge saddle of muscle across his upper back, and his biceps were like thighs, practically, and there must have been some muscle in there, just by volume, even if they did look kind of chubby. And his gut wasn't a flabby gut, exactly; even his fat looked hard. His weapon was weird-looking enough—it was a pole with a big curvy cross of sharp metal on the end—that you just knew he could do something really outstandingly dangerous with it.

505

The Lorian army went nuts for him when he stepped forward. They bashed their swords into their shields and looked at each other as if to say: yes, he may look a little funny, but our fellow is definitely going to kill the other fellows' fellow, so three cheers for him, by Crom or whoever it is we worship! It almost made you like them, the Lorians. They had a multicultural side to them that Eliot wouldn't have expected.

But there was no chance that their champion was actually going to kill the Fillorian champion, Eliot's champion. Because Eliot's champion was Eliot.

There had been some debate, when the idea was first mooted, about whether it made sense to send the High King of Fillory into single combat with the hand-picked designated hitter of the Lorian military. But it rapidly became clear that Eliot was serious about it, and when the High King was serious about something, people had learned to shut up about it pretty quick. Partly because the High King didn't tend to change his mind, so you might as well skip the whole futile-protest stage, but mostly because people had figured out by now that the High King knew what he was doing.

High King Eliot stepped forward from the front rank of his army, that, predictably but gratifyingly, also went nuts. He smiled—the smile was twisted, but the happiness was the real stuff. The sound of the king's regiment of the Fillorian army going nuts was unlike anything else in the known universe. You had men and women shouting and banging their weapons together, good enough, but then you had a whole orchestra of nonhuman sounds going on around it.

At the top end you had some fairies squeeing at supersonic pitches; fairies thought all this military stuff was pretty silly, but they went along with it for the same reason that fairies ever did anything, namely, for the lulz.

Then you had bats squeaking, birds squawking, bears roaring, wolves howling, and anything with a horse-head whinnying: pegasi, unicorns, regular talking horses. Griffins and hippogriffs squawked too, but lower—baritone squawking, a horrible noise. Minotaurs bellowed. Stuff with humans' heads yelled. Of all the mythical creatures of Fillory, they were the only ones who still creeped Eliot out. The satyrs and dryads and such were cool, but there were a couple of manticores and sphinxes that were just uncanny as hell.

And so on down the line till you got to the bass notes and the subsonics, which were provided by the giants grunting and stomping their feet. It was silly really: it only just occurred to Eliot that he could have just picked a giant as his champion, and then this thing would have been over in about ten seconds flat, pun intended. But that wouldn't have sent the same message.

At first, when Eliot had gotten the news that the Lorians were invading, it had seemed grimly exciting. Rally the banners, Fillory's at war! Antique formulas and protocols were invoked. A lot of serious-looking non-ceremonial armor and weapons and flags and tack had come up out of storage and been polished and sharpened and oiled. They brought up with them a lot of dust and a thrilling smell of great deeds and legendary times. An epic smell.

The invasion wasn't a complete surprise. The Lorians were always up to some kind of bad behavior in the books. Kidnapping princes, forcing talking horses to plough fields, trying to get everybody to believe in their slate of quasi-Norse gods. But it had been centuries since they actually invaded. They were usually too busy fighting among themselves to get organized enough to come down across the Northern Barrier range in any significant numbers.

Moreover, the peaks of the Northern Barrier range were supposed to be enchanted to keep the Lorians out. Eliot wasn't sure what had happened to that; when this was all over he'd have to remember to figure out exactly why those spells had gone pear-shaped. For now here they were, in force, and it was a tricky business, because while Eliot was determined to repel the invaders, he also found that he was very reluctant to kill any of them.

Eliot was familiar with the literature on the subject, or at any rate with the movies of the literature on the subject, or at any rate with relatively short sections of one of the movies. As far as he had gleaned, in Tolkien the hordes of orcs and goblins and trolls and giant spiders and whatever else were all so evil that you were free to commit genocide on them without any complicated moral ramifications. They didn't have wives and kids and backstories. But the Lorians weren't like that. They looked human enough that killing them would be basically murder, and that wasn't going to happen. Some of them were even kind of hot. And anyway those Tolkien books *were fiction*, and Eliot, as High King of Fillory, didn't deal in fiction. He was in the messy business of writing facts.

So he was going to roll them back, but with minimum casualties. It was tricky. There was nothing—in Eliot's admittedly limited experience—more tedious than virtue.

It was also tricky because the Lorians didn't give a shit about any of that stuff. Death was inevitable, and they seemed to think dying in battle took some of the sting out of it. They were one hundred percent Klingon about it. Which, whatever, Eliot wasn't about to impose his twenty-first-century American worldview on them. But he didn't have to go over to theirs either.

Fortunately the Fillorians had an advantage, which was that they had every possible advantage. They totally outmatched the Lorians in every stat you could name. The Lorians were a bunch of guys with swords. The Fillorians were every beast in the *Monster Manual*, led by a clique of wizard kings and queens, and Eliot was very sorry, but you knew that when you invaded us.

It was late spring when the Lorians came pouring—they didn't really march, they weren't that organized—through Grudge Gap and onto Fillorian soil. Some rode big shaggy horses. They didn't wear matching outfits, but they all seemed to have chosen from the same menu: steel caps, mail shirts or leather armor, round shields, long tunics, bare legs, UGG-type leather boots with fluffy interiors. In their hands or over their shoulders they carried straight double-edged swords of varying lengths, modest-sized but vicious-looking war axes, countless spears and bows. They were met by a nightmare.

See, the Lorians had made a mistake. On their way down from the Northern Barrier they set some trees on fire, and an outlying farm, and they killed a hermit.

Even Janet was surprised by Eliot's anger. I mean, she was

furious, but she was Janet. She was pissed off all the time. Poppy and Josh looked grim, which was how they got angry. But Eliot's rage was towering. They burned trees? His trees? They killed a *hermit?* They *killed* a *hermit?* His heart went out to that weird, solitary man in his uncomfortable hut. He'd never met him. They wouldn't have had much to say to each other if they had met. But whoever the hermit was, he obviously despised his fellow man, and that gave him some credibility in Eliot's book.

And now he was dead. Eliot was going to destroy the Lorians, he would annihilate them, he would murder them! Not *murder* murder. But he was going to fuck them up good.

He was tempted to let the Lorians try to cross the Great Northern Marsh, where the sunken horrors that dwelt there would deal with them, with extreme prejudice, but he didn't want to give them even another day's march on his grass. Besides, there were a couple more farms in the way. Instead he let the Lorians march part of one day, till noon, till they were hot and dusty and ready to knock off for lunch. Probably it was blowing their minds how easy it was all turning out to be. They were going to do it, lads, they were the ones, they were going to fucking take fucking Fillory, dudes!

He let them ford the Great Salt River. He met them on the other side.

Eliot stood alone, disguised as a peasant. He waited in the middle of the road. He didn't move. He let them notice him gradually. First the guys in front, who when they realized that he wasn't moving called a halt. He waited while the guys behind those guys got crowded into them, soccer-stadium style, and they called a halt, and all the way back down the line in a ripple effect. There must have been, he didn't know, maybe a thousand of them.

The man leading the front line stepped out to invite him—not very politely—to kindly get the fuck out of the way, or one thousand Lorian linebackers would pull his guts out and strangle him with them.

Eliot smiled, shuffled his feet humbly for a second, and then punched the guy in the face. It took the man by surprise.

"Get the fuck out of my country, asshole," Eliot said.

That one was on the level, no magic. He'd been taking some boxing lessons, and he got the drop on him with an offhand jab. Probably the Lorian wasn't expecting what amounted to a suicide attack from a random peasant. Eliot knew he hadn't done much damage, and that he wouldn't get another shot, so he quickly held up his left hand and force-pushed the man back so hard he brought six ranks of Lorians down with him, much the same way Asterix took down entire files of centurions.

Eliot dropped the cloak and stood up straight in his royal raiment, so they could see that he was a king and not a peasant. A couple of eager-beaver arrows came arcing over from back in the ranks, and he burned them up in flight: puff, puff, puff. It was easy when you were this angry, and this good, and God he was angry. And good. He tapped the butt of his staff once on the ground: earthquake. All thousand Lorians fell down on their stupid violent asses, in magnificent synchrony.

He couldn't just do that at will, he'd been out here all day setting up the spells, but it was a great effect. Especially since the Lorians didn't know that. Eliot allowed it to sink in.

Then, to mix things up, he undid a spell: he made the army behind him visible, or most of it. Take a good look, gentlemen. Those ones with the horse bodies are the hippogriffs; griffins have the lion bodies. It's easy to mix them up.

Then—and he indulged himself here—he made the giants visible. You do not appreciate from fairy tales how unbelievably terrifying a giant is, at all. These players were seven-story giants, and you did not mess around with them. In real life humans didn't slay giants, because it was impossible. It would be like killing an apartment building with your hands. They were even stronger than they looked—had to be, to beat the square-cube law that makes land organisms that big physically impossible in the real world—and their skins were half a foot thick. There were only a couple dozen giants in all of Fillory—even Fillory's hyper-abundant ecosystem couldn't have fed more of them. Six of them had come out for the battle.

Nobody moved. Instead the Great Salt River moved.

It was right behind them, they'd just crossed it, and the nymphs took it out of its banks and straight into the mass of the Lorian army, like an aimable tsunami. A lot of the soldiers got washed away; Eliot had made the nymphs promise to drown as few of them as possible, though they were free to abuse them in any other way they chose.

Some of the ones who weren't swept away wanted to fight anyway, because they were *just that valiant.* Eliot supposed they must have had difficult childhoods or something like that. Join the club, it's not that exclusive. He and his friends gave them a difficult adulthood to go with it.

It took them four days to harry the Lorians back to Grudge Gap—you could only kick their asses along so fast and no faster. That was where Eliot stopped and called out their champion. Now it was dawn, and the pass made a suitably desolate backdrop, with dizzyingly steep slopes ascending on either side, striped with spills of loose ruck and runnels of meltwater. Above them loomed icebound peaks that had, as far as he knew, never been climbed, except by the dawn rays that were right now kissing them pink.

Single combat, man to man. If Eliot won, the Lorians would go home and never come back. That was the deal. If the Lorian champion won—his name for some reason was Vile Father—well, whatever. It wasn't like he was going to win.

The lines were about fifty yards apart, and it was marvelously quiet out there between them. The pass could have been designed for this; for all Eliot knew it had been. The walls made a natural amphitheater. The ground was perfectly level—firm packed coarse gray sand, from which any rocks larger than a pebble had been removed overnight, per his orders. Eliot kicked it around a little, like a batter settling into the batter's box.

Vile Father didn't look like somebody waiting to begin the biggest fight of his life. He looked like somebody waiting for a bus. He hadn't adopted anything like a fighting stance. He just stood there, with his soft shoulders sloping and his gut sticking out. Weird. His hands were huge: they looked like two king crabs.

Though Eliot supposed he didn't look much less weird. He wasn't wearing armor either, just a slightly floppy white silk shirt and leather pants. For weapons he carried a long knife in his right hand and a short metal fighting stick in his left. He supposed it was probably pretty obvious that he had no idea what to do with them, apart from the obvious stabbing and whacking motions. He nodded to Vile Father. No response.

Time passed. It was actually a teensy bit socially awkward. A soft cold wind blew; it was freezing up here even in May. Vile Father's brown nipples, on the ends of his pendulous man-cans, were like dried figs. He had no scars at all on his smooth skin, which somehow was scarier than if he were all messed up.

Then Vile Father wasn't there anymore. It wasn't magic—he had some kind of crazy movement-style that was like speed skating over solid ground. Just like that he was halfway across the distance between them and thrusting his blade, whatever it was, straight at Eliot's Adam's apple at full extension. Eliot barely got out of the way in time.

He shouldn't have been able to get out of the way at all. Like an idiot he'd figured Vile Father was going to swing the blade at him like a sword, on the end of that long pole, thereby giving him plenty of time to see it coming. Which would have been stupid, but all right, I get it already, it's a thrusting weapon. By rights it should have been sticking out of the nape of Eliot's neck by now, slick and shiny with clear fluid from his spine.

But it wasn't, because Eliot was sporting a huge amount of invisible magical protection in the form of Fergus's Spectral Armory, which by itself would have saved his life even if the blade had hit home, but in addition to that he was sporting Fergus's A Whole Lot of Other Really Useful Combat Spells, which had amped his strength up a few times over, and most importantly, had cranked his reflexes up by a factor of ten, and his perception of time down by that same factor.

What? Look, Vile Father spent his whole life learning to kill people with a knife on a stick. Was that cheating? Well, while Vile Father was doing his squats and whatever else, Eliot had spent his whole life doing this: magic.

When he and Janet had first finished up the casting, a couple of hours earlier in the chilly predawn, he'd been so covered in spellcraft that he glowed like a life-size neon sign of himself. But they'd managed to tamp that down so that the armor was only occasionally visible, maybe once every couple of minutes and only for a moment at a time, a flash of something iridescent and mother-of-pearly.

The time-reflexes part of it worked a bit like that bullet-time effect in *The Matrix*, which is to say that it worked exactly like that. The trigger was Eliot twitching his nose like Samantha on *Bewitched*. He did it now, and everything in the world abruptly slowed down. He leaned back and away from the slowly, gracefully thrusting blade, lost his balance and put a hand down on the sand, rolled away, then got back on his feet while Vile Father was still completing the motion.

Though you didn't get to be as big and fat as Vile Father was without learning a thing or two along the way. He didn't look impressed or even surprised, just converted his momentum into a spin move meant to catch Eliot in the stomach with the butt of the pole. I guess it doesn't pay to stand around looking all impressed on the battlefield.

Though Eliot was impressed. Watching it slowed down like this, you had to admire the athleticism of Vile Father's style. It was balletic, was what it was. Eliot watched the wooden staff slowly approaching his midriff, set himself, and all in good time, hammered it down as hard as he could with his metal baton. The wood snapped cleanly about three feet from the end. Fergus, whoever you were, I heart you.

Vile Father course-corrected once again, reaching out with a free hand to snag the snapped-off bit while it spun in midair. Eliot batted it away before he could get to it, and he watched it drift off out of Vile Father's reach, moving at a graceful lunar velocity. Then, seeing as how he had some time to kill, he dropped the baton and slapped Vile Father's face with his open hand.

Personal violence did not come naturally to Eliot; in fact he found it overwhelmingly distasteful. What could he say, he was a sensitive individual, fate had blessed and cursed him with a tender heart; plus Vile Father's cheek was really oily or sweaty. Eliot wished he'd worn gloves, or gauntlets even. He thought of that dead hermit and those burned trees, but even so he pulled the punch. With his strength and his speed all jacked up like this, he had no idea how to calibrate the blow. For all he knew he was going to take the guy's face off.

He didn't, thank God, but Vile Father definitely felt it. In slow motion you could see his jowls wrap halfway around his face. That would leave a mark. Emboldened, Eliot dropped the knife too, moved in closer, and delivered a couple of quick body blows to Vile Father's ribcage—the hook, his instructor had told him, was his punch. Vile Father absorbed them and danced away to a safe distance to do some heavy breathing and reconsider some of his life choices.

Eliot followed, jabbing and slapping, both ways, left-right. My mother, my sister, my mother, my sister. His blood was up now. This was in every way his fight. He hadn't come looking for it, but by God he was going to finish it.

Vile Father was moving in again, still without much expression on his stolid, hoggy face. Eliot felt as though he ought to be inspiring a little more terror in his adversary, but whatever. He flipped time to normal speed for just a second, coming up for air; Vile Father was whirling his abbreviated pole arm in a tricky cloverleaf pattern, much good may it do him. Eliot slo-moed again, ducking under it, working around it, pounding the man's body like a heavy bag, hoping to knock the wind out of him.

He ought to have been more careful. Eliot had seriously underestimated how much punishment Vile Father could take, or maybe he'd overestimated how much he was giving out. He'd definitely underestimated how quickly Vile Father could move, even relative to Eliot's massively accelerated pace, and how completely he had sized up his overconfident, inexperienced opponent. Gently, even as he sucked up a hail of body shots, Vile Father barged into Eliot and managed to get his arms around him.

Never mind, Eliot would just slip out—hm. You'd think you could just—but no. Ah. It was harder than he thought. A moment's hesitation had cost him. Vile Father's smooth baby face and yellow teeth and beefy breath were right up next to him now, and those ham hock arms were starting to squeeze and crush.

Vile Father had evidently assessed the situation and decided that it didn't matter how fast your opponent could move when he couldn't move a muscle, so you took whatever damage you had to to get the other guy in a bear hug. He had, and now he was trying, slowly but strangely inevitably, to get his teeth into Eliot's ear.

Enough. This guy was strong, and he had all the leverage, but he wasn't superhuman. Eliot felt like he was practically encased in Vile Father at this point, and he hadn't taken a proper breath in about thirty seconds. He set himself and began to pry himself free.

It was still a lot harder than you'd think, and Vile Father was not at all kidding about his personal vileness, but Eliot slither-wrenched his way out of Vile Father's arms and staggered a few feet back. He was still getting his balance when he felt something poke him painfully behind one shoulder. He arched his back away from that fiery hot point and shouted:

"Fuck!"

Nothing the Lorian was carrying should have been able to get through the Spectral Armor. He spun away, still ahead of Vile Father, but not nearly as far ahead as he expected; in real life both their movements must have been a blur. This guy was running magic weaponry; Eliot should have looked at the blade on that thing more closely. Vile Father was packing something that could actually cut him.

It must have been Fillorian metal. Magic metal. I bet he took it from that hermit, Eliot thought. I bet that thing's made from a Fillorian plough blade.

Oh, that is *it*. Eliot snapped.

On his feet again, Eliot spun around the blade and grabbed

what was left of the weapon's shaft and wrenched it out of Vile Father's hands. That probably took some skin with it, he thought. Good. He threw it as hard as he could, as hard as Fergus could. It was still rising when it disappeared into a low-hanging cloud.

He skipped back and set himself the way his boxing instructor told him to, then he shuffled forward. The boxing thing was mostly just for the aerobics, plus it was an excuse to enjoy the company of the boxing instructor, whose amazing upper body was enough to make Eliot not even miss Internet porn in the slightest, but it had some practical value too.

Jab, jab, cross. Hook, hook. No more holding back, he was snapping this shit out crisp and firm. He was rocking Vile Father back on his heels now. Eliot found he was baring his teeth and spitting words with each punch.

"You. Killed. A. Hermit. You. Weird. Sweaty. Bastard!"

Don't go down, cocksucker. Don't go down, I want to hit you some more. They were practically back against the Lorian front line when Eliot kicked Vile Father in the balls and then, indulging a personal fantasy, he swept the leg and watched Vile Father rotate clockwise in a stately fashion and simultaneously descend until he crashed, thunderously and with a lot of slow-motion blubbery rippling, onto the packed sand.

Even then he started to get up. Eliot kicked him in the face. He was through with these fucking people.

He dropped all the magic at once. The strength, the speed, the armor, all of it.

"Go."

Well, he didn't drop *all of it* all of it. His voice echoed off the stone walls of the pass like thunder. Leave a man his vanity, and his sense of theater. It was just good PSYOP. He picked up the broken stub of Vile Father's weapon and threw it into the sand. Fortunately for his sense of theater, it stuck there upright.

"Go. Let this shattered spear mark the border between our lands. If any man cross it, or woman, I make no guarantee of their safety. Fillory's mercy is great, but her memory is long, and her vengeance terrible."

Hm. Not exactly Shakespeare.

"You mess with the ram," he said, "you get the horns."

Better leave it at that.

Eliot scowled a terrible royal scowl at the Lorian host and turned and walked away, speaking a charm under his breath. He was rewarded with the soft rustle and creak of the little stub of wood growing into a little ash tree behind his back. A bit of a cliché. But hey, clichés are clichés for a reason.

Eliot kept walking. His breathing was going back to normal. The pass ran north-south, and the sun was finally cracking its eastern rim, having already been busy lighting the rest of Fillory for at least an hour now. The ranks parted to let him go through. God he loved being a king sometimes. There wasn't much of anything better in life than having your own ranks part before you, especially after you just delivered a bona fide public ass-kicking to somebody who deserved it. He avoided eye contact with the rank-and-file, though he did point two fingers at the most senior of the giants, acknowledging that he'd done the High King a personal favor by showing up.

The giant inclined his head toward Eliot, slightly, gravely. Their kind played a deep game.

It was a funny feeling, coming back to real-time after having watched the world in slow motion. Everything looked wildly accelerated now: plants waving, clouds moving, people talking. It was a beautiful clear morning, the air an icy coolant washing over his brain, which was overheated by combat. He wasn't angry at all, anymore. He decided he would just keep on walking—he would walk the whole half-mile back to the Fillorian encampment by himself. Why the hell not? A lot of people tried to fuss at him about his punctured shoulder, which was probably still leaking some blood, and now that the adrenaline was wearing off it had started to sting pretty furiously. It felt like the point was still stuck in him.

But he didn't want to be fussed over. Not quite yet. Plenty of time for that. Like a lot of people, he'd had a pretty difficult childhood. But his adulthood was just getting better and better.

TERRY BROOKS

WELL, WHAT CAN I SAY ABOUT THIS?

I guess I could say that it was cut from the book in which it was originally intended to see the light of day. Too repetitious. Already covered. Unnecessary. I don't tend to argue a lot with my editors, and especially with Lester del Rey, when I didn't have a strong fortress of arguments in which to fling down my spears and arrows of objection.

I could say it represents the only face-to-face meeting between the two in which a conversation, of sorts, took place. The two most important figures of their respective eras, but the one was already dead and reduced to shade form, and the other was struggling with whether or not becoming a Druid was a good idea.

I could mention that this brief encounter was not uncovered by yours truly, who, in all honesty, had forgotten it even existed. Instead, it was dredged out of the mire of words written and discarded over the years by none other than Shawn Speakman, my faithful Web Druid, who thought it would be fun to include it in this otherwise fully realized anthology of stories.

Or I could admit I am uncertain about most of the above (well, not the Shawn part) and just ask you to read this short excerpt and accept it at face value. Think I'll go with that.

Terry Brooks

WALKER AND THE SHADE OF ALLANON

Terry Brooks

The shade of Allanon did not answer Walker at once, but remained silent and unresponsive, hovering like a dark cloud over the roiling waters of the Hadeshorn, all size and blackness against the starlit sky. Steam sprayed from the lake surface in sharp geysers, as if the dead trapped below were seeking to catch anew the breath of life. The moon was down, hidden behind the peaks that cupped the valley, a wary passerby on its way toward morning. Where he knelt at the water's edge, solitary and motionless, silence cloaked the shattered landscape.

Walker blinked away the droplets that clung to his eyelids. In the midst of ghosts that found blind release in the legendary Valley of Shale, he must remember to see clearly. It occurred to him that coming here was a mistake, that asking for help from the dead was foolish. What help they offered was forever couched in obscure references and double meanings, words that fostered confusion rather than understanding. Better to know nothing than to be misled by false interpretation. Yet whom else could he turn to besides the shade? If even a tiny glimmering of understanding could come from their meeting this night, he must not pass it by.

Allanon stirred within his spectral trappings, cowled head inclining slightly toward the supplicant.

—Ask what you would of me—

Walker stared fixedly into the blackness of the cowl, into the void that opened through it. "I have been shown a way to return the Druids to the Four Lands, to rebuild the Council at Paranor, and to bring to pass all that Galaphile hoped to achieve in the rebirth of civilization so many years ago. A map of another land has disclosed magic born out of the Old World. The magic is the key. But the way to the magic is uncertain and marked with dangerous twists and turns. It requires a journey to an unknown land. It requires great risk of me and of those who will go with me. I would know more of what to expect."

Wind brushed his face, hot and strangely dry, blown off the surface of the Hadeshorn in a sudden gust. It caught the robes of the shade and caused them to billow like smoke.

—If you would know the future, you would try to change it. If you would try to change it, you would damage your soul. Do you ask me to allow this—

"No. I ask you to better prepare me for the choices I will be asked to make."

—You are a Druid. You cannot be better prepared than you already are—

"Then give me a reason to think that what I do is right!"

Walker heard the desperation in his voice and was displeased with it. The shade seemed equally so. The waters over which it hovered spat and hissed in sudden fury, boiling up like a hot kettle heated by fresh fuel. Walker felt the familiar uncertainty, the unease of speaking with the dead, of confronting one who even in life had been so much more capable than he, of one who had known no equal and experienced no defeat.

—Take the map and follow it. Follow it as you would a thread unraveled from a cloak of darkness. Wind it about your finger and when you reach its end, weave it back together once more. You will know what to do—

It was an unsatisfying response that told Walker nothing, and in a mixture of disappointment and frustration, he came to his feet.

"What am I to do with the magic I seek, once it is found?" The Hadeshorn hissed anew, but Walker ignored it. His voice tightened. "Yours is the collective knowledge of all the Druids. You must know of the magic's potential, of its power. It can destroy everything regained if it is not used well."

—Everything—

"Then tell me how to prevent that from happening! Am I to take everything I find—all of it? What part am I to give to the races? What should be held back and what put to use? I can't see far enough into the future to comprehend the answers!"

A booming cough shook the ground beneath his feet, and a growl rose from within the earth.

—A shade has no right to tell the living what they need. Only the living can make that decision. You must make it for all, because that is what you are given to do. On your shoulders hangs the mantle of responsibility for those with lesser insight, courage, and vision. Druids are charged with no less, Walker. Be what you have been given to be—

Walker shook his head in dismay. "I am not what you say—not smarter or braver or more insightful. I have never been that. I am simply the bearer of a blood trust bestowed on Brin Ohmsford long before I was born, a trust I carry not because I want to, but because I must and because by doing so I might one day see a time when there is no further need for Druids!"

He leaned toward the dark shape, his voice building. "I am no better than those I seek to help. I am a poor answer to their difficult questions. What are you, then? Where is the vaunted Druid power that should give me the insights and understandings I lack? Where is that power, but buried in the pit from which you rise to taunt me! If I am to be the way, then show me something of the path!"

Lightning crackled before him, streaking down into the Hadeshorn from the heavens. It was followed by a thunderclap of such fury that he could feel it reverberating in the air about him. He stepped back from the brilliance and the sound, shielding his face. In the aftermath, everything went completely black, and he was suddenly alone, stranded in an inky void.

He could feel the shade of Allanon draw close to him then. He could hear the hiss of his anger.

—You travel to secure a treasure, Dark Uncle. You journey to fulfill a dream. What you accomplish will cost you and those with you. For some, it will cost everything. Lives will be lost and dreams shattered. None of those who return will be the same again. Ever—

A slow hissing began to build from somewhere within the invisible black that shrouded them. It came from everywhere at once, slow and steady and terrifying.

—Of the things you seek, you shall find them all. Of what you would know, only some will be revealed. Of what you retrieve, nothing will you take away. The future is fluid and ever changing, and so it will be here. Give yourself over to it. If you would accomplish what you most desire, let go of what most weighs you down. Recognize when you have exceeded your reach. Give heed to what is meant to be and do not question or regret or try to subvert it—

From a collage of images that formed in his mind, Walker caught a glimpse of what he was being told, yet the particulars remained just out of reach. He shook his head in confusion.

—One dream, Walker, of those you embrace is all you are allowed. The rest, you must release—

Allanon's voice was a dark, sad hiss of warning. Walker caught the inflection and the tone.

"Which dream?" he whispered. "Which one?"

But when the suffocating void fell away and the night sky reappeared overhead, the Hadeshorn lay before him as still and empty as dark glass clouded by smoke, and Walker was alone.

SHAWN SPEAKMAN

I KNEW I HAD MORE STORIES TO TELL BEFORE I FINISHED WRITING *The Dark Thorn.*

Worldbuilding is an important aspect of writing. The world must be believable; the world must feel real. That takes planning and requires posing a lot of questions, with some answers left unresolved in the book. When I sent my spiritually broken knight Richard McAllister into Annwn, I knew he would only be able to explore a small part of that world, leaving many questions unanswered and numerous stories yet to tell.

"The Unfettered Knight" is one such story. It takes place many years before Richard McAllister has taken up his knighthood. Instead, the tale features knight Charles Ardall and his trusty fairy guide Berrytrill, who are mentioned briefly in *The Dark Thorn* and who have been called to Vatican City after a great evil has infiltrated the home of the Catholic Church.

Since I was confronted with cancer and all of its uncertainty in 2011, I wanted to write a story that took a look at life, death, and the meaning of both. I also know that at no time will vampires play a role in the Annwn Cycle. But like any self-respecting urban fantasy writer, I wanted to take a stab—pun intended—at writing a unique vampire story.

"The Unfettered Knight" is that stab.

I hope the story surprises you. It did me.

Shawn Speakman

THE UNFETTERED KNIGHT

Shawn Speakman

When Heliwr of the Yn Saith Charles Ardall stepped from the portal into the catacombs beneath St. Peter's Basilica, he entered a massacre from Hell.

He had seen many like it during his tenure, but none quite so gruesome.

"Unbelievable carnage," Berrytrill whispered, the fairy flying at his ear. "This fight, the knight did not back down."

"No, he didn't," Charles agreed. "Then again, Bruno Ricci wouldn't."

"Indeed. A tougher knight, I have not seen."

The Heliwr nodded, looking around. No immediate danger presented itself. Instead, broken bodies littered the rock bank of the Tiber River's underground branch, the dead spreading to the far side of the cavern. There were three dozen bodies in all. With the light of the portal highlighting the bloodied environs and the subterranean chill seeping into his bones, Charles knelt beside the first corpse he came to. The man's chest was blasted open, his black uniform free of insignia and his slackened fingers still attempting to grip a rapier. He stared upward through the knight, soul absent.

Charles shivered. It was a face frozen in shock and pain at how life had ended.

The warrior's last minutes were not what drew Charles though. The dead man was pale like milk, almost translucent, and had been long before the battle.

On a hunch, the Heliwr pulled back the man's lips.

Two fangs poked free, brought short in death.

"Vampire," Charles noted.

"Stickfick," Berrytrill cursed. "My princely crown, I would bet the others are vampyr as well." The fairy flew over a few more dead bodies. "Myrddin Emrys says where one vampyr exists—"

"Others do too," Charles finished. He looked about the cavern. "They all are wearing similar garb. They were a company of warriors with intent. But what intent beyond breaking into St. Peter's?"

Berrytrill returned and, landing upon the corpse, more closely examined the vampire. Lightning had torn through its chest and exploded the creature's heart—the power of Bruno Ricci at work. After his scrutiny, the fairy pointed underneath the torn uniform near the cauterized wound.

"What is this?" the fairy asked.

Charles peeled back the uniform shirt. A small Celtic rune tattoo had been inked into the unmoving chest.

The work appeared fresh, the skin still inflamed.

"Check the others. Are they similarly tattooed?"

Berrytrill did so and returned. "They are. What does the symbol mean, Charles?"

"It is an old symbol. It means 'life after life's death.'"

"Failed rune magic then," the fairy grunted. "The ink did not keep them safe."

"Guess not." Frowning, Charles examined the mark more closely.

"You see something else," Berrytrill noted.

"The rune is slightly . . . altered."

"How so?"

"It has a much longer fore stroke than it should."

"It matters not. It failed to keep the vampyr safe. It is not the worry of the moment, Charles," Berrytrill said, looking around for emphasis. "Did Bruno give any indication where their leader went?"

"He barely had enough strength to draw me here, let alone tell me what happened," Charles said, standing. "First we must find him and the Cardinal Seer. Then we hunt the one who orchestrated this."

"With care," the fairy said pointedly. "Your wife and forthcoming child would not appreciate a hunt that ended in your death. Nor would she look favorably upon my royal personag—"

"Hold!"

Charles located the command's source as Berrytrill hid his presence in the folds of the Heliwr's cloak. Across the cavern, men wearing the blue, red, orange, and yellow uniforms of Vatican Swiss Guards came into view from the entrance of the catacombs, aiming rifles and pistols at the newcomer. Charles cursed inwardly. If they were present, it meant the portal knight Bruno Ricci had fallen—perhaps was even now dead. It also meant the Vigilo and likely even the Pope knew of the vampiric incursion from Annwn, making the role Charles carried all the more difficult.

A tall thin man wearing all black with the Swiss Guard crest sewn into his sweater stepped to the forefront, no fear in his icy eyes. Pistols remained holstered on his hips, hands near enough to draw but far enough away not to provoke. Charles knew the role the man fulfilled for the Vatican despite having never met him.

"I give no cause for alarm," Charles greeted, raising hands in supplication. "I am here to set right the wrong that has transpired today."

"I will be the judge of that," the man said gruffly. He raised his chin ever so slightly. "Cardinal Seer Ramirez said a man would exit the portal, one bearing a black staff." He paused. "I do not *see* a staff."

"Who are you?" Charles questioned sternly, bringing his own authority to bear.

"I am Beck Almgren, Captain of the Vatican's Swiss Guard."

"And bearer of Prydwen," Charles said. "Shield of Arthur."

Surprise flickered in the other's eyes but it was quickly banished.

"I am."

"Captain, I am Charles Ardall. I am no threat to you. I am the Heliwr of the Yn Saith. It is my responsibility to ensure this world and that of Annwn remain separate if a portal knight fails in their duties. That failure occurred, so I am here to end the threat that has entered your home." He paused. "Please, have your guards lower their weapons."

"That may be," Beck Almgren said. "But I still need to see that staff."

Charles nodded, slightly annoyed. He reached into the ether between his world and that of Annwn, calling the badge of his office, drawing the fount of his power. It happened easily. The staff materialized, the wood black and comforting in his hand, its top gnarled like a cudgel. Faint white light pulsed along its length. The Dark Thorn had been his now for many years, the responsibility he carried become such a part of him he couldn't remember a time without it. It aided his hunt for those who wrongfully crossed; it also kept him safe against creatures his world knew nothing about.

The guards didn't lower their weapons, though. Instead, fear filled the cavern. Remembering the panic he had felt the first time Merle had shown him magic, Charles kept the power of the Dark Thorn between him and the Vatican forces.

In case one of them did something quite foolish.

"Stand down, Captain," Charles ordered. "I am no threat."

Beck Almgren immediately understood the gravity of the situation. The men under his command knew nothing of Annwn and the responsibility he carried, the need for secrecy vital in keeping the two worlds separate. None of them knew he possessed Prydwen, an Arthurian relic fifteen centuries old that protected him no matter the damage visited on his person. They also did not know the duty Charles carried. They were pieces in a secret chess match privy to a chosen few.

With a curt order from their captain, the guards lowered their weapons, although the distrust did not disappear.

"I think the Swiss Guard should remain here," Charles said.

"To ensure nothing else enters from Annwn," Beck Almgren agreed. "I will escort you to the Cardinal Seer's chambers then."

Charles crossed the cavern, stepping carefully around the corpses. Berrytrill kept hidden, wise to the necessity of secrecy. The Swiss Guards may have seen the Heliwr call magic, but seeing a real fairy—the fey creature blasphemous to the Catholic Church and those who followed it—would likely have been more than many could bear.

As the Heliwr drew close, Beck Almgren pulled free a single pistol and clicked the safety off.

"I won't hesitate to use this if your intentions are ill."

"Then there won't be need to use it."

"Cardinal Seer Ramirez awaits. If you truly are the one he has called, Charles Ardall, I believe you know the way."

Charles did. With Beck Almgren walking behind, pistol at the ready, the Heliwr made his way through the underground, the Dark Thorn striking the stone of the cavern with every other step. The tunnel wound like a snake through the bedrock of Italy, the walls chiseled smooth by stonemasons more than a millennia dead. Charles shuddered. The chill infiltrated deep, and the odor of stale death surrounded him. It was a world few had seen, one as unchanging as a graveyard. After minutes, they stood in a large room where a well had been driven deep into the Earth, a winch and bucket ready to draw water, the only evidence that someone lived in these environs. The room had three other doorways leading to different parts of the catacombs, two snaking beneath Rome and the other cutting up toward the city.

Charles took the left-hand corridor and continued onward. Beck Almgren followed. The passageway sloped gradually upward, the air growing warmer with each step. Sarcophagi and skeletal remains lay within holes bored into the path's walls. The dead slept a long slumber here, the catacombs housing some of the most important members of the Catholic Church.

Like other catacombs above, this was a necropolis of history.

It didn't take long for the Heliwr to come to an open oak door banded in rune-etched iron, the warm glow of light welcoming.

Letting the Dark Thorn vanish, he stepped inside with Beck Almgren.

The room was a simple space, orderly—a reflection of the person who lived in it. Candles chased the shadows and a fire blazed warmth from a hearth in the corner of the room, casting its glow over two plush chairs and a bed pushed up against the wall. Books of various sizes and colors lined the shelves of several bookcases. A Bible as old as any Charles had seen sat upon a pedestal in the middle of the room, open, while the Fionúir Mirror, a talisman the Cardinal Seer used to view Annwn, hung upon one of the walls, the seeing glass shrouded in black velvet, its secrets hidden.

Charles took it all in but was suddenly filled with dismay.

Upon the bed lay Bruno Ricci. Clothes bloodied and torn, the most powerful of the portal knights had taken a beating to protect Rome from the vampires who had entered it. One arm lay crooked, clearly broken; gashes rent his flesh everywhere else, bleeding into new bandages. Smaller abrasions already purpled. He breathed strongly though, his chest rising and falling regularly, giving Charles hope he would recover sooner rather than later.

And Bruno appeared not to have been bitten.

Charles breathed a bit easier then. There were worse fates than defeat, and vampirism was one of them.

Two other men stood at the foot of the bed, looking down on Bruno. Cardinal Seer Donato Javier Ramirez stroked a thinly bearded chin, his body stooped and pate shiny in the candlelight. He lived in the chamber, his role as Seer of the Vigilo keeping him close to the portal. He had lived eight decades and, while blind, had survived countless invasions from Annwn. Charles had befriended him years before, the animosity between the Catholic Church and the pagan-empowered knights holding no influence over the relationship the two men shared.

Beside the Cardinal stood a man who appeared younger than the Seer but was infinitely older. Merle, once known as the ancient wizard Myrddin Emrys, looked upon Bruno with worry, his hair and beard white, and his ever-present pipe held in his right hand. Charles had never seen him in Rome, let alone on Church grounds. Merle was directly responsible for taking control of the portals from the Vigilo centuries earlier and empowering his own knights—those without political or religious gain—with Arthurian relics of old, a last act of magic to balance the various powerful influences in the world.

If Merle risked the ire of the Church by entering the Vatican—powerless as he now was—the situation was dire indeed.

The Cardinal Seer turned toward Charles, his milky eyes seeing more than most.

"Lower your weapon, Captain," he ordered. "Before yeh doom us all."

Beck Almgren did so without hesitation but gave Charles a final glance that dared violence of any kind.

"Thank you," Cardinal Ramirez added.

"It is good to see you well, Cardinal Seer," Charles greeted, stepping forward to grasp the older man's hands firmly. He was saddened at the lack of strength in the return grip. "It is unfortunate we have met again under circumstances such as these."

"Yer role is one of peril. And peril calls it," the Seer cackled sadly. "The last time was that particularly nasty troll who tore up the Sistine Chapel, was it not? One day, perhaps we will continue our debate on if God created the fey Tuatha de Dannan."

"It is one I will win yet," Charles said, smiling. He turned to Merle. "I'm surprised to find you here."

"I am where I am needed most, always," Merle said, a twinkle in his light blue eyes. He wore his usual khaki pants and white dress shirt. He raised his pipe and looked toward the Cardinal Seer. "Donato, may I?"

"I prefer not, Myrddin," the Cardinal said. "Other than my fireplace, ventilation does not come easily down here. My apologies."

"None to give," Merle said a bit sadly, pocketing the pipe.

"He should not be here," Beck Almgren growled lowly, clearly annoyed by the ancient wizard.

"Captain, yeh are new to yer role and have much to learn," Cardinal Ramirez chastised, ignoring the man's irritation. "Heliwr Charles Ardall is one of the bravest men I have met. He has carried the Dark Thorn now for several years and does so with conviction and wisdom." The Seer paused. "Charles, the Vigilo is largely absent from Rome at this time, the other seven Cardinals attending their flocks. Only the Pope is within Vatican City."

"Has he been notified?" Charles asked.

"His Excellency has not, nor should he be," the Cardinal said. He narrowed blind eyes at the captain, preemptively silencing him. "I speak with God's love, but Pope Urban has a tendency to be rash when affairs of Annwn arise."

"You wish this taken care more discreetly then," Charles affirmed.

"Just so."

Beck Almgren mumbled darkly under his breath.

"How is Bruno?" the Heliwr asked, looking at the bedridden knight.

Merle took a deep breath. "He lives. He is a tough man with a hard spirit. Even with the healing draught I gave him, he will awaken soon, I think."

"Who . . . or what . . . did this to him?"

"Before he called yeh to Rome, Bruno confided that a vampire of extraordinary power led the warriors in the catacombs," Cardinal Ramirez said. "The creatures that lay dead before the portal? They are but toddlers to this monster. I think his wounds are evidence of that."

Charles took note of the damage done to Bruno, a resolute pit of anger growing within. Vampires were dangerous, but not normally to the knights who warded the seven fixed entrances into Annwn. The guardians carried weapons imbued with fey magic and most knew spells from Merle to keep safe. The vampire who had overpowered Bruno had to be ancient and strong beyond recall.

The Heliwr found one aspect strange though. If a vampire had overcome Bruno, why did the knight still live? Especially without having been bitten and turned?

"Did anything else get past him?" Charles asked.

"Two or three others," Merle said. "You will need Berrytrill to keep you safe."

"Speaking of, where is yer guide, Charles?" Cardinal Ramirez asked. "I have not heard a whisper of his wings on the air since yeh entered."

Charles removed the cloak he wore. He would look out of place if his pursuit took him topside into Vatican City anyway. Before he finished folding it, Berrytrill flew free like a sparrow released, the fairy hovering in midair, his wings a blur and his twig arms folded crossly as if to defend himself.

"We waste time, Charles," the fey creature said.

"There he is," the Seer said, smiling.

"Get that abomination out of here!" Beck Almgren snarled.

"He is only a fairy, my able companion and guide. He will remain, whether you like it or not, Captain," Charles said pointedly. "You have my word that he will cause you no harm nor be observed by Rome's denizens."

"Cardinal Seer Ramirez, you have gone too far!" the captain grated. "To welcome such a creature onto holy ground is a sin beyond a sin. It is my duty to keep that creature out of Rome! If that thing gets near me, I'll—"

"Do what, asssqueak?" Berrytrill sniffed. "Why I would want to sully my royal person with the likes of you is quite beyond my understanding."

Beck Almgren reddened. "You little vermin—"

"Enough of this," Merle cut in. The room went silent. "Ancient arguments and animosities do not serve us this day. An emissary of the Swiss Guard returns bearing news for all to hear."

To this, a guard stormed into the room, bowing quickly. "Captain, we have it cornered!"

"Where?"

"It's in the Vatican Secret Archives."

"Whatever for?" Captain Almgren questioned. "What would it want with archaic writings and crumbling parchment?"

"Knowledge," Merle said.

"How do you know that?" the captain asked.

"If I traveled from one world to another at great risk to visit a library, I'd be after information," Merle said darkly. He looked to Charles. "And only one of us can assure the vampire is still there."

Charles nodded and called the Dark Thorn. Magic infused the room. Moving to a rarely used corner, the Heliwr brought the staff up and stabbed it into Italy. Although fashioned from the Holy Thorn at Glastonbury Abbey in England, the butt of the Dark Thorn entered the rock easily, the magic pushing aside the physical boundaries of stone even as it connected with the world. Bringing his will to bear, Charles focused on his quarry, seeking what was hidden. It did not take long. The magic snaked upward from the Seer's quarters, into the catacombs, to the surface of the Vatican grounds.

It ended within one of the buildings to the north of St. Peter's Basilica.

There Charles would find the creature.

"I have my way," he said.

"Is he in the Vatican Secret Archives still?" Cardinal Ramirez asked.

"He is."

"What will you do?" Beck Almgren questioned Charles.

"What I must," Charles said. With a hint of a smile, he added, "Talk first, I would think. Ask him to return to Annwn. If that fails and he won't, I will . . . improvise."

"One more thing, Captain Almgren," the guard said. "It's taken three prisoners. Cardinal Archivist Cesare Farina and two of his night interns."

"That makes things more dangerous," Cardinal Ramirez said.

"I say again," Beck Almgren pushed. "The Pope must be told."

"And he shall be, due to where this vampire has gone," the Cardinal Seer said impatiently. "Our Eminence is willful, though, and sometimes it is our role to protect him—even from himself. If this vampire has designs to kill him, we must take all caution possible to prevent that. That means keeping him from knowing. Keeping them separate. If Our Eminence knows, he will confront this vampire directly. And we know not if that is exactly what the vampire wants." The Seer paused. "The better question is, what is it hoping to discover *in* the library?"

Charles straightened. "That is what I intend to find out."

"Captain Almgren, I have ordered the Swiss Guard to surround the room—and not to enter," the guard said.

"You will have to wield your power with care, Heliwr," Beck Almgren added, giving Charles a dark look. "The Secret Archives is a sealed area, holding some of the most precious parts of the Catholic Church's history. Violence of any kind could damage that history."

"Noted, Captain," the knight said.

"We must speak, Charles," Merle said, moving away from the others.

Charles frowned but followed the old wizard toward the burning hearth. The Churchmen let them go, although Captain Almgren stared after with daggers for eyes.

Merle turned his back on the others and stepped close.

"You must be careful, Charles," he said.

"I know that, Merle."

"You don't understand," the wizard said, his blue eyes intense. "You are to be a father. With that comes a responsibility just as great as that which brought you to Rome. Do not underestimate this vampire. It is imperative you survive this day and many afterward. I know I criticized you when you wedded, even more so when I learned of the conception. But that is past. The future holds more than you know."

"If I didn't know better," Charles said, grinning. "I'd think you are apologizing and now happy I am having a child."

"The future calls upon that scion, Charles," Merle said seriously.

Charles became just as serious. Merle always knew more than he let on. The wizard had been alive since the fifth century, his demon ancestry slowing his aging but his early baptism making him an instrument of good. With his unique lineage came the ability to see aspects of the future. He described it as seeing probability, with some future lines more prevalent in his sight—and therefore more likely to occur. The lines were rarely certain, leaving Merle cautious and the portal knights nervous more often than not.

For Merle to suddenly warn Charles meant the once confidante of Arthur the Eld was not entirely sure of the outcome this hunt would have.

Uncertainty filled him like ice.

"I will remain here, for a time anyway," Merle said, eyeing the knight on the bed. "Bruno needs his arm set. Best to do that now before he wakes from the draught I gave him. That kind of pain is not pleasant while awake."

Charles nodded soberly. Merle turned to the fairy.

"Keep him safe, Berrytrill. That is *your* task."

"I will, Myrddin," the guide said earnestly.

Unsure of what had just happened and not having the time to mull on it yet, Charles turned back to the Seer and captain. "With the portal knight bedridden, I think it best the Captain of the Vatican Swiss Guard watch the entrance into Annwn and ensure nothing else comes through."

"Sound reasoning," Cardinal Ramirez admitted.

"I will return," Charles said simply.

The others nodded. Charles and Berrytrill left the room, knowing the eyes of the Vigilo watched him leave. Such meetings, though rare, always left him annoyed. Add what Merle had shared, and anger seethed just below the surface. At least none of the other Vigilo members were in Rome. Throw in the confusion of having a child on the way, and Charles now questioned whether or not he had made the right choice in accepting his knighthood.

"I am still amazed by the friendship you have built with the Seer," Berrytrill cut through the knight's dark thoughts, flying slightly ahead as they made their way quickly through the catacombs. "Given the hatred the Church has for your kind, especially."

"My *kind*?" Charles grunted. "Well, sometimes the enemy of your enemy is your friend. And once you look past the ideology that separates us, we want the same thing. It helps that he is a bit more . . . philosophical . . . about life and God. He is not as extremist as most in the Vigilo. Probably stems from being forced to view all sides."

"He would never do anything to harm you?" the fairy asked.

"He wouldn't," the Heliwr said. "Now, the Captain of the Swiss Guard, I don't trust."

"That tittweak smelled of wanton power."

Charles said nothing more, thinking on what had just happened. Berrytrill gave the knight a frown but flew ahead. Climbing up through the catacombs, the Dark Thorn held before him, Charles cursed the situation. Myrddin Emrys. Some days, the knight reviled the name. For the wizard to share his concern and the truth so openly meant his auguries were nearly split. The day could be won; the day could be lost with his death. There was no way of knowing which.

That wasn't what bothered Charles though. He had accepted his knighthood and its danger. His wife knew the risks as well. The unborn child she carried did not, though, and the fact that Merle had already seen a future where that child played an integral part in the wizard's machinations left Charles more than unsettled. It left him frightened—and angry—of what else he didn't know.

Could he fulfill his duty as Heliwr safely? Ensure his child had a father? And teach that child to be wary of Merle? Or was it time to step down from his role as the unfettered knight?

No answers were forthcoming.

Eventually Charles came to a fork in the tunnel. Berrytrill, guiding the Heliwr, nodded and flew ahead. Charles knew the subterranean depths better than most alive and had been here twice before on hunt. His guide had too. The first time, a leprechaun had managed to trick Bruno and invaded the Vatican just to drink ale on Church grounds—an outrageous blasphemy to the Vigilo but great fun for the fey creature. During the second incursion, a troll with fists the size of cinder blocks had battled its way destructively upward into the Sistine Chapel.

Both times, Charles had saved the Vatican and kept his world ignorant about the Tuatha de Dannan. That was the role Merle had bequeathed him.

Now something far more dangerous called his attention.

He had taken several different passages, following the path

the Dark Thorn had shown him, when his sixth sense blared in warning.

"Wait!" Berrytrill screamed at the same time.

The warnings came too late.

Behind large sarcophagi interred in the walls, two vampires leapt from the shadows upon Charles, teeth bared and powerful grips forcing him down.

The knight barely had time to react. The magic of the Dark Thorn burst from him like a solar flare, driven by the adrenaline of fear and surprise, the power from two worlds infusing his entire being. The white fire flung the vampires aside like rag dolls, slamming both against the tunnel walls. They did not stay down long. Even as Charles fought to regain his balance to counter the threat, they were already on him again, one trying to gain his neck through sheer force and the other attempting to wrest the Dark Thorn from his grip.

Even with the staff's power lending him more than mortal strength, the vampires were stronger, stronger than anything Charles had encountered. He had become the prey.

All would have been lost if not for Berrytrill. The fairy zoomed out of the darkness, yelling the battle cry of his clan. He attacked the vampire grappling for Charles's neck, ripping dust out of the tiny pouch on his back and throwing it upon the undead horror.

The silver dust fell upon its face and golden daylight erupted. The creature screamed, falling back and pawing at its former face, the radiance blinding and flames licking its pale, dissolving skin.

"Now, Charles!"

Sudden half-freedom bolstering his desperation, the Heliwr rammed the other vampire against the wall. Rib bones shattered. Snarling in pain, the creature lost its grip on the Dark Thorn but fought to grasp Charles anew. He did not let it. He clubbed the vampire across the face, driving it to its knees, and in one fluid motion swung the staff like a sickle at the other vampire.

The butt of the Dark Thorn penetrated its chest, killing heart and life.

Years of battle training coming to his aid, Charles yanked the Dark Thorn clear of the dead undead and spun to confront his last enemy. It didn't matter. With broken bones and a jaw that hung awkwardly to one side from the strike Charles had delivered, the vampire had not moved from where it had slumped to the catacomb floor. *Beaten*, Charles thought. Berrytrill hovered nearby, fists full of silver dust if needed. It wouldn't be. The creature from Annwn looked up at the knight, a broken thing, the hatred filling its eyes the only lively aspect about it.

"Geht et ovah wit, knight," the vampire mumbled, barely able to speak.

"That's what I do," Charles said coldly. Without waiting for a reply, the Heliwr drove the Dark Thorn through the vampire's chest like a stake.

The creature died with a hollow gasp.

"Thought you were done for," Berrytrill said.

"No time for applause," Charles said, catching his breath. He gave the fairy a dark look. "Don't let that happen again, Trill."

"My fault, no doubt," the fairy agreed, already guiding up the passage.

Given angry purpose at being caught off guard and pushing his family worries aside, Charles reduced the corpses to ash with the Dark Thorn and then chased after his guide. It didn't take long for the Heliwr to navigate the underground world. Upward they traveled, not speaking, the fairy watching for further ambushes and Charles ready for one if it happened. The world of the dead began to fade away, fewer burial holes chiseled out of the living rock. The grade leveled eventually, the fire in his legs matching that in his heart, and he finally came to a dead end in the passage where a set of stairs vanished upward into a stone block.

"This vampire we hunt knew how to get out," Berrytrill noted.

Charles nodded. "So it would seem."

"It knows more than it should."

The knight did not stop to contemplate how the vampire knew the inner workings of the Vatican. Instead, Charles unlocked the secret door by touching hidden catches in the wall designed by

Leonardo da Vinci—entering the correct combination just like the vampire would have had to do.

The response was immediate. A series of clicks filled the tunnel and the stone door at the top of the stairs dropped several inches and slid silently aside.

Charles took the stairs two at a time into the musty odor of parchment and ancient ink. The Heliwr stood within the lowest levels of the Vatican Secret Archives. More than fifty miles of shelving contained tens of thousands of volumes, prints, engravings, coins, and parchments, most from ages past but all of great importance. It was daunting to imagine reading it all. No one had, as far as Charles knew. The Cardinal Archivist and his prefects knew the library better than anyone and the secrets it held. Occasionally Charles had inquired after that knowledge when needed for his knightly role. He was lucky in that regard; only a select few were granted research access to the Secret Archives every year.

There were secrets hidden here no one had laid eyes on in centuries. Had the vampire fought for entrance into the archives for information, as Merle believed?

Or for something far more sinister?

Charles stomped the stone tile to the right and the door closed behind them.

"Being a prince or no, there are some marvels in this world I do so care to quietly observe," Berrytrill sighed. "I could spend years and years reading here."

"Do not forget why we are here, Trill," Charles chided. "Keep a lookout. The two vampires below were left there for a reason, and we are close now. The object of our hunt is on the other side of this bunker. Can't fall prey now."

"Good point," the fairy said, speeding ahead.

Charles watched him go, extending his own senses into the faintly lit area. The vampire was not far away. He knew that. He could also feel the groups of people above enjoying Rome's night and all its wonder, wholly unaware of the evil that had infiltrated the city. Vampires were relegated to myths, legends, and sappy romance novels that left middle-aged women aquiver. None of those people knew the truth. Ages past, very real Tuatha de Dannan fey and other magical beings had fled this world for Annwn to begin life anew. The Church had driven them out with iron and the sword.

Those Catholics above knew nothing of that. And if they had known, such creatures would have been labeled blasphemously evil.

When Charles had crossed half the distance to the far wall, passing hundreds of rows of books and gathered scrolls, Berrytrill came flying hurriedly back.

"Swiss Guards ward the restoration room," the fairy shared.

"And beyond?"

"The vampire."

Charles quickened his pace. Time was of the essence and Berrytrill would have cleared the way of traps—magical or otherwise. It didn't take him long to traverse the rest of the room. The path the Dark Thorn showed him fully realized, Charles slowed as he peered around a last set of bookshelves to assess the situation on his own.

Berrytrill was right. Almost twenty Swiss Guards stood at the entrance to the restoration room of the Secret Archives, weapons aimed through the glass that comprised the room's long wall. The guards did not concern him though. Beyond, in the room, he could just make out the unruly white hair of Cardinal Archivist Cesare Farina, his lined face drawn with fear, and fresh bruises blooming where he had been struck.

And at his side the unmistakable presence of the vampire.

Charles did not waste time. He strode into the middle of the Swiss Guard as if he commanded the entire world. A guard moved to obstruct the knight almost immediately.

"Halt! Now!" he demanded.

"I am here to speak with the Cardinal Archivist," Charles said, loud enough for the occupants in the restoration room to hear.

"Only those given leave by Captain Beck Almgren can ent—"

"Let him pass!" Cardinal Archivist Farina yelled.

The guard frowned but moved aside. The others of the Swiss

Guard let the Heliwr pass as well. Striking the floor with the Dark Thorn to gather all attention to him and with Berrytrill hiding in the crux of his armpit, Charles strode through the glass door designed to keep moisture and contaminants out and into a situation he immediately did not like.

Cardinal Archivist Cesare Farina, also a member of the Vigilo, sat next to the vampire at one of the dozens of tables used for the maintenance of the Secret Archives' precious documents. He did not move. The vampire had fingers about the old man's neck, his grip absolute, one that could end the mortal's life instantly. The creature had also taken two other prisoners; two restorers, undoubtedly working the late shift with their Cardinal, sat at the rear of the room, both men staring blankly as if in a trance.

"Charles Ardall," Cardinal Cesare Farina greeted with a weak smile.

"Are you three okay?"

"We are," Cardinal Farina said. "The vampire has not harmed us."

With Berrytrill now hovering nearby, Charles gazed then at the subject of his hunt. The intruder from Annwn was definitely a vampire. Thin skin. Prominent fangs. Eyes set within gaunt features. But he was unlike any Charles had seen too. Instead of possessing the northern European features that marked those who had entered Annwn millennia ago, the vampire had a dark Middle Eastern aspect to him. It told Charles that this vampire was likely not bitten and turned in Annwn, but in this world long before the fey had left, and had ventured to Annwn at a time much later.

Knowing that, it made the creature ancient beyond belief. It did not stop there. The eyes proved the theory if his heritage did not. The entity that stared back at Charles bore the weight of ages, a depth of soul the knight had only seen in the eyes of Merle. It was more than that though. Power radiated from the vampire, old power derived from centuries of experience that reverberated the air like a high-tension power line.

Charles had encountered several vampires in his time as Heliwr but none like this.

"Who are you and what do you want?" he questioned finally.

The vampire smiled, fangs born. It was a smile that lacked humor. "I want what you want, knight."

"What would that be exactly?"

The vampire cocked his head. "For me to gain that which I desire, of course."

"You have broken into the home of the Catholic Church," Charles said unflinchingly. "You have killed many men this day, your own as well as those from the Swiss Guard. My fellow knight lays wounded. Not the best way to ensure aid in your quest."

The creature shrugged. "I had to gain *your* attention, Heliwr."

Charles did not like the sound of that.

"Why do you have need of me?"

"Besides the ancient wizard who yoked you into service, Heliwr, you are the only one with the respect needed to enter areas of this city that I wish admittance to," the vampire said. "You and you alone."

"Hate to break it to you, vampire," Berrytrill chimed in smugly. "But the Knights of the Yn Saith are despised by the Church."

"That may be, fairy," the other said. "I still have need of your master."

"My master, he is *not*, not at al—"

"I am Charles Ardall," the Heliwr said, cutting his guide off before the conversation turned ugly. "And this is my *quiet* guide, Berrytrill. Who are you and why are you here?"

The vampire grinned self-mockery. "I have been called He Whose Life Dies Not. The Sable Warlock. The Fatal Revenant of Scarl. In this land, long ago, I was Mortuis, The Dead Who Walks. The world has wept ever since those days. Because that was not my birth name. Once, I was dead, the result of illness, and entombed for four days before being resurrected and returned to sunshine, a light that holds no love for shadowkind. A miracle some called my return. The miracle turned to ashes in my mouth long ago. I have learned to hate that day I entered the world with a second life."

It didn't take Charles long to realize what the vampire's true name was but he could not believe it.

It was impossible.

"You are Lazarus of Bethany," Charles said finally. "Or you think you are."

The vampire nodded. "One of many names, but that was my first."

"Blasphemy," Cardinal Cesare Farina growled.

The vampire squeezed the old man's neck, snarling. "The only blasphemy, priest, is what your God did to me that day. Do not believe me? Open your mind."

The Cardinal Archivist squawked in sudden pain and his eyes rolled back into his head as magic filled the room. Charles could feel it, ancient and potent. Unsure of how the knight could even act to prevent what was being done, Cesare Farina breathed in suddenly, eyes returned to normal, body shuddering and fear twisting his features.

"It is true. He is Lazarus," the Cardinal Archivist whispered, shaking still. "I saw . . . that day. Christ . . ."

"But that would make you millennia old," Charles argued.

"I have witnessed much," Lazarus said. "Through the blood of Jesus I was returned to life after four days of death. It was a blood that changed me forever, just as my blood is a plague to all who meet me. He did this to me, called me to help fulfill His will and convince the world to believe in Him. A will that has cursed me for centuries."

Cardinal Farina shuddered anew. "Proof. Real proof. In my mind," he whispered, rubbing at his temples. "I saw your sisters there, that day . . ."

"Martha and Mary did right by me," Lazarus continued. "My sisters sent for the Christ, whom I followed out of devotion and love. I saw the truth of His will even then, the reasons for it, even if I knew not its implication for my own soul. I followed God, to see right done in a world that yearned for it. The truth could not dispel the judgment—the jail time—that was given to me though." The vampire sneered, eyes flashing pent rage. "I was not asked if this is what I wanted."

"He returned you to the living though," Charles said, putting a small bit of trust in what the Cardinal Archivist had seen. "Some would call that an incredible gift."

"They have not walked my life," Lazarus said. "Destroyed lives. Families decimated. Spread evil."

"Of course. You are a true vampire," the knight said. "A killer."

"I am that. Make no mistake."

"But you blame Christ for your actions since then?" Charles said. "I am sorry, but even vampires have a choice."

"Therein lies the irony," Lazarus growled, his eyes grown darker. "After my resurrection, I learned He waited two whole days before making the journey to Bethany, days I still lived my mortal life. Two whole *days*," the vampire seethed. "Choice, you say? You mock. By that time, I had passed beyond into . . . beauty. Absolute peace. I have since learned hatred for the reason of my rebirth. 'I am the resurrection, and the life: he that believeth in me, though he were dead, yet shall he live: And whosoever liveth and believeth in me shall never die.' Christ, I curse those words, words that I have read more times than breaths I have taken, unable to ignore the bloodlust with which I was cursed. I no longer believeth yet I live. Through His blood. Choice? What choice? It took centuries of searching for an answer to counter my existence—a hunt that has led me here."

"And Jesus wept," Cesare Farina added, tears filling his eyes. "But not for the sorrow of your sisters at your passing or for the lack of faith some in Bethany felt but instead for what He would do to you."

"Perhaps this Cardinal Archivist is not as dumb as I took him for," Lazarus said. He patted the old man's bearded cheek like a child's. "No, He wept for the atrocity that I would become, for the travesty of life I would reflect, for the hypocrisy of His cause. He needed the miracle for the Word and his everlasting Church. He knew what he created, the miracle that would grow his flock. And for that I am forever damned." He paused. "If He had only arrived two days earlier, thousands of lives I have taken would have not known my bite, my curse. If only He had let me lie in my cave and remain in the peace and tranquility of death. If only He—"

"Life is filled with ifs, Lazarus," Charles said. "They don't allow you to revisit and correct. Ifs are best forgotten."

"That is where you are wrong, Charles Ardall," the other whispered. "I will set right this wrong. Tonight.

"An *if* shall set me free."

Charles could barely comprehend the historical gravity of what he found himself in. Let alone the danger. He knew the Bible and the main writings that comprised the doctrine Catholics adhered to. The creature across from him didn't just know history that had shaped the world. Lazarus *was* history. The vampire possessed knowledge that every scholar would desire; he also undoubtedly knew information that could be used for his evil purposes. If Charles had already been on edge, he was even more so now.

Yet the Heliwr felt a growing sense of sympathy for the vampire. Of pity. The man that had been Lazarus of Bethany was something else now, betrayed by the very goodness he had followed, had loved. The act that the Word had enacted—if what Cesare Farina had seen was true—was an evil far more virulent than what the vampire had become since his first death.

"You mentioned a hunt that has led you here," Berrytrill said.

"Matters such as these require a certain decorum, fairy," Lazarus said. "Today is the most important day of my life. It necessitates a longer explanation so that history may be made whole again. Let my reason for coming here and the bargaining for what I want begin." He paused, looking directly at Charles. "I will let these two workers free, *if* the Cardinal Archivist takes me to a very specific text I know exists in these Secret Archives, a writing so old and so ancient that only a handful have ever laid eyes on it, let alone read its pages."

"You shall not lay your sinned hand on a single page under my care," Cesare Farina muttered, his steel returning. "This library is owned by His Eminence. No creature of Hell has ever been given leave by the Pope to do as it pleases here. Not ever."

"And yet here I sit, priest, in your home," Lazarus said, taunting Cesare Farina with a sharp shake. "The Pope won't mind giving me his leave. This is in his best interest, after all."

"Which text would you be after?" Charles asked.

"The Bible."

"I could have given you one from any hotel in Rome," the knight snorted.

"No. *The* Bible. The first Bible," the vampire said. "The Bible that is unsullied by editing fingers and biased purpose by those in power. The Bible that exists with the full text of the Word. There I will find what I seek."

"Blasphemy," Cardinal Farina croaked. "The Codex B is the oldest edition here and its contents are well documented outside these walls."

"The Codex B, as you call it, is shyte," Lazarus said, running a sharp fingernail down the man's cheek, but his eyes never deviated from Charles. "That came into existence centuries after the original. There is another text, one I have been assured exists, and in it I will confirm my salvation and set right the wrong done me."

"No such book is here, Lazarus," the Cardinal Archivist said.

"You dare twist words with me. I smell it on your breath," the vampire mocked. He grabbed a fistful of the old man's white hair and yanked his head back. "It is not a *book* but a set of scrolls, more the like." Charles could only watch the vampire's fangs inch closer to the exposed neck. "Answer me!"

"It's not a book!" Cesare Farina screamed, feeling death on his neck.

"What is it then, priest?"

Eyes rolling in panic, terror won. "A series of vellum pages and scrolls! Very old. Very fragile."

"Of course they are, fool," Lazarus said, smiling triumphantly.

The Cardinal's fear filled the room like a stink. Charles hated the situation. He was unable to intervene without jeopardizing Cesare Farina's life. No wizard spells or power from the Dark Thorn were faster than Lazarus; in the split second it would take to call his power and strike, Lazarus would have already sensed it and acted. If the vampire wanted to kill the Cardinal, there was nothing Charles could do about it.

That wasn't his only worry. There were questions raised now, questions that needed answering. The original text of the Bible. An *unedited* edition. The information was daunting in its reality. Why would the Bible be edited? What could the Church gain? What was it protecting? Other editions of the book had been altered but they were common knowledge. Thinking about his debate with the Cardinal Seer, what if the Apostles knew of the fey? Had originally written about them? What if the Word called the fey good? What truths did the Bible hide in its first edition? Mentions of lost relics and places of power? What control did the Church keep by its revision work?

And most importantly, what did Lazarus hope to find?

"If we agree to give you access to this Bible, what will you give in return?" Charles asked, ignoring the protestations of the Cardinal Archivist.

"As I said, the lives of these Churchmen, to start," Lazarus replied. "They are not the reason I came here, a mere means to an end. I will give you something more as well, something you as the unfettered knight want."

"What is that?" Berrytrill questioned.

"My death."

"I can do that for you right now," Charles said, gripping the Dark Thorn tighter for emphasis.

"The badge of your duty through my heart, right?" Lazarus said, grinning the same humorless smile that began to grate on the Heliwr's nerves. "Undoubtedly the same death you dealt my companions in the passageways below."

"That's right," the knight said.

"Stakes do kill the progeny of my curse," Lazarus said. "I would know. I have killed enough of them over the centuries when needed. No, as the first vampire, I am immune from such acts of wooden violence." When Charles did not immediately respond, Lazarus learned forward. "Do not believe me, Heliwr?"

"Hard to believe, given those of your kind I've killed."

Lazarus stood, still gripping the Cardinal Archivist close. He ripped open his shirt, baring his chest. In one fell kick, he shattered the ancient chair he had been sitting on. Wood shrapnel exploded. He bent to pick up a piece more than a foot long, its end sharpened to a murderous point.

"Tell me, fairy, how do you kill a vampire?"

"A stake to the heart," Berrytrill said. "The best way."

"Exactly," the vampire said. He handed the stake to Cesare Farina. "Kill me, Cardinal of these Secret Archives."

"I will not," the Cardinal Archivist muttered, gone as pale as the vampire.

Lazarus painfully squeezed the old man's neck again.

"Do it. Or you die."

The old man took the makeshift stake, his hand palsied. Charles could see the fear that threatened to overcome the Cardinal.

"Do it!" Lazarus roared.

In a jerky motion, Cesare Farina succumbed and brought the stake downward. The Cardinal's aim was true. The stake penetrated deep into the vampire's chest where his heart would be. Cesare Farina shakily let go of the stake. Lazarus snarled in pain but did not fall, his eyes dark like terrible midnight, maintaining his grip on his prisoner.

The creature did not die. Instead, Lazarus pulled the broken piece of chair free.

The flesh mended instantly as if nothing had happened.

"I am not dead, Heliwr of the Yn Saith," Lazarus said, breathing hard but made whole. "Explain it."

"I can't," Charles said, bewildered.

"There is only one thing that can kill me," Lazarus said. "And the knowledge can be confirmed in the only true Word."

"You did not know of this first Bible until recently," Charles remarked, still unsure what had just happened. "Otherwise you would have tried to see it earlier. Why now? Who shared its existence with you? Who is aiding you?"

The eyes of the vampire narrowed briefly in indecision. "A witch," Lazarus said finally. "She is extraordinarily powerful for her kind, not like those who populate many of the towns and cities of Annwn. She has lived almost as long as I have."

Charles did not like that. Witches did not offer help without gaining something.

There was more to this than the knight knew.

"No," Charles said. "You have come here for more than information."

"I trust witches even less than you do," Lazarus said. "Centuries of unexpectedly entering their company have taught me that."

"Witches give and then collect. What have you promised?"

"Nothing yet. She too wishes my death."

Charles had to admit that could be a possibility. A vampire as powerful as Lazarus would make a formidable enemy in a world that was not that large. Even though the breadth of Annwn was controlled by despot Philip Plantagenet at the behest of his father, King Henry II, the removal of the vampire would be a boon to any witch desiring to carve out her own niche without the meddling of one such as Lazarus.

"I see you are leery of me, Charles Ardall," Lazarus said. "You have my word I have not come with sinister means or purpose. I do not plan to harm anyone in Rome this day or those after. Look before you. I could have easily killed these men if I so desired. Look at your earlier point about choice. If I intended to be an assassin, I would not have come to this underground library. My word is given."

"Bulldingle. A false word, no doubt," Berrytrill snorted.

"My word matters, at least to me, fairy," the vampire growled.

Silence filled the room. The eyes of Lazarus met those of Charles. The Heliwr could sense no lie in them. The purpose that drove the vampire made him all too willing to give up to gain what he required.

"Let the archive interns go free now," Charles said.

"I will do that, as a gesture of good will."

The two young men suddenly came awake, their eyes blinking as if from a long sleep. Then terror at what had been done hit them. When the vampire nodded in their direction, the two students fled the room, the whoosh of sterile air through the closing door following after as the Swiss Guards grabbed them and escorted them away.

"Are you a learned man, Heliwr?" Lazarus asked.

"I've done my share of reading."

"Then this will interest you. Lead the way, priest. Or that neck will be mine and I will turn you into the very thing you despise, to spend eternity in Hell alongside me."

Grown paler, Cesare Farina turned and walked toward the back of the room. Charles and Berrytrill followed. Working their way around a labyrinth of shelves, the Cardinal brought them to the far side of the room where a desk older and heavier than any Charles had seen before sat pushed against a wall. Over it, a tapestry depicting Old St. Peter's Basilica hung. Various folders and paperwork sat on the desk, the bureaucratic aspect of the Cardinal Archivist's work for the Vatican.

"It is here," Lazarus whispered. "The Word. I can feel it."

"The desk must be moved," the Cardinal said.

"Then move it, priest."

"It takes at least seven men to—"

Lazarus did not wait. He grabbed the corner of the desk and flung it into the interior of the room. Paper and pens went chaotically flying.

"Open the door now!"

Cesare Farina did not wait. He gently moved the tapestry aside and placed his aged hands on the stone of the wall. The Cardinal closed his eyes and began to whisper words in a language Charles did not know. Long moments passed. Then a soft white light began to expand from his fingertips, growing in intensity even as it spread outward. It glowed faintly, forming the lines of a door. Then a soundless explosion of light became a dim entryway. Lazarus entered, dragging the Cardinal Archivist with him.

Charles gave Berrytrill a curious look before following.

Stale air smelling of parchment met the Heliwr even as tiny orbs of bluish light blossomed in the corners of the room, magic coming alive to illuminate deep shelves lining the walls. Scrolls, parchments, and books sat upon them, carefully organized. That was not all. Power felt only in the world's more ancient places thrummed within Charles. He shivered from the feeling, having only experienced it a few times during his travels. An entity or object of great influence existed in the confines of the room.

"I will make this easy on you, priest," Lazarus said, his pale skin tinged blue beneath the orbs. "You know this book. Better than anyone alive due to your position. Show me the book of John."

Cesare Farina pulled two cotton gloves from his pocket and put them on. He then slowly moved to one of the walls, eyes betraying the anger he felt at the situation, and carefully removed a series of loose pages from a shelf. The Cardinal took his time, unwilling to damage the ancient text, careful in every movement. He extricated one page in particular and placed it upon a metal and glass table that sat in the center of the room, designed specifically so as not to contaminate the documents.

"Be gentle, please," the Cardinal Archivist said, producing another set of gloves for the vampire. "If I am to make a guess, what you wish to see is halfway down the page."

Lazarus did not take the offered gloves. He instead carefully touched the page as a lover would his love, as if by doing so lent him an intimacy with the object. He began at the top, eyes skimming, looking for something in particular.

Charles leaned in to look but it was in a language he did not know.

"I cannot read it," Berrytrill observed, hovering over it.

"Not many can," Cesare Farina said.

"I have been alive a long time, fairy," Lazarus said, still skimming. "When you have been alive as long as I have, you learn many languages that exist to eventually die. Of course, *this* is my native language."

Charles watched the vampire closely. Something still nagged at the knight. Long moments passed. Lazarus continued with his reading, almost as if he had forgotten the others in the room. The Cardinal Archivist stood nearby, his fear replaced by worry for the priceless document the vampire pored over.

Then Lazarus stopped, his eyes doing a reread of a particular passage.

He closed his eyes, a satisfied smile crossing his lips.

"It is true," Lazarus breathed. "I am set free."

"Set free of what?" Berrytrill asked.

"There is much in this life that those such as yourself may never know, little fairy," Lazarus said. "You live a finite life. As does your Heliwr there. Life holds meaning when it is short. Given a disease that robs a man of his life in a matter of years, that man will travel, see the world, eat and drink things he never would have considered before. He drinks life like a fine wine and becomes more than he was. He dies but he dies happy, knowing he has fulfilled as much of life as he possibly can.

"That does not exist for me," Lazarus continued. "Life steals from me even as I live forever. I am an abomination. A mistake by the Word."

"What do you now seek to end that mistake?" Charles questioned.

"The weapon bathed in the blood of Jesus Christ."

"And what's that?" Berrytrill asked.

"The Holy Lance," the Cardinal Archivist answered.

"The priest has the right of it. The Spear of Longinus. It punctured the side of the Christ," Lazarus said, nodding as if to validate what he had just discovered. "Whether the Word intended it or not, the spear has been endowed with power upon coming in contact with the Christ's blood. It states it simply here while it has been omitted in all Bibles since the Church took control of its message. Just as the Cup of Christ has the power to grant life—and that particular aspect of the Word's story has also been stripped out—the spear can undo that life. I require the spear. Nothing more. And the witch who augured its place in this world is certain it is being housed here, in the Vatican."

"How can you be sure the Holy Lance will kill you, Lazarus?" Charles asked.

"There are no assurances in life, Heliwr," the vampire admitted. "But it is one of the last options that I possess."

"How do I know this is not a trick to steal the relic? What assurance do we have?"

"As I have said, you have my word."

"You would die—quietly and cleanly—and that is all?"

"It is," Lazarus said. "I only wish to die on consecrated ground. I have no designs to kill you, this Cardinal Archivist, or anyone else for that matter, in so long as I am destroyed and released from this perpetual bondage." He paused. "But if you do not give me what I desire, I will see the entirety of Rome made vampire."

"You threaten Rome now?" Berrytrill asked.

"If it prompts you to action, yes."

Charles stared hard at the vampire, thinking. There was desperation to the creature that could not be denied. He wanted to die. The knight had seen frantic hopelessness in people before, and Lazarus possessed it. But there was a danger in letting the creature near such a powerful relic. The Holy Lance had a storied past, filled with coronations and war, with legend recounting that whoever held it controlled the fate of humanity—for good or ill. To the knight's memory, it had vanished centuries earlier and had never been located, its whereabouts even a secret from Merle.

A previous Pope had obviously discovered it, authenticated it, and kept its power secreted away within the Vatican.

And now the witch had sent Lazarus to find it.

"If the spear is here, why did your witch not simply tell you the precise location of the spear, Lazarus?" Charles asked finally. "Surely she could have if she could divine where the Bible was located for you. Why involve the Cardinal Archivist and the book he protects at all?"

"I wished that, Heliwr," the vampire confessed. "But she would not share that knowledge, not for any reason I could give."

"Why not?"

"In her words," Lazarus said, disgust on his face. "Letting the wolf loose among the sheep is far more interesting." The vampire darkened. "My coming to these Secret Archives did have a benefit though. I now know the Spear of Longinus is the best hope of ending my curse."

Charles weighed the dilemma. Lazarus was a formidable opponent, a creature of great power. Given the spear, he could prove insurmountable. Charles possessed the Dark Thorn and other magical abilities but were they enough to defeat the vampire if it decided to turn against him? He did not know. And given Merle's prophetic worries earlier, Charles was even less certain of the situation's outcome.

"You cannot be seriously considering this, Charles Ardall!" Cardinal Farina argued, as if reading the Heliwr's mind.

"It is my role to consider all options," the Heliwr said.

"I do not have the authority!" the Cardinal erupted. "I know not where the Holy Lance is in any case!"

"But *I* do."

Everyone in the room turned.

With a look of absolute disapproval, Pope Urban IX stood flanked by guards at the entrance to the hidden room, Beck Almgren just behind. The pontiff was a middle-aged man, one of the youngest to come to the highest position within Catholicism, and while Charles had not met him, he knew Urban to be head-strong and rash in his beliefs and how he conducted them. The Pope looked at each of the room's occupants, conviction burning in his eyes, before his gaze settled on Lazarus.

Disgust fought at the corners of his mouth. "What has entered my home?"

Charles cursed inwardly. The captain had notified the Pope. And put one of the world's most powerful men in harm's way.

"Your Holiness," Cesare Farina said bowing.

"I will see this done, Cardinal Archivist," Pope Urban said. "I have heard enough. The creature before us is evil, an evil that brings darkness on the world. I doubt God or His Son would create such a being. Lucifer has done this in some way. But it is God's will that has brought him here and if he wishes to be destroyed, so be it. God will pass judgment on his soul, and the world will be free of an enemy of the Word."

Lazarus said nothing but nodded to the Pope.

"But my Grace," the Cardinal Archivist began. "It is my duty to protect you. Should you be this involved? I have to say this might be a ploy, and you should leav—"

"I will see this done. Myself," the Pope declared. He gave Charles a look that challenged argument. "Heliwr, do you believe

557

this abomination? Can the Spear of Destiny destroy it? Can such a one be killed in this manner?"

"Lazarus believes it to be so," Charles said, unsure of how the pontiff would affect the situation now that he was involved. "Cesare Farina and I both witnessed a stake enter his heart, to no avail. He lives. So I don't know if he can be killed. But I think it likely if the Holy Lance possesses the power legend accounts."

"What does your wizard believe?"

"Merle is ignorant to what has transpired in these Secret Archives."

Pope Urban chuckled meanly. "I doubt that."

"Now that you are here, this is a choice *you* must make," Charles pointed out.

"And if I hadn't been?" Urban said, lightning in his eyes. "No, don't answer. You are mantled in your demon wizard's wayward wishes. God is not so easily fooled. He put me here. I *will* make the choice. This is not *your* home after all."

"Where is the spear?" Lazarus broke in.

"It is safe, protected," the Pope said, eyes narrowing upon the vampire. "I will retrieve it. But first, creature of Hell, you will remove yourself from these archives. I will not tolerate your taint here, among such importance." Urban turned to his Cardinal Archivist. "Cesare Farina, return the parchment page to its safe placement, please, and close the room."

The Cardinal of the Secret Archives did just that and, once finished, nodded for the others to vacate the room.

Lazarus did not object but went willingly.

Once the room emptied, Cesare Farina spoke a few ancient words and the wall reformed, cloaking its priceless contents in secrecy again.

"I have ordered the Swiss Guards not of my retinue to return to the catacombs below, just in case this is a ruse," Pope Urban notified, turning to leave. "Follow me. This should not take long."

Cringing beneath the imprisoning grasp of Lazarus once more, the Cardinal followed his pontiff out of the Secret Archives, through several bookcases and doorways, and up flights of stairs.

The Swiss Guards once outside the restoration room were indeed gone. The Pope led but he did so slowly, his personal Swiss Guard detail still protecting him, Beck Almgren a step behind. Even though he led, Urban kept an eye on the vampire almost as closely as Charles did from the rear of the retinue. All the while, the Dark Thorn was an assurance of warmth beneath his hand.

It did not take long for the odd group to leave the ancient building and enter the cool night air of Rome. Charles knew the area. The Cortile della Pigna surrounded them, the courtyard bounded by other Vatican buildings, the walls featuring alcoves filled with tall statues from antiquity and more modern artwork placed sporadically about the grass lawn. To the south through the library, the Borgia Tower stood, its heights a sentinel over the Cortile del Belvedere. The Sistine Chapel lay just on the other side with the dome of St. Peter's Basilica lording over all. Charles could feel the portal thrumming nearby, deep in the catacombs, far from where they stood if one did not know the secret passageways that littered Vatican City.

With the high walls of the courtyard boxing them in, the Pope had brought the vampire to an area that was not easily fled.

"Wait here," Pope Urban instructed.

"Where is the spear?" Lazarus asked again.

"That is none of your concern," the pontiff chided. He looked at Charles and then at Beck Almgren. "If the vampire attempts to flee or cause other mischief, Heliwr, I trust you and the Bearer of Prydwen can subdue him until my return. The Thorn and the Shield should be enough, correct?"

"I would accompany you, Your Eminence," Captain Almgren said.

"You will not. This I must do alone."

Not waiting for a response, the Pope strode south toward St. Peter's Basilica, his guards remaining a shield about him. Charles waited like the rest beneath the stars. None of them spoke. The Cardinal Archivist prayed in whispers, an act that clearly unnerved Lazarus. Captain Almgren scowled nearby and did not take his eyes from the vampire. Berrytrill sat upon Charles's shoulder, arms folded, his leafy face scrunched up in barely contained irritation.

Charles felt as his guide did. No matter his desire to see Lazarus destroyed, he did not like that the vampire was near to getting what he wished. That wasn't all though. The knight did not like the deadly sin of power craved in the eyes of the Pope. He did not like being effectively removed from decisions, Urban now in control. And *was* the Pope in control? A vampire as ancient as Lazarus undoubtedly had duplicitous tricks to use when it suited. Even though the Cardinal Archivist had corroborated the identity of the vampire, something felt missing, a truth that could haunt them for days yet come. The feeling they were being misled grew like an angry itch.

One Charles could not scratch.

He mulled on that, still trying to unravel the puzzle that was Lazarus. After long minutes, Pope Urban returned and strode toward them across the courtyard lawn, bearing a long item wrapped in white cloth. Without a word, he unwrapped it and brought free a spear from antiquity, its design clearly Roman, its long tip glinting in the weak starlight.

"The Holy Lance," the Pope presented, letting the cloth fall to the ground.

"It looks new," Berrytrill observed.

"The wood shaft has been replaced several times, fairy, but the point has never lost its edge in all the centuries since that day it punctured the side of Christ."

"What now, Your Holiness?" the Cardinal Archivist asked.

"I will speak with the Heliwr. In private."

Unsure what Urban wanted to discuss, Charles followed the Pope deeper into the courtyard where distance and night cloaked them in privacy. As a precaution, Charles gathered the magic of the Dark Thorn to his use and spoke three simple words, the spell keeping their conversation private.

"Do you sense any intention other than what the creature said in the depths of the Secret Archives, Charles Ardall?"

"I do not know," Charles said, glancing back at Lazarus.

"Something is not right. The vampire speaks true but not. There is something in all this he is not telling us."

"The Holy Lance cannot fall into its hands. Do you understand?"

"As wielder of the Dark Thorn, I agree."

"I wish something of you then," Urban continued. "I do not want to be parted from the spear, not for any reason. There must be a spell you can weave to make this so. My forbearers have protected the Holy Lance for centuries. I must do so as well."

"That could be very dangerous," Charles said, apprehension filling him. "Magic is not something to be taken lightly. Merle has been very adamant about situations like you suggest. For a knight to enact magic on another person is a grave risk. Magic can go wrong; it can be unpredictable. And you being the Pope with great responsibility and with intense public scrutiny makes it—"

"An even graver risk," the Pope finished.

"It is my role to keep the two worlds separate. If something happens, it will be obvious to the world, more than likely." Charles paused. "To be blunt, you should not be taking part in any of this."

"I must accept that risk," Urban said, ignoring the Heliwr's warning. "It is my job to end creatures like this. I *also* cannot lose the spear. It is one of the foremost relics in my possession and under my protection." When Charles did not immediately agree, the Pope stepped closer. "You *will* do this. I take full responsibility for the magic employed upon my person. It is a necessary evil and burden I must bear," he whispered.

Charles said nothing, simply nodding. The proper spell came easily enough. He had bound elements many times during his tenure as Heliwr, and it was not a difficult way to fulfill what the Pope requested. It still bothered him to enact magic on another person though. The warning Merle had given him remained.

Even so, it had been many years—since the beginning of his apprenticeship under Merle—that his own magical abilities had gone awry in some fashion.

But that did not mean it could not happen now.

"Hold the spear as you would when striking Lazarus," Charles said.

Pope Urban did so. Charles called upon his magic, the Dark Thorn bolstering him. He wove a spell from the ether, from ancient words, calling on the power of the world through his heels as well as the power connecting him to Annwn through his staff.

It did not take long. The Pope's right hand began to glow a warm blue where it held the shaft of the spear.

After he finished the spell, the glow disappeared.

"The staff cannot be taken from your fingers," Charles said, the flush that came with enacting magic gone suddenly. "I can undo it once we are finished. The magic has bound the carbon atoms in the staff's wooden shaft to the carbon of your hand. Test it. Try to release the Holy Lance."

"I cannot let it go," the pontiff said, all too pleased. He turned his back on the knight and strode back toward the others. "Time to end this evil's life."

Charles ended the privacy spell and followed, still wary.

"Kneel, creature," Pope Urban said, holding the Spear of Longinus before him for emphasis. "I bring the death you have asked for."

Lazarus released Cesare Farina and knelt as asked.

"Slay me, Pope Urban the Fingerless," Lazarus whispered.

The leader of the Catholic Church hesitated a moment before raising the Holy Lance to strike. The warning that had been growing in Charles's heart shrieked to sudden life.

"No!" he yelled. "Wait!"

Before Charles could intercede, it was too late. As the spear began to fall toward the vampire, the weapon suddenly vanished.

As did Lazarus.

Charles and the others stood frozen, unsure what had just happened. Then the horrified howls of Pope Urban filled the courtyard with chilling clarity. Blood spurted into the night from a right hand suddenly maimed, lacking every digit, the Pope bent over in wild-eyed, pained terror.

"Charles, Lazarus flees!" Berrytrill yelled.

"Follow him!" the knight roared.

Berrytrill had already done so, vanishing almost as quickly as the vampire. Charles chased after, ignoring the pain-racked sobs of the Pope and surprised anger of his captain and guards. As his guide hunted for Lazarus, Berrytrill left a trail of fairy magic dust—a trick of Heliwr guides centuries old—and Charles followed this, having already called on the spell that would allow him to do so.

It became quickly apparent what path the vampire had chosen. The trail glowed on the air before Charles, for his eyes only.

And it led into the Vatican Library.

Back the way they had come.

Charles sprinted, the Dark Thorn still called forth. The Heliwr could not believe what had just happened. Knowing he could not help Urban, he followed the magic trail back into the Library. The magic Berrytrill employed showed Lazarus retracing his steps toward the Secret Archives—and likely back through the passageways beneath Vatican City the vampire had used to gain the archives in the first place.

Lazarus planned on returning to the portal.

The vampire might have had another destination in mind but that did not feel right. He had come from Annwn; Annwn is where he'd return. Charles could locate the creature every few minutes with the Dark Thorn but those were precious minutes he would not lose, minutes that could make a difference.

It was a risk Charles would have to take.

He broke from Berrytrill's glowing trail and, rather than entering the Secret Archives, sprinted into the Cortile del Belvedere toward St. Peter's Basilica. He ignored the parking lot, the Borgia Tower, and the Sistine Chapel. He instead tore through corridors both secret and well traveled during the day, hoping he did not make a mistake. The only chance he had was cutting the vampire off before he entered Annwn. If Lazarus did, Charles would have a much harder time tracking him, killing him, and retrieving the powerful relic. The creature was unnaturally fast, able to cover distances with great speed. But the tunnels beneath the city were long and meandering. Charles had to hope he was quick enough to take advantage of a more direct route. He had one chance, and speed was his only ally.

Charles burst into St. Peter's Square. The grandeur of Vatican City met him, ornate buildings of architectural beauty dwarfing humanity. Several dozen people still milled about the Square, some walking hand in hand, others photographing the splendor of the city at night. Charles ignored their surprise and eventual pro- testations at his erratic appearance with the Dark Thorn. He left them all behind. In seconds, he entered the heart of Catholicism, St. Peter's Basilica, purpose driving him. Down through the nave he ran, into the heart of the massive structure. No one stopped him. Soon the Papal Altar and Baldacchino rose over him, the tomb of Saint Peter beneath. There Charles gained the entrance to the Secret Grotto that held the hidden door into the catacombs beneath, sweat freezing his burning skin even as he ran faster into the world's depths.

After numerous twists and turns through the catacombs, Charles came to the corridor that led to the Secret Archives in one direction and the portal to Annwn in the other. Breathing hard, he peered around him with spell-empowered eyes.

The trail Berrytrill created had not yet reached these corridors.

Which meant Lazarus likely hadn't either.

Hoping that was true, Charles waited.

Just when the knight thought that he had made a mistake and was about to use the Dark Thorn to locate the vampire, he sensed movement coming toward him from the direction of the Secret Archives, a disturbance of air, a quiver of sound that could mean only one thing.

Calling the fire of the Dark Thorn to bolster his need and senses, he waited.

When Lazarus tried to pass in a blur, Charles tackled him.

Both of them went flying.

The vampire's momentum threw them down the corridor a dozen yards. Magic kept Charles mostly safe as he skidded to a halt beneath Lazarus, lashing out with fire born of anger, determina- tion, and need. Caught by surprise, Lazarus fought back imme- diately. The vampire was faster than the Heliwr and quickly had the knight by his front clothing, fangs bared in anger. He brought

564

the Holy Lance up in defense against the Dark Thorn, the dead fingers of the Pope still attached to it, both of them vying for an advantage.

"Give this up, Lazarus!" Charles roared.

"I go to fulfill a debt that comes with my death!"

Charles sent the fire of the Dark Thorn into the vampire's face. Hair singed, Lazarus roared like a lion caught in a grassfire. He tried to flee. The knight did not allow it. He tripped the vampire with hastily drawn magical tethers, sending the other sprawling to stone. Charles was on him in a second. He slammed the cudgel of the Dark Thorn into the vampire's jaw, a strike that did nothing but anger the vampire more, and pressed the head of the staff into the other's chest, to pin the night creature against rock.

"This does not concern you, Heliwr!" Lazarus said, unfazed. He held the Holy Lance at his side but did not use it to attack. "I go to my death!"

"I no longer believe your lies!"

"I have not lied," Lazarus growled lowly, fangs fully extended. Charles could see in the other's eyes a desire to kill the knight, to rend him from limb to limb—that need eroding the creature's control and only a moment away from reality.

Charles realized this was the moment Merle had portended.

"You stole the spear, Lazarus," the Heliwr argued more calmly.

"I did," the vampire admitted, the fire in his eyes banking a bit. "But I promised I did not intend to kill anyone. I still do not. You are safe and I have killed no one. I did purchase a service though. And that service must be paid in full."

Charles kept the magical pressure on his opponent. "Not today. I will fight you to the end. Do the right thing. Give up the Holy Lance."

"I smell your wife on you," Lazarus growled. "Your soon-to-be son! I sense you are worried you will die fulfilling your knightly duty. Do not. Not this day. But neither should you devastate their lives with your loss by pressing me, Heliwr! You have greater deeds to fulfill! And I will not take another life!"

At that, he heaved Charles backward, sending him flying.

He slammed against the wall with such force it would have killed a normal man. The Dark Thorn saved him though, softening the powerful brunt of the assault, though his magic could not prevent it entirely. His head hit the wall hard, the breath in his lungs left like a gale, and all went dark as he slid down to the ground against his will, struggling against unconsciousness.

He had no idea how much time had passed when a shrill voice filled his ear.

"Where'd he go?!" Berrytrill screamed.

"The portal," Charles mumbled, shaking his head. "Follow him!"

The fairy guide did, leaving the Heliwr behind. Sweat pouring freely, Charles regained his feet, battling the wave of nausea and weakness that threatened to overcome him. He fought both and won. Soon rage took over—at what had been done to him and how the situation had unfolded—strengthening his resolve.

Stumbling a bit at the start, he went after his guide. The catacombs took him back to where it all had begun. As he followed the fairy's trail, a cacophony of broken sounds rolled through the underground tunnels, getting louder with every step. Then he realized what it was.

It was the sound of echoing gunfire.

Another battle raged. Had the portal been compromised again? Or did the Swiss Guards fight only against Lazarus? When Charles finally burst into the portal cavern, he was not prepared for what he saw.

A new threat had not entered Rome.

A dead threat had.

The vampire corpses that had littered the cavern were now reanimated through dark arts, attacking dozens of Swiss Guards, trying to break through to the entrance where Charles now stood. In front of him, Bruno Ricci fought, arm slung, looking every bit as dead as those he faced. But Carnwennan was blinding white-hot power, the magic of the Arthurian knife bolstering its bearer's strength and resolve. The portal knight sent swaths of lightning deep into the zombie midst, keeping them at bay long enough for the Swiss Guard to form a counterattack.

The vampiric zombies came on, an unending torrent that felt no pain. Charles hadn't seen it in time. The runes tattooed on their skin.

Life after life's death.

"Are these vambies?" Berrytrill mused. "Or are they Zompires?"

"Be careful," Charles growled, ignoring his guide's poor attempt at humor. "To get caught by one would be your certain death."

"Look to the portal!"

Charles did so. Lazarus stood before the Annwn gateway, calmly, still holding the Holy Lance. He had either made his way through the melee or enacted the rune magic after he had gained the portal, creating a zombie diversion while he waited. But for what?

Or whom?

Then Charles saw movement within the shimmering portal.

An old woman stepped free of the void, ratty gray hair hanging limply about a pinched, wrinkled face. Her clothing was destitute like a beggar's but rings with various priceless gems that would have made the greediest coblynau miner envious sat upon every finger of her hands, verifying her identity.

The witch Lazarus had made his bargain with.

Charles suddenly understood.

"Don't do this, Lazarus!" he roared.

The vampire ignored him. He handed the Holy Lance to the witch and knelt. Raising it and wasting no time, the old crone struck. Lazarus met the thrust with his entire being as if offering himself in sacrifice to the witch. When the metal pierced his heart, every muscle in his body snapped taut. He leaned back and, coughing crimson into the air twice, gasped several unintelligible words before going limp.

He then slowly slid off the spear to the cold stone floor as the witch wrenched the weapon free.

The vampire did not move.

The witch straightened and finally looked at the cavern and those within it for the first time. Charles locked eyes with her. Like Lazarus, she was ancient, her eyes shining victory and malice.

Charles saw a fire there that burned eternal. It was clear to him the witch had a plan, and a major piece of it had just come into her possession.

With a smile devoid of humor, she vanished into the portal with her prize.

After what felt like an eternity, the Swiss Guard finally created a hole in the wall of zombies. With Bruno Ricci keeping the undead at bay and Beck Almgren finally returned to lend his own fey power, the Vatican soldiers shot their rifles and pistols into the skulls of the zombies. Charles did not wait for the inevitable victory. He ran through the din, keeping clear of the danger surrounding him, encased in an armor of magic in case the Swiss Guards were incapable of hitting only their targets. Soon, he was free of the horde and running full out for the gateway into Annwn.

"Where are you going, Ardall?!" Bruno Ricci yelled over the din, his knife lightning-infused war.

Charles did not stop. "After the spear!"

Within moments, he and Berrytrill won the shimmering void. The knight did not enter immediately. He gave the body of Lazarus a quick, wary eye. The spear had worked. The vampire lay dead, eyes filled with wonder.

The man Jesus Christ had brought back to life had finally found death.

With a nod to Berrytrill, Charles entered the portal. The power of the gateway engulfed them. Even as Charles walked forward into the void, the smell of mulch-fueled growing plants accosted him, a sweet, heady odor leading him to Annwn. Berrytrill was nowhere in sight, but Charles knew the fairy was flying close behind. Soon the knight began to be reduced in size, the air being forcibly drawn from his lungs. Even though he had grown used to passing between the two worlds, it never got any easier.

Just when he thought he would pass out, Charles crossed into Annwn.

He stood upon a massive finger of granite extending out of an emerald carpet of grass plains to the west of the Forest of Dean.

The sun sat overhead in an azure sky, and the hum of insects surrounded the Heliwr and his guide even as the day's warmth chased the catacomb chill from their bones. To the northwest, the massive spikes of the Snowdon Mountains were in evidence in the far distance, a last bastion of freedom for the Tuatha de Dannan; to the west, Charles knew Caer Llion sat on the ocean, the capital city of the self-crowned Philip Plantagenet controlling most of Annwn.

Flanked by two dead trees, the portal to Rome shimmered behind him.

Charles did not dwell on the beauty of the day or the political imbalance in Annwn. With Berrytrill watching, he called the Dark Thorn and sent its butt into the soil, searching for the Holy Lance and the witch who had machinated it from the Vatican.

"The witch has disappeared," Charles said angrily, the Dark Thorn in his hands matching the heat in his heart. "Cloaking herself in magic, knowing we would come after her, no doubt. I cannot track her or the Holy Lance."

Berrytrill flew in midair before him and frowned.

Long moments passed. There was nothing more Charles could do. He was the Heliwr, given a grave responsibility and gifted with great power, but even he could be bested at times.

"That's that then," Berrytrill said at last.

"Why did the vampire aid the witch?" Berrytrill asked.

The two stood again on the outcropping of rock that held the portal to Italy, the sunshine warm and inviting. Once Charles had realized they were powerless in regaining the Holy Lance, they had returned to Rome, to set right many of the wrongs still there. The zombies had been dispatched with few losses; the portal was once again protected. Retracing his footsteps, Charles ensured all aspects of the invasion were put right. With the help of Bruno Ricci, he had wiped clean dozens of guards' memories, Beck Almgren watching to ensure it was done properly. It had taken hours of work but it was done.

Bruno Ricci would heal. Pope Urban had the worst of it, but even the Church would construct a plausible reason for the loss of his fingers. Italy and the world knew nothing of what had transpired. And life would go on much as it had for centuries.

"It was a means to an end," Charles answered finally, still thinking on it.

"The end of the spear, literally."

Charles couldn't help but grin. "I suppose so."

"Still. The Spear of Longinus is out there. Somewhere."

"It is," Charles said, the notion sobering. "The witch had other intentions, of that we can be sure. Perhaps Merle will have an answer. Until we locate the Holy Lance, we must be vigilant and look for it whenever we tread Annwn. It is too important—and powerful—of a relic to remain in the hands of such a creature. The witch sent Lazarus into the Vatican to secure it for her own reasons. Few could have crossed into Rome and bested its portal knight, especially one as strong as Bruno Ricci. Fewer still would have enough knowledge of our world and that of the Bible's history to make his way to the Vatican Library and eventually gain the staff from the pontiff. No, it was a bold move and well orchestrated. We will hear from the witch again."

Berrytrill grunted. "It never ends."

"I just hope we are up to the task," Charles added. "The witch has been alive a very long time and has learned patience. We will have to do the same."

"We will," Berrytrill said, before looking off toward the Snowdon. "There are good qualities, like patience, learned by the passage of time—but darker qualities too." The fairy paused. "Humans are fascinating. There are Tuatha de Dannan who live for centuries but who never succumb to the madness that clearly had taken hold of Lazarus. Why did the vampire choose death?"

"Humans aren't meant to be long lived, I guess," Charles reflected. "Besides, life is much more than longevity. Quality of years is more important than quantity. Lazarus learned that all too well. No quality could be gained from his continued existence—at least that's how he felt. He therefore decided to end it on his terms."

"What does quality mean to you?"

Charles did not answer immediately.

"A loving wife," he said finally. "Looking into her eyes and knowing peace as I've never known. Sunlight on my face in spring, when the world is escaping winter in Seattle. A kind gesture from a stranger. Traveling to Annwn and seeing what this world has to offer. Having a baby on the way and all the anticipation that brings." He smiled and looked to the fairy. "Enjoying friendship like ours at every possible moment."

"And Lazarus no longer had those things?"

"I suspect he did. He just could no longer see them."

Berrytrill hovered in the air quietly, thinking on that.

"There are souls who fight to live," Charles added, also mulling it over. "And there are those who give up all too easily."

"Do you think he has found peace with his God?" Berrytrill asked. "Or is he in that place of fire and brimstone you mention all too often when you curse?"

"Hell," Charles said. "We won't know until our reckoning day, I suppose."

"Your reckoning," the fairy admonished.

"Oh?"

"*I* plan to live forever."

"You just may," Charles said, smiling. "But you'll miss me if you do."

Berrytrill looked toward the horizon, frowning deeper, as if trying to see that day and not liking what he saw. Charles grinned inwardly at his private joke and followed his guide's gaze. Several ravens swirled in the distance, upon currents of air from Annwn's ocean in the south. They settled back to one of the sentinel trees outside of the Forest of Dean before taking flight again. The dark birds were free, much like Lazarus. They had no reason to fear the world around them. They were unfettered but, unlike the vampire, they were enjoying the life they had been given.

"Bran," Charles whispered.

"What?" Berrytrill questioned.

"Bran means 'raven' in Welsh," the knight said and continued to watch the birds. "It's a good, strong name for the baby."

"Bran Ardall," the guide tested. "I like it."

Charles nodded.

"How do you know you are having a boy child?"

"Whether he knew it or not," Charles said, smiling sadly. "Lazarus shared with me a gift before his death."

"A boy child. You should name him Trill instead. A more regal name the boy child could not have," Berrytrill mused with a sarcastic sniff before becoming smiling bits of leaves. "Where do we travel now?"

"Home," he said. "And, if he has returned, for a long discussion with Merle."

The Heliwr of the Yn Saith took a step down the steep trail that led to the plains below the granite outcropping, already removing the light cloak from his pack that would hide his world's odd attire in the foreign territory. With Berrytrill flying ahead to keep their passage safe, Charles strode west toward Dryvyd Wood where the Seattle portal thrummed entrance to a city that held his heart.

Home to his expecting wife and their forthcoming baby boy.

And a life worth living.

ACKNOWLEDGMENTS

Unfettered would not exist without some extraordinary people helping in various and different ways. I am indebted to one and all of them.

Richard and Kathy Speakman
Who taught me to never back down from a fight

Todd Speakman
Who showed love from great distance

Jeff, Becky, Payton, and Kendall Lawson
Who are my second family and love like it

Rachelle Longé McGhee
Whose talent is in every page of this book

Thomas Malpass, MD
Who saved my life not once but twice

Minh-Trang Thi Duong, Marion Tiongson, Jennifer Callahan, and Patricia Liming
Who bring love and light to every patient they care for

Terry and Judine Brooks
Who checked up on me incessantly

Todd Lockwood
> Who rendered beautiful art and better friendship

Peter Orullian
> Who kept me company on the worst of days

Harriet McDougal and Nat Sobel
> Who gave a turn of the Wheel of Time

Bill Schafer
> Who advised how the experts do it

John Joseph Adams
> Who shared knowledge with a novice

My story contributors
> Who rallied to me and wrote tales filled with wondrous magic

And finally, the readers
> Who supported a fellow reader in need